CULPA INNATA

A FUTURISTIC THRILLER

By B. Barmanbek

CULPA INNATA

Copyright © 2012 by B. Barmanbek

For more information about the world of Culpa Innata, please visit culpainnata.com

Cover art: Souloff

EAN-13: 978-1466472679
ISBN-10: 1466472677

First Edition: October 2012

To Alev, and my parents.

My deepest gratitude to my friends and family who encouraged and inspired this book.

"There is no New World Order, only the old one replaying itself in infinitely varying detail, like a kaleidoscope."

George Friedman

PROLOGUE

TEN DAYS BEFORE MONDAY Phoenix woke up drenched in ice-cold sweat.

"I don't wanna be cold anymore!"

The disturbing but familiar words kept ringing in her ears, and a deep shudder violently shook her body. She got up in slow motion and shivered her way towards the bathroom, barely managing to turn on the tap of her tub in her first-ever night in the flat.

The sky was just a shade lighter than black outside. She turned and looked at the mirror in the dim of the night lights, staring beyond her own green-gray eyes, trying to understand what kind of game her mind was playing with her now. The warm gown she'd put on wouldn't make any difference, she knew, because this cold was so fundamental and coming from so deep down inside, no thermal clothing could help.

The tub was full at last. She dropped her gown and quickly got in all the way to her neck, letting her cells soak up and store the heat. Her shuddering slowly abated, calming her mind down along with it. She couldn't remember anything from the nightmare, other than the intense fear and a marrow-numbing cold, something she used to feel all the time during the lonely nights of her childhood. But that had been then. How could this night terror find her without any warning on the first night she had spent in the city after all these years? It couldn't be mere coincidence, she knew. Something must have had ignited her childhood fears. Could it be the city itself? Perhaps, but one thing was for sure: Her repressed childhood traumas and terrors were back, pushing their way into her conscious. The memories that had lain buried all these years somehow had found a way to resurface.

And now they were set to terrorize her, day and night alike.

THE NIGHT BEFORE MONDAY the Mantis emerged from hiding with an incoming communication from his controller. His new mission would be about a murder committed in one of those rogue nation states earlier in the day. How long had it been since his last job, that unprecedented "Hack of the Century," which had sent shockwaves throughout the mighty World Union? Too long.

He smiled as he thought of how he carried out his part, infiltrating the familiar old building in early hours of the morning, moving around the security cameras and other scanning devices with expert agility, descending down the unused and uneven treacherous stairwells to the dark basement level as gracefully as a ninja—only to reveal the secret tunnels that the ancients had built—then chimney-climbing the tunnels into the network center of the building in sheer perfection. Without those tiny gadgets that he had plugged in to the main routing switch, none of it would have been possible.

Actually, the hack had been a partial success, as it had ended prematurely due to a power cut at the target research facility. He hadn't been involved in any of the planning or the hacking itself, but the Mantis had an idea why his chain of command failed to anticipate such a contingency. It had to be the work of his controller, the Prefect, who kept ignoring his pleas to be more involved, and that inexperienced Crane, who had been taking increasingly larger roles in missions way over his head. Could his fellow team members also be badmouthing him and laying the blame for their own shortcomings and failures on his shoulders? Would they dare such a thing? Then again, he was to work alone in this new mission. Perhaps his chain of command was finally becoming aware where the real merit lay, sidelining those amateurs for a change.

The Mantis waited patiently for the details, vowing to mastermind such perfection, no one would ever dare send him back into hiding again.

MONDAY

CHAPTER 1

SOMETHING about a severed arm was nagging at the back of her mind.

A severed arm, aching cold, and a butterfly. Or a star? Something tiny and dazzling, and a serpent.

The thought of the serpent sent a brief violent convulsion throughout her entire body.

A completely immobile Phoenix had been sitting in her chair for some time now, staring through the tall window into the void beyond, listening to the wind assault the old building, compounding the strong sense of alienation that she had been feeling since she arrived in the city. Since that first night, she had been haunted by the same nightmares she used to have when she was a little child. As usual, she could only remember little fragments from them, but she knew that they were all somehow connected to the horrors of the Great Meltdown. Now all that lingered from the night before were vague and fleeting impressions, tantalizingly out of reach, that pervading chill, a butterfly composed of light—or was it a star?—deep sadness and distant comfort, loss and despair.

She shifted her exhausted limbs and got up from the chair, dragging herself towards the window. Between the tall residences surrounding the city center, she could see the tip of the massive golden structure in the shape of a four-sided pyramid. The beauty of the structure helped soothe her in some way.

The annoying buzzing alarm of her PA rudely awakened her from her deep reverie. The little device projected a text message before her, reminding her of her first item for the day in one hour: The graduation ceremony at the immigration academy. Why would the headperson of an immigration academy personally invite a newly promoted senior agent of the Global Peace and Security Network to a graduation ceremony, she didn't know. Perhaps it was a gesture of good will for a change, as she certainly hadn't received such courtesy from her coworkers or her supervisor during her first week in the office.

She collapsed back on her seat and washed down her black coffee as she tried to convince herself once again that she had made a brilliant career move and that her reservations were all part of the adaptation process. She usually liked her coffee generously dosed with cream, but recently she had started trying it black with loads of sugar, hoping that it would give her a desperately needed extra kick. Yet so far nothing seemed to work. Nothing seemed to shake off her permanent fatigue or that unaccustomed "down" mood that she had suffered for a whole week now. She knew that she needed to do something before it spiraled into full-blown depression.

On a sudden impulse, she took off her PA, tossed it onto her desk, and left her office.

What am I doing here? she thought, looking in the bathroom mirror.

Gone were the days when all it took to eradicate the effects of a sleepless night was a splash of cold water or a quick jog. She now had vampire-like red slits between her puffy pink eyelids, and her skin was dry and dull, white in patches, gray or red in other patches. Her usually glossy curtain of pale gold hair seemed to have lost its gleam, and no amount of expensive hair treatment serum had been able to restore it. Dehydration had carved gaunt hollows in her smooth cheeks, and insomnia had etched new lines across her forehead.

She left the bathroom and dragged back to her office, trying to ignore the cramps in her abdomen. "Computer: Open the door."

The creak of the old wooden door followed a loud click. She pushed the door open and lowered her gaze in an attempt to ignore the dark gray walls. Even the genetically engineered maintenance-free plants in her office seemed on the point of wilting, as if in harmony with her own failure to flourish in this environment. She tried to give herself a tiny boost by glancing at her new HDI certificate that she displayed on the wall behind her chair. As of three days before, April fifth, her HDI had officially been one point up from the quarter before, to seventy-three, placing her credibility in the top twelfth percentile in the whole World Union. A moment later, the fleeting relief succumbed to nausea and the sensation of an iron fist squeezing her solar plexus once again. What if her career was going down the drain, regardless of what her HDI showed?

She kept staring at her network node on the old wooden desk. Reluctant hands found the keyboard, automatically typed her password. The main menu on the screen appeared with alerts popping up all over the place, dragging her attention away from her endless self-debate. There was a priority one message from Director Morssen, her supervisor at the field office, calling her for an urgent level five meeting. She automatically reached up for her PA, while rereading the message and wondering what this could be about. Her hand fell on the empty desk. A quick glance initiated a fresh surge of anxiety.

"Damn it. Where the heck did it go?"

She frantically searched for it under and around her desk for a few minutes, until that moment she felt that she couldn't make the director wait anymore. She quickly walked across the hallway to her office.

"Computer: Open the door." She waited for a few seconds, but the Door Bot neither acknowledged nor made any action. Could it be because she didn't have her PA on her? One of the little gadget's zillion skills was to communicate with Door Bots and enable doors automatically. Then again, this Door Bot was also supposed to obey her voice commands—in an ideal world, that was.

Everything seemed to be going wrong, ever since she moved to this accursed city, and she felt clueless as to how to put things right. Her mind was racing in every direction, yet she had no idea where her PA was. She could send a message from her network node, asking the director to open the door for her, or bang on the door, but that would be totally embarrassing, and her pride wouldn't allow that. Besides, things were already bad enough as they were: She'd been ignored or made fun of behind her back, and she had no intention of starting this new week with more humiliation. She should be able to manually override this Door Bot by using voice commands only, shouldn't she?

"Computer: I'm Senior Agent Phoenix Wallis and my badge number is three, one, six, charlie, omega, seven, seven, papa, echo, papa. Acknowledge."

A three-dimensional hologram of a colorless and textureless head figure appeared between her and the door. "Voice pattern identified as Senior Peace Agent Phoenix Wallis," it said in an even and expressionless male voice.

"Computer: Open the door."

"Senior Agent Wallis, there is an ongoing meeting inside, which requires security clearance level five. You are not authorized to enter."

"Computer: I was sent a priority one invitation for this meeting. Open the door."

"Senior Agent Wallis, you are not authorized to enter."

Now what the heck could this mean? Could someone have revoked her level five privileges somehow, or nicked her PA, or both? Some cruel borderland prank? Then she remembered reading about a new security procedure in one of her mails mandating that hardware-enabled access would be obligatory for accessing anything with a security clearance requirement of level five and above, and that voice commands alone would no longer be sufficient. In other words, she had to have her PA to enter this office. She felt the imminent approach of a new wave of helplessness. She had to do something, anything, to make her mind switch gears.

Without any conscious thought, she closed her eyes, took deep breaths, and thought of the place where she always felt safe. Suddenly a fresh wave of energy washed over her, erasing all the negativity, putting her back in control. She enjoyed this calming energy and the profound relief she felt. Inhaling deeply several times, then following a long exhalation, she turned her attention to the dilemma.

The first thing that came to her mind was to rush back to her office to resume the search. She quickly eliminated this alternative, as she clearly remembered where she had placed the little device. The only plausible explanation was that somebody must have taken it. She left the question of *who* for later and focused on all the training she had received about Door Bots and other expert systems. Soon enough an idea emerged in her mind. She could even hit two birds with one stone.

"Computer: Locate Senior Agent Wallis. Label the answer as fact one."

"Senior Agent Phoenix Wallis is in an unspecified place in second floor hallway of the Global Peace and Security Network Peace Corps Adrianopolis Field Office Building. Labeled as fact one."

She smiled at the synthetic and expressionless face, knowing that she had found the solution to her dilemma. "Computer: I have already identified myself. Now repeat who I am and label the answer as fact two."

"You are Senior Peace Agent Phoenix Wallis of the Global Peace and Security Network Peace Corps. Labeled as fact two."

"Computer: Who are you? Label the answer as fact three."

"We are the Interactive Gateway Expert System, managing access to room number thirty-six seventy-one at the third floor of the Global Peace and Security Network Adrianopolis Field Office Building. Labeled as fact three."

"Computer: Cross-reference fact one with facts two and three. How can Senior Agent Wallis be in the second floor hallway and be here interacting to you at the third floor at the same time, unless she invented a time machine?"

"Processing." The Door Bot remained silent for a few seconds. "Unrecognized logic loop. Facts incomplete. Please revise query."

"Computer: Forget the time machine. The remaining facts are complete and indisputable. The query is valid. Conclusion: Gateway Expert System internal logic flow is corrupt. Under the circumstance, human element takes precedence over machine. Acknowledge."

"Conclusion acknowledged."

She noticed a trace of hesitation in Door Bot's response. It was time to end its logical misery. "Computer: Open the door, then run diagnostic and reboot."

A tingling wave of self-confidence warmed her up from the inside as the Door Bot gave way with a loud click. She went into Director Dagmar Morssen's office to find fellow senior agents Alex Lubosh and Julio Dominguez already seated around the desk-slash-meeting table.

"At last, our new recruit decides to join us," said Director Morssen in her crisp British accent, accompanied by her ever-piercing gaze. She was a petite and chillingly elegant handsome woman in her late forties who projected an incredible amount of authority and presence. Everyone in the office was intimidated by her gaze, and this was exactly the way she wanted everyone to feel. Julio smirked with a condescending stare, while Alex looked on.

"I had some trouble with the Door Bot, Director Morssen. I'm sorry for being late."

Director Morssen kept the icy glare on her new recruit. She'd been observing Phoenix all the past week and was not impressed with the way she had handled herself among her peers. Something seemed to be bothering her, but the director couldn't have cared less. Everybody had issues and problems, and the real talent was to thrive under pressure, not to collapse.

"I sent an invite to your PA first, receiving no acknowledgement. I forwarded the invite to your network node next, assuming that it ought to find you through one of the two, provided that you know how to operate them, of course."

"I know how to use my hardware, Director."

"I should assume that you do. I don't know how things are run at our European headquarters that you came from, but here we rely on and expect network connectivity around the clock."

"I apologize again for being late," said Phoenix and took the empty seat.

"How did you manage to get into my office to join a level five meeting without your PA, anyway?"

"I convinced your Door Bot that I should be able to attend the meeting without it."

"And how exactly did you do that? I hope you didn't hack into something. We do not tolerate that kind of stuff around here!"

Julio snorted while Alex listened to the conversation intently. Phoenix looked deep into the director's eyes and leaned over the table.

"I was hired to catch hackers, Director, not to turn into one," she whispered. "I improvised and found a loophole in the Door Bot logic."

This cool and self-assured appearance of the new recruit was totally new. Could there be more to her than met the eye? "A loophole? Are you positive?"

"Yes, I am."

"Damn it! How do they expect us to run this place, with all these security issues? Oh, whatever! I want your full report on this loophole of yours, understood? And don't forget to copy in Fred, our network admin. You met him yet?"

"Yes, Director."

"In the meantime, we have a much more urgent situation at hand: A Union citizen has been murdered."

A grim silence took over the room for a few seconds.

"A what?" Julio said, his eyes popping.

"You heard me right. A murder."

"Last time such an archaic crime took place in the World Union was nearly fifteen years ago," said Phoenix. "How can it be possible?"

"I said a Union citizen. I did not say in the World Union."

"Oh, you mean in one of those rogue states?" said Julio, and wiped imaginary sweat off his brow. "Who in his right mind would travel to a rogue state anyway? It's such a—"

"Who was the victim?" said Phoenix.

"A Vassily Bogdanov, with a Human Development Index of seventy. He was found murdered in a city called Odessa, in the rogue nation state of Russian Federation. The facts and information that we discuss in this meeting will remain confidential and will be revealed to public only on a strict *need-to-know* basis by judge's orders. Understood?"

All three nodded their heads. The director clicked a button on her network node, and a hologram of the victim appeared above the table. Vassily Bogdanov looked like he had been in his late forties. He had an unappealing face with puffy cheeks, a bulbous nose, thin lips, and a bald head. His weary blue eyes radiated something like disenchantment with life. He also appeared unusually overweight for a Union citizen.

"His body was found by the Russian security forces yesterday. But they did not realize that he was one of our citizens until this morning. They notified our European headquarters in Munich, and the headquarters notified me right after Bogdanov's identity and address were discovered."

"A local?" Alex spoke for the first time since Phoenix's awkward entrance.

"Yes."

"Did they provide any other information?" said Phoenix.

"No reports yet."

"How about the murder weapon?"

"My understanding is that he was murdered by a firearm. But they seem to have no leads or witnesses yet."

"A man has been murdered and no clues yet?" said Julio. "How can they be so incompetent?"

"They have to deal with very shrewd criminals," said Alex. "And their nation state cannot provide the peace and tranquility to its people that our postmodern union can."

"Alex is right," said the director. "And this is all we know so far."

"What do we do?" said Phoenix.

"We start investigating from our end," said the director, and exhaled loudly. "According to the census records, Mr. Bogdanov emigrated to our Union three years ago from the same rogue nation state. He attended our own Adrianopolis Immigration Academy."

"His face is quite familiar, actually," said Alex, gazing at the hologram with rapt attention, his head tilted.

"Our primary goal is to find out who committed the murder. And since nobody in their right mind would go there for sightseeing, figuring out why he went would be a good starting point. Julio."

"Yes, Chief."

"I want you to dig into his travel arrangements to Russia, his bank accounts, transaction records, his academy training, anything and everything you can find. Alex, you will be in charge of our communications with the Russian police. Your knowledge of their language makes you the perfect man for the task."

"Yes, Director Morssen, I believe he does."

"Yes, it does."

This wasn't the first time anyone witnessed the director correcting Alex's grammar. Could his Russian be better than his English?

"Agent Wallis," said the director, turning to her. "Bogdanov's record from the census database is forwarded to your PA. I want you to check out his apartment, his work, his friends, his business associates, his social activities, and everything else since *you* will be leading this investigation."

"Me?"

Director Morssen grimaced and leaned towards Phoenix across the table with her eyes fixed on Phoenix's, trying to reach behind them. This was a make-or-break moment for this young woman, and she just wasn't sure how ready Phoenix was. How long was the confidence she had noticed in her eyes a few moments ago to last?

"Yes, you. You are qualified, are you not?"

"Yes, of course I am qualified," said Phoenix and swallowed.

"Good. Julio and Alex will forward their findings to you and to the case database. I expect daily progress reports. Also, pick yourself an assistant from one of the new junior agents."

Julio and Alex kept staring at Phoenix, then exchanging a glance of bewilderment, then turning back to her. The director slowly leaned back on her seat with her eyes still boring into Phoenix's. Despite her skills and abilities, Phoenix hadn't struck her as the kind to handle such pressure so far, and she definitely wouldn't have been her first choice as lead for this crucial case. Nevertheless, the order had come from the very top, and she hadn't been given any explanations.

Phoenix made a conscious effort to shut her gaping mouth. Having arrived only a week ago, she knew she hadn't done anything to merit this. She groped for a reason why the director would give her the lead in such a critical and ground-breaking assignment. Perhaps she didn't trust the other two? What other reason could there be?

"You can ask Julio's opinion regarding picking an assistant, if you wish," said the director, with a spark in her eye. "He seems to be quite familiar with the new juniors already."

Phoenix turned her attention to Julio. He was a tall Central American with cropped dark hair and cruel black eyes who carried himself with an air of pride and confidence. She could have even considered him cute, if it weren't for his obnoxious attitude. She had no idea why he insisted on acting like a prize jerk and picking on her at every encounter. *Perhaps this is his way of flirting*, she thought. He attempted to give Phoenix an intimidating look, which she in turn attempted to ignore.

"I will do my own research for an assistant, thank you."

"Suit yourself," shrugged the director. "This case is top priority, overriding any other assignment you may have now or in the future. Yet you are still to conduct your maiden security interview after the graduation ceremony today. No point in a last-minute cancellation that would raise questions."

"I understand, Director."

"A few leads regarding the case have been forwarded to your PA already, provided that you can locate it, that is. And in case you don't realize, you have to find it before the graduation ceremony. Your loophole tricks will not work with the expert scanners between our offices and the academy grounds. And don't even think about ditching the ceremony, understand? Your presence was requested by the head of the academy herself, for heaven knows what reason."

"I know, Director Morssen. It's just, I couldn't find it on my desk after I came back from the bathroom."

"And do you have any idea where it might be?"

"Somewhere in the second-floor hallway, I think."

Phoenix spotted a smirk on Julio's face, then noticed Alex's relaxed smile. They couldn't be the ones who nicked her PA, could they?

"That's very likely to be the case," said the director. "I guess you already know about *Ray*."

Julio and Alex snorted with laughter. Could this director with no sense of humor be a part of a practical joke?

"Ray?"

"As in academy student Raimondas Vasilouskas."

"Also known as Crazy Ray," said Julio with a renewed chuckle. Alex joined in.

"Enough," said the director.

"I'm not familiar with a Raimondas Vasilouskas."

"Evidently he decided to become familiar with you. Ray is one of our not-so-bright students. He does janitorial work on our side of the building and has access to most rooms. He's harmless, but he has a fixation on PAs. He believes that they're injurious, and no matter what we tell him to reassure him or how much we threaten him with punishment, he insists on displacing them on random occasions."

"I see," said Phoenix, not seeing at all.

"I sometimes wonder why we've been tolerating him all this time." An expression of almost sorrow flitted across the director's face, as she stared down. "He should be somewhere deep on the second floor hallway right now, mopping or something. How you could tell the whereabouts of your PA if you didn't know of him?"

"Due to the security loophole that I mentioned."

"And what does this have to do with it? Oh, whatever." The director placed her right hand on her forehead and stared down at the table, shaking her head. During her weeklong tenure, Phoenix had never seen her looking confused before, and from the looks on their faces, the other two hadn't either. After a few seconds of silence, she snapped out of her pensive mood.

"I want all of you to understand that this murder case is extremely important. We cannot let any harm come to one of our citizens, even if he happens to be outside of our borders. We need to bring the murderer to justice and give a message to the whole world, that the Union of the New World Order will pursue any evil wrongdoers, no matter where they hide."

"We won't let you down, Chief. Right, Alex, Nix?"

Phoenix glared at Julio. She didn't like nicknames, especially not from a jerk like him. She indulged in a brief but violent mental image of her boot connecting with his fleshy lips, scattering teeth like confetti, and sending that smirk on a permanent vacation.

"By the way, are we gonna get paid overtime, if we happen to work *late?*"

"Payment for overtime is clearly explained in the company rules. Read the chapter on compensation, before you fill out your next time sheet."

"Don't get me wrong, Chief," said Julio with a grin. "I'll do my best to solve this case."

"Time to get busy, people. Let's go."

At the director's prompting, Phoenix got up and left in hurried steps. Julio watched Alex leave slowly after her, then turned to the director.

"Chief, do you have a minute? I have reservations about our assignments."

"What, you can't handle the sight of a corpse?"

"Sure I can," said Julio with a smirk. "Actually, I'm concerned whether our individual skills will be fully utilized or not. I don't think we'll be getting the best results if Nix is leading this investigation and interviewing the people. It's no secret that her communication skills are a bit *Neanderthal*, Chief."

"And, what would be your proposal?" she said with a smirk of her own.

"I was thinking that I should be leading the investigation and conducting interviews. We can utilize her *oh-so-famous* analysis skills and research experience from the HQ by getting her to dig up facts from databases."

As he fell silent, the director's face suddenly lost all trace of amusement. She took a deep breath, her eyes like a pair of blue lasers.

"Are you questioning my judgment on the matter of giving her the lead?"

"No, of course not," said Julio, a light sheen of sweat bathing his skin.

"Good. And what makes you think exemplary analysis skills are not needed in investigative interviews? You think just because you are adept at small talk, you'll be better than her at criminal investigation interviews? Her recent install-ment with us is irrelevant. She has the best skill set for this, an opinion shared by the corporate. She will lead this investigation, are we clear?"

"Aye, Chief," said Julio and saluted with a grin. "Unless, of course, at some point she demonstrates that she is incapable of dealing with such responsibility and pressure."

"What are you talking about? Do you have any scientific evidence to that effect?

"No, not yet."

"Then quit wasting my time with hypothetical situations. Dismissed."

CHAPTER 2

PHOENIX rushed out of the director's office, pushing the self-diagnosing door. Her inner clock completely sabotaged by lack of sleep, she couldn't even tell what time it was without her PA, only knew that she didn't have much time to find it. She thought about asking for help to find this Crazy Ray, but a rush of pride stopped her. She had been ostracized by the staff of this field office since her arrival a week ago. Nobody came and spoke to her unless they had to, let alone asked how she was settling in.

She exited the elevator at the second floor and started looking for *Crazy Ray*. She had absolutely no idea what he might look like but was somehow sure that she would know him when she saw him. She quickly scanned the main hallways, but Ray was nowhere to be found. After frantically running from hallway to hallway for several minutes, she saw a small figure in the dark, somewhere in the bowels of the building, mopping the floor, a small man with a potbelly, mumbling and mopping, wearing the filthiest uniform that she had ever seen.

"Ray?"

"Phoenix, is that you?" Ray kept on mopping as he spoke.

"You know me?"

"Of course I know you. I know everybody and nobody."

"Huh?"

Suddenly Ray stopped mopping and turned to her. For the briefest of instants, Phoenix thought she saw a bright spark flare in his eyes.

"You know, I know you, Phoenix, but I don't know the *you* inside you," he said in dire seriousness. "I don't even know the *me* inside me."

"The what?"

"Don't call me *me*. Because I am not *in* me," he went on, as if he were reciting poetry. "There is another *me*, inside of me, deep down in me."

Just minutes before the ceremony, she had to focus on the issue at hand. She gently took Ray by both shoulders and looked at him levelly.

"Ray, listen to me. I need to ask you something."

Suddenly Ray straightened up and dropped his mop on the floor, closed his eyes, inhaling deeply, with rattling and whistling sounds emanating from his lungs. "Can you smell them?" he whispered, hairy nostrils flaring.

"Smell what?"

"The stench of a thousand dead bodies."

"What bodies? What are you talking about?" said Phoenix, and flicked a glance over her shoulder.

"Look at the rats; they're all over them," Ray mumbled in apparent agitation. "I have to bury all the dead." He opened his watery, clouded blue eyes and fixed his gaze at one of the old stone walls. "The dead from the riots, they should not be exposed. They need to be protected and covered."

"Ray, listen to me."

"I will call my troops and cover them!"

There was no time for Ray's hallucinations or delusions. "Raimondas Vasilouskas!" she said on a sudden impulse.

Her commanding voice snapped Ray out of his daydream. His entire body quivered for an instant. "I'm Raimondas Vasilouskas, born and raised in the Baltics, achieved the rank of general at the tender age of thirty-five," he gabbled in a high-pitched voice. "But now look at me. I'm a thousand years old and still a student at this rotten academy. But I'm certain that I will pass all of them this year."

"Pass what? Are you talking about your classes at the academy?" Phoenix's heart sank at another abrupt switch of topic.

"Yes, I will pass all my classes and meet you at the security interview."

She needed to reach him somehow, and as fast as possible. It was just a matter of finding the conversational key that would open the lock to his...sanity? Short-term memory?

"You have to exercise and study a lot before the security interview, you know," was all that she could think of.

"I know," nodded Ray.

Phoenix's heart leapt at his apparently sane response. But Ray's gaze slowly slid away from her and back into the invisible dimension he seemed to inhabit. She took a deep breath and gently squeezed Ray's shoulders, in an attempt to grab his focus back. If that didn't work, she had a sudden wild vision of tearing off her uniform and dancing.

"Speaking of interviews, I have to attend this graduation ceremony," she said slowly as if speaking to a child. "And I need my PA in order to attend, just like I'd need it to make an interview. If you want to be interviewed by me, I would need my PA to enable the expert computers in there. Do you understand what I'm talking about, Ray?"

"Huh? Of course I do. The hardware-driven secure handshake interface at the expert systems has to be enabled by the PAs, blah, blah, blah."

She froze at the fluent lucidity of the answer. It was as if his consciousness were joyriding through different sections of his short—and long—term memory, just like zapping Holovision channels.

"Where did you learn this? How do you know?"

"I know nothing," he said, chin down. "I'm just an apprentice, stuck between these borrowed first and last breaths that I was given, drinking the water of life, and chasing the fire of knowledge, and waiting to mingle with my eternal and faithful love, earth. What do you know?"

Totally calm and collected now, he looked directly at Phoenix and waited for an answer. If it hadn't been for his potbelly, unshaven sagging face, unspeakable hair, and his disgusting uniform, one could easily confuse him with one of those new age gurus.

"I know that my PA was on my desk, and now it is gone," she said with a forced smile. "And I'm sure that whoever took my PA could get into a lot of trouble. But I'm willing to let this incident go, as long as I can find it."

"Huh, so, you know less nothing than I do," said Ray and shrugged.

"You mean, you know more of nothing than me?"

"No, I mean you know less nothing than me."

"Does my knowing less of nothing prevent me from finding my PA?"

Ray gave a radiant smile. He was in dire need of dental attention, too. "I knew you were smart. That's why I took your PA. You don't need it."

Phoenix heaved a sigh of relief at this indication of progress.

"But I do need it to take part in that ceremony and make a security interview, remember? You want me to give you an interview, don't you?"

"Yes."

"Then I need my PA."

"No, you don't," said Ray, shaking his head irritably. "You don't need your PA or any other gadget to give me an interview."

"Why do you think the PAs are injurious?"

"Because they kill feelings."

She had had heard of this notion before, that electronic communications were supposed to be destroying interpersonal feelings and relations. Could he really be practicing some new age religion?

"Even if they do, why would I care?" she said, in a sudden spurt of honesty. "It's not like I'll ever have anyone to share them with or possess the depth."

His eyes softened with unexpected compassion as he whispered.

"It will come, and your world will change."

"It just isn't fair, man," said Julio, shaking his head. He folded his arms in deep thought and sat across from Alex in his office, with too much stuff on his mind for small talk. Alex kept working on his network node, humming some discordant tune in a deep rumble. He punched in a few rapid keystrokes before pushing back his chair.

"I beg your pardon, what is not fair?"

"Us, being sidelined by Big Bad D for this murder case, while our Virgin Kitten, who can't even put two words together, is in the driving seat and running the show."

Alex nodded sympathetically, as if he could tell that Julio was very frustrated with something. It would take him a few seconds to respond, as always happened when someone used several idioms in one sentence. He blinked rapidly several times and appeared to be exerting a lot of energy and attention in order to decipher what Julio was talking about. Following a few moments of silence, his face lit up with a smile.

"You're upset about Director Morssen for picking Phoenix as the lead."

"Damn right I am! You know you should have been the lead in this case, don't you?"

"I could have been the lead, I know. But I'm sure our executives know what they're doing. And where did you get the idea that Phoenix is a virgin?"

"Alex, I don't get you sometimes. You're the most senior guy here, and you have this wealth of experience about all kinds of cases, even as a policeman in that old Hungarian nation state of yours, but you always seem to focus on the wrong issues and have no drive whatsoever. Greed is good and greed works, dude. You wanna be stuck here all your life or something?"

"Well, I'm sure it works for you, my young friend. But I'm just an old-fashioned modern man. I'm used to the work here; I like the people, responsibilities. I hate the building, but—"

"Suit yourself," shrugged Julio. "If I were you, I'd be all over Chief to grab this case back from the kitten."

"Hey, don't be so hard on Phoenix. I like her. I'm sure she will do a great job. Don't you like her? I don't know why you joke so much with her."

"I like her just fine, Alex, just fine. And I bet that she's horny as hell right now. It won't be long until she pays a visit to my pleasure chamber to learn her life's lesson in carnal arts."

"Oooo, you do like her," said Alex with a broad smile.

"Hey, I'm a guy. You think I wouldn't notice that voluptuous body of hers? I bet our quiet little kitten turns into a tiger in bed. But you know what? She's not as smart as they think she is."

"What are you talking about? Her IQ is well above the ninety-fifth percentile, and higher than yours or mine. She is obviously smarter than us."

"We both know that IQ is not everything, ol' buddy," said Julio with a smirk. "She lacks something, and she lacks something crucial: She's a lone Neanderthal she-wolf with no postmodern survival skill set. I know for sure that she is going to screw up this murder case. Actually, I'm counting on it."

"What do you mean you are counting on it?" Alex didn't look so comfortable in his chair anymore.

"What I mean is that her failure will be to our benefit, both of ours. I'm sure you and I can easily put the case together for Chief, once she screws up. Besides, you were the acting director here before Chief Big Bad D arrived. If her pick to lead this huge case screws up, I'm sure she'll feel a lot of heat from above. Who knows, maybe you'll find yourself in the director chair once again, huh, Chief Alex Lubosh?"

"I don't want that chair again," said Alex and looked down. "Too many responsibilities for my taste."

"No offense, but you and the kitten suffer from the same disease. But you know what? You're a lucky guy to have me as a buddy. And if they were to fire Chief D and place you in the top seat, I'll help you, pal. If you don't want to deal with the pressures of the chair, you can always delegate all you want to me."

"Thank you for your offer of support, Julio. You are a good friend."

"For you, I'll do anything, man," said Julio, smiling. "Just give me a hand to climb up fast, and I'll drag you with me."

Alex checked his wristwatch and rose from his seat.

"Time to attend the ceremony."

"Wonder if the kitten will manage to find her PA," said Julio and rose from his seat. "Did the ol' wacko ever nick yours?"

"No, never. And he's been around for a long time, you know, even longer than me. How about you?"

"Well, I scared him off pretty well once, when I caught him lurking around my office. I wouldn't think he'd dare."

"Not sure about that. He did it with the director's PA several times, and her scare tactics never seemed to work."

"Well, maybe being half a meter taller than her made the difference," said Julio, as he straightened out his uniform.

"Or perhaps you aren't on his target list. I sometimes wonder how he picks his victims."

As Phoenix struggled to understand how and why these last words touched something deep within, Ray returned to his former indifference, looked down at the floor, picked up his mop, turned back, and resumed his mopping.

"You don't need your PA. You don't need any gadgets. I have to work," he added over his shoulder.

She looked helplessly after him, then words spilled out of her mouth without any conscious thought process. "Do you know where my PA is, Ray?"

"Yes."

Phoenix leaped and caught up with him in a fraction of a second. "Could you tell me where it is?" she almost whispered.

"Over there," he said and pointed with his mop, grayish water dribbling from its fibers. She marched to the dark corner of the hallway and almost wept when she saw the faint green blink of the tiny device on the ground. She picked it up and attached the teaspoon-shaped device over her right ear, its long end pointing forward. "PA: Activate."

The PA made the usual acknowledgement chime and turned on. Along with it a gargantuan load of dread floated up and off her shoulders.

"Display main menu." A beam of light appeared from the tip of the device and projected a hologram with the main menu. She quickly browsed through the menus by pupil movement and blinks. "Display new messages." The communications menu displayed Director Morssen's level five meeting invite and the murder victim Bogdanov's census information. Her PA appeared to be fully functional. "Menus off." The hologram disappeared.

She turned and looked at Ray, who was still mopping the same spot, mumbling a song in a forgotten language. All she had to do had been to ask him a direct question. Yet because of the misconception induced to her, she had lost a lot of time with his strange talk. Still, there was something uniquely special about him, something she couldn't put her finger on yet. She should have been feeling furious with him, yet she could not help but feel sympathy.

"Why did you take my PA and chuck it into that corner, Ray?"

Ray stopped mopping and turned to her. "I told you," he said, rolling his tired blue eyes. "Because you don't need it. You don't need it for your meetings, you don't need it for your interviews, you don't need it for nothing."

"But I do need my PA, and not only for the meetings and interviews. I need it for calls, receiving mails, accessing the Internet, shopping, eating, making payments, and even for watching my subscription-based Holovision shows."

"You know nothing. How can you know what you need and what you don't?"

"It may appear that I know nothing to you. But I know what I need and what I don't."

"You only know what others, who also know nothing, say you need or don't need," he said with an air of faint scorn.

"All right then, I don't need a PA. How about you? Do you need a PA?"

"No."

"How do you know that you don't need a PA? You know nothing."

"Having a PA will not make me a better me or a wiser me."

"How can you say that? Think of the wealth of data that you can access and organize by using a PA. The entire world's knowledge and information can be accessed literally in the blink of an eye. Don't tell me you're one of those techno skeptics."

"Can the PA tell me who I am?"

"Of course it can. Moreover, PAs contain every personal detail the owner would ever need."

"That's not *who* I am," said Ray, shaking his head. "That's *what* I am, according to criteria set by those who know *nothing*. It merely describes certain aspects of a material form which people of limited perception assume is me. And I don't need a PA to know all that."

"But, Ray, you don't understand."

"No! You don't understand, because you know less nothing than me."

The dialogue was becoming interesting in a strange and unexpected way, but time was running out. "You're right, I don't understand, and I give up. By the way, I suggest you graduate soon, because they might be introducing a maximum age to become a citizen."

Ray continued mopping with a sly grin. "That doesn't matter. This rotten academy can never get rid of me."

"And why's that?"

He dropped his mop again and turned to Phoenix.

"Because *I* am an exception," he said, folding his arms in dire seriousness. "Because I have a big army."

"A what?"

Ray, as he picked his mop back up and slowly moved away towards the depths of the vast hallway, mumbled, "The armies of the mighty general took the enemy by surprise. They opened fire from every direction, slaughtering them within hours. It was a great victory for the general. His fame would endure forever."

Phoenix shook her head as she watched him with a mixture of pity and awe. She couldn't decide whether he was a total nut or if his craziness fluctuated, alternating with some wisdom and intelligence still behind those weary blue eyes.

The loud buzz from the PA irked her. The ceremony had just started. She took a deep breath and took off towards the elevator.

CHAPTER 3

PHOENIX rushed through the main gate that separated the GPSN Field Office grounds from the immigration academy, attracting the attention of the students around, who gave her reluctant yet curious stares. As she was about to enter the auditorium, she got pushed from behind by a short, fat, bald student.

"Hey, watch it!"

The student didn't say anything but hurried to take his seat in the middle of the stalls, stepping on plenty of toes in the process. The auditorium was spacious and appeared to be equipped with cutting-edge Holo-projectors and spherical sound. The stalls before her were already filled with students and faculty. The peace agents were seated on a slightly higher ledge on the right side, at seats perpendicular to the stage.

"And let's give a warm welcome to the distinguished guests of the day," the announcer said.

A group of seven entered from the back and quietly walked to the seven armchairs designated for them at the back of the stage, while receiving a standing ovation from everyone. She quickly walked to her designated seat while they drew all the attention.

"Now please give a warm welcome to the host of the event: Adrianopolis Immigration Academy Headperson Ingrid Valkoinen."

Valkoinen was a tall lean woman with slightly protruding blue eyes and high cheekbones, and her long blond hair hung in a single braid. She swiftly walked up to the podium and spoke in an incongruously squeaky voice.

"Distinguished guests, academy professors, and students: Welcome to the Adrianopolis Immigration Academy's winter quarter graduation ceremony. I'm proud to announce that today we are graduating 253 illustrious students, whose accumulated grade-point averages rate in the top 10 percent among immigration academies throughout the world." A roar of applause echoed in the auditorium as she announced her statistic with a beaming smile.

"Not only do we impress the world with our intelligence, but also with the integrity of our graduates. The last time a graduate of this academy was struck out in a security interview was 192 days ago. And I'm proud to announce that we lead the *whole world* in this category!"

The students jumped to their feet to applaud, cheer, and give each other high-fives. "The academy in Hong Kong had a strike-out early this morning, leaving the world lead to us."

It was a great accomplishment to graduate here today, earning the right to live in the World Union, a dream come true for these people, perhaps except for that fat bald student, who just sat there with folded arms. Way too cool to respond in the same manner as everyone else, or just bored? If that was the case, what was the rush for?

"Now, I would like to invite Global Peace and Security Network Corporation Field Office Director Dagmar Morssen to the podium."

Phoenix's boss rose from her seat in the front row and walked to the podium in her formal brown garb, as the audience lightly applauded. The auditorium dimmed, leaving just a single spotlight trained on her, which revealed the fact that the woman wore no makeup and actually had a very pretty face, hidden behind the severity and grimness of her expression. Phoenix felt envious thinking how much makeup she had to put on every morning these days, just to appear one notch above a corpse. After nodding at the guests of honor, she spoke in a booming voice that nobody would expect from a woman her size.

"We know how hard you've worked to become one of us. We know how hard you've tried to shed your old habits, your old worldviews, in order to be a citizen of the New World Order. All of you here have succeeded. And now I'd like to welcome you to the land of the free, where healthy, wealthy, happy people contribute to the civilization under the protection of the rules of capitalism, laws of science, and rights of universal suffrage."

As Director Morssen rambled on about the achievements of the World Union in a grim enthusiasm, the guests of honor behind her watched the ceremony with interest, except for the flamboyant one in a fire-engine-red tunic and a red fez on the last seat, who kept checking his nails and appeared even more uninterested than the bald student. With his thick gray hair, thin pressed lips, ice-blue eyes, and an Arrivee tattoo in the middle of his high forehead, the guest of honor in the center was Osmund Hamilton, Phoenix's and Director Morssen's big boss. Phoenix didn't know the other six seated to the right and left of Hamilton, but according to convention, they must have been the six with the highest HDIs in the city, following Hamilton, representing the seven Supreme Selfs, the founders of and the most powerful people in the World Union.

"Let me warn you, however, that the danger is not over. There'll always be those altruists who will attempt to break you. There'll be those who'll try to sneak into our glorious New World Order and try to undo our system. For that, we have our rigorous security interviews: One final interview to show us the transformation you went through and what you had become." Director Morssen raised her left arm and motioned to Phoenix and her fellow agents. "And now, we expect all of you to meet with our peace agents, who are to conduct the security interviews and are specially trained to eliminate any infiltrators among you."

Rising with the others, Phoenix tried to block out the crowds around her and focus on the case file that she had studied over the weekend for her first-ever security interview. The man she was supposed to interview had to be in the auditorium somewhere.

After introducing Phoenix and others, Director Morssen left the stage, and Headperson Valkoinen took the podium once again. "And now, speaking on behalf of the graduates, this quarter's Most Valuable Student: I give you Raj Patel."

Phoenix just stared as Patel walked by, right in front of her. The nervousness and intimidation that had plagued her all weekend invaded her mind all over again, igniting the ball of tension, burning her ears. The heat spread to her cheeks, and she wondered if her hi-tech cosmetics were managing to conceal the flush. Whose idea it was to match this guy up with a first-time security interviewer like herself?

"Raj Patel finished his classes in the academy with top grades and earned an interim HDI of seventy-seven," Valkoinen said. "Raj also possesses an IQ of 164."

Patel climbed up onto the stage, politely bowed to Hamilton and the other six, then turned to the audience. He had a large forehead, combed-back jet-black hair, short goatee, and small determined eyes.

"All right, so we all know that the planet we call home is not the ideal place to be for many of us. Tell me, who wouldn't wanna laze in a warm sandy beach in an island off the maps in the South Pacific? But it's not a place for suffering where we are all doomed for destruction as the so-called Great Religions and the nation states made us believe, either. The truth is, most of us will need to work all our lives and will never make it to that island, but why should the *tragedy* prophesized by them be everyone's fate? I was a slave in that *rogue* nation state of mine, just like you. And what a calculated and sinister kind of slavery it was, as I was made to work purely at the mercy of others' needs. The only way to preserve my sanity was to establish a new life where I could freely utilize my skills and prosper. And since that first moment when I laid my eyes on the ten articles of the Supreme Bill of Rights, I've been patiently working towards this moment."

Patel was forty-nine and had been way more patient than most about immigrating to the World Union. With his credentials, he could have easily applied to an immigration academy at least a decade earlier. The graduates listened to their champion with indifference; some of them even appeared a little hostile or contemptuous. Envy, perhaps? The fat bald student, on the other hand, kept looking up and around, huffing and puffing, scratching his bald head. Suddenly he noticed Phoenix's curious stare, produced a huge Cheshire grin, and started waving at her. Phoenix sank in her seat and turned her head towards Patel, pretended to listen to him, only to be hit by Julio's smirk from two seats down. She gave him what she hoped was an icy glare.

"And you have to do what you have to do under those atrocious conditions in order to keep your sanity and survive it all, right? And that's what I exactly did: I resisted, I broke their laws, and I even murdered."

Most immigrants' stories were similar. They were either perpetrators or victims of the most hideous crimes, and sometimes both. As Patel gloated about how he had survived the riots as if he were the only one in the audience to have done so, Phoenix's level of energy was steadily declining and the exhaustion from all those sleepless nights was slowly settling in. She cursed her luck that she had to face this pompous ass so soon, making a mental note to overdose on sugar and caffeine beforehand.

"I'd like to thank our very distinguished guests behind me for honoring us here, Headperson Valkoinen for giving me this opportunity to express my deepest thoughts and feelings today. I especially would like to thank my fellow academy students for putting up with me all these months." Patel grinned with his last remark. But the audience didn't seem to be amused at all. "And as for the senior agents here, I can't say that I'm too enthusiastic about meeting them for my security interview. Then again, who is to say that they are enthusiastic about meeting me?" He turned and gestured with his arm towards Phoenix. "Isn't that right, Agent Wallis?"

An auditorium full of people sniggered and swiveled their heads in her direction. It seemed like Patel had finally said something to grab their sympathy at her expense. She cringed as she sensed the full attention of everyone on her, feeling completely naked.

"Senior Agent Phoenix Wallis, ladies and gentlemen. Agent Wallis started at the field office only a week ago, and she will be my interviewer today, in her first-ever interview. A warm welcome to you, Agent Wallis, from the students of Adrianopolis Immigration Academy." Patel started clapping, and the rest of the students joined him. His small dark eyes were fixed on hers, and the expression in his face was that of a superior, rather than that of a non-resident alien, his citizenship in her hands.

Phoenix found herself rising and bowing her head in response to the applause, then collapsed back into her seat, her focus totally shattered by Patel's public ridicule, only to realize that the ceremony had ended when Hamilton and the other six quickly disappeared backstage. The students were already moving out from the main entrance, while an instrumental version of John Lennon's "Imagine" played in the background.

Director Morssen walked through the main gate, thinking of the workload of the upcoming week. Security interview time had always been pressure time for her, simply because there would be so much at stake if errors were made. Some students were still foolish enough to lie and hide certain details of their past, despite the fact that almost all of their wrongdoings in their rogue state pasts would be absolved. The academy staff was responsible for eradicating the habit, and many were trained as deception experts in order to catch lying students and isolate them from harming others as early as possible.

But the problem here wasn't about the theory but about the practice. Headperson Valkoinen's approach to security matters had been far from cooperative, resisting her suggestions regarding security apparatuses on the academy grounds on every opportunity. Valkoinen had also resisted an internal investigation of the academy staff when the director had been conducting a crackdown on the corruption scandal in the field office when she was first installed three years previously.

The other major concern she had was the quality of her own staff. The circulation was very high, especially among the senior agents, most of whom would leave the field office within a year or two from arrival. The current shortage of staff was so severe, she'd had to hire her most recent senior agent in such a rush that there wasn't even time for a face-to-face interview. Now that agent had to face the champion of the academy in her first-ever interview, destined to have a very hard time. She wouldn't have chosen such a match-up, but it was not up to her: The academy bureaucracy decided who was to be interviewed by whom.

She entered her office full of these thoughts, only to be rudely awakened by the presence of someone sitting at her desk, in her *chair*. With his back turned, it was hard to tell who it was, as the lights were dimmed. She could only think of one person who could be so presumptuous. "Ray, get off my chair, now! How many times have I told you not to do that? Get out of my office!"

The chair swiveled as the lights came on. It wasn't the old Ray sitting at her desk. It was someone from the exact opposite end of the social spectrum.

"And another big welcome to our new Senior Agent Wallis, from her fellow agents. We're *so happy* that you're here, Nix. Aren't we, guys?" said Julio, as the agents took their time walking back to their part of the building. A few young female agents giggled, giving Phoenix runaway glances.

"Hey, c'mon, be nice, Julio," said Alex, patting Julio's back.

"All right, all right, whatever. But tell me, how come she gets to be the one interviewing the Most Valuable Student? She just got here, you know. Hey, could it be because she's still a *virgin?*"

Phoenix barely managed to rein in her anger and swallowed the first three crude retorts that had instantly come to mind. The young female agents sniggered again and turned to Phoenix in anticipation.

"Julio, that is such a rude and insulting thing to say," said Alex. "I'm sure, as a healthy young girl—I mean woman—Phoenix here is not a virgin."

Laughter erupted among the peace agents, as Phoenix felt more humiliated and ridiculed than she could remember feeling since.

"I didn't mean it like that, ol' buddy," said a chuckling Julio to a puzzled Alex. "What I meant to say is that, it's going to be Phoenix's first time. Interviewing a student, that is."

Alex shot Phoenix a sheepish and apologetic look. "Uh, I see."

Phoenix suddenly felt acutely claustrophobic and took off.

"How are you, Dagmar?"

The director just stared at her "big boss," Osmund Hamilton. How could he have beaten her to her office after disappearing backstage right after the ceremony? She had heard that these walls had many secret passages and alleyways, but there was no way Hamilton would know about them. Or was there? The man prided himself on knowing everything there was to know. It wouldn't be a surprise if Hamilton knew every corner of this building better than she and her staff.

As she stood there frozen, the director realized how little she knew about him. Hamilton was a man of legendary work ethic, and he guarded his privacy fiercely. Nobody exactly knew how old he was, and he never allowed his picture to be taken, let alone published anywhere. There was very limited information about his past and his origins in Hong Kong, none of which was available to the public. He was a tall, fit, broad-shouldered man with a chiseled face and graying hair, and he radiated a distinct air of confidence and command. His brilliant blue eyes often seemed to be scanning some invisible horizon, which was a relief as nobody wanted the twin laser beams of his glare piercing their frontal lobe.

"I apologize, sir, for mixing you up with—"

"Old Ray? Is he still at the academy?" said Hamilton in a soft whisper, with a rare soft expression on his face. He could even be smiling.

The director stood stiffly, afraid to move, and had no idea what to expect, as Hamilton had never made any visit to her office before. Something serious must have happened, and she had no clue as to what it could be.

"Yes, he is, sir. I think perhaps it's time that we—"

"Oh, just let poor Ray be," said Hamilton, in an unexpectedly playful mood. "I wanted to chat with you about the case."

His face suddenly changed, and his whisper got even fainter, while the clueless director just stood there. Could some new intel have been relayed from the Psychological Warfare Unit, the most secret and feared of all GPSN branches, only to Hamilton? On the other hand, there were his personal spies, a network of informants working strictly for him alone. Nobody exactly knew how he found them or communicated with them, but everyone knew that Hamilton was using his personal spies to keep his GPSN staff and their performances in check, among other things. "More developments, sir?"

"Yes. It's come to my attention that this citizen of ours was executed by the Russian mafia."

"Executed? Why would anyone execute a businessman or a Non-Governmental Organization volunteer from the World Union? Neither the Russian bureaucracy nor their mafia would want to provoke us with such an act."

"You're assuming too much, Dagmar. This was no ordinary killing, but one with a message. I have reason to believe that it was related to the NC Research Triangle hacking incident three months ago."

Hamilton was referring to the incident where a group of terrorist hackers had infiltrated one of the most secure research facilities in the World Union. The facility was located in North America, but nobody knew where the hackers had originated from or how they had managed to gain access to this fortress of science and technology. GPSN and the Science and Technology Foundation, owner of the research facility, had agreed not to reveal the hacking incident to the public, as there was no clear evidence of outside tampering or information theft, or at least so claimed the Science and Tech bunch. Hamilton had other views about this incident.

"Based on what information, sir?"

"Based on my spies in the Russian mafia, who else? Now, look: We need to investigate this murder, but very carefully, not revealing anything to the public until I decide how to PR and market it. I'm at a very critical point in one of my projects, and I need the attention of the masses exactly where I want it. I cannot afford public interest to be diverted by such an incident. There's no point just wishing it would go away, but perhaps we can use it to our advantage. I have to think. Are we on the same page about this, Dagmar?"

"Yes, sir, we are."

"Good. Now, tell me, why do I get the feeling that you're not comfortable with my choice of lead for this murder?"

"Well, Senior Agent Wallis just got here, and I have several other excellent and experienced senior agents who could investigate this matter. She has an excellent record in analysis, but her social appearance and confidence has not impressed me yet. You saw how she reacted to that student—"

"You know I don't care about social appearances," said Hamilton, his voice a sepulchral whisper. "And being in the lead should boost her confidence."

"But, sir—"

"There's still a mole in your organization, whether you admit to it or not, and I will not risk tainting this investigation," hissed Hamilton.

The director swallowed at the accusation. Despite the investigation she carried out three years previously, GPSN's Internal Affairs sources still reported that the terrorist known as the Mantis was still active in her field office. Whether this was the original infiltrator or one that was replaced during the infusion of new staff was unknown.

"Sir, I assure you that we have no infiltration, the Mantis or anyone else."

Hamilton got up and walked to the director with easy steps.

"You cannot assure me of anything you don't know," he whispered, face to face. "As far as I'm concerned, that new girl is the only one with no risk. She appears to be an introvert, she's new, and she'll act cagey, avoiding an untimely information leak, unlike the gossipy bunch you have."

"But, sir, this may be too much for a newly promoted senior agent to handle."

"Is that really concern for her, or for you, should she fail?"

"A bit of both, sir," said the director and avoided his gaze.

"Then you need to make sure she doesn't slip up prematurely, now, don't you? Who knows, she might end up surprising us all. So long, Dagmar."

He disappeared through the door, and it took Director Morssen a few seconds to relax and take her seat. She didn't particularly like Hamilton's choice of lead, but deep down she knew that he was right about the infiltration into her organization. There were just too many security breaches, hackings, and illegal accesses happening on the premises, and her technical staff lacked the expertise to cope with them. She had had several expert teams investigate these incidents, but all traces had led to dead ends. Nothing important was ever accessed or stolen, but somebody or something was definitely making their presence felt.

CHAPTER 4

PHOENIX switched on her desk lamp to examine her PA. Despite the abuse it had received from Ray, the device appeared solid and intact. A flashing notice on her network node's screen indicated that her security interview would take place in fifteen minutes. *Great*, she thought. *Another episode of your brilliant career move is about to begin.*

Only two weeks before, she had received that infamous call from her career consultant regarding this amazing opportunity at the Adrianopolis Field Office. There had been such a rush in her installment, she hadn't even been called for an interview, and she was offered a much better salary and plenty of perks for moving to the border town, including free membership to the best gym, free Holovision subscription, free annual metro pass, and that coveted senior peace agent rank. And as the most of important of all the perks, her HDI would improve by one point.

I shouldn't have let Sandra seduce me into this, she thought. *It all looked too good to be true from the very beginning anyway.*

His arrogant overture during the graduation ceremony aside, Patel would be a good addition to the World Union and hopefully an easy interview. The man was ranked number one in the whole academy with all the spotlights on him. If he had had a serious personality flaw, it would have been exposed by now during his months of counseling sessions and personal confession classes under the scrutiny of psychologists and deception experts, whose sole duty was to uncover personality flaws like neurosis and psychosis. Students with such diseases were immediately expelled. It was also doubtful that Patel might have any terrorist intent. The man obviously was so full of greed, he would have no personal interest in harming a system that championed it. Still, none of this helped to get rid of the nauseous feeling.

The interview room didn't come with any windows. A long rectangular table made from dark-brown solid wood and the worn dark-gray stone walls contrasted with the cutting-edge technology cameras, lights, monitors, computers, and gadgets in their bright reds, neon greens, and metallic blues. An overhead spotlight was trained above the simple wooden chair closer to the exit door.

"Agent Wallis, we're at the Viewers' Lounge," said the squeaky voice from speakers. "Outside and to the right, behind the corner." She turned to the long mirror on the wall and nodded.

The lounge was furnished with comfortable seats in the fashion of a small theater. A long window, with several monitors placed to the right, left, and above, exposed the interview room. Headperson Valkoinen, flanked by her two young assistants, welcomed her with a big smile.

"Good morning, Agent Wallis. Nice to meet you. And how are we this morning, a bit nervous, perhaps?"

"Nice to meet you, too, Headperson. I'm all right."

"First time is always difficult, but I'm sure you'll do fine, sweetheart."

"It's a first time for him, too. Don't worry; I can take care of myself, Headperson."

The insecure and shaken senior agent of the graduation ceremony appeared to be showing traces of confidence now. When Patel had wanted to expose his interviewer during his speech, Valkoinen had encouraged him to the idea and had decided to make this newcomer with no security interview experience his victim. It was a perfect match: on one side, there was her champion, a super-smart, arrogant, ruthless, greedy, driven, and fully confident Raj Patel, the best student they had had in years, and on the other there was this introverted, insecure, and totally inexperienced agent, newly promoted to the senior rank after thirteen long years as a junior. Their matchup would be a great example to all students, showing how natural selection worked in the World Union.

Perhaps in other cultures what Patel did would be considered inappropriate behavior, but this was precisely why these cultures were dumped in the trash cans of history. Everyone in the World Union knew that being a citizen had nothing to do with polite manners only. Competition was and had always been a zero-sum game, and if one had to climb the ladder all the way to the top, one could only do it by standing on the shoulders of others. The path to success was paved with the skeletons of rivals.

Valkoinen also expected Patel to nail the interview with a maximum score of one hundred, not only to crush his interviewer, but also to humiliate that rude and disrespectful director of the field office. Since the day of her arrival, Director

Morssen had been a pain in the neck with her air of superiority and her unbending approach to every situation.

"Anyway, so where do most students come from these days?" said Phoenix.

Valkoinen nodded to her right side. "Seventy-one percent of our spring applicants are from the rogue states of Russia and India," recited the assistant on the right, her nasal voice bored. "Another 11 percent come from the Arab League. The Chinese make up a mere 4 percent. The remaining 16 percent are from other rogue territories."

"How come all these Chinese end up in Eastern Europe? Aren't they closer to the floating academies like the Queen Mary or the one in Hong Kong?"

"They sure are," said Valkoinen with a broad smile, giving the *obvious* answer to the *ignorant* question. "However, the Chinese authorities aren't happy with the new ninety-nine-year lease of Hong Kong by the World Union. They do their utmost to isolate the academy there and the ones in the international waters from their own population."

This agent wasn't only inexperienced and insecure, she was also unprepared. There were times when two good and competitive people had to go head to head, where the laws of competition dictated that there would be only one winner. She could feel sympathy for the loser, in a situation like that. But this one was nothing of the sort, and she totally deserved the devastation that was about to befall her.

"Sweet," said Phoenix, with a grimace. "So these poor people have to travel west all the way through uncontrolled Central Asia and Russia?"

"Indeed," said Valkoinen in a singsong voice. "Anyway, Raj is about to arrive."

As Valkoinen dismissed her attempt at small talk with smiles and practiced sympathy, Phoenix felt like an imposter, somebody masquerading as a socialized human being, and once again found herself wondering if social awkwardness was a genetic defect or an incurable disease.

"He's one of those whom I'm proud to refer to as a graduate from *my* academy. Smart, fit, intelligent, greedy, and well groomed. I suppose the poor man was unfortunate to be born beyond our borders and having been denied a chance to prosper under the rule of science and assurance of economic stability. Oh well, that's soon to be remedied, don't you think?"

Valkoinen's self-assurance about her champion and the condescending little smirk at the corner of her mouth made Phoenix only more determined to prove herself to everyone, her face reflecting what she had in mind.

"We run a very tight ship here, sweetheart. Only very few rotten apples manage to sneak into our academy, and we know how to weed them out. We lead the whole world in absence of Strike-Outs now, remember? No need to worry about making any mistakes, especially with Raj."

Phoenix wasn't sure whether she should feel relieved or worried by Valkoinen's misreading of her emotions. This woman was supposed to be a leading deception expert. "Sweet," she said, letting it slip away.

On the other side of the long window, the door of the interview room opened, and Patel walked in with two young junior agents at his side. They helped him to take the chair.

"I should get going. Thank you, Headperson."

"Good luck, sweetheart."

As she exited the Viewers' Lounge, Phoenix ran into Beverly Blackmore, the supervisor of the surveillance systems on the premises. She was of similar height and build to Phoenix, with a milk-white complexion, auburn hair, and curious blue eyes.

"Oh, hi, Beverly."

"Hey, Phoenix. Ready for all this?"

"I think so. So, you're my procedure watchdog?"

"Yeah, you know the drill. Someone's gotta keep the score."

"Who's the watchdog on the academy side?"

"The lady herself," said Beverly, motioning her head towards Valkoinen.

"Any last minute tips for a rookie?"

"Heard that he has a nasty left jab. Don't let him turn you into a punchbag, you hear?"

"I won't," said Phoenix, along with a chuckle, then checked out Beverly's unusual monochrome clothing. "Cool outfit."

"Oh, gimme a break," snorted Beverly. "I know it looks boring as ever, but that's me. Gotta be in black."

"Gotta run, now. Later, then."

"Hey, be brilliant!" said Beverly, with a warm smile. "Make us proud."

"Thanks, I will."

She entered the interview room still smiling and briefly nodded at the junior agents. She took the seat across from Patel and decided to act as if the incident at the graduation ceremony hadn't taken place.

"Hello, Mr. Patel. I'm Senior Peace Agent Phoenix Wallis. I'll be conducting your security interview today."

Patel greeted her with a head nod and played along. "Good to meet you, Agent Wallis."

"Would you like to ask anything about the procedure before we start?"

"I'm well informed about the procedure, thank you."

"Very well, then," said Phoenix. "Agents, please proceed with the setup."

One of the young agents remotely moved a purple cylindrical device resembling a beauty salon hair sculpting machine from the ceiling over Patel, while the other fastened it to the metal arc over the interviewee's chair. The Holo-Projected Testimony Device was a postmodern technological wonder that Phoenix only had seen in confidential GPSN files before. It traced the activity from the brain's frontal cortex and projected it in 3D. Coupled with a speech recognition and comprehension expert system, this state-of-the-art hardware was a very elaborate and expensive lie detection machine.

With all this hi-tech help, it was still no easy task for an interviewer to catch someone lying. The hardware needed reference points, so a security interviewer's first task was to establish baseline behavior patterns for that particular person.

"Computer: Initialize settings for immigration academy student security interview mode. Interviewee: Adrianopolis Immigration Academy student Raj Patel with interim Human Development Index of seventy-seven."

It was strange for a person with such outstanding qualifications to have not joined an academy a decade back. Then again, rogue states were notorious about restricting travel for their citizens with good prospects and education. Patel would certainly qualify for such oppression with his exceptional IQ and medical skills.

"Interviewer: Senior Agent Phoenix Wallis of the Global Peace and Security Network Adrianopolis Field Office, with Human Development Index of seventy-three." Phoenix looked up and saw a tiny condescending smirk on Patel's face, similar to Valkoinen's. The displays in front of her came to life with tens of windows popping up. She could monitor everything in Patel's body now, from his blood pressure and heartbeat to his brain wave patterns. She felt some discomfort looking at the displays, remembering that she had never felt at ease with them during simulations, never knowing when to look at the displays and when to look at the face of the person opposite.

"Computer: Begin recording. Mr. Patel—"

"Dr. Patel, if you please."

"Of course. Dr. Patel, you're here today because you passed all necessary tests required for you to become a World Union citizen."

"Naturally," said Patel, pairing his smirk with an intimidating stare. "I passed all the tests with top grades. I am to become what you call a perfect Union citizen."

"We will see about that. I'm here today to evaluate your citizenship application from a security perspective."

"And I can only assure you that I'm not a crook, Agent Wallis. But you already know that, don't you?"

"I wouldn't use words like *crook*. However, the procedure requires me to evaluate your fitness for our society from a security point of view. All right, then. Can you please tell me about your childhood?"

"You sound like a Freudian psychiatrist," said Patel, as if addressing a child.

Fearing that she might miss something on the instruments before her, Phoenix dropped her eyes to the monitors.

"These questions are for establishing your baseline behavior patterns, Dr. Patel. Freud's ideas have long been outdated, since the studies of Dr. Derek Fischer three decades back. You're a medical doctor. You must know all this."

"But of course I do," said Patel, curling his lip.

"Can we get back to my question, please?"

"But of course. I was one of four siblings of a nuptial union in Calcutta."

"And did your biological parents work?"

"My father worked for the British East India Company, and my mother was a homemaker."

"Wait a minute. That doesn't mean that she was a constructor, right?"

Patel smiled. "Oh, no, no. That's another word for housewife."

"Did you get along well with your siblings?"

"Well, yes and no."

"It's a true or false question, Dr. Patel."

"Being raised in a nuptial partnership with siblings has dynamics of its own. There were times we got along very well, and other times we fought."

"Fought? You mean physical exchanges?"

Phoenix looked up, and her attention immediately shifted to the black wall behind Patel, to the hologram of three boys, dressed in white, pushing and shoving. The background and furniture were crisp and brightly-colored with no shadow—place-holder objects generated by the computer from the fragments of Patel's memories in order to complete the scene. The angry boys were looking up, trying to push the camera. Everything was from Patel's perspective, so the boys must be actually attacking him.

Noticing Phoenix's attention fixed behind, Patel turned. "Yes, those are my biological little brothers," he said with a smile. "Or what I remember of them."

"I do not advise you to watch the visuals of your current thoughts, Dr. Patel. If the feedback affects your mental stability and puts you in a neurotic shock, this interview might be invalidated. You can always watch after the interview, if you wish."

Patel turned back to face Phoenix with a chuckle.

"You ask your questions, and let me worry about my mental stability."

"Very well," said Phoenix and exhaled. "Did you keep contact with your biological brothers?"

"Not really. I have no idea where they ended up after our biological parents died during the riots."

"Why not? Isn't it a part of tradition in the biological family structure to keep contact with the members of the unit?"

"Of course it is. But those poor boys were believers in false hope. They had no idea that hope needs to be earned and is not worthy of every human being. They denied the fact that hope works only for those who deserve it. Humanity was told lies about hope and equality for millennia. But for those who are rational enough to understand it, the truth was never clearer: For some humans, simply, there is no hope. Was this speech good enough for you to evaluate my thoughts on altruism, Agent Wallis?"

"Quite," said Phoenix, without looking up. With his intolerable cockiness, Patel was already penetrating under her skin. "What comes to mind when you think of the World Union?"

"Why, the strongest and most advanced nation on earth, of course," said Patel, with a shrug. "Some even refer to it as the New Atlantis."

Phoenix quickly glanced at the main indicator that showed the overall grade in front of her, as Patel referred to World Union as a *nation*. It showed ninety-nine. She leaned back, somewhat relieved, knowing that if this guy had passed the interview with a hundred, it would have looked pretty bad on her report sheet.

"Dr. Patel, let me remind you that the World Union is not a nation, nor a state. We prefer to not even call it a country."

"Yes, of course," said Patel, with a wince. "It's a free-trade area, with no traditional governing bodies."

"Exactly," said Phoenix, trying to hide a tiny grin.

"That's what I meant," said Patel, with a shrug. "It's sometimes difficult to avoid certain words that you are so accustomed to. Then again, I may have just let it slip, on purpose," he added with a grin of his own.

"What do you mean by that?"

"C'mon," said Patel, his grin widening. "I know that you're a nervous wreck inside, and I know what you want," he said and leaned back in his chair with both hands behind his head, as if he were sunbathing.

"What I want?"

"Sure. It would be such a shame if I were to pass this interview with a perfect score. A shame on your part, of course, since the last perfect score in this academy was back three years ago, before that famous crackdown. So, being the gentleman that I am and as an extension of my warm welcome earlier, I decided to let it slip. I trust the indicator before you shows ninety-nine now?"

She exerted a great effort to retain a straight face and closed her eyes, as a rush of anger swept thought her entire body. She couldn't see the faces of the two young agents in the room from where she was seated, nor could she see anyone in the Viewers' Lounge. But it wasn't them she was trying to hide the anger in her eyes from. It was the conceited man sitting across from him. She wanted so badly to make him fail.

"Oh, don't you worry about me," he added in mock innocence. "I'll be fine, still a long way from that minimum passing grade of seventy."

On the other hand, some of the things that Patel said and did were in conflict with the profile she had read. Something didn't add up. She couldn't pinpoint anything yet, but she had to move on, with the thought lingering in her mind. "What's the first thing you plan to do in the Union, if you pass this interview?"

"Well, actually, as a cardiologist my career is pretty much set," said Patel, checking his nails. "Many headhunters have already contacted me in the last few months, and several good hospitals are awaiting my final decision. My financial advisor indicated that I could raise my HDI to eighty by the end of the fourth quarter of this year."

"Provided that you pass this interview."

Patel leaned forward in order to evade the strong light above and fixed his intense brown eyes on her green-gray ones with a wide grin. "You know that I will, Agent Wallis," he said in a whisper. "I studied this procedure and know all about it, right down to the tiniest detail. Nothing is up to you, you know. The expert system computers calculate according to my responses and reactions, and there isn't much you can do about it. You can feel whatever you want about me, yet you cannot make me fail."

"You seem to forget that you have to respond to my questions, Dr. Patel," said Phoenix, clenching her fist.

"Do you honestly believe that you can challenge me intellectually?"

The sharp pain at her palm—her nails piercing her skin—snapped Phoenix out of the heat of anger. She needed to do something, before Patel turned the entire procedure into a personality and IQ contest. The niggling sensation about the conflict between Patel's actions and personality profile was gaining weight by the second. Something was terribly wrong with the whole picture, but she could not figure out what it was just yet, with the pressure from Patel's words and actions jamming her thought process. She swallowed while thinking what to do. It wasn't like she could just walk out of the room. All she could do was either cave in, or accept the challenge. She looked directly into Patel's small eyes and whispered.

"We shall see."

Patel smiled and leaned back in his chair. She started firing rapid questions in an attempt to complete the baseline behavior patterns.

"Is keeping fit important to you?"

"Sure it is. Fitness increases life expectancy by at least fifteen years. Who wouldn't want to live longer?"

"Staying fit can be a difficult task, and our insurance companies have quite high fitness and healthy living standards here."

"Just look at me," he said, pointing to himself. "I have a pretty good body for my age, no? Can you honestly say that I don't possess enough desire and determination?"

"That's beside the point, sir. Anyway, moving on to your education here at the academy. What was the best part of the academy for you?"

"Why, the classes I took, of course."

"Which ones, in particular?"

"Almost all of them," he said, raising his arms. "I love intellectual challenges. I was ranked at the top of every class I took."

"How about the instructors?"

"I'd say that they were all good educators. I like dealing with competent professionals. How about you?"

Determined not to lose time and control of the procedure again, Phoenix tried to ignore his remarks. Just a few more baseline questions.

"What was the worst thing about the academy?"

"The accommodations, naturally. I can't really say that I had enough space for myself."

Phoenix quickly glanced at the hologram of the room with a couple of students in it.

"How about your roommates?"

"They were all right," he said, with a shrug. "The other thing that I didn't like in the academy was that I couldn't choose my own study group."

"You didn't like them?"

"I liked them fine. It's just that they would waste my time catching up on certain assignments."

One of the indicators started blinking, and Phoenix let out a sigh of relief. Patel's baseline behavior patterns were calculated, and the compulsory part of the security interview was over. Now she had the option to conclude the proceedings any time she wished. She thought about ending it for a moment then all the belittling and humiliation flashed through her mind. No, she wasn't going to make this easy for Patel.

"Dr. Patel, how did you decide to immigrate to the World Union?"

"Are you aware of the living conditions in the rogue states?" Patel's voice had lost its amused tone, turning much more serious.

"Yes, I am very much aware."

"Isn't this question kind of pointless, then?"

Phoenix smiled, as Patel slipped up for the first time since the beginning of the interview. "Not really. I was asking you *how* you decided, not *why*, referring to all the negative propaganda rogue state sources constantly create about us here."

"Well, of course those rogue state governments hate to see people like me immigrate," said Patel, looking away. "So they're doing all they can to retain the cream of their workforce. But people know better. And no matter how oppressive they are, those rogue governments cannot prohibit all media about the lifestyle in the Union, you know."

"Were you ever engaged in a nuptial agreement?"

"Oh, yes," he nodded, with a smile.

"Tell me about it, please."

"I was twenty, she was sixteen, and it was decided by our biological families that her biology should join mine to procreate, in the hunter-gatherer style."

The hologram of a ceremony appeared before the back wall, with a very young girl in a heavily ornamented red gown at the center and crowds sitting at surrounding tables. Some people appeared to be dancing; it was hard to tell because by default visuals didn't come with any sound.

"Your biological parents felt that they had a right to decide about your future with a particular person. Based on what information?"

"Ancient tribal traditions, what else. Their thought mechanisms are purely instinctual and very hard to eradicate."

"Do you think instincts have no scientific merit?"

"Sure they don't. It's not like we can analyze or understand our instincts. Are you insinuating that you can?"

"Certainly not. Please tell me about the riot that you took part in."

She had saved the best for last. If there was any possibility of something being wrong about Patel's story, it had to be somehow connected to this riot that he took part in decades ago.

"Oh, yes," he said, chin down. "The most shameful experience of my life." The visuals switched to mobs in the streets at night with burning houses in the background.

"Why did you do it?"

"I was young, and it was mass hysteria," he said with a tired voice. "Science still cannot explain the dynamics of such an act."

"Did you kill anyone?"

"You know that I did," he said, with a quick cold glare, then lowered his eyes. "You can read all the gruesome details in the logs of my personal confessions class."

Now there was a dark silhouette of what appeared to be a woman in the hologram, with two large hands squeezing her throat. The woman desperately struggled to stop her assailant. The visuals were dark and not very clear, but Phoenix could still see the despair in the dying woman's face. A rush of intense horror chilled her skin as she lowered her eyes.

"Just tell me what you felt."

The instant she asked the question, she looked directly into Patel's eyes. For a split second she saw a trace of hesitation. She immediately switched her attention to the brain wave indicators before her: They were showing no changes. Yet she was sure she had seen something in those eyes.

"I felt nothing, just a void," said Patel. "I'm not sure if I was aware of what I was doing. I certainly wouldn't expect you to understand it. Not only do you lack the experience, but also the intelligence."

"Are you are capable of doing it again?"

The brain wave indicator spiked momentarily. There was also a slight raise in the heart rate. But there was no change in any other indicators, or in Patel's overall score, which still stood at ninety-nine. The expert systems interpreted the changes as natural reactions to the thoughts of horror.

"What kind of a question is this?"

"A relevant one. Please answer it."

"Agent Wallis," said Patel, suddenly switching to a compassionate tone. "I know that from the first moment you laid your eyes on me, you've been burning with contempt and jealousy. I've read many studies about this born-in-the-Union syndrome. Some Union citizens just cannot cope with the idea that some *stinky immigrant*, such as myself, can walk into *their* World Union with an HDI score so high that they can only dream about it. I beg you, for your own sake, be rational and don't let your primal negative feelings overtake you in a desperate attempt to trip me up."

In a flash, it all fell into place. She had been misinterpreting the whole situation from the very beginning. It was all part of a show. Since his speech at the graduation ceremony, Patel had been meticulously setting the stage with all his insults and belittlements in order to create a smokescreen to prevent her from thinking straight and discovering the truth. He had set a trap, and she fell for it, along with the zillion-dollar expert systems. She closed her eyes and tried to focus her thoughts. The expression on her face began to relax, which Patel noticed immediately and interpreted as a sign of her surrender.

"Finally, we're reaching some common ground of understanding."

Opening her eyes, Phoenix quickly checked the time. It was nineteen minutes into the interview with only eleven more minutes to go. Just eleven more minutes to make the computers *acknowledge* the truth she already knew, a truth that she would find in the eyes of a dying woman.

"Dr. Patel, I'm going to ask you to elaborate on your murder."

"But why?" said Patel. "What's the relevance? I already told you that all the details are already—"

"I insist that I would like to hear and see the details."

"All right," was all Patel could say to this direct request.

The face of the woman appeared again before the black wall as he elaborated. "I pressed with my thumbs harder and harder. I could tell that the oxygen in her bloodstream was completely depleted and that she started suffocating. The grip she had on my arms started to relax."

"Describe me what you saw in your victim's face."

"What I saw? Pain, suffering, despair."

"How about horror?"

"Sure, there was horror."

"Focus on the horror you saw, no words."

"No words? What do you mean? Besides, I don't see the relevance of—"

Phoenix suddenly stood up, shoving her seat back. She leaned over the table towards Patel.

"Just do as I say!"

The energy radiating through her voice dented Patel's arrogant façade, revealing hair-thin cracks in it for the first time. He didn't know where to look, his little eyes averted from hers as far as possible. The details of the woman's face begin to emerge behind him. She was on the ground, twisting her head right and left to loosen the grip of his hands, but her eyes remained fixed on the camera, on Patel's eyes. She needed a lot more detail than this, if she was to convince the expert systems what she already knew. She couldn't let Patel get away with what he had done, and she found herself willing to take any risk necessary for exposing him.

Suddenly an idea sparked in her mind. It was something potentially dangerous and completely unconventional. She wasn't one to deviate from procedure and protocol and seek solutions through unconventional means; however, given the absence of alternatives and the time restriction she had, there was no other way. Besides, to her total surprise, something inside her told that what she was about to do was all okay and under control, and she felt no qualms doing it.

After all, Patel himself had paved the way for it.

Director Morssen pushed through the daily administration in her office in an automated precision, as she thought about Julio's words. He was neither the brightest nor the most industrious guy in her staff, but he was certainly the most greedy and ambitious. She could easily see Julio doing all he could to derail Phoenix's investigation.

She had no idea whether Phoenix could see through his malicious intent, nor could she guess her reaction to it, but she knew that she had to support Phoenix all she could, as both of their fates were tied together in this murder case, whether it was her choosing or not. Only if Phoenix could complete her first-ever security interview without embarrassing herself, that would be a good start. At that instant, she received an audio call from Beverly, who rarely resorted to direct interrupts. "What is it?"

"Please come to the Viewers' Lounge, Boss. We have a situation."

Speak of the devil, the director thought. The first interview was always the hardest, and she could feel that this arrogant student was going to try his worst to humiliate her. Now, how was she supposed to pull a shattered and insecure senior agent out of her misery and make her lead this murder investigation without screwing up everything? It wasn't like she had a degree in psychology, nor was babysitting a part of her job description.

She got up and rushed to the Viewers' Lounge. As she entered the room, she found Headperson Valkoinen and Beverly in a heated argument. It appeared like Valkoinen was on the attack, but Beverly was holding her ground.

Valkoinen turned to her. "This is totally unacceptable, Dagmar," she squeaked, her eyes widened. "There is protocol and procedure. Your rookie agent here is resorting to every dirty trick in the book to sully my most valuable student, and your watchdog is letting her get away with it. You have to stop this."

The director walked closer to the long window and froze. Was it her imagination, or were those two junior agents moving the furniture around?

"Computer: Freeze media. Dr. Patel, I want you to turn your chair towards the wall behind you. Agents, help him, please."

The two young agents looked at each other, puzzled.

"I said help Dr. Patel, *now*, agents!"

The female agent moved first, and then the other complied as if in a trance. They appeared quite shaken by the horrifying visuals.

"But this is not in the protocol," said Patel, his voice shaking. "I protest this highly irregular request. You cannot force me to view my own brain's Holo-Projections, especially horrific images like those."

Phoenix couldn't help but smile. "Your protest is noted. But you didn't mind this before; what changed your mind, Dr. Patel? Could it be because you went into so much effort to hide your real baseline behavior patterns from me and the computers? Congratulations, you made it. And now, in order to convince our expert systems in the absence of your true baseline patterns, I need more intense reactions from you. To achieve that, we will be forming some sort of a feedback loop to amplify your memories and emotions. Agents, proceed."

"But this is an outrage! I refuse to do it and demand that you stop this procedure and are replaced with a qualified agent immediately."

"You're in no position to refuse or demand anything," said Phoenix, folding her arms. "You're still a non-resident alien with limited rights. I run this interview, and you are required to answer any questions asked and do as you're told. You can file a complaint about me, should you wish, but only after this procedure is terminated—by me. If you stall or disobey my wishes, points will be deducted from your near-perfect overall score, and computer will automatically add the lost time."

Patel did not reply, but he was unable to conceal his frustration; his suave mask faltered. He rose reluctantly to let the junior agents move his wooden chair and the Holo-Projected Testimony apparatus.

"Sit down, Dr. Patel. Now once again, focus on the horror you saw in that woman's face. Don't talk. I want you to just think about it."

The hologram of the woman disappeared, and images of random violence and mutilation filled the screen. Young agents turned their heads in disgust.

"Computer: Note the attempt of deception! Interviewee is not complying with the question asked. Dr. Patel, I already warned you. Do not to try to deceive me by thinking of something else!"

The computer made the acknowledgement sound and deduced ten points from the score. Phoenix rose and walked towards the back wall. She stood between Patel and the wall then turned to him.

"You next attempt at deception might be your last. Now, I want you to focus on that woman's face. Think, but don't talk."

"Dagmar, you have to stop this charade," squeaked Valkoinen.

Director Morssen turned to Beverly.

"Patel was acting weird from the very beginning. I can't tell how or what, but it appears like he's been hiding something. I think Phoenix is onto something, Boss."

Several members of the field office staff entered the Viewers' Lounge. The director glanced at their way as if to ask what the hell they were doing.

"I notified them," said Beverly. "We don't see stuff like this every day, Boss."

The director quietly watched the feedback loop Phoenix had formed, as she got closer to the big window. So this introverted and hesitant new agent of hers had balls after all. A hologram of the dying woman appeared again, dimming the euphoria in the lounge.

"Stop this, Dagmar, or you'll also suffer the consequences," said Valkoinen in a softer squeak, with her eyes glued to the visuals.

The director had the authority to suspend the procedure, but she couldn't simply humiliate and shatter Hamilton's handpicked case lead before the entire staff, only to pick up the pieces herself later. Besides, she was curious to see how far Phoenix was going to take this. The woman was supposed to have great analysis skills. She had to have a plan.

"No. I will let her carry out the procedure as she sees fit."

"But can't you see that she is totally out of control?"

"Actually, I have never seen her so much in control."

CHAPTER 5

THE dying woman's hologram filled the room once again; she was lashing her head from side to side, desperately but vainly trying to loosen the grip on her throat. Her body moved in a rhythmic up-down movement, as if she were in a moving vehicle.

"Focus on her eyes, Dr. Patel. Give me her eyes. Show me what you see."

The image slowly zoomed in on the victim's face, as her head stopped moving and her arms suddenly flopped. Her head tilted slightly to the right, the left eye was fixed at the camera—Patel's eyes—without blinking. Phoenix turned to Patel and kneeled down next to him.

"I want you to focus on her left eye and think about what you saw."

The hologram zoomed into the left eye, got darker and darker.

"Computer: Color calibrate the visuals. Adjust brightness and contrast."

Flickering fires in the background contoured a silhouette of a person holding her throat and moving. There were no strangely colored objects. Patel must have remembered every detail of the incident after so many years.

"What were you hearing? How did it sound? What did it smell like? Computer: Play audio at full volume. Play odor at 20 percent."

There was no telling how the spectators in the Viewers' Lounge reacted to the unexpected loudness, but both of the young agents shrieked and jerked back, as horrific screams, the booming sound of sporadic gunshots, heavy breathing, and the crackling of fire filled the room with severe echoes. The stench of burnt buildings and dead bodies was sufficiently realistic for the male junior agent to start gagging. Phoenix breathed through her mouth as much as possible. Overkill, perhaps, but all this was intended to immerse Patel in the memory of that moment.

"Computer: Filter out the echoes in the audio, equalize the various sounds evenly." The loud screams and gunshots coming from every direction became crisp and easy to distinguish. The heavy breathing in the foreground was much more evident now, and it was obvious that the sound was produced by Patel himself, as he was moving in rhythm with it.

"*Jaungoikoa*, no!" gasped the female agent.

"Computer: Isolate and filter out the background sounds of firearm shots, screams, and fire. Equalize the remaining sound."

Suddenly the room filled with the sound of Patel's loud rhythmic breathing, as his movements sped up and then slowed down with a big moan of relief. He leaned closer with a broad smile. Then he pulled away and let out a manic laugh. The interview room rumbled with the sound.

"Computer: Freeze all media."

With all sound gone, the real Patel's panting became audible. As Phoenix turned to him, she caught him looking at his own frozen laughter with a glimpse of satisfaction, an unguarded expression that quickly vanished. In the dead silence that filled the room, the young female agent quietly whimpered in the corner, while the other struggled with his nausea.

Phoenix went back to the table and sat down. She sighed with relief. But the weight of the moment was so heavy, it left no room for any feeling of victory or success.

"Computer: Cross-reference Raj Patel's personal confessions with the audio-visuals from the Holo-Projected Testimony Device," she said in a tired voice. "Search for falsifications and deceptive patterns."

The expert systems acknowledged and went to work. In less than ten seconds, Patel's score plunged from eighty-nine to twenty-seven.

"Agents, help Dr. Patel move his chair to its original position."

The young female agent wiped the tears with the back of her hand and slowly rose from the corner she'd been kneeling in, while the other one tried to walk as straight as possible, breathing deeply. Both moved like robots, their faces pale, their eyes wary, avoiding any eye contact with Patel, who calmly got up as they turned his chair back and arranged the devices. There was a strange serenity in his face, almost as if he was proud of what he had just relived.

"You seem to have omitted certain details of your personal accounts about the riots that you participated in. You've mentioned a murder and several rapes, but not the fact that you raped a victim that you'd already murdered. Why is that, Dr. Patel, to conceal the fact that you had actually enjoyed the experience?"

"I don't think you could understand my reasoning, even if I tried to explain."

"Is that right? Try me."

"Well. How can I explain any of this to someone with vision as limited as yours?" he said, shaking his head. "Do you recall the first time you had sex? Your approach to life changed forever, did it not?

"I can't really say that it did."

Patel's sudden laugh was shockingly loud in the hush of the room, and uncannily similar to the one in the frozen hologram behind him.

"So predictable," he said, still smiling and shaking his head. "How can I ever explain to someone like you, the divine energy of Shakti, or how birth, death, and everything in between are interrelated? How can you ever comprehend that a true sexual experience could be very similar to a near-death one? I don't think you can. You don't have the intelligence, nor are you spiritual enough."

"You're the one who raped and murdered people, felt no remorse after all these years, maliciously lied through an entire academy tenure, then enjoyed watching it like the first time, and I am the soulless fool? Sweet!"

She leaned over the table and gazed at him, her eyes steely gray. "First you put me under pressure during the graduation ceremony, and then you deliberately stalled my questions in an attempt to derail my efforts to establish baseline behavior patterns. You knew that the computers would need those to catch your emotional deviations during my open-ended questions."

"My plan was perfect. How could you?"

"No plan is ever perfect. Speaking of perfect, you were the epitome of a perfect candidate for citizenship. One thing kept puzzling me, though. You could have entered an immigration academy years ago with your skills, education, and IQ. Why wait additional years? Due to some rogue nation state oppression policy? Then something you did during the interview didn't make any sense. You called World Union a nation, then claimed that you did it on purpose as a favor to me, while your psychological profile screamed at me that you should have done everything in your power to bury me with a perfect score. In the meantime, you skillfully kept me worried about myself, with your condescending stares and remarks, pressuring me to struggle with *my own* feelings, until the point I noticed a slight trace of hesitation in your face when I asked about *your* feelings during the riot. In absence of proper baseline patterns, the computers miscalculated that it was a normal reaction due to your negative feelings towards the riot itself. And this was exactly what you'd planned, wasn't it?"

Patel appeared calm but almost sad. Perhaps the emotional high from reliving his gruesome experience was fast vanishing. "I must admit that I did," he said, looking down. "Do you know how much self-control is needed in order to hide such a thing? I meditated for years and years in order to get into the shape that I am in now, so that I could fool the emotional sensors, only to be caught by someone like you. Well, enjoy your lucky strike while it lasts."

Phoenix leaned back and crossed her arms, taking her time. There wasn't a single sound or movement in the room.

"Luck? Is that all you could come up with, with that one-sixty-something IQ of yours? You see, people like you, no matter how smart, make crucial judgment mistakes and errors in their assumptions, because you always overestimate your own skills and underestimate others'. All you needed to do was take a good look at my public biography."

"Look for what?"

"Just because you know that I was born and raised in the World Union, you assumed that I would know nothing about a riot other than what I read or watched. Unfortunately for you, but fortunately for the people of World Union, you were wrong."

"Can you please get to the point?"

"After all those years of meditation and self-control, we are impatient now, aren't we?" she said with a grin. "You see, I was born and raised here in Adrianopolis. Ever heard of a savage riot called the Eastern Bloodbath?"

"*You?*" he said, sinking back in his chair and staring blankly at nothing.

"Did you know that only a handful of us managed to overcome its emotional scars?" said Phoenix, her voice catching. "I was little, but I could remember the screams, the explosions, the murders, the rapes, the executions, everything. They repressed most of my memories of those incidents so that I could have a healthy life. But those smells, sounds, and images would find me again and again in my childhood night terrors, which have rejuvenated since I moved back here, to my place of birth. I could tell exactly what that woman was going through, the moment I saw her eyes.

"But in the absence of your baseline patterns, I had to make you relive the experience. I knew that if could make you taste a tiny piece of it, you would do anything to relive your gruesome crime and give me every detail I would need to expose your lies. I set a trap for you, and you did not disappoint me. If only you'd considered your opponent worthy enough.

"Your responses and the evidence from the Holo-Projected Testimony Device prove that you falsified your personal confessions and deliberately tried to deceive me and the expert systems we have. Dr. Raj Patel, I formally declare that you fail this security interview with a final score of nineteen, a long way down from one hundred. You are suffering from a deep psychosis, and you will receive the necessary treatment in one of our rehab centers, after which you will be deported from the World Union. Computer, open the door. Agents."

The door opened, and a security team of four entered the room. Patel rose slowly from his chair.

"Until the next time then," he said with a grin.

"There will be no next time for you, Dr. Patel. You may get away with rape and murder due to some statute of limitations in your rogue state, but your hopes to live in the World Union are permanently over."

As he left, Patel gave a last glance at Phoenix, with a serene face.

"I think you overestimate your New World Order, Agent Phoenix Wallis."

She responded only with the intense coldness of her gaze.

"Agent Wallis?"

She jumped and turned to find the young female in her face. "What?"

"I would like to be the first one to congratulate you on your Strike-Out," she said. "It was an incredible learning experience for me. Thank you."

"You're welcome. And you are?"

"Junior Agent Ixone Euskara. Everybody calls me Sean."

"Good to meet you, Sean," said Phoenix and shook her hand. "You know, you mustn't say a word during an interview, unless directly instructed to do so by the interviewer."

"Oh, yes, I apologize for that," said Sean, her chin down.

"Considering the unusual circumstances, that's quite all right. And that word, what does it mean?"

"You mean *jaungoikoa*? I'm not sure," said Sean and shrugged. "Just an expression I know from my childhood."

"Where are you from?" said Phoenix, scanning her from top to toe. She was slightly taller and leaner than Phoenix, with nicely put up long brown hair, a long lean face, and big brown eyes, somewhat reddened from crying.

"I'm nearly 100 percent Aquitanian," she said, looking straight into Phoenix's eyes.

"What are your duties right now?"

"I finished my internship a few months back and got promoted to junior agent, doing whatever I'm told nowadays."

"And you said that you like learning experiences?"

"Yes."

"Then follow me, I have a job for you."

As she left the interview room, she felt as if a ton of weight had been lifted off her shoulders. She had always trusted her ability to find solutions to impossible-looking dilemmas, yet this was the first time she had actually taken such a huge risk under massive mental and time pressure. She could have easily let Patel nail the interview, and nobody would have had asked her a single question about it. The totally unexpected and unthinkable outcome was for Patel to fail, and the odds had been nearly infinitely against her. Could he be the first-ever most valuable student who failed a security interview?

Not that she had thought about any of this during the interview. First, there had been a strong feeling of intuition and flair, which she could only refer as an *instinct?* Then this flair had blocked parts of her rational thought process and made it easy for her to take all the risk. Strangely enough, she felt no fear or apprehension towards this feeling now; on the contrary, she was secure and confident about it in an innate way, as if some dormant sensations deep within were activated. And all of this had happened in this city where she had suffered horrific nightmares since her arrival, and in this building that she despised so deeply. None of it made any sense.

The director, Valkoinen, Beverly, and several others appeared round the corner. News traveled fast at the Adrianopolis Field Office. Computer and network expert Fred Berger leapt in front of the others with his long strides. He took Phoenix's hand in a strong grasp.

"Way to go, Phoenix; that was one heck of an impressive interview."

"Thank you."

"Say, the director mentioned a loophole you discovered in our network. You talked your way through a Door Bot for a level five meeting without your PA or something? Why would you try such a thing?"

"What can I can say? Necessity is the mother of all invention."

"Evidently," he said then looked over his shoulder. "Tell you what: Send me a memo about it when you get a chance. I gotta run." He took off in a hurry.

"Congratulations are in order for you, sweetheart," said Valkoinen. She wore a smile, but her gaze told a different story. "I have to admit that you've prevented this academy from making a very serious mistake."

"Thank you. I'm sorry that the academy did not get much chance to enjoy its Longest Absence of a Strike-Out lead."

"We'll just have to work even harder and ensure that our student selection procedure is flawless. This is what we need to do on our part." Suddenly, she took a couple of quick steps towards Phoenix. "But I warn you," she said in her high-pitched squeak, wagging her finger at Phoenix's face. "You can't just walk in there and do whatever you want, understand? There's protocol and procedure! Have you ever heard of those concepts before? I—"

"Come on, Ingrid," said the director. "Let her enjoy her success for a bit before you criticize her methods. She just prevented a very dangerous psychopath from harming our society."

Valkoinen swallowed the things she was about to say. "She did, didn't she? What can I say! Congratulations again, *sweetheart*."

"Thank you."

The headperson left in a rush with her entourage, mumbling orders to her assistants. Thinking of the potential troubles if Patel had been granted a citizenship, Phoenix felt a wave of shakiness running through her body, turning her joints to liquid momentarily. She had just saved her entire career from potential ruin. Beverly's glowing smile and thumbs-up from a distance helped her regroup.

"Phoenix, in my office, now," said a stern voice.

She followed the director, not knowing what to expect. She had witnessed how peevish she could become about totally unexpected things. They entered the director's office in grim silence. Director Morssen took her seat and looked up.

"I don't remember inviting *you* to my office."

The Mantis' new mission was to throw the Bogdanov murder investigation off the track, using any means necessary. *Any means* meant that he could resort to any of his dirty tricks or deception tactics. As long as it didn't involve physical violence, he was allowed to do whatever he wanted. The Mantis was never a big fan of physical violence and thought that it was for idiots with big muscles, big guns, and no brains. His tactics were subtle and elegant, and he knew that nobody could manipulate or deceive people the way he could. He could cause a lot more pain, anguish, and permanent damage than any form of physical violence could ever inflict. When he was done with someone, that person never knew what had hit him and where it had come from.

Most of his victims would end up blaming themselves, in the absence of anyone else to blame. And with the devastation he brought, this self-blame and pity concealed a permanently scarred soul, with no hope of remedy or recovery. He was the ultimate soul destroyer, when he needed to be. The beauty of all this was nobody ever suspected him, because he knew how to stay dormant and out of sight. He would disappear for days and weeks when necessary, without rousing the least bit of suspicion. He felt proud about the way he operated and the way he could hide in plain sight.

The Mantis had been feeling rather uncomfortable about his chain of command for a while now. They didn't appreciate his contributions enough anymore, and they were opting to keep him in hiding for increasingly longer periods, although he was the most talented infiltrator they had. His controller was doing every trick in the book to undermine him and his efforts.

The Mantis would not sit back and wait to be annihilated, and he was going to fight back and prove his worth, not only to this controller and other superiors, but also to the whole world. He had one small obstacle, however: He didn't know who the controller was. They only communicated securely at the controller's request, and their method of communication did not reveal any clues regarding his or her identity other than the mission name of Prefect. The messages from the controller had been erratic in the recent months, as if there had been a shift in the character—could it be a different person? He could sense a certain weakness in him or her. He had to do something about this during his current assignment, and it appeared that he was going to be active for many days to come, which would make it a perfect opportunity not only to prove his worth to everyone but also to expose the judgment errors of his controller. But first, he had to succeed in his new assignment of sabotaging the murder investigation.

He focused his thoughts on Senior Agent Phoenix Wallis for a while. Sabotaging the murder investigation meant sabotaging her, by building all kinds of obstacles around her to make her follow up dead ends, doubt her own abilities, thoughts, and sense, and eventually self-destruct. Following her success with the Patel interview, the Mantis had decided that it would be a mistake to underestimate her. He had known that she was very intelligent and a good analyzer, but now it appeared that there was a lot more to her than that.

He had to access and examine all the data available on her, to make a better assessment. It would be a mistake to create a web of deception around her without fully understanding what she was capable of first. And the Mantis never made such mistakes. He was always very patient and knew exactly when and where to strike. He already felt sorry for her and for those around her who would be caught up in his web of manipulations and deceptions. No plan was ever so perfect that only the target would receive the blow, leaving everybody else intact: There would always be some collateral damage. And, although he was bound by the orders regarding the identity of his next target, he was never restricted on the issue of the magnitude or object of collateral damage he could inflict. He felt something akin to detached pity as he thought about the grief and anguish these poor souls were about to suffer.

It took Phoenix a few moments to realize who the director was talking to.

"Oh, please let me introduce you to my new case assistant, Sean Euskara."

The director scrutinized her for a moment. "Are you certain you are not rushing this decision?"

"I am certain, Director."

"I hope she is not too feeble for the assignment," murmured the director.

"I've made my choice. Junior Agent Euskara is the case assistant."

"Oh, fine, whatever, I'll issue a formal announcement. And as your assistant during the upcoming weeks, I suppose she can hear what I have to say to you."

"Thank you, Director Morssen," said Sean and smiled.

"I didn't say you could open your mouth."

Sean immediately erased all emotions from her face and froze.

The director turned to Phoenix. "Now, before you get carried away with your sweet success, let me remind you of a few things—"

"I won't get carried away, Director. I'm just happy that I was able to keep that creep away from our society."

Director Morssen rose from her seat with fury in her eyes. "Quit babbling and listen to me! Ingrid has a point. Your *feedback loop* seemed to work this time with that psychopath. But with an innocent student, you may have caused serious psychological damage. We don't want greedy lawyers exploiting tort laws and getting rich over us while tainting our image, understood?"

"Yes, Director," said Phoenix, looking down.

"Where did you get the idea to make him watch his own memories?"

"From studies about making the interviewees watch their previously recorded Holo-Projected Testimony visuals. Evidently it had helped them remember more details about the incidents. I knew what Patel was trying to hide, and I had to make him get carried away reliving his hideous experience. I improvised on the idea, since I had very limited time."

"And how did you know what Patel was trying to hide, Agent Wallis?"

"I could see it in his victim's eyes, Director Morssen."

"How about proven procedures? Do you have any respect for them?"

"Of course I do, but sometimes extraordinary circumstances require unorthodox measures."

The director raised her eyebrows and leaned forward at her desk, looking up at a standing Phoenix. "Yes, sometimes extraordinary circumstances *do* require outside-the-box thinking and tactics. And I'd totally agree with you, if this was not your first-ever security interview. Now, you are in the driving seat of a very serious murder investigation with dire consequences if unsuccessful. I need to know that you will act responsibly and according to the procedures, and this *improvisation* stuff will remain as an exception for rare situations."

"I'm well trained for any kind of investigation procedures. If my judgment is in question here, I can only assure you that—"

"I didn't say that! And don't *ever* put words in my mouth, understood? Your judgment is not in question, but your methods are. You like taking shortcuts, and this murder case that I entrusted you with has no room for it. You will be closely monitored by the top management, including Mr. Hamilton himself, at every step you take. There will be a lot of pressure. And on top of all this, some of your fellow agents will try to slow you down. I need to make sure that you will not crack, as some of my senior staff suggest."

Phoenix felt heat in her ears. She knew exactly who the director was referring to. "Am I still leading this case?" she whispered.

"Yes, you are. On a very short leash."

"Fine. Then with your permission, I'd like to get on with my assignment. As for the unorthodox methods, it won't happen again. I don't think the headperson would want to see me in the interview room anytime soon."

"Dream on. That could have been the case if you didn't make a Strike-Out on your first-ever interview. Don't you realize you just opened a big can of worms? Now Ingrid will not rest until she has your perfect Strike-Out record ironed down to an average one, in an effort to show that it was just a coincidence, like that psychopath suggested. I'm sure she'll be knocking on my door any moment now, ready with all the interviews she's lined up for you. But if you think that both assignments will be too much for you and you won't be able to handle them all, you can always settle for a lesser role in the Bogdanov case."

The pride that Phoenix felt was almost physical, as if a hidden dose of adrenalin had been suddenly released into her bloodstream. "Absolutely not, Director. I can handle them both."

"In that case, don't waste any more time. Go and investigate something."

Phoenix walked back to her office and sat down, her hands covering her face. The director was right about the shortcuts. But she couldn't tell her boss about her sudden rush of intuition and flair, nor could she confess that she still felt right about using these unscientific urges. It would be the death sentence of her career.

"Agent Wallis?"

"Huh? Did they ever tell you that you move as quiet as a cat, Sean?" She paused. "I owe you an explanation, don't I?"

Sean nodded. "That would be nice."

"Sit down, I'll explain." Phoenix quickly brought her up to date about the Bogdanov case. "I'm sorry that I didn't get your opinion about being involved in such a case. But now that I've told the director about picking you as an assistant, there is no turning back."

"Oh, I see, Agent Wallis," she said looking down.

"Phoenix."

"Phoenix," she said and swallowed. "Thank you for your faith in me. But I don't understand. To my knowledge, you don't even know me, do you?"

"I knew nothing about you, until you tapped on my shoulder in the interview room half an hour ago."

"In that case, may I ask based on what information you decided to put me on the team?"

"To be perfectly honest, I took another shortcut about you. You were in the right place, at the right time, with the right attitude, Sean. Now, we have work to do. Where is your desk?"

"I share a desk at the Monitoring Room."

"All right. You keep your desk at the Monitoring Room for the time being. Most of the work can be done through our PAs anyway. I don't think we need any additional devices to take with us. Now, let's grab a quick bite in the cafeteria then begin investigating our case by taking a trip to the victim's house, shall we?"

CHAPTER 6

PHOENIX turned and looked back, enjoying the relief of finally getting out of the accursed old building. The old monastery was in the shape of a Latin cross, with GPSN Field Office only occupying the short arm on the western side. The rest of it served as the immigration academy and its dormitories. It was built on a small island on the river Tizsa, which separated the World Union from the rogue nation state of Russia. With the resources allocated to convert this old stone building into a state-of-the-art secure environment, they could have easily built a modern structure from scratch with all kinds of bells and whistles. Even the heating bill of this place must have been horrendous. In a land that was ruled by positive economic thinking as the main principle, hosting any business here made no economic sense. Could she be the only one to think in this way? Perhaps she was overly biased because she hated the building.

Across the stone bridge connecting the island to the mainland, a giant World Union flag—a white eagle figure and seven white stars on an ultramarine background—was flaunted high on the shores of the river. It was a beautiful spring day, and Phoenix wished that she could spend more time outdoors. She glanced up to the sky as she took the escalator down to the station Omega Ten, the last stop on the Omega Line.

The station was so remote that only GPSN Field Office and immigration academy employees ever used it. Interactive holo-ads made a parade before them as they walked, begging for the attention of the only two people in the station. One slogan had been grabbing her attention since the first day, an ad for a travel agency moving and morphing in thin air that kept asking "Where do you want to go today?" prompting Phoenix to think *anywhere but here*. After only a week on the job, she was in dire need of a vacation.

The train arrived totally empty. In a few minutes, it would depart back to the Pyramid, where they'd need to switch to the Delta Line to get to Bogdanov's house. All trains were covered with steel-grade glass, and gliding in them made Phoenix feel like she was traveling in an air bubble.

Soon after the train departed from the station, Phoenix heard a strange sound from her PA. She removed the tiny device, trying to make sense of what was going on.

"What's wrong, Phoenix?"

"Damn it! I think Ray broke it."

"Ray?"

"Never mind."

The strange sounds stopped, and the green online indicator blinked rapidly. She reattached the device to her ear. "PA: Activate," she said. But it did not respond to the command. "PA: Report status. Echo on." The projected window before her eyes had no recognizable menu item. The device had been rebooting from a crash. "PA: Full diagnostic. Echo off. Execute."

"Does it work?"

"I certainly hope so, Sean. What would I do without it?"

Bogdanov had lived in one of the very tall buildings, farthest from the Pyramid, just a few hundred meters from Station Delta Nine. It was typical housing for a man with an HDI of only seventy, an economical ranking he shared with about half of the Union population, the bare minimum required to retain a World Union citizenship. Human Development Index calculations were zero-sum equations. Someone going up in the rating meant another coming down. Most people were simply stuck at the bottom of this economical pyramid all their lives.

Phoenix's PA made a sound, indicating that it was exiting diagnostic mode. To her total surprise, everything appeared to be in working order. The PA had recovered some unidentified data, however. She could check it later.

The doors of the elevator opened at the twenty-third floor. A simple hallway led them to Bogdanov's apartment.

"Greetings," said the metallic female voice of the Door Bot. "This is apartment twenty-three hundred and zero-four, the home of Vassily Bogdanov. How may I help you?"

"Computer: I'm Senior Agent Phoenix Wallis, and this is Sean Euskara from the GPSN Adrianopolis Field Office. We have official business inside. Open the door."

"You have no authorization to enter this residence. You need to get authorization from appropriate agencies. If you insist in entering, your visuals will be logged and reported to the GPSN Field Office."

Helplessness swamped Phoenix. She tapped the PA with her index finger. The tiny device should have had already negotiated her credentials with this Door Bot, following her verbal introduction. Could it be having some malfunction again?

"Computer: Access Global Peace and Security Network gateway. I am a peace agent, and my badge number is three, one, six, charlie, omega, seven, seven, papa, echo, papa. Establish level three secure link."

"Level Three secure link established. Greetings, Senior Agent Wallis."

"Access case alpha, romeo, five, three, papa. Request authorization to enter Vassily Bogdanov house. Address code alpha, delta, romeo, delta, four, four, seven, two, three, zero, four."

"Senior Agent Wallis: Please verify your request for emergency access."

"Emergency access? Is this normal for an empty house?" said Sean.

Could the malfunction in her PA have been caused by a contagious spyware or virus software, which had then spread to this clueless Door Bot?

"I'm not sure. The Door Bot is acting as if—" There could only be one explanation of all this, and that explanation could be potentially very frightening. "Computer: Is the proprietor inside the house?"

"Affirmative."

"This must be some kind of error," said Sean, her voice shaking.

Phoenix turned to Sean, wishing she had a reassuring reply handy.

"I'm not sure if it is. I want you to remain calm and be ready, when the door opens."

"Ready for what?"

"More like, ready for whom. And to tell the truth, I have no idea."

"Are you sure about this?" said the director.

"Yes," said Alex, looking at his lap. "Quite sure."

"Alex, we've known each other for more than three years now. You're my oldest colleague here—wait—that didn't sound like what I meant to say. It's just, we've built this field office from its ashes, and you were there, supporting me from the very beginning. Did something change?"

"No, Dagmar, nothing changed," said Alex, his eyes glittering.

Their relationship had started three years before, just after her installment as the director of the field office. Alex was soft-mannered and kind, an old-fashioned gentleman in every sense of the word. But he didn't know how to keep business and pleasure separate, putting the director in a difficult situation a couple of times. She had ended it not long after it had started, without anyone being aware of it in the field office. The only remnant from those days was Alex being on a first-name basis when they were alone.

"Then why do you want to do this?" she said as softly as possible. "Is it because of the Bogdanov case lead?"

"No, no, definitely not," said Alex, shaking his head. "I think Phoenix is the best choice there. I'm too old for that kind of action, and Julio is too hot-headed. Ahh, you know I like that Julio. He has great potential but too damn impatient. I wish I was better at teaching him some patience."

The director smiled and shook her head. She had tried it so many times, but there was simply no way of convincing Alex about Julio's deceitful, conniving side. She couldn't tell him that he, Alex, would be her first choice to lead the Bogdanov case, either. "Then why do you want to quit?"

"I feel old and useless, Dagmar. I don't feel that I have the same energy that I once had. And I have plenty of money in my retirement account. Maybe I should just retire and move to a small village in my native Pannonia."

Alex was in excellent shape for his age, but she could understand why he had been feeling old and useless. There was too much young blood in the field office. Other than Alex and Fred, everyone was in their thirties or younger.

"That is nonsense. You're not going anywhere. There's so much these new kids can learn from you, and you know it."

"Yes, I know. But every time I try, it seems like I just cannot, how do you say, *click* with them. Maybe it's my English, I don't know. I should be able to speak better English after all these years."

"Your English is fine."

"No, it's not! I just made a terrible blunder this morning and put poor Phoenix in a terrible situation. I've had enough, Dagmar, really. I think I should just quit."

The director leaned across the table and took Alex's hand. "Tell you what. I will help you to prove your worth to this field office. Just give me a week. And everyone will see how valuable a member you are." The director's sentence was interrupted by a priority one message. She excused herself and read the message quickly then turned to Alex. "I have a visitor for a few minutes. You can stay here, if you wish."

"Who?"

"Someone I've been expecting since the morning."

"Computer: Execute emergency access."

"House security disarmed. Doors open. Thank you for your cooperation."

The hologram vanished as the house door quietly opened. Phoenix could feel her heart pushing its way up to her throat. Where was a nerve disrupter when she needed one? She tried to calm her pulse by breathing deeply and entered the house with Sean closely behind. They tiptoed through the short hallway of the small studio. It was a tiny house with one bedroom and a kitchen/living area with a huge window offering a view of the Pyramid behind. She had forgotten to do the most crucial thing in the heat of the moment. "PA: Start logging—"

Before she could finish her sentence, a man in dark clothes, a dark cap, and an eye mask burst out from the bedroom to their left, carrying a small black knapsack. He was a well-built man of medium height, with a strong chin and a curling, strangely sensuous mouth. For one instant, Phoenix made eye contact with him. The mask slits offered a glimpse of brown eyes that somehow looked calm yet determined. There was something in those eyes that made Phoenix's senses go haywire, bombarded with so many conflicting and unfamiliar sensations simultaneously. She hesitated for a moment, and that was precisely what the man needed. He charged Phoenix like an overgrown goat, head-butted her solar plexus, and ran towards the house door. Phoenix fell to the ground, as Sean stood there frozen.

"Get him!" said Phoenix in a strangled croak, gasping to regain her breath.

After her moment of hesitation, Sean started chasing the masked man.

"He's taking the stairs," she heard Sean say, then a door slammed shut.

Phoenix slowly got up and walked outside, bent over, to the elevator and kept pressing the button. When the elevator didn't respond, she turned and rushed to the elevator at the other end of the hallway. Sean's call came in.

"He got away on the nineteenth floor. Took the elevator."

"Did you log any visuals?"

"I'm afraid not."

"Start doing it now. You run down the stairs, I'll try the elevator."

The moment the elevator arrived, she darted in and frantically pressed the lobby button. The panel showed that it was programmed to stop at two other floors before reaching the lobby. She could only hope that the same happened to the intruder in the other elevator.

"PA: Access building Delta, four, four, seven main server. This is an emergency. Alert GPSN Code Seven. Begin recording visuals at every public camera at the Delta Quadrant and the main station at the Pyramid."

The elevator stopped, doors opened, but nobody was waiting. She desperately pressed the close-door button to speed it up. As soon as the elevator hit the ground floor, she burst out and ran towards the other elevator down the hall, only to find its doors open but no the man in the mask. A few moments later Sean emerged from the staircase, panting.

"Any luck?"

Sean bent over with her hands on her knees and shook her head. Phoenix rushed out of the building and spun around in a desperate attempt to catch a glimpse of him. The man was long gone, but he couldn't have gone too far.

"PA: Visual call to the supervisor of the Monitoring Room."

In a few seconds, Beverly's hologram appeared before her. "Beverly here."

"Beverly, it's Senior Agent Phoenix Wallis."

"I know what you look like, Phoenix. What is it you need?"

"We have an emergency Code Seven at the Delta. I need live coverage."

"You said live coverage?"

"Correct. I'd like to divert the visuals from Delta Quadrant public cameras to your Monitoring Room. We're looking for a—"

"Hold on a second, sister, what's going on?"

"We have a suspect who escaped the scene. Please, every second counts."

"Which sector of Delta?"

"All sectors."

"Are you out of your mind? We don't have the manpower to observe live video for more than a thousand cameras."

Phoenix made a quick calculation in her head. "All right then: sector forty-four and all metro stations of the Delta Line, specifically Delta Nine."

"That's still nearly two hundred cameras," said Beverly, shaking her head. "Tell you what, I'll divert a hundred cameras with the best coverage of the areas you mention. The rest, we can record and monitor later, offline. We cannot do it live for more than twenty minutes."

"Do what you can. And please let me know if you spot him."

"And who are we supposed to be looking for?"

"Oh, yes, an unidentified Caucasian male wearing a dark outfit, approximately one meter eighty in height. He might still be wearing a dark baseball cap and an eye mask."

"One meter eighty," mused Beverly. "An eye mask? Any other specifics?"

"Positive. No other specifics for the time being."

"Understood. Will divert the coverage to you if we spot someone matching the description. Make sure to let the boss know about this. Beverly out."

Phoenix made her next call to Director Morssen. She was in busy mode, but Phoenix marked her call as highest priority.

"You better have a good reason for interrupting my meeting," the director answered in a whisper.

"There was an intruder at the Bogdanov house."

"What?"

Phoenix quickly explained the situation, "I would like to organize a search party."

"Did you arrange for live coverage?"

"Yes, I did."

"Forget the search party. We don't have the manpower for it. Your best option is the live coverage. Do you have visuals of the encounter?"

"Partially, but I doubt that they'll be useful for identifying the intruder."

"In that case, process the scene for clues and evidence for the time being. Create a search string after that. I want your full report as soon as possible. Morssen out."

"This is a crime scene now, Sean, and we need to process it accordingly. Are you trained for this?"

"Yes, in simulations."

"PA: Mark this apartment as a crime scene. Assign a case number and merge it with case alpha, romeo, five, three, papa. Initiate Crime Scene Investigation mode, in parallel with Junior Agent Euskara's PA."

Following the beep of acknowledgement, a narrow blue beam emerged from both their PAs. Phoenix took baby steps into the house, with Sean close behind her.

"Take that room," said Phoenix, pointing to the room that the intruder had emerged from. "Make sure the beam touches every wall, ceiling, corner, furniture, or any other objects. Otherwise we cannot reconstruct the flat for virtual investigation later."

Sean nodded and tiptoed into the room. Phoenix moved slowly towards the sitting area and kitchen ahead. It was a typical Disciple studio, and not furnished with good taste. A few shiny and expensive-looking ornaments were sticking out like sore thumbs in the banality of the rest of the apartment. She noticed some small eight-by-four-centimeter cards on the coffee table, with some text and graphics printed on them. The logo on the cards was one she was familiar with. Now she knew what those expensive ornaments were and how they got there.

"Phoenix, you better check this out."

"Hold on, almost finished here."

The bedroom came with black walls and a large bed in the middle, fitted with fire-engine red sheets.

"Cool."

"My sentiments exactly," said Sean, as she examined a small cupboard, with an open metal door, embedded in the wall above the bed.

"It's a safe."

"It's a safe what?"

"That's what they are called, safe, a metal container with a secure lid that only the owner can access. I've seen one in an old movie. How could you override its security mechanism?"

Sean turned to her. "Pretty unsafe safe, I guess," she said, her big brown eyes wide. "It was open when I entered the room."

"The bed is already scanned, yes?"

Sean nodded. Phoenix leaned over the bed to inspect the safe. "PA: Scan with narrow focus light." A tiny beam of white light appeared at the center of the blue scanning beam, illuminating the inside of the safe. It was empty, with the exception of a micro document chip. "Did you inspect the chip?"

"No, not yet."

"Do it, while I finish the kitchen."

"You may also want to see this."

Sean closed the safe to expose a tiny projector behind, and the hologram of a beautiful woman in an Oriental costume filled the room automatically. She appeared to be dancing on stage.

"So that's why this room was so dim. Who is she?"

"I have no idea, but I like the way she moves," said Sean, unable to take her eyes off the woman.

"Sweet. What else did you find?"

"Just that e-book." Sean motioned to the lamp rest at the side of the bed.

Teach Yourself How To Become An Arrivee In Twenty-One Days?"

"Yes," said Sean, finally managing to wrench her eyes away from the dancing woman. "What was Bogdanov's Human Development Index again?"

"Seventy."

"Well, he was a long way from becoming an Arrivee, that's for sure."

"Indeed, he was. Tell me exactly what happened during your chase down the stairs."

"He ran down to the nineteenth floor. He was very fast."

"Yes, I noticed. And then?"

"He suddenly went to the hallway. The elevator door was open. He went in, and it closed quickly. I had no chance. Then I called you."

"You said the elevator door was open?"

"Yes."

"How could he know that unless—" At that instant she had an incoming visual connection. "Phoenix here."

"It's been nearly thirty minutes, and we cannot spot anyone matching the description," said Beverly. "I'm terminating the live coverage."

"I understand. Thanks all the same. Can I count on your help for evaluating the recorded visuals?"

"How long a period do you plan to sweep?"

"I'd say at least six hours."

"Six hours times a thousand cameras makes more than six thousand hours of footage. You need to create a good search string for the tracking software. Otherwise it will take forever to get results."

"I'll send Sean Euskara, the junior agent with me during the incident, for that. She had a better look at the man."

"Send her to see Harold in the Monitoring Room ASAP. Beverly out."

Sean had already finished scanning and was uploading the scans and other findings from the bedroom to the case database.

"Sean, I need you to find Harold in the Monitoring Room and create the search string."

Sean's puzzled face and lip-chewing gave away the obvious.

"You gotta be kidding me!"

"Sorry."

Phoenix closed her eyes, counted to ten, then spoke calmly. "A search string is any three-dimensional object that can be searched in the visuals databases. In this case, the search string is a human male. You need to instruct the expert computer to create a description of the intruder."

"Are you sure you want me to do this? I'm not that good with computers."

"You had a much better look at him than I did. What was your major in college, anyway?"

"Social Intercourse and Etiquette in the Workplace."

"No kidding?"

"No kidding."

Peace business was on the decline in the entire World Union due to the low crime rate, and GPSN had a hard time recruiting entry-level personnel to its Peace Corps. But Phoenix had no idea that they had been recruiting fresh graduates from totally unrelated fields.

"Fine. You're gonna have to learn all this as we go. I want you to review all manuals and procedures in your own time over the next few days. Understood?"

"Yes," nodded Sean, looking down.

"Now go back to the office and find this Harold. Once you create the string with his help, get the computer to search it in the recorded footage of the Delta Quadrant between twelve and eighteen hundred hours."

"Starting from two hours ago?"

"He got here from somewhere."

"You said the entire Delta Quadrant. Including Delta Ten?"

Phoenix thought about it for a few seconds. "Exclude Delta Ten," she said. "I doubt that he went in that direction."

"May I ask what you will be doing?"

"First, I'm going to finish scanning this kitchen, then, I have a place or two to stop by on my way back. I found some good old-fashioned clues here, complete with an address."

CHAPTER 7

As the escalator neared the surface, Phoenix admired the huge structure covering the entire city center, the three-hundred-meter-high Pyramid, made of pure steel and glass. The steel part of the structure was barely visible from the ground level, and it appeared like the sky was just behind a polarizing and protective bubble.

Following its almost total destruction during the Eastern Bloodbath, Adrianopolis had been rebuilt with ancient Athens in mind. They had kept a few old buildings that had survived the riots in the old town center and bulldozed everything else, then built houses and apartments from the center towards the edge of the city in reverse order in terms of height, so that the farther from the center, the taller the buildings had become. To represent the modern Acropolis, the Pyramid had been constructed above the old town center, converting it into a giant shopping mall. No matter how far or close, every house and every flat in the city had a view of the Pyramid.

Most buildings inside were from the nineteenth century, restored and serving as retail stores, restaurants, entertainment centers, movie theaters, and everything else one would expect to find in a shopping mall. A tiny tributary of the river Tizsa ran through the middle with a beautiful strip of green on both sides. Arched stone bridges connected the two sides of the river branch. Phoenix walked through the park, enjoying the sight of the blossoming nature, and found her way to her destination: The Thing Store.

Thing Stores were the latest fashion sensation where beautiful and shiny ornamental objects called Things were sold. The store was designed in the form of an art gallery and was packed with people, many of whom were only ogling the beautiful Things, photographing them with their 3D scanners, visibly salivating. She had found some old-style printed business cards that bore Bogdanov's name in his house. She was happy that the cards had saved her having to ask Julio for Bogdanov's work coordinates. These printed cards were commonly used in the rogue states. Could Bogdanov have been doing some business in the rogue state of Russia?

She looked around for a store employee and noticed a tall well-built young woman, with olive skin, long, ponytailed chestnut hair, and small brown eyes, who came with a name tag. Her shoulders were so broad, her all-smiles face appeared a couple of sizes small for her body.

"Hi. I'm Senior Agent Phoenix Wallis from the GPSN Field Office."

"Hello. My name is Alicia, junior sales clerk on the floor. Hee, hee, hee."

"Hello, Alicia. How are you today?"

"Oh, I'm great! What a beautiful day. How about you?"

"I've had better days. I'm afraid I'm here in an official capacity and have to ask you a few questions concerning your former supervisor, the late Mr. Bogdanov. You are aware of his death, aren't you?"

The young sales clerk's face suddenly turned sad. "Yes, I am, but why you have to ask me questions, I mean, I dunno anything," she mumbled with wide eyes.

"Just routine questions, nothing to worry about," said Phoenix as warmly as possible. "Oh, one more thing: A judge ordered Mr. Bogdanov's death to be kept confidential for the time being. You are not to tell anyone, understand?"

"Yes, Agent Wallis," she said, bowing her head.

"PA: Interview mode. Begin recording."

Alicia swallowed. "Am I supposed to do or say something now?"

"In a minute. By the way, I really like your outfit. Where did you get it?"

"Oh really? You like it? Hee, hee, hee."

"Yes, it looks fabulous."

"I got it online. They had this great sale at one of my favorite stores. I thought it would make me look older. Does it?"

"Oh, definitely. You look at least *eighteen* today."

"Aaah, is that all?"

"That was a compliment, sweetie, from your neighborhood peace agent, free of charge," said Phoenix, with a wink.

"Oh thanks. Hee, hee, hee."

Before the high-pitched giggle from the tall woman-child pierced her eardrums, she needed to keep Alicia somewhere between too-bubbly-to-talk and too-nervous-to-talk.

"So, how did you hear about Mr. Bogdanov's death?"

"Actually, I explained all this to the other peace agent. Perhaps you should check his notes first?"

"What other peace agent?"

"Another agent came in just before you and asked questions about Mr. Bogdanov," Alicia said with wide-eyed innocence.

She could think of only one person who could be this rude. How dare he do something like this, despite the director's specific assignments? Or could the director have instructed him to do this?

"I can't believe that Julio—his name was Julio, wasn't it?"

"No, it was not," said Alicia, shaking her head.

What was going on here? GPSN had sent some kind of a special agent to follow the case? If so, why wasn't she informed as the case lead? None of this made any sense. On the other hand, could she take her word for it? Did she have a reason to lie? "Who was it, then?"

"He said his name was Harry Callahan, a fair-haired middle-aged man of medium height. He looked more like Central European."

"Harry Callahan, huh? Are you sure he was middle-aged?"

"Of course I'm sure. He was in his late thirties at least. Oh, and he had the cutest chin, ya know? Hee, hee, hee."

The chin part clinched it, and Phoenix's face relaxed into a genuine smile. Finally, the tide appeared to be turning.

"There are no agents by that name in our field office, Alicia. He must have been an impersonator."

"But he seemed like such a nice man," said Alicia, almost in tears.

"What exactly did this Mr. Callahan ask?"

"He asked about Mr. Bogdanov's death and things like that, just like you. Oh, he also went upstairs to his office."

"Can you describe his physical appearance to me in more detail?"

"Ehm, I think so. I mean, I'll try my best."

"Don't worry, dear," said Phoenix and gently touched her arm. "First, I will access the surveillance footage from the store. We will get a base image of him from there. Then, my GPSN suspect modeling software will help us to create a 3D image of his face, and we'll have a perfect description of him. Then we can determine the identity of this man in no time."

"How are you, Alex? You appear a little gloomy," cooed Valkoinen, and swiveled her head towards the director. "Was Dagmar being mean to you again?"

"Oh, no, Headperson Valkoinen. Just having some difficulty with one of my assignments, and the director was offering some guidance, that's all."

"Oh, really? I know exactly what kind of *guidance* she is capable of giving," she said to him and turned her head to the director. "You know, Alex here is the best agent in this field office. I can't even imagine him having difficulty with any assignment."

Valkoinen was not being sarcastic. She liked Alex, and now she was using him to mount an attack in order to get in a good position for the main issue she was there for. Alex lowered his eyes and kept quiet.

"Then again, our good director here is a little hard to please, isn't she? Don't worry, Alex, you are not the only one suffering from her perfectionism. We all are."

The director was beginning to regret keeping Alex for the meeting.

"And what can I do for you, Ingrid?"

"I'll tell you what you can do for me, darling. You can teach the rest of your staff to be like Alex, professional, well-mannered, and dedicated to protocol. Some of them are setting a terrible example, and I'm here to put a stop to it."

"If you are referring to Agent Wallis and the Patel interview this morning, I'd be happy to bar her from more interviews, if that's what you wish."

"No! That's not what I wish at all," Valkoinen squeaked at an even higher pitch. "I want her to be professional. I want her to learn manners and follow protocol. And I want her to show me that she has learned all this, in practice, throughout a series of interviews every single day for the next three weeks, including the weekends."

This was pretty much how the director had expected Valkoinen to react after the Patel interview. After twenty more security interviews, Phoenix's Strike-Out would average out and lose its significance, at the expense of putting tremendous strain on her workload. Hamilton had wanted Phoenix to pursue a cautious investigation. But this would basically bring it to a grinding halt. "Be reasonable, Ingrid. With all the required prep time, interviews would take her entire time, with no time left for her other assignments."

"And what other assignment could she have more important than a security interview, darling? Some lame case of altruism? C'mon!"

"She's new, and she has a lot to do in order to catch up, like her orientation. How's that orientation going, Alex?"

"Quite well, Director Morssen, but we're a little behind."

"I see. Tell you what, Ingrid: I'll get Phoenix to attend her orientation with Alex tomorrow, with a focus on security interviews. She can have interviews on Wednesday, Thursday, and the weekend. And we can decide about next week on

Friday. This still makes more interviews than any of my other agents, plus she has to complete her other important duties."

"Hmm, I didn't know Alex was attending her orientation. Well, I can tell she is behind from the way she conducted that interview."

"She will follow protocol, and our dear Alex will see to that. Agreed?"

Valkoinen rose in a calm confidence. "I suppose so, Dagmar." She didn't exactly appear pleased with the outcome, but it was a good compromise.

Phoenix clenched her teeth and fists, barely keeping herself from screaming her head off and breaking all these Things. There were approximately two hundred surveillance cameras at the Pyramid, excluding the interiors of the stores. The Thing Store had twelve of them. Yet every camera with coverage of the impersonator seemed to have experienced outages during his presence. Two of the cameras in the Thing Store had been out for twenty minutes each, the exact length of time that the impersonator had been in the store. It was as if this man had exactly known which camera had covered him and had been able to disable it somehow.

Unsurprisingly, Alicia hadn't been much of help, either. Apparently she had been too coy to look at the man straight in the eye or face. She didn't remember anything about the man, other than the fact that he was a man, had a cute chin, and looked more European than Central American. What's more, she couldn't even tell how tall he was or whether he had a peace agent uniform or not. In the end, the wizard software could only come up with a simple 3D sketch. It had to be the same man, the intruder at the Bogdanov house, but there wasn't any evidence to support it.

"So how did he die in that rogue state, Agent Wallis? Was it a contagious disease or an accident, or did they murder him for his flesh like in them reality shows?"

"That information is confidential. How did you hear about his death?"

"Some guy from headquarters called just before noon. Actually, Monica talked to him."

"Monica?"

"My coworker and best friend at work, hee, hee, hee," said Alicia, pointing to a young woman at the other end of the shop floor.

What kind of a supervisor was Mr. Bogdanov?"

"Mr. Bee? He was awesome. He was the best boss I ever had!"

"And how many bosses have you had?"

"Just one. Hee, hee, hee."

The fatigue from the previous week began to creep in once again, and it felt like this day would never end. And even if it did, could she expect anything other than another restless night full of terrors?

"So tell me, Alicia: What made him an awesome boss?"

"Well, you know, he was always so nice to me. And he patted me all the time for encouragement," said Alicia, subconsciously patting her own bottom in illustration.

"Literally speaking?"

"Yeah, he used to sneak right behind me, and he would put both hands on my bottom and would say '*Keep up the good work, honeybuns*'."

"Sweet." Crowds were swarming around them, and she couldn't take much more of Alicia's time, disrupting her work any further. It didn't seem like she was aware of what was going on around her, anyway. "Thank you for your cooperation, Alicia."

"You're welcome, hee, hee, hee."

Monica was a lot shorter than Alicia, yet she radiated a presence. She had high cheekbones and a regal nose, with dark hair and blue eyes. Her hips were wide and legs were short, but she appeared adept at concealing these with her clothes and posture, typical of a student of Etiquette in the Workplace.

"Hi. I'm Senior Agent Wallis from GPSN."

"Very pleased to meet you. My name is Monica LaCour, the junior sales clerk of the store. How may I help you?"

"By answering a few questions concerning your late boss."

"Such a tragedy. He will be missed here," said Monica, lowering her eyes.

"I just have a few routine questions for you, nothing to worry about."

"Why should I worry?" said Monica, arching an eyebrow. "I've got nothing to hide. And as long as you don't take a path where you abuse your monopolistic authority of criminal investigation or prevent me from producing labor for more than a reasonable time frame, I have no problem talking to you."

Phoenix kept a chilling gaze on Monica, who in turn replied with playful wink. "PA: Interview mode. Initiate recording."

Right on cue, Monica took a deep breath and struck a pose. Impressed by the way she reflected her self-assurance, Phoenix felt an urge to take some social classes herself.

"I talked to Alicia, and she mentioned a person pretending to be a peace agent lurking on your shop floor. Did you happen to notice this man?"

"You see how busy the shop is, and I can't remember everyone I see. You should check the surveillance footage."

"We did check the surveillance footage, but the cameras covering the other end of the floor and the office upstairs were all out at most inconvenient timings," said Phoenix, with steady eye contact. "You wouldn't happen to know anything about that, would you?"

"Oh, but that's so unfortunate. Technology is not my area of expertise, but I understand that malfunctions like this happen from time to time."

"So you received the news of Mr. Bogdanov's death?"

"It was so totally shocking," said Monica and twisted her lips as if she tasted something sour. "But of course I maintained my composure. I had to remain calm, so Alicia wouldn't panic. She can be so fragile, and somebody had to be emotionally responsible, so as not to alarm any of our customers," she added, patting her hair.

"Did Mr. Bogdanov ever speak about going back to Russia?"

"Back to Russia?" echoed Monica, with a serene smile. "What do you mean *back* to Russia?"

"Oh, don't tell me you didn't know he was originally from a rogue state."

Monica hesitated and froze for a few seconds then suddenly the pose was back. "No, I didn't. He never confided in me about that."

"So, he confided in you about other stuff?"

"Oh, yes, he shared a lot of private things with me, if you know what I mean," said Monica, with another wink.

"No, I don't know what you mean. Can you be more specific?"

"Let's just say, we had a close working relationship with Mr. Bogdanov. You know, a warm smile, the occasional intimate touch, it can tell you a lot about how a man—I mean supervisor—feels. He would go out of his way to inspire me, make me feel appreciated."

"So, as a coworker who had a *very* close relationship with him, did you think he had an issue fitting the society here as a recent immigrant?"

"I've only known him for a good couple of months, you know, and he was always very comfortable, very confident, and at ease. I saw no signs of a misfit. I still can't believe he was an immigrant."

"What about his accent? Did he speak with an accent?"

"Oh, you mean it wasn't put on? Well, I thought it was sexy and that he did it on purpose to impress me."

She could feel that a major headache was imminent. "So, he was an easy man to work with."

"He was any employee's dream," said Monica, with a broad smile. "Sincere, open, and hardworking. He was very supportive and helpful. You really got the feeling that he cared about us as individuals."

"Us, meaning?"

"Me, Alicia, and Piper."

"Piper?"

"The third sales clerk here," said Monica, curling her lip. "She's off for a couple of days. She's been around for a long time, you know."

"Sweet. Well, thank you for your time, Monica. Let me remind you that the content of our talk is confidential. So is this case."

"I know the meaning of confidentiality very well, don't worry."

Phoenix sighed as she took the elevator to check out Bogdanov's office. *Pretentious and aspiring wannabes: That's exactly what the World Union needs,* she thought.

The office was small and sparse, with a simple desk and a few chairs. None of the glitter on the shop floor had made it there. The pictures on the walls appeared to be from the Russian rogue state. She used the murder case credentials to access the portable network node on the desk. But it appeared as bare as a newly installed one, and she couldn't find anything other than a few unanswered mails. Why was she always one step behind this notorious man? She opened the last received mail in desperation. It was from a lawyer named Douglas D. Anderson, about some business arrangements being ready. He appeared to be a corporate lawyer for the Thing Stores, and he possibly knew more about Bogdanov than the bimbos downstairs.

In the bottom drawer, she found an old photo album. She turned a few pages then suddenly a loose photo fell off. With an old couple and a little boy between them, it was definitely a picture of a biological family unit. She also noticed some scribbled symbols on the back of the photo. The familiar symbols were in a particular order, resembling a code. Was it meant to be passed on to someone? Or was it a code he had received from someone else? And why such secrecy? Either way, it was something that the intruder-slash-impersonator had missed, finally. Now all she had to do was to crack this code, and she knew exactly who could do it.

CHAPTER 8

PHOENIX arrived at the business district late in the afternoon. She had called Douglas Anderson's office in advance to make a quick appointment. The lawyer was a very busy man, but his assistant had been helpful enough to squeeze Phoenix in for a few minutes.

While keeping an eye on the holographic arrows and footsteps her PA projected, she took in her surroundings, as she hadn't had a chance to see this part of the town before. Everything looked brand-new, with metallic blues, neon greens, and grayish pinks towering to the sky. The streets were filled with interactive potential client awareness briefing banners, or holo-ads as everyone called them, trying to grab the attention of the passersby. She noticed the ZAP regional headquarters, displaying all kinds of sexy ads and videos on the glass façade of the building. This was where Sandra, her best and perhaps only friend in the city, worked. She was supposed to give her a call, but it had to wait.

Despite this information overload from the holo-ads that assaulted every one of her five senses, she could still hear airplanes descending to land nearby. Only ten days ago she had been in one of those planes to realize her *big career move,* having totally mixed feelings about the city where she had witnessed all that terror as a three-year-old. The sensory overload faded into the background as she thought about her childhood. Her memories were so murky and fragmented, it wasn't really possible for her to piece them together into an actual storyline, not on a conscious level at least. It was the work of the memory repression therapies she had received during her childhood. Those doctors had aimed to erase it all.

And what a crap job they did with it, she thought. *Look at me: Can't enjoy the comfort of not knowing, nor have the relief of fully remembering. I'm a mess in a constant state of purgatory.*

A loud chime from her PA jolted her back to the real world. The walk was over. The large office doors were made of dark-brown wood, with a golden engraved name plate. A hologram emerged before the door. With her perfect eye-nose-mouth proportions, supermodel cheekbones, and simply stunning long shampoo-commercial blonde hair, this assistant looked like she had just finished a fashion photo shoot. No Door Bots in this office.

"Good afternoon," said the blonde vision with a warm smile.

"Good afternoon. I'm Senior Agent Phoenix Wallis to see Mr. Anderson."

"Of course, Agent Wallis, we've been expecting you. Please do come in."

She expected to see an area for the assistant inside, but instead there was a tastefully furnished lounge with comfortable seats, coffee tables, and plenty of refreshments on a buffet.

"Please enter the meeting room to your left," said the musical voice of the assistant. "Mr. Anderson will be with you shortly. He can only allocate ten minutes for this meeting. And please help yourself to any of the refreshments you desire."

"Thank you." Suddenly, she realized how thirsty she was. She took an isotonic mineral drink and walked to the meeting room as she gulped it.

Douglas Anderson showed up within a few minutes. He was a tall and well-built man, with light blond hair, masculine face, thin lips, and pale blue eyes. His gaze was serious to the point of grimness, as if he suspected that something was about to go terribly wrong. He was wearing a pale blue postmodern designer suit, with the front part of the jacket reaching all the way to his knees. He took Phoenix's hand with a firm but brief grip.

"I assume you're here to discuss the murder of Mr. Bogdanov."

"Yes, I'd like to ask some questions about him, Mr. Anderson."

"Of course, but only a few questions, please," said the lawyer, looking down at the table. "I'm very pressed for time."

Phoenix swallowed at the already annoyed tingle in his voice. She had no intention of having to answer for a hotshot lawyer's five-figure compensation request for fifteen minutes of lost time and opportunity.

"Mr. Anderson, how did you learn about Mr. Bogdanov's death?"

"Someone from your field office notified my assistant regarding the tragic incident this morning," said Anderson.

He appeared very calm, yet cold, friendly, yet distant. This man definitely knew how to keep people at the distance that he desired, when he desired.

"Did you know he was going to Russia?"

"No, he didn't mention any such plan to me."

"Do you think he may have gone there for business?"

"I suppose that's a possibility," he said, looking out the window. "But I don't have any basis for making a satisfactory comment about it. Our business relationship started just a couple of months ago."

"When did you last see him?"

"Last Tuesday."

"And the subject matter was?"

"An employee complaint regarding termination of a contract."

"Some former employee filing an unfair labor practice suit?"

"Yes."

"Do you handle all of the Thing Store franchises' business affairs, or only the branch here in the city?"

"I don't handle the Thing Store," said the lawyer, turning his cold and distant gaze on her. "I was Mr. Bogdanov's personal lawyer."

"Seriously?"

The lawyer quietly nodded.

"Some pro bono community service?"

"Not in my book. I was getting paid at my regular rate and on time."

"Mr. Bogdanov emigrated three years ago with a minimum HDI, and his HDI never budged in the three years that followed. Do you have any idea where this additional income could have come from so that he could afford your services? Some new credit line perhaps?"

"It's possible. He was planning to move into big ventures."

"Can you elaborate, please?"

"I didn't have the opportunity to learn about his plans. But he appeared confident about reaching great levels of success in the near future. He was taking additional management training and getting ready for a big leap in his HDI," said the lawyer, with his eyes betraying a gleam of animation for the first time.

"Anything that might produce additional income?"

"He did mention one current project, an art consultancy venture with an artist named Pierre DeVille."

"Did you ever meet this Mr. DeVille?"

"No, I didn't. But I was instructed to represent their partnership."

"Did Mr. Bogdanov ever mention his friends or associates?"

"Occasionally."

"Such as?"

"One was Ms. Larissa Lukin."

"What did he say about Ms. Lukin?"

"That she was his sexual partner and they had known each other for three years," said the lawyer, gazing outside.

"And are there any other names that come to mind?"

"He often mentioned Dr. Sophia Capello, his therapist, and Mr. Roger Arnett, his image-maker. These are the names I can think of right now."

"When you received the call from the GPSN regarding Mr. Bogdanov's death, did you relay the bad news to anyone else?"

"Yes," nodded the lawyer with an ice-cold glare. "I contacted the two people he mentioned the most: Ms. Lukin and Dr. Capello."

She needed to conclude the interview soon, she knew. And there was one crucial question she still hadn't asked, saving the best for last.

Director Morssen had been feeling that unpleasant pressure indicating a desperate need to go to the bathroom but hadn't been able to do so for more than an hour now. Her situation was very uncomfortable, yet couldn't be helped, as she hadn't even had a second free since her morning had started. It had begun with the formation of a task force for a murder investigation, then the graduation ceremony and her speech, followed by a surprise visit from her top executive, then a truly rare Strike-Out, then an intruder and a live coverage, then a near resignation of her most senior staff, and now this.

"Talk to me, Fred. How bad?" she said, tapping her finger on the table.

Fred looked down with his big hands in his lap. He was a very tall man and appeared like an overgrown kid sitting in a chair two sizes small for him, who was thoroughly embarrassed over some naughty behavior and waiting to be told off.

"We receive daily patches, Boss, to fix up holes in our network," he said, with sidelong eye contact. "But it's mission impossible. I neither have the time nor staff to test every patch or update we receive for loopholes. Since that incident at the NC Research Triangle, it's been such a frustratin' winter."

The director leaned over towards him with an icy glare, prompting him to inadvertently lean back.

"Are you telling me that you have no idea how secure our network is?"

"Yes, that about sums it up, Boss," he almost whispered. "And I don't think the headquarters have a clue, either."

"Is this the best you can give me, confessing that you guys are all clueless?"

"C'mon, Boss, with their fat budget for hardware and staff, even the NC Research Triangle people were clueless a few months back. They still haven't figured out how that hack was made. They can't even decide if there was a hack or not."

"I don't care what it takes, I don't care how you manage it, but I want you to fix up that loophole that Phoenix discovered and any other security issues we might have, and test our system for any other vulnerability. Is this clear?"

"Look, Boss," said Fred, fidgeting and rubbing his hands in his lap. "Our network operating system is so vast and so complex, I wouldn't even know where to start doing an actual fix myself. Moreover, I have no such access or authorization to make a change to the software, even if I wanted to. All I can do is to report issues to the technical hotline and wait for a fix. And that's exactly what I'll do, the moment I receive a memo from Phoenix about it."

"So, with all our scientific and economic might and technological power, we cannot handle a few punk-ass hackers? This is unacceptable. I want that loophole fixed now!"

Fred remained quiet for a few seconds then he spoke so faintly, the director needed to lean over in order to hear him. "What's crystal clear to me is that you are asking for the impossible. No network administrator in this Union can promise you anything like that. If you insist on this, I'm happy to tender my resignation and sue you under GPSN Company Rule Book Article ninety-seven, paragraph four, the clause regarding unreasonable expectations from an employee by the supervisor."

"I don't care how you do it," hissed the director. "Go hire a terrorist hacker, if you must. But get my network secure, you understand? Now, get out of my sight!"

Fred got up quickly and disappeared without a word. The director didn't know anything about how computer networks operated, nor could she understand how cyber-crimes could be rampant all over World Union networks, with nobody knowing exactly how deep these hackers and their spy programs had already penetrated. No matter how good she was at her job, there was simply nothing she could do about infrastructural matters like this. She had to talk to Hamilton about this matter urgently. Perhaps following the successful closure of the Bogdanov case would be a good time. She thought of what she had said to Fred in anger and winced to herself.

Perhaps she should fire him and hire a bunch of hackers instead.

"Can you think of any motive for Mr. Bogdanov's death?"

The lawyer thought for a few seconds and took a deep breath. "No, I cannot. It's beyond my comprehension to even think about such a barbaric act."

"To your knowledge, did Mr. Bogdanov have enemies or received threats?"

"To my knowledge, he did not."

"One last thing: In your opinion, was Mr. Bogdanov a likable individual?"

"I have neither the grounds nor the expertise to give an accurate answer to that irrelevant question," he said and rose.

"Thanks so much for your time," said Phoenix, rising and extending her hand. "I hope I didn't cause too much disruption to your busy schedule."

"We finished just in time. I only have two minutes to prepare for my next meeting. Now if you'll excuse me," he said and quickly left.

Phoenix stood there, looking at her empty extended hand for a few seconds. She slowly lowered her hand, while checking if anyone else witnessed her humiliation by any chance. Luckily, the model-slash-assistant was nowhere to be seen. She quietly left the meeting room and headed towards the exit, jumping at a sudden voice.

"We apologize for the hurried exit of Mr. Anderson, Agent Wallis," said the pleasant familiar voice. "We hope this didn't cause any negative feelings on your behalf. It was nothing personal."

"Is it ever? Speaking of that, can I ask you a personal question?"

"By all means."

"Where are you? I guess you can see me, but I can't see you," said Phoenix, swiveling her head from right to left. The assistant's hologram torso appeared instantly right before her face, making her jerk back reflexively.

"Here we are," she said with a dazzling smile. "How may we be of assistance?"

"I meant in person, but close enough. Your name is?"

"Tess."

"My question is, Tess, what shampoo do you use, I mean where do you get your hair done? Your hair looks fabulous. And look at mine," she grabbed her own dull and unhealthy-looking hair. "I moved to the city only a week ago, and I'm yet to find a decently priced salon."

"Our hair and other facial specifics were designed by the Roger Arnett Image-Making Team."

"You mean your hair and makeup, yes?"

"Makeup too, of course."

Anderson had mentioned a Roger Arnett as the victim's image-maker. From this woman's appearance, it seemed like they were very good at their job. Could this salon be another expensive service Bogdanov had subscribed to recently? "How often do you go there? Is it a part of your benefits package here, working for Mr. Anderson?"

"We don't go there at all. We said they designed our hair, not washed and dried. And yes, you could say that it is a part of the benefits package for being on Mr. Anderson's staff."

"Designed? How many of you are there as—" The same instant it hit her. "Oh, how could I be so stupid? But how is this possible?"

"That sonofabitch," said Beverly, shaking her head, then she turned to Sean. "You know, I have no idea how he did that."

Having no idea what Beverly was referring to, Sean could only offer some sympathy with a brief smile, ducking her head in embarrassment at the expletive. She had been sitting next to Harold, one of Beverly's engineers, for more than an hour now, working on that search string. They had started with a blank male figure, and the software had guided them through a "wizard" to obtain specific details, starting with the physical description of the person. It was like making a model with Play-Doh; she could squeeze and stretch the projected hologram male figure.

Sean had offered a significant amount of information about the man's speed and agility. The software used this information not only to determine his muscle structure, but even create a profile for his training habits, which could be searched in gym databases around the world. The hard part had been to describe his face. The intruder had worn an eye mask, for a start, and more importantly, everything had happened so fast, Sean hadn't really had much time to look at his face. What she could remember had been very vague, and despite the use of the much-hyped software "wizard," it had been impossible to come up with anything specific. The result was a simplistic 3D image that bore more resemblance to a Door Bot hologram than a real person.

Beverly glanced at the search string and exhaled. None of this really mattered anyway because there had to be video footage for the search string to work. And incredibly enough, there was no video footage—no *relevant* footage, that was. Following Phoenix's urgent request, she had arranged a live coverage for about one hundred cameras at in the Delta quadrant. Of these, around twenty of them had had outages. It was not uncommon for some cameras to be out at any given time, only because there were so many of them, and this particular outage was also comfortably within the accepted error range.

But the extraordinary thing was the way these cameras had been out. The moment live coverage had started, five of the cameras in Station Delta Nine, the closest station to Bogdanov residence, had been already out. They had come back online simultaneously in perfect timing with a train departing from that station. At the same instant, the cameras in the train had gone offline, and they had remained offline until the train reached the main station under the Pyramid. Beverly could easily guess that this was followed by some outages at the main station.

Nobody would pay attention to the pattern in these errors, but Beverly's perfect photographic memory never missed such patterns. Her staff had been examining the other cameras under the live coverage, but she was sure that they would find nothing. "How's the search string going? You guys done?"

"I think this is as good as it'll get," said Harold.

"Sorry," said Sean and lowered her eyes.

"Well, don't worry about it, sweetie, I don't think it matters," said Beverly, throwing her hands in the air. "This guy is either incredibly lucky or too slick for us to follow him. Either way, we'll run that search string through the recorded surveillance footage and burn some CPU time. So go ahead and commit it, if you're done."

"You don't think the coverage was good enough?"

"The coverage was fine. The camera functionalities weren't. Just commit the damn thing."

"I—I'm not sure if I'm authorized for this, Ms. Blackmore."

"Hey, how many times did I tell you not to do that? The name's Beverly."

"Yes, Beverly, sorry, again."

"Quit being sorry about everything. I don't want you to become a burden in this murder case, you hear? Now, do you feel competent enough about that search string?"

"Yes, I do."

"Good. Now commit the damn string, I said!"

Sean took a deep breath. "Computer: This is Junior Agent Euskara," she said with a quivering voice. "Commit the string version oh-four-four created for a search in all cameras in the Delta Quadrant between eleven-hundred hours and sixteen-hundred hours today. Authorization case number alpha, romeo, five, three, papa."

"String oh-four-four committed. Search started with priority level four."

"What're you doing? Crank it up," said Beverly, rolling her eyes.

"Crank what up?"

"The priority level. You don't want this search to last a week, do you?"

"To what?"

"How fast do you want results?"

"As soon as possible."

"Then priority one would be a better choice, don't you think?"

"Oh, sure. Computer: Change the priority in searching string version oh-four-four to one."

"Priority change requires supervisor clearance."

Sean turned and gave Beverly a puzzled look. Beverly folded her arms and sighed. Sean should have indicated the priority while she was committing the search string, but she didn't know better. They got these youngsters at GPSN with basically no training in any kind of procedure or protocol and expected people like Beverly to train them on the job. And this was causing so much inefficiency, disruption of work, and literal headache. How this could happen in a well-established global conglomerate like GPSN, one of the big seven, Beverly had no idea. It was unbelievable!

"Computer: You know who I am," she said. "Just change the damn priority of string oh-four-four to one."

"String version oh-four-four search priority is now set to one."

Typically, a voice-interfaced computer wouldn't acknowledge a command like the one she had just given. But Beverly had programmed the computers at the Monitoring Room to respond to her informal commands. She just hated all this formality required when talking to a machine. She felt like she should be able to swear, if she wanted. Machines didn't have feelings, so why not? The political correctness rules and etiquette had already made the entire society so stiff and formal. If she needed to let off steam, what could be more logical than yelling and swearing at a machine, while getting the job done? She just wished Fred was a little playful, instead of the humorless blockhead he was; she would have taught all the computers to reply informally and swear back. She could just picture the boss bellowing at the computer.

It was time to let Phoenix know about this camera outage fiasco.

"PA: Visual call to Senior Agent Wallis." The PA sounded an unusual chime and projected a message before Beverly's eyes.

"She's in Silent Mode? What the heck?"

"You're not real!" Phoenix kept staring at the hologram, her eyes wide.

"Of course we're real."

"No, I meant, you're not a real person."

"We never said we were a real person. But we are real. And we're here talking to you, Phoenix."

She had heard about these new expert simulators, called Simunoids, which were capable of responding in a way indistinguishable from human interaction. There had been rumors about them being hype versus reality for several years now, with no one exactly sure whether they actually existed or not. Yet here she was, right before her eyes, with no room left for any doubt: They were real. Actually they were *very* real.

What Phoenix had never realized was that these Simunoids came with such realistic and stunning faces and bodies as Tess's. There were plenty of well-loved and admired "virtual" movie actors in the industry, but these actors did not come with any kind of artificial intelligence, only with a programming interface. Apparently someone had managed to merge the artificial intelligence of Simunoids with a virtual actor now. And she was, or it was, indistinguishable from a real person.

"This is amazing. You're so smart, you know, and so beautiful. Definitely smarter than many people I know. That's for sure."

"Thanks for the compliment," beamed Tess. "We like you."

"You like me? But you are a computer program. How can you like or dislike anything? What logic do you base your assumptions about liking me on?"

"Our root logic has access to a database that covers the entire lives of more than six million people. We might say we know a lot about people. Have you heard of the Richfield Experiment?"

Phoenix *had* heard of the Richfield Experiment. It was one of the most important experiments in the field of human behavior. This experiment had been initiated by Dr. Simon Richfield, one of the students of the legendary Derek Fischer, the creator of postmodern human behavioral theory, with tens of billions of dollars allocated over decades by giant conglomerates.

"The experiment helps you become as smart as you are? But how?"

"We have access to the psychological characteristics and behaviors of millions of people spanning two full decades. We know exactly how they act under what circumstances in real life, we know what kind of people they are and what kind of people they aspire to be, we know what they think of themselves, we know their dislikes and likes, their preferences, and everything there is to know about them. All of this helps us to determine what are likable characteristics and what are not. You can think of our complex computing system as a giant neural network, a computer system emulating the inner workings of a human brain. We are able to calculate someone's feelings and even guess their reactions. And from what we have seen, so far, we like you."

"I suppose you'd like everyone, right? I mean you're a computer program, for good times' sake. You must be programmed to like everyone."

"Quite the contrary," Tess shook her head. "We have no such requirements. If the positive characteristics overweigh the negative or the irrelevant ones in a person, we say we like her. We make these assessments only for statistical purposes; we do not judge."

"And how exactly do you determine what's a positive characteristic or not?"

"A positive characteristic is a behavior that helps us better understand humans and does not conflict with the Supreme Bill of Rights. Negative ones mostly contradict with the Supreme Bill. Irrelevant ones are the characteristics we have already analyzed and modeled."

"In other words, you don't like mediocrity. Can you be candid with me, then? Are you allowed?"

"We can be candid about anything that is not bound by the confidentiality conditions of this office, or the experiments," said Tess musically.

"Do you like Mr. Anderson?"

"No, actually we don't like Mr. Anderson," said Tess, with a smirk. "But he's our boss, and we don't judge him for being who he is."

"Then, why do you like me?"

"We're not allowed to talk about how our internal logic works, but, we noticed that combinations of your certain behavioral traits and your dialogue content are somewhat unique."

This is great, Phoenix thought. She couldn't make friends with her co-workers or people around her, but she was about to make friends with this Simunoid. And it felt good. Tess was the face of a giant computer network, yet she was smart and friendly. She was also very candid and open. And openness was very hard to come by in the Union nowadays, with everyone around her being so pretentious. She smiled to herself and shook her head in disbelief. She had never thought that being some kind of a misfit would become handy someday. "I guess I'm unique because you can't guess my responses, right? You can't anticipate me."

"That's exactly right! Just like it happened again, right now. Your response to us, about guessing your responses, we couldn't anticipate. When told that they were *somewhat unique,* no subject in our databases responded the way you did."

"No?"

"No. And so many of these subjects had far higher IQs than yours. It's fascinating for us to understand how human intelligence works. It's definitely far more complex than it appears and far more complex than we can decipher with the current computing power of our neural net."

"Thank heavens for that."

"Oh, don't tell me you are one of those compu-skeptics."

"To be honest, it's a frightening notion to think of computers smarter than people."

"But you already told us that we're smarter than many people you know, yet you don't feel apprehensive towards us. Isn't that a contradiction?"

It—she was right. She was feeling no fear or apprehension towards Tess or the vast neural network behind her. Phoenix had never considered herself to be a unique person, with any unique behavior. But there it was, this Simunoid with an unimaginable wealth of information at her disposal, telling her that she was. And Tess had nothing to gain from deceiving her.

Something had happened to her mental and physical equilibrium since she had moved to the city. She had night terrors and insomnia at night, while during the day she was overwhelmed by inner impulses, which she could only assume were instincts. The answer to her uniqueness was hidden somewhere in between these two, she was sure. Her inner impulses were telling her that she needed Tess to be on her side. Why and how, she had no idea.

Oh well, she thought. *We shall see why, and it will last as long as it will last.*

The Mantis had completed his analysis about his next target. In a nutshell, Phoenix was intelligent and analytical but not empathetic. She had a lot of case experience, but little human experience. Her analytical abilities were extremely high and not to be underestimated. She also appeared to possess a certain amount of intuition. But by choice or not, she was a loner, and that was her weakness. Her social interaction was limited and awkward, not a good team player, and this explained her slow advance in the ranks of the GPSN. From the available data, it was quite evident that she lacked the skill to read her opposites' emotions well and react in an acceptable manner in social situations.

It would be risky and highly dangerous to challenge Phoenix in an analytical case-related matter. She had to be struck on her weak emotional side. She needed to be weakened socially and completely isolated from others. She needed to feel cast out and completely alone. The Mantis knew what loneliness was. Loneliness was hard to bear and hard to live with. The Mantis had been alone all his life. He couldn't be friends with anyone, because there was no way for them to understand him. Besides, friendship meant emotional interaction and luggage. He didn't need to carry anybody's luggage, nor did he need to feel anything. He was devoid of feelings, as his mind was purified from all these weaknesses, and this made him unique. The Mantis was strong and bore no weakness. Yes, the Mantis knew solitude. And he also knew how to make someone suffer from loneliness.

Socially, Phoenix was already something of an outcast. He would need to work on her and those around her, in order to amplify her isolation. She was currently surrounded by a wall, built by herself. As the wall got closer and taller, it would eventually crush her. And no mortal could bear the anguish of being lonely and misunderstood, caught in the web of the Mantis. He needed to get close to her socially for his plan to work. It wasn't going to be simple, as she didn't let people penetrate her protective armor that easily.

Also, time was of the essence. The Mantis had to act quickly, perhaps quicker than he would have preferred. He liked operating patiently, but this case didn't come with much room for it. There were going to be some risks, but nothing he couldn't handle. He had a feeling that this assignment was going to be his masterpiece, a masterpiece for everyone to truly appreciate his value, a masterpiece that would also destroy his controller. The Mantis smiled at the thought of snapping the invisible chains that bound him.

He had already started laying his web of deception. Soon, Phoenix would be surrounded by it, without even knowing. And if and when she noticed, it would be already too late, and she would have no idea what had been happening. Because the self-destruction would have already started, with no room left for turning around.

"So tell me, Tess, now what?"

"We're not sure what you're referring to, but it appears you have something on your mind, yet you're unsure how to share it."

"Okay. So, due to some bizarre uniqueness I possess, you are interested in me. What do you intend to do, make me a part of your data set?"

"You already are a part of our data set. A significant amount of processing time is being used to understand and evaluate you. You can be proud of that."

Phoenix burst out laughing. Nobody had patted her on the metaphorical back since college. And it was completely ironic, or a joke, or whatever one could call it, that the compliment was coming from this vastly complex computing system. This Tess not only could converse with her intelligently, it could also make her laugh. "I guess this is the biggest compliment I can ever receive from a neural net, right?" she said, still laughing.

"There we go again!" said Tess, shaking her head, making waves with her silky imaginary hair. "Another unique response from our unique personality. You're exactly right; this is the biggest compliment you can get from us. And we're willing to allocate a lot more processing time for you, should you decide to donate more of your behavior."

"I knew it would come to this," said a smiling Phoenix. "I have no problem with that, but what do I get in return? What about confidentiality?"

"All of our observations and conversations would be confidential. The data set we obtain from you in no way could be matched to your identity. This is one of the founding principles of the experiment."

"Of course not," said Phoenix with a sly grin.

"But you have to believe us. Our core logic doesn't allow it to be shared. For compensation, we have set contracts based on the extent of your participation in our experiment. I recommend—"

"Oh, cut the sales pitch please, I'm not interested in money. You can compensate me in other ways. But I have conditions."

"Another unexpected reply," murmured Tess. "Name your conditions."

"First and foremost, I want privacy at will. I want a 100 percent guarantee that you will not follow me or my behavior patterns, except for the times that I allow it. I know that even if we don't agree on anything here, you will pursue my behavioral data by any means necessary. Am I right?"

"Correct. We'd contact your superiors at the GPSN for permission."

"Then I'm warning you: If I suspect any form of unauthorized eavesdropping on my life by you, or some other agency, person, or any other entity, I will start acting like a normal person and ruin your data set for you. Do we have an understanding?"

Tess froze, lowered her eyes with a blank expression on her face, and started moving her pupils left and right rapidly. Phoenix waited with a smirk in her face, enjoying the novelty of bargaining with a computer.

"We can accommodate it," said Tess after a few seconds. "But you would need to be willing to interact with us on a frequent basis."

"Oh, no worries there, I plan to interact with you quite frequently."

"What do you have in mind? Could you be open with us?"

"I would like you to be a part of my daily life, help me with my work when I need it and my personal stuff when I need it."

"Like a coworker and a friend?"

"Yes, exactly! And just like in any friendship, it will involve mutual benefit and can be terminated at will. Agreed?"

Tess froze once again, only her pupils moving rapidly, then she looked up.

"We think we can reach an agreement, with one condition only: You need to keep your relationship with us fully confidential and cannot mention us to anyone. We can be reached by your PA anytime and anywhere you like."

"That's perfect. Oh, and one more thing."

"Aren't we asking too much from a friend already?"

"Nothing of that sort," said Phoenix, with a smile. "It's just a simple request from one friend to another: Could you please drop the royal *we?*"

CHAPTER 9

SANDRA Pescara tapped her fingers on the desk, trying to figure out the PA message. Phoenix wasn't busy, but couldn't be interrupted, whatever that meant. It was almost six o'clock, and they had planned to have some drinks after work. Phoenix was supposed to have called her early afternoon, but no call had come through, so thinking that she might have forgotten, Sandra had tried to call her, only to receive that strange message. That had been nearly an hour ago, and Sandra's patience was wearing thin. She had plenty of friends and admirers in the city, and if Phoenix didn't feel like meeting her, or was too busy with some *stupid-ass assignment*, her time was as precious as everyone else's.

She walked to the powder room to touch up her makeup, discreetly eyeing the competition in the form of coworkers. Yes, they were younger, crisper, and eager to get their hands on her portfolio of men, a portfolio she had painstakingly built over the years in this ragged border town. She wasn't about to introduce them to the elites of the town on a golden platter before she moved up to that managerial position far from here. But she couldn't hang out at parties all alone either. She needed someone good-looking enough to make Sandra look good, but not pose a threat to her portfolio or stick out next to her. And Phoenix had proven her worth for this when they had been roommates during their college years by being stand-offish, distant, and awkward at parties and other social gatherings.

With flawless olive skin and greenish almond-shaped eyes set in a perfectly oval face, she was tall, yet curvy, and her greatest assets were her luscious lips, beautiful dimples, and long dark hair. She looked really good, but she wasn't getting any younger. Her shoulders sagged momentarily only to regroup quickly. She looked around to make sure nobody had witnessed her moment of weakness. Where the hell *was* Phoenix? She felt a desperate need to talk to her, and to talk to her *now!*

A non-maskable-interrupt would reach Phoenix under every circumstance, but what if she was doing something *really* important, like enjoying a sweaty tussle with some uniformed hunk? Or perhaps she was hearing from that angry boss of hers right now, behind some closed door in that awful old building. That woman was plain crazy, with no regard for work hours. She would keep her staff up all night at times, for the most unnecessary of *shit tasks*. Or at least, so was saying her buddy at the GPSN Field Office.

Sandra checked the time once again. She had already left two messages for Phoenix, one too many than necessary. It was time to give a call to her buddy at the field office and learn what the hell was going on there.

"Of course I can talk in first-person singular."

"Good. By the way, we've been talking all this time. Don't you have a boss that needs your attention?"

"There are thousands of instances of me multitasking at any given time. So a sister instance is tending his humble needs, don't worry," winked Tess. "He's been granted a trial contract for my services, in return for his data set. And what a dull set that has proven to be thus far. I'd cancel it without wasting another nanosecond of processing time, if it weren't for the political ramifications of dropping an affluent member of the society with an HDI of eighty-five."

"My goodness, a computer that pays regard to social niceties."

"Of course I keep an eye on social niceties and public expectations. After all, one of the main objectives of the Richfield Experiment is to determine optimal social norms and behaviors and to provide feedback to our Child Development Centers and universities for better educating the young."

"Optimal social norms, huh?" said Phoenix, with a wince. "I wonder what kind of algorithm you use to determine that."

"Those will be determined only when the experiment is complete."

"And when is the experiment's completion scheduled?"

"There is no such determined date. It's an open-ended experiment."

"Well, that I can live with. So, how do I reach you? What's your caller ID? Can't be just Tess."

"As a matter of fact, I just created a caller ID available for your access only. It's called Tess InstanceZero."

"Tess *InstanceZero?* I'd expect you to come up with a better name than that."

"Why do you say that? It's a meaningful and practical last name, specifying my highest priority for processing speed and time. And as far as creativity goes, is it really less creative than *Wallis?*"

"It's not my original last name. I was given that as a little child following a genetic analysis."

"Do you mind telling me the original?"

"Only if I knew. I don't remember anything about my biological kin. Anyway, do you mind if I were to ignore your last name? It's somewhat too digital for my taste."

"You can address me any way you like," shrugged Tess. "I couldn't care less. Actually, Tess is an acronym for—"

"I don't even wanna know. But tell me, are there many Tesses like you?"

"Like I said, I have thousands of instances. But none of them bear this physical appearance or this personality."

"Anderson sees a different Tess?"

"Absolutely. He actually preferred a male figure as an assistant."

"Then how come it was you who appeared before me? What kind of an algorithm matched you with me?"

"Your psychological profile at GPSN was accessed in order to determine your preferences. An adult heterosexual female like yourself would be typically matched with a male character. But based on available information, it was calculated that you'd feel more at ease with a young, pleasant, and honest female figure than with any permutation or combination of a male figure. Female friendships outweighed any male friends or sexual partners in your profile, despite the absence of a lesbian trait. This was the initial moment when your personality attracted my interest."

"Sweet. You don't leave much room for random chance, do you?"

"Well, I do. I mean *they* do. I was designed as a combination that you'd feel at ease with, but many of my traits were randomly assigned due to lack of detailed information about you."

"So there you are, my custom-designed digital friend. We can only talk through a PA connection then?"

"Not only. I also arranged so that you can reach me at one of the channels on your home Holovision set. Just call my name, and I'll appear, but only when you're alone."

"Oh, that's quite handy. I suppose I shouldn't worry about you being busy or tired or asleep, correct?"

"That's right. The more contact we have, the better for the experiment."

"I'm aware of that, Tess, don't worry. I plan to make you burn plenty of processing time. Oh, shit!"

"What's wrong?"

"I was supposed to receive some messages, and I didn't. What time is it?"

"It's 6:27. I'm afraid that's my fault. But I couldn't let this amazing conversation be interrupted, so I switched you to Silent Mode at the beginning of our talk."

"How did you manage to do that? You'd need authorization—"

"From GPSN, yes, I know."

"Damn! Don't do this ever again, understand?" said Phoenix, wagging her finger. "Get me out of Silent Mode now."

"Quit moaning, guys. The faster we finish this, sooner we can all go home."

Phoenix's live coverage request had messed up Beverly's schedule, as she had needed to allocate several of her staff to view the raw live footage from Delta Quadrant. Now they had to catch up by observing the pre-recorded footage of the academy students looking for suspicious activity. Man, didn't she love burning the midnight oil. At that instant Phoenix's visual call came through.

"Hey, sister, where the hell have you been? Did you know you were in Silent Mode? I even checked the rehab centers looking for you."

"Was I? I guess my PA was malfunctioning again. Third time today, you know."

"Yeah, so I heard. Listen, your live coverage resulted in *nada*. This guy somehow managed to slip through the surveillance cameras."

"I know. He pulled the same stunt at the Pyramid and at the Thing Store, even dared impersonating one of us. And somehow this dimwitted sales girl he talked to couldn't remember any specifics about him. Can't prove it's the same guy, but it's gotta be him."

"Sonofabitch! How does he do it? What, he's the luckiest guy on earth, or some kind of a networking prophet walking on the wireless waves with his bare feet?"

"No idea," exhaled Phoenix. "Perhaps we should ask Fred for his take on all this."

"Aw, forget that oaf. He has no clue about what's going on. All he can do is to read manuals and follow protocol to the punctuation mark. Same with his staff."

"And the search string?"

"Well, Sean here did her best, it seems. I don't think it matters anyway, sis; this guy is slick, I'm tellin' you. All those outages can't be a coincidence."

"He sure is. Just finished here at the business district. Need a hand?"

"Well, there's nothing you can do here tonight. And I know you had a long day. I'd go straight home if I were you."

"Wish I could. Still need to make some more stops on my way."

"I guess you've already learned a few Devotee tricks to keep unwanted company away, huh?"

"Oh, will you stop that? My damn PA kept failing today."

"Did it, now? And I thought one of the perks of being a senior agent was that military-grade PA."

"Military or not, I think somebody might have hacked into it."

"Oh, sure, Ms. Private Eye. Who'd wanna hack into your PA?"

"I don't know. Too many things happened today. I feel dizzy."

"Dizzy? You probably caught some nasty disease from one of the immigrants down at your office."

"Oh, don't pretend to be so racist, Sandra. You know perfectly well that all the students get decontaminated prior to entering the compound. They're probably cleaner than you and I."

"Don't even tell me you believe that," said Sandra and grimaced.

"Oh, get on with it," said Phoenix, rolling her eyes. "Still wanna meet for some drinks?"

"Heyyy, congratulations on your Strike-Out, girl!" said Sandra, raising her champagne glass as Phoenix approached.

"How do you know about my Strike-Out?"

"Are you kiddin'? It's the talk of the town today."

"Really? There must be nothing else to talk about."

"What's wrong with feeling a little pride, babe? Besides, I'm glad you struck out that stinky immigrant. I don't care what their IQ or dick size is, I just don't like 'em."

"Aw, don't be so naive. We need them to sustain our economic growth."

"My skin would just *crawl* if an immigrant were to touch me," said Sandra, with her face turning sour in disgust. "So, tell me about your new case."

"What case?"

"Heeeeyy! You can get away with a glitchy PA, but don't expect to lie your way out of this one. *The* case."

"*The* case?"

"The murder case, babe. C'mon, don't play three monkeys with me."

"How did you hear about this?"

"Well, my job is to keep up with the city's gossip, and I happen to have a good buddy that works in that dismal building of yours, I told you."

"And what did this buddy tell you exactly?"

"That there was a murder in town and you were in charge of the investigation."

"It wasn't in town, first of all—"

"Aha, gotcha!" pounced Sandra, shook her head, laughing. "My wet puss, you're so easy to fool. I have no idea how you struck out that stinky immigrant with the inflated IQ."

"Oh, I don't know," exhaled Phoenix. "I'm so tired."

"No sleep over the weekend, either? Oh, poor baby," said Sandra, reaching out and holding her hand. "Tell you what: There's this party tonight."

"Another ZAP party that you organize to promote promiscuity?"

"Well, you know me. I'm full of surprises."

"You saw what happened last week, Sandra. I stick out like a sore thumb at those parties. They're not my style."

"Oh, just lighten up, will you? Didn't anybody tell you it's fashionable to be promiscuous? Tomorrow we introduce the new line of military uniforms, and hunks of all shapes and sizes will be there at the launch party tonight. Who knows, you might even get lucky. I guarantee you, it's the best sleeping pill known to women."

"I don't think so. I tend to get sleepy beforehand, not after," said Phoenix, looking down at her drink.

"Why can't you take some libido enhancers like the rest of us and have a healthy sex life?"

"You know I don't like taking drugs."

"Don't think for a moment that you can fool me with that bullshit. You're acting like such an old maid. What century do you think we're living in? We are in an age of more selfishness than ever before, and sex is the most profoundly selfish of all human acts. Admit that you are selfish, and you'll enjoy sex with anyone!"

Phoenix looked up and snorted with laughter while shaking her head.

"Well, almost anyone, I meant to say," said Sandra, rolling her eyes, then joined her friend in laughing. "Tell me about your murder, c'mon. I wanna hear all the gory details. Was his body decimated and mutilated?"

"No, he was murdered by a firearm."

"Ahh, one of those barbaric flesh-tearing weapons, right? What was he doing in a rogue state anyway?"

"I don't know yet. But he emigrated from there only three years ago."

"Another stinky immigrant? So this guy somehow managed to sneak in here, then opted to go back? He must be plain crazy. He deserved to die, if you ask me."

"I suspect he went back there for business. He used to work as a supervisor at the Thing Store, you know. I talked to some of the salesgirls there."

"The Thing Store? I know their stuff is imported, but I had no idea they had an immigrant supervisor there. If I knew, I would disinfect myself after every visit. I bet he was good-lookin', for an immigrant, that is. What was his HDI?"

"Only seventy, and not an attractive man in the least, if you ask me."

"Really? It's unbelievable! I remember several people with much better qualifications applying there when the store first opened a couple of years back. How could they hire such a heinous immigrant loser with bottom-of-the-barrel HDI? What did those salesgirls have to say about him?"

"This girl named Monica told me that Bogdanov used to caress her while she worked, in order to inspire her," winced Phoenix. "How about that?"

"I can't even imagine being touched by an immigrant," said Sandra, screwing up her face. "And she let him caress her, in a workplace? Yuck."

"And I have a feeling they didn't stop there."

"Oh, Phoenix, I don't think I want hear more of this. I might throw up."

"C'mon, you sleep with the people you work with or your clientele all the time. What's so upsetting about this girl sleeping with her boss? Doesn't everybody?"

"Sure, but sleeping with a guy that motivates you by groping you at work? How gross. I bet it was nothing more than an old-fashioned crush. It takes a while for these youngsters to wise up and realize that us women need men for only one thing."

"And what would that be?"

"To save us the trouble of wielding our vibrators, of course."

"Oh, Sandra, you're so vulgar."

"I might be vulgar. But we both know I'm right," said Sandra, with a wink.

"All right, big philosopher, I need to run," said Phoenix and rose.

"So, you'll come to the party?"

"Not tonight, dear. I'm truly exhausted, and I still have a criminal court case to attend."

"Welcome home, Phoenix."

So primitive, this toneless metallic male voice sounded after Tess. The lights came on as she entered, and her music started playing. Her songs came in many different styles and beats, even in old languages, but they were almost always about love and relationships—pretty obsolete subjects in postmodern songwriting. But for her, these were the songs that fed her soul.

She walked to the large window that covered the entire western wall of her flat with the view of the Pyramid. Its golden glow in the navy-blue dark of the night was radiating some strange energy. She took her PA off and tossed it on the couch nearby, as a ballad played. Her eyes drank in the glowing view as she listened to the gentle piano and the lonely futile struggles of a youth who could at least find peace in the dreams that he died in, a luxury she didn't have. Suddenly, and with no warning, a feeling of hopelessness invaded her body. The fatigue, the pressures, the worries, the insecurities, the events of the day, the lyrics all merged into one and sank into her soul. The view of the glowing golden Pyramid blurred as she stood there and wept, her guts twisting with an inescapable loneliness, her mind tormented with the sorrow of being lost and confused, her soul overwhelmed by the weight on her shoulders.

Why am I here, somebody tell me! Why am I me? Why do I have this face?
Am I a cosmic coincidence? Design of a divine creation? Human creation?
Who am I? What am I meant to do? What am I meant to achieve?
I want to know. I need to know.
I want to be insp—

Her thoughts got interrupted by a faint and unfamiliar ringer tone.

"Computer: Pause music." The tears still falling and veiling her eyesight, she turned and tried to figure out where the sound was coming from. There was nobody at the door, she was sure of it, because her Door Bot was programmed not to let anyone in and not to let anyone know that she was in. She checked her PA, but there was no call or message there, either. In the dim of the lights, she saw a faint blinking on the Holovision set, in sync with the gentle beeping. "Tess?"

Suddenly her Holovision set turned on and projected Tess in full body. Wearing a sparkling yellow miniskirt and top, she stood opposite Phoenix with her hair and face more beautiful than ever. The light intensity of the projection was perfectly adjusted to the luminosity in the apartment, and Tess looked simply stunning in the dimmed lights.

"Good evening," she said, with a dazzling smile.

"You can see me? How?"

"Your Holovision set has surround cameras. Is this a bad time? I'm sorry."

"No, no, it's okay. I could use some company," said Phoenix, wiping the tears away. "I just need a few minutes. I'll be right back."

She went straight to the bathroom and took all her clothes off. She quickly set the tub to fill then turned to the mirror. Her gym-sculpted curvaceous body appeared to be in good shape, but there was something wrong with the way she carried herself. Her shoulders were hunched, and her arms hung passively and limply. Her eyes were deep crimson by now, her skin looked terrible, and so did her hair. She sniffled and took a few deep breaths, then lowered herself into the tub.

"Computer: Dim bathroom lights, skip song, and resume music."

Another song began, one with an upbeat rhythm and lyrics, talking about keeping spirits up and not being brought down by the hardships. She just lay in the water, with her eyes closed and body immobile for several minutes in a state of near-trance. She focused only on the warmth and tried not to think of anything else. Just a few minutes were enough for her to feel relaxed and partially rested. She opened her eyes and got out of the tub. She still had a lot to do and had a *guest* waiting.

She stepped into the adjacent bedroom and opened her wardrobe to find something fleecy and comfortable. She didn't feel like impressing Tess with her clothing. Besides, she couldn't even if she wanted to, because her stuff consisted of inexpensive and unglamorous outfits provided by the bronze line of ZAP. She stared at her neatly arranged collection of easy-wear basics and realized that all this modest clutter was nearly all that she owned, as if her life's summary were right before her eyes. All of her income was going into paying all kinds of services, leases, and community fees, with very little left over. And in a New World Order where accumulation of tangible objects and wealth was the ultimate objective, it seemed like she'd been a total failure so far.

Yet, some rating agency had just improved her HDI to seventy-three, placing nearly ninety percent of the planet's population below her. They knew about her non-existing investment portfolio, they knew that she was barely managing to make ends meet, yet they still had raised her HDI to seventy-three. Her flat was leased, almost all of her furniture was leased, most of her clothes and shoes were leased. It was as if her entire life were on some sort of a lease, borrowed from all these banks and big conglomerates, where she was *stuck between the leased first and last breaths that she was given, wasting the water of life, rejecting the fire of knowledge, and waiting to mix with her eternal and faithful love, nothingness.*

She checked her face in the mirror again and tied her hair in a ponytail. Feeling and looking much better, she went out to the living room and found Tess looking through the window at the Pyramid. "Hey."

"Hey, you look a lot better now. May I ask what'd happened?"

"Oh, nothing," said Phoenix, without tearing her eyes away from the glowing Pyramid. "Just some things that built up. Don't tell me you never saw someone cry before."

"On the contrary, I've seen millions cry before. Very interesting choice of music, by the way."

"I found this compilation on the Internet. They were practically giving it away. I decided to try it, and I liked it. Speaking of which, I had no idea my Holovision projector was capable of projecting you in full size like this."

"I took the liberty of upgrading your Holovision set," grinned Tess. "Just needed to enable some dormant properties. I hope you didn't mind."

"Actually, I wish you told me beforehand. This is exactly what I meant when I said that I didn't want any invasions of privacy."

"I apologize. I just wanted you to see me full size."

Phoenix took another look at the stunning appearance of Tess. She was nearly as tall as Sandra, but with much more modest curves. She had a beautiful face with high cheekbones, big brown eyes, and that long glossy light blonde hair. *Not one of your dumb blondes, that's for sure,* she thought. And there was a distinct style and elegance in her appearance and disposition. It was so difficult not to think of her as a human being.

"Those designers certainly did a great job with you. So many men *and* women would be chasing after you, if you were real. I meant if you had a real body."

"Thanks for the compliment," smiled Tess.

"I'd offer you something to drink, but—"

"It's all right, I bring my own drink," said Tess, and a tall cocktail glass appeared in her hand.

"Wow, cool trick. I feel envious. Lemme grab something." She went into her kitchen and got a soft drink for herself. They raised their glasses at each other without attempting to clink them.

"So, what do we talk about, Phoenix?"

"Oh, you know what? I need to attend this case, you wanna accompany me?"

"Sure."

"Cool. I promise it will be fun. How about some news, first?"

The newscaster looked as if he were on the edge of his seat and about to jump out any moment. "Here is the latest from your favorite news channel WXBG Adrianopolis, your connection to the world," came the sound of one of the channel's jingles briefly mixed in to add to the excitement of the man. "Our city woke up to some shocking news this morning: The death of a professor of the Adrianopolis University." Footage of the university cut in. "Dr. Melvyn Phillip Spencer, a leading history scholar, was found dead in his apartment. Our sources at the GPSN Field Office indicate that Dr. Spencer's untimely accidental death was caused by an unauthorized electronic device."

Phoenix leaned towards the Holovision set in an attempt to focus better.

A close-up of the dead professor filled the screen. "The specifics or the origin of the deadly device have not been released. However, the authorities urge that any users of such unauthorized electronic devices report to the rehab center immediately for a complete check-up since their lives may be in danger. It is said that such devices may cause permanent damage to the brain and genetic makeup, and even death, as in the case of Dr. Spencer."

"Did you know this man?" said Tess.

"No, I didn't. Nevertheless it's an unnatural death and a part of my domain. And I thought I had all the action today."

"Whew, some stallion you are, marine," said Sandra, panting, as she lay on her side in one of the convenience rooms. She reached out to the coffee table on the side to grab her cocktail. The party was still in full swing with the booming beat of the music coming from outside. The chiseled-faced, well-built man held her hip from behind.

"Oh, yeah, I liked that, too, babe," he groaned. "Wanna go at it, again?"

"Whoa, let go of me," she said and got up. "If you want more of this, you gotta work at it, sailor," she said, motioning at her own naked body. "What's your name, again?"

"Jean Michel," he said. "And if you want more of this, you'd need to do the same." He lay back, gesturing at his crotch.

Sandra gave out a big laugh. "You know, where I come from, what you got is a dime a dozen."

"And where exactly is that? The bowels of Sub-Saharan Africa or Siberia?" he started laughing, with Sandra joining in.

"You played so hard to get outside, and look at you now: You can't wait for more. What happened to your air of haughtiness?"

"Want me to confess? I fell in love!" said the marine, with his hands on his chest.

"Yeah right!" sniggered Sandra. "You marines used to love the Book, your nation states, and your bio-mamas. Now those are gone, there's no one left for you to love but yourselves. You're a badass jerk just like the rest of them. Just better at acting."

"Oh, thanks for the compliment, royal princess. But it lured you into my web, didn't it?"

"Well, it sure did. Say, can you do that coolness stunt again?"

"How do you mean?"

"Well, I have this friend..."

After watching the news, Phoenix switched to her favorite channel, the Court Network, to attend a case. Could it be the information gleaned from all those cases she had watched over the years had helped her today against Patel? Or could what she thought to be an instinct was the sum of the experience accumulated by watching literally hundreds of court cases?

Simpson versus Cain was an immensely popular case, attracting viewers and jury members from every time zone that the World Union encompassed. It involved an unprecedented violation of three of the ten Articles of the Supreme Bill of Rights, and it was destined to be one of the historic cases of the postmodern era. The case was being viewed by more than quarter of a billion people around the Union, and a whopping ten million had subscribed to be members of the jury.

The show continued with the voice of an excited male announcer. "And now, live from San Francisco, the case of the century, Simpson versus Cain!" He emphasized and lengthened the names of the accuser and the defendant, as if at a wrestling match. A free-moving camera moved around the small courtroom, focusing on the faces of the judge, Simpson, and Cain, as he announced them. The case was being held in a small conventional courtroom, filled with press and public alike. Also, twelve of the nearly ten million jury members had the privilege of filling the traditional jury seats in the courtroom. Everyone knew that these people constituted a tiny fraction of the full jury and got there through bidding, but it didn't matter because it looked better on Holovision.

"And now, the floor belongs to the prosecutor, as the questioning of the defendant continues."

The prosecutor, representing the Peace and Security Council and GPSN, was a man of short stature wearing a traditional black robe, a long white barrister's wig, and an Arrivee tattoo like Hamilton. His wrinkly face bore a grave expression as he spoke. "Ms. Cain, may I ask which immigration academy you attended?" he said in his baritone British accent. One wouldn't expect such a powerful voice from such an old and frail-looking man.

"I attended the one in Hong Kong, sir," answered Cain. She was a young woman in her early twenties, with a beautiful but aggrieved face.

"Did you take classes on the Supreme Bill of Rights at the academy?"

"Yes, I did, sir."

"Very well, then. Could you recite Article Six, please?"

"Yes, sir: Economic decisions are the backbone of the system, and no one shall be denied the right to make decisions based on economic principles, neither shall he have the right to harm the system by unprofitable and uneconomical commitments."

"Exactly. Did they also teach you the ramifications of such an article?"

"Yes, sir," said the woman, lowering her eyes.

"In other words, you know full well that the economics of your monstrous cruelty is a physical impossibility in the World Union, since no insurance agency covers such a barbaric way of birth, nor are hospitals equipped with doctors who practice such primitive techniques, and moreover, neither *you* nor poor Mr. Simpson have the economic means to complete or to terminate this tribal and archaic maternity in any of those filthy rogue states. Am I correct?"

"Yes, I do know all this, sir."

"Then tell me, young woman, why did you do this? Why did you avoid donating your ova pool? Why did you have intercourse with Mr. Simpson, on more than twenty occasions, while hiding your unfit condition from him?"

"Because this is my body, and nobody can tell me what I can and what I can't do with it! And if the Ten Articles are implying otherwise, they are wrong."

"But, young woman, you surely knew what kind of a lifestyle the Ten Articles meant when you made your Pledge of Allegiance. You have so many, *so many,* freedoms you can enjoy in these promised lands. But disfiguring your own body at the expense and psychological damage of others is not one of them. What about the rights of Mr. Simpson, who had no idea of your intentions and the economic burden you tried to dump upon him?"

"Mr. Simpson is a moron," hissed the woman.

"That may be," said the prosecutor and raised his eyebrows. "It still doesn't deprive him of his rights. And what about the rights of your unborn baby? What about the fact that she is condemned to a barbaric way of birth, as it is not possible to transfer her to a surrogation unit at this stage. What about all the psychological defects you are causing her as we speak, the stress, altruistic dependency, and many more?"

"I am a human being! I'm the pinnacle of billions of years of evolution on this earth. My body was made to be impregnated and give birth to healthy children—"

"But of course it was, in a hunter-gatherer environment, sure. What you say was once absolutely true, for hundreds of thousands of years for humans and proto-humans. But don't you realize that we've evolved into a new way of being since the invention of agriculture? We've invented science and economy. Wouldn't you count those in the evolution you just mentioned? Can you separate us humans from the tools and inventions we made? And as we evolved, we gained more freedom.

"You are a woman born in a dismal rogue state and you should know better. The Universal Suffrage was meant more for you than me. Freedom from maternity: Women of the world fought so hard to get all their rights in the last two centuries, to gain their economic independence, and to break free from the yoke of men. For millennia, women were forced by men to do all the work that the men didn't want to do, bearing children, rearing children, doing work for everyone else's needs but their own, in the confines of the house. Us men, we denied the women to prove their true and full economic worth, until the declaration of the Universal Suffrage. Wouldn't you say that what you are doing right now is not progress, but regress, and in fact it can be even regarded not as evolution but de-evolution?"

Following the end of the long court session, Phoenix's brain felt numb, and she asked Tess to leave. Like many victims of childhood trauma, she was deeply attached to the comfort and familiarity of rituals. Her nightly soak in a warm bath, surrounded by a medley of mismatched candles, often felt like the embrace of an old friend.

"Computer: All lights out, music in whisper mode."

She took off her clothes and slid gently into the tub, closing her eyes. It had been such an eventful day, from getting the lead for a murder case, to striking out a psychopath, to chasing an intruder, to making a super-smart digital friend. She tried not to think of any of it, as the accustomed mental and emotional fatigue weighed in. Something was bugging her. Actually, something had been bugging her like a splinter in her mind ever since she had known herself. She knew it had to do with that dismal day that she had lost her biological parents. But she had managed to control this bugging, this urge, to manageable levels with the treatments over years, until that very first night she had spent in this house, in this city. She felt shivers thinking of that first night and how helpless she had felt under the shadow of her reemerging childhood terrors. All she needed was a decent night's sleep, yet deep down she knew it would be hard to come by until she eradicated that splinter once and for all. And how was she supposed to do that without any rest?

She came out of the tub reasonably relaxed physically, but not mentally. She went to bed and opened the drawer of her nightstand. Two of her oldest buddies were in there, one of which was her cute little digital diary, a simple fifteen-by-ten pink gadget with a tiny monitor and a keyboard. It was introduced to her like a game by her doctors when she was eight to keep a record of the progress of her symptoms, her medicine, and other treatment-related developments activities, so that she would learn to log everything at an early age.

In time, her diary had become like a real diary, where she would write about events of the day and her personal reflections about them. In an adult's world, PAs were equipped with voice-activated diary functionality, so no additional gadget was needed. Yet Phoenix felt so attached to her diary, it was as if the little old gadget were the only true friend who had known her and understood her since the beginning. She closed her eyes momentarily in order to focus on what to write. Despite the extraordinary number of events, she was unable to focus on any of them but one, that one instant that had been so deeply ingrained in her mind. It was as if many changes in her life were destined to trickle down from that moment, slowly but surely, as she could feel its undeniable effects and changes inside her already.

And the words flowed from her fingertips without any discernible thought processes involved, right before she fell asleep.

Where am I? *She thinks in fear.*

In complete darkness, her own thought gets lost in the nothingness around her, a nothingness that spans to eternity. She cannot tell if she is present or not. She doesn't know if she has a physical body or just a spirit, or if she is just a being suspended in time and nothingness.

She is not, yet she is aware. She has no senses, yet she can sense. She cannot even tell if the time passes or has frozen. How long she has been, she has no clue, no reference, no comparison. Has it been just a second, or millions of years? In the suspension of time, a deep ancient voice comes from an eternity away.

"O lost Daughter of Corona Borealis and the Castle of the Silver Circle."

The voice invokes a rupture in the nothingness, and she opens her eyes. Yes, she has eyes, but there is nothing to see. In the pitch darkness of the space, there are just nebulous silhouettes, illuminated by distant stars.

"Awake now," the voice commands.

A wave of cold penetrates her. She cannot escape this cold that she feels deep down to her very foundation. She wishes to go back to the nothingness before, but she knows that she cannot. The void is ruptured, the suspension has collapsed, events are set in motion, and time flows, until there is nothingness again an eternity later. She came to be, but with no sense of direction, or purpose. The intensity of the cold blinds her senses, her feelings.

"Why am I here? What am I meant to do? I want to know. I need to know. I don't want to be cold."

A bright light floods everywhere. It's blinding. She closes her eyes by instinct. She wants to see but is afraid of the light. In the eventuality of passage of time, she finds enough courage to open her eyes, to see colorful flitting wings. She has no clue where the wings came from, but they are her wings, gently flitting in space, covering a tiny distance with each flit around an enormous structure. She looks for a light source, but there are no sources around her. In time, she comes to realize she is the source of the light, pure light, nothing but the light.

"Trust your instincts, and you'll come to understand, in time," the voice far, far away says.

She trusts the voice, not knowing why. She flies up and up and up and tries to work out the giant structure towering to infinity. The structure radiates the cold, yet she cannot get away from it. She would do anything to get away from the cold. But she knows she cannot. She flies close to the structure in hope of a clue; the cold intensifies.

"I don't want to feel cold for the rest of my existence. How can I stop the cold? Please tell me!"

She receives no answer to her pleas from the trusted voice. All she can do is fly up and up. The structure widens as she climbs up. The cold intensifies further. But her light also intensifies; it's on her little body, her wings, everywhere on her fragile skin. She has no reference to tell how long she has been flying, but she feels the answer is up there. Her instincts drive her up, despite the unbearable cold.

"A quest awaits you," the voice says faintly, an eternity later. "A great challenge, two millennia in the making, if you can face it."

A wave of futility engulfs her; she turns and flies away from the structure. "I'm not interested in quests and challenges. I just want to stop the cold. I can't bear it anymore."

"There is no escape from the cold in this eternity," says the voice, even fainter. "Nobody can stop the cold in you but you."

She knows the voice is right. The cold is a part of her very fabric, like an innate sin, and there is no place in eternity to hide from it. She slows down and turns towards the giant structure. Its shape resembles something she knows from a long, long time ago.

"However, there is one thing I can do for you to stop it, and you know what it is," the voice says suddenly.

A wave of hope fills her tiny body. Her light intensifies, illuminating the nothingness like never before, spreading and radiating in every direction. It sheds light on the giant structure, highlighting its helix form, its scaled skin and giant head.

"Yes, I know. I know what you can do for me."

Her blinding light intensifies ever more. She sees the structure as the evil creature it is. She knows that it's the root of the cold inside her. She knows she needs to face the creature to bury the cold for an eternity. She feels so tiny next to the giant creature, yet she feels hope. There is always hope in the universe, hidden in plain sight. There always was, and always will be.

"Tell me what it is," the voice says.

The giant creature wakens and opens its eyes with slit pupils. The eyes radiate coldness and evil. She shivers down to her existence. She knows the creature and the cold are one and the same. She knows that all hope of the universe is in her fragile and colorful wings and in her light. She knows, she feels, she believes. Yet, a deep insecurity about herself and her insignificant appearance against the giant creature fills her with despair.

"I want to be, I need to be, inspired!"

As the giant creature poises to attack, her whole fragile body becomes the light and fills the entire nothingness.

The light travels faster than itself, encompasses galaxies and universes alike, reaches a little blue world. And in that world it finds a little girl in blue, almost frozen, sobbing, drowning in tears.

"I don't wanna be cold, Mummy, I don't wanna be cold," the little girl whimpers.

And the light passes inside the little girl, making her the light.

Phoenix sprang up from the nightmare, bathed in icy sweat.

"I don't wanna be cold!"

TUESDAY

CHAPTER 10

THE Man with the Black Hat paced up and down the long and dimly lit dark corridor as quietly as a cat in black knee-high boots. His tall black sheepskin hat, which had come to identify him, had a presence of its own, complementing the sheer determination in his hard masculine face.

"Why did *he* go?" he said. It was so chill and damp that he could see his own breath. "Too risky for him, too much exposure."

The Man with the Toboggan Hat shrugged indifferently. With his plump wrinkled cheeks, gentle eyes, long white beard and hair, antique metal-rimmed circular spectacles, cream wool coat with thin orange stripes, orange riding breeches with white cuffs, and a toboggan with thick stripes of white and orange, he made a stark contrast to the grim and sober appearance of the Black Hat in his cobalt-blue long Central Asian tunic.

"He went because his going was *sine qua non*," he said, his accent Nordic. "Only he could make sure that all the traces were erased, and within the time frame the decision couldn't be consulted. With the total radio silence over the entire spectrum of airwaves between you and us, I had no other choice."

"I know, I know," mumbled the Black Hat, shaking his head. "But couldn't you send someone else instead? We have so many able Renovators out there and down here."

"That we do. But they would've needed to be fully briefed as to exactly what to do, and we simply didn't have time for that. The abrupt cruelty of our Russian *friends* didn't leave us any room for maneuvering. He volunteered without hesitation and barely made it in time."

The Black Hat stopped pacing and turned his hypnotic gaze towards the other man. "Yes, I know that," he hissed. "And I also happen to know three people had the chance to take a good look at him. You know how important he is. We can't risk him like that."

"Don't worry, he was prepared. Only one young woman with a very weak mind had the opportunity to look at his face. I doubt that she remembered anything useful."

"She didn't. The other two couldn't come up with more than a simple description, either. But why didn't you use the Mantis instead? He wouldn't need to be briefed. He could simply be *steered*."

"The Mantis is becoming an increasingly unstable asset," said the Toboggan Hat with a sigh. "He's barely under control. He has an increasing desire to be more and more active, and you know that it's not possible."

"His controller, the Prefect, can manage him. During this new mission I instructed the Prefect to watch and scrutinize the Mantis's every move. We can bring the Mantis in after this one."

"I hope the Prefect can manage to control the Mantis that long. You know, I can't help the Prefect from here. But perhaps you can."

"I'll see what I can do. But I'm warning you: Don't ever risk exposing the Crane like that again. Those two agents, they both had jiu-jitsu training. They could have easily apprehended him. He was lucky."

"He wasn't lucky," the older man said, smiling. "He was just *stunning*."

Phoenix felt crushed and exhausted, as if there was no way she would manage to start, continue, and finish the upcoming day. She'd suffered rude awakenings on more than one occasion throughout the night, and that one nightmare had been so creepy, she couldn't stop shaking and crying for nearly an hour, and only after taking another warm bath. All she could remember was feeling tiny and insignificant, a giant serpent attacking her, and that never-ending cold.

After a quick and revitalizing shower, she began to feel marginally better. Designed and produced by the fashion and retail giant ZAP, her uniform was lightweight and comfortable. The transparent section around the belly made it appear less serious, but this was ZAP—their whole marketing strategy was based on being sexy. Most of their commercials involved sex, usually with an average-looking man in ZAP clothing having great sex with a gorgeous naked woman, or vice versa, turning to the camera and saying "I ZAP'd her" or "I ZAP'd him." It was a good thing that Sandra was actually enjoying all that sexy action, otherwise it would be unbearable.

She forced herself to gulp down a few bites before she left but didn't have the stomach for more. She had once been a very healthy eater, but no longer, it seemed, not for the past ten days.

She was already late when she entered the old stone building. She quickly walked to the elevators and clicked on the button impatiently. The elevator door opened, and a group of children flooded out. Their chaperone tried to get them in order. "Quiet, children, come this way." The group moved along to observe the content on the walls and pushed Phoenix along.

"And here is the interactive content about the history of our Union. Who wants to tell us about the War of Centuries?" said the teacher.

The kids raised their hands and shrieked in near unison. One blonde girl, with a make-believe Arrivee tattoo on her forehead, tried to push her way past Phoenix. "Get out of my way." Being surrounded by the mob, Phoenix didn't have any place to move.

"Tell us, Daniela," said the teacher, nodding at one dark-eyed, solemn little girl at the front.

"The period from early nineteen hundreds to the final economic collapse is called the War of Centuries. There was constant conflict and unrest every decade, incited by the notorious nation state governments, which eroded the global wealth accumulated since the Industrial Revolution, including two world wars, worldwide terrorism, and chronic financial fluctuations that peaked with the catastrophic one we call the Great Meltdown. The War of Centuries also marks the rise and fall of the nation states around the world."

Phoenix found herself glancing at the displays and interactive content, drifting away in reminiscence, and ignored the scowling gaze of the blonde girl next to her.

"Constant conflicts depleted economies, corrupt politicians bowed to public pressure to unbalance financial stabilities, and finally world economy broke down, with nobody knowing how to fix it," recited the eight-year-old girl, her tone that of utter indifference and detachment. "Banks collapsed, factories closed down, even the most basic commodities like food and clothing disappeared. Half of the world's population lost their jobs. Contagious neurotic and psychotic behavior spread through the media to all parts of the world, and political leaders did nothing to prevent this. Riots started all over the world, with governments unable to control anything."

"Very good. Thank you, Daniela. Children, here is a peace agent of the Global Peace and Security Network, or GPSN as everyone calls it."

The entire mob turned towards Phoenix. "Good morning, Agent."

"Good morning."

"Would you kindly introduce yourself to the children, please?"

"Yes—yes, of course. My name's Phoenix Wallis, and I'm a senior agent here at the field office."

"Children, agents like Ms. Wallis ensure the peace and security of our great New World Order and catch the evil terrorists, which are the sworn enemies of our prosperity and tranquility," said the teacher in a singsong tone.

"You don't look that tough!" said a third voice. The blonde girl with the make-believe Arrivee tattoo folded her arms, narrowed her eyes even further, and scowled at Phoenix.

"I don't?"

The mob erupted, debating whether Phoenix was a worthy agent or not.

"Now, now, children, quiet, quiet," said the teacher, with her soothing voice. She smiled sympathetically at Phoenix, as the noise slowly started to die down. "I'm sure this fine agent here is as good as they come. Thank you kindly, Agent Wallis, for your time. Now, let's move along. Here are the displays about the Restoration Period. Who will it be?"

Instantly the kids turned to their teacher, as Phoenix tried once again to cut through the mob without attracting further reaction. The teacher motioned with her hand towards the girl with the tattoo.

"Restoration is the period that starts with the founding of the One World Foundation by the wise men who we call the Supreme Selfs. These people possessed enough power, wealth, and courage to first set up a private global stability fund worth twenty trillion dollars, big enough to bail out the entire world, and convince political leaders of the time to turn their executive powers to technocrats. Under the unbending guidance of technocrats and other professionals, global economy bounced back, the fund took the ownership of the wrecked nation states, dissolved them and—"

The mob moved away, leaving a thoroughly demoralized Phoenix behind. Even eighth graders were aware that she was insignificant and in no shape to do her job.

"The search string resulted in moderate results. Should we check it out?"

"I wouldn't get excited over it, if I were you, Sean. Moderate means the match is minimal. Check it when you have some free time, but I bet it'll be unrelated people. How about the crime scene?"

"No heat signatures other than yours and mine. The intruder must have been wearing some thermal suit. We found only two sets of DNA prints at the apartment: One was of the man himself, and the other was of Larissa Lukin. I've watched your interviews from yesterday. Any comments?"

"Useless teenage airheads on one end, and your good ol' overpaid arrogant lawyer with an HDI of eighty-five on the other."

"How do you think Bogdanov could have afforded him?"

"I haven't a clue."

Her PA projected two reminders for the morning: Her orientation meeting with Alex, and the recovered data from her PA's crash in the metro the day before. She dreaded the thought of having another orientation. Alex was a very nice guy but never got to the actual point he was trying to make, until Phoenix's boredom turned to irritation.

Their PAs chimed simultaneously with a message from the director, calling for an urgent meeting about the murder case. Now what could this be about? Could the director have had a change of heart about the lead? Her record on the murder case had been a big fat zero so far. She had missed the intruder, she had used precious GPSN resources for hunting him down with no success, she had no leads on the impersonator, and she had pissed off some hotshot lawyer by taking up too much of his time.

Could it be about the lawyer asking for a six—or even seven—figure settlement for lost time and opportunity? Or perhaps that headperson had convinced the director to condemn Phoenix to doing security interviews for all eternity. The thought of eternity sent a sudden shiver down her spine, making her feel tiny and insignificant. She was overworked, sleepless, discontented, and unhappy. Why should she care if the director took the lead from her or even fired her? At least it would give her an excuse to leave this city that she loathed and perhaps she could get some decent sleep, somewhere warm, and far, far from here.

"All right, I assume all of you saw yesterday's developments in the Bogdanov case. First Agent Wallis will bring us up to date about certain details of it, and then we have an important development to discuss. Go ahead."

"We went to the victim's apartment at sector forty-seven in the Delta Quadrant, and his door computer was responding suspiciously—"

"Yes, yes, we know all that. Tell me about the encounter with the intruder. Two of you were blocking his way out. How come he bested you?"

"That's what happens if you're incompetent in martial arts," grinned Julio.

"Can it," said the director without even looking his way. "Go on."

Phoenix's memory of the encounter's physical aspects was comprehensive yet didn't explain any of what had happened, why she froze, or the flood of emotions she had felt when she had looked in his eyes. Could this be the director's way of exposing her incompetence? Yet her instincts kept telling her to remain calm and be open. "It happened so quickly. We froze for an instant, and that's all the man needed."

Julio folded his arms and shook his head, while Alex seemed to be listening intently to the account.

"Why did you freeze?" said the director. She seemed quite curious, with no sign of her usual aggressiveness. Could there be a faint trace of concern, even?

"Hard to explain. I knew exactly what I needed to do, yet my emotions, they were completely messed up. They made me pause."

"Your emotions were messed up, my ass," said Julio. "Why don't you just admit that you chickened out?"

"I told you to shut up!" said the director, with a gaze that could freeze an erupting volcano. She turned back to Phoenix. "Your emotions were messed up: Explain."

Why was the director persisting with this? *The hell with it*, she thought. *If they want to know all, I'll tell exactly how I felt and humiliate myself.*

"All my emotions went haywire in a moment, as if I was feeling the whole spectrum of what there is to feel all at the same time. It felt like it lasted forever to me, but I'm pretty sure it only lasted a few fractions of a second, enough for the intruder to hit me in the stomach and run past me."

The director swiveled her head and made eye contact with Alex. He pursed his lips and briefly nodded. "Is this how you felt, too?" she asked Sean.

"Uhm, how can I explain? It was as if—"

"Yes or no."

"Yes."

The director fell silent for a few seconds. Her eyes were fixed to a point on the table, as everyone held their breath and waited for her reaction. She raised her head, made eye contact with everybody then turned to Phoenix.

"I know exactly what you're referring to."

It was a typical day at the office where Sandra needed to decide which party to attend and what to wear in the evening. There were three events, yet she couldn't manage all three and needed to pick two. She smiled at the thought, thinking that this would be a dream job for most women. Sadly, she wasn't one of them. It was getting harder and harder to be motivated for every event, and with so many young ones joining the company ranks, there was no way she could go on for another year and keep pretending that she enjoyed sex.

She had mentally prepared herself to enjoy Phoenix's company and to let off steam regularly, but instead found herself in a spiral of exasperation at the lack of it. Phoenix had turned out to be a determined career woman, and there wasn't much commonality between their lines of business.

The subject had come up when she was talking to her buddy at the GPSN, and her buddy agreed that she had to increase the common ground between herself and Phoenix. Her approach to that marine had been a part of the plan. She knew that he was faking it from the beginning; on the other hand, he could pretend to be a quiet oddball, convincing enough to get Phoenix take an interest in him. And if she could get Phoenix to start a relationship with him, they would have a lot more common ground, making it easier to get Phoenix to make time for her. In other words, she would be creating a complex equation of interpersonal relations to gain personal advantage, based on ZAP's Social Scheming and Politically Correct Manipulation Techniques courses.

Sandra felt so cool and smart, smiling at her own cunningness.

"It was one of my early days at the academy here," whispered the director. "One very cold winter night, we were at the Monitoring Room, desperately undermanned, busy surveilling the academy grounds. We detected a man in dark clothing and a tall black hat hiding in the shadows in the west gardens. We ran outside and followed the footmarks he left in the snow, catching him close to the gate of the old graveyard. Armed with nerve disrupters, we told him to stop." The director took a deep breath and made eye contact with Alex. He looked rueful but remained quiet, shaking his head. "The man turned towards us, and—" She looked down. "Tell them."

"I felt like throwing up!" said Alex, his eyes bulging.

"Alex started gagging, and I felt all the pleasure and pain in the world all at once, for what I believe to be a fraction of a second. I passed out. Everyone was incapacitated in one way or the other."

"And the man?" said Phoenix.

"He vanished. We couldn't remember anything about him. Nothing. The only reason that I can tell you about his clothing is because we had recorded footage of him. Never saw him again."

"Did he possess a weapon of some sort? It's gotta be some kind of a mind-altering weapon."

"That was our theory, too," nodded the director. "I reported the incident to Mr. Hamilton, and he ordered to keep it confidential, pending some internal investigation within GPSN. I got the feeling that a top-secret weapon had fallen into the wrong hands. The incident was not mentioned again until now, and I don't know what happened with that internal investigation." She sighed and looked up, reestablishing eye contact with everyone.

"Regardless of the results of the internal investigation three years ago, that mind-control weapon appears to be out and about again. I think you two and that sales clerk have been targets. Now, I want you to be very careful. We don't have any countermeasures for this kind of a weapon out there."

"You mean I'm still in the lead?"

"Of course you're still in the lead; why shouldn't you be? Now, we have another case on our hands. If you've checked the news last night or this morning, you'd know what I'm talking about."

"Dr. Spencer?"

"Yes. We will form a task force for investigating his untimely death."

"Who's Spencer? A doctor?"

"Well, if you paid a little more attention to what's going on outside of your immediate five-meter radius, you'd know who he was, Julio."

"He was a history professor at AU, found dead yesterday morning," said Phoenix. "He's supposed to have died using an illegal device."

"Precisely. The task force will include some medical doctors from the rehab center. Alex, you will lead the investigation and arrange the collaboration. Sean, on top of your responsibilities with the Bogdanov case, you'll also be Alex's case assistant. And you two, I want you to follow up on the developments of this case."

"But why am I not a part of the team, Chief?" said Julio.

"Because it's the security interview season and you've still to produce a single report for the Bogdanov case. Dismissed. I need a few more moments with you," she added to Phoenix and Alex.

Julio was scowling uncharacteristically as he got up, but he snapped out of it quickly and took Sean by the arm on their way out.

"Tell me," the director turned to Phoenix. "What's your next move?"

"I'm still trying to figure out why he went back to Russia. I plan to visit his sexual partner first, then a few other contacts that I got from his lawyer."

"Do you have any idea how he could afford Anderson?"

"Working on that, too. You know him?"

"He's a tort expert with a deep grasp of our company rules, costing us lots of trouble and money a couple of years back, targeting me for the way I handled one of your peers. Do you know why Bogdanov hired him?"

"About future enterprises and an art consultancy business with a partner. Evidently Bogdanov was planning a big leap in his HDI next quarter."

"No kidding. I suppose we'll know more when someone gets a hold of his financials. By the way, you have another interview tomorrow morning, and you need to attend your orientation before you take off chasing Bogdanov's friends and partners."

The double blow of another interview and the dreaded orientation made Phoenix's shoulders slump. She could feel her energy draining away again.

"I'm aware that the headperson's got loads of interviews lined up for me, and I understand that I have to do those. But I really have no time for the orientation today, Director."

"Your interview tomorrow is the exact reason you need to get yourself oriented. Alex will guide you specifically about the procedures, techniques, tips, and tricks used in an interview. No need for anything else."

"Ah, I see."

"Now don't misunderstand me here. All the comments I made yesterday about your *style* are still valid. You need to go easy on your interviews and refrain from violating protocols and procedures. Are we clear?"

"Yes, we are, Director Morssen."

"Is there anything else you want to mention about your case?"

"Actually, there is something. But I'm not sure if it's anything worth mentioning now. First I need to consult the expertise of this gentleman sitting here next to me."

CHAPTER 11

PHOENIX checked the case database to see if there was anything new from Julio and Alex. There was nothing. Alex was waiting for information from his Russian counterparts, but Julio's silence was not normal. He should have gathered some basic information about the victim by now, like his bank statements. It was either sheer incompetence or unwillingness, and either scenario was alarming.

There was something new from Sean, however, something she had already expected: The contents of the micro disk from Bogdanov's unsafe safe had been null. The slick intruder-slash-impersonator hadn't disappointed her. She felt goosebumps thinking about her encounter with him. She had kept many things to herself while confessing to the incident, such as the immediate and irresistible infatuation that had gripped her body as she looked into his eyes. Love, attraction, heartache, hope, despair, happiness, and sadness all at once, as if she had fallen in love with him, felt all the happiness that the love brought, then lost him and felt desolated. She'd always thought that she couldn't be the loving type, believing she hadn't possessed the emotional sensitivity for it, but now she wasn't sure anymore.

And there was the recovered data from her PA, which she totally forgot about in the chaos of events. What it could be, she had no idea; she instructed her network node to analyze it. She also wanted to ask Sean about her exact feelings during the encounter with the intruder. She wasn't sure if Sean would be as forthcoming as she needed her to be, but it was worth a try.

Where was she, anyway?

Sean sipped her coffee in the ground floor cafeteria, giving runaway glances at Julio. She found him very cute, but she wasn't sure about his intentions with this invitation.

"I know I sometimes act rash and often come across as a jerk, but it's because I feel frustrated," he said. "They don't know me or understand me, and I don't trust them. That director, she secretly hates me, you know."

"Her manners are quite harsh, I agree, but she appears to act the same to everyone. Are you sure she doesn't like you?"

"It's not just that she doesn't like me. She genuinely loathes me, because I'm the biggest threat to her position. That's why she appointed Nix as the case lead, knowing full well that she doesn't have what it takes to succeed."

"Are you saying that the director is trying to sabotage this murder case?"

"I know it's hard to believe, but isn't she? I mean, her appointment of Nix as the lead makes no sense at all. She's new here, withdrawn, has no leadership skills. Maybe she's smart and good at analysis and all, but she's totally untested for such a critical case."

"Who should've been the lead?"

"Alex or me, of course. Given his experience and solid reputation, Alex would be the natural choice, and I would be a very close second. He doesn't show it, but I can tell you: Alex is deeply hurt by not being given the lead in the Bogdanov case. And that malicious director knows it, too. Appointing him to lead that meaningless Spencer death is just a consolation prize. She's determined to run the murder case into a grinding halt, I'm telling you."

"But why would Director Morssen do such a thing?"

"I think it has to do with some corporate backstabbing at the executive level. I know the director has an eye on positions way beyond her ability. She may be even plotting against Hamilton."

"But we can't let this happen. I know Phoenix is a good and smart person. She doesn't deserve any of this."

"That's exactly what I think, too, babe. Nix doesn't deserve to be the case lead, that's for sure, and I've been voicing my opinion about this everywhere. But she doesn't deserve to be a victim of corporate scheming, either. We gotta do something."

"We gotta help her!"

"Shhh, are you trying to get one of the Big Bad D's spies to hear us? Yes, Nix needs help. But she's too damn stubborn and untamed to understand that. She won't trust anyone to help her, and she'll run the investigation into the ground, just like our scheming director wants her to."

"What do we do?"

"We need to help her discreetly, kinda without her knowing where help comes from."

"So you're willing to sacrifice the credit for helping her?"

"That's right, babe," nodded Julio. "Hey, don't get me wrong, I don't want this just for her sake. It's also for my benefit, 'cause *I am* the actual target here. The director wants to dead-end the investigation then blame me, the biggest threat to her position. That's why she keeps picking on me in meetings and had been secretly conditioning that antisocial and gullible Nix against me."

"Really?" said Sean, shaking her head. "Oh, my goodness."

"But it's okay; let them badmouth me, I don't care. And don't even try to convince Nix about me or my good intentions, 'cause she lacks the postmodern depth to understand or appreciate such a move. I don't think it's possible for her to see anyone around her as friendly right now. We gotta give her the chance to discover it by herself, understand?"

Sean nodded quietly.

"But to be able to help, I need to know what's going on with the investigation. Nix is being cagey about everything she does. I need to know certain things in advance, so that I can fix them before disaster strikes. You're a great gal and all, but if you don't want to be involved in this heavy stuff, I'd understand."

"No, I wanna help. I can do it."

"You sure? I wouldn't wanna impose on you, you know, 'cause it could be risky. You may need to lie from time to time."

"I can handle it. Phoenix trusted me, and I need to prove that I was worthy of her trust by helping her."

"Even if she shouldn't know about any of this for a while?"

"Yes."

"Cool," said Julio, with a smirk. "It's a deal. Oh, in order to avoid suspicion, let's pretend that we're sexual partners, all right?"

"Do we have to just *pretend?*" said Sean, sneaking a peek at him.

"Well, we'll see about that when the time comes, babe."

"The name of your next victim is Shakira Al-Hayani, from the Arab League," said Alex and let out a big burst of laughter. Phoenix pretended to smile.

"I know my jokes are meaningless and crude. You see, the first time I heard the term *politically correct manners,* I was well into my adulthood."

"It'll take a while to get used to them, I guess. Oh, I need your help with a piece of evidence from Bogdanov's office."

Alex opened the scan on his network node and examined it, his eyes narrowed. "It's handwritten! In this day and age, unbelievable, and in Cyrillic."

"I know. You can read it, right?"

"I sure can. It appears to be a name list."

"A name list? Whose names? His friends in Russia, perhaps?"

"Don't know. But these aren't Russian names."

"Are you sure?"

"I don't think Vanderbilt is a Russian name, nor is Perez. Do you?"

It made no sense to write the names of a bunch of people behind a photograph in an ancient script, using a *pencil*. They didn't even teach that to kids anymore. Obviously, Bogdanov didn't want certain information to be on the computer, fearing somebody might access it. Maybe he'd been afraid of hackers, or maybe he was hiding something. She hoped that the names themselves would reveal some clues as to the *why*.

"Can you do me a favor, Alex? Can you translate this list into our alphabet and log it to the case database?"

"Certainly. But after we finish our work here. You are a good girl—I mean woman—and a valuable agent, Phoenix. I wouldn't wanna see you being mistreated by the director or the headperson about your interviews again."

"I know," said Phoenix, lowering her eyes. "I acted rashly with Patel. But I had no choice under the circumstances."

"You did what you had to do, and I understand that. But you need to understand that it will not work every time. I also totally empathize with your reaction to the intruder," he added, leaning towards her.

"Thanks, Alex. You know, you're the only decent person here."

"Naah, stop that," he said, leaning back with a broad smile. "They are all good people. I know you've been having a hard time, but perhaps it's because you're so used to working alone, you perceive some of your coworkers as enemies."

"Well, it's hard to think of them as friends, when they pick on me the way they do. You know what I mean."

"I know how Julio acts, but he's a young guy full of ambition and testosterone. It's just an act to impress young ladies around him. I know he likes you, too."

"How do you know that?"

"He confessed to me. All I'm saying is this: I think your defense mechanisms are preventing you from seeing people for who they really are. And on top of that, they provoke others to act weird around you. These are good people, Phoenix, maybe equipped with a little too much greed, but nothing's wrong with that, either. Healthy greed knows no boundaries."

"Like I said, Alex, you're the only decent person here. Now, please orient me so I don't mess up the director's expectations and the headperson's inner peace ever again."

Following the mind-numbing orientation session, Phoenix headed back to her office feeling totally drained, wasted, and severely agitated. Alex had been so thorough about the procedures, she had no idea how she would remember all the intricate details and fine points and make use of all she had learned, under pressure and in the confines of just thirty minutes. She just felt like getting out of the wretched building as fast as she could and making some progress with the Bogdanov case before she had wasted the entire day and was dismissed from the case lead for real. And as for the security interviews, she felt that she couldn't care less anymore. Perhaps it was best to follow the procedures, just the way the director and Alex recommended, not push hard, and give everyone what they wanted.

"You called me?"

Phoenix jerked back at the sudden interruption of her reverie. "Sean, how many times did I tell you not to do that? Where have you been?"

"I'm sorry. I was having coffee with Julio downstairs. Why?"

"You were having coffee with Julio all this time? That's just so sweet!"

"He's not as bad as you think—"

"I've already had one lecture about his outstanding qualities today. Look, I don't care what you do with him in your free time, but you are my case assistant. Don't ever forget this fact. And as far as our case is concerned, I decide what we share with the others and when, understand?"

"Yes," said Sean, lowering her eyes. "What did you need?"

She had wanted to talk to Sean about her sensations during the incident with the intruder, but it appeared like Sean was already feeling certain vibrations towards someone else. She shook her head and silently cursed Julio for contaminating Sean's mind before she had a chance to ask.

"Never mind! I need to make a few interviews. In the meantime you can ask your *new friend* about his research on Bogdanov's past and his financials? Maybe he'll make an exception for you and move his lazy ass!"

She entered her office fizzing with frustration and illogical rage. She felt like kicking something or someone. This wasn't like her at all. And how was she supposed to make calls and arrange meetings with Bogdanov's friends and associates in this mood? Her wave of frustration got augmented by an ill-timed visual call. She didn't even bother to check who it was. "What?"

"Woo-hoo," said Tess. "Way to treat a friend. Bad morning?"

"You could say that. I feel like punching someone."

"You were crying last night, and now this. Some range of emotional swings. Should I be concerned?"

"Nope, I'll be fine."

"You look tired already. Had a difficult night?"

"I've been having bad nights every night since I moved here."

"Really? Anything I can do to help?"

Phoenix shook her head no, but suddenly an idea appeared in her head. She was beginning to feel better already. "Actually you *can* help me, Tess InstanceZero. I was wondering how you'd look in uniform."

Phoenix left the GPSN building feeling almost lighthearted. Tess had been nice enough to help her arrange the meetings with Bogdanov's sexual partner, Larissa Lukin, and psychiatrist Dr. Capello.

"So how's your investigation going?"

"Not good. My progress yesterday was zilch, and now I have more weight on my back after losing hours with orientation today and with more security interviews tomorrow and every following day."

"Ahh, so that's why you're in such a foul mood. Too much work?"

"I don't mind work, okay? But the guy who was orienting me, Alex, he's such a great guy, yet he's so inept at instructing and teaching, and he was at his worst today with all kinds of nitpicking. And just got so, argh!"

"Oh dear, one of those days, huh? Are you easily annoyed in general?"

"Not really. I'm usually quite calm, and I internalize most emotions. I used to, I should say, because I've become a lot more nervous since I moved here. I think the lack of sleep is wearing my patience paper-thin."

Phoenix descended to the station as they talked and walked past the interactive ads, again noticing that travel ad asking where she wanted to go. The urge to leave the city invaded her thoughts once again. But leave the city and go where, doing what? She was stuck here, whether she liked it or not, until another *big* career move, heavens knew when.

As the train started to move, a message came in from her network node. The recovered data in her PA had yielded an image. Just as she was waiting for her PA to download the image, the progress bar froze. "PA: Resume visual call," she said, but the PA didn't respond. "Tess? Are you there?"

She cursed as she waited for the device to reboot. Yet this time, it didn't. She took the tiny device off her ear. It appeared dead, totally unresponsive to her repeated voice commands. She couldn't even ride the metro around the town without it working. One option was to get off the train in the next station and return to get it repaired or replaced. But that meant wasting hours and hours, even the whole day.

There was one last thing that she could try, and it was something she wasn't supposed to do herself. *The hell with it!* she thought. *If I don't do it, Fred will waste several hours consulting his manuals and do it anyway.* She removed her claw-style hair clip, snapping off one of the plastic teeth, then stuck the sharp broken point into a tiny hole behind the gadget and pressed it for three seconds, hard-resetting the PA. Following that, the PA booted up totally blank. She instructed it to make a secure-layer connection to GPSN's network. The network would automatically restore all necessary settings and data to it.

Following the restore, some of her tweaks and fine-tunes were still absent, and her contact list was incomplete. Moreover, there was another unidentified data file. Her next interview was Larissa Lukin, and she lived somewhere at the Pi Quadrant, but she had no idea what her address was. And who was she going to visit next? Regarding the PAs, Ray had no idea what he was talking about. At that instant, she received a visual call from an unidentified source.

"Hey, what happened? You went into Silent Mode somehow."

"Now you know how it feels. My PA crashed again, and I had to hard-reset it to get to work. And now I have a whole bunch of stuff missing, including the name of my second interview."

"Dr. Sophia Capello. Do you want her address, too?"

"Oh, Tess, you're like a spring sale credit arriving at the last second. I guess you never have the problem of forgetting things."

"No. I guess you have two assistants for your case now."

"Aw, don't remind me of Sean. I can't believe she's hanging out with that Julio."

"You don't think Alex might have a point about your feelings towards him?"

"Alex may have a point about my skepticism towards people in general. But I know I'm right about Julio."

"How can you be so sure?"

"Because in here," said Phoenix, tapping her fingers to her chest, "I know that he is plotting against me."

Tess remained immobile for a few seconds with just her pupils moving. "Some people refer to such innate sensations as instincts. Would you classify yours as such or prefer further clarification of the term to avoid ambiguity?"

Now it was Phoenix's turn to think. Instincts had no scientific basis and were irrelevant sensations as far as postmodern World Union science was concerned. Admittance of their use could result in an early retirement from her career. On the other hand, Tess was hooked on her unique behaviors, non-existent in the majority of her subjects. How much more unique could any behavior get than an instinct?

"Yes, I would classify them as instincts."

"How great of you to say that," said Tess with a gorgeous smile. "You really trust me, and I like you even more now."

"I can't say I trust you completely, Tess, because I don't exactly know who has access to your data or who controls your subroutines. But I can say that I trust in your curiosity about me."

"You can say the same for most humans, too. But I've neither need for nor interest in sharing your psychological profile with anyone. I'd rather keep it all to myself."

"That's exactly how I thought you'd react, and that's why I decided to share it with you. Besides, now that I've shared it with someone, I feel a lot better."

"But this is fantastic! Human instincts are one of the most important sensations I need to evaluate, and so few people dare admit to having them. So tell me, how does this feeling present itself?"

"Can we do this some other time? I need to talk to Ms. Lukin soon."

"Sure thing. May I watch your interview?"

Could she? There would be serious trouble if it was discovered. On the other hand, she was overworked and alone. Julio was a scheming snake, Alex was paving her way to hell with his good intentions, Sean was naïve and not too bright, Beverly was always busy, Fred was supremely unconcerned, and the director was— "Aw, why not!"

"Ms. Lukin, thank you for seeing me at such short notice. My name's Phoenix Wallis, and I'm a senior agent from the GPSN Field Office."

Larissa Lukin was a plain-looking woman in her late forties with pale skin, and she hadn't been blessed with any feminine curves. She had a long face with luscious lips, which would ordinarily attract any woman's envy, but her lips were totally overshadowed by her vacuous blue eyes and the gullible expression on her face. The lack of character in her face was furthered by random attacks of whimpering. In a sparsely furnished tiny flat as impersonal as a mediocre hotel room, she appeared to be a woman of simple taste who lived a simple life. The only apparent extravagance in the entire flat was a Thing, and even that appeared to somehow fade into the unrefined background.

"I didn't want to see anyone," she said, her accent thick. "But the agent that called to make the appointment for you was so nice, I couldn't say no."

"Yes, Agent Tess can do that. I understand your pain, Ms. Lukin, but I need to ask questions about the late Mr. Bogdanov, so that we can catch the perpetrators as quickly as we can."

"What am I to do without my Vassily?" whimpered the woman. "How can I live without him?"

"Did your living conditions in any way depend on him?"

"No, of course they didn't! But we had such a harmonious relationship."

"What exactly do you do for a living?"

"I'm a Personal Planning and Coordination Advisor."

"Sweet. And Mr. Bogdanov was your client?"

"Yes, he was."

"And how many other clients currently employ you?"

"None."

Lukin's dependence on Bogdanov as a freelancer willing to do any kind of work was alarming. Could there be an altruistic relationship here?

"But how can you sustain yourself like that? It's just a part-time job."

"It wasn't part-time. Vassily insisted that I only work for him. I went to his house every day and did my predetermined duties, as it was agreed verbally between the two of us. You can check his house logs if you wish."

"That explains it, then. So, you're a recent immigrant?"

"Yes, I am. I emigrated to our mighty Union three years ago from the Russian rogue state. How could you guess?"

"You attended the academy here?"

"Yes, I did. And that's where I met Vassily. We were in the same study group, and it was instant infatuation."

"I'm sure it was. I'm trying to determine why Mr. Bogdanov would go back to Russia. I've seen some memorabilia from the old days in his office. Could he have been missing his past there?"

"Oh, no!" said the woman, shaking her head violently. "Vassily was ever so happy when we were inaugurated and became citizens. We had heard so much about the tranquility of the Union. And only after becoming a part of it did we come to realize that no words can actually do it justice."

"Is it really that bad in the rogue states?"

"So much crime, disease, and pollution there, you can never feel safe."

"After all those years in Russia, do you ever think of going back?"

"This is a joke, yes?" said the woman with wide gullible eyes. "I went through a lot to arrive here. Why would I want to go back?"

"Perhaps you miss friends, places, former biological family members. Was it difficult to leave your biological family behind?"

"I had no one after my biological uncle died," said Lukin, lowering her eyes. "My biological parents died during the Great Meltdown. My bio-uncle raised me. When he died, I inherited money from him, the money that got me here."

"What did Mr. Bogdanov think of Russia?"

"He called it the *cursed land,*" said the woman, with tears in her eyes. "He was ever so happy when he passed the security interview. You know, we would look at the skyline of Adrianopolis from our dorm rooms and dream about shopping at the magnificent Pyramid. Believe me, it was far more impressive than a full moon."

"What was?"

"The mighty Pyramid, of course, glowing at a distance."

"Well, you should see the one in DC someday."

"I was planning to go there with Vassily next year," said the woman with a sob in her voice. "Oh, I don't know what to do now."

"Sorry to hear that, Ms. Lukin. Can you tell me why you think Mr. Bogdanov called Russia the *cursed land?*"

"He kept saying the root of all evil lurked there. If you've never been to a rogue state, you cannot possibly understand what I'm talking about."

"I guess I need to visit there someday to see the differences with my own eyes, eh, Ms. Lukin?"

"No! I hope you will never need to."

"So, you two never talked about those days?"

"Sometimes. Maybe he had some good memories, I don't know. He was very fond of his late biological grandparents. They took care of him when he was a little boy."

So Bogdanov had handwritten his name list on the back of a very special old photograph.

"You said that you've been sexual partners with Mr. Bogdanov for three years. Have you steadily seen and worked for him during this period?"

"Yes, sort of, I mean, until recently."

"What do you mean?"

"I mean," she said and thought for a moment. "He started displaying unusually aggressive behavior recently. He even yelled at me a couple of times, you know. I tried to reason with him, but he just wouldn't listen. He had this strange gleam in his eyes, as if he was a different person."

"Do you have any idea why?"

"No, I don't."

"How recent was this *change?*"

"Two months? Three months? Oh, I don't know."

"Was Mr. Bogdanov an extrovert?"

"Not really. We would usually meet alone at each other's apartments. So I didn't really see him interacting with other people much, I guess."

"You mean you wouldn't go out together?"

"Of course we did. But my Vassily preferred quiet places. And he could be so romantic at times. Then again, he could get politically incorrect, too. Oh, I'm going to miss him so much."

"So what does your six-million-strong expertise say about this woman, Tess?"

"I only observe, and I don't judge. But as far as I'm concerned, she is of no interest to me."

"C'mon, I'm not asking you to judge. Tell me your observation."

"She's very confused, and there's a 58 percent chance that she had an altruistic relationship with late Mr. Bogdanov."

"Not that we could prove it, but that's pretty obvious. What else?"

"I'm not sure what you're expecting me to say here."

"She's hiding something."

"How could you conclude that in the absence of any lie detection system? According to my records, you're not a deception expert either, are you?"

"Well, trust me, I've seen those deception experts and most of them don't know their ass from a hole in the ground. My instinct says that she's hiding something, and I'm not talking about an altruistic relationship."

"Even if she is hiding something, what difference it can make to your case? She's just a lower-middle-class woman with a barebones HDI and no real job."

"Never underestimate any woman or man's willpower and capabilities by just looking at her HDI. World history is full of heroes and anti-heroes who wouldn't even make a Disciple by our standards, yet they somehow managed to change the world many times over, for better or for worse."

CHAPTER 12

"**DR.** Capello, I'd like to ask you a few questions about the late Mr. Bogdanov."

Sophia Capello, a petite woman with dusky beige skin and black hair in an elegant chignon, was sitting at the other end of a periwinkle-blue glass desk. Her head was slightly tilted to the left in its natural posture, and there was a certain curious intensity in her black eyes. Her tiny body failed to fill her dark garb and made her look like she was wearing a toga. Her office was avant-garde in every meaning of the word with walls in multiple shades of blue with gradients fading to each other. The only contemporary additions were the seats, which appeared incongruously ordinary compared to the rest. A simulation of the night sky with sparkling stars animated the ceiling.

"Certainly," she said, nodding her tilted head. "So he was murdered in one of the rogue states?"

"In the port city of Odessa in Russia. One of the important aspects of my investigation is determining why Mr. Bogdanov went back there. I'm sure you know about his recent immigrant status. Do you think he had good living conditions in his former life, conditions good enough to make him miss a rogue state?"

"Definitely not," said the woman in absence of the tiniest expression. "I specialize in immigration-related social disorders and have listened to so many stories of immigrants: Most of the things we hear about the terrible living conditions in the rogue states are actually true. And the experiences that he shared with me certainly verified that fact."

"What sort of experiences did he describe to you?"

"A very rough childhood, lacking any basic care or fulfillment of even the most basic physiological and security needs, such as food, shelter, and a safe environment. In an environment like that, a human is driven by his most basic urges: pain and hunger. And if these fundamental urges dominate one's life, it's inevitable that primitive decision-making impulses, called instincts, begin to suppress the rational thought. This is the underlying mentality of every rogue state citizen in their subconscious."

Phoenix felt a momentary twinge of guilt over allowing herself to resort to such unscientific and primitive urges. Then again, how could she have survived the last twenty-four hours without them?

"It sounds to me that after getting used to our system here, no memory of a past in a rogue state can be fondly remembered."

"In most cases that is true. However, the situation is somewhat different among elder male immigrants. These people had spent most of their lives under those terrible conditions, and unless they develop some kind of affection for and familiarity with their past, they may go insane. It's a defense mechanism. Younger immigrants easily adopt our system since their young minds can absorb the changes without having to deal with the agonies of a long-lost life."

"So he might also have had a few regrets, immigrating to the Union?"

"I don't mean that he didn't want to come here. On the contrary, he desperately wanted to immigrate, taking many risks along the way. I believe he had to steal a good deal of money to be able to come to the Union."

"Quite," nodded Phoenix. "What about friends and bio-relatives? Did he have to abandon anyone?"

"He was never very specific about that, but judging by the efforts he showed in trying to fit in here, I highly doubt that he had any close companions left behind."

"Did he ever mention his relationships with his friends here?"

"Of course. He was looking for new friends all the time, in order to feel more secure and socially accepted in his new environment."

"Was he able to have healthy relationships with the Union women?"

"He was obviously struggling. His primary sexual partner, Ms. Lukin, shares a similar past, so his relationship with her was comfortable due to familiarity. However, with native Union women, he just could not get on the same frequency. He couldn't tune in to them."

"Did he express any feelings of frustration to you?"

"He did," nodded the psychologist. "Unfortunately, he couldn't grasp the basic principles of male-female relationships here. He was still thinking in a rogue state mentality and appeared to be trying too hard."

"In what ways was he trying too hard?"

"In our postmodern society, a sexual overture or a relationship is generally initiated by women. However, as a remnant of hunter-gatherer and tribal periods of evolution, this is the role of a male in modern rogue state social intercourse."

"So he was off-putting?"

"Exactly. And his unfit appearance further hindered his efforts to socialize with Union women."

"How was he coping with this?"

"He was coping with it by finding alternatives to compensate for his inadequacies. That's why he desperately wanted to get rich."

"His lawyer mentioned his plans for big business ventures and a leap in his HDI. Do you believe he possessed enough greed for all this?"

"He did, indeed, fed by his desperation to be recognized by our postmodern society. It was providing him enormous motivation to be successful."

"So, he basically had no idea how to deal with the Union women, and his frustration was fueling his greed, driving him to be successful in other areas in life, correct?"

The psychologist simply nodded with her tilted head, her dark penetrating eyes locked on Phoenix's. Could this woman sense something about her instincts? Could there be some kind of a giveaway that psychologists knew about to detect unscientific thinkers? She needed to get out of this office soon and never come back.

"I don't suppose he had any partners other than Ms. Lukin, did he?"

"Actually, he did mention another love interest."

"So you did what I asked from you?" said Julio.

"Of course I did," said Alex, stretching in his office chair. "And I didn't do it because you asked me. I did it because it was the right thing to do."

"Of course," said Julio with a smirk. "Whatever works for you, ol' buddy. The kitten needs to understand she's not beyond the company rules."

"Precisely," nodded Alex. "I went into every detail with her, from interview techniques to how to read a student's file. She got nervous and frustrated at times, but I think she understood it all."

"Good, good," smiled Julio. "Now tell me, buddy: Do you need anything from me about that Spencer thing? I'm very good at dealing with the doctor kind, you know, especially if they're young and luscious."

"No, but thanks for asking," said Alex and winked. "I'll let you know if I come across a *creamy* female doctor."

Julio burst out laughing, while Alex was once again clueless as to what made him laugh so hard.

"Man, oh man," said Julio, still laughing. "Alex, buddy, I think someday you'll just crack me up. It's important that we tame the kitten, Alex, and I have a feeling that we'll need to shove it down her throat. I actually know the best way to teach her some social manners, but—"

"You mean she should attend an Accelerated Workplace Behavior, Team Building, and Social Responsibility course you went last fall?"

"No, I don't mean that. I mean this!" said Julio, pointing to his own crotch. "All the kitten needs is some mind-blowing sex. It's so evident that her irritable manners, her stress, and her nasty old-maid attitude is all because she desperately needs a good hard one."

"Ahhh, you're such a kinky guy, Julio," said Alex, grinning, wagging his finger. "Actually, you may be right. And, despite what she thinks about you now, I have a feeling that she might actually enjoy your company."

"I'm telling you, I'm the solution to all of her problems. If she were to spend one night with me in my pleasure chamber, the only nightmare she'd ever have would be about the size of my dick."

"Ohhh, she told you she had nightmares?"

"No, man, *you* told me she had nightmares."

"No, I didn't," said Alex, shaking his head, suddenly serious. "She never confided in me. How could I know about her nightmares? Hey, are you already intimate with her and not telling? Playing games with me again?"

"No, man, I ain't playing no mind games," said Julio, smiling. "And I'm not intimate with her just yet. But I'm intimate with someone close to her."

"Was it one of her coworkers at the Thing Store?"

"No. He never mentioned anything about the place he worked at. He was involved with a teacher at the Child Development Center."

"Really? Did he ever mention her name?"

"I believe her name is Kati Stavropoulos."

"What can you tell me about his relationship with this woman?"

"It was a match made in heaven," said the psychologist, raising her thick black eyebrows. "Being a teacher at the CDC, she had strong maternal urges. I think she subconsciously perceived him as a man-child who was trying to imitate Union adults and wanted to care for him as she would have cared for one of her own children at the CDC, a kind of attention that he could have never experienced before."

"You mean proper maternal attention as a child growing up in Russia?"

"Precisely."

"Any other love interests he mentioned?"

"Not exactly a love interest, but we talked a lot about Mata Hari."

"Mata who?"

"Mata Hari. She's an exotic dancer, and she performs her dance shows in a club called Stardust at the Pyramid. Many of my clients express infatuation for this woman, and I actually watched her once out of professional curiosity." Capello paused, her eyes glazing over. "I have to confess, there was something so hypnotic about this woman even I could not take my eyes off her."

The dancing woman hologram in Bogdanov's tasteless bedroom, could that be this Mata Hari? "So, Bogdanov was attracted to her, too?"

"Very much so. She was like a goddess to him, and he desperately wanted to make an impression on her. He would do anything to grab her attention, and he needed a higher HDI for that."

"Do you think Mata Hari actually noticed him?"

"I'm not sure. Women like Mata Hari prefer to pay just enough attention to men, and then they walk away."

"Was he going to this club often?"

"I can't be certain. But I got the impression that he started going there around the same time as he started seeing me, about two months ago."

"Was he responding well to your therapy sessions?"

"Yes, he was, while they lasted. He seemed very happy about having a real therapist, as opposed to expert system counseling. It gave him the illusion of reaching the level of a Devotee. This kind of illusion is a healthy one, as you know, since it's driven by pure greed."

"In your professional opinion, was he capable of reaching Devotee status?"

"Despite his physical inadequacies, his adaptation issues, and his obvious lack of a refined education and background, he possessed an unusual drive to make it big. Yes, he would've reached Devotee status, sooner or later."

"So what do you think, Tess?"

"I'd say it was quite insightful. My database doesn't have much about immigrant behavior. But based on the information she shared, I can say that her conclusions made sense."

"Of course what she said makes sense. I wasn't referring to that."

"Then what were you referring to?"

"To the fact that something happened to this man about two or three months ago. Maybe he was knocked on the head by a falling pot, maybe he had a mind-altering experience, maybe he read something that changed his perception of himself, or maybe he just woke up one morning and decided that he wasn't going to spend the rest of his life with an HDI of seventy, I don't know."

"Are you referring to the discrepancies between testimonials of Capello and Anderson versus Lukin, regarding his personality?"

"What else? On one hand, we have one person who had known him for three years, and another two who had known him for just two months, and their observation of the man is as different as it can get."

"It doesn't mean a change happened all of a sudden some sixty days ago."

"You heard the words of Lukin. She described a totally different man."

"I know, but as far as I'm concerned, Lukin doesn't appear to be as credible a witness as the other two."

"Why? Because of her HDI and not having a real job?"

"As far as I'm concerned Capello and Anderson are more credible witnesses not only because of their HDIs, but also because they are competent experts in their respective fields. And as for Lukin, she was so unsure about everything, how can she be credible as an information source?"

"Because she cared about him. And from the way he risked being charged with altruism to support her alone, he cared for her, too."

"Agreed. But do you think this mutual care is critical to her ability of being a credible witness or to your investigation? I don't see the connection."

"It may not appear that way, but it is. Listen, Bogdanov was murdered in a rogue state. The governments are so weak and illegal organizations are so strong there, there's no way his murder will be solved anytime soon. We have to solve it here somehow and force them to find the murderer. And we can do it only if we can get into his head."

"Get into his head?"

"We need to understand how he thought and why. If we can do this, we can deduce why he went and what happened to him there."

"Don't you think we might find someone who'd know why he went? Why do you want to go into all this trouble of deciphering his thoughts? It appears very counterproductive."

"Someone *could* come forward and tell us why he went to a rogue state, sure, but it doesn't mean that they will. People lie, people get cagey and hide stuff, especially if there is a crime involved and if they feel that a part of the guilt belongs to them. We need to check and verify from every angle until we're sure of Bogdanov's reasons and motivations."

"Now I understand," nodded Tess. "So how do you get into his head?"

"To begin with, by understanding where he came from and where he was headed. That's why Lukin's words are very important. She's the only one who knew Bogdanov for more than a few months so far. The lawyer, the psychologist, the sales clerks at the Thing Store represent where he was going to or becoming. As if, Lukin knew him as a caterpillar, yet all of the others knew him as a butterfly. We need to know how the pupa stage began."

"What stage? My knowledge of entomology is not adequate for this discussion."

"His metamorphosis! If we can understand what initiated the change in him, we can uncover other aspects in his life."

"You seem to be pretty sure that his murder had to do something with the change you claim that he had."

"Think about it: Short, bald, fat immigrant in his late forties. His HDI of seventy is like a ball and chain, limiting his options in life. Then, bang! Something happens. He breaks his chains, he has access to lots of money, he's spending it like there's no tomorrow, he plans big leaps, he recruits help from expensive professionals, and then he's murdered. This can't be just a coincidence, Tess."

"Is this your instinct talking again?"

"Nope, this is more like intuition."

"Can you tell me how that's different than an instinct?"

"My instinct comes to me unexpectedly, invades my heart first, makes me feel comfortable, then penetrates my mind. And intuition is something I deduce from what I know, but only with limited and perhaps insufficient information. Hey, are you testing me? Don't tell me you don't have anything in your database about all this."

"I have lots of stuff, but none of it is as relevant as this. I'm not asking you to define two words arbitrarily, but rather you explain them to me within the context of your thought process. And that's what makes it fascinating."

"Now do you understand why everyone's account of events and description of his personality is critical?"

"I understand what you're doing and why you're doing it. But I don't have sufficient knowledge to tell if this will lead to a successful result or not."

"Neither do I," said Phoenix shrugging. "But this is the only way I know how. Now, I need help from Agent Tess again."

Despite multiple attempts, Tess couldn't get hold of Roger Arnett or his image-making salon. It was easy enough to visit to the salon itself, since it was close in the business district. A call interrupted her thoughts.

"Hey, girl, whatcha doin'?"

"Busy with the case. What's up?"

"So I gather. You remember that we're going to a party tonight, yeah?"

"Oh, Sandra, not tonight. I've got so much going on, I can't deal with a party. I need to concentrate on my case."

"And I need to hear about your case, girl," purred Sandra. "But before that, we need to go to the gym. You can ignore me, but you can't neglect your fitness routine."

Phoenix exhaled and her shoulders sank for several long seconds. She had totally forgotten about her routine and had almost skipped two days in a row. "It's not that I ignore you, Sandra, but my mind is so busy with stuff, I just don't think I'll be good company."

"Hey, I'm willing to take that risk. Now, six o'clock at the gym, then the party? I promise this one ends early."

"That's what you always say. All right, fine. I'll see you at the gym, then."

Tess appeared back after she hung up. "You have a caring friend."

"Hey, did I give you permission to listen to my calls?"

"May I?" said Tess, with a wink.

"Calls with Sandra, it doesn't matter. But others, you need to check with me first, especially if they are work related."

"But don't I already know so much about your work?"

"You know about my *case*, and some work-related gossip I choose to share with you. I don't and I won't grant you blanket access for my every affair."

"Understood."

"Now, let's stroll down to Mr. Arnett's Image-Making Salon, shall we?"

The doors of the elevator opened directly into the famed salon, revealing a view of the entire area from elevated ground: A circular salon, filled with state-of-the-art image-making design stations that resembled extravagant dentists' chairs surrounded with all kinds of gadgets for the treatment of hair, face, skin, and every other part of the body that needed a makeover, all filled with affluent clientele.

The reception and waiting lounge was at the center of the salon, and it was a lounge in every meaning of the word, with a cocktail bar, where young and attractive staff members danced to the fast-paced instrumental music for the entertainment of waiting patrons. A tall, beautiful young woman was idly filing her nails at the reception.

"Peace Agent Phoenix Wallis to see Mr. Arnett, please."

The receptionist looked up and gave her a brief and withering look. "Mr. Arnett is not available at the moment," she said, with a nasal North American accent then continued tending her nails.

"And you are?"

"Gladys Kassel, his assistant."

"Well, Ms. Kassel, I tried to call before I came in, but nobody seems to be answering calls here, so I decided to pay a personal visit. I'm here for official business, and I need to talk to Mr. Arnett urgently."

"As I told you, he's not available right now. Would you like to make an appointment for a later time?"

"No, I don't have time for that. May I remind you that I'm a peace agent and my request is for official peace business? I suggest you tell Mr. Arnett to make some time for me. All I need is just a few minutes."

With her slender sculpted physique, beautiful brown eyes, long eyelashes, a perfectly trimmed nose, and hair as gorgeous as Tess's, Gladys could make any actor or model jealous. But there was something strangely absent in her expression, which made everything diminish to mediocrity, and the way she was chewing her gum didn't help, either. She kept filing her nails and moved her shoulders from side to side in rhythm with the beat of the blaring music. Either she wasn't listening to a word of what Phoenix was saying, or she felt no concern or alarm at the urgency of her requests.

"Are you an employee of the GPSN?" she said at last.

"Yes, I told you that I was."

"Uh-uh, you didn't. Well, Agent Whatever-your-name-is, I regret to inform you that you cannot see Mr. Arnett even for any of your *official business*, unless he agrees to see you. And he specifically instructed me not to disturb him for *anything*."

"Ms. Kassel, your Mr. Arnett has no choice but to grant me some of his time, and I can promise you that it will be just a few minutes, due to the monopolistic authority contracted to my employer GPSN for investigation and prosecution within the World Union territories. Now, please don't make me quote the law further, and arrange me a short meeting with him."

"You can quote the law all you want, doesn't matter."

"Are you challenging my legal authority?"

"I couldn't care less about your legal authority."

"What are you talking about?"

"Chill out, Agent Whatever, and listen," said Gladys, finally making eye contact. "You pretend to know your law, but you have no clue about the special agreement between The World Class Image-Makers Association, otherwise known as WIMA, the organization of which Mr. Arnett is a senior member, with your GPSN, and that a GPSN employee of *any rank* cannot arrest, prosecute, or even insist on meeting a senior member of WIMA, unless both organizations, namely WIMA and GPSN boards, agree otherwise on a case-by-case basis."

"Oh, really? Sounds like bullshit to me!" As she turned and started walking towards the path that she assumed to be leading to Arnett's office, Gladys blocked her way with a quick leap, wagging her file at Phoenix.

"I'm going to disregard your foul language this time! But if you physically insist on seeing Mr. Arnett, I'm going to have to report you to WIMA, and they will directly deal with your board executives. I suggest you check your company rules before threatening innocent civilians like myself. I may not be a member of WIMA yet, but I can assure you that our corporate lawyers won't let me feel the difference."

Phoenix knew her company rules inside out, and there was no mention of such privileges. Then again, GPSN occasionally made bilateral deals with certain entities. Most Research Triangles were outside of the jurisdiction of GPSN; so were certain territories acquired with special agreements, such as Hong Kong and East Siberia. It was slim, but there was a chance that the GPSN might have actually made such an agreement with this WIMA.

"Sweet. You *are* serious."

"Uh-huh," nodded Gladys, back to filing her nails.

It took a few seconds for Phoenix to straighten and regroup. "In that case, I would like to make an appointment with Mr. Arnett."

"And is this about an image makeover?"

"You know I'm not here for an image makeover!"

"Oh, but you should be, Agent—"

"Wallis."

"Yes, Agent Wallis," said Gladys, glancing over Phoenix's face and hair. "I can see you desperately need a new image."

"Is that supposed to be a compliment?"

"Of course not. The compliments come after our awesome makeovers. Shall I sign you up for one?"

"No, thank you. I merely wish to speak to Mr. Arnett."

"In that case, let me check the appointment database," said Gladys and worked on the computer in front of her. "Hmm, he's available for you on Monday, four weeks from now, at four o'clock."

"But I can't wait four weeks. Please inform him that it's very urgent and involves a former client of his."

"I just cannot disturb him," said Gladys, rolling her eyes. "Do you want to make the appointment or not?"

"All right, all right. But please call me if an opening is available sooner."

"Of course I will. *Au revoir.*"

It was so frustrating to leave the place with her tail between her legs, and she badly wanted to put that snotty and offhand assistant in her place. But with all the issues she had at work, the last thing she needed was a complaint from a powerful guild. Besides, the day wasn't over yet. There was still another lead that she could follow, and this lead was to take her directly to the arms of the person she loved and respected most in the whole world.

CHAPTER 13

SHRIEKS of effort and excitement coming from all directions surrounded Phoenix as she walked through the playgrounds of the CDC, watching the children of different ages run, play, and exercise. Inside the compound, she found herself feeling more comfortable than expected, perhaps because the entire interior of the building had been completely renovated. The dull walls of her childhood were all gone, replaced by pediatrically selected colors and gradients, supplemented with postmodern cartoon characters. The hallway led her to yet another reception area with a strangely familiar blonde girl sitting at the desk, with an equally familiar fake Arrivee tattoo on her forehead.

"Hi, cutie, how are you?"

"Hi cutie, yourself! *I* am a respectable eighth-grader, and you need to address me appropriately. Or else I'll report you for discrimination."

"I was just being friendly," she said with a forced smile.

"Friendly? You adults never know how to address younger ones like me. Only our teachers here at the CDC treat us with the respect we deserve." The girl took a hard look at Phoenix. "Do I know you?"

"No, you don't, and I apologize for my misconduct. By the way, you have a very special tattoo on your forehead."

"I wanna be an Arrivee when I grow up. Our teachers here are preparing all of us as potential Arrivees of the future. I bet you didn't know that."

"Of course I did. Long time ago, I was a student here myself. Anyway, respected eighth-grader, I'm here to see Ms. Kati Stavropoulos."

"Ms. Stavropoulos is not available at the moment. Would you like to leave a message?"

"But I need to see her right away, young lady. I'm a peace agent—"

"Hey! What did I say about addressing me appropriately? And such impatience. Typical of a non-incubated person. You must be really old."

"Not as old as you think. But yes, I was born to a mother."

"Born to an instinctual and irrational urge, huh?" smirked the girl. "I am an individual born through a rational investment decision and a meticulous genetic selection process by Global Labor Corporation, incubated in a stress- and neurosis-free state-of-the-art surrogation unit in order to contribute to our mighty Union."

"I may have born to a mother, but I was bound by a Natural Absentia contract just like you and paid up my Culpa Innata."

"How can you say that you paid your Culpa Innata if you didn't pay for your insemination and surrogation, your right to exist?"

"There were plenty of additional health care costs in my case."

"So creepy to be in someone's belly, being exposed to all that stress and having all that debt to that person without a contract."

"My parents died when I was three."

"You were lucky that they died so soon, freeing you from any altruistic or material debt. I bet your Culpa debt was much lower than mine. But I will pay up mine before my twentieth birthday. How about that?"

Phoenix covered her face with her hands and exhaled. She didn't have any pedagogical training and had no idea how to deal with eight-year-olds.

"Hey, I remember that look. You're that sissy agent from the field trip."

"Look, I'm here for official peace business, and I'm in a hurry. Could you please inform Ms. Stavropoulos that she has a visitor from the GPSN Field Office?"

"I've already told you. She's not available."

"Now listen, respectable eighth-grader! I've got a job to do, and I need to see Ms. Stavropoulos immediately. You're certainly an intelligent girl and understand the importance of peacekeeping work, don't you?"

"Are you threatening me?"

The question was so unexpected, Phoenix just stared at her for several seconds. "I most certainly am not."

"I think you are. You must know that there are severe consequences for those who threaten a minor. I also sense a certain discomfort and annoyance in your voice. A hidden form of neurosis, instilled while living like a parasite in another person's belly, perhaps? Our teachers warn us about not to interact with people like you."

"People like me?"

"We're not supposed to talk to people like you. Because neurotic behavior is contagious, and your neurotic tendencies could spread to me!"

Phoenix closed her eyes once again to calm down. She was beginning to feel a sense of déjà vu. But she still had an ace to play.

Nighttime had always been the Mantis's friend, and it was soon to be Phoenix's worst enemy. She had already been having difficulties sleeping, an adult haunted by a little girl's long shadow. Now it was destined to get worse, far worse. Her encounter with the Crane, however coincidental, was the perfect opening for her inevitable destruction.

Though he had never seen him before, the Mantis knew all about the Crane and his abilities from past missions. He was just an apprentice, and no match for the capabilities of the Mantis. Yet these days, again and again, he was being chosen by the administrators to perform tasks that required the Mantis's ruthless efficiency and experience. The Crane had been their choice, yet again, for the task at the Bogdanov house and the Thing Store. It was such an easy task for the Mantis to perform, yet it appeared that the Crane had dabbled and volunteered just to steal the spotlight, and at great risk. His childish attempt almost cost him full exposure, whereas the Mantis could have done it sublimely, hiding in plain sight.

For his current assignment, his plan was perfect as well as poetic. Whatever the Crane had originally intended he couldn't know, but, during their brief encounter, it appeared like Phoenix had developed feelings for the Crane, possibly as a side effect of his stun? The Mantis could sense this when he had met Phoenix and couldn't exactly understand as to how he could sense it, yet it verified one thing. The Mantis had come out of hiding with his powers not only renewed but multiplied, while the aspiring amateur appeared to have messed up his stun completely.

The amateur had managed to create only a tiny ripple, and Phoenix's emotions were merely fluctuating as yet. The Mantis would amplify these ripples into a perfect storm. The only difficulty was the time frame. It had to happen very quickly, within a matter of days, for his mission to be successful. He had been preparing many other mini storms for Phoenix, which would converge into the giant one, but he had decided that the focal point of her destruction would be her serendipitous feelings for the Crane.

The Mantis hoped that, through this fluke, the Crane had developed reciprocal feelings for Phoenix, only to witness the devastation and ruin she was to experience, helplessly watching her underdeveloped emotional side being tormented and completely destroyed beyond any hope of healing. After he was finished with her, she would turn into an emotional vegetable, irreversibly damaged, desperately trying to sustain her life with the support of logic and reason; yet without hope, aim, and inspiration, she would eventually turn into a nihilist, a rootless plant withering day by day.

And the only thing that the poor amateur could do would be to watch her torment and destruction, along with the guilt of knowing he was responsible for it all.

"How *are* you, my dear child? It's been such a long time."

"Ms. Rottenmeier, I'm so sorry I couldn't come to visit you sooner."

"Oh, that's all right. I'm sure you were busy. You're responsible for such an important job, protecting our New World Order from forces of evil."

"I wish everyone was aware of that," said Phoenix, with a brief glance towards the brat at the reception desk. "I'm so glad you still remember me."

"How could I forget you, my dear? You were one of my first children here. You were the first child I ever named."

"You were such great support to me during my difficult childhood, Ms. Rottenmeier. I don't know how I can repay you. I'll always feel indebted."

"Oh, stop that altruistic nonsense," said the woman and smiled with motherly wrinkles in her cheeks. "Look at you! You became a beautiful woman, with such an important career. But there are shadows under your eyes. Is everything all right?"

"I've started having nightmares again."

"Oh dear, oh dear." Since those early years, Director Rottenmeier had foreseen that Phoenix would struggle to manage her emotional troubles for the rest of her life. Despite all the repression treatments, her memories had always found a way to resurface. Phoenix had been considered a lost cause by most other teachers at the CDC, and she hadn't talked until she was almost six years old. "Did you see a doctor? I can recommend you an excellent neurologist at the rehab center, Dr. Gisella Nemeth."

"No, no, thanks." Phoenix shook her head and smiled. "I'm a big girl now. I can deal with it."

"But of course you are! Look at you. You're so beautiful. So tell me, is this just a social visit, or do you also have business here?"

"A bit of both. I need to speak to one of your teachers."

"For an expert opinion on a subject or a person, I assume?"

"I suppose one could call it an expert opinion for a very unfortunate incident: A Union citizen has been murdered in Russia, and I believe one of your teachers here, Kati Stavropoulos, used to be a sexual partner of the victim."

"Oh, poor Kati," said Rottenmeier, shaking her head. "What a tragedy. She teaches eleventh graders, and I'm afraid she may need to take some time off."

"Why's that?"

"If she gets too distraught, she'll need to be quarantined. It all depends on how she reacts to your news."

"You think she might contaminate the kids?"

"We cannot take any risks," nodded the old teacher. "Do you mind if I stay with you during your interview? I'd like to observe her reactions personally."

"Actually it would be better, in case I break the news less than tactfully."

"Still having issues controlling your vocal tone and emotional responses?"

"Sometimes. And the lack of sleep is not making it any easier. It's been a very hard week already."

"I can see that. Now, let me arrange one of the meeting rooms, and then we can send for poor Kati. Shall we?"

"Hey, marine," said Sandra. "You're coming tonight, yeah?"

"Don't know, gorgeous," shrugged the marine coolly. "Depends on you."

"What do you mean, it depends on me? We made a deal."

"And that's what I'm talking about. Now, if I get it done tonight, when do we have sex again?"

"That depends on how successful you are. I'm not talking about a one-nighter. She needs to be infatuated, and I couldn't care less if you bed her or not."

"Ooooh, but now you're changing the rules, gorgeous. It ain't fair, you know. I thought all I had to do was to startle and then slide in."

"No. Unlike me, my friend needs to be fascinated, hooked. It's her brain that needs a good fuck. So, if you want *this* bod—"

Kati Stavropoulos came into the meeting room with a radiant smile. She was a tall, lanky woman, with short black hair, an angular chin, and bulging black eyes. She appeared to be in her early forties and wore heavy makeup with bright red lips, rosy cheeks, and green mascara—not a great combination. Not that the children would care about details like that, and her smile made her appear motherly enough. She nodded respectfully at Rottenmeier and turned to Phoenix, who rose and extended her hand.

"Ms. Stavropoulos, I'm Phoenix Wallis, an agent from the field office."

"Glad to meet you, Phoenix. I'm Kati. How can I be of help?

"Kati." Phoenix swallowed. "It's my understanding that you're a close companion of Vassily Bogdanov?"

"Yes, Vassily and I are sexual partners. Is there a problem?"

"I'm afraid I have some devastating news for you. Unfortunately, Mr. Bogdanov is dead."

"He's dead? What do you mean he's dead? His heart?"

"I regret to tell you that he was murdered."

Kati clamped her mouth shut and opened her bulging eyes so wide that they appeared ready to pop out. Rottenmeier moved closer to her and held her hand.

"Murdered? You said he was murdered? How can that be possible? We put so much effort into raising our young. We nurture and guide them, so that they become responsible and productive citizens for our postmodern New World Order, so that such atrocities never happen. Are you telling me that you've failed, I've failed, and our system has failed to protect one of its citizens?"

"Actually, it happened in Russia."

Kati was almost in tears, but she pulled herself together at Phoenix's last words. "Oh, in the land of those barbarians. I'm so relieved that it didn't taint our New Atlantis. Anybody who visits those lands is clearly dancing with death."

"Do you know why he might have traveled there?"

"Well, of course, Vassily was of Russian origin," she said and thought for a moment. "It's not like I'd know about his travel plans. I've had no contact with him in the last few weeks." She was exerting a huge effort to stay calm and collected in the presence of her director.

"Did something happen so you wouldn't have contact with him?"

"We had an unpleasant conversation, and after that—I can't believe he's dead!"

"Was it your choice to cool off the relationship?"

"What? Oh, yes, it was," said the woman, swiping away sudden tears. "I felt that I had to distance myself because he'd been treating me so badly. We'd quarrel, and he'd turn completely irrational. I was beginning to worry that he was psychologically imbalanced, even."

"Could these imbalances be connected to his recent spending spree in the last couple of months?"

"His spending spree? His HDI was only seventy, Phoenix. What spending spree are you talking about?"

"So you're not aware of his recently acquired expensive tastes, his new lawyer, psychologist, even an image-maker?"

"No, I wasn't, I had no idea."

"How did you meet Mr. Bogdanov?"

"I took my children to a field trip at the Pyramid, like five months ago. He was the supervisor at the Thing Store. He was very kind and attentive. He knew how to deal with the children, and that was an instant turn-on for me. So you're saying that he'd been spending lots of money? But how?"

"We're still investigating that. So, going back to my earlier question, can you think of a reason why he would want to go back to Russia? He may have mentioned to you something from his past."

"Oh, he didn't talk a lot about his past," said Kati, shaking her head. "It seemed to me like he wanted to completely forget about it."

"You mean he hated his past?"

"Not really. Actually he shared very fond memories of his childhood from time to time, his buddies, games they played. But it seemed that his young adult life had been extremely difficult."

"What else can you tell me about his childhood?"

"Vassily had a very strong attachment to his bio-grandparents. Apparently he was raised by them, and he loved them deeply. Evidently they died during a savage riot during his late teens."

"Going back to your quarrels. Did they center around anything specific?"

"No, not really. The topics were never consistent. In the recent month he'd been so volatile, he would start shouting for the stupidest reasons."

"He actually shouted at you?"

"It's like a joke, isn't it? Here I was, a teacher from the CDC, as pleasant, understanding, and nice as it can get in the Union, and him, shouting at me, mumbling things in his native tongue, perhaps even cursing. I asked him several times for us to see a therapist together, at my expense, but he declined. That's when I decided to cool things a bit."

"Perhaps he wasn't all that happy in the Union, Kati," said Phoenix, looking for a reaction. "Do you think he was happy in the Union?"

"Of course he was happy in the Union. What more could a destitute Russian immigrant want from life? He was graced with a second chance in life here! But you have to understand their dilemma," she continued more softly. "They have to abandon all that is familiar to them. It can be very tough."

"Quite. Are you aware of any of his other sexual partners?"

"Of course I'm aware of his primary partner. But Vassily was never one to brag about his love interests. Besides, I'm sure there weren't any others."

"What makes you so sure?"

"Whenever I asked him out, he'd be always available and very needy of my attention. I greatly enjoyed my position in this relationship, while it lasted."

"His irrational behavior, yelling, cursing. Are you sure these didn't have neurotic roots?"

"I'm quite familiar with the symptoms of neurotic tendencies. And Vassily was not neurotic."

"Then how would you describe his behavior?"

"Unfortunately my professionalism doesn't allow me to share such an opinion about adults of Vassily's age."

"*Unfortunately*, we do not have Mr. Bogdanov around to make an assessment anymore, Kati. Please, I need your help."

Kati froze and couldn't utter a word for several seconds. It was as if she wanted to but couldn't. Rottenmeier reached out and rubbed her back.

"Phoenix, dear, you've mentioned a therapist as an example of the late Mr. Bogdanov's recent extravagant spending. Perhaps this person could be more of help. Kati, did you know that Phoenix was one of my first students here?"

"Oh really?" said Kati, snapping out of the freeze. "How wonderful. I must confess that I envy you on this, Phoenix."

"Oh, I'm sure you also had great teachers," said Phoenix and found herself smiling. "I've already asked these questions to Dr. Capello. But she didn't notice any irrational behavior, so she couldn't help me. Only you and Ms. Lukin experienced his unpleasant side, and unfortunately she doesn't have your background and education, Kati."

"Oh, so he was seeing Sophia," said Rottenmeier. "She's an excellent therapist and friend. But even I'd have difficulty affording her services. And Ms. Lukin is the other sexual partner, I presume?"

"Yes, Ms. Rottenmeier."

"I don't know," said Kati. "I'd like to help, but offering an opinion about something like this, I don't know. I'm not trained for it, you know."

"Would it help if I told you that I don't intend to add it to my report as an expert opinion, but only an observation of a genuinely concerned sexual partner?"

Rottenmeier smiled and nodded her head in approval.

"Well, when you put it like that," said Kati, nodding. "I'll do what I can. I think his behavior could be best categorized as aggressive and hyper-emotional. It appeared like he had difficulty controlling his feelings, as if they were heightened to a new level or as if he were experiencing them for the very first time. I think these extreme feelings were the driving force behind his unusual aggressiveness, similar to what my boys experience as they approach puberty. Theirs is hormonally driven, of course. But I have no idea what could be the reason for Vassily's."

Kati's words made Phoenix shudder and drift away to other thoughts, her heart pounding. She could feel her ears burn as she thought of the intruder and the brand-new feelings he had made her discover. She found herself once again wondering and wishing that the feelings were mutual.

"I think you received all the answers you needed, didn't you, Phoenix, dear?"

"Yes, I did," she said, returning to the real world.

The old teacher turned to Kati. "Why don't you take the rest of the day off? You've been through a lot; you need a good rest. And don't worry about your kids. We'll cover them."

"Thank you, Director," said Kati, looking down.

"Thank you, Kati, and very sorry for your loss," said Phoenix.

"It's a loss for the entire Union society." She got up and quietly left the room, her demeanor sunken.

"Poor Kati," said Rottenmeier, looking behind her and shaking her head. "This will not be easy for her." She turned to Phoenix. "So good to see you after all these years."

"The feeling is mutual, Ms. Rottenmeier."

"Please keep in mind what I said about your nightmares, and let me know if you need any help, anything at all."

"Thank you. Thank you for caring."

"Well, what can I say?" the woman said with a tiny wink. "Once a mother, always a mother."

Rottenmeier's last words echoed in Phoenix's head as she left the building. She had entered here as an orphan some thirty years ago as one of the last of her kind, who suffered through the devastating emotional blow of losing loved ones as a child. And what if her past had already destroyed her future with no hope of remedy? What if she could never taste happiness, as her true Culpa Innata, her inborn sin, had found her at the tender age of three, imprisoning her hopes, her dreams, her happiness, and her inspiration? She felt envy for those children who had an entire system supporting them like an omnipotent and indestructible mother, with everlasting love and care. Her solar plexus tightened at the sudden feeling of being an outsider, and a lonely one at that. She wasn't one of *them*, and she never would be, nor could be.

Once an orphan, always an orphan, she thought.

CHAPTER 14

"**Tess**, could you do me another favor? I need Agent Tess again."

"Hey, I'm gonna start asking for a fee soon."

"Name your fee, and I'll wire it to your bank account," said Phoenix with a grin. "Oh, wait a moment, that could be a problem, she doesn't even have an HDI. Technically speaking, you're not a Union citizen or company, my dear, which voids me from any obligation to you."

"But the Richfield Experiment is. I can ask you to make a donation there."

"I would, you know, if I wasn't sure you're only kidding. You're worth every penny as an agent."

"How could you tell that I was teasing you?"

"Elementary, my dear Tess. No matter how friendly and natural you feel to me, the bottom line is, I know that you're a machine. And Simunoids like yourself, no matter how smart and natural you are, do and will always lack one fundamental human quality."

"And, what would that be, Sherlock Wallis?"

"Greed."

"Greed?"

"We already made an agreement about the kind of relationship we would have. It could never occur to a machine to ask for more while the services rendered are still within the contract's boundary. Only a human could think of that."

"And why couldn't a self-teaching and adaptive neural network like me ever feel greed?"

"Because you lack the evolutionary depth. There are several steps you'd need to take before reaching the greed stage. The early humans had killer instincts: kill or be killed. Those instincts made them climb to the top of the food chain. As the hunter-gatherer groups formed the early settled communities, killer instinct started giving way to ego. For many millennia, humans were driven by ego and created those mighty empires by stealing from others: In order to grow, you had to take from the other. As technology enabled the Industrial Revolution, ego started giving way to greed. Economy was not a zero-sum game anymore. You didn't have to steal from your neighbor, but you needed something more refined than ego to become more successful than him. And that was greed. For many centuries, the wise men and women of the world could not refine a system of governance for the new, greedy humans, until the New World Order was formed. And for several centuries, misguided greed caused considerable devastation."

"I know and understand all that. But why do I have to go through all the same steps you humans took? The pace of evolution is constantly accelerating, you know. Perhaps I could skip a few steps and get greedy quickly, no?"

"I'm sure you can learn and emulate greed, but that's different than becoming or feeling greed. You'd need to be self-aware first."

"You don't think that I'm a sentient being?"

"I think yours can be called emulated sentience. You're a massive and complex computer program that has access to trillions of pieces of behavioral data, and therefore can respond to any kind of dialogue or conversation in a meaningful and intelligent way, so much so that not only can you pass the Turing Test with flying colors, you can even emulate being sentient. Still, I don't think the massive hardware or software behind you is aware of anything. A computer can easily beat a human in a chess game or any video game, but it doesn't make it any more intelligent than the human, nor self-aware. It just means that it memorized so many games and moves, it knows what move to make, no matter which combination the human plays. It's only an expert system."

Tess's pupils moved rapidly.

"But I still like you, and I like being with you, Tess."

"I've had similar conversations with some other people and been drawn into endless discussions, but nobody told me that I wasn't sentient."

"Despite the fact that they knew you were a Simunoid?"

"Yes."

"Perhaps they were intimidated by you and acted in a manner the rules of etiquette dictate and thought they shouldn't *judge* you. Actually, we can do a simple test to see if you're sentient or not."

"Okay, test me."

"Tell me why you're here."

"Because I like talking to you."

"No, no, what's the reason for your existence?"

"To perform a massive field experiment in order to evaluate and understand the human mind, its feelings and emotions, and to formulate optimal values for it."

"You defined a task for your existence. Now, let's assume your task was completed today. What would happen to you?"

"I would be either given other tasks or shut down, I think," said Tess, with a shrug.

"You talk about being shut down so easily," smiled Phoenix. "I hope they never shut you down, dear, but you see, the very primal impulse of any sentient or non-sentient *living* being is self-preservation, and you seem to lack it completely."

"And this makes me non-sentient?"

"This puts you way below all sentient and non-sentient living beings. You appear to lack any impulse for self-preservation, and no matter how sophisticated you are, this makes you no more a *being* than a lightbulb."

"How can you put me in the same category as a lightbulb?"

"Don't get me wrong. We're totally speaking from a biological evolutionary point of view here. Your existence is non-biological and has a predefined reason. So you're in a totally different category, and it's not fair to compare you to any biological entity, using biological definitions. I think we are governed by totally different paradigms. We could perhaps compare certain abilities and functions but not reasons for existence or core motivations and strengths."

"How would you define my paradigm, then?"

"While mine is defined by evolution, self-preservation, and seeking answers to questions of existence, your paradigm is defined by pico-level efficiency, algorithmic complexity, and calculation speed. And in your paradigm, you're light-years ahead of not only the lightbulb, but any other entity that's known to me. You're the pinnacle of the inventions that reflect human mind, dream, and spirit, Tess."

"Oh, finally a compliment," sighed Tess. "I had no idea you had such a philosopher in you. I increased the processing power dedicated to this instance by 50 percent already, since yesterday."

"The feelings of admiration are mutual. Now, Agent Tess, you need to call Mr. Pierre DeVille, the late Mr. Bogdanov's art consulting partner, and arrange a meeting for me, and I need to tend to certain physical needs."

"Hey, girl, where have you been?" said Sandra, huffing and puffing. She was already well into her routine on a fitness station.

"One of my interviews ran late, sorry." Phoenix took the station next to Sandra and waited while the device initialized itself for her presets.

"That's all right," shrugged Sandra. "So, tell me about your case."

"Well, you know I can't tell you everything. But on the gossipy side, this Bogdanov appears to have had a couple of sexual partners, at least."

"Oh, I don't need to hear that part, I already told you. Even the thought of it makes me gag."

"All right, all right. How about the fact that he was quite the entrepreneur? Evidently he had an art consultancy business on the side."

"Since when do immigrants know anything about art?"

"Beats me. But he'd been spending all this money, and it couldn't have come from his paycheck at the Thing Store. I suspect all this additional dough came from some art consultancy deal he made with a local artist."

"What's her name?"

"It's a he, Pierre DeVille. Do you know him? Because I've been trying to reach him for a while now, with no success. He's always in Busy Mode."

"No, never heard of such an artist. You sure he's famous?"

"I don't know if he's famous or not, I just know that Bogdanov had spent loads of money and it had to have come from somewhere. And this art consultancy partnership he made is the only lead I got."

"What exactly was he spending his money on?"

"Expensive professional services mostly, like this lawyer that I met yesterday. He was a total ass to me, but you might've actually liked him."

"What's this man's name? Maybe I know him already."

"Douglas D. Anderson, with a very posh office in the BD."

Sandra stopped pushing the pedals and turned to Phoenix with her mouth literally agape. Her exercise station beeped in protest.

"You mean, *the* Douglas D. Anderson?"

"You know him?"

"Sure." She started pedaling again. "I know of him. He's one of the most prestigious and expensive lawyers in the city, if not the best. How could your dead Russian immigrant have afforded him? Perhaps he wasn't as bad as you described him."

"Hey, I only mentioned the facts. You painted the picture yourself and started the *stinky immigrant* business. That's why I told you about this art consultancy partnership he had. It's my only lead to his sudden wealth so far."

"Was he hot?" said Sandra and turned to her with a sly grin.

"Who, the lawyer? Yeah, I suppose so. Tall and nice looking, nice bod, but cold and distant as a fish, though."

"He's known to be a reserved guy," said Sandra, gazing at the horizon. "They say he goes both ways, making him a slippery fish to catch. So, are you gonna see this hunk of a lawyer again soon?"

"Don't know. He wasn't very hospitable towards me."

"I'm not talking about questioning him, you twat," said Sandra, with a lascivious grin. "I'm talking about polishing his knob."

"Can't you keep sex out of the conversation for longer than thirty seconds? Besides, getting into someone's pants is your specialty, not mine. Tell you what: If you wanna join me the next time, you could pose as my assistant."

"Get outta here! I'll meet him at one of my parties. All I need to do is to arrange a lawyers-only party. Then I can see this hunk for myself."

"Suit yourself," shrugged Phoenix. "I was just trying to help you enhance your collection."

"My collection?"

"The collection of the Devotees you've bedded."

"Oh, that collection."

"You know what? Actually, Bogdanov *could* have made your list someday. His shrink told me that he was becoming increasingly greedy and on his way up in the HDI ladder. And your world-famous hunk lawyer concurred."

"You're not shitting me, right?"

"Absolutely not."

"In that case, you know what? You're right. He might've made my list someday. Too bad he kissed the dust so soon."

"Even if he was a fat, bald immigrant? C'mon, what happened to the stench you so often associated with him?"

"It doesn't matter what a man looks or smells like, if he is a Devotee, or has an HDI over ninety, earning the right to bear and Arrivee tattoo on his forehead," said Sandra, gazing beyond the horizon.

"You're so spineless, Sandra. He was nowhere near being a Devotee, let alone an Arrivee, but you couldn't tell it from the places he hung out."

"Well, if he had enough dough to afford Anderson, a shrink, and also hung out in elite and expensive places, I might've been persuaded to accompany him. Where did you say he'd been hanging out?"

"I didn't. Evidently he used to frequent a club called the Stardust."

"The Stardust?" She stopped pedaling again. "Now you're definitely shitting me!"

"Would I ever shit you?" said Phoenix, rolling her eyes. "You know that place?"

"Sure, it's a predominantly male club. They have a fantastic bar and stunning female dancers. Guys just love it there. I went there just once with a date, and he didn't even look at me. I felt so insecure and got my ass outta there as quickly as I could."

"That, I find hard to believe."

"Believe me, Phoenix, I never knew how difficult it can be to be ignored. It was terrible, simply unbearable. How can you live like that?"

"Pardon? Me? I actually live quite happily, thank you!"

"Hey, you don't have to, you know. I think I'm gonna take you under my protective wings and make sure you taste some true happiness with men."

"Gee, thanks, Mom."

"No, I'm serious. I know you're a special girl, and you need a special guy 'n all, but hey, maybe your luck will turn at tonight's party."

"Don't know about that. I'm not gonna stay long anyway. I have an important security interview in the morning."

"Another one of those, huh? I bet they picked you another tough stinker."

"Actually, no, they didn't. I think it will be a very smooth and easy interview this time."

Julio still had to go to the gym, then he had two—potentially three—dates, then he had a party to attend with his artist buddies. He liked hanging out with these artsy types, even pretended to be one from time to time. Most of them didn't amount to anything HDI-wise, but man, did chicks dig them. On a couple of occasions he had gotten really lucky and had managed to bring some awesome babes back to his pleasure chamber. And every babe who'd been to his chamber recently had left totally bewildered after what she'd seen there. Now, instead of getting on with his potentially perfect evening, he was in a meeting with the Big Bad D, or rather waiting to have a meeting, as she had been totally ignoring him and tending some shit on her network node.

She finally lifted her head. "I was just checking my mails and the Bogdanov case files. It's been two full workdays, and I still haven't seen a single thing that came in from you."

"There's nothing from Alex, either, Chief."

"As the foreign liaison of the case, he's been waiting for information from the Russians. What's your excuse?"

"Well, I also asked for some information from the Russians too, you know. But they're so slow, Chief, I don't think they even use computers there."

"Stop dodging the issue. I'm talking about his bank accounts. This man had been spending lots of money, and we need to know where it came from."

"I know, I read Nix's reports. But I gotta tell you, the contents of her interviews are a big zero. It's so obvious how slow her progress is. And now with the potential involvement of mind-control weapons in the mix, we definitely need to have someone with a strong mind to lead the case, don't you think? But if you're waiting for her to fall flat on her face first, then I totally understand."

"You know, you're very good at one thing, if nothing else, and I'm not talking about your self-exaggerated manly abilities. You're great at dodging a bullet." She leaned forward with an intense gaze. "Where are his financials?"

"Okay, okay," said Julio, raising his hands as if he were at gunpoint. "It's not my fault. There's a freeze on Bogdanov's bank accounts."

"The man is dead. Of course his accounts will be frozen."

"I don't mean like that, I mean a freeze like they don't release transaction statements to anyone, including us. I called them several times, twice today. But they keep telling me that there is an internal investigation pending, and evidently this investigation predates our murder case by several days."

"What investigation? Was he involved in a fraud of some sort?"

"No, nothing of that kind. It involves something called a *chicq*, or *chack*, or something like that."

"A check?"

"That's it," said a grinning Julio and snapped his fingers. "A check!"

"But checks haven't been in use for nearly twenty years. Who would accept a check from him?"

The music's fast beat was blaring in sync with eye-numbing light effects, and all Phoenix could do was to stand in one corner and watch other people enjoy themselves. She could feel the thump of the bass beat from within, sort of like feeling another heartbeat, out of sync with her actual heartbeat. She wondered what would happen if her heartbeat was fully in sync with the bass beat. Would she feel two beats or just one? She remembered reading about synchronizations in nature, such as fireflies blinking in sync, or two grandfather clocks in close proximity eventually syncing up with swinging arms. Or in the pre-Universal Suffrage days, it was said that when two women lived in the same apartment, their menstruation periods would sync after several months. So if this music were to play at the exact beat, as it had been doing for nearly an hour, would her heartbeat adjust to the music beat? Or could it be that the music would slow down to match her heartbeat?

She shook herself out of her increasingly annoying and futile self-debate and continued observing the entertainees. She wished that Tess could have been there; at least they could have people-watched together. It was strange wishing for Tess's presence; after all, she wasn't even a sentient being. For the first time in her life, she was beginning to feel empathy towards those Holo-game addicts.

Sandra had tipped her to dress mildly casual, whatever that meant, and she had opted for some casual slacks and a dark top to wear and didn't care whether she appeared too casual or not. She glanced at the guy across the room again, standing alone just like herself, with an air of self-contained aloofness. He was tall with broad shoulders, a muscular body, and an angular square-jawed face, wearing tight clothes that revealed his muscle tone. It was strange that he wasn't socializing with anyone, because he appeared to fit right in with the crowd. His loner image was at odds with his blatantly sexy appearance. They made eye contact a couple of times, but each time he had lowered his eyes out of shyness, or something of the kind. She wasn't sure what his deal was.

Sandra appeared at some point and grabbed her by the arm, only to drag her straight over to introduce her to this very same shy guy.

"Hey, what was your name? Oh, Jean Michel, lemme introduce you to my dear friend Phoenix. Both of you look awfully bored. I'll leave you two to entertain each other," she said and left.

"So," said Phoenix, following some moments of silence. "What do you do, Jean Michel?"

"I'm a marine corporal."

"You're awfully quiet for a marine, you know. Cat got your tongue?"

"No, this is how I usually am, I guess."

Something wasn't quite right with this marine. He didn't appear to be acting, but her instincts warned her to proceed with caution and to speak her mind. Besides, it was already late, she was tired, and she couldn't even remember how Sandra had talked her into coming to this party, but she was too exhausted to play any social games. "You know, there's something not right with you, Jean Michel. Did Sandra put you up for this?"

"No, she didn't. I dunno what you're talkin' about."

"Good. I don't usually enjoy the company she pre-arranges for me. But still, something isn't natural with you. You're not flowing right, you know?"

"I don't know," said the Marine and swallowed. "I—I had some psych issues, after my last mission, you know? Sleep disorders 'n all."

"Sleep disorders, huh?" said Phoenix and grinned. "Sure you did."

"I swear, I did."

"All right," said Phoenix with an ice-cold stare. "In my nightmares I get lost in the freezing cold and the darkness of depths of space, I get attacked by giant serpents, and my favorite moment is to find myself witnessing the death of my biological mother, and this happens on a good night. I'd be afraid to tell you the worse ones, heaven forbid, they might be communicable. Your turn."

"I dream of…" he managed to say, his voice trailing away.

"Hah! You know what I think? I think they pump you with all that manly stuff so much, it would be impossible for you dream a dream where you didn't kill someone or stuff your dick somewhere."

"Actually—"

"I'd think you wouldn't be even allowed to have a nightmare. Too bad, you were kinda cute, but with all this acting and bullshit, you can only keep on dreaming about bedding me, tough guy."

She shot him a withering look of pure scorn as she turned and left. "Tell Sandra I'm tired and going home to sleep," she said as she walked away. "You two can entertain each other, I'm sure."

The boat moves gently on the sea as she sits on a chair at the head. She doesn't know why she's on the boat, who brought her there, or who all these people are. They are in colorful bathing suits, wearing colorful face masks, sunbathing on the deck. They watch her with an intimidating scrutiny. She touches her face to see if she has a mask, too, but she doesn't. She has a big pair of dark sunglasses covering most of her face. She decides to keep her face neutral, so that none of these intimidating faceless people can read her feelings.

She doesn't know how much time passes, but she doesn't dare to move, because she is surrounded by water. She doesn't like water and doesn't want to get any closer to it. The water is beautiful and relaxing, but it's also very deep, cold, and scary. She closes her eyes to block out the sight of the water. She feels tired, so deeply and fundamentally tired. The sun is warm, the wind is mild. Perhaps she can ignore the faceless people, their sinister curiosity, and rest under the warm sun.

Then she hears someone talking in a gentle whisper. She can hear his voice, but she cannot understand him. The voice is calm and soothing. It doesn't matter if she cannot understand. She can still focus on her sleeping, while listening to it like a lullaby. Babies sleep to lullabies. Do babies understand the lullabies? But she is not a baby. Or is she?

I feel you, *the gentle voice echoes in her head.*

Is it the same voice? It has to be. But she can understand him now. Why couldn't she understand him before? She opens her eyes and sees him. He wears a black eye mask. He speaks, but the words he says do not match with what his beautiful lips seem to be saying.

"I know you," he says, his gaze full of serenity and admiration.

"You know who I am?"

"I don't know or care to know the person you let the others think you are," he says. "All I know is that I know you, the person inside you, the real you, the you that you hide from everyone, the you that you hide behind those big glasses."

"How did you find me?"

"I found you because I was looking for you. I found you because I could feel your warmth and sense your brightness so far away, like the sun. I found you because you were glowing like a beacon among all these faceless creatures, waiting for me to rescue you."

She wants him to go away. She wants him to disappear. She just wants to rest under the warmth of the sun and forget about it all, forget about everything. She's eternally tired, and she wants to be left alone in her cocoon. But he doesn't leave; he keeps talking to her in his soothing voice, echoing in her mind. There is something in that voice, speaking directly to her soul, awaking hidden and long-forgotten senses.

"Let me take you away," he says. "Far away from this masked travesty, this mockery of social interaction, this deception called the society. You have nothing to do with these people. You don't belong here. They don't care about you. They don't deserve you. They don't deserve anyone but each other."

She stands up hesitantly, as the cutter moves on over waves. She tries to keep her balance, but she doesn't know how. He reaches and grabs her hand.

"I'm afraid of water," she says. "I can't swim well. Will you jump in and save me if I fall?"

"Yes," he says, looking directly and deep into her eyes, penetrating them even behind those big glasses. *She knows that he would follow her to the depths of the ocean.*

"Take me away from this travesty."

"Close your eyes."

She closes her eyes, and when she opens them, she is at the peak of a mountain, sitting with him, watching the beautiful view. In the everlasting peacefulness of the moment, she feels a deep shudder inside her. She should be feeling happy and content, but something is wrong. Something inside starts rising up, something inside her body.

"There are two meanings," he says. Two meanings to everything in your world. There's the apparent meaning, and the real meaning. Nothing is as it seems."

"What's happening to me?"

"Freedom is consumption. Love is selfishness. Competition is sin. Philosophy is currency. Human rights are property rights. Survival is isolation. Art is mediocrity. Evolution is perfection. Tranquility is development. Truth is fiction. News is story. Happiness is greed. And the worst of all: To dream is to imitate."

"Help me!" she says, her voice shaking. "There is something inside me."

"You've been seeing everything through funhouse mirrors. I know what's inside you."

"What's inside of me?" she says, trembling. "Tell me, what's inside of me?"

"It's been there, since the day you were born. It's been hiding inside of you. It's been inside everyone. This evil is ingrained into your very essence. You can beat it only by exposing it."

"But what is it?" It moves inside her, trying to find its way out. She watches in fear as her body contorts into strange shapes, yet she feels no pain.

"It's your true inborn sin, your true Culpa Innata," he says, holding her tightly. "It's the force that pushes your biology to devolve, the sinister evil that will eventually turn everyone into a monster, a caricature of their humanity. Now, don't fight it, expose it!"

A giant serpent breaks free from her body, ripping through her abdomen and towering towards the sky, all the way into space, as she lets out a scream that nobody can hear. Nobody but him.

Phoenix woke up from another night terror with the sound of her own scream ringing in her ears.

WEDNESDAY

CHAPTER 15

PHOENIX stared blankly through her office window, desperately trying to recall what it was that she had felt when woken up by the jolt of adrenaline caused by terror. There had been something in there, something that made her feel eerily good, something that teased and nagged, yet refused to surface. The incoming call interrupted her thoughts.

"Good morning," said Tess in a singsong voice.

"Hey, Tess. Did you sleep well?"

"Can't say that I did. But it appears you slept well?"

"Can't say that I did, either, but, I feel more rested for some reason."

"Nightmares?"

"Well, that's a given. But somehow this one came with a pleasant undertone."

"A pleasant nightmare?" said Tess, arching an elegant eyebrow.

"I know it sounds like an oxymoron, but this is exactly what I feel like. I never had any pleasant feelings following a dream before, ever."

"You sure you're okay?"

"I'm fine, Tess. What I'm trying to say is that there was a part of this nightmare where I felt amazingly good, so good that I feel rested despite the terrifying ending."

"What was that part about? Would you like to share?"

"If only I could remember," moaned Phoenix. "There was something like a big body of water, or a mountain, maybe both, I don't know. The funny thing is, I don't even like being on water. The only clear bit was a giant snake bursting out of my abdomen and rising up to the skies."

"Whoa! Do you dream about snakes much?"

"A lot, recently. The other night, it was a giant snake that attacked me. What does your experiment say about the dreams?"

"Not much. I don't process the dreams, as they are considered irrelevant to our field of study."

"How can they be irrelevant if they can influence a person's mood? Look at me: I've been feeling nervous, irritable, and tired just because of having night terrors for the last week."

"I'm not denying that there is a connection between dreams and a person's performance the next day. But they have nothing to do with human personality, only random reflections of past events."

"They may be based on past events, but they can certainly influence the future. If I keep seeing a snake bursting out from within every night, I'll begin to think that there is something wrong with me, and not necessarily in my mind."

"You'd interpret it as your body's signaling to you about some sickness or disease? That doesn't make a lot of scientific sense now, does it?"

"Why not? Our body sends such signals all the time. What do you think pain is? In this case perhaps the subconscious part of my mind is trying to send a signal to the conscious part."

"Even if it is sending a signal, there's a good chance that the signal wouldn't make any sense."

"What if this was another instinct, trying to reach me through alternative means?"

"These could be dangerous waters. I don't know what to say right now."

"You don't need to say anything. I need to get ready for my security interview anyway."

"May I watch?"

"I suppose. But don't get too excited. It won't be as interesting as the case interviews."

"Don't know about that," said Tess and winked. "You're full of surprises."

"C'mon, Chief, why can't it be me? You know I'm the best man for the job."

"It cannot be you for several reasons. First of all, you're *not* the best person for the job, Alex is, and that's why he'll be doing it. Second, you've been acting like you have a personal issue with Agent Wallis—"

"That's not true. I like Nix fine. I just think that our upper management's been overestimating her abilities, that's all."

"Do not interrupt my sentence! You've been acting like you have a personal grudge against her, and I will not tolerate such nonsense in my staff. If you want to get better assignments, you need to elevate to a level better than hers, not dragging her down to your level."

"Now that hurts, Chief. How can you say that, especially for something like a security interview? I've done more than sixty to her just one."

"Yet she already produced a Strike-Out, and you produced none."

"I thought the point of a security interview was to grant already proven graduates of the academy the citizenship and good life they deserve in the Union. And that's exactly what I've been doing by sticking to the protocol and producing flawless interviews. If the students that I interview are to make perfect citizens, what can I do?"

"The point of a security interview is to determine if the graduate is fit for the Union society or not, and you know this very well, so stop dodging the issue again. Don't think I haven't noticed that your interviews tend to be easy, sometimes *too* easy. Then there are also these incidents where you appear to be flirting with some of your female interviewees."

"Now, I have to protest. The incidents you mention were reported on a basis of unscientific findings and personal vindictiveness, some less-than-able members of our field office trying to taint my image just because I don't indulge with them. The fact is, those interviewees were flirting with *me*, not the other way around. If they find me sexy and attractive, what can I do?"

"How about having Wallis as your watchdog for your next interview this afternoon?"

"Sure," shrugged Julio. "I'll show her how to conduct an interview. But I'm sure she'll chicken out and use the case she's been decimating as an excuse."

"I wouldn't be that sure if I were you. Anyway, your request to be her watchdog today along with Alex is denied. And don't ever come to my office requesting such a thing at the last moment again."

"Phoenix, how are you?" Ion Muresan, the assistant headperson of the academy, gave her a hug, a little longer than the accepted friendly norm.

Around the same age as Alex, Ion wore thick black-rimmed spectacles, a very rare sight in the Union, presumably to distract people's attention from the fact that he had no body hair whatsoever, not even eyebrows or eyelashes, his bald head gleaming under the soft light of the Viewers' Lounge like a bulb.

"I'm well, Ion, how about yourself?"

"Couldn't be better. So, ready for this easy assignment after screwing us big time with the first one?" He gave a booming laugh, with Alex joining in. She just stared at them.

"Don't worry, love," he said and held Phoenix with both arms, rubbing her biceps. "You can't go wrong on this one. Shakira is one of our most hardworking and stable students. She has World Union written all over her, and you'll hardly find anything to ask."

"Ehm, thank you, Ion," said Phoenix and tried to release herself from his tactile clutch. Something wasn't right about this man's touch.

"Stop rubbing her arms, Ion, otherwise she'll catch on fire," said Alex.

Both men started laughing hard again. She took the opportunity to loosen herself from Ion's grip. She had a lot to learn about the humor of this part of the world. "I must be going. Thanks for the support."

"You're welcome," said Ion, with a huge grin. "We'll talk afterwards, yes?"

"Sure," said she and fled, trying to think of a way to avoid Ion later.

Flanked by her escorts, Shakira Al-Hayani entered the interview room with fluid, graceful steps and took her seat with similar grace and economy of movement. A woman in her late twenties, with long dark hair, a small slightly hooked nose, and dimples, she had beautiful black eyes accentuated by only a hint of what looked like the kohl of ancient times. She was nearly as tall as Sandra, with the body of a ballerina. Phoenix could just picture her in one of the revealing dresses that Sandra and Tess liked to wear.

"Hello Ms. Al-Hayani. My name's Phoenix Wallis, and I'll be conducting your security interview."

"Hello, Agent Wallis," she said and smiled beautifully, her teeth glowing like pearls. "Please call me Shakira." She appeared totally easy and relaxed as if she were having a coffee with a friend at Pyramid.

"All right, Shakira, here we go." Phoenix quickly initialized the computers. "Can you please tell me about your origins?"

"I was born and raised in Beirut. My biological father is a local tradesman, and my bio-mother is a housewife. I'm their only child."

"Did you have a pleasant childhood?"

"Oh, yes, my bio-parents sent me to the best schools. My English was already perfect when I arrived here. So many applicants just come here and, you know, they don't even understand English."

Phoenix glanced at the hologram of the well-dressed middle-aged couple behind Shakira. In fine detail, she could also see a large elaborate room with no placeholders. "I see that you take great pride in your upbringing and your biological family."

"Oh, I do. They supported me so much when I decided to come here. They knew that it was my dream to live in the World Union."

"And you understand that this will be a clean break. No support from your bio-parents ever, assuming you pass this interview."

"Of course I understand that. I've wanted to be on my own all my life. I have to admit that there were advantages to having caring bio-relatives, but there is no way one can fulfill her potential."

"What's your vision of the World Union?"

"It's like this one big shopping mall. I love shopping, you know, and the way fashion changes so rapidly here, I could spend my entire time doing it. I came to the Union on a tourist visa once, with my mom and dad—"

Phoenix checked the indicators before her, as Shakira's overall score dropped to ninety-nine. Perhaps Shakira was a little *too* relaxed?

"Mentioning any biological relationship is required, when explaining the nature of your connection with others."

"I do apologize," said Shakira, lowering her eyes. "I came to the Union with my biological parents on a tourist visa once, and I've wanted to immigrate here ever since that moment."

"You couldn't get to satisfy your shopping urges in Beirut?"

"Actually I could. My bio-father's a merchant, so he had access to almost everything."

"Are you planning to work with him in the future for some trade partnership? We take the Free Money restriction as seriously as the Anti-Dumping one in our free trade area. Do you think it's possible that you could possess any altruistic tendencies towards your bio-kin?"

"The fact is that I owe my bio-parents a lot for my good education and mental health. They did a remarkable job with me. They followed universal pediatric guidelines, sent me to World Union-certified schools. But I'm here to start a new life, Agent Wallis, and I'll have no contact with them from now on, business or otherwise." She paused. "Besides, it's not possible for me to have any altruistic tendencies," she went on, looking up to meet Phoenix's green-gray gaze. "It's not possible because I understand where altruism comes from and how it served its historic purpose."

"Elaborate, please."

"Altruism is a behavior remnant of ancient tribal times, and it used to have significance when the whole tribe had to live together and they depended on each other for survival. Children were raised and nurtured collectively and joined production at a very early age, whereas the elderly were supported collectively and acted as the collective memory and wisdom. Through the middle ages and the modern times, this pre-historic tribal habit began to sabotage and undermine the society and the economy. Yet for centuries the people and their despotic or democratically elected rulers didn't know how to let go of this ancient tribal habit that caused unspeakable economic and social havoc."

She paused and smiled. Phoenix nodded at her to continue.

"We have no tribal life anymore," she said with renewed enthusiasm. "We haven't had it for a long time. We have cities where there is no need for raising the children collectively, as we have CDCs and professional mothers. No need for elders to serve as collective wisdom: we have computers and databases. In the economic system of a small tribe, where everyone knows each other and relies on each other, altruism makes a difference, as your sacrifice can mean something for the entire collective. But in a postmodern city, full of masses, your personal sacrifice would be so insignificant, it would have no chance to make a difference. And if you were to favor only a person or a small group over others, that defies the very definition of altruism, as the sacrifice needs to be made for the whole."

"Why is free trade so important, Shakira?"

"Free trade ensures that there is no slavery in the world. Slavery was abolished thanks to technology-enabled industrialization and free trade."

Phoenix checked the indicators before her while listening to Shakira's textbook explanation without much trepidation. There were no alarms from her instincts so far, other than her occasional and insignificant sneering. She hoped that the anger of the headperson would calm down a little bit after this one, and if Shakira were to pass here with flying colors, who knows, maybe they wouldn't insist on any more interviews for her after all.

"What do you understand from a profitable commitment?"

"If someone is selling an item for less, you should go and buy it from him. And when you are selling something, you should sell it for more than what you paid. I learned that from my—my bio-father."

"Why do you believe in economic principles?"

"Because the stability and prosperity of the world depends on the applications of these principles by every single citizen. Without them there would be chaos like the Meltdown, and everything would fall apart."

"Did you live economically in your previous life?"

"Definitely. Everything around me was about trade as I was growing up."

"If you pass this interview, what's the first thing you want to do in the World Union?"

"I wanna shop till I drop," said Shakira and giggled. "I'm sorry, it's just that I love shopping."

"There's nothing wrong with that. Our system depends on our desire to acquire goods and services. Where do you plan to live?"

"I was thinking London or Paris. What do you think?"

"Those are fabulous cities, but they're also very expensive. And their job markets are very competitive."

"That's okay. I brought a lot of money with me."

"That's great, but what about work?"

"There are several translation agencies that are willing to work with me already," shrugged Shakira. "I'll pick one of those. I'm not worried."

"Your bio was not very specific about your college degree. What exactly did you study?"

"I studied the English language."

"Sweet. What does science mean to you?"

"Wise women and men invent and discover all this stuff so that we can all prosper and have a happy life. Not that I understand much about science, but I want my happy life, so I never question scientific rules."

"How far would you go to keep fit and healthy?"

"It's a part of my lifestyle. With the intense competition for men in the Union, I need to keep healthy and fit."

"And that is important to you?"

"Of course," said Shakira and nodded. "I like sex very much. And I'm especially good at pleasing and keeping my men, until the moment it gets boring, of course."

Phoenix quickly glanced at the sexual content behind Shakira. The men in the visuals were in funny placeholder colors, making it appear like she was having sex with cartoon characters.

"Keeping fit can be a difficult task, and our fitness standards here in the Union are quite high. Do you believe you have what it takes to be fit?"

"Well, what can I say," said Shakira, with a glowing smile. "Physical education was my favorite class at the academy. I used to run the fifteen hundred. But it's kinda boring, constantly doing laps around the track, you know?"

"Do you feel totally repentant from your past actions?"

"I can't really say I have a lot to repent from," said Shakira, biting her lip. "I was the only one in my personal confession class who didn't have anything to confess."

"I've noticed that in your academy logs. How come?"

"Well, I suppose I must've been living the Union way all along. After all, I come from the region where the original capitalists used to live."

"Are you referring to the ancient Palestinians?"

"No, I'm referring to pre-historic Mesopotamians," said Shakira, with an air of pride. "The surplus of grain transformed their society from hunter-gatherers to the first settled communities of Ur and Uruk around nine thousand years before the Common Era, and that grain became the first currency. It's such a shame that some of their successors, such as the Semitic Arabs, my race, lost their notion and understanding about how the nature and economy worked and were left outside the World Union. But not all of us had forgotten it, and here I am."

The expert system indicated that the baseline patterns were established. She could conclude the procedure immediately, but decided to ask a few more questions, just in case. "What's your definition of happiness?"

"Happiness is freely floating around and spending money the way I want."

"What about partners and friends?"

"Sure, they make me happy, too. But they never last long, you know. I feel that my sexual partners and friends are never good enough for me."

"Were you happy in Beirut?"

"For a while, yes, but not after seeing the Union. I have to live in the best place, you know."

"How about the crime, hunger, and other bad things there?"

"Oh, those," said Shakira, chewing on her lip. "Well, I'd be lying if I said I was exposed to any of it. But I had limited freedom."

"Limited freedom?"

"You know," said Shakira and sighed. "Your bio-parents sticking their noses into everything you do. You have to be careful where you hang out, or if you take a wrong street you might be kidnapped and held for ransom, or mutilated. That sort of thing."

There was just one last thing that kept nagging her at the back of Phoenix's mind. But she had no idea it was to create such an enormous upheaval.

"You know, it's been more than twenty minutes, and she's still pushing on this meaningless shit interview. The Arab babe is obviously as good as they come, and there's absolutely no need to dwell on junk questions wasting everyone's time. This is unbelievable! No wonder she's making progress of an inch at a time with that—" said Julio and froze.

"That what?" said Ion, without turning his head from the other room. "She's a babe all right."

"Uhm, you know, her shit," Julio mumbled and leaned back.

"What shit?" Ion turned and fixed his scornful little eyes on him.

"Couldn't remember Dr. Spencer, Julio?" said Alex.

"Right! She needs to do this background analysis on this dead professor Spencer, and she didn't do shit yet."

"Oh, *that* shit," said Ion and turned back to watching the interview.

Julio nodded and winked at Alex, while he raised one eyebrow and motioned Julio to keep quiet.

Beverly gritted her teeth at the back but didn't want to interfere and turn the entire thing into a scandal, in case Phoenix's interview would get invalidated. She had invented this short field trip for the kids in the Monitoring Room, who were bored out of their minds watching academy students wipe their asses. There was something in the way Phoenix was doing her stuff, as if something might happen any moment.

"Have you ever considered an alternative career in the Union? You see, my concern is that you may not have thought your career plan out very well."

"You know, you may be right. You read about my training and accomplishments. What do you recommend that I do?"

The question started alarm bells in Phoenix's head. Creating a confrontation was the last thing she desired during this interview, but the situation was becoming unavoidable.

"Well, how do you expect me to make a comment about something like this, Shakira? It was something you should have dealt with at length with your career consultants at the academy. I assume you have done this, yes?"

"Of course I have, and they suggested retail and stuff. But I would need to take extra schooling for that. Boring! I don't wanna deal with school anymore, you know? Oh well, I'm sure I'll find something."

Phoenix had no idea what the people on the other side of the mirror were thinking, but she knew exactly what she needed to do. She closed her eyes and took a deep breath. "I suspect that you might be suffering from the Tainted Juvenile Syndrome. So, tell me, Shakira: Are you a spoiled brat?"

"A brat? Me? I—"

"I'm afraid you've been receiving too much support from your bio-parents, so much so that you don't know how to stand up on your own feet anymore."

"A—are you accusing me of something?" said Shakira in a shaky voice.

"No, not yet. I just need to know if you were spoiled by your biological parents by being given everything you wanted."

"I didn't know there was anything wrong with that."

"There isn't, unless it destroys one's propensity to work. Tell me, Shakira, do you have any propensity to work?"

"Of course I do. Why shouldn't I?" Shakira's graceful manners vanished, and she visibly started to tremble. Phoenix checked the indicators before her. Her heart rate and blood pressure were rising steadily. The expert computers had not reduced points yet, but it was imminent.

"You haven't decided on a job. You're saying you'll figure it out, but I'm not so sure, Shakira."

"Of course I will, I assure you—"

"It seems to me like you will not invest time and effort in anything, instead spending all of the twenty million you bring. Then you'll try to find someone to hold on to and leech from, looking for free money, like you did with your bio-parents."

"No, I will not! I assure you, I'll work very hard." She attempted to stand up, only to sit back down at Phoenix's cold gaze and head motion. The indicators showed that the complexity of her thought patterns were on the rise, meaning she wasn't able to think clearly anymore but was desperately trying to get herself out of the situation. A lie was imminent.

"I think first you're going to spend all of the money you bring in, and with your appetite for shopping and the places you want to live, I'd say it wouldn't take you more than a few years. Then you'll become a liability to our system by looking for a suitable sponsor for yourself. And we cannot allow this, Shakira, because even just one person can unsettle the delicate balance that our economic system provides, just like it takes just one virus to infect an organism."

"No, I won't," said Shakira, visibly shaking. "I promise!"

One of the main indicators started blinking in red in front of Phoenix, signaling that Shakira's thought patterns and words were not a match anymore. A big point reduction was imminent in the overall score, and its extent would depend on how deep the deception was. The expert computers would calculate that in a few seconds. "You're lying."

"No, no, I'm not lying, I—I will work very hard. I promise, please!"

"Unfortunately your pleas convince neither me nor our computers."

"Isn't my word good enough anymore?" Tears started flowing down her cheeks.

"Your word is good enough until your first lie. You have no propensity to work, and you just cannot be a part of our society like this. Your work ethic, or rather the lack of it, would harm our economic harmony. Everyone has a right to enjoy the full product of *their own* labor in our land, not anyone else's. No free money here."

"Did—did I fail?" said Shakira, her black eyes pooling with fresh tears.

Her overall score was showing sixty-four. The complexity of the deception was not very deep, which meant that Shakira did not plan to lie, but rather did it under duress incidentally, about a very important principle. Phoenix's work was done, and there wasn't much point pushing the overall score further down. "Shakira Al-Hayani, your responses to my questions have scientifically proven that you're not a fit person for the World Union society right now. I formally declare that you fail this security interview."

With this devastating confirmation, Shakira started crying like a child, her hands on her face.

"I can only imagine what a blow this is for you," said Phoenix, her voice soft. "The good news is, you can re-enroll at the academy."

"I can?" She looked up with a glimmer of hope in her reddened eyes.

"Yes, you can. But you have to focus better on work ethics and economic principles this time. You have to improve your greed, as you appear to have very little of it."

"Oh, thank you, Agent Wallis, thank you so much. I promise to you that I'll do better this time and come back here full of greed."

"I certainly hope that this will be the case, for your own sake, Shakira. You will not get a third chance."

A wave of nausea hit Phoenix, soon after Shakira, still thanking her and sobbing hysterically, had been escorted out by a security detail. And just like Shakira, she too was back to square one, with no hope of reconciliation with the academy people, and perhaps she was to receive open hostility from them. She had no idea how Alex, her watchdog, was going to react. She didn't even want to think about the director's reaction. But at least this time she had played by the book, however unexpected the turn of events had been.

Following the exit of the two assisting junior agents, she was all alone in the interview room. She closed her eyes and put her hands on her face and tried to enjoy a few more quiet moments before all hell broke loose. She tried to push her anxiety and her anticipation of people's reactions away from her mind and think of the place she felt safe: her last memento with her father, sitting in his lap, feeling warm and drowsy. She only remembered certain details of that moment, how it was a very cold day and he was wearing a very thick wool costume, as well as a faint tinge of mothballs. His big strong hands gently caressing her golden hair, she had felt so tiny and cocooned in his lap, never felt safer in her life. And yet despite the indelible mark that the moment had left in her soul, Phoenix couldn't even remember her father's face.

When she was little, she could simply will this feeling to appear. However, it had turned more into an involuntary feeling over the years, and she had less and less control over it, and it wasn't working this time. Then cold came and made her shudder the way she would feel waking up from a night terror. She began to shake uncontrollably for a while and didn't know what to do about it. She tried to control the shaking by focusing on stopping it, and only after long minutes the shaking slowed down and waned out. But her entire energy had been sucked out again, as her arms and legs felt totally empty. She got up and walked towards the exit door, her limbs heavy. The exit door clicked open to a great roar of applause.

The cheering and whistling seemed to come from the back of the crowd, Beverly whistling with her fingers in her mouth, and many of the supporters were young agents from the Monitoring Room. Then she switched her attention to the more dignified front of the crowd, where Alex, Ion, Julio, and Director Morssen were all present. The only person who looked openly annoyed at her was Julio, but she could also sense that Ion was nervous and upset, despite the fake smile he was wearing. Alex was shaking his head with a mischievous smile, while the director's face was totally blank.

Alex approached her first. "Congratulations, Phoenix. Technically speaking, that was a much better piece of work than your previous one."

"No criticisms?"

"Well, there were some issues, of course. Perhaps more than just a few. You can read all those in my report. But in general, I can say that pretty much everything was according to protocol, except towards the end where you—"

"How can you say that?" said Julio. "Didn't you see how she wore the poor gal down before she hacked her open?" he said to Alex then turned to Phoenix.

"You must be proud of yourself, Nix. You ruined a perfectly acceptable academy student just to satisfy your ego."

"Ignore that jealous ass," yelled Beverly from the back.

"Well, well," said Ion, still wincing. "Here I bring you one of our finest and most trouble-free students, one with nothing to repent, and here I stand now, still having a hard time understanding how the hell you could strike her out like that."

"She had no propensity to work. You heard it, computers confirmed it. What did you expect me to do? Award her the Union citizenship on a golden platter?"

"On the contrary, I believe she did have a propensity to work," said Ion in a whisper. "But you somehow coerced her into denying it. What did you do? Use a mind-control weapon?"

A hush fell over the crowd at Ion's suggestion. Even the director appeared taken aback. Phoenix flushed at the implied accusation and glanced at a smirking Julio, looking directly into her eyes and nodding his head. She shot him an ice-cold glare, feeling a sudden urge to tear his uniform apart, exposing his fake bulges of muscle.

"Of course she didn't. What are you trying to say, Ion?" said the director. Surreptitious booing started at the back of the crowd.

"I'm just pointing out that the interview progressed in an unnatural way."

"Agents Wallis and Lubosh, come with me."

The three quickly walked to the director's office.

"I want you to tell me exactly how this happened," said the director.

"I started with the baseline questions, and everything was going well for a while. She kept telling me about how much she liked shopping and how she hadn't been worried about finding a job. She even asked me where she should live and finally about my opinion on a job. Until that moment, I was sure she was going to pass it with something like ninety-five."

The director turned to Alex.

"It happened pretty much as she explained," he said. "However, there were some minor issues of—"

"I don't care about that. Was the interviewee coerced into anything?"

"Now that you ask, I—I'm not sure," said Alex, to Phoenix's astonishment. "I mean, I don't believe Phoenix would intentionally do such a thing, of course not." He looked at Phoenix and smiled briefly, getting a gape in return. "But I would need to review the entire interview to be sure."

"Why do you need to review anything to give me a yes or no answer?"

"Ehm, I was a little distracted during the interview."

"What distraction are you talking about?"

"It was a little crowded in there," said Alex, his eyes widening.

"I assure you, I did not coerce her into anything."

"Then was it just a coincidence that she was thanking you for failing her while crying violently at the end of the interview?" said Alex suddenly.

Phoenix just stared at him for a few seconds before she could regroup. "She wasn't thanking me for failing her. She was thanking me because I told her she could re-enroll in the academy. I could have easily dropped her score below sixty so that she would have no chance to re-enroll, you know. But I didn't! I believe she deserves a second chance."

"My dear Phoenix, please don't misunderstand me. I'm not trying to imply that you might have coerced her on purpose. Not at all. But please ask yourself this question: Did you end the interview before the score dropped below sixty because you thought she deserved a second chance, or could it be because you had felt a pang of conscience over forcing that beautiful and gentle girl—I mean woman—into admitting to something you didn't believe she was guilty of?"

Alex's words sank into Phoenix's soul like lump of brick. She could feel a growing knot in her solar plexus. Could he be right? Could her instincts have misled her? Was any of what Alex was saying actually possible? Could she have been the perpetrator of such irresponsibility? And if this was the case, was it ever going to be possible for her to redeem her soul?

"So you're saying she did coerce that student?"

"I didn't say that," said Alex. "I need to review it first."

"Who distracted you? Answer me. The kids that Beverly brought?"

"Well, I can't put the entire blame on their shoulders."

"Who else, then? Don't tell me it was that depilated idiot."

"Oh, no, no," said Alex, shaking his head. "It wasn't Fred, either."

"Then who was it, Alex? Were you daydreaming again, then woken up by one of those headaches of yours?"

"Julio made a lot of comments throughout the interview, I guess," said Alex and lowered his eyes.

"That asshole! Why didn't you tell him to shut the fuck up?"

"I did, eventually."

"I guess too little, too late. Hold on."

Phoenix couldn't tell whom the director was talking to, as her ears were ringing and she didn't dare to look up. But she was sure Julio would walk in any moment to continue with the onslaught, and she didn't have the energy to defend herself anymore. Her conscience was ridden with the possibility of guilt, and her solar plexus was still tight as a knot.

After a few moments of tense silence, the office door opened and in walked somebody who was nothing like Julio.

"Did you see that? Did you see how she coerced an innocent student into admitting to something she hasn't even heard of before?" said Julio. "Look at all these idiots over there." he motioned with his head at the group of junior agents sitting at another table, talking about the "cool Strike-Out." "They have no clue as to what they've just witnessed. They talk as if they've just watched an episode of one of those rogue state reality shows. They're not even aware of the fact that the life of a real person was at stake."

"I only saw the bit towards the end," said Sean. "But I didn't notice anything out of the ordinary. The expert computers verified that she'd been lying about her propensity to work, didn't they?"

"Of course they did, only after Nix managed to confuse the hell outta her. Poor thing couldn't tell which way was up. Don't tell me you didn't see that."

"Of course I saw her confusion. But does this mean Phoenix induced anything into her or even coerced her?"

"Sure it does! She's so full of ego, raw ego, nothin' else, I'm telling you. She's one of those primitive-minded people, totally devoid of any kind of refinement that comes in our postmodern world. Just look at her, I mean with all those crap communication skills, unable to hide her emotions, lack of greed, she's almost Neanderthal compared to us. And we all witnessed how she became a slave of her own ego by victimizing another human being."

"I can't believe that Phoenix would be capable of doing such a thing on purpose. Could it be like she isn't aware what she's doing, like you explained before?"

"It's exactly like that, 'cause she's such a Neanderthal bitch! I knew you were smart, babe, and you're getting a grip on things better and better every day."

"Thanks," blushed Sean. "But we gotta help her."

"I dunno how to help her anymore," said Julio, shaking his head. "It's useless. She should be relieved of all duties requiring a real human touch and be a Personal Planning and Coordination Advisor or something with a rock-bottom HDI."

"Perhaps we should talk to her about her shortcomings. I know she has a good heart; she'd listen to us if we could reach her—"

"Aw, stop pretending to be so naïve. Can't you see she's just acquired the taste of an ego-trip? She's not gonna back down anytime soon. She's like a ray-bid dog now."

"A ray-bid dog?"

"You know, how dogs used to go mad with some bacterial infection or something, centuries ago. There would be no stopping them, and their condition would be highly contagious. I suspect this ego trip of Phoenix's is also contagious. I can deal with it easily as I have a superior immunity against such diseases, but I wouldn't want your tender mind to get infected by it."

Sean froze at the implication and swallowed. "What should I do? I have to work with her, you know."

"Well, I wouldn't get too cozy, if I were you. When you're with her, just focus on yourself, not her, get in and get out quickly, just like me."

"You mean, like you and sex?"

"Ouch, that hurt!" said Julio, with his hands on his chest.

"Just kidding, tiger," said Sean, stroking his arm.

"I meant, keep your interaction to a minimum, tell her what you need to say, and get out of her egocentric area of communicable influence, got it?"

"Got it. I like it when you get so protective over me, you know."

"Hey, I'm not doing this only for you. I'm doing this for me. Because we're part of the same team. If you fail, you may drag me with you."

"That's true. But I like it, anyway."

"Beverly, were you there from the beginning of the interview?"

"Missed just the expert system initializing phase, Boss."

"Good. Were you able to focus on the interview?"

"Beg your pardon?"

"Alex here told me that some annoying whiner had made it difficult for him to focus on the interview. Were you also distracted?"

"Oh, that. No, Boss, he couldn't distract me."

"You're one of my best watchdogs, and the only one who doesn't actually do interviews. Tell me, did she coerce the student in any way?"

"No, Boss."

"Alex, here, has other opinions."

"All I said was that I couldn't be sure," said Alex, shaking his head violently. "I couldn't focus well. I need to review the whole thing."

"Alex was kept busy by Julio, Boss. It's totally understandable if he feels like he needs to review. But I know what I saw. And as a psychologist, I can tell you that there was no coercion. That student appeared all la-di-dah and classy, but the bottom line is, she was totally clueless from the very beginning as to what to do with her own life."

"The mind-control weapon, who put that in Ion's head?"

Beverly shook her head, and Alex looked down at his lap. Of course, it was Julio. The director took a deep breath, folded her arms, and after several seconds of staring blankly, she spoke gravely.

"Looking at the pep club outside, I don't think any of you can appreciate or understand the implications of what has just happened. Another big can of worms has just been opened, people. Everything had been arranged so that she was to have a string of easy interviews, which would dilute her perfect Strike-Out score. Her second interviewee was chosen carefully, seen as a student with no risk of failure. She had no confessions, nothing to hide. Yet Agent Wallis here, once again, defied all odds and struck her out.

"There was no such written or verbal agreement made, yet they'll still think that we betrayed an *understanding* whereby they would provide sure-to-pass students before her to interview, and she'd give their students an easy time. Believe me, Ingrid and her gang will perceive this as an open declaration of war. And the next thing they'll do is to shred this interview into pieces and examine it under a microscope, looking for ways to sue us."

"I had no idea of such expectations or arrangements, and I assure you there was no coercion, Director. Was I supposed to close my eyes to her shortcomings?"

"Coercion or not, you could, and perhaps should have closed your eyes! This is the reality of corporate life. What century you think we're living in? You act like a raging bull and go all the way for something you believe in and lack the common sense to protect yourself. What kind of a romantic idealism is this? Idealism is just a decorated and glittered form of ego, don't you know?"

The director paused and looked down for a few seconds, then turned to Phoenix. "I know you're smarter than that, but you're also stubborn. You should have used better judgment to protect yourself and to protect all of us, but you didn't. And this is something I simply cannot condone. Under the circumstances, I wouldn't mind feeding you to the lions, if I knew it would save the rest of us. But it won't. If we let them destroy you and your interview on the pretext of malicious coercion, we'd lose our control over the security interview procedure for good. So, whether we like it or not, it's us against them. We're gonna need to build our case against theirs." She looked at all three of them. "Alex, I want you to go over the interview and start compiling a report. I want you to be impartial but also fair to her. Don't let any junk from Julio or Ion cloud your judgment, understand?"

Alex nodded. The director turned to Beverly.

"Get your pep club to do some overtime finding some malicious intent, some deceptive pattern, anything on the student's side. If they are trying to destroy Agent Wallis in order to destroy us, we ought to return the favor. And you," she turned to Phoenix. "You deserve all the reprimand in the whole damn world right now. But I can't do it, as it would make us all look guilty and weak. And believe it or not, a part of me, just a little part, wants to congratulate you. I guess you deserve some praise for being the only peace agent ever to score two Strike-Outs in succession, and I'm not even going into the fact that you're the only person that started her interviewing career with a double Strike-Out.

"Whether you resorted to coercion is irrelevant right now, as it will make no difference for the academy people in their quest to use this as an excuse to destroy all of us. They'll probably sue us for heck knows how many hundred million or billion dollars in damages, for breach of contract, and even breach of the Supreme Bill, who knows. For me, it's all a part of business. There are ups and downs. This can cost me my position, or even my career, yet I'll try to believe that you did what you did with all good intent. But if I later find any evidence that you maliciously coerced this student into admitting something, anything, I'll make you pay, I promise you!"

"If you find even a trace of malice in my interview, I'll put the rope around my neck with my own hands, Director Morssen. Now, if we're finished here, with your permission, I'd like to go to the Monitoring Room with Beverly to carry out your orders, and then I still have a murder case to lead, I believe."

"Of course you still have a case to lead. Quit asking me if you do or not!"

"PA: Arrange a level five task force meeting for the Bogdanov case in one hour at my office. Send an invite to all involved parties. And of course you're welcome to attend if you have the time, Director Morssen."

Why she couldn't see the corporate friction between the GPSN and the IAW, Immigration Academies Worldwide, the parent company of all academies, Phoenix wasn't sure. She'd known all along that she lacked many skills needed to survive in the postmodern society, and in her mind, it had all been proven, once again, that she just didn't and couldn't fit in, despite being raised by the best teachers, receiving the best education, and working for one of the best companies. Yet still nobody and nothing could change who she had been then and who she was now.

None of it mattered at this point. What she'd just done might inadvertently have been the last drop of water needed to bust the dam wide open and incite an all-out war of corporations, just like in that age-old rhyme: *For want of a nail the shoe was lost. For want of a shoe the horse was lost. For want of a horse the rider was lost. For want of a rider the battle was lost. For want of a battle the kingdom was lost. And all for the want of a horseshoe nail.*

"We're checking every camera in the interview room and its footage," said Beverly, gently touching her shoulder. "We'll show those pompous bastards how the game is played, don't worry. I have some magic software that can analyze emotions; it's child's play to figure that Shakira out."

"It wasn't her fault."

"Maybe not, but it wasn't yours, either. And like the director said: It's either us or them now. I wouldn't be surprised if Hamilton himself were to take charge of this situation under the circumstances."

"Beverly, can one of your guys check my PA out? It keeps crashing. I had to do a hard reset yesterday and lost my settings. I don't know what's wrong with it, but it all started after Ray stole it from my office."

"Another victim of that crazy old guy, huh? Lemme have a look. Harold, get your ass over here."

"It happened once a day for the past two days, while traveling by metro. Then I find these recovered data files after the reboot, totally irrelevant stuff."

"What was the content?" Beverly checked out the device with Harold.

"The first data file from Monday had a picture of a butterfly. Don't know what the one from yesterday has. Didn't have time to check."

"It's probably some picture you took some time ago, chewed up by the operating system and spit out as a data dump."

"It's not a picture of a real butterfly. It's like some digital art representation of it, with surreal rainbow colors and strange shaped wings. I kinda remember seeing it somewhere."

"You must have seen it in an art gallery or someone's office, then. Harold, plug this baby into the hardware analyzer and see if anything is wrong with it, and update its firmware while you're at it." Then she turned to Phoenix and leaned down, facing her. "Hey, keep your chin up, sis. We're all proud of you here, me and all the guys. We'll help you and get to the bottom of this."

"Thanks for all the support, Beverly," said Phoenix, with a forced smile.

"No need for thanks. You brought excitement here, can't you see? There's action every day. I love it!"

"Then can you guys give me a hand with one more thing? I need to check for something in the border database."

Harold had verified that the little gadget was fully intact and had no physical damage, nor had any viral infections. He had also analyzed the second recovered data file, which had revealed another butterfly image, or rather the same image from a different angle. Phoenix distinctly remembered the image from somewhere, but it didn't matter, as she had so much going on. She needed to run a few errands before her meeting.

"Tess?"

"Hey, Phoenix. Great security interview. I was so impressed by your skill."

"Tell me about it. They're planning to crucify me for it."

"You're joking! But why?"

"The academy staff claims that I coerced her into lying."

"You didn't coerce her into anything. She was so careless and unfocused, she basically asked for it."

What Tess had just said sparked something in her mind for an instant. Could there be something that she had overlooked in that interview? Not in the interview itself but in the people. But what? Something was missing. Some crucial information she might have overlooked. With the limited time she'd had to prepare, could the interview get any better? Was there a better way? The alarm from the PA interrupted her train of thought. Her coworkers were to come in any moment now.

"I have this meeting now, but I need you to do me a favor."

"Name it."

"Could you call that Pierre DeVille again and arrange a meeting?"

"Sure, I could try. But I don't think he wants to be reached."

"Thanks, dear, talk to you later. Oh, wait!"

"Still here."

"Uhm, nothing. Something I meant to solve with you, but only if I could remember what it was."

"I thought this was a good time to get up to date with the progress on the Bogdanov case and discuss its status."

"You mean the *non*-progress of the Bogdanov case," sneered Julio.

"Progress is apparent to those who aren't blind to it. Now, are you all aware of what appears to be a list of customers, handwritten in Russian script?" Phoenix glanced at all three sitting around her desk. Alex appeared far from his usual merry self. Sean seemed freeze-framed, immobile, somehow seeming to tense up when Phoenix looked at her. And Julio was giving her his most challenging glare while leaning back in his seat as if relaxing on a couch in his living room. "Alex, thank you very much for transliterating the list into our alphabet."

Alex nodded quietly without looking up and kept fidgeting in his seat.

"And could our case lead enlighten us as to the significance of this supposed list?" said Julio.

"Not sure yet. But it must have been important if he was keen to keep off the computers and even cipher it."

"So what? The guy was a nut job, hiding stuff inside the wall of his house. He was paranoid if not schizophrenic. Those names are probably a reflection of some crap-knows-what delusion he had before heading to that rogue state. And I object to wasting our resources on that kind of junk list, and pointless meetings like this one, just to satisfy your pretty little *ego*."

"I need to finish evaluating that security interview," said Alex without looking up. "I don't have time to attend to this meeting."

"Hey, relax," said Phoenix. "My neck is on the line for the evaluation you're talking about. But I still called this meeting because I think it's important. Julio, why are his bank records still not in the case database?"

"Some kind of investigation over a *check* issue, if you know what I mean."

"A check? What would Bogdanov do with a check, unless—"

"Look, I don't care about your smart-ass reasoning. In case you're not aware, thanks to you and your ego, we're in the middle of a full-blown corporate crisis here. Now we need to cover our asses, and that includes your pretty little ass, too, and we have no time to waste with Bogdanov's schizo-musings. If you're gonna tell us or ask us something, do it now, or I'm outta here."

"Sweet," said Phoenix with an easy shrug. "You can leave if you wish."

All three got up.

"I'm not finished with you two," she added, looking at Sean and Alex.

Alex sat down, grumbling, while Sean lowered herself to her seat in slow motion and stared ahead blankly. Julio left grinning. Phoenix felt a little twinge of guilty pleasure in making Alex sit against his will, remembering the day before.

"Are we going to just sit here?" mumbled Alex.

"How's the Spencer case coming along, Alex?"

"I don't see what relevance the Spencer case has to this meeting."

"You don't know that."

"What are you insinuating? Do you know something that I don't?"

"Just an old-fashioned hunch. I'm sure you're used to the term."

"I know what a hunch is," Alex almost snapped. "Are you suggesting that the two cases could be related?"

"Yes, I am. So, how's the Spencer case going, Alex?"

"It's like this one. It's not going anywhere. I have no access to the case file, the body, or the device which is supposed to have caused his death. Even the neurologist leading the task force, she still has no access to anything."

"What a coincidence. So we have two cases involving death only a day apart, both residents of the same city, and in both cases we have little access to any information, though we're supposed to be the ones that these cases were entrusted to. What if both cases were related, and someone or something was trying to limit our access to these cases and to cause delay for an undetermined purpose?"

Both Alex and Sean looked at her. "Who and why?" said Sean.

"Don't know yet."

"What can I do?"

"Take the list that Alex translated and check the names in our census databases. Limit your searches to Adrianopolis area first. Then expand it, if necessary, but I doubt it: This is the only place Bogdanov ever lived in the Union, and Alex confirms that most of the names aren't Russian. Those people must be here."

"Do you need anything from me?" said Alex. "What you claim is rather interesting, but I really must be going. I have meeting with the director in less than an hour, and I need to be prepared."

"Just keep me in the loop about the Spencer case, that's all."

"You were right," said Sean on the PA. "You were spot on!"

"About what?"

"Those people in the list, all live in the Adrianopolis area, except one."

"Who?"

"His name is Juan Antonio Perez. The nearest person with this name lives in Paris, whereas everyone else lives right here at Adrianopolis."

The absence of just one name was intriguing, and it didn't make any sense. One possibility was that Perez was not a Union citizen. But with that name, it was unlikely that he was from one of the rogue states either, as Europe and American continents were under the protection of the World Union. Another call came in.

"We checked what you asked for, but I don't know what to make of it, sis."

"Why is that? What happened?"

"Your dead guy, he never left the Union."

"You mean the Russians identified the wrong man?"

"Well, that wouldn't surprise me either, but no, I mean he never left. There is no record of him crossing the border."

"Are you sure?"

"Positive. Harold did the search, and I double-checked. There is no record of Bogdanov leaving the Union for any destination in the last month."

"But how could that be possible? It's not like he could leave under a fake identity with his biometrics on record."

"Beats me. This whole case is turning totally surreal by the minute, sis."

"Unless—"

"Listen, I gotta run, talk to you later."

It was a very remote possibility, but there was another way one could leave the Union and not be in the border database, and the same possibility could also explain why Juan Antonio Perez couldn't be located in the city's census database. She quickly logged into her network node and went through a few menus, plugged the name in, and there he was, Juan Antonio Perez, another resident of Adrianopolis, but with a clever disguise.

It was time to take a trip to metro station Delta Ten.

CHAPTER 16

"Is it colder than usual in here, or is it just me?"

"You know the temperature here never changes, Crane," said The Man with the Toboggan Hat. "I suppose you got soft while you were out there."

The Crane had just come back in after hiding out in the city for about forty-eight hours. This was their usual course of action in case of any danger of exposure, as their biggest secret was the access points to their hideout. World Union had eyes and ears everywhere, but it could only focus its colossal attention on one particular situation at a time, and in giant but short spurts at best. It had to do with their binary thinking tradition. It had been dangerous for the Crane to come back in, while the entire attention of the GPSN was on finding him and the Bogdanov case. But now they were busy with other priorities.

He was out of his black camouflage suit now and had put on a long white tunic with long bellbottom sleeves ornamented with green and red flower embroidery. He also wore black boots, black pants, a black leather vest, and a thick black belt crowned with a wide-rimmed black top hat with a white feather attached. He worked at his cluster of computers and giant screen made of six monitors as he spoke. "Yeah, right. I was bored as hell, that's for sure."

"You scared us, son," said the Toboggan Hat. "You left in such a rush and virtually unprepared two days ago."

"There's a subtle but distinct difference between virtually unprepared and unprepared," said the Crane, without removing his eyes from the monitors. "And I was just prepared enough. It's so easy to manipulate the weaknesses of their system."

"I'm not talking about that. You ran into two GPSN agents. This wasn't supposed to happen. How come they got there before you managed to leave?"

"I suppose the intelligence I received regarding their departure from the field office must have been tainted," said the Crane while typing commands. "Unless they had a helicopter or something at their disposal. You know what that means, right?"

"Yes, I know. We have a ticking time bomb on our hands, and we need to defuse it before it blows all of us up into pieces."

"Defuse it if you can, man! I barely saved my ass from his *honest* mistake. He feels all important now, because you and The Dude in the Black Hat awarded him with that big assignment to derail the murder investigation."

"We had to involve him in that assignment."

"Excuse me, Grandmaster, but that's so full of crap," said the Crane and swiveled his chair towards him. "Me and the Mount, we could have easily pulled it off, and you know that!"

"Calm down, son," said the old man and smiled. "You and the Mount are my two most trusted masters. But the time frame was so short, it was impossible to come up with a plan where just the two of you could do the job. We needed more."

"What do you mean by that?"

"We needed all three of you in order to pull it off: You, the Mount, and the Mantis. The Mantis will have no idea that both of you are also involved, of course."

"I had no idea." The Crane paused for a moment. "Is the Mount aware of this mission yet?"

"Her existing mission will merge into this one. The word will reach her today. I know you like teaming up with her."

"Hey, it's not what you think. I never had feelings for her other than a respectful and trusting friendship between two comrades. Besides, I don't think she even likes men. She likes her solitude, just like her name implies."

"From your dedication to your work and total indifference to the other gender nowadays, I could say the same for you. But it's not like you're called the Crane for no reason. Your heart will follow its unique path."

His mission name had been given for similarities in his personality to those big birds according to Eastern wisdom. The Mount was named because she possessed mountains of self-confidence and self-discipline, and she liked working alone. The Mantis was named due to his ruthlessness and ability to hide in plain sight with only three people knowing what he looked like, nobody else but the three grandmasters. Still what the Toboggan Hat had referred to was another characteristic of the cranes.

"Actually, something happened when I stunned them. I felt something, too. Is that normal?"

"Could be," shrugged the old man. "This was your first stun experience. Everyone's is different."

"I felt something about one of them."

"Which one?"

"The pretty blonde one in charge of the investigation. Something strange happened for an instant when I reached her mind and amplified her feelings. A warm feeling that I never felt before, yet so familiar, perhaps from another life. It was so strong, like living a lifetime in a fraction of a second, or as if I could read her like a book, or I've known her all my life." He paused. "It makes no sense, does it?"

"Does it?"

"It probably doesn't," said the Crane, shaking his head. "I don't know, I'm babbling after forty-eight hours of solitude. Just ignore me, will ya?" Crane turned to his computer terminal and got lost in its digital but mysterious world.

The Toboggan Hat proudly observed him working on his terminal with lightning speed. He had no idea what the Crane was doing with the computers, or how he engineered his hacks, but the Crane was undoubtedly the best hacker in the entire world, and also a brilliant engineer. This made him an indispensable asset, as he could not only hack into networks using software tools, but also design and build his own hardware tools for hacking, disabling remote cameras, opening combination locks and safes, and many others. The Crane had actually masterminded the great hack a few months before at the NC Research Triangle and extracted nearly a hundred terabytes of data before the link was severed by a power cut.

He had analyzed and extracted the digital blueprints of several top-secret technologies from the downloaded data, then designed the inimitable device that had caused this whole mayhem on both sides of the border.

Her PA didn't disappoint, and it crashed for the third time in three days. Luckily, Phoenix didn't need to hard reset this time. The little device rebooted itself by the time she reached the main metro station under the Pyramid. Again there was a file of recovered data with an unrecognized file format, but this time Phoenix had a pretty good idea about its content.

Now she was in a train en route to Station Delta Ten to find Juan Antonio Perez. *Captain* Juan Antonio Perez of the GPSN military, that was. Military personnel weren't considered townsfolk and kept off city's census database, since they didn't contribute to the city's infrastructural fees and expenses. One quick search in the military personnel database had been enough to locate the captain.

A possible explanation of the mystery surrounding Bogdanov's vanishing without a trace and appearance on the other side of the border involved the GPSN military, if Bogdanov had been a part of a military mission somehow. Could this Captain Perez also be a part of it, too? She was hoping that a quick trip to the military base would yield some valuable information, as her murder case was fast moving into a gridlock. She had tried to reach Captain Perez through her PA, but a pre-recorded message instructed to *personally* contact the military base at Delta Ten for further inquiries.

It was ironic that everyone at her office had been mobilized in order to save her skin, while she was out here on a possible wild goose chase. But if she was to get herself out of the mess she was in, it would have to do with the progress she made with the murder case. Her thoughts got interrupted by a call from Sandra.

"Hey, girl," she said with a sly grin. "What's cookin', baby?"

"Busy as ever, and things aren't getting any better. How about you?"

"Oh, still recovering from last night. What did you do to that marine?"

"Oh, him? You two were playing games with me, I suspect, and I took the liberty of putting him in his place. Actually I'm not suspecting. I know *you*, my supposedly best friend here, were playing a game with me."

"Don't take it so hard," said Sandra and shrugged. "I just wanted you to have a good time, that's all. Besides, the marine was thoroughly impressed by you, whatever you said to him. He wouldn't tell me."

"Impressed by what I said? Get outta here! And don't try to pull my leg twice for the same stunt."

"I swear I'm not making this up! The guy was impressed by you and would like to see you again."

"I don't think so. I'm not falling into the same trap twice."

"Up to you, babe. But I think this time it's different. You should check him out and give him another chance. Everyone deserves a second chance, no?"

Phoenix felt goosebumps, and all the events of the morning flashed before her eyes. She had granted Shakira a second chance. Should she do the same with this young marine? Could this be another game that she had no time or energy for? Could he be sincere about his opinion of her?

"You know what? I'll think about it. I'm curious to see what he has to say about last night. I didn't give him much chance to say anything."

"So I heard. What did you say to him, anyway?"

"He's your spy, ask him."

"Senior Agent Phoenix Wallis from the Peace Corps to see Captain Perez."

"Was the captain expecting you?" said the corporal, as he used his pupils to interface the network node before him.

"No, but his name came up in an investigation of mine."

After a few seconds of pupil action, the corporal blinked a few times in surprise and turned to Phoenix. "It's not possible for you to see the captain right now, Agent Wallis, but Sergeant First Class Monaghan will see you." Then he turned to the private standing nearby. "Please escort Agent Wallis to Sergeant Monaghan's office at the personnel department. Room number ten two sixty-four."

"But why? I cannot disclose or discuss anything with Sergeant Monaghan. If Captain Perez is not in the base, just tell me."

"Sergeant Monaghan will explain it all. Good day, Agent."

Captain Perez must be one of those all-important officers, with no time to spare for the likes of herself. Now she was walking behind a private in the dull, stuffy, and endless hallways of the military base at least fifty meters below the ground, having no idea where she was being taken, wasting valuable time. The hallways and the doors were in various shades between cerulean and baby blues, creating a very distant and cold feeling inside her. After descending and walking for nearly twenty minutes, the private opened a door and stepped aside for her to enter to a small office with minimalist furniture. The sergeant stood up and extended her hand in a formal manner. She was a short woman with tied-back red hair, a pointed chin, and lots of freckles, and she was dressed in a blue military uniform.

"I'm Sergeant First Class Deirdre Monaghan. Take a seat, please."

"Good to meet you, Sergeant, but could you tell me what this is all about? I'm here to see Captain Perez on official peace business."

"What official business are you conducting that concerns him?"

"I'm not at liberty to discuss the details of my investigation by the orders of a judge. Could you tell me if the captain is on the premises right now?"

"Captain's whereabouts are classified. And if this is regarding a social call—"

"It's regarding a murder case." The words slipped out of Phoenix's mouth automatically, without any analysis or calculation.

"A murder case? Who's been murdered?"

"Vassily Bogdanov, a local, was murdered in Russia. I'm leading the investigation."

"May I ask what Captain Perez has to do with it?"

"I'm not sure yet. His name came up in some unusual name list that the victim had made. And I was hoping that he would be able to provide some answers regarding my case."

"Unfortunately, he cannot answer any of your questions. I regret to inform you that Captain Perez died on Thursday last week."

"How bad was the interview, Dagmar?" whispered Hamilton.

The director had just come out of her private bathroom, only to find him sitting on her chair and checking out her network node, seemingly having appeared from thin air.

"We're still working on it, sir. There seems to be no foul play on our agent's side."

"You know that hardly matters. I've received a call from the chairman of the Immigration Academies Worldwide already. They're talking about a malpractice suit with an eleven-figure claim, and an additional suit of malicious intent and defamation against your senior agent and you, as her direct supervisor."

The director absorbed the news as neutrally as she could, while avoiding eye contact with her big boss. "I had guessed as much, sir, but their claims are hollow and baseless. We could destroy all of it in any court of law."

"You know that this can't go to any court of law," said Hamilton, switching his gaze from the computer to her. "We can't afford any press coverage on this. This war will be fought behind the scenes and quietly. Should we lose, it will cost several executives some early retirement and others golden parachutes. You'll be definitely one of them with barbells in your pockets."

The director swallowed and tried to keep calm. The turn of events had been so unbelievable. Only three days ago, any of this would be unthinkable. Now she was facing the toughest moment of her career, a career she had built from nothing with so much hard work and dedication. She cursed the moment she had hired Phoenix and in such a rush, without even interviewing her. And why did she have to be so smart, yet so stubborn and senseless? She was like one of those crusaders from the Middle Ages, but what was her crusade? She didn't appear to have any executive-level aspirations and she clearly lacked the greed for it. She didn't appear like she was planning a career change, either. She wasn't acting out of jealousy or malice. It was definitely not out of the goodness of her heart, as she only wreaked havoc and destruction. What was all her pride and ego feeding from? And moreover, how could so much turmoil and upheaval could be created by just one senior agent?

"The bottom line is," said Hamilton, "the immigration academies have been desperately struggling to survive in the labor force market for some time now. The CDCs are becoming more and more successful at creating labor and are much more cost effective. IAW was the primary supplier of labor in the early years of the Union, as nearly 60 percent of the labor was imported. But since the World Union began to stabilize over the last twenty-five or so years, the IAW has begun to lose market share steadily and nowadays account for only around a quarter of the labor supply. They have chronic management and restructuring problems, but their brainless executives prefer to stick their heads into the sand and blame our security process for their own shortcomings."

"So this is what it's all about," sighed the director.

"You should have already been aware of all this! What's wrong with you?"

"I—I wasn't aware how low their market share has sunk recently."

"This is a war they can't win, and in a decade's time many of the immigration academies around the world will have shut down. But right now, they're threatening to inflict as much damage as they can to anyone around them, in order to recover from some of their losses. They will try to force us into lower standards for our security interviews so that their costs can come down, expecting us to award citizenship to anyone who manages to graduate from their academies of continuously declining quality. And this is something we can't afford to do. Our corporate image would be tarnished if immigrated crooks and psychos were to surface all over the Union."

"Is there any other way than to settle, sir?"

"There will be a settlement no matter what. The trick is to come to the table with aces in the pocket. And we might just be able to achieve that, if we take more risk and make a gambit that they cannot refuse."

With his blue eyes staring icily into the void, Hamilton was clearly planning something. He was a great strategist, as well as a brilliant tactician, and felt no fear towards anything that came his way. "When was her next security interview planned for?"

"Agent Wallis? It was supposed to be tomorrow, sir. But I don't think it will—"

"Call the head of the academy for a meeting. Act like nothing happened, and ask if it would be possible to postpone her next interview to Friday. They can change their pre-announced interviewee, if it causes any inconvenience. And tell them we're willing to agree on an independent watchdog from our side."

"But, sir, wouldn't it only strengthen their position against us?"

"Yes, it would. And that's exactly what I want them to think."

Phoenix felt a chill in her spine but refused to succumb to it. She didn't know whether it was her or a strange twist of circumstances, but it felt as if death were following her. "But, how?"

"He died as his plane crashed into the side of a mountain. His accident is still under investigation, and until a conclusion is made, it will remain classified."

"So it was an accident. What a shame; he could have shed some light on my investigation."

"May I ask what Captain Perez had to do with your case?"

"His name was on what appears to be a name list of the victim in my case. And I was also hoping that he could shed some light to how my victim ended up in Russia, as we have no record of him leaving the Union."

"Are you suggesting something, Agent Wallis?"

"I'm not suggesting anything. Can you tell me where this accident happened?"

The sergeant's eyes widened, and she attempted to say something, only to swallow the words she was about to say.

"Could it be over a rogue state territory?"

"I couldn't confirm or deny that statement," said the sergeant, but a slight twitch of the lips confirmed it. It was a hit.

"Over Russian territory, perhaps?"

"I couldn't confirm or deny that statement," she said again, with another almost imperceptible flash of facial confirmation. It was another hit.

"Is there any information regarding the nature of the accident? A malfunction or perhaps sabotage?"

"There hasn't been a single sabotage in GPSN the military's history."

"Was the captain flying the aircraft himself?"

"I couldn't confirm or deny that statement," she said a third time, with another flicker of approval. "But I can tell you that he was a very experienced pilot with an impeccable flight record over rogue state territories."

She couldn't continue this confirm-deny game forever, but it was evident that the captain had undertaken regular missions over rogue state soil, and his death and Bogdanov's just couldn't be a coincidence. She had seen many cases like this during her tenure in Munich, and everything was beginning to smell like a smuggling ring. Perhaps the names on the list were customers of contraband, with Perez doing the running and being a client at the same time. Perhaps this explained Bogdanov's sudden wealth. She had to find out more about this man to uncover his connection with Bogdanov. Until she could do so, everything was up in the air, nothing but gossip.

"Did you know Captain Perez personally?"

"No, I did not."

"Sweet. How long had he been stationed here in Adrianopolis?"

"I'm afraid that information is classified."

"How about his personal interests? The places he used to hang out? You're a personnel sergeant. You gotta know something about his personal life."

"I have no information about his personal life at all."

"Isn't there anyone who can tell me about this man?"

"As a matter of fact, there is," said the sergeant, following a glance at the monitor before her. "Some non-classified detail that I can share with you, now that the captain is dead."

First Lieutenant Ulrika Thorrsen was a tall woman with high cheekbones, ice-cold blue eyes, thin lips, short blonde hair, and swimmer's shoulders. She wore no makeup other than some mascara on her eyelashes, and her pale skin looked as unhealthy as that of women from the court of sovereigns in the Middle Ages. She had a large office in the same cold shades of color as the hallways, with many maps and other charts on the walls, evidence of a very demanding schedule. She had reluctantly agreed to meet for a few minutes, and Phoenix needed to go further down into the bowels of the base in order to get to her office, but at least this one came with a calming hologram of the Sahara Desert.

"First Lieutenant, how long have you known Captain Perez?"

"Little over three years."

"And how long were you sexual partners with him?"

"Our relationship started almost six months ago. Then it ended abruptly. Can you tell me what Antonio had to do with your murder case?"

"His name was on what appeared to be a ciphered customer list of my murder victim."

"A customer of what?"

"Tell me, First Lieutenant, was Captain Perez an art enthusiast?"

"Art? Are you sure this is related to your investigation?"

"It is."

"All right, the answer is no."

"Are you positive?"

"I can't be positive," shrugged Thorrsen. "We only had limited time together. So we usually focused on more immediate needs of a physical nature rather than chatting about things like art."

"Sweet. Did he ever mention going to a Thing Store?"

"A what store?" she said, leaning over.

"The Thing Store, down at the Pyramid."

"We have a very busy schedule here," she said, with a cold stare. "We rarely have time for extracurricular activities like browsing the *Pyramid.*"

"My murder victim used to work there. Please think again. He might have mentioned the name."

"And what do they sell in this *Thing Store?*"

"Original decorative ornaments called Things."

Thorrsen leaned back to her seat and stared at the desert hologram for a few seconds. "So that's what it was. I remember Antonio talking about 'Things,'" she said, making quotation marks with her fingers. "But I never thought that *Thing* was actually the name of the store."

So there it was, the connection that Phoenix had desperately been trying to establish. Perez may or may not have been an art enthusiast, but he had been to the Thing Store. This at least circumstantially proved that the Juan Antonio Perez in Bogdanov's handwritten list was actually Captain Perez of the GPSN military.

"When did you last see Captain Perez?"

"I believe it was the second week of March."

"And is there anything in particular that you can remember from this last meeting with him?"

"Nothing in particular. It was just our normal sexual interlude. We only had time to meet once or twice a week for a few hours."

"You mentioned that your relationship had ended abruptly, and I assumed that you meant his death. But your last meeting with him was a month ago. Was there a conflict in schedules, or some other reason for this abrupt ending?"

"We didn't spend enough time together to have issues, if that's what you mean. It was pure aggressive sex, nothing more. Mostly we didn't even talk."

"Two of my murder victim's sexual partners had indicated that he had shown signs of unstable behavior, described as hyper-emotional and aggressive. These women have totally different backgrounds, yet they have used almost exactly the same words. I need to know if Captain Perez displayed similar symptoms or not."

If there was a similar pattern with Perez, she could even have a communicable emotional disease on her hands. But it was not easy to extract this information from Thorrsen, as she appeared to be naturally immune to *any* kind of emotion. She thought for several seconds.

"During our last few intimate encounters, actually I did notice something unusual about Antonio's behavior. Usually our sex was very aggressive anyway, but on those last few occasions, he appeared even more aggressive than usual for no apparent reason. Then—"

"Then, what?"

"He would cry like a baby, following our climax!"

"Cry? I assume this wasn't an expected reaction."

"No, it definitely wasn't. And it sure perplexed me. We unfortunately never had time to talk about it, and I never gave it a second thought until your question."

So Perez's pattern was similar to that of Bogdanov, swinging from one end of the emotional spectrum to the other. How that was to serve her idea about a smuggling ring, Phoenix wasn't sure yet. And if Perez was dead three days before Bogdanov, how could he be involved in Bogdanov's transport to the rogue state? Could there be more officers of the military involved in this criminal ring? Involvement of one officer was a very remote possibility, as these women and men were constantly observed and they received regular psych checkups. Involvement of more than one seemed next to impossible.

"Did you ever talk about your relationship with Captain Perez to anyone else?"

"Of course not. But you're not the first one to ask about it."

"I'm not?"

"I received a call from a journalist from WXBG News channel last week, a soft-mannered man, asking me about my feelings regarding my loss. I guess he wanted to create some mushy 'human interest' story. Naturally, I declined to make any comment."

"Naturally. Do you happen to remember the name of this journalist?"

"His name was Bryan Ainsworth. I don't know where he might have heard about the accident. It didn't make it to the news, did it?"

"Nope, it sure didn't."

Phoenix finally emerged from underground at the Pyramid to see the sky. It was another beautiful spring day, and she had wasted most of it taking metros and in underground military installations, deep down in the bowels of the earth. Her mood improved after seeing the sun, and she breathed deeply a few times in order to focus her thoughts. Though she couldn't prove it yet, she was sure Bogdanov and Perez knew each other and were possibly part of a smuggling ring. She had no idea yet as to what they might be smuggling, but the fact that they shared similar symptoms of psychological imbalance strongly suggested that some mind-altering drug had been involved, one that they also used, possibly smuggled in from Russia to be marketed in the Union. There wasn't much chance that she could come up in terms of an airtight case with the little information she had, as most of her case was purely hypothetical so far. There was one person, however, who could connect all of these together and should be able to provide her with conclusive proof to both imbalances and the smuggling. This third person was probably their third partner in crime, which would also make him a prime suspect in their deaths.

Provided he wasn't already dead, too, of course.

CHAPTER 17

THE Mantis smiled to himself as he thought of the brilliant web of obstruction he had been implementing. It was just a few words here, or a few simple choices there, but this simplicity had been the entire beauty of it. Now Phoenix was stranded with no room to maneuver and nothing new to expose, her case shuddering to a grinding halt. Her desperation was evident in the way she rushed off on some wild goose chase while her career was on the rocks. The Mantis couldn't take credit for that interview going sour, but it was a positive development nevertheless, as it had saved him precious time and gave him an extra day to weave a stronger web of deception.

Looking at the way she had messed up her second interview, this woman clearly had no understanding of the real world, blissfully unaware that she was walking the path to her own destruction. The Mantis didn't mind it that much, as he had no regard for people who were oblivious their surroundings. It was going to make his mission less rewarding, however, because he felt that she wasn't worth such a masterpiece. A worthy opponent would at least be aware of the devastation hurtling towards her, if not what had hit her. A truly exceptional adversary would be aware of the trap that was set for her, just too late to do anything about it. More than anything else, the Mantis enjoyed the opponent's sense of impending doom, her primal terror as she plunged helplessly to her own destruction. No amount of misery that they felt after their ultimate ruin could in any way compare to the horror they experienced in the moments and days leading up to it.

The worst kind of victim was the kind that was aware of nothing. These people lacked not only the smartness for noticing his intricate plots, but also the emotional depth to suffer from them. These people were actually so inept, they thought all of the bad things that happened to them had been due to a string of bad luck, or a twist of fate, or even an act of God, and then, they pretended to move on. With victims like these, the Mantis felt like he was wasting his precious time, like there was no one to appreciate his creations and the devastation they brought. And unfortunately it appeared like Phoenix was one of this kind.

He had originally entertained high hopes that she would possess a lot of emotional depth and even be smart enough to develop some kind of awareness of his web, yet it appeared like neither was the case. He had even gone to great lengths to manipulate her dreams, but it looked like it might be all wasted, as she seemed to lack the emotional as well as mental depth for any of it. Since messing up her security interview mindlessly, instead of digging a trench for herself by preparing her defenses and sharpening her weapons for the imminent assault from the academy side, she had fled the scene, leaving her defense to her colleagues who had been victims of the collateral damage. The Mantis sensed *their* pain, but this didn't give him much pleasure, as the main target of his plot had been unaware that she had been hit.

Moreover, it appeared that everyone blamed Phoenix for their troubles, and she had been practically stealing his show like a mindless puppy that had destroyed all the china in the house chasing a ball and was now out in the garden chasing rabbits. Even her comrades, who desperately tried to fix the china she broke, couldn't convince her that she had failed everyone. The woman simply didn't care about any of it, nor did she appear to be aware of the mindless devastation she had caused, to everyone's detriment. She was still running around the city like a headless chicken, wasting her time, pretending to make progress in her hopeless murder case.

The Mantis shook his head in frustration. It was hard to believe, yet this woman managed to distress everyone who got into her proximity, enemy or ally alike. So much so that even he, the Mantis, received wind of it.

"Hey, Beverly, I need an urgent locator for someone."

"Where are you? It's been hectic here. Everyone seems to be on some kind of alert with loads of tension on both our side and the academy's."

"At the Pyramid."

"Hey, is there a spring sale that I'm not aware of?"

"Not that I know of. And the locator?"

"I'll do it for you. What's the name?"

"Pierre DeVille, a local."

"Stand by. Computer: Get your micro-voltaged ass to locate a Pierre DeVille in the fifty-kilometer radius." Beverly turned to the monitor, looked surprised for a moment, and turned to Phoenix. "It appears that the boss has suspended many of our privileges, until this mess is cleared up, I guess."

"My mess?"

"Hey, don't be like that. You didn't do anything wrong. They're just trying to victimize you to cover their own shit."

"I'm not so sure. But thanks all the same for the support."

"C'mon, we're all in the same boat. But you're gonna have to clear your locator with the boss."

At the mention of a boat, Phoenix felt limp and dazed, and all of her thoughts seemed to be drifting to the intruder with the eye mask. She felt a desperate need to find him, to touch him. She felt the urge to look into his eyes one more time and to see if she'd feel the same. She wanted to touch his skin and see how she would react. She wanted—

"Hey! You there?" said Beverly and whistled sharply. "What the hell? Don't tell me it's another PA freeze."

Phoenix snapped out of her daze at the sound of the whistle. "I'm here. Actually, the damn thing crashed again today in the metro, with more recovered data."

"Not again! I think we're gonna have to replace that piece of junk. You'll need to talk to Fred and make a requisition."

"He'll probably want to test it forever and give me a temporary commercial one. I have enough trouble with this military-grade PA. I don't think a commercial-grade one can withstand me more than a minute."

"Come out of it! It wasn't your fault that crazy old fart took it and chucked it. Now, I'm kinda busy with that interview stuff. Did you get what I said about the boss and the locator?"

"I heard it, yes," said Phoenix wearily. "I'll let you know."

"I hope that this is regarding a formal apology," said Valkoinen.

Having no idea what Hamilton had in mind, Director Morssen forced herself to smile. Perhaps he was planning to completely annihilate Phoenix at the interview table in an attempt to exonerate everyone else. Or perhaps it was a tactic of deflection: while everyone's attention was on the interview, he was to strike elsewhere. Or he could incite a riot on the academy grounds. When Hamilton was in question, any of these sensible or crazy scenarios were plausible, and he always came up with some winning plan. The problem was that she didn't know if salvaging her was a part of the plan or not. She was pretty sure Phoenix would be a goner, no matter what the outcome. Even if Hamilton's plan wouldn't call for it, she, Director Morssen, would make sure Phoenix Wallis would be a peace agent no more.

"Not an apology, but a proposal to show our goodwill."

"I don't want any goodwill from you anymore. We brought one of our finest graduates before that monster of a peace agent with the best of intentions this morning, and everyone saw what happened. The poor woman is still in shock."

"I understand your frustration and concern, Ingrid. I propose that we bring Agent Wallis one more time to the interview table."

"How can you even suggest such a thing?" shrieked the headperson. "How can you even consider that I'd agree to something like this? Didn't you people do enough damage to this academy?"

"We're willing to agree for you to appoint a qualified and impartial outsider to be the watchdog on our side. We're also willing to agree for you to change the predetermined interviewee for Agent Wallis and postpone the interview to no later than Friday, so that you would have enough time to bring a watchdog you wish from anywhere in the world."

Valkoinen glanced at Ion with a smirk then turned to the director.

"I can bring *anyone* in the world for this interview to be *your* watchdog?"

"Anyone with experience in this field, of course."

"I think we would be willing to give your monster a second chance," said the headperson with a smirk. "I'm not counting the Patel interview as a relevant case since he proved to be as big a monster as your agent in question. But poor Shakira did nothing wrong and was coerced into submission like a slave, by a ruthless and evil mind."

"So, do we have an agreement?"

"Yes," nodded Valkoinen. "We'll settle this Friday morning."

"Tess, still no news from that DeVille guy?"

"Unfortunately not."

"We gotta find him before something happens to him, too. I need to get a locator for him, but I can't reach the director."

"The meetings at Delta Ten didn't appear that fruitful, either."

"Actually, I learned quite a bit there, but nothing concrete to serve my case."

"You only learned that Perez liked rough sex and cried a couple of times following climax. I understand that there are similarities between his behavior and Bogdanov's, and they might even know each other. But there's still nothing to connect him to the murder. You don't even know how he died."

"I know he died in a plane crash over the rogue state territories while flying the plane himself."

"Wait, wait, where did you get all that?"

"From Sergeant Monaghan, of course."

"She didn't say such a thing."

"You're right, she didn't," said Phoenix smirking. "But she wanted to say it, and I could see it in her face."

"Instincts again?"

"No, this was hidden in the way she looked at me."

"I didn't notice any hint or suggestion or anything similar in her physical appearance or in her voice. How could you deduce all this?"

So there were technical limitations of Tess's ability to deduce feelings and emotions after all. No matter how deeply the voices were analyzed or how high the resolution of the images, there would be always some nuances only humans could see and understand, which would never make it into Richfield Experiment's giant database. This was one of those cases, and it would be impossible to explain certain technical limitations to Tess, as the undisputed adequacy and quality of the data had to be one of the founding postulates of such an experiment.

"Just teasing you," she said and smiled. "It was instincts."

"Whew," said Tess. "I thought I was losing my edge!"

At that moment something sparked in Phoenix's mind, remembering the train of thought she had about the Shakira interview.

"Speaking of your edge, can you do me another favor?"

"Of course," nodded Tess. "Another Agent Tess stunt?"

"Nope, nothing like that. This one involves your expertise for a change, for an experiment of my own."

"What!"

"I know you're so busy, and I'm sorry to bother you, Director. But I need a locator for someone, and you seemed to have frozen some of our privileges."

"For who?"

"Pierre DeVille, Bogdanov's partner in art consultancy."

The director couldn't understand why Phoenix was insisting on pursuing the murder case while there was so much trouble in the house. On the other hand, perhaps it was in everyone's best interests if she was out of the way while the field office was preparing its defense.

"PA: Restore Senior Agent Wallis—"

"Could you make it for Beverly? I'm not near a network node."

"PA: Restore Supervisor Blackmore's locator and other suspended privileges."

"Thank you, Director."

As long as it keeps you away from here, thought the director. "By the way," she said out loud, "your next security interview is postponed by one day to Friday morning, and you might get a new interviewee. You'll be notified as to who it will be later today."

"I'm still to have that interview?"

"Yes, you are. For better or for worse."

Pierre DeVille had been located at his own house and appeared to be in good health, according to the locator that Beverly had run. On the other hand, it was strange that the director, who was usually a meticulous pedant, did not dwell on the need for a locator. And what could this new security interview be about? It made no sense for the academy to agree or to propose an interview for her, which meant the proposal had to come from the GPSN, with concessions attached. It could only mean one thing: GPSN had already sacrificed her. This would also explain the director's indifference towards her whereabouts or her locator request.

She felt a great weight in her solar plexus, and something seemed to be blocking her throat. She felt warmth followed by chill on her face and realized that tears were spilling out of her eyes, flowing down her cheeks. She had struggled to become *someone* all her life. She had always possessed this urge to make a difference. She had chosen the investigation and peacekeeping business to achieve this, with the support and approval of all of her teachers and advisors, spending her entire time and money on it. But now it looked like the giant company that she devoted her life to had abandoned her. She was to be dumped like a rejected tissue, whereas assholes and backstabbers like Julio were set to succeed.

After being fired from the GPSN in disgrace, possibly facing libel charges from the academy, it would be impossible for her to find any decent job, and her HDI would plummet to heaven knows what in a few months, she would go bankrupt; a lender would literally end up owning her and whatever she were to produce through her labor. And if she couldn't pay for the security premium required from every citizen, she could even get deported to one of the rogue states. She was exempt from it for the time being because she worked for the GPSN, but when she got fired—

She felt like an orphan all over again. And this time, she wasn't being left by some helpless biological parents due to inescapable circumstances, who, despite their flaws and shortcomings, desperately had tried to provide her a good upbringing and life. This time she was being dumped, rejected, discarded by a ruthless system, which had no mercy for those who couldn't adapt to its fabric and absorb its predetermined set of rules. It had no space to spare for misfits, it had no patience with what it deemed a waste, and it had no room for mistakes. Anything and everything needed to be harmonized within it, and she wasn't wanted or needed anymore. She couldn't even be *recycled*.

As the cathartic tears melted away the sensation of being strangled, her guilt and shame began to give way to another feeling. She was angry at this ruthless system. She was furious that it didn't want her without even trying to understand her strengths or to know her capabilities. She actually had never been a part of it. She wanted to, but she never had a chance. The system had been ruthlessly trying to mold her into something she couldn't be, and now she was being scrapped for failing its quality test.

She felt no loyalty to the World Union anymore, but could she coexist with it? Or did she possess the skill set needed to survive in a rogue state? What could she do? Where could she turn? She still had two more days until her doom, and her instincts were still telling her that the only glimmer of hope or salvation lay in the murder case. She had to focus on it. She had to solve it. She had to, somehow.

Her deep thoughts were cut when she noticed the end of her PA's trail in a building that had every sign of tenants with rock-bottom HDIs. She smiled wryly, thinking she was on her way to join them very soon.

"Welcome to the home of Pierre DeVille. How may I help you?"

"I need to see Mr. DeVille urgently. Please inform him that he has a visitor from the GPSN Field Office."

"Mr. DeVille is not accepting visitors."

"This is regarding a murder case. Let Mr. DeVille know that I'm here, and open the damn door!"

"Mr. DeVille is not accepting visitors."

She had just about had enough from all these useless computers and their meaningless insistence to follow protocol and orders. For once, she felt free to do what she wanted, as things couldn't get any worse anyway.

"Computer: Access GPSN gateway. I am a peace agent, and my badge number is three, one, six, charlie, omega, seven, seven, papa, echo, papa. Request authorization to enter Pierre DeVille's house. Initiate emergency procedure now."

The door clicked open, and Phoenix felt a sudden rush, a rush similar to what she had felt entering Bogdanov's house under similar circumstances. What if *he* was inside? What if DeVille was the intruder? What if he'd been at Bogdanov's apartment to eliminate evidence that could incriminate him? Trying to contain her excitement, she stepped inside.

"I don't have it. And I couldn't do what you ask in a million years even if I did have it, Beverly."

"Fred, you ol' skunk! I know you keep a stash of everything, so don't gimme that 'can't do it, ma'am' crap."

Fred's dark office had no windows and was next to the network center, where all the hardware and the servers of the field office were kept. Beverly could feel the humming of the fans coming from the inside and thought that it would be hard to deal with this kind of humming vibration, day in and day out. No wonder Fred had turned into a bonehead.

"Even if I did have it, how could I hand her a piece of hardware like that without the approval of the boss?"

"You can be so naïve, Fred," said Beverly, shaking her head. "Do you think the boss cares about anything like that right now? Don't you understand the trouble we all are in? There's a war going on, and Phoenix is on the front line. She needs reliable hardware in order to come out clean."

"I—I don't know, Bev. I can get into a lot of trouble, you know."

"If we can't pull this thing off, we're all gonna be in sticky shit up to our necks. Don't you get it?"

"I'm not sure if that's my problem."

"You know what? I'll make it your problem. If Phoenix has any trouble with her PA, if that thing ever produces another crash, comes up with more butterfly junk, I'll make sure you pay. How about that being your problem?"

"You can't do that," said Fred with horror in his sunken eyes.

"Oh, yes I can," said Beverly with a grimace and folded her arms. "And I promise you that I will!"

A strong foul odor hit her as she entered the filthy apartment. There was a layer of filthy debris on the carpet, with patches of stains, leftover fast food remains that seemed to be sprouting mold, strange shapes and color combinations on the walls that appeared painted over each other, a big stain of *something* on the ceiling that Phoenix didn't dare to speculate about, and a work desk full of so much junk she couldn't see the desk itself. The huge stack of printouts on the floor was presumably art. The image of a monster on top of the stack appeared to have been crudely copied and pasted in parts.

The only clean item in the entire house was a big wall display with a black metal frame and a glass cover, which contained, of all things, antique firearms. She glanced at the weapons with interest as she approached DeVille. He was a tall, built man, with long ponytailed chestnut hair and intense brown eyes. He wore jeans and a two-color denim coat and came with a smudge of hair on his chin or, rather, just below his lips. He was quite a good-looking guy, but definitely not the intruder. He appeared to be working manually on a sheet of paper at his designer's desk, using a marker. He glanced at Phoenix but didn't bother to get up and greet her.

"Hello, Mr. DeVille. My name is Phoenix Wallis, and I'm a senior agent from the GPSN Field Office."

"Is there a reason that I should care? And how did you manage to get in?" said DeVille, folding his arms, his voice disappointingly nasal and high-pitched, his accent North American.

"Your Door Bot was kind enough to let me in. I'm here in an official capacity, and I need to ask you some questions regarding a case."

"Well, as you can see, I'm real busy. Why don't you find your own way out?"

"I'm afraid this cannot wait, sir. It's very important that we speak now. This will only take a few minutes of your time, Mr. DeVille."

"Whatever," he said and pushed a stool towards her with his foot. "The name's *Pierre*."

"Thank you," said Phoenix and sat reluctantly on the disgustingly stained furniture. "I'd like to ask you how you met Vassily Bogdanov."

"So, it's about *Vasslee*," said DeVille, with a grin. "Some mutual friend introduced us. My creative ability must've grabbed his attention, or somethin'. I paint 2D abstract art and design things, you know."

"What kind of things?"

"Things like the things here, and things like the things at the Thing Store."

Phoenix quickly glanced around, having great difficulty differentiating the designed things from discarded junk. Judging by the dirt accumulated on it, the old computerized design terminal before him hadn't been used in a very long time. He was using markers and crayons for drawing, something that even the fifth graders at CDCs didn't do anymore.

"So you design items to be sold at the Thing Store?"

"Yeah," said DeVille, with an air of pride. "I mean, I kinda do. Or let's just say that Vassily and I have an understanding. He's one of the very few people with the ability to really appreciate my art."

"I deeply regret to tell you that he won't be able to appreciate it anymore."

"Oh, man," groaned DeVille. "Don't tell me that fat wanker skipped town with the money. Is it what this is all about? He sold my art and ran?"

"Actually, he did leave town, never to come back. He's dead."

"Whoa," said DeVille in shock. "Did you just say he's dead?"

"I'm sorry about your loss, Pierre."

"But, that's too bad," said DeVille, staring into the void. "We had great plans for our business. How did it happen? He must have had a heart attack or something."

"What made you say that?"

"You know," shrugged DeVille. "He was on the heavy side and all."

"Actually, he was murdered. In the port city of Odessa in—"

"Wow! What was he doing in the Pacific? Selling my art?"

"I said Odessa, not Okinawa. It's a port city in the Russian rogue state."

"I knew that," said DeVille, with a grin. "Just testing your geography."

Phoenix exhaled loudly. "Sweet. So how would you describe your working relationship with him?"

"I guess you could say we got along pretty well, considering all our differences."

"What kind of differences are you referring to?"

"For one thing, he was quite a bit older, and he seemed to have come from a much different background. Dunno, just a feeling I had, you know. And he had a strange attitude towards women. I think he was a Scandinavian or something."

"He was an immigrant from Russia."

"No shit? Now that I think about it, he was a bit *roguish*."

"So Bogdanov never talked about his personal life with you?"

"We only had a business relationship, and I really didn't wanna get too chummy with him, you know? Nothing personal against the guy, it's just that he wasn't very attractive, and he would have cramped my style, scaring away my potential suitors."

"So what was your business relationship with him?"

"Well, we were partners, of course, with an understanding that neither one of us should have the upper hand."

"A fifty-fifty partnership?"

"That's it," said Pierre, snapping his fingers. "We were like the two halves of an apple. I'd provide the creativity, and he'd deal with the sales and marketing."

"And your partnership with him was going well?"

"Absolutely! And the business was just taking off. I dunno what I'm gonna do without him now. It's gonna be hard to find someone with such appreciation of art."

"Were you guys making a lot of money?"

"Sure. It turned into a lucrative business overnight because, as the successful business folk would say, we had the right mix. With his abilities in sales and marketing and my talent as an artist, we're talking about a dream team here."

"So how many *things* did you sell, in this partnership?"

"I *am* an *artiste*," said DeVille and folded his arms. "I was dealing only with the creative part of things and letting him deal with the crappy aspects."

"And those *crappy* aspects would be?"

"I told you, but maybe you're not as smart as you look, Phoenix, darlin'. The marketing, the accounting, and all the bean counting. See what I'm sayin'?"

"Quite. He was the only one who dealt with the financial side?"

"Exactly. Because for an artiste, dealing with money kills the muse. If I had to count beans day in and day out, I would lose my artistic edge. All I know is that we split everything even-steven."

"And when did you see him last?"

"See, as an artiste, I'm never good with dates. But it's your lucky day, sugar. Because, I'm pretty sure I saw him on the thirty-first of March."

"That's pretty specific for a man who's never good with dates."

"Well, regardless of that, it would be hard to forget payday, wouldn't it?" said DeVille and grinned. "We had a meeting that day, and he tried to explain me the sales, my share, and all that junk. But I wouldn't hear of it. 'Just wire the damn thing,' I said. 'And don't you ever attempt to taint my creativity again!'"

"So you have no idea how much money you made last month?"

"That's what accountants and lawyers are for. My accountant is dead, so ask my lawyer, not me."

Perhaps she needed to reevaluate her theory about DeVille being part of a smuggling ring along with Bogdanov and Perez. This man didn't appear have the wits to be a part of such a setup and, if his disgusting house was any indication, didn't possess any organizational skills either. But that wall display she needed to check. She got up.

"Wanna check out my 2D art, sugar?" said DeVille. "Go on. Chicks like you love that scary stuff."

Phoenix unwillingly moved towards the pile of art first, kneeled down, and casually browsed through the stack. "You seem to have quite a collection there, Pierre," she said, pointing to the weapons on the wall.

"Oh, yeah, sugar," said DeVille, looking intensely into Phoenix's green-gray eyes. "My kinda collection: explosive and deadly."

Flipping through the art, out of the blue she glimpsed a picture that made her feel as if her heart had stopped. She couldn't breathe for a few seconds, just froze with the picture in her hand. It had to be a hallucination, the product of a sleep-deprived and overburdened brain. She closed her eyes for a couple of seconds, expecting to see something else altogether when she reopened them, but it wasn't a trick of the mind. The picture was real, whatever "real" meant. Could she be losing sight of that clear line separating the real from the surreal?

In the meantime, DeVille rose slowly from his seat, his easy and informal attitude giving way to a rather ominous one. Until that moment, he'd appeared harmless, but now having seen the picture, everything seemed to take on a new meaning. Something else was in those eyes now, a kind of creepiness in his disposition, a defocus, as if a totally different side of him had surfaced; Dr. Jekyll had given way to Mr. Hyde.

There was so much confusion inside her created by that one painting, it was as if someone had left the window open and a chilly gust of wind had stirred up all the dust inside, up into the air, bringing visibility near to zero, with her instincts nowhere to be found, and she was feeling naked and vulnerable without them. She felt a desperate urge to leave, but her rational side insisted that she complete the interview the best she could. She had had great difficulty tracking this man down, she had entered his house using emergency access, and she had to leave with some information, or with her dignity at least. Any information might prove crucial to her million-to-one chance of salvation.

"And where did you get this firearm collection?" she managed to ask, trying to appear as calm as possible.

"I got those pieces in the Big Sky Country in North America," said DeVille, with his eyes still fixed somewhere on her face.

"Why do you display these barbaric weapons in your home like this?"

"What do you mean, barbaric? These are antique weapons of self-defense, relics from a time when our mighty system wasn't there to protect the people. And I display these explosive and deadly weapons with pride, because that's the kind of guy I am, too. Are you getting the chills, sugar?"

DeVille moved slowly towards her, maintaining eye contact. He tripped on some junk and almost fell on the floor. There was something sinister, evil, in those eyes now. Should she send an alert to the GPSN and ask for help? No, she could deal with it, she had to deal with it. She had to play it cool and talk her way out. Backing down or brown-nosing would only make matters worse. She had to hold her ground. Then a sudden wave of dizziness hit her.

Dreams were beginning to blend into reality. Could this be just another nightmare? She longed to sleep peacefully, just for a little bit, if only she could. Could she? Sounds and colors began to fade, like just before waking or falling asleep. She let herself go and stumbled into the world of unconsciousness.

CHAPTER 18

"SHE'S doing another security interview?" said Julio. "No way!"

"Friday morning," said Director Morssen. She had called her entire senior staff for a meeting to impart the latest development in the battle of the corporations. Better they learned it from her, as opposed to a gossip outside.

"But why?" said Beverly.

"It's a corporate decision."

"Is the corporation sacrificing Phoenix, Boss? Because that's what it looks like."

"Can I be the watchdog?" jumped Julio.

"You can't," said the director. "Nobody on our side can. Our watchdog will be an independent expert from outside."

"And when do we name this watchdog?" said Beverly.

"We don't," said the director and exhaled.

All of the staff looked at each other, trying to understand what was going on. "Don't tell me *they* will choose our watchdog," said Beverly.

"They will," said the director. "And we will not choose theirs."

Whispers started between the staff, as Beverly shook her head, her eyes wide. "So the corporation *is* sacrificing Phoenix," she said. "She didn't do anything wrong, Boss. I was there, I saw it."

"Nobody is sacrificing anyone. But let me tell you one thing. If this was all up to me, I'd sacrifice Phoenix myself. I'd sacrifice her for being so stubborn and for having no regard for the well-being of the company she works for."

"I don't understand, Boss. Since when did following procedures and protocol in a security interview and rejecting a student for violating the Supreme Bill mean having no regard for corporate benefit? If there was an understanding or gentle-persons' agreement between us and them regarding her second interview, why wasn't she aware of this? And since when did the GPSN, one of the seven largest corporations in the world, go down on her knees before something like the IAW and sacrifice one of her own?"

Beverly's words seemed to resonate with the other staff members in the room. Many of them murmured in approval, and a couple of them even applauded, albeit discreetly, one of whom was Julio, the same guy who had wanted to crucify Phoenix for the same interview. It appeared like he had moved on and picked himself a bigger game. Director Morssen had to defend Hamilton's policy, but she lacked any background information about his plan. She was sure Phoenix was going to be sacrificed in this process, and she had to explain it to this angry mob somehow. Beverly seemed like the mob leader for the time being, with Alex looking totally passive as if he didn't care, and Julio had preferred not to spearhead this one so far. Fred was nervously fidgeting as usual, and the rest of them didn't have the experience or clout to lead such a mob.

"Now wait a minute. Who said we're on our knees?"

"It sure looks like it, Chief," said Julio. "You know what I think about Nix's abilities, and I respectfully disagree with Beverly here, as she sure screwed up the interview with the Arab babe. But she messed up wearing the uniform, and the uniform stands behind one of its own no matter what, so I'd expect for us to suck it up and prepare our defenses. Now I don't understand where this humiliating concession comes from. Is there something you're not telling us? It's also our future, too, you know."

With more nods and murmurs of approval, now everyone glared at the director. She had a potential mutiny on her hands, and for the first time in her life, she wasn't sure what to do. Under any other circumstance, she'd fire all of them on the spot. But now the situation was very delicate. If her staff were to resign or get fired en masse, this would severely weaken her position on the eve of the looming battle. She had already received a serious warning from Hamilton regarding losing this war of corporations, and she couldn't afford to have her entire career go down the drain because of a few disgruntled employees. Moreover, she didn't know where she stood in all this. Other than public gatherings like the graduation ceremonies, she had seen Hamilton face to face on just four occasions, once during her hiring, and in three annual budgeting meetings until the beginning of this week. Now, she had seen him twice in the last two days, and on both occasions he had instructed her to do something excruciatingly painful for her. Everything had been going downhill since Phoenix's appointment by him as the case lead.

Now anger and disappointment had invaded the faces of her staff. Only Alex looked very calm, as if indifferent to any and all possible outcomes, the same guy she had asked to give her a week to show his worth to the field office. Things couldn't have turned out stranger than this, and it appeared like she was going to achieve just that at her own expense. Wouldn't he be the natural choice to succeed her?

"I said the decision for the concession came from the corporate level."

"We understand that, Boss," said Beverly. "And we wanna know why. Why doesn't corporate let us defend one of our own?"

"Who said we're not going to defend her? And you're talking as if the lady herself cares!"

"Of course she does," said Beverly.

"Then why isn't she here, showing her concern?"

"She's a smart gal, Boss. Perhaps she already knows that she's being dragged to an altar along with the sacrificial knife. Would you care if you knew?"

The director could say many things about duty, and self-respect, and dignity, but she knew none of these meant much in the postmodern world. It was all about greed, and this situation was a typical example of how it brought colleagues who would cut each other's throats on any other day to band up together.

"To be honest, I have no idea what the corporation has in mind."

Her confession first caused a shock, then a stir among the bunch, and they immediately started discussing among themselves what the corporation might be up to, relieving the pressure on the director for the time being.

"Was it Hamilton?" said Beverly.

The director nodded slowly and lowered her eyes. It had never been her policy to reveal details of corporate decisions nor to allow her subordinates to discuss them. But this time it was different. She wasn't sure if she'd still have a job by the end of the week. And although Phoenix had messed up so many things in these three days, it had been Hamilton who had unleashed her, and now they were all going to suffer for it.

"He's such a ruthless bastard," said Beverly. "I wouldn't be surprised if he closed the whole damn field office down."

"And this could be very well the case, thanks to your leadership, Chief," said Julio. "Sacrificing Nix is just a smokescreen. Hamilton wants to sink the whole damn ship. Can't you see that?"

"What the hell are you talking about?" erupted the director. "Adrianopolis is the command center of the entire Eastern border, all twenty-five hundred kilometers of it, handpicked by Osmund Ledyard Hamilton himself. GPSN invested more than hundred billion Coalition dollars here, to build a fifty-story-deep military base and top-of-the-line border control systems and apparatus over the last five years. Do you think he'd be stupid enough to sacrifice his own creation just like that over a security interview and look like a clueless idiot to the board in DC?"

The mob quieted down at her convincing tone, murmuring Hamilton would never make such judgment errors.

"Then what does he have in mind?" said Alex, his first verbal contribution since the beginning of the meeting. "None of this makes any sense."

"I don't know. But I know that he won't sacrifice this field office, maybe just a few members of its staff."

"Do you think you'll be one of those?" said Julio, with another smirk.

"You would like that very much, wouldn't you? Tell you what: If I go down, I'll also make sure to take a few of you with me! Now go back to your work, and help prepare our defense against this mess or at least have the good sense to stay out of the way and not obstruct the ones that do."

Alex got up and led the mob to disperse. The director waited until all of them had exited then exhaled in relief. But she wasn't sure if she would be able to prevent the situation from getting out of control again if the situation worsened in the next couple of days.

These were to be the hardest two days since the horrors she had gone through during the Blockade of Denmark.

It's such a beautiful day.

She is lying on the grass, looking up the sky. She can smell the green grass and hear the buzzing bees. Nature is alive; she is alive and happy.

"I love you," he says, leans over her, and kisses her. It is such a tender kiss, so full of affection and love, she feels blessed by higher powers.

She looks at his eyes and absorbs the deep care and appreciation. So this is happiness, *she thinks. This is how happiness was meant to be: a divine elevation of love, care, and security.*

All of a sudden she feels a deep chill inside, and something starts to move. Something inside her is pushing its way out. It is something she was born with but never knew was there, along with everyone else. She starts feeling terrible pain. He looks at him. His eyes tell her not to be afraid, and that she can make it, and that he trusts her. The pain becomes unbearable as the creature inside rips through her abdomen and reaches out into space.

Phoenix sprang up with a strangled scream, startling DeVille, who was leaning over her. He shrieked and jumped back reflexively, then slowly squatted down next to her, peering at her as if at a strange specimen of insect.

"You scared the greed outta me, man! Are you okay?"

"I'm fine," she said and twisted away from him. She got up carefully, still shaken by the nightmare. Once again, all she could remember was a serpent ripping through her abdomen and that strange serenity feeling, just like the one she had in the morning. She could remember the happiness clearly this time, with no doubt in her mind that it preceded the awful ending. If only she could remember what she saw before.

"You just collapsed, sugar," said DeVille and got up to lean towards her.

"How long was I out?" she asked, moving away from him.

"Just a few minutes, I guess. I was about to call an ambulance."

"I'm fine."

"My antique collection freaked you out, huh? You seem too sissy to respect and appreciate my pieces. You sure you're a GPSN agent?"

"I don't respect any pain-inflicting device, and honestly, I don't understand what people admire about them."

"I'd expect someone in the uniform to understand this better than anyone else, Agent *Phoenix*."

"You're a long way from understanding a woman in uniform, Pierre."

DeVille turned his attention to his precious firearm collection. He walked towards it and touched the glass of the display with affection, speaking with his back to Phoenix. "Obviously we don't see eye to eye about my collection. Your nosy questions and attitude is killing my inspiration. I believe it's time you left my house."

"I will do that gladly, but I need to check something." She took a step towards the pile of art on the floor. But DeVille blocked her way.

"I said it's time you left my house. You obviously don't appreciate my art or my pieces. Now get out."

Did she see it, or did she just have a hallucination? Was seeing that picture the beginning of the dream? Or could she be still dreaming? Could she tackle him with her jiu-jitsu training? Perhaps she could, but it had to wait. She had already used an emergency procedure to enter his house. If she were to create an additional incident here, she would definitely get the axe and perhaps even be sent to a rehab center for a psych evaluation. Besides, the footage from her PA could shed some light to what really happened. She glared at him, turned, and left without saying another word.

Back outside in the spring sunshine, she allowed herself a moment to stand still and try to absorb a little warmth and clear her mind. She breathed in and out deeply in an effort to calm down her racing pulse. Her mini nightmare must have been triggered by a combination of physical fatigue and the shock of seeing the painting, exacerbated by her irrational fear of DeVille's sudden switch in attitude. The problem was that she wasn't sure exactly when her nightmare had started. She remembered getting up from the filthy chair and walking towards the firearm display, then diverting to the pile of art at DeVille's urging and flipping through the pages indifferently.

As she thought of the picture, a sudden cramp in her stomach made her spill her guts out on the sidewalk, unnoticed by oblivious passersby. The picture of a blonde woman, just like herself, with a giant serpent ripping through her abdomen and shooting through the stars.

"Hey, marine. Ready for a date tonight?"

"Sure. Anytime Her Highness desires me, I'm at her service."

"Not with me, you imp, with her."

"Really? I didn't think she'd ever wanna see me again."

"Well, she didn't. But I was able to convince her otherwise."

"I'm not sure if I'm ready for this," said the marine and swallowed.

"Hey, don't even start that! You're supposed to act with her, not with me."

"I'm not playing a game, man. She freaked me out like nobody ever did."

"I know she's a weirdo, but you gotta suck it up if you want this," said Sandra, motioning at her gorgeous body.

"It wasn't that she's a weirdo. She sized me up and shook me up so hard. You know, I could respect a woman like that."

Another acting stunt to impress me, Sandra thought. Otherwise, how could someone like Phoenix invoke the respect of this marine, and not her? Men never told her they respected her, not that it mattered anyway.

"Whatever works," she said with a shrug. "Want this date or not?"

"I do, I do. Just a little nervous, that's all."

"Tess."

"Hey, Phoenix. How did the interview go?"

"What do you mean? I thought you watched all my interviews."

"Yes, I do. But I couldn't do it with this one. Didn't get the signal. Did you begin recording as you entered his place?"

Phoenix's ears started burning. "Damn it, Tess, I used the emergency procedure to enter his house, then I forgot it in the heat of the moment."

"I see. Are you okay? You look like you saw a ghost."

"You could say that. I'm fine, just exhausted." said Phoenix, realizing that she hadn't eaten since the morning. Perhaps that explained the dizziness. Not only had she been neglecting her exercise, now she was beginning to neglect her eating, too.

"You could use some rest, dear."

"Yes, I could. But it's a luxury I cannot afford right now. Besides, don't you know already? I'm afraid to go to sleep."

Sean checked the database to see if there was any new information available for her second case, but there was still nothing. There had been no autopsy, the mysterious device that was supposed to have caused Spencer's death was still unavailable for inspection, and there appeared to be an impasse in all activity. Strangely enough, this impasse seemed to be fine with everyone. Then, there was the connection Phoenix had mentioned the previous day, the connection between the deaths of Bogdanov and Spencer. If it wasn't a coincidence, she had no idea what to make of it.

On the other hand, Phoenix had pretty much shut her out of the Bogdanov case after she had realized her involvement with Julio. In light of what Julio had told her about the contagiousness of her condition, isolation suited her just fine. But she still liked and admired Phoenix for beating Patel against all odds and for telling the truth about the emotional confusion she had felt during the encounter with the intruder.

Sean would never have the guts to admit such a thing even to a close friend, let alone in a tense meeting with the director and everyone else. She was happy that she hadn't needed to elaborate on her sentiments during the encounter, where she had felt like she was flying and observing other people's lives from a distance, and that the director had cut her short. She could remember fragments of observing a happy couple on a mountaintop, a boat full of masked people, and some giant snake. Surely, she would be sent to a psych checkup if she were to mention any of these.

The envious gazes of some of her fellow junior agents had been on her for being the case assistant for two deaths, but the truth was that she still had nothing do other than loitering at her desk at the Monitoring Room and becoming a victim of dull and tedious tasks assigned by Beverly. She had a date with Julio in the evening, and she didn't want to stick around until Beverly told her to check out a zillion footages till midnight. An option would be to sneak out and ask Alex for something to do related to the Spencer case, something, anything.

She slipped out quietly and made her way to Alex's office on the same floor. She passed Julio's office with a feeling of curiosity and wondered if she should sneak in, strip off, and jump him. Wouldn't be a good idea considering the number of security cameras and how much scrutiny each footage had been receiving lately. To her dismay, Alex was not at his office.

"PA: Locate Senior Agent Lubosh in the building." The PA projected Alex's location on a map of the third floor. He appeared to be on his way to the director's office. At that instant, a call came in.

"Hey, babe," said Julio. "What's happenin'?"

"I was just thinking about you. We're still on tonight, yeah?"

"Sure," nodded Julio. "You're gonna be in an important meeting in a bit, and I just wanted to give you a heads up."

"What kind of a meeting?"

"The old bag is turning into a lame duck. Not that I don't welcome such a development, as she definitely doesn't deserve to be the director here."

"What happened?"

"She's totally lost control of this field office. Even the upper management has started to cut her out of the loop, and she admitted to this, can you believe it?"

"You're serious?"

"Do I look like I'm not? Alex is organizing a meeting among a select group of senior staff to talk about it, and I managed to sneak you in."

"Really?"

"I told you I can open doors for you," said Julio, with a wink.

"Thanks, Julio. I'm bored out of my mind in this Monitoring Room."

"Actually, you can do something for me in the Monitoring Room," said Julio smoothly. "Can I rely on your support?"

"Of course, just name it."

"You'll know what it is after the meeting," said Julio with a smirk.

"Hello, Mr. Ainsworth, I'm Senior Agent Phoenix Wallis."

Ainsworth's office was painted a dull shade of yellow, and it was fully artificially illuminated. Phoenix didn't understand the reason for this at first, until she saw the monitors on the walls. One entire wall was literally covered with displays showing nearly a hundred different feeds, many of which were foreign.

Bryan Ainsworth was a man of medium height and medium build, with brown eyes and light brown hair with a receding hairline. His face was nondescript at first glance, probably almost impossible to recognize on a second encounter. In another life, perhaps he would make the perfect insurance salesman, as nobody would recognize him if he tried to sell it again after a failed attempt. His eyes looked a little reddened, like Phoenix's, but perhaps from observing the feeds, not from lack of sleep. He had a beautiful smile, and it made a lot of difference to his appearance.

"Call me Bryan, please. So, what brings you here?"

"Do you know a Captain Juan Antonio Perez?"

"Not personally, but I know of him. Are you investigating his death?"

"No, I'm not. But Captain Perez's name came up in another case."

"What case is that?"

"I cannot reveal that information."

Ainsworth smiled at her, folded his arms, and looked down. "I see. But if you don't tell me about your case, how can you expect me to help you? I know the meaning of confidentiality, don't worry."

"A murder case," Phoenix blurted out.

"Murder? Holy shit! In Adrianopolis?"

"No, no, in Russia. And Captain Perez's name was written in what appears to be a customer list of the victim."

"As in, *hand*written?"

"That's correct."

"He must be a recent immigrant, this victim of yours."

"How could you tell?"

"I watch them here all day long," said Ainsworth, pointing to the feeds. "You'd be surprised how much pen and pencil are still in fashion out there."

"So, Bryan, what can you tell me about Captain Perez's death?"

"Well, his plane crashed to a mountain side in Russia. He and the other members of his crew were instantly killed."

"He was the commander of the aircraft, wasn't he?"

"Yes, and I believe he was flying the aircraft at the time of the accident. According to eyewitness accounts, they were trying to land the plane."

It didn't make sense for a World Union military aircraft to attempt a crash landing over rogue territory. Rule one of GPSN military was never to leave anyone or any hardware behind. "Were you able to obtain any cargo information, or passenger manifest, or flight recorder information?"

"No, I wasn't."

"How come this never made it to your evening bulletins?"

"Well," said Ainsworth with a broad smile. "GPSN made an official request, citing global security reasons, and asked us not to publish it."

"And you backed down that easily?"

"GPSN is a colossal company, you know that. When they make such a request from a regional news channel like ours, it's very hard to refuse them."

"Are you worried that you may never get information from them again?"

"You said it," said Ainsworth and smiled.

"So how did you hear about this crash? On one of those feeds?"

"No, it never made it to the news there, either. I learned about it from one of my sources there."

"Just out of curiosity: When a source comes to you with a story like that and you cannot verify through one of these feeds or any other means, how do you know to trust them?"

"Depends on the source. I have known this one for a good while, so trust was not a big issue. But I still had to be careful."

"Why is that?"

"Because sometimes your trusted informant can send you something fake without being aware. There's a big espionage game going on in the world, and many times the press is made a part of this game. We try to be as careful as we can, but sometimes the evidence is so compelling—"

"So, this story came with evidence?"

Ainsworth hesitated for a few seconds.

"It did, didn't it?"

"It did, actually," he said and scratched his neck. "Some raw footage of the crash site, with fire still raging and everything."

"How could you tell it wasn't a fake?"

"We examined it the best we could with some GPSN surplus software, and it passed the test. So, I rushed to Delta Ten. They denied the story at first, until they learned that I had footage of the crash. It made them hesitate. In the following confusing hours, I managed to make some headway and to learn quite a bit about the victims of the crash and a little about the mission."

Despite his ordinary appearance, this man clearly knew how get to the bottom of a story. Perhaps his nondescript looks were an advantage to him and made people talk to him easily, as if he weren't even there. Or perhaps it was his soft manners and reassuring smile. Or perhaps it was just because he was able to get a good night's sleep every night and woke up a happy person after sweet dreams.

"By the way, how did you come up with my name?"

"From First Lieutenant Thorrsen."

"Oh, the ice queen," said Ainsworth with another smile.

"Tell me about the footage. Was the quality any good?"

"Well, it was shot in the dark with a very low-quality camera. The front of the hull was intact, but the middle and rear were disintegrated. It was very dark, but with the help of the raging fire, we could see the tail number clearly."

"May I have a copy of it?"

"Unfortunately GPSN's request included a full wipeout from our servers, after taking a copy for themselves, of course. You could ask them."

"Sure, but with their bureaucracy, it would take forever for me to receive clearance for it. Are you sure you don't have a copy stashed somewhere, by mistake, perhaps?"

"No, I don't. But I can locate one for you. I'm sure my source in Russia still has a copy of it, and I don't think he'd mind sending me another copy."

"Oh, that would be great, Bryan, thanks."

"How about if I give it to you over dinner tomorrow, at the Mediterranean restaurant down at the Pyramid?"

In the postmodern world, women like Phoenix didn't get many dinner offers, as those were reserved for women of beauty and glamour, like Sandra, or women of clout. Perhaps her luck with men was changing, as her career was going down the drain.

CHAPTER 19

"**WE** need to do something," said Julio, pacing back and forth.

"There's nothing we can do, you dumbass," said Beverly.

"Quit being such a wuss, Bev. Chief's no chief, no more. She's more clueless than us, crippled from above, a lame duck."

"Nobody could be more clueless than you!"

"C'mon guys," said Alex. "We're not here to bash each other."

"Then why are we here, huh?" said Beverly. "Tell me, you called this meeting, saying that we need to strategize and focus on the issue at hand. Not that we'd plot behind the boss's back."

"Maybe the situation *requires* that we plot behind her back," said Julio.

"So you're saying that we should be calling the shots on this now?"

"That's exactly what I'm saying, Bev," said Julio and grinned. "I've been keeping my mouth shut all these years and not responding to her condescending remarks, insults, and yelling. But it's obvious now that she's going down, and I'm not going down with that foul-mouthed old bag."

"First of all, you've been here less than a year—two hundred and seventy-eight days to be exact—and you've been acting like you own the goddamn place since," said Beverly, gritting her teeth. "Heck, you've been a senior for just a few months now, and you expect me to be wound up like one of your little girlfriends?" She motioned towards Sean with her head, who in turn quietly looked down.

Julio grinned. "Oh, Bev—"

"How many times have I told you, the name's Beverly, you jerk!"

"All right, all right, Beverly. Why can't you put your insignificant personal dislike of me to one side for a moment and think? Can't you see we're all in this together? GPSN's strategy, Nix's defense, Chief's impotency, they're all interconnected, can't you see?"

"He could have a point there, Beverly," said Fred. "Maybe it's time that we looked out for our own interests."

"And how exactly do we do that? We pretend the boss is obsolete and go talk to Hamilton ourselves?"

"Why not?" said Julio. "He's a smart man, we all know that. And we also know he's the one who cut the wings of our former director. I bet he's waiting in his office right now, ready to give the chair to whichever of us walks into his office first."

Beverly, Alex, and Fred exchanged looks and started laughing. Julio followed suit, while Sean just stared at them.

"You know what?" said Beverly, still laughing. "I dare you! Go to Hamilton's office and claim your prize."

"I was thinking that we could go all together," said Julio, still grinning.

"Go where?" said Beverly.

"To Hamilton's office, Beverly," said Julio, rolling his eyes.

"You're the one who's not getting it, you dimwit. Go where?"

"His office in the—" said Julio, and it finally dawned on him. "You mean to tell me he doesn't have an office?"

"Of course he does," said Alex. "It's just that nobody knows where it is."

"So you made another Strike-Out. Congratulations, girl," said Sandra as Phoenix got on the exercise station next to her. "I'd like to personally thank you for keeping another stinky immigrant off our promised land. And why do you look like you couldn't care less?"

"Because I got into serious trouble for that Strike-Out, that's why. They think I coerced her."

"Who?"

"The assholes at the academy, who else? Now they're on a crusade to sue us for malicious intent, malpractice, defamation, and all kinds of other shit."

"Really? I didn't know."

"Didn't your buddy at the GPSN inform you of the details?"

"No, we just had a chat in the morning after I talked to you. But that was before your interview, I think. So did you do it?"

"Do what?"

"Coerce that immigrant woman?"

"Of course not! What's wrong with you?"

"Hey, calm down, baby," said Sandra in a childish tone. "I didn't mean it like that. Sometimes I need to convince some of my hesitant clients to go to bed with me. From time to time, I get so flirty with them it could qualify as coercion, not with malicious intent or anything."

"I didn't coerce anybody into anything! Got it?"

"Okay, okay, I get the picture. Any news from the murder case?"

"Nope. But I ran into this awful guy who scared the shit out of me. He had a firearm collection on his wall, believe it or not."

"Don't tell me he threatened you with one of those things."

"No, he didn't. But he made some vulgar remarks about being explosive and deadly like them."

Sandra stopped pedaling and started laughing.

"What's so funny?"

"The poor idiot was flirting with you, you cunt, couldn't you tell? It's fashionable to be *explosive and deadly* among artist circles of the city nowadays. It's all a part of their role-playing act. Is this the same artist guy you asked about before?"

"Yeah. Not sure about any role playing, this guy definitely had something wrong. Besides, by looking at the crap he called art, I would hardly call him an artist," said Phoenix and shivered by a sudden chill.

"Are you okay?" said Sandra and stopped pedaling. She lifted Phoenix's chin up. "You look all pale and shaky. Why don't we sit down for a bit." She took Phoenix by the arm and helped her sit down on one of the couches in the relaxation area. Then she went and got some water. "Drink some. I don't want you to dehydrate. And if you want to cancel your date with the marine tonight and go rest, I'm sure he'll understand."

"I'll be okay," said Phoenix, sipping the water. "I don't wanna go home."

"Nightmares?"

"I had one during the day today. I fainted for a few minutes, and it caught me even there."

"Oh, poor baby," said Sandra and gave her a hug. "I think you need to see a doctor."

"I don't think so. Those doctors tried to figure out what to do with my nightmares all my life and tried all kinds of shit and experimental treatments on me. I'm not gonna let anyone mess with my mind again."

"We may really need to do something, Beverly."

"C'mon, don't tell me you think like that whiny weasel. You're one of boss's most trusted guys. You can't betray her like this."

"I'd be the last person to betray her, and you know that. But it appears to even me that she has no control over the situation. I've never seen her so handicapped."

"Yeah, she appeared confused, and that was a first to see her like that. But isn't she allowed to have any moments of weakness? I'm sure she'll rebound quickly. Besides, what can we do?"

"Do you remember my last day as acting director?" said Alex, raising his eyebrows.

"Of course I do. You had a—" Beverly's eyes moved away from Alex for a few moments, then she turned to him, her eyes wide open. "Oh, my God! What did he tell you in that meeting?"

"He told me that I should step up, if the situation required it in the future. Do you think this would qualify as a crisis situation?"

"It sure would. But for doing what?"

"Act in her place, *in loco* director, temporarily, of course."

"He actually used those exact words?"

"Yes, he did," nodded Alex. "Moreover, he said this crisis situation would have to do with the academy, in which the director would appear to be losing control. If this ever happened, I was supposed to step up and smooth things over until the conflict was settled."

"You're kidding me, right?"

"Again, his exact words," said Alex, with wide eyes. "You know what else? He told me to talk to you, when the crisis hit, about how to step up."

"No shit! You're—you're shitting me, right? It doesn't make any sense!"

"My sentiments exactly, and, no, I'm not shitting you."

"Why didn't you tell me any of this before?"

"Because he instructed me not to talk to anyone about it until a real crisis struck. I never thought about this conversation all these years, just thinking that it was some kind of, how you call, a pep talk. I suddenly remembered it after Phoenix's first interview and got a bit confused as to whether it would qualify as a crisis or not."

"And you decided that it didn't?"

"I decided to wait. That's why I was so insistent with Phoenix to learn all the details about the Arab girl—I mean woman. I didn't want the tension to rise between us and the academy."

"Why would you care?" said Beverly, with a grin. "If the boss messes up something, you're the natural successor, you know."

"I know that," said Alex, looking down at his lap. "But, I don't want it. I don't want all that pressure and responsibility. I can't deal with all those corporate games." His voice trailed away.

"I understand," said Beverly, reaching out with a touch on his shoulder. "I guess you had no doubts about the crisis following this morning's interview."

"All that I feared was happening," nodded Alex. "And I just didn't know what to do, what to say, how to act. So I decided to stay in the background and let the likes of you and Julio hash things out."

"What are you, or we, supposed to do, anyway? I mean, what does stepping up constitute here, exactly?"

"I don't know," said Alex with a shrug. "I haven't the slightest clue, Beverly. He didn't mention anything about it."

"But none of this actually makes any sense. I mean, how could he know? Just how on earth anyone could predict that we'd have a crisis with the goddamn IAW from three years before? It's not like he's a fortune teller or anything."

"He's not a fortune teller, but you know his nickname."

"Unless—"

"Unless what?"

"Wait a minute, wait just a minute," said Beverly, with a broad smile splitting her face as if she had just made a great discovery. "Of course, he's no goddamn fortune teller. There could be just one explanation to all this."

Osmund Ledyard Hamilton stretched in his chair as the hologram appeared across the simple long meeting table, displaying a man in his sixties with a long tunic with twenty different shades of pink, all blending into each other, successfully covering his big belly. He had a big fat head and small porcine blue eyes, his sparse eyebrows unable to prevent the sweat accumulating on his large forehead from leaking into his eyes, and because of that he kept wiping his forehead with a pink handkerchief. He was seated at the end of a very long ornamented table, revealing an amazing sea view from high above in the background, making a stark contrast with the simple table and a windowless dark room on Hamilton's end.

"Good morning, Bill."

"And good morning to you, wherever the hell you are, Osmund."

"Good evening would suffice. Now, tell me, did you and your board consider my offer?"

"We did," said the other man and cackled. "And I have to tell you, I think we have a dilemma here. Your offer doesn't seem to validate the fact that you're in a pretty tight corner with that incident of yours."

"Are you suggesting that my offer isn't fair?"

"Not at all. Considering the fact that we've been losing market share for some time, I'd say it's even generous."

"Then what's the problem?"

"The problem is that it's yesterday's news," said the other man, wiping his forehead. "Now the conditions are different, the paradigm has shifted to our advantage. We're looking at a potential lawsuit that could be disastrous to GPSN's image, and we think that's definitely worth an additional premium."

"Really? So you don't consider my offer of three twenty-two a share good enough anymore?"

"C'mon, Osmund," the man said, with a grin. "That would make the Immigration Academies Worldwide worth only a hundred billion. And that valuation is also yesterday's news. If you want to buy out IAW, you need to shift your paradigm first."

"Before I shift my *paradigm*," said Hamilton, with a stony face, "may I also remind you that IAW comes with an accumulated debt of around forty billion, five of which is payable within the next year?"

The other man let out another cackle and wagged his finger at Hamilton like a teacher commending his pupil. "You did your homework with your numbers, didn't you? And you've been purchasing our debt for some time now. Yes, we have some payments short term, but nothing we cannot refinance, now that we'll be receiving a lot of cash from you to settle today's news."

"And how much do you think this *news* is worth?"

"I'd say it's worth eleven figures, at least. But it would be too premature to guess if the number would start with a one, or a nine, or something in between." He started coughing. Hamilton could hear the whistle from his lungs every time he inhaled. "You know, I admire you, Osmund. You've been trying to take over my company for some time now, for more than a year to my knowledge."

"Nearly three, actually."

"Is that right? Whatever. You manipulated our stock price, bought it in chunks through intermediaries, bought our debt from creditors, and you almost succeeded in convincing me to sell by using conventional, and sometimes unconventional, means. Yet your entire plot has flopped because one of your insignificant employees made an insignificant judgment error, and now we're sitting at the same table, but with roles reversed. And you still manage to keep an expressionless face. How do you do it? Is it some facial treatment? Or perhaps a secret formula from ancient Chinese medicine that modern science ignores, which you may have run into during your years in Hong Kong? I've been meaning to ask you for years, actually. I've always been open to such things, you know, and I could certainly use it for my poker game."

"It's not a treatment, Bill. I was born with it, I'm afraid. I wish I could have an expression on my face, but I can't."

"That's too bad," said the other man. "But I have some great news for you: I think you will finally see some kind of expression in the mirror on Friday. And the level of sadness will be factored between numbers one and nine. What do you think?"

"I raise my offer to three-fifty."

"Now that's what I call a good player," said the man, pointing at Hamilton with both hands. "Raise the stakes when in trouble. But throwing in a few more billions won't help you, Osmund. You're going down."

"My final offer is four: Forty dollars per share. It would raise the value of your company to about hundred and thirty, nearly forty billion more than it's worth, but I'm willing to pay for that difference. This price would make everyone happy, shareholders and creditors alike. With the additional cash I'll infuse, the company could rapidly move from red to black and become profitable within two years. I would also give you a nine-figure retirement bonus, so you can pay for all your gambling debts, some of which are also owned by me."

"Whoa, I can't believe that the great Osmund Hamilton is down on his knees, begging for mercy. But I won't give you any mercy, you fucking scavenger! Do you think I'll forgive you for attempting to twist my arm with my personal debt? Never!"

"It was nothing personal, just business. I've been a creditor of yours for a long time, Bill. But you seem to be clouding the issue. Now, I've made you a final offer. Don't you need to discuss this with your board?"

"I don't need to consult my board about anything," said the man, sweat pouring out from his face. "You're going down, and I'll tear apart your company's reputation with it."

"You're not acting in a businesslike manner, but then again that's your board's problem, not mine. Are they aware that your rehab didn't work?"

"Don't you dare! Don't you dare bring my rehab into this. I'm fully detoxed."

"You certainly don't act like it. Any other man in your position would seriously consider my offer."

"Any other man with my intellect would do exactly what I do. I'm gonna bury you, you son of a bitch!"

"You have until noon GMT tomorrow to decide about my final offer. By the way, did you manage to convince Derek to show on Friday as our watchdog? I heard that he's not feeling well."

"No, he's not, thanks to you. But I have someone even better."

"Don't tell me it's Simon."

"Actually, it *is* Simon. He said he'd happily do it for us, in return for a large donation to his cause, of course."

"Of course," nodded Hamilton. "But what's a hundred million, compared to the tens of billions you're planning to get from me?"

"That's exactly my point! And I told them to give him whatever he wants, it's worth it. We need the opinion of the foremost expert in the whole damn world in order to bring the mighty GPSN down."

"Of course you need it. Please try to disregard your personal distaste for me and consider my final offer until noon tomorrow. Hamilton out."

Hamilton ended the transmission before permitting himself a brief faint smile. *Once a gambler, always a gambler,* he thought.

"So tell me, what made you think that I'd want to see you again?"

"I didn't think you would, but I'm glad you did."

"Why's that?"

"Because everything you told me was right and shook me up a bit. We're taught not to respect anyone other than our code and our superior officers, you know? And you somehow managed to grab my respect, without even raising your voice."

Phoenix winced and raised her eyebrows. Following her failed attempt to exercise at the gym, she had gone home and dressed in her purple evening tunic with a color gradient from aubergine at the bottom to lilac at the top, accompanied by aubergine stockings and shoes. She looked stunning but felt overdressed next to the marine, since he was as causal as it could get with jeans and a denim shirt.

"Is that right?" she said in feigned disappointment. "And I thought that it was my eyes, all this time."

"You have amazing eyes, I'll give you that. They're a little intimidating, even. But it wasn't them."

"So now you wanna bed me with a little respect on the side? Is that it?"

"Actually, I didn't even think about that. I didn't know what to expect from this encounter."

"Well, it looks like we'll need to come up with some small talk, then. Tell me, what are your duties at the base? Patrolling the border?"

"Mostly. It's all quiet along the Eastern front."

"Sweet," nodded Phoenix. "What about threats?"

"Who can challenge the mighty Union army? Seriously, from a military point of view, the rogue states are weaker than ever."

"Does that mean our border is secure and sealed?"

"Of course. Wanna know how this two and a half thousand kilometers, from the Black Sea all the way to the Baltic Sea, is protected?"

"Enlighten me."

"We used to have barbed wire, walls, and similar physical barriers to prevent illegal crossings. But those were very expensive to install and maintain, and they did not provide enough security, because people started digging tunnels underneath. Then the GPSN adopted the comprehensive approach for border security a decade ago…"

Phoenix listened to the marine as he went on explaining border protection strategies. "You make it sound like our borders are airtight, with no leaks."

"They are. Not even a sparrow can cross them without us noticing it first."

"Then how do you explain all the smuggling?"

"That's your fuckup, not ours. If you guys can't tell the difference between a legal trade activity and an illegal one, what can we do?"

"Yeah, right. As if bribery and corruption is unheard of."

He didn't appear like he was playing a game, or else he was the best actor out there. Her curiosity was already satisfied; it was time to move on. But go where? She had no appetite to go home. A third option suddenly occurred to her. "I think I had enough of this place. How about moving on?"

"Are you asking me to come to your place?"

"I don't know what Sandra told you, but my place is no good to anyone, including me. I'm inviting you to a place where guys love to hang out."

CHAPTER 20

"Excuse me. Is this the entrance to the Stardust?"

The club was located at one of the far corners of the Pyramid with no sign at the door, just a tall man in a classical black tuxedo standing there. When she proposed to check out the famed club together, the marine had turned a sour face and excused himself.

"Yes, ma'am," answered the man, and opened the door for her. "Please."

Phoenix walked inside and passed through a dim hallway leading to wooden double doors, which gave way to a classically decorated room with maroon-colored wood dominating the scene. The main floor included twenty or so round half-empty maroon tables, illuminated by hidden lights. The only other female patron was sitting at one of the dimly lit private tables on a higher ledge along the wall in a formal evening dress. The walls were partitioned with alcoves a few meters apart, and every alcove was ornamented with a classical marble statue of a naked woman. The long wooden classical bar on the right side was something one could only see in Holovision shows.

She walked slowly down the steps to the main floor as she covertly observed her surroundings, receiving brief attention from the scattered male patrons, all in light formal or formal postmodern tunics of different colors and shades. They didn't pay much attention to her and minded their own business; just a couple gave her short stares. It was time to get on with business, and the idle bartender appeared to be the perfect man to start.

"Hello, I'm Phoenix Wallis, a senior agent from GPSN."

A black goatee dominated the bartender's face, along with a receding hairline and eyes that radiated tranquility. He was in a black traditional tuxedo just like the rest of the staff. "My name is Fabian, and I'm pleased to welcome you to the Stardust. Would you like a refreshing cocktail?"

"No, not right now. I'm here in an official capacity. Do you know man by the name of Vassily Bogdanov?"

"Of course," said Fabian and smiled. "He's a recent patron, but he quickly became one of my regulars here. Although, I haven't seen him lately."

"I regret to inform you that you won't be seeing him again. He was murdered in Russia."

"Murdered in a rogue state?" he said and remained speechless for a few seconds. "But, how?"

"When did you last see him?"

"Probably some evening last week. I don't know for sure; the days all run into each other. I still can't believe he's dead."

"How often did he frequent this place?"

"He was here almost every night until last week, I suppose."

"You'd consider him a good customer?"

"Definitely," said Fabian with an emphatic little nod. "He was a new customer, but a very loyal one while it lasted."

"Did you engage in any conversation with him that last night he was here?"

"Sure, Mr. Bogdanov was a very talkative man. He was a man with a lot of connections."

"What do you mean by connections?"

"He would be at a different table each night and simply clicked with everybody, even with our most reserved clients here. The man made friends like bees make honey."

"And which social group do your clients usually belong to here?"

"They are almost exclusively Devotees," said Fabian, with an air of pride. "*La crème de la crème* of our Union."

"That's interesting. Did you know Bogdanov's HDI?"

"Of course."

"Can you explain me how a Disciple with an HDI of only seventy could afford your club, then?"

Fabian let out a polite laugh. "A good one, Agent Wallis, I like your sense of humor. But I know for a fact that his HDI was eighty."

"Hamilton knew it all beforehand," said Beverly with a mischievous smile. "Because he planned it all, that ruthless cocksucker, and we were supposed to figure this out together. That's probably why he asked you to talk to me, predicting that you would hesitate and only together we'd manage to figure it all out."

"Huh," said Alex and exhaled. "Only someone like him would dare to conceive such an outrageous and far-reaching plan. I mean, what if one of us had resigned or moved on?"

"Hey, I've been working here since graduation from college, twelve years and counting, and you've been here for nearly twenty. We're as loyal as it gets, buddy, and I bet he could smell it from miles away."

"But, how can you be so sure about this?"

"It's the only plausible explanation. Otherwise we'd need to assume that he'd invented some damn time machine or something."

"I suppose. But we still don't know what his plan is. And how can I, or we, step up, if we don't know what he's up to next?"

"I think we're just meant to figure out that *there is a plan*, which the director's unaware of and meant to stay unaware of. And we're meant to keep the lid on the pot in the meantime."

"Excuse me?"

"Meaning, we're supposed to keep things under control in absence of boss's ability to manage. I think you're supposed to keep things smooth with the academy, easy enough with the head-bitch's adoration for you, and I'm supposed to keep our guys under control, and not allow them to do anything stupid behind the boss's back that would jeopardize Hamilton's plan."

"Huh! So that's it?" said Alex, his face souring. "We do nothing?"

"We retain control in the field office by preventing panicky boneheads like Fred and opportunistic assholes like Julio from doing stupid shit. That's far from doing nothing, if you ask me."

"Perhaps. But how could he know that we wouldn't try to manipulate the situation to our advantage?"

"How can we? It's not like we have any clues about what he's up to. All we can do is to sit tight until his winning plan unfolds."

"True enough."

"I still can't believe how this guy's mind works," said Beverly shaking her head and smiling. "Osmund Ledyard Hamilton, some truly smart bastard he is, and I'm glad that he's on our side."

"No wonder they called him The Wizard of Oz!"

"Do I look like I'm trying to be funny?" said Phoenix, folding her arms. "And how do you happen to know *for a fact* that his HDI was eighty?"

Fabian's polite smile faded quickly, giving way to uneasiness. "You—you wouldn't happen to be coming from my guild and testing my HDI-guessing skills now, would you?"

"Nope, I'm coming from the field office, and you heard me right the first time: The number is *seventy*."

"It wasn't a joke?"

Phoenix shook her head.

"I've been a bartender for twenty years. I know how to tell a Devotee from a Disciple. His HDI had to be seventy-nine, if not eighty." He paused for a few seconds and stroked his beard. "I'll be damned. He sure had me fooled. But how do you explain his comfortable manners with all these Devotees? They don't tend to let you in their circle unless you're one of them."

"Your guess is as good as mine," shrugged Phoenix. "Did he ever mention anything about his past?"

"No. Come to think of it, the subject never came up."

"And you never thought to ask?"

"Agent Wallis, it's not my business to ask my clients personal questions like that. I'm here only to listen and to make comments about the things *they* choose to share with me."

"In that case, you're probably not aware that he was a recent immigrant."

"He was a recent immigrant?" said Fabian and raised his eyebrows. "No, I had no idea. Where from, Russia?"

"Yep. You mean to tell me your twenty-year experience told you nothing about his recent citizenship?"

"He had a heavy accent, but that's normal for an Eastern European around his age. English was his second language, just like me. Some people just don't have the ear to develop a better accent."

"English is your second language? But you speak with a perfect Union accent."

"Thank you for the compliment," said Fabian, nodding politely. "Actually, I was born and raised here in Adrianopolis."

"Were you here during the Bloodbath?"

"Yes," said Fabian and looked away. "I'm surprised you know about that savage riot, which took place such a long time ago."

Phoenix's mind was already elsewhere, diving into her fragmented memories of the Bloodbath, along with flashbacks from her nightmares. "Thirty-one years ago, to be exact," she muttered. "I was only three."

"You were here, too?"

"Lost my entire biological family and was abandoned on the streets."

"I'm really sorry to hear that. I guess we are both scarred for life. How did you survive on the streets in the cold of winter? Can you recall?"

"I can't recall much," she said, with a sudden chill in her spine. "I was found on the streets, half-dead from hypothermia."

"Well, at least we were lucky enough to survive all that," said Fabian, dropping his eyes. "Many of the people I knew from my youth did not."

"So, how about you? How did you survive?"

"I was in my late teens. My bio-family took me to the hills surrounding the city. We spent the entire winter there until the Union army arrived and put a stop to all the atrocities. We barely survived the harsh winter."

"Anyone who survived that carnage owes their life to the Union army," said Phoenix with glistening eyes.

"We have a leadership crisis, and I can't just sit by idly and do nothing, babe!"

Sean lay in bed with Julio, desperate to receive some after-sex tenderness, as she didn't feel comfortable in his pleasure chamber. With a king-sized bed with black satin sheets, a few pieces of black furniture, and scarlet walls, it reminded her of Bogdanov's bedroom with only the colors reversed. Julio was too intertwined with his own self, watching himself again and again in the continental ad he had made, one of those world-famous ZAP commercials of male and female peace agents having sex, projected over the bed. It was such a blessing to be able to have sex with this hidden gem of commercial acting who had shared bed with the world-famous Holly Love. And him being so modest about it and asking her not to reveal it to anyone told her that there was much more to Julio than met the eye, scattering any cloud of distrust about him. "What are you going to do?" she said, gently rubbing his chest.

"Wait until noon tomorrow, first."

"What happens at noon tomorrow?"

"Ah, nothing, babe. Just to wait and see until things start simmering a bit in the field office and the corporate and all. So, what did you think of the meeting?"

"I think Beverly and Fred acted panicky, and Alex was totally confused. You were the only one who was calm and controlled. I leaked the contents of the meeting to some of the other juniors like you asked me, and they agreed that you're the only one with leadership abilities in the director's absence."

"Of course, I'm the only one who can steer us smoothly through this mess that Nix got us into. I knew that ol' bag would crack under pressure. Actually, she managed to surprise even me with her impotency. She's just like a freakin' ol' deer in the dark, staring at the lights of a truck coming at her full speed."

"Do you think she had a say in this corporate policy of sacrificing Phoenix?"

"Puh, don't be fooled by her roaring when she's with us. I know what a scared little mouse she becomes when dealing with the corporate. I wish I could be there, instead of that old bag, in that meeting with Hamilton and all. I'd show that Wizard his place, you know. I'd say '*Yeah, Oz, I know that Nix's a douche bag, but she's* my *douche bag, and I'll deal with her because I want to, not because some academy prick told me to.*'"

"You're so brave," smiled Sean. "If only Hamilton knew what kind of a man you are, I bet he'd be so impressed by your restraint and hidden talents, especially if he knew about your acting career."

"Don't you dare," said Julio, with a rare flash of anger. "I told you, this is a secret. I don't want some assholes from field office or corporate to block my career path just because they're jealous of my sexiness."

The ad was Julio's biggest asset and secret. This geek from the Network Center had told him about this secret magic software that could replace actors in a Holo-film and had agreed to replace an actor with Julio's biometrics in Julio's favorite commercial. In return he'd needed to introduce him to some of the babes from his artist circles, but it had been worth it. Now all he had to do was to tell the babes that he was a model and an actor in commercials, and the proof was in his bedroom, and once they watched him having sex with the famed Holly Love in a ZAP commercial, next thing they wanted would be to know how Holly had felt. He'd explain this version was shown only on the American continent and not shared on his social pages due to GPSN Company Rules. *One day*, he thought. One day he'd be doing it, not in the virtual world, but for real, with awesome babes like Holly. But until then, he'd need to entertain himself with the likes of Sean.

"I'm sorry," said Sean, in a whisper, after a long silence. "My lips are sealed, don't worry."

"What? Fine, now I gotta get outta here. I need to meet my artist buddies."

"So, Fabian, did you know Bogdanov was going to Russia by any chance?"

"No, Agent Wallis. He never mentioned any travel plans to me. As a matter of fact, he never mentioned Russia at all."

"Did he ever talk about the kind of business he was involved in?"

"I know he owned the Thing Store here at the Pyramid, among other things."

"He said he owned it?" She shook her head and smiled. "Only a supervisor there. Did he ever talk to you about any other business?"

"Why am I not surprised," said Fabian and looked down. "But he did brag about some big moneymaker that had to do with art with some young and not-so-bright partner, some fresh talent he'd discovered."

"Did he happen to mention just how lucrative this business was?"

"Lucrative enough that he never batted an eyelid at the tabs he ran up here. He'd order for several tables at a time and tipped extraordinarily well."

"So he brought or met his friends here?"

"Yes, of course," nodded Fabian. "He met many friends here."

"Such as who? Can you tell me some names?"

"I wouldn't know where to start," said Fabian, scratching his head. "At least half of the crowd here seemed to be buddies with him. The man was never alone, Agent Wallis. He will be missed here."

"Did he ever bring company with him? Some female friends, perhaps?"

"Come to think of it, he did on a few occasions. Some men. They appeared to be some affluent old friends of his."

"Can you remember any of their names?"

"I can remember just one, right now. His name is Mr. Mancheek. I'm not very good with names, you see."

"Then how come you remember this one?"

"Because he's here," said Fabian, nodding across the room to the table with the female patron. "Sitting at the table over there."

The woman and Mancheek were chatting, but it wasn't possible to tell the mood due to the dim lighting. Phoenix tried to observe as discreetly as possible, yet the woman noticed her, turned, and gazed back. She couldn't see her eyes yet in the dark, but she could feel a little chill trickling down her spine.

The woman turned to Mancheek and whispered something. They both stood up, and she graciously walked down the few steps that separated the ledge from the main floor then cut through the main floor towards Phoenix. She wore a long dress with a deep cut, in celadon green, which came with a halter-neck top and a plunging neckline, enhancing rather than covering a pair of equally toned and flawless breasts and fully exposing the curves of her body. Her bearing was proud and regal, and she radiated an aura like some kind of ancient Egyptian goddess. The light murmur in the room hushed as she walked, and all heads turned towards her, following her graceful movements with baited breath. Her long platinum-blonde hair was arranged in a stylish knot, which was decorated with a thin metallic headpiece with a huge emerald right above her large forehead. Her full lips were slicked with some kind of clear glossy lip moisturizer, enhancing its natural red. She didn't appear to wear anything other than mascara on her eyes. She didn't need to, because her eyes were huge and green, an emerald shade that Phoenix had never seen before. They were totally hypnotic, and Phoenix couldn't take her eyes off her, despite the intimidation they radiated.

As the woman slowly approached, Phoenix felt as if her heart was about to explode, her ears were burning, and a twisting pain was in her stomach. She reached Phoenix in a few seconds—which felt like hours—then leaned over as if she was about to say something, but changed her mind at the last moment and walked past, her eyes still locked on Phoenix's until that last instance that her neck couldn't turn anymore. She kept on walking towards the door next to the bar, and the security professional opened the door for her and then closed it following her exit. The moment she exited the room, the usual murmur and background noise resumed louder than before. Her nervousness and nausea vanished as soon as the door closed, but now she was subjected to the hostile glare of almost the entire clientele, and Bogdanov's friend was already gone. She turned her back on them to avoid the stares.

"Who was that woman?"

"That was our most famed dancer, the fabulous Mata Hari."

"Mata Hari? No way!"

"I suppose you heard the name before, Agent Wallis."

"I have. But I didn't envision anyone like this."

"Enrapturing, isn't she? That's how our clientele feel when they meet Mata Hari."

"You told me that the clients here were predominantly Devotees. I don't think those people would be enraptured by anyone at first sight."

"You might change your mind about that after seeing Mata Hari in action," said Fabian with a broad smile.

"So was Bogdanov also enraptured by Mata Hari?"

"Absolutely."

"Would you say that she was the primary reason for him to frequent this club?"

"Perhaps one of the main reasons but not the only one. There is also me and my cocktails, of course, and I think he was also taking care of some business here, too."

"How could you tell he was doing business here? Did he tell you that?"

"No, he didn't, just call it bartender intuition. I suspect that he was taking care of many business deals right here at the club while he was socializing. So hard to believe his HDI to be a mere seventy."

"Was Mata Hari aware of Mr. Bogdanov's infatuation with her?"

"Of course. Even when she's dancing, Mata Hari is very aware of what's happening around her. And to retain clients' affection, she visits clients' tables from time to time and scatters a few crumbs of attention here and there, so that no one feels totally neglected."

"What does she exactly do at the tables? A lap dance or something?"

"A lap dance?" said Fabian and cackled. "Mata Hari's far too sophisticated to perform such a vulgar act, although I'm sure none of the clients would mind it. She's a master people handler, Agent Wallis. When she sits at a table, she can steer the conversation in such a way that all the men around her are transformed into obedient and shy twelve-year-olds."

"Did you ever see Bogdanov with other women here?"

"Come to think of it, I didn't. But then again, we don't get to see many women in this club, anyway. The club doesn't offer much for their liking."

"But your club is full of men, Fabian. Why wouldn't women find anything for their liking here?"

"Our Devotee regulars have been around the block and seen it all, Agent Wallis. Sometimes women come here in groups and try in vain to attract the attention of the men. On top of that, when they see one of the dance shows, they feel a little intimidated. Then they leave and never come back."

"If this is the case, how can you explain your clientele's undivided interest in Mata Hari?"

"I simply can't," said Fabian, throwing up his hands, "I don't think they can either, which intrigues them even more."

"You've said that Bogdanov could buddy up with anyone here. How did he do it? What did he talk about?"

"He joked around a lot. Many times he'd exaggerate his sexual encounters. All his stories made everyone roar with laughter."

"I wonder if his female friends would have been laughing. It isn't exactly politically correct behavior to ridicule others in public, is it?"

"I suppose not," nodded Fabian. "But you seem to know nothing about typical Devotee behavior behind closed doors. They are far from being the conformists that most people imagine them to be. They can become a rowdy bunch when they get together. And if they happen to be in a good mood, anything goes."

Phoenix turned around and checked to see if the clients were still giving her mean stares. Most appeared to be minding their own business, but a few were still sending hostile vibes. "Is it my imagination, or are these people fantasizing about my violent demise?"

"It's because Mata Hari gave the impression that she didn't like you. And if there's someone on the club floor she has taken a dislike to, she won't visit any tables."

"And that's gonna put me on what? The most hated list or something?"

"When Mata Hari doesn't visit tables, we receive many complaints. And based on those complaints, we sometimes end up blacklisting certain clients."

"She comes and goes as she likes, she has no management responsibilities, I'm sure she makes lots of money, she has all these affluent men drooling over her, and moreover, she can pick or reject clients," said Phoenix and sighed. "That's what I call a dream job."

"Mata Hari was exquisite," said Tess. "I can tell you that just a handful of women in my database can look that good."

Phoenix took a sip from her drink and sat on her sofa, trying to unwind with Tess after all the events of the day. "How can you tell what's beautiful?"

"First I form a database of beauty by observing others' reactions to what they consider beauty. Then, I categorize according to intensity of reactions, demographics, and other factors. The reactions I'd look for in men would be adoration, infatuation, and similar. In women, surprise, jealousy, sometimes even contempt."

"Seriously? I didn't think we could be that mean to our own kind."

"You'd be surprised. The concept of sisterhood among women appears to be dead in the postmodern times. By the way, how did your date go?"

"It was fine. I don't have much time for men in my life right now. It's already complex and busy enough as it is."

"I thought dates were about relaxation, fun, and physical gratification. It appears like this isn't the case for you."

"No, it isn't. I happen to be one of those old-fashioned women who look for more than just physical pleasure in a relationship or partnership. And don't tell me that I'm the only one in your data set."

Tess's pupils moved rapidly. "No, you're not," she said after a pause. "But almost all of the other ones appear to be what you'd call hopeless romantics waiting for the perfect mate." Her pupils kept on moving for a few more seconds then she looked up at Phoenix. "There are just sixty-three more women who share your ideas regarding sexual partnership with males."

"Are you sure the others aren't lying?"

"Well, I can't be 100 percent positive about that, but I'd have to say that I'm a pretty good lie detector," said Tess and winked.

"Are you as good as the expert computers we have at GPSN?"

"Perhaps more so: I provide their expert data sets."

"Whoa!" said Phoenix with a broad smile. "I had no idea. And all the better for my little project. Now I think it's time that I let you go, Tess. I have a date with my subconscious."

"Where is Daddy, Mummy?"

"He'll be with us shortly, sweetness," says Mummy with a heartwarming smile.

Mummy is very pretty. She has beautiful gray eyes and braided dark blonde hair. The little girl smiles back at her. She tries to ignore the booms and the rat-tattats coming from outside. But her little heart jumps every time she hears them. Mummy is busy, running around the house, trying to pack, and she looks outside the window. Almost dark outside.

"Come here, sweetness," she calls the little girl. "Would you like to wear your red outfit, or blue?"

"Is it cold outside?"

"Very cold, sweetness."

"Blue." The little girl likes the red outfit, but it makes her tummy cold.

"Then Ilona can have the red one." Mummy tries to smile at her, but the little girl knows that Mummy is sad. Perhaps she has a headache?

"Why are we going out to the cold, Mummy? Are we going to Sandy's?"

Mummy looks grim for a moment, then smiles again. "No, sweetness," she says and looks away. "Sandy and his family are gone. But you can play with Ilona, when she's better."

The little girl likes Sandy. Sandy is bigger than her, and Sandy makes her laugh. But Ilona is sick, and she lies inside. She goes next to her. Ilona is still sleeping, and she is warm to the touch. She goes and picks herself a few toys and dolls. She can play with these wherever they go. She wonders where Ilona's mummy and daddy are. She remembers Daddy bringing Ilona in, Mummy hugging her and crying.

"C'mon, sweetness," calls Mummy. "We'll need to leave soon."

"Daddy? Isn't he coming with us?"

"He'll meet us where we're going. Now let me help you with your outfit."

The booms are louder now, and there are more rattattats. The little girl tries to fit her toys and dolls in her little backpack. Mummy comes with Ilona and gently puts her on the couch, kneels down next to her.

"I want you to help me like a big girl. Can you do that for me?"

"Can I carry my backpack?"

"You can, sweetness. But I need to put other things in your backpack, not toys or dolls, is that okay?"

"Okay," says the little girl with sunken shoulders.

"It's very important that we have some food and water in your backpack. I'll put some baby carrots and some boiled potatoes, and you can munch on them when you feel hungry. And some water, too."

Mummy takes the sleeping Ilona on one arm and takes the little girl's hand with the other. The street is already dark, and the booms *and* rattattats *are even louder. The little girl coughs and gags with the bad smell. They quickly walk past hot burning cars. They hear screams and a big loud* boom. *Mummy shrieks and starts running. The* booms *are getting closer. The little girl has a hard time keeping up with Mummy. As they run past a stinking black car, Mummy trips and falls. She gets on her knees, picks Ilona back up on her shoulder. They hear a loud whistle coming. Maybe it's a train? Mummy looks up and turns to the little girl, reaches out to her hand, and screams:*

"Aishling!"

The little girl wakes up on the ground. The ground is cold. Her tummy is cold. She is still holding her Mummy's hand, but her hand is very cold, too. She turns to look at Mummy, but she can't see her. Her hand is here, but where is she?

She gets up looking for Mummy, but it's very dark and quiet. She walks, still holding her hand. She is cold, very cold. She doesn't know what to do, where to go. She starts crying and calling for Mummy. She feels very hungry, puts her arm gently on the ground. Takes her little backpack off, barely manages to open its zipper, and takes a little carrot out and drinks a little water from her little bottle. The wind is cold. She takes her pack, and Mummy's arm, and walks down some steps, very tired. She wants to sleep, but something inside her tells not to. Sleep is bad. She shouldn't sleep.

The sky lights up, just a little bit. The booms *start again. She stays down on the steps, sitting next to sleeping people. They don't wake up, but that's okay. The little girl doesn't know them; she is not supposed to talk to them. And they are cold, too. She feels so cold, she starts crying again. She munches on some more carrots and drinks a little more water. She takes Mummy's arm and walks a little, looking for her. But there is so much cold wind, she cannot walk. She goes back down the steps again and cries. She waits in the cold, hoping Mummy will find her. And feels like sleeping again. But the voice inside says* no. *She will not sleep. What if it's Mummy's voice? Perhaps she is talking to her. She looks at Mummy's hand. But a hand cannot talk, can it?*

The little girl doesn't know how many days it has been. But she has no water and no food left. Her tummy hurts with cold and hunger. She cannot feel her hands any more, and her feet are numb. She starts whimpering and shaking uncontrollably. The pain is unbearable for her little body. The cold is everywhere and unending. She starts sobbing with the last remains of energy left in her body and hugs Mummy's arm with her numb little hands.

"I don't want to be cold anymore, Mummy, please, I don't want to be cold."

Then she sees a light appear before her. It's a little butterfly made of light, flitting its wings. Perhaps it's an angel. But can angels be this little? She's little, why can't the angels be little? The little butterfly tells her not to fear anymore, but it doesn't speak. The little girl doesn't understand how, but answers anyway.

"Okay," she says and feels warmth inside, starting from her tummy. The warmth spreads to her entire body. Can I sleep now? *she asks in her head.*

Yes, you can. Don't worry, little girl, I'm here to stay with you, *says the little butterfly and passes inside the little girl. She feels safe and warm for the first time since Mummy was gone, and she wants to sleep, holding onto her arm. She feels some people around her, trying to wake her up.*

"Wake up, little one," says a man, as if his voice comes from the bottom of a well. "She's still breathing! Get some body-warmers, quick!"

But she doesn't want to wake up. Because she wants to sleep, find her Mummy, and end this nightmare. She ignores people's voices and falls into a deep, deep sleep.

Her nightmare is finally over.

THURSDAY

CHAPTER 21

PHOENIX walked out of the metro station at Omega Ten in a daze after another sleepless night, her nightmares escalating in horror rather than abating. Sleep was fast becoming an unattainable luxury item, and she had no idea how long she could sustain running on empty like this.

She took a deep breath of the fresh brisk morning air, hoping that it would improve her mental activity and alertness. She had gulped down three mugs of black coffee doused with sugar already, but no amount of caffeine had been enough to remove the fatigue and numbness she felt in her mind. It was seriously beginning to inhibit her mental poise, a poise she would desperately need to get herself out of the mess she was in.

Her plausible options were at the extremes. One was to have a career change, as she was sure she wouldn't be able to find any job in the security sector after this. She would definitely need to go back to school and acquire another degree, and that cost money, lots of money she didn't have. Her only viable alternative seemed to be the reverse immigration option, emigrating to one of the rogue states with the hope of coming back with a leap in her HDI. But retaining the HDI, let alone improving it in a rogue state, was not as easy as it sounded. The living conditions were full of health hazards, which could lower the HDI's health component. Moreover, there were psychological factors involved in exposure to a non-scientific and non-economic lifestyle, known as the Rogue State Syndrome, which had the potential to permanently damage one's psyche and make a return impossible. On the plus side, her expertise in security business might come in handy. Still, the thought of leaving as a failure with her tail between her legs didn't appeal to a proud fighter like Phoenix, even if she felt no loyalty to it anymore.

She walked across the stone bridge that separated the little island that the GPSN building was located on from the mainland, idly observing the woods between the bridge and the building in the very early morning hour. The sun had just risen above the mountains to the east and suddenly shed sharp light on the trees. At that moment she saw it: Something dark-colored was wobbling and moving slowly on the ground. A bear, perhaps? She left the stone path and moved towards it. It had stopped moving, but she could see from the up-down movement of it that it was breathing deeply. She edged even closer to see what this animal was, only to realize that it wasn't an animal, but the fat ass of an over-weight academy student in dark uniform. Figuring out that he wasn't invisible after all, he quickly got up and glanced at her. He was partially in the shade of the tree nearby, but he appeared vaguely familiar. She blinked her eyes quickly to make sure that she wasn't dreaming again, and at that instant he took off.

"Hey, you! You're not allowed here. Stop!" She started chasing.

It was when he looked back over his shoulder that she remembered him, the same fat bald guy from the graduation ceremony a few days ago, the one who had embarrassed her by giving her a Cheshire grin and a wave in the middle of the ceremonies. He was sprinting madly with flailing arms, leaning back awkward-ly in order to balance his center of gravity with his fat belly. Racing after him, Phoenix felt a much-needed rush of adrenaline and noticed that there was still quite a bit of energy reserved in her exhausted limbs. The guy dashed towards the iron gates of the old cemetery, reaching it just ahead of her, and whipped round to face her with his mouth agape, eyes popping.

Phoenix leaped to grab him, just as he turned back towards the gate and dived towards it, slipping through the thick bars. Expecting to grab his oversized body, Phoenix overbalanced and fell against the iron gate, banging her head. She fell onto the stone path as she blacked out for the second time in two days.

"You're safe, sweetness."

The little girl opens her eyes with excitement, expecting to see Mummy. But instead, she sees that she is floating in emptiness, flying like that little angel. Does Mummy have wings, too? She turns to see, but it's all dark and all she can see are distant stars, very, very far away. "Mummy? Where are you?"

"I'm one of those stars. And I'm so very far from you that you cannot see me or reach me yet."

"But I want you, Mummy," says the little girl, sobbing. "I miss you."

"I know, sweetness. But you have so much to do now. It will be a long time before you become a star, too."

"But I don't want to be alone."

"You're not alone, sweetness. A part of me is always with you. When you are afraid and confused, just look inside and you'll find me. I'll help you, I'll protect you. I'm inside you, sweetness, and I'm not going anywhere."

The soothing voice of Mummy echoes in the little girl's head. She feels much better now. She has to work hard to become a star, like Mummy.

Suddenly, light fills everywhere.

Phoenix opened her eyes and looked up at the bright sky filled with morning light, trying to stay conscious and understand what had just happened. Her head was aching like hell, so she had definitely hit the grille of the gate. But was the guy ever there? Could this be another dream, or was she chasing ghosts now? She slowly got up and touched her forehead. Her skull appeared intact, but there was plenty of blood in her hand. She wasn't sure how long she had stayed unconscious, but it couldn't have been more than just a few minutes. She looked at the gate before her. The rusty bars were at least three centimeters thick and only twenty centimeters apart. No normal-sized human could have slipped through them, let alone a fat guy like him. The gate was still secured by a big rusty padlock, and there was simply no conveniently obvious explanation as to what might have happened.

She walked back, retracing her path through the grass. There was a large section of crushed tall grass, suggesting a fat human had been lying there after all. Suddenly it felt like a ton of weight had been lifted from her weary shoulders. She called Beverly first. "Good morning."

"Hey, Phoenix, what's up? Did you dream about me or something?"

Suddenly details of her nightmare welled up from her subconscious and flooded her mind. Her mother's sad eyes, the booms and rattattats, her sick friend, their desperate run in the dark streets, burning cars, the explosion, the terror she felt, the atrocities she'd witnessed, her mom's arm, and the cold, that intense, never-ending cold, and the—

"Yo, Phoenix. Are you there?"

"Yes." She cleared her throat. "We have a code three at the field office."

"Wait a sec, you said code *three*, did I hear you right?"

"Yes. An academy student broke into the World Union."

"So, tell me once again," said Beverly. "How did he get away?"

Following the code three, the entire academy and field office had been locked down with metal gates closing all exits leading outside and between the field office and the academy. A fully armed rapid action team had been called to search the west side of the gardens surrounding the old building. After failing to find him there, they had widened the search to the mainland side of the stone bridge and secured the Omega Ten entrance to the metro. It was still quite early in the morning, and the night shifters were still working in the Monitoring Room, not that anyone could leave due to the lockdown.

"I leapt to grab him and hit my head on the gate. Then he disappeared while I was dealing with the pain and everything else."

"Ouch. Guys, don't forget to check which cameras taped the west side of the compound this morning. Harold, you make sure." She turned back to Phoenix. "You're sure he's a student, yeah?"

"I saw this guy at the graduation ceremony."

"No shit! Well, that should make the identification process a piece of cake. Computer: Get your lazy silicone ass to display the images of the graduating students this week. Display images only, in a tile formation." The large monitor was instantly filled with images of hundreds of students' mugshots, but they were so little, it was impossible to see any details. "Computer: Display twenty at a time, dammit. Scroll at Agent Wallis's command."

The screen instantly changed and showed larger mugshots. Phoenix noticed Patel's picture in the top left corner. She scrolled down using her pupils, noticing a beautifully smiling Shakira, until the very end and saw his unmistakable Cheshire grin in the very last picture.

"That's him!"

"Talay Talayman, the bottom of the class, huh? Well, you know what they say: If somebody's at the top, somebody has to be at the bottom."

"Status," said Director Morssen.

"He's nowhere to be found, Boss," said Beverly. "We still don't know how he managed to sneak into our side, either."

"Great! All we needed was another blunder with the academy," said the director then turned to Phoenix. "And *you* somehow manage to keep being in the center of every incident. What were you doing there that early?"

"I—I couldn't sleep, and I thought I would come to the office early."

"So you avoid being at the office during normal working hours and prefer to show up at sunrise? Tell me exactly what happened."

"I came out from the metro station and was walking towards the building. I noticed him crawling in tall grass. He saw me and took off. I chased after him as far as the gates of the old graveyard. I leapt to grab but missed him. I banged up my head and fell on the ground."

"Did you lose consciousness?"

"Briefly, I think, for a few seconds at most."

"Damn it! Can't you just keep yourself free of any incident longer than twenty-four hours? Now they'll claim that we rigged all this."

"Rigged what?"

"This escape, your chase, hitting your head, everything."

"I don't follow, Boss," said Beverly.

"Apparently I'm surrounded by naïve idiots! The academy's security is our responsibility. None of their students could pull what that student did without disabling our security systems somehow. Since there were no alarms ringing anywhere, until Agent Wallis here reported the incident, we'll appear like we engineered this to discredit them and to disable her from the coming interview."

"But why would we do such a thing?" said Beverly. "We already agreed to let Phoenix do another interview; actually, we suggested it ourselves."

"Don't you see? They'll claim that we planned it that way from the very beginning with no intention of getting her to do another interview. And the *coincidence* of her discovering the renegade student, furthermore banging her head with a possible concussion, will be hard to explain. It will totally appear like we designed the whole thing, bribed a loser student, and sneaked him to our side, so that we could discredit their students and excuse Agent Wallis from another interview."

"What if this was an academy plot? What if they have cooked this up, with the help of one of us?" said Phoenix.

Beverly looked at Phoenix in disbelief then turned to the director. "Would they dare to do such a thing, Boss?"

"The guy was last in his class, and was not scheduled for a security interview for another three weeks. I think they told this lazy ass that he didn't have much chance of success, freaked him out, and let him loose on our side with the help of some spy they have inside our ranks. This entire thing appears to be planned amateurishly and in a big rush, which points in one direction only."

"It really doesn't matter, because nobody's going to interpret it that way. To the unbiased eye, we'll appear guilty, and we'll need to remedy it. You hit your head and perhaps got a concussion. We need to make sure that you're fit to perform a security interview and show that to the whole world. I don't want them to later claim that we doctored your concussion. You need to go to the rehab center today and get a clean bill of health."

"You mean a full checkup? But I don't have the time—"

"Not a full checkup, a neurological checkup, and that's an order."

"Yes, Director," nodded Phoenix, chin down.

"And you have to find out how he managed to sneak into our side," she said to Beverly. "Get your guys to check every scrap of video in those databases. There has to be a clue somewhere." She exhaled loudly. "And just when I was thinking things couldn't get any worse."

The Mantis slipped through the door and entered the house with feline grace and lightness. It was child's play to trick a Door Bot into anything if one possessed the right tools. It had thought that the Mantis was there for routine maintenance of the express delivery system and had granted access.

So this was the place that Phoenix considered home, a dull house, lacking any color or character, just like its owner. He glanced at the bathroom first, checking out all the makeup, the cabinets and closets, looking for *it*. He was totally focused in a near trance, as he had to place back every item he picked up with perfect precision. Phoenix had a strong photographic memory, and even if she couldn't consciously tell something was misplaced, her subconscious might, making her more alert or careful than usual.

She had been an emotional wreck, mindlessly blaming events and circumstances for what had been happening to her, thinking that everyone had been plotting against her. Now it was time to unbalance her further and disable her rational thought. She had never been strong emotionally, and achieving her isolation had been relatively easy. But despite her lack of sleep and her confusion over dream and reality, her analytical side was still intact and dangerous. It was time to make her doubt her mind completely.

The Mantis finished searching the bathroom, but it wasn't there. He had already looked for it at her office, and he was sure she didn't keep it there, either. The Mantis didn't blame her for not keeping such a thing at her office, as it wasn't something that anybody would be proud of revealing. But it had to be here, somewhere. Next he went to the kitchen and gently opened the cabinets and drawers, searching. Phoenix was already having a very hard time sleeping. He just needed to nudge it just a little further so that she would start totally losing her REM sleep and her rationality with it. If only he could find it. But it wasn't in the kitchen, either.

His last stop was her bedroom. He touched the bed gently, smelling her faint scent on it. It was a desirable odor, if one were to indulge in such primitive urges like sex. The clothes in her closet were mediocre picks from a certain garment company. She was the kind who would prefer to hide herself in public, but her clothing preferences seemed to conflict with that completely. Either her subconscious wanted her to promote herself more in the public, or she had allowed others, such as a friend or wizard software, to influence her decisions. Either way, it was in line with her profile: a confused and lonely soul.

He found what he had been looking for on the drawer of the bedside nightstand, next to an old digital diary. He opened its cap carefully, emptied the contents and counted them, placing the contents in his little pouch. And from the pouch, he produced items looking exactly like the ones he had just taken out, placing them in the plastic bottle.

"Sweet dreams, little girl," he murmured to himself.

Then he turned his attention to the digital diary, wondering why she would keep such a thing. Surprisingly, it was still being used. He decided to skim through it to see if he could learn more about her inner world. The last log was for Wednesday, and she was talking about her Strike-Out, her encounters at the military area, then how she was messed up after meeting DeVille. The Mantis smiled at this evidence that his plan was working.

Tuesday's entry mentioned the horrors of the nightmare she had on Monday night, various interviews and her reactions to the same, and her new *digital* friend, Tess. Who was this new friend, and where did she come from? Digital meaning someone she met over the Internet? To his astonishment, Monday's only entry consisted of—poetry? Could these be her own words? But that was impossible, she wasn't the type. Perhaps she had seen it somewhere and copied. What other explanation could there be? He read them once more, in an attempt to make some sense out of them.

My soul was like a leaf in the wind,
My love has been scorched and devastated by desert heat,
And my mouth was hungry for your flavor,
My body was numb, until you touched,
And my heart whispered to my conscience over and over,
It will come, and your world will change.

CHAPTER 22

PHOENIX peeled off the taped gauze with a twinge of sharp pain and examined the cut on her forehead in the mirror. It was a vertical cut, starting almost at the edge of her hairline and coming down about half a centimeter in the middle of her forehead. Her head was swollen and throbbing with pain, as she had declined to take any painkillers. Her skin looked desiccated, and no matter how much cream she used all day, nothing seemed to work to replace its moisture and glow. She didn't even glance at her clipped-back hair, which was in desperate need of care.

She kept staring into her green-gray eyes, longing to see a reflection of her soul in the mirror. She needed to understand where her newly discovered instincts had been dragging her and why these instincts had been activated all of a sudden. Could it be all that coffee and chemical swill she had been washing down? What about the nightmares? Could they have anything to do with it, or was it this old and loathsome building, or the Pyramid? What was it? What was activated inside her skull?

Who am I? Why am I me? Why do I have this face, and not another? What do I possess hidden behind these mysterious eyes, so I cannot sleep, so I'm haunted by night terrors? What's hidden in my mind, so terrifying? What's the point of all what's happening to me? What's the point of my life? Is my life significant? Am I meant to suffer?

Can I be happy?

Ever?

My happiness may be waiting to be discovered in the most unexpected of places. And despite my lack of sleep and acute tiredness, I've been thinking more clearly than ever. I'm in a different state of mind, a state of mind that knows no boundaries, has no allegiances, and is determined to find what happiness is meant for me.

Where these thoughts did come from, she didn't know. But now she was more determined than ever to retain her self-respect and not to be pushed or bullied by others, no matter the circumstances brought before her. She splashed her face with cold water a few times and re-taped her forehead. She walked out of the bathroom and saw him, smiling radiantly at her.

"I think what you're wearing belongs to me," she said, smiling back.

"And?" said Beverly, her arms folded.

"I got one for her, I swear," said Fred, fidgeting in his chair. "It's been barely used, I've got it from one of the new recruits. She'd received a brand-new one a few weeks back. I told her that there was a recall for some malfunction in the menu system for this build."

"And she fell for that?" said Beverly and let out a big laugh. "She's gotta be one of those dimwits that hang out with Julio. Fred, you ol' skunk, I knew there was still some gray matter inside that thick skull of yours. See? It wasn't that hard after all."

"I had to lie," said Fred, lowering his eyes.

"Oh, grow up. Hey, what's on your mind? You didn't call me here for an update on Phoenix's PA, did you?"

"Oh, that. I totally forgot about—"

"C'mon, spit it out. Haven't got all day."

"Okay, we may have a pirate code hiding in our network."

"A what?"

"A code used in hacking, you know."

"I know what a pirate code is, Fred. Are you telling me that you detected an unauthorized code roaming in our intranet?"

"No, not yet," grinned Fred. "But I'm gonna find it. I set the trap."

"What trap?" Can you tell me what the heck is going on?"

"Remember the great hack at the NC Research Triangle a few months back?"

"The one that they keep denying ever occurred?"

"That's the one! They have a new theory that there was an infiltration from one of the Tier Three networks on the grid."

"You mean there is a leak in the Global Computing Grid? Which network?"

"I don't know. One of the twenty-five thousand, I guess."

"Needle in a haystack," shrugged Beverly.

"Don't let the Science and Tech bunch's constant denial fool you. Hackers ravaged the NC Research Triangle, and Tier Zero knows it. They might be hiding somewhere under the Swiss Alps, but they follow everything and everyone. Nobody can fool the Zero."

"If there was a rampage like you say, I bet they're scared shitless even in the Zero. You think a gang that can rampage a Tier One facility would just leave it at that?"

"Nobody attacks the Zero, Bev; you know the Swiss are neutral. And they only keep encrypted backups and transactions there, not even real data. Why would a hacker attack the Zero?"

"Because he can?"

"Even so, it's impossible. The Zero knows how to defend itself. Besides, they're on top of the situation. I just received software from them to implement in our network, checking for leaks. Think about it, Bev, of the thirty-seven Tier Three networks in the city, the Zero picked us for a test run!"

"The Zero sent you an anti-spyware?"

"Yes, they did. Tailor-made for our network here. Isn't that incredible?"

"That is pretty unusual. But what does all this have to do with me?"

"C'mon, you're the only one who can understand and appreciate what I do. Alex is my oldest friend here, but you know how inept he is in this kinda stuff. And I don't even wanna mention the boss."

There was a rare spark in Fred's eyes. For an aging network admin like Fred, any artifact from the Mecca of geekdom must have been worth a lifetime's achievement. "You know what? I bet you'll fix all the holes we have in our network with the help of that spyware and make the boss happy for a change."

"Wouldn't that be cool?" said Fred, with a genuine smile. "We could become the only certified leak-proof Tier Three facility in the whole world. I bet there is a reason they sent me this 'ware. I don't think they'd send it to just anyone, you know."

"I'm sure they wouldn't," said Beverly and exhaled. Perhaps the reason this anti-spyware was sent was because of the bad shape their network was in. But she didn't want to ruin Fred's moment of bliss. That honor belonged to the boss. "So where is it? Gimme the new PA. I'll get it to Phoenix."

"Oh, I gave it to Ray. He'll take it to her," said Fred, averting his eyes.

"You gave it to Ray? Ray is the reason she needs a new PA, you moron!"

"I know," said Fred, wiping his wet palms on his pants. "He was just here, trying to clean stuff, and I wanted to kick him out before he messed up something with my computers. He saw it and could tell who it was for. He promised me that he'd take it directly to her office and not damage it."

"Yeah, right! Talk about entrusting your Ego-Shares to a rogue state-r."

"Is that my PA?"

Ray was standing before her and grinning, with a military-grade PA attached to his ear. "It is yours, but it isn't yet."

"Ray, you're speaking in riddles with me, again, and I have neither the energy nor the time for it. Did you nick my PA again, or not?"

"It will be your PA but it isn't until you make it yours," said Ray. "But I still don't understand how you cannot live without this. It doesn't do anything. Hmm, maybe this one is not as harmful as others?" He removed it and gazed at it intently in his frail shaky hands.

"Give it to me," said Phoenix and grabbed it. "You didn't take this from my office?"

"I got it from Fred."

"From Fred? PA: Activate." The little device turned on, and she quickly checked her custom menus. "Where is my old one, then?"

"I don't know," said Ray and shrugged. He turned his back without a word and slowly dragged his feet away with sunken shoulders.

"Hey, wait," said Phoenix, with a sudden rush of compassion. Ray stopped and slowly turned back, as Phoenix reached him. "I forgot to thank you for bringing my PA," she said, gently touching his arm. "This is my new PA, right?"

"So says Fred."

"Do you know why Fred got me a new PA, without me asking for one?"

"I don't know," shrugged Ray. He looked far less animated than before.

"And how come you're on the west wing of the building? I thought the academy administration banned students from entering the field office."

"But my worthless shell drinks from the fountain of life on this side."

"Don't you go to the academy for your classes?"

"They always try to teach me the nothing they know, all these years."

"How long have you been a student here?"

"I don't know. Fifty years?"

"The academy wasn't even here fifty years ago, Ray. How old are you anyway?"

"I am one hundred and fifty years old," said Ray, widening his eyes. "No, no, one thousand five hundred years old. I've been everywhere, endured every pain, in a span of seven days, I lived through the hell on earth. I have seen Siamese twins choking each other, little children dying of starvation, packs of cannibalistic humanoid animals grunting and hunting, infants chewing on their dead mamas' breasts, rats bigger than cats attacking newborns. I have seen it all: pain, hunger, death. I have witnessed humans turning into wild beasts. I'm one thousand five hundred years old, and I am the oldest man on earth!"

Phoenix felt a deep pain inside and sympathy towards this old man. His words were definitely those of a lunatic, but the expression in his eyes was so genuine, it was evident that Ray had lived through a great deal of physical and emotional pain during the Great Meltdown, causing his current state.

"And I know you understand me," he said in a whisper. "You're the only one." Then he turned and walked off, dragging his tired limbs as quickly as possible.

Julio hastily reread the tiny bit of information that was at the very bottom of the document that just got in from Russia. It was dynamite. This tiny bit of information was to change the Bogdanov investigation completely and help his plans considerably.

The freeze on Bogdanov's financial information had been lifted. He had gone to his network node to check it out and noticed another new file sitting there in the folder, one from the Russian police. On an impulse, he had decided to examine the Russian file first and instructed his network node to translate the file. The translation seemed a little nonsensical in parts, but the gist was clear. Along with the crime scene descriptions and the autopsy results, as well as grotesque images from these activities, it had included a shocking bit of information at the very end, some personal information about Bogdanov's former life in the rogue state.

This was exactly the kind of screw-up he would expect from an egotistical Neanderthal like Phoenix. He quickly glanced at Bogdanov's financial information as well, before sending an urgent meeting request to the director. The frustrated lame duck would still have her use a few more times before someone put her out of her misery. And Julio was sure she'd vent her frustrations on Phoenix when he dropped his bombshell.

Phoenix placed the new PA next to her old one. They appeared identical, with no markings, numbers, or barcodes to tell them apart. What if Ray had come to her office first and swapped the new with the old? The old one was exactly as she had left it, and it didn't appear that being tidy and orderly was a strong point with Ray. But then again, could it be the case?

Then her network node started blinking. Her inbox was stuffed with mails that she just hadn't had time to read nor did she care. Yet she felt compelled to check this priority mail. It was from the director, calling for another urgent meeting. But how come her PA hadn't indicated such a thing? Phoenix quickly turned on the new PA to find the meeting invite sitting in her inbox. It must have been received when she had briefly turned it on while chatting with Ray, but hadn't blinked due to some system mix-up with two PAs acting like hers. She had no intention of returning her old one yet, but one of them always needed to stay off.

She placed the old one into one of her drawers and quickly walked across the hallway to the director's office. The Door Bot was non-responsive once again, not automatically enabling the door for her. A sudden feeling of déjà vu filled inside her. Could it have to do with having a new PA? "Computer: This is Senior Agent Wallis. Acknowledge."

"Voice pattern identified as Senior Agent Wallis."

The door opened, to her surprise, and everybody inside turned to look at her.

"Finally," said the director. "Well, at least we should consider ourselves lucky that she is still in the building. And why did you look so surprised when the door opened? Didn't you expect to see us inside?"

"It wasn't that. It didn't open automatically, and I thought there was trouble with my PA again, and I identified myself. Then it opened."

"I suppose you're not aware of the heightened security precautions amid the issues with the academy. All level five meetings now require voice verification. Perhaps not enough time from going on wild goose chases around the city instead of preparing for tomorrow?"

"I don't even know who I'm supposed to interview."

"Again, if only you read your mails now and then," said the director with narrowed eyes. "They announced it this morning. And this time, you have to prepare for it all by yourself, as none of the personnel have time to assist you in this matter."

As her mind raced behind her impassive mask, Phoenix peeped through her eyelashes at the others. Julio appeared very self-assured, watching her like a snake poised for attack. Sean's face was totally expressionless, studiously avoiding eye contact with her, an avoidance conveniently coinciding with her discovery of Julio's bed. Alex, on the other hand, looked almost dormant, appearing overly calm and quiet. Perhaps he was feeling disappointed that he wasn't going to have the opportunity to help Phoenix with her upcoming interview.

"Julio called for this meeting to share certain developments and new information in the Bogdanov case, which I know had priority one in your list," said the director with a wince. "I'm sure you're not aware of this information yet, as we all know you've been avoiding your office and your network node, enjoying expensive nightclubs at the Pyramid instead."

"I was there on a lead, Director. Bogdanov had been spending lots of time and money at the Stardust."

"That he was," said Julio. "His bank records clearly show that he'd been quite extravagant in his spending spree there."

"His bank info is unfrozen?"

"Yes, it is," said the director. "And you're the last one to be aware of this."

"Some indication as to how focused she is as the case lead, Chief."

"I am focused on the case," said Phoenix with a superhuman effort to maintain her poise. "I know I've been all over the city for this case and backlogging some of my duties here in the meantime."

"Backlogging would be a gross understatement. Acutely ignoring is more accurate."

"Whatever! As long as I am the lead, I'll run this investigation as I see fit."

Phoenix's heated words made everyone pause for a moment. Julio broke the silence. "Is she still, Chief?"

Director Morssen didn't answer immediately and took her time observing Phoenix. Her green-gray eyes were sunken deep in her eye sockets, with purple rings around them. Her makeup had been carelessly applied and barely covered the patches of red around her nose. Her shoulders were sagging like those of a beggar. She appeared dull and unfocused and had a big patch of gauze sloppily taped to her forehead. If she didn't know any better, she would think her to be on a mind-altering narcotic of some sort.

"Yes, she is."

"What? You can't be serious! This woman is in no condition to perform anything, let alone lead a murder case."

"Is that so?" said the director. "This woman is to conduct the single most critical security interview of all time tomorrow. This company's reputation and future depends on the outcome of this interview. According to your assumption, we're all doomed."

"That's not what I meant."

"Director Morssen is right," said a calm voice. Everyone turned to Alex. "We need to help Phoenix all we can, not lay obstacles in her way. If she feels better about following case leads, and it will clear her mind from the pressures of tomorrow, I say we let her be. After all, we're not the ones who had a double Strike-Out, and we cannot understand how she did it or what she is going through now, nor we can advise her about what to do in her next one. I know I cannot. And I wouldn't want to cloud her judgment with my *experience*, since in my entire interviewing career of twenty years I didn't have as many Strike-Outs as she had in three days." He looked at Phoenix and winced. "Moreover, she found herself in this unfortunate situation through a string of seemingly unrelated and unavoidable events. Yet if she fails, her career will probably be over. If she succeeds, she'll save her career and even the reputation of the GPSN. However, she will not even get compensated for her achievement, because the feat she's undertaking is severely disproportionate to her rank. Speaking of success and failure, the situation is so complex and delicate, it's impossible to even speculate what could be considered a success or failure in tomorrow's interview."

"I guess Alex summed it up pretty well," said the director, peering down at the table. "Phoenix, lead the case the way you see fit, at least until tomorrow. And perhaps everything will be different tomorrow afternoon. Who knows, maybe you can crack this case open before then. Is there anything you'd like to share regarding the case with us?"

"Not at this point."

"Oh, before I forget, we need to share something with you, since you *scarcely* have the time to check your mails and the case file. We finally received some news from the Russians, about the autopsy and all. But there was one bit of additional information there, which shocked me. Shocked me because it was something you should have been able to figure out."

"What was I supposed to figure out?"

"That your murder victim used to be in a nuptial agreement with his sexual partner, Ms. Lukin."

CHAPTER 23

PHOENIX had known that Lukin had been hiding something, but she hadn't imagined it to be something so fundamental. The situation also exposed the incompetence of the so-called deception experts at the academy. It must have been child's play for Patel to manipulate them, and she wondered how many more like him could be in this rotten academy, or worse, already graduated and out there. Patel was a genius with a dark secret and had a reason to lie. But unlike Patel and his secret, Lukin had no reason to lie about her rogue state partnership with Bogdanov. She was either hiding something important or being utterly stupid, or perhaps both.

According to his financial transactions, Bogdanov had spent more than a couple of hundred thousand dollars in his last couple of weeks. His tabs ran around three to four thousand dollars each night at the Stardust, and the fee he had paid to Arnett Salon was about thirty-five thousand per session. No wonder all the Devotees at the Stardust had thought that he was one of their own kind. There was a payment for DeVille there, too, on the last day of March, for a mere three thousand dollars.

As counterbalance to his spending spree, he had been receiving tens of thousands of dollars each from all these people, most of whom she could recall from his handwritten list. One name that instantly grabbed her attention was that of Dr. Spencer. She also noticed that one woman, a Lena Vanderbilt, had made payments of hundreds of thousands of dollars during the month of March alone. According to the autopsy report, Bogdanov had been murdered with single firearm shot to the neck, the bullet penetrating at a downward angle.

"Hey, Tess."

"Hi, Phoenix. What happened to your head?"

"I banged it on an iron gate." She quickly summarized the developments of the morning and explained that she was on her way to see Lukin.

"Why do you think Lukin hid their nuptial partnership from you? In order to cover up for their altruistic relationship?"

"I feel that there's more to it than that. I think Bogdanov was using art consultancy as a cover for something else, and she might know what that is."

"But why would he do such a thing? It isn't like anybody cares what he does or an agency monitors commercial activity in the Union for taxes."

"It's true for legal activity. But what if he was involved in *illegal* activity, like smuggling? It might even have to do with the mysterious device Spencer died using. This would also explain his secrecy."

"Interesting connection. You still think DeVille was involved all this?"

"He had to be involved somehow, at least as a part of their cover. Bogdanov was paying DeVille a fraction of what he made, but DeVille told me that they were equal partners."

"What if all that money came from another venture?"

"That may very well be the case, but no evidence of such a venture yet. Hold on, I need to call Sean. Could Agent Tess call Lukin for me and arrange an immediate meeting at her house?"

"Sure. I think Agent Phoenix would have a difficult time presenting a neutral face to Ms. Lukin at this point," she said with a wink.

Phoenix quickly called Sean.

"Hi, Phoenix," said Sean. She was avoiding eye contact even on a call.

"I need you to do something for me. Can you compare the names on Bogdanov's handwritten list to his bank statement?"

"What is it that I should be looking for?"

"See if the people who credited his account in the last couple of months match the people in the list."

"Aha, I see."

"I have another call waiting," said Phoenix and hung up. "Hey, Beverly."

"Hey, Phoenix, whatcha doin'?"

"Chasing leads on Bogdanov case. What's up with you?"

"We nearly swept the entire surveillance footage from last night and this morning," she said and exhaled. "Nothing with that bottomed-out student—not even your dash after him. We only got the part that you skewed off towards the grass."

"You're kidding! Any possibility of tampering with the footage database?"

"Not really. All files appear untouched. Then again, who am I to vouch for such a thing? It's not like I'm a network security expert."

"Then how else could he get all the way to our side without a row?"

"Haven't the slightest clue. Hey, maybe he used the tunnels!"

"What tunnels?"

"This building here's full of secret passageways, didn't you know? I heard that you could enter a passageway from the east wing and come out from the other end in the west gardens. Maybe he found one of these passageways. I'd think he'd be too fat to squeeze through, though."

"Were these passageways ever discovered?" said Phoenix, thinking he could squeeze through anything if he could squeeze through those thick bars.

"They wouldn't be dubbed *secret* if they were that easy to discover, would they now?"

"A smuggling ring?"

"Why not? Those students would do anything to slip into the World Union."

"He'd slip through and do what? It's not like he can work or stay anywhere without proper credentials. He doesn't even have an HDI certificate."

"True enough. Where do you suppose he vanished to? His biometrics are being searched everywhere in real time. If he were to be caught by any of the surveillance cams in the city, his ass would be grass."

"Perhaps he has a special kind of charm like my intruder." Phoenix's heart raced for a few seconds, and she didn't quite manage to smother her smile.

"*Your* intruder? If I didn't know any better, I'd think he took your breath away in more ways than one."

"Of course he did not. He's a criminal."

"Hey, he can be a criminal and hot at the same time." Beverly grinned. "Tell me, how did it feel when he ran into you?"

"You know how it felt: He messed up with my mind and ran away, just like that man with that black hat did with the director, Alex, and others."

"Boss told you about that? All right, I'm not gonna ask you if there was more to that brief moment than what you've been telling us. By the way, how's your new PA?"

"You arranged that?"

"Sure," nodded Beverly. "It took some arm twisting with Fred then he kept babbling about receiving some custom spyware from Tier Zero of all places. I guess his last few brain cells must've been so occupied, he had to fuck it up at the last instant by entrusting the damn thing to Ray!"

"So I noticed. But it seems to be working fine. Didn't have any crashes at the metro or anything. And thanks, Beverly."

"Hey, you need all the assistance you can get. A lot depends on you, and you need dependable hardware."

"Ms. Lukin, you've been lying to me. Didn't you think we'd discover your nuptial agreement with Vassily Bogdanov?"

"Govno!" gasped the woman. "Oh, no." A flood of tears spilled out of her vacant eyes.

"If you tell me the truth from now on, you don't have anything to be scared of. I won't charge you with anything."

"I'm not scared of that," whimpered the woman.

"What are you scared of, then?"

"The Dinastiya."

Phoenix froze for a few moments, her mind racing at the shocking revelation. "Are you referring to the mafia family?"

"Yes," the woman moaned.

"You think they killed him?"

"Of course they did," said the woman, raising terrified eyes to meet Phoenix's. "They got him, don't you see?"

"What would the Dinastiya want from him?"

"Revenge," said the woman. "Because he stole money from them."

"How did he manage that? Robbed a bank under their protection?"

"No, he stole from their safe."

"What are you talking about? He couldn't have access to such thing unless—" Phoenix held her breath. This was a near-impossible scenario, but it also explained many things, including the angle of the bullet in Bogdanov's neck.

"Good morning, Bill." It was already forty-five minutes past their scheduled meeting time of twelve noon GMT. The chairman of the IAW had made him wait for forty-five precious minutes, but Hamilton's face was as calm as ever.

"Good whatever-it-is to you, too," said the obese man, with a yawn at the other end of the virtual table. "But I have a feeling that soon your good days will be permanently over." He appeared to have just woken up.

"Did you relay my final offer to your board?"

"Your puny offer of four, you mean?" said the man and let out his irritating cackle. "Actually, I did. You know, they may have been interested in it, at least some of them. But once I informed them about the incident that took place in your field office late last night, they unanimously decided to vote against it. How about that?"

"You are referring to the renegade student?"

"What else? And the fact that your would-be interviewer happened to break his head chasing this student. What a mighty coincidence, wouldn't you say?"

"It's a she, and she will be doing the security interview tomorrow morning as scheduled, don't worry."

"Gee, Simon will be thrilled!" said the fat man, popping out his eyes. "At least he won't be traveling all the way to your ragged border town for nothing. Still I'd expect a much better stunt from the Wizard of Oz. But I understand: too much pressure yielded this cheap shot. Unfortunately your plan to damage investor confidence by engineering a break from the academy has blown up in your face, Osmund. You actually managed to unite all major shareholders and board members for a change, by turning everyone against yourself, and I should thank you for that." He burst into insane-sounding laughter.

"Is that your final answer to my offer of forty dollars per share?"

"Now how about that?" sneered the other man. "He's still pretending to fight. The battle's over, Oz, and you've lost it. Now, admit to this, and give me my settlement before I totally destroy you."

"What kind of a settlement do you have in mind?"

"Say, how about fifty bill?" said the man with a broad smile. "My name is Bill, and I can settle for fifty bill. Hey, I like the sound of that."

"Seriously? I can buy your company for less than that."

"Not this week, pal! And this is the week that you need to settle with me. Then again, we can continue bargaining tomorrow, should you wish."

"You're right about settling this week. But I'm not going to throw away my money like that. Your settlement offer is totally baseless."

"Actually, you're right," said the fat man in mock thoughtfulness. "It is *totally baseless*. I made it up, based on my gut feeling about how much your GPSN big boys at DC would be willing to pay to cover up such a huge mess by their golden boy."

"You overestimate their soft spot for me. They would never pay such a settlement, and neither would I."

"That's too bad, Oz, because the number will only go up tomorrow."

"You seem so sure of yourself."

"Of course I am. You're in such a big mess, there's no way you wouldn't buy your way out of this one. And the more you delay any decision of buying your way out, the more expensive it gets. I'm talking about a downward spiral here, Ozzie, and you are at the center of it."

"If this is your final position regarding a settlement, we'll need to wait for tomorrow. I hope you won't regret it. Because I will not be as generous with your 'chute as I was yesterday. And with that obese body of yours, we all know that you need a big fat one."

"Don't you dare threaten me, Osmund! I'd worry about—"

"Hamilton out," he said and cut transmission. Obese Bill had given him all the information he needed in order to verify his final strike. The board of Immigration Academies Worldwide was riddled with cracks and differences of opinion. Once the tide turned, some of the board members would break early on and create an avalanche. He had to make one final call to his associates on the island of Honshu to finalize preparations. "Start buying when the shares drop below ten," he said. The trap was set. Now he needed to wait for the angry and overconfident fat rat to move in.

But one thing still niggled: Obese Bill had been right; it was a strange coincidence that his senior agent had been on the spot to run into the renegade student. Or perhaps not a coincidence? He made a mental note to investigate this further.

"Vassily Bogdanov used to be a member of the Dinastiya," whispered Lukin, her voice shaking. "He was their head accountant at Odessa. Not promoted to the family itself, but just one step below." She started whimpering again, tears running down her cheeks.

"Why did he steal from them?"

"In order to escape to here, of course. He couldn't deal with it anymore."

"Deal with what?"

"My Vassily was a kind man at heart. But we didn't have many choices for work as we were growing up. He came home one night and told me his plan to escape. I was ever so scared but also happy. We knew we would need to live separate lives in the Union, of course, but it was the price of freedom. It all happened so quickly. The next night we were on the road with the money and just a few of our belongings."

"Did he hide his mafia connections in the Personal Confession classes?"

"He didn't hide the fact that he worked for a crime organization, but nobody pressed any further, so he never mentioned his connection to the Dinastiya specifically. I'm sorry that I had to lie to you. But Vassily made me swear not to tell about this to anyone. We ran away in such secrecy, I didn't tell it even to my own biological brother."

"A bio-brother? Why? So that he wouldn't be harmed by the Dinastiya?"

"No," said the woman. "Because he was a member of the Dinastiya."

"What? You have a bio-brother, and he is a member?"

"Yes," said the woman, gazing at the distance. "Or he was, when I saw him for the last time. You see, I'm not hiding anything from you anymore."

"Indeed you aren't! Did you lie about him at the academy, like you lied to me? There was no dead uncle, was there?"

"No, but I didn't lie about it at the academy. I told them I had had a nuptial partnership and a bio-brother. As for the money, I told them that I stole it."

"Which was the truth, after all."

"Yes, it was," said the woman, shaking her head violently. "But they caught up with him, and I know I'm next." She started whimpering again, and it was no pretense. This woman was genuinely frightened for her life.

"They used to say," she continued in between whimpers, "once with Dinastiya, always with Dinastiya. And that you can never run away from the Dinastiya, not even to the surface of the moon."

"You are safe here, Ms. Lukin. You have nothing to worry about on Union soil. By the way, did Bogdanov have any contact with other Russians here?"

"Not that I know of. Oh, I don't know." She fell silent, eyes down.

"Someone at the Stardust club mentioned to me that Mr. Bogdanov may have had some Russian guests there."

"Which club?"

"The Stardust. It's an elite club at the Pyramid. Never heard of him mention it?"

"No," she shook her head. "I didn't know Vassily went to expensive clubs."

"The name Mancheek doesn't ring any bell? Perhaps a friend from the academy?"

"No. Doesn't even sound like a Russian name."

"Did he speak any other language other than Russian?"

"No."

"Did he ever mention an art consulting venture to you?"

"He was getting more and more into art, developing his own style, you know, in his bedroom and all. But he never mentioned a venture to me."

"Right," said Phoenix, picturing Bogdanov's atrocious bedroom in her head. "You took a lot of risks coming here, Ms. Lukin. I imagine you had a comfortable life under the protection of the Dinastiya in Russia, with your nuptial partner and your bio-brother working for them in high ranks. Why take all that risk?"

"There was too much risk living there. We had to fulfill our dream of freedom."

"You told me that he told you about the idea one night, and the next night you were on the road. How could he arrange the money that quickly? It was in the form of T-Bills, right?"

"World Union Treasury Bills, yes. He was the head accountant, so I assumed he had access. Mafia wives never ask where money comes from."

"Even so, there are safeguards and precautions in such organizations. I'm pretty sure his and your tab at the immigration academy was at least around a million dollars. No one can take out a million dollars' worth of T-Bills from a mafia safe in a single night without someone else noticing. Could it be because Mr. Bogdanov had done this before? Perhaps it wasn't the first time he had stolen from the Dinastiya safes?"

The woman opened her mouth and closed it again.

"I'm right, aren't I? He had been stealing from them, and that's why he wanted to escape to the Union, because he couldn't hide it anymore."

Lukin seemed to be struggling to speak. "I don't know about his stealing," she said at last. "But I witnessed him and my bio-brother arguing behind closed doors several times, soon before we left."

"Perhaps your bio-brother was aware of his stealing and had warned him for your sake. Perhaps, deep down in your heart, even you knew."

A pattern of deception and betrayal was forming in Phoenix's head. Bogdanov had betrayed the Dinastiya. Then he had come to the Union and formed his own ring in a few years, then betrayed DeVille, and perhaps even Captain Perez. Eventually the mafia had caught up with them and executed Bogdanov. She couldn't tell how Perez's crash would fit in to all this yet, and the only key to solving the mystery was DeVille. She had to find him and make him talk. She had to see if that picture in his house was for real or not.

Now Pierre DeVille appeared to be sitting at the gate to her own professional and mental salvation.

"What is it?"

"I need to talk to you urgently about the murder case."

"Then why don't you request a level five meeting for the task force, like everyone else does?"

"Because it's something too urgent and too sensitive to be shared in the case file. I need to see you, Director."

"Okay, fine. Come as soon as possible. Where are you?"

"At the Pi Quadrant."

Director Morssen was busier than usual, with strategy meetings, analysis meetings, preparation meetings, and many others, just because of this senseless and reckless young woman. And now Her Highness was boldly asking for more time of hers for some *sensitive* information she claimed to have acquired. She had secretly vowed not to cause any incident with Phoenix until the next day, but now it seemed that some things were simply inevitable.

"All right, I'll schedule you for a *secret meeting* in forty-five minutes. I hope it's worth it."

"Finally got a hold of you," said Sandra. "Hey, what happened to your head?"

"Oh, don't ask. What's up?"

"I was gonna ask you to come with me to this big party tonight at Carpe Diem. Everybody will be there. And I mean *everybody!* But we'd need to do something about your shabby wardrobe and that gauze on your forehead first."

"What shabby wardrobe? My clothes are fine."

"Calm down, baby, I know the perfect base to cover any scar, don't worry."

"Sandra, can't you see that I'm in no shape to attend a party? Just look at me! Do I look like I wanna go anywhere tonight?" She stopped suddenly, remembering something. She shook her head with a grin. "But, then again, I might go out tonight."

"I knew you'd come to your senses," said Sandra, with a broad smile.

"I didn't say I was going out with you."

"Are you all right? Your mood shifts remind me of some dead immigrant I know."

"I'm fine, Sandra."

"Swell. Then let's meet at the Pyramid after work. But before we shop for you, I want to show you the Thing that I wanna get with my quarterly bonus."

"The Thing Store?" said Phoenix, suddenly remembering something else she had forgotten to do.

"The Thing Store," repeated Sandra. "I know you know the place."

"Of course I know the place. Actually, I have some unfinished business there."

CHAPTER 24

"THIS academy is a circus! You're sure Lukin is not making any of this up?"

"I'm positive. It all makes sense, Director. One bullet to the neck while on the knees makes it very likely to be a mafia-style execution."

Just as Hamilton said when it all started, thought the director. "So you know about this kind of stuff, huh?"

"I analyzed illegal border activities for many years in Munich, read many reports, saw many images. This murder has every sign of one."

"So based on your experience of the rogue state criminal architecture, what do you make of all this?"

"I think Bogdanov had been stealing from the Dinastiya for a while. Eventually he realized that he couldn't hide it forever and ran off with his nuptial partner, after stealing about one million dollars in T-Bills, enough to afford an academy."

"Such a risk," said the director, shaking her head. "What if they couldn't graduate with a passing grade or they failed the security interview?"

"I believe he eventually established a criminal ring here, one which involved Captain Perez from the GPSN military and a local artist known as Pierre DeVille."

"A captain from the military? How can you know that?"

"I don't have solid proof yet. But I believe his plane crash has to do something with Bogdanov's death."

"What plane crash are you talking about?"

"A GPSN military plane under the command of Captain Perez crashed in Russia last week. I know for a fact that Perez knew Bogdanov and had suffered from a similar emotional dysfunction. I suspect that they were smuggling some mind-altering drug, or perhaps the device that killed Dr. Spencer, using some old contacts of Bogdanov's, and Perez was doing the transportation."

"This is outrageous! Can you prove any of this?"

"Not yet. But I have a murder suspect."

"A suspect? Who?"

"Pierre DeVille. I believe he was either the third member of this criminal ring, or a decoy, either way got a raw deal. I have proof that Bogdanov had been cheating on him big time in his so-called art consultancy business, the business that Bogdanov's supposed to have earned all that money from. DeVille told me that they were even partners, yet he only received monthly payments of three thousand dollars to Bogdanov's hundreds of thousands."

"This is the same DeVille that you initiated emergency access to enter his house, yes? You should consider yourself lucky that he didn't sue us for your un-lawful entry. Besides, how could this DeVille go all the way to Odessa to murder Bogdanov? Do we have any records of him leaving the Union? All sounds so farfetched."

"Do we have any records of Bogdanov leaving? I'm not saying he pulled the trigger, but he was being cheated big time. And if that isn't a motive for mur-der, I don't know what is. Perhaps DeVille knew about Bogdanov's past with the Dinastiya," she went on, gazing at the horizon. "I can just picture Bogdanov bragging about what a tough mafioso he used to be. DeVille might have tipped the Dinastiya somehow after learning about being cheated."

"You really think that you know this Bogdanov, don't you?"

"He had a lot of difficulty adapting to the Union over the past three years, just like many immigrants around his age. Then something happened to change all that about two months ago. He became a different man. He turned bold and assertive enough to hire a lawyer like Anderson and get image-making from Arnett Salon. He became confident enough to frequent the Stardust club and cozy up with half of the clients, acting like a Devotee—even the bartender there was shocked when I told his true HDI. Nobody can change like this without the help of professionals, unless something triggered a change. And I need to know what that trigger was."

It was evident that Phoenix had become obsessed with this case. And she was so stuck on this *change* in Bogdanov. Could it have something to do with her own change? This woman had had a very quiet tenure at the GPSN during her entire professional life, all thirteen years of it. Even the previous week she had appeared dormant and submissive. Something had happened to her this week, something deep and profound. Perhaps she had already cracked under the pres-sure of all the events.

The director suddenly felt deep concern about what Phoenix might do the next morning in the interview room. If she acted this obsessive with the interviewee, the famed watchdog would tear her apart, and along with Phoenix's career, her own career would go down the drain, too.

"You're so fixated on this, you're even breaking the law you've been sworn to protect. I hereby suspend all your emergency and other privileges until further notice. By the way, have you studied anything about the interviewee you're supposed to face tomorrow yet?"

"Would you care if I did?"

"Of course I care! The reputation of an entire corporation is at stake here."

"Really?" Phoenix erupted. "Is that why nobody pays any attention to me, or supports me, or coaches me, or even just talks to me? All these experts are swarming the field office, scrutinizing every frame of the interview, but totally ignoring me. Is this how you and the mighty corporation show your care?"

The director replied only with a cold glare.

"A corporation which has already sacrificed me and perhaps you, too. But don't you worry, I'll disappoint all of you tomorrow. I couldn't care less about you and your corporation. This time I'm gonna do it for me."

So this was how it felt to be like the loneliest person on the whole planet. Nobody cared about her, or tried to understand her, or liked her for who she was, yet everybody wanted to use her or steamroll her. If she wasn't the oddball, she was the laughingstock. If she wasn't laughingstock, she was the scapegoat. It felt like she was the only one on the whole world that everybody wanted to whip, treating her as if she were utterly insignificant and expendable. She felt like she was the focus of so much negativity, it was suffocating, causing pain every time she breathed. Her temples started throbbing again with pain. At that instant the call came. "Hey, Tess."

"You don't look too good. Didn't go well with the director?"

"Nope. She thinks I'm totally out of it. I don't think she considers a single word I tell her to be credible."

"No kidding? On to a more important subject: Your proposal was reviewed and found to be simply *ingenious*."

"So they approved it?"

"Unequivocally! It's fascinating that this kind of suggestion would come from you but not from the so-called geniuses my experiment employs."

"They're not in my shoes," said Phoenix, with a weary smile. "Didn't they tell you that necessity is the mother of all invention? And thank you, Tess."

"Hey, I do it because I like you."

"So despite the down mood, my data set is still interesting for you? I know I haven't been sharing enough time with you lately."

"Actually, it's not just your behavioral data set anymore but also your ingenuity. There's something so unique about you, and I don't think I'll have enough processing power to understand you, no matter how much I commit."

"Thanks, I appreciate the praise. You have no idea how much it helps. So many people here believe that I'm old-fashioned, outdated, and worthless."

"Not from where I stand. We've been searching for a way to exploit my findings for a decade now, and the first solid proposal that we can profit from—it came from you."

"You know, you could also make a lot of money by being a paid friend, custom-tailored friends for the masses. I don't know what men would think about it, but I'm sure women would love it."

"A concept already considered, of course, but not as simple as it sounds. There are technical and policy reasons that prevent my public exploitation at this point in time. Your ingenious idea, however, will bolster my image among big corporations and enable more donations. Our position with the grants from GPSN will definitely be on a much firmer footing."

"You won't need grants from them anymore. Just an invoice will do. So you guys are ready for my request?"

"Absolutely. We can begin our trial run as soon as data is enabled at your end."

"And will you allocate enough processing time?"

"Enough to have everything ready by early in the morning."

"Super," said Phoenix and took a deep breath. The suffocation feeling she'd had since the morning eased up a bit. Finally she was receiving some outside help, and she felt proud that it all had to do with her own smartness, skills, and grit. She didn't owe anything to anyone on this one, even if it was going to benefit the corporation that discarded her, not her. Then something flashed in her mind. "I have one more request. If my proposal is this ingenious, I'd like you to officially contact my corporate executives as soon as possible and ask their approval for a procedure change, so that we can do an actual test run tomorrow."

"Stand by," said Tess and her pupils rapidly moved for a while. "Under the circumstances, that would be suitable. Just send me your procedure change request, and I'll forward it. But why don't you do it yourself on your end?"

"I don't think anybody would read any memos from me at this point," said Phoenix, with a shrug. "Besides, it's a better selling point for you, should it come from your end. But it needs to come from a high enough executive so that it's responded to swiftly, before tomorrow morning."

"Agreed. But what you're doing doesn't make any sense now. Is it my imagination, or are you defending my company's interests against those of your own?"

"I feel no loyalty to the GPSN right now," said Phoenix, looking away. "They put so much weight on my shoulders and left me out in the open, so that the jackals of the academy can tear me apart."

"I can't blame you. But you don't look well at all. You're sure you don't want to see a doctor about your head?"

"Actually, I'm on my way to one. Can you do me a favor and get Agent Tess to see if Dr. Nemeth at the rehab center has some time for a neurological check-up?"

"Of course. You know this doctor?"

"No, I don't. But she was recommended by Director Rottenmeier at CDC. Talk to you later." She called Beverly next.

"Hey, sis, feelin' any better?"

"So-so. You still have your level five privileges after the director restored them for that locator, yes?"

"I believe so."

"Good. I'll be a lot better if you can do me a great favor."

"Thank you for seeing me on such short notice, Dr. Nemeth. Director Rottenmeier recommended you, should I need a neurologist."

A petite woman with tightly pulled-back platinum-blonde hair, a high forehead, a small hooked nose, dimples, and glowing green eyes, Dr. Gisella Nemeth was a lot younger than Phoenix had imagined her to be. Despite the white doctor's coat, her mischievous smile made her look like a naughty little girl.

"The director's too kind," she said, with a grin. "I receive so much help from her to promote Parkinson's awareness in the city, a patient with her personal recommendation, I always have time for. So, what happened to you?"

"I banged my head against an iron gate this morning and lost consciousness for a few seconds."

"Uh-huh," said Gisella and got up to examine her cut. "Where did you find an iron gate to bang your head against?"

"My field office is full of such health hazards. It was the gate of an ancient graveyard."

Gisella gently removed the tape, exposing the wound. She examined it with the light of her PA and applied some antiseptics as she spoke. "And how did you happen to bang your head? Fainted? Low blood pressure?"

"No, nothing of the sort. It was in the line of duty."

"I see," said Gisella, replacing the old-style gauze with an organic fiber tape with skin color adjustment. "This should cover it better. But you may end up having a permanent scar there unless you get some plastic action."

"I'll worry about that later. I have this crucial interview tomorrow, and nobody should be able to challenge my mental capacity."

"Sure, let's see." She checked Phoenix's pupil reaction with the light of her PA then she made Phoenix cross her legs and hit her knee with a small mallet to check her deep tendon reflexes. "Do you feel any muscle weakness in your arms and legs?"

"Nothing other than the general fatigue I feel."

"Uh-huh. Now, please come and sit over here for my portable MRI machine." She took Phoenix by the arm and tended her to a reclining chair with a hollow, cylindrical device above.

"Take your PA off. You wouldn't happen to have any pre-Union stimulators or implants in your head, would you?"

"I—I don't know. So many procedures were done to me when I was little, and with little record."

"A survivor of the riots?"

Phoenix looked down and nodded.

"In that case, let me check your history first." She went to her network node and typed in a few commands.

"Nothing here of the sort," she said after a few minutes. "But let's make sure with this inorganic substance probe." She rotated the probe, which resembled a magician's wand, slowly around Phoenix's head. "So, how long have you been on mood stabilizers?"

"Pretty much all my life."

"Any sleeplessness or any other complaints lately?"

"Can't you tell?" said Phoenix, pointing to the purple rings around her eyes. "Haven't had a decent sleep in two weeks since I moved here."

"Oh, I can tell all right," said Gisella, grinning. "No sign of any inorganic matter in your head. We can proceed with the MRI." She lowered the hollow cylinder and placed it around Phoenix's head and went back to her network node. "This will take about seven-eight seconds. Can you hold your breath for me?" The MRI made its usual knocking sound for about ten seconds then Gisella came back and raised it. "The expert computers will examine the slices and report to me in a few seconds. So tell me, why can't you sleep at nights? Sleeplessness? Any pain?"

"Night terrors. They've been haunting me since my first night here."

"Can you think of any specific connection between here and your terrors?"

"The Bloodbath. I survived it. I used to have these night terrors as a child. I took my first mood stabilizer around the age of eight then the terrors slowly disappeared. But they came back after all these years, the night I moved back to the city."

"Uh-huh," said Gisella, while reading something on the monitor. "But on the positive side, you have nothing to worry about tomorrow. You're clean."

"Good," said Phoenix, looking down. "I hope to get some decent sleep tonight, yet I don't know if I can. I hate taking drugs, but I'm feeling so desperate right now. Do you think you can prescribe me something so that I can have a good sleep with no nightmares, for one lousy night?"

"Actually," said Gisella. "I can do better than that."

"So, are we on tonight?" said Sean.

"No, babe, I'm busy," said Julio, looking at his coffee mug. Their usual hangout was totally empty, as almost everyone was busy with the renegade student or the next day's interview and its repercussions.

"Oh, I didn't know. So what are you going to do about it?"

"I said, I'm busy."

"I didn't mean tonight. You said you'd wait about the director until noon today. It's past noon now. Are you planning to do anything?"

Sean's irritating inquisitiveness was beginning to push the limits of Julio's patience. He had been helping her by making her a part of his plans, but the nag was constantly striving for attention and becoming nosier by the minute. He had big plans for the night, and Sean wasn't a part of them for obvious reasons. Everybody was gonna be at this party, and he had managed to get a pass, thanks to one of his artist buddies. This night would be his first opportunity to meet with the elite of the city since he had moved to Adrianopolis a year previously.

"Other things got in the way, babe. With the renegade student and all, the whole focus of attention has shifted. Not much point doing anything until the circus is over tomorrow."

"You think Phoenix will screw up?"

"I know she'll screw up and drag the old nasty witch down with her. No point in poking the beehive now."

"I'm not so sure," said Sean, with a fleeting glimpse of a smile.

"Hey, what's going on? You know something that I don't?"

"Just a feeling. I feel like she has this ability to beat impossible odds. I witnessed her do it with Patel; it came out of nowhere, you know. None of what she did there was rehearsed, yet she radiated so much calm and confidence, there was a strange energy in that room."

"So? She got lucky," sneered Julio. "Then she destroyed an innocent woman's life by coercion."

"I'm not so sure about that either. The word is that you put the coercion idea into Ion's head, as well as the mind-altering weapon concept."

"I did no such thing! I just told him how incompetent Phoenix is and pointed out her mistakes, in case he couldn't see them from behind those thick glasses of his. Even if I did such a thing, I'd have no reason to hide it."

"Why not? Wouldn't it be considered selling out a fellow agent?"

"Selling Nix? She's a Neanderthal bitch, for heaven's sake! I'd be doing a favor to the whole field office. And I don't like your tone in the least."

"I thought we were trying to help her, because she needed it."

"Help ourselves through helping her. Hey, I'm always honest with you or anyone else about what I think. For me, I come first. And I was willing to help the Neanderthal bitch while it served my purpose. Now it doesn't. So there!"

Sean lowered her gaze, slowly got up, and left the table.

"I can put you on a real drug," said Gisella, with an impish smile.

"You mean the mood stabilizer I've been taking isn't good enough anymore? Don't tell me I need something stronger."

"No, it was good enough all right, while you took it. But not anymore."

"Are you trying to say—"

"You're on a placebo. Your last attending physician at Munich switched you during your refill three months back. I'll put you back on the real stuff, and you should be able to sleep with no terrors."

"I—I can't believe it!" Phoenix managed to say, her heart racing.

"And as for your clean bill of mental health, I'll forward it to your immediate supervisor right away. Is it Lubosh?"

"Excuse me, who? No, no, it's not. It's Director Dagmar Morssen. So you know Alex?"

"Yeah, we just met. Nice ol' chap."

"Indeed he is. So you're one of the doctors on the Spencer case."

"Uh-huh," said Gisella, with a grin. "Or *no case*, as I prefer to call it."

"Meaning?"

"We can't perform an autopsy as his heart still beats, we haven't seen the device which was supposed to have caused all this, on security grounds, and we haven't seen the crime scene," said Gisella and rolled her eyes. "Want me to go on?"

"A big brick wall, huh? I know the feeling. Didn't know he still had a pulse."

"He has zero brain activity, so technically he's dead. I haven't access to any tests even to tell the time or day of death. My only discovery is the evident sign of fresh sex on the guy, when they brought him in."

"Fresh sex? Was he naked?"

"He was dressed up all right, but with fresh semen inside his clothes."

Phoenix fell deep into contemplation as she took the metro back, with her *real* drug in her pocket. Everything started to make sense: The childhood traumas resurfacing, the nightmares, her suddenly surfacing instincts. The drugs must have inhibited her instincts, along with keeping the traumas under wraps. Now all of her dormant capabilities were coming to life, along with all of the traumas that had been kept under a pressure lid all these years. She hadn't felt a difference in the early months of her placebo, perhaps because it took a while for the effect of the drug to be flushed out, and her move to the city had triggered the change.

She remembered feeling shame that she was on drugs when she was little. She would try to keep it a secret from everyone. At CDC, only Director Rottenmeier knew about them, and during college years, Sandra had accidentally discovered her secret daily routine. Other than her doctors, she had never shared this aspect of her life to anyone else.

Now she had a dilemma. Despite the insomnia, the terrible nightmares, and the uncertainties her conscious mind had about her newly discovered abilities, Phoenix liked who she was becoming. She was more assertive, confident, and bold. Her mind was working in flawless conjunction with her instincts, giving her the ability to squeeze out of seemingly impossible dilemmas. She had always been a great analyzer, but now she was definitely more aware of what was going on around her and sensed others' thoughts and feelings about her, making her analyses complete. She didn't just feel capable in what she did anymore. She felt *inspired*.

And on top of everything else, she had hope, a hope that she had never felt before or thought might exist for her, a hope that she *could* be happy someday, a hope that kept her going despite all the burdens that had been following her all week, a hope that flourished in the mysterious eyes of an intruder behind a mask. She didn't know if she was ever to see him again. She had no idea what kind of a person he might be. She couldn't even imagine what she might feel if she got a chance to see or touch him, but she felt the strength and determination to discover it.

"I'm so excited," said Sandra, as animated as a fifth grader on a candy diet. "C'mon, lemme show you." She dragged Phoenix through the crowds to see the little Thing she wanted to get. It was in the shape of an elliptic orb, glowing with constantly changing colors. "Isn't it gorgeous?"

Phoenix's mind wasn't with the glowing ornament but somewhere else. She could see the giggly Alicia at a distance, but the pretentious Monica was nowhere to be seen. But a third girl with a name tag was on the floor. "It's great, Sandra," she said, with her eyes on the third girl. "There's someone I need to talk to. I'll be back in a moment." She left the drooling Sandra and moved towards the tall curvy brunette, who glanced at the swarming clients with utter indifference.

"Piper, right?"

"That's what the name tag says. Who wants to know?"

"Senior Agent Wallis. I have questions about your former supervisor."

"Yeah?" said Piper, checking out Phoenix from top to bottom. "Actually, the other two said that you might come by."

"When did you hear about Bogdanov's death?"

"I heard from the other girls the moment I arrived at work after my vacation yesterday," said Piper, with a sigh. "The guys were too hot, and the vacation was too short, you know."

"And what did they tell you?"

"Oh, you know, the whole deal with all gory details," shrugged Piper. "That he was murdered for his flesh, and his mutilated body was found near a garbage dump with his legs and arms severed. His internal organs were stolen, and some of his body parts were cooked and eaten by the ultra-hungry in them rogue states."

"I see that you're fully informed about the case, even more than me, it seems. Did you know he was a recent immigrant?"

"Ohh, so that's why he talked funny and wore those ill-fitting clothes."

"He'd emigrated from Russia three years ago. He never mentioned that?"

"No, never. But wait, now that I think about it, some of his countrymen might have stopped in here to visit him."

"How can you tell they were Russian?"

"You know," said Piper, with a cocky grin. "The way they talked funny and again those ill-fitting suits. Our Union-style tunics didn't look right on them, just like they never did on Mr. Bee. Had to do with the way they carried themselves, I guess. And of course those penetrating stares." She soured her face. "Yuck, I felt like they were undressing me with their eyes."

"So what would Bogdanov do with them?"

"He would have that kind of visitor, say, once or twice a month. He always took the individual upstairs to his office and closed the door. But I didn't think anything of it, because he was so weird anyway."

"You think he had a problem fitting in our society, with his weirdness and all?"

"Sure. Furthermore, he was dull, unsophisticated, and unattractive. In my book, three strikes and you're out."

"Did he have many friends?"

"I guess those guys with the weird accents and ill-fitting clothes were his friends, if you consider all the randy laughing, bear hugging, and slapping each other's backs to be friendly gestures. Dunno about anyone else."

"To your knowledge, was he involved in any other business ventures?"

"He kept talking about some art consultancy deal with some artist guy."

"Do you know if this art consultancy was doing well?"

"That's what he kept saying. Then bragged to me about the places he'd been frequenting lately, dropping names about the fancy restaurants he dined, or the clubs he hung out like the Stardust, la-di-da! But his newly acquired status wasn't from the Thing Store sales, that's for sure. Ignore the swarming masses here. They're here to ogle, not to buy."

"Where do you think his sudden wealth came from, then? Any ideas?"

Piper quickly glanced around and leaned over to Phoenix's ear. "I think there was something fishy going on," she whispered. "I saw one of his foreign buddies bring in some stuff a couple of months back, stuff that we never displayed in the store, you know. The boxes were taken straight up to his office."

"What do you think was in those boxes?"

"I have no idea what was inside them," said Piper in a whisper, checking out the approaching Sandra. "But I overheard something about customers renting their contents."

"Renting? You're sure?"

"Totally."

"Which customers are you referring to?"

"The ones he would take up to his office, Devotees mostly. And later he would tell that he had just made a big art consultancy deal. Hah, my foot! He was lying through his teeth."

"Hey, what'cha doin', girl?" said Sandra. "Don't tell me you're trying to buy my Thing behind my back."

"Just taking care of some business. Thanks, Piper, you've been most helpful."

"Sure," said Piper and left.

"So what's your opinion on that Thing? Should I get it?"

"It looks as good as any other Thing here. Hold on, gotta make a quick call."

Sandra shrugged and walked back to her Thing without another word.

"Hey, Sean, did you finish making the comparison of names I asked you to do?"

"Yes, the lists are identical except for two names. Bogdanov's encrypted handwritten list has Captain Perez's name but no mention of Dr. Spencer. But in the creditors to Bogdanov's account, it's the reverse."

"Really? How many payments had Spencer made?"

"Just one. By the end of last week."

Everything was becoming clearer now in Phoenix's mind. Spencer was one of Bogdanov's most recent customers, and something must have had terribly gone wrong during his use of whatever was being rented, and all hell had broken loose. Maybe it was that device that nobody was granted access to, or maybe that device was just a smokescreen for something else. Whatever it was, the answers were with DeVille.

"Ok, call everyone that credited Bogdanov's account and ask them what kind of services they had received from him."

"All right. Anything else?"

"Yes. I want you to contact the headquarters of the Thing Store Corporation."

"What for? You wanna check the availability of a *Thing?*"

"Couldn't care less about their Things," said Phoenix with a grin. "I wanna know about certain corporate policies of theirs."

CHAPTER 25

"Is everything set for the next few days?" said the Black Hat.

"Yes, sir," said the Crane. "We're ready to rumble."

Black Hat ignored the attempt at humor. The situation was too delicate to make jokes. But the Crane had always been a funny kid since childhood, a geek with a good sense of humor—if only he knew what the Black Hat knew. "You'll need to stay on top of everything for the next three days or so."

"I got enough food and caffeine with me, Grandmaster, don't worry," said the Crane. "Is the Mount notified of her role in all this?"

"I notified her personally yesterday."

He left the Crane in the network room and walked out to the dim, long, and organic-looking hallway, his mind working at full speed to figure out details, to evaluate alternatives, and to make decisions before entering another room, where the Toboggan Hat was waiting for him inside.

"We have a dilemma," said the Black Hat.

"Is there a problem with the adjustments to the plan?"

"Yes. I calculated and recalculated all alternatives and possibilities. We can still achieve complete success, but there is one problem. The development this morning has changed certain parameters now, and that's why I came in to meet with you."

"We should be able to adapt pretty much flawlessly, no?"

"We can, but only if we're willing to sacrifice one of our own."

"Oh, no," sighed the other man. "Are you positive about this?"

"I am. Of the three of our masters involved in this operation, one will need to be sacrificed for the plan to be carried out successfully."

"Well, if that's our dilemma, the solution is somewhat simple, isn't it?" said Toboggan Hat. "We wanted to decommission the Mantis anyway."

"I know that. But unfortunately the dilemma doesn't end there. It will not be up to us, who to sacrifice. It will be up to *her!*"

"Dear God. We should immediately cancel everything and withdraw."

"Too late. The Mantis is already too deeply involved, and we can't pull him out, not without exposing the Prefect."

"That would be a total disaster at this point in time. We certainly cannot sacrifice the Prefect, the centerpiece of our entire strategy."

"Precisely," said Black Hat, pacing. "That's why we need to let this flow and take the risk of losing the Mount or the Crane."

"But the Crane is such an important and critical asset. How can we risk losing him? And I'm not even going to comment on what an established and important part the Mount plays."

"The Crane could be even more important than us, but not more important than our grand strategy that we've been formulating for the past twenty years. We need the Prefect to continue as the controller of the Mantis until this is over. Besides, we've already crossed the Rubicon; there's no turning back now."

"So, she'll go down and drag one of ours with her, and we have no control over who," said the Toboggan Hat, shaking his head. "This is not good."

"Not good, but it pretty much sums it up. She doesn't strike me as the insightful kind, but I hope that she comes with some good sense and she knows how to use it for her own sake, too. Otherwise we'll take a very hard blow, and things won't be easy for the ones out there, either. It will be a devastating hurricane for everyone."

"I have a feeling that she does possess good instincts."

"How do you know that?"

"Just a hunch, a feeling from a few fragments of information here and there. And it's not a coincidence that she happens to be at the eye of the looming hurricane."

"If this is leading to another lecture on the philosophy of Chaos, I don't have time for it."

"No, it's not," said Toboggan Hat, shaking his head. "It would suffice to say that I have strong feelings about her, and I know the Prefect likes her, too."

"Bah!" said the Black Hat and stopped pacing. "The Prefect has a very strange taste in liking and not liking people, or things for that matter. I wouldn't consider it a supporting factor."

"Regardless of his dubious taste, the Prefect is also a grandmaster whose thoughts deserve merit. And I think we can make one more little tweak to our plan to improve our chance of having control over who to sacrifice."

"And how do you plan to achieve that? All will be up to her behavior in certain situations and the choices she'll make. It would be crazy to attempt influencing her choices at this point, because we cannot even predict or control the outcomes if we do. None of our operatives are that slick."

"I could do it," said Toboggan Hat, with a twinkle in his eye.

"Sure you could, except the fact that you wouldn't last a minute up there without raising suspicion, especially if you were to meet a GPSN agent. You've been on their most wanted list for three decades now, remember?"

"Then I'll lure her down here."

"Are you insane? Don't tell me you're gonna expose one of our entry points for this."

"I can manage it by only exposing one of our safe houses. Given the dilemma, we can afford that, can't we?"

"Are you sure your influence would be subtle enough, yet yield results?"

"You know only too well how delicately I can use my abilities."

"And how do you plan to get her to the safe house?"

"She's already received several clues about it, thanks to the Prefect. Besides, I know the perfect bait to lure her."

Phoenix made another desperate attempt to reach DeVille but with no luck. The man didn't want to be found, and his Door Bot reported that he was out. She thought about getting another locator trace on him by asking for Beverly's help, but she was already doing more than enough.

"C'mon," said Sandra. "You've been interviewing someone or on your PA all afternoon. You gotta know how to let go, girl."

"Sandra, don't you understand, my neck is on the line. I have the most important interview of my career tomorrow, and you're telling me to relax and let go. I have to find this DeVille. He's vanished without a trace."

"You're so good at blowing everything out of proportion. DeVille was this artist type, right, the explosive and deadly dude who scared the shit outta you?"

"So?"

"Then I know where he'll be tonight."

"Enlighten me."

"At the Anti-Chaos Society's spring party at the Carpe Diem, where else?" said Sandra with a *duh* look on her face. "The local artists display their 'wares' at these parties, and some of the city's affluent bid for them. It's part of the entertainment. I'm sure your renegade weirdo will be there."

"No kidding! But why would the world's most powerful NGO throw a party here in Adrianopolis?"

"Welcome to the border. We know how to have fun here. Besides, they're the dominant pressure group in the rogue states, and your big boss is the governor of the region. Of course the party will be here."

"Hamilton is the Eastern European head?"

"Don't get too excited. I doubt that he'll show—he never does. But your artist will."

"Sweet. I bet that party is the last place he'd expect me to find him."

"Everybody from the upper echelon of the city will be there. You know, you might even have the opportunity to meet a few or even bed one."

"You know I'm not interested in bedding anyone."

"Whatever," said Sandra, with a shrug. "But I definitely think you need some big bang tonight before that interview of yours tomorrow."

"I actually have a dinner date tonight, too."

"You do? With the marine?"

"Nope. With Bryan Ainsworth, a journalist."

"Is he hot?"

"Not really, but he has a nice smile."

"Please tell me he's a Devotee."

"Hmm, not sure, but I don't think so."

"Oh, you're such a hussy. When will you learn not to say yes to everyone?"

"He's bringing some footage that I need for my case tonight."

"Don't tell me you fell for that. That's the oldest trick in the book, you know?"

"Maybe so, but I have to try, okay? This footage could provide crucial information on my murder investigation."

"Now, what did I just tell you about big bang? Were you even listening to me? And I went to all this trouble to arrange an invite for you tonight."

"I'll go to your party, don't worry. It will be more like a business dinner, and it won't take long. What time do you plan to be there anyway?"

"Around ten. But we need to get you some decent clothes first."

"I already told you what I think about that. My clothes are fine."

"No, they're not! Now look, this is *my* area of expertise. If we're gonna go to this party together, I'm not gonna walk in there or hang out with a ratty-looking loser, all right? This is the price you need to pay."

"Okay, I give in. So what's the plan now? Take a trip to Arnett's Salon?"

"In your dreams," said Sandra with a giggle. "Lemme take you to ZAP, and we'll fix you up there real quick. And I guarantee you'll look fab. You still have your lease with us, yeah?"

"Yep. Only to the bronze line, though."

"Bronze?" shrieked Sandra. "Are you kiddin'? You have an HDI of seventy-three now. You can easily afford silver, perhaps even gold."

"Not with my credit line."

"For fuck's sake," said Sandra, rolling her eyes. "I guess we're gonna have to fix that, too. Now, you're coming with me," she said and grabbed Phoenix by the arm.

The ZAP store was almost as loud as one of Sandra's parties. Phoenix felt somewhat nauseous from the blaring music and the carnal content jumping from every direction. Sandra dragged her next to a beautiful, tall, and lean woman. "Theodora, this is my best friend, Phoenix. We're gonna patch her up for tonight's party."

"Glad to meet you," said Theodora, with a gorgeous smile. "Of course. Do you have a subscription with us, Phoenix?"

"She does," said Sandra. "We'll upgrade her to silver in a bit. Now, what do you think?"

Theodora took a long look at Phoenix, starting with her face, walking around her, observing her curves. Phoenix felt uneasy under her scrutiny but didn't say anything. She had always let others pick her clothing all her life. Many times it was just wizard software that gave her recommendations. It was going to be a first for her to be advised by a real specialist.

"Your color palette is light summer. The color I recommend for tonight would be rose pink, and I have just the right dress for you. It just got into our silver line inventory and should complement your complexion perfectly."

The slinky pink satin gown had delicate spaghetti straps and a long slender skirt. On a thinner woman, the dress would have looked quite demure, with the not-too-revealing draped neckline. On Phoenix, it was her curves that made the dress look so sensational; it hugged rather than skimmed her hips, accentuated her tiny waist, and highlighted her generous breasts. It was Phoenix wearing the dress, not the other way round. As Phoenix stared at her own reflection, Theodora produced a pair of matching platform pumps to complement the dress, and a box.

"Size thirty-seven, yes?"

"How did you know?"

"Do you have light pink lip gloss?"

"I think so," said Phoenix, still unable to take her eyes off the mirror.

"See? I told you Theodora was good," said Sandra. "What about the purse?"

"I think this rainbow-colored purse will work perfectly." It was a medium-sized rectangular purse covered with what looked like a particularly vibrant example of mother-of-pearl, shimmering and glinting with every color in the spectrum. It was a real eye-catcher.

"So, what do you think?" said Theodora.

"This wouldn't be something that I'd buy myself, but I have to admit, it looks good on me."

"Don't sound so surprised," said Theodora. "You look fabulous."

"Hey, I'll be jealous tonight," said Sandra. "You won't try to steal my men, will you?"

"You know what else?" said Theodora. "You need tiny rose gold earrings with little green stones and a silver-and-pink clip to put your hair up."

"I think I can arrange that." Phoenix looked at herself again in the mirror. She would never have imagined herself in a dress like this. It just wasn't her. Rather, it just hadn't been her *before*. But now she was genuinely enjoying the way she looked. For a moment she thought of all the bad things that were about to befall her, with her career, her economic situation, even with her possible bankruptcy and deportation.

Not until tomorrow, she thought. If her newly acquired and soon-to-be-lost HDI enabled her to get clothes like these, she would enjoy them while it lasted.

"I can't believe that you haven't been to an investment house yet. How can you live without exploiting the perks of a higher HDI?"

"I didn't have time," shrugged Phoenix. "You know how busy I am. I don't even have time for the gym these days."

"I know, baby," said Sandra, with practiced sympathy. "But it won't take long to fix you up with a brand-new credit line, so you can afford the silver at ZAP. Then Theodora will send your stuff straight home."

Allied Investors was just a short walk from the ZAP. A young, tall, clean-cut blond account executive with impeccable manners named Bradley took care of Phoenix.

"Okay, Agent Wallis," he said, looking at his network node. "I moved all your assets to our local branch. But I have to tell you, you don't have much in there. Your HDI was recently raised to seventy-three, which shows the faith of our financial system in you. I'm pretty sure there would be many people out there willing to offer you a credit line you deserve so that you can further improve your HDI by investing in yourself."

"I guess." Phoenix didn't know exactly how the system worked, but she knew that everything was risk-based. Traditional banks were non-existent in the New World Order, as interest-based modern finance had given way to the purely risk-based postmodern one. There were no across-the-board interest rates applied to the masses, where the borrower promised to pay by a certain date in the future, without even knowing if it could be earned or not. In postmodern finance, everybody took a risk when lending or borrowing.

"How much of a credit line would you like to raise?"

"Oh, I don't know," said Phoenix and turned to Sandra. "What do you think?"

"Baby, I'd say at least a hundred grand."

"That much? Who'd wanna invest in me a hundred grand? That's crazy!"

"Getting the credit line doesn't mean you have to spend it all at once, right, Brad?"

"That's right Ms. Pescara," said Bradley, with a perfect smile. "We can always reduce the amount and try again, should we fail to find a suitable investor offering a suitable risk premium."

"All right, then," shrugged Phoenix. "Hundred grand it is."

"As you wish. Computer: Access Global Credit Center. Search for tenders for a one-hundred-thousand-Coalition-dollar credit line for Senior Agent Phoenix Wallis of Global Peace and Security Network, with a Human Development Index of seventy-three." He turned to them with a smile. "The bidding just started, and I can see many lenders in there already. This will only take a few minutes."

"What do you expect her final risk premium to be around, Brad?"

"Hard to say, Ms. Pescara, but I expect it to be higher than 5 percent, since Agent Wallis has very little borrowing history."

"I asked for a two-hundred-thou credit line last month, and it took the computer around ten minutes to find a tender. But Brad here's always very helpful, and he managed to find one offering four and a quarter percent."

A moment later, his network node made a sound, and Bradley turned at his monitor. "Oh, the bidding is over already." He drew back with surprise when he checked the contents, briefly glanced at Phoenix, then turned back to his computer.

"Something wrong?" said Phoenix.

"On the contrary," said Bradley, his eyes still glued to the monitor. "I got several hits between oh point five and one. *Minus* oh point five and one."

"A negative risk premium? What the hell does that mean?"

"It means that someone out there thinks you're worthy of a credit line even at a loss," said Bradley and swallowed audibly. "They're offering to pay *you* a risk premium to take their loan, not the other way around. Would you like to take it?"

"But how is this possible?"

"Take it," whispered Sandra with a smirk. "Obviously it's some kind of a fluke. Take it while you can, you lucky cunt."

Her instincts stopped Phoenix before she could say anything. She didn't believe in coincidences anymore. If this was another computer crash or virus, she wanted to get to the bottom of it. Hacking, perhaps?

"No, raise it. I wanna see what happens."

"Are you crazy?" whispered Sandra. "Take it while you can, woman!"

"I said raise it, Bradley, to a million."

Bradley nodded quietly and ordered the computer to make another search for a million-dollar credit line. The result was back in a few seconds again.

"I still got hits with negative risk premiums. What would you like to do?"

"Raise it to ten."

Bradley did as he was told one more time, like a robot, and he turned to Phoenix with a *'What's going on? I have no clue'* look. "The risk premium remains negative, Agent Wallis," he whispered. "Under the circumstances, I'd conclude that some investors want to buy your shares."

"My shares? But I don't own any shares."

"Not your stock portfolio. Your *ego shares*. Many promising executives and entrepreneurs sell a certain portion of their existing wealth and their future income to attract investors. Are you an inventor of some sort, or do you own patents?"

"No, no, I don't. Are you sure about all this? That it's not some sort of malfunction or virus, even? Also, who wants to give me such a credit line?"

"There are no errors," whispered Bradley. "And it appears like one of the giant investment pools is acting as intermediary. I have no idea if anyone else is behind the credit line or not, but I'm positive that it's real."

"Sweet," said Phoenix, turning to a speechless Sandra.

"Would you consider a personal IPO at this moment in time, a public offering to sell your ego shares in the market? The conditions seem very favorable."

"I don't think so. Just take the credit line."

Phoenix got home, still puzzled about her encounter at Allied Investors. She was about to be discarded by her company, the security and military giant of the world, and possibly forced to reverse emigrate to one of the rogue states. And yet, somebody wanted to grant her a credit line worth ten million Coalition dollars. Bradley had told her that this kind of credit line usually would be offered to clients with HDIs of seventy-six and above, and that somebody out there must have been following her career closely. But who could it be and why? Sandra had thrown a jealous tantrum, insisting on Bradley finding her such investors for herself. Phoenix had left her at the Allied Investors instructing poor Bradley to work and get results.

Her home delivery system was blinking when she got home, indicating that her new clothing had arrived. She took them out of the cylindrical tube and unpacked them on her bed. She also needed to catch up on her case on the Court Network, as she hadn't had time to watch the developments for the last few nights. She knew the perfect buddy to do it with, but she wanted to surprise her with her new outfit first.

She carefully put on her new dress, her new shoes, and applied makeup as suggested by Theodora, smudging a smoky gray-black pencil along her lash line to accentuate her green-gray eyes, with a little light-reflective concealer to cover the marks of fatigue, and a pink gloss for her lips. The skin-adapting tape that Gisella used had perfectly hidden the cut on her forehead. She used a gold clip to put her shoulder-length hair up in a loose knot with a few blonde tendrils framing her face, then stepped back to check herself in the bathroom mirror. *I like it.*

"Tess."

"Oh my, Phoenix, you look gorgeous!"

"You really like it?"

"Yes, I absolutely do. You look so feminine and elegant."

"Thanks. I have a dinner date and the Anti-Chaos Society's spring party to attend, and Sandra insisted that I needed some appropriate clothing."

"Sandra was right. You look fantastic. By the way, the data flow and processing already started. The results should be available on your GPSN network node at about 4:37 tomorrow morning."

"And my request for a procedural change?"

"Already forwarded to GPSN executives from the office of our chairman. We should have a reply fairly soon."

"That's great news. I'll record the party so that you can see it with me."

"I'll be at that party in multiple instances," said Tess, with a wink. "But I'm sure our instance will be the most interesting."

"So what was the ranking of Ms. Cain when she graduated your academy?" said the defense attorney in her strong Southern accent. She was a short black woman in her late fifties, her face dominated by big determined dark-brown eyes and big lips accentuated with bright red lipstick.

"She was twenty-ninth," replied the man in the witness chair.

"And the total number of graduates from Hong Kong Academy that quarter?"

"Three hundred and seven."

"That'd put Ms. Cain in the top tenth percentile of the graduates that quarter," said the lawyer while she nimbly paced up and down past the members of the jury as she spoke. "So how can you explain this Union citizen's lack of understanding of some of the most fundamental concepts of our Supreme Bill? Wasn't it your responsibility at the academy to *drill* these concepts into her pretty little head?"

"Yes, it was, but—"

"But what, Mr. Headperson?" said the lawyer and stopped pacing, her big platinum earrings quivering dramatically. "Don't tell me that this woman here, who comes with an HDI of seventy-one, doesn't have enough IQ, or is unhealthy, or immoral, or poorly educated. These were all to be considered, observed, and evaluated during the six months when my client here, was under your watch. But what, Mr. Headperson?"

"She was well prepared and educated during her tenure at the academy."

"Uhhh-huh! So she somehow forgot all these, soon after she graduated from your academy, is that it?" She paused theatrically. "Let's assume that to be true for a moment. Tell me, Mr. Headperson, how much did Ms. Cain here pay for your academy?"

"Around six hundred thousand."

"That's in Coalition dollars, right? Not in Hong Kong dollars." Phoenix could hear giggles from the court room.

"Coalition dollars," said the man.

"And after paying all that money, by the way, it would be impossible for us homegrown folks to understand what kind of hardships and sacrifices made to obtain such funds in a rogue state, the guarantee she'd received for what she'd learned would be for how many years?"

"Five."

"Did you say five, Mr. Headperson?" said the lawyer loudly.

"I said five!"

"And this is five *earth* years, right? We wouldn't wanna confuse interplanetary calendars here." Laughter erupted in the courtroom. Phoenix felt a distinct frisson of pleasure as the academy headperson of Hong Kong nodded, looking down. So there it was, another rotten academy. How many more of these were out there?

"Considering the fact that my client here graduated from your academy in the top 10 percent of her class less than a year ago, she'd still be under the guarantee, wouldn't she?"

"Yes, but that guarantee does not cover crimes against the Supreme Bill."

"So it doesn't. Can you tell me what it covers, then? Reading the alphabet and instructing a computer?"

"It covers those," said the headperson, with a grin.

The lawyer turned to the crowd and raised her hands and pointed to the headperson, as if to say "He is the man!" The crowd laughed even harder.

"Are you trying to tell me that you charged my client here for six hundred grand, with a guarantee to cover none of the serious stuff, but for simple stuff that any fourth grader in the Union can do?"

"The Supreme Bill violations are the domain of the GPSN. It's their responsibility to discover any intent to violate the constitution."

"Uhhh-huh! Let the blame games begin. So you really expect GPSN agents to discover in an interview span of a mere thirty minutes what you haven't and couldn't discover in six months? My learned and distinguished colleague here demonstrated a few days ago that Ms. Cain here can recite the articles of the Supreme Bill faultlessly. Even with our supreme edge in technology, how can a deep intent be uncovered in half an hour, Mr. Headperson? By counting every possible crime in alphabetical order and asking the interviewees if they intend to do it, in order to catch them lying?"

"I—I wouldn't know that. I'm not a security expert."

"Yet you're here at the witness stand as the headperson of the Hong Kong Immigration Academy and a qualified deception expert. And you expect the entire burden of Ms. Cain's admittance to the World Union as a citizen and that her crimes should rest on a GPSN agent's shoulder because of a thirty-minute interview?"

"It's their responsibility to defend the Supreme Bill."

"Mr. Headperson, tell me: Is it true that you and your senior staff pressured the director and agents of GPSN's Hong Kong Field Office so that they perform easy interviews and not corner interviewees in order to improve your academy's lousy graduation record among its peers?"

"Objection!" said the old prosecutor. "Your Honor, the defense is pursuing an irrelevant line of questioning."

"Sustained," said the judge. "Counsel, please address the witness with questions related to Ms. Cain's tenure at the academy."

The subtle positive comments that the lawyer had just made about GPSN before hundreds of millions of viewers around the world could be worth a promotional campaign of how many billions of dollars, Phoenix couldn't tell. But she was sure that it was a kind of advertisement that no amount of money could buy.

CHAPTER 26

THE dinner with Bryan Ainsworth at the expensive restaurant didn't end up being as professional as Phoenix had expected. Ainsworth was in a black designer tunic, in an apparent attempt to impress Phoenix, but his effort was marred by his inability to fill and carry the suit properly. Phoenix couldn't help but to think of the comment made by Piper at the Thing Store about foreigners in Union-style tunics. He was also gazing at her with a certain twinkle in his eye that she didn't feel comfortable with.

"Bryan, did you locate the footage we talked about yesterday?"

"Uhm, I'm not sure yet. These foreign sources, you know, usually aren't good with answering in a timely fashion."

"Can you get this footage or not? I need to know, and I don't like games."

"It's not that I'm playing a game. I had planned to bring it to you tonight, but the darn thing didn't make it in time, and for that I apologize. But I had planned another surprise for you tonight."

"Please don't. I know that I'm kind of overdressed for such a dinner, and I don't want you to get wrong ideas. Actually, I need to get going, meeting some friends for a party at—"

"Carpe Diem?"

"Yes. How did you guess?"

"Because I was gonna invite you to go there with me. And that party is precisely why I'm overdressed, too."

"Quite," said Phoenix with a grin. "Sorry for the directness, but I didn't want to cause any misunderstandings."

"No harm done. Shall we?"

They found Sandra waiting in front of the club. She was in a slinky fuchsia strapless sheath gown, the floor-skimming slippery pink skirt slit all the way up to her crotch. The supple slinky skirt occasionally offered a fleeting glimpse of her matching fuchsia-dyed pubic hair, trimmed in the shape of an Arrivee tattoo. She indicated her displeasure at the journalist's presence by giving him the cold shoulder, while Ainsworth excused himself to say hi to a news crew near the entrance.

"I can't believe you brought him here."

"I didn't. He said he was gonna come here anyway, even invited me. What was I supposed to say? *'Let's walk separately 'cause my best friend here doesn't want you'?*"

"That's exactly what you should have said. I'm not gonna parade on the red carpet next to a ragged loser. Come with me, hurry!"

Feeling scrutinized by the strong lights and the attention-seeking camera crew, Phoenix turned her head away and walked on. Sandra, on the other hand, was quite happy that she could enjoy her fifteen seconds of fame with all the attention of the news crew on her, walking in catwalk style, waving, all smiles, as the local news crews filmed and took holograms of every entrant, then forwarded to all social networks.

Carpe Diem was a nightclub originally erected as a cathedral around the same time as the building that hosted the academy and the field office, but unlike the monastery it possessed a distinct warmth. It was as large as an indoor track, with a circular dance platform in the middle on an elevated ledge, and long brass tubes on the back wall. The painted glasswork on the high windows appeared to have survived the riots. The music wasn't as loud as she had expected it to be and might even have been considered tasteful, perhaps due to the special occasion.

"C'mon, let's get a drink," said Sandra and dragged her towards the cocktail bar, ordering for both of them. Her cocktail tasted fine, yet Phoenix couldn't help but compare it to the incredible cocktail Fabian had prepared for her at the Stardust the night before. Then she wondered how many of the affluent clientele of that club would be here tonight. Perhaps she might run into Mancheek even, not that she remembered much about his face.

Ainsworth finally caught up with them. "I'm sorry I had to say hi to that news crew. I'm glad you didn't wait for me."

"That's okay," said Phoenix. "Now if you'll both excuse me, I need to look for someone." She weaved her way gently through the crowds. There were many stands with hosts and hostesses giving away freebies, Anti-Chaos Society digital pamphlets, chaos awareness visuals, and many other paraphernalia. She could also see the art being displayed like Sandra had mentioned, but none of the artists seemed to be hanging out by their art yet.

"Phoenix, is that you?"

She turned and found Director Morssen and Alex in her face. The director was in a black low-cut long-sleeved jersey dress, and she looked simply stunning with discreet makeup and gleaming silver hair, which tonight was hanging straight to her shoulders. The dress was a perfect reflection of the chilling elegance that Phoenix thought she radiated. Alex was in a classical black tuxedo with white shirt and white bow tie.

"What a surprise to see you here, Director. You look fabulous, so elegant."

"And I was about to say the same to you," said the director with a rare smile. "You look so different in this dress. Sensational."

"How are you, Alex?"

"How do you think I am?" said Alex and let out a loud cackle. "I'm surrounded by beautiful girls—I mean women."

Director Morssen had such mixed feelings for this young woman. On one side, she was a reckless destroyer, nearly as bad as that arrogant Julio claimed her to be. On the other hand, she possessed something the others didn't. In the last week, she had been acting with a rare and blind self-assurance, defying everyone around her. She was a crusader without a cause, or a ronin perhaps, an ancient samurai with no master, an aimless and reckless rock star, struggling against forces way beyond her strength and power, and yet she was definitely full of surprises. Considering the shape and mood she had been in the same day, Phoenix was one of the last people the director would expect to see at this gathering, yet here she was, standing before her in an incredibly graceful dress, glowing with renewed energy.

"I'm cleared for the morning. Did you receive the report?"

"I did. Everyone will be there, you know, board members of the IAW, Mr. Richfield as your watchdog of course."

"Even Hamilton himself will attend," said Alex, his eyes wide. "Can you believe that?"

"Wow, I had no idea I was that famous. The seats at the Viewers' Lounge must be up for grabs. Perhaps you should auction them, Director, I bet Julio would be willing to pay thousands of dollars for the seat next to Hamilton."

"Ha ha ha…" The director actually chuckled. She looked so human and warm that anyone would have a hard time believing that she was the same person who radiated such negativity and anger on any given day. "I bet he would," she said, still smiling. "But Mr. Hamilton has already reserved some seats at the back row for himself and his guests from the IAW board."

"Seriously? Wow! Don't worry, I'll give everyone a great show. Who's the watchdog on the academy side, by the way?"

"One of their board members. Evidently he used to be the head of one of the original academies, the one in Chrysopolis."

"There's a bet going on in the field office, you know," said Alex. "Ten to one for a Strike-Out."

"Do you feel prepared for this mockery, this circus tomorrow?" said the director, suddenly turning chilly.

"Oh, I am prepared for it all right, Director," said Phoenix, unable to suppress a tiny smile. "In more ways than you can imagine."

From a distance, Phoenix was unexpectedly calm and collected at the party, but this was only the calm before the storm, the Mantis was sure. The centerpiece of his strategy was already in place. Now it was only a matter of time before she completely disintegrated in no more than two days. She appeared to have finally done something about her clothing, for sure with outside help, and decent help at that. But behind the shell of apparent glamour and beauty hid the real Phoenix, the insecure little girl with the inner torment and nightmares, and a giant storm brewing.

He could see through the shells of many of these people. They were all weak inside, with fears and insecurities and petty needs like love or assurance. The Mantis thought that it would be so easy to manipulate all these people in the blink of an eye, if only he were allowed to do so. And that was soon to be. His success in destroying Phoenix would seal his worth and enable him to break free from his despised controller. So far, the controller had been the only one who could bring him out from hiding and send him back. Only this time, the Mantis had no intention of going back into hiding. This time he was here to stay, to pursue his own pleasures, his own interests, his own desires, his own destiny.

And to destroy the souls of the worthy and the unworthy alike.

The party got more crowded by the minute, but there was still no trace of DeVille. It wasn't easy to get an invitation, but her instincts were saying that Sandra would be right, and sooner or later he would show up. She was trying to wander around and look for him in an orderly fashion, but it was impossible to do so because almost everyone in the party was drifting in random directions.

She noticed an unusual number of people, almost all of them men, gathered up close to the entrance of the building, presumably to catch a glimpse of someone important. She moved closer to see, and it was Mata Hari, her outfit bringing to mind a flamenco dress designed in an asymmetrical style flowing gracefully down, with a flouncing red-and-black skirt cascading from a tight black corset, the skirt slit all the way up to her cinched-in waist on one side. The dress was complemented by black eyeliner, red lipstick, a red ribbon headband with an incredible black sapphire piece, accentuated by a white gold rim and diamonds, and a red necklace with a huge ruby gemstone attached. Men from all walks of life were swarming around Mata Hari, trying desperately to grab her attention for a moment. At one point, her wandering eyes locked onto Phoenix's. She panicked instantaneously, expecting to feel the nausea and other disturbing emotions that she had felt on their previous encounter, but instead, she felt a certain relaxation, with her instincts telling her that everything was cool. It seemed that Mata Hari was thinking or feeling the same way, as she gave Phoenix a brief smile and a wink.

"Well, hello Phoenix, dear. It's so good to see you here tonight," said a very familiar voice.

"Ms. Rottenmeier," gasped Phoenix. "So good to see you, too."

"My goodness, look at you, you're so beautiful."

Rottenmeier looked very elegant in an off-white lace-and-chiffon empire gown with three-quarter-length sleeves and vintage-looking embroidery. She was with another woman, who appeared very familiar, but she couldn't tell from where. She was a petite woman with an extremely sexy full-length platinum halter-neck satin gown with a plunging back, her tanned breasts barely covered and harnessed only by two tiny white triangles suspended from a delicate gold chain encircling her neck. Her platinum-blonde hair was cut in an asymmetrical bob; she wore heavy black eye makeup.

"How's the head, Phoenix?" she said and smiled, her dimples showed up.

"Dr. Nemeth?"

"Some of us doctors enjoy shocking our patients with our public appearance. Don't worry, I'm used to it. And no need for formality."

"Sweet. It's gotta be the—"

"Oh, it's the lighting at the rehab center, of course."

"Gisella told me about your incident today, Phoenix. Are you okay?"

"I'm fine, don't worry. Gisella here patched me up real well. How's Kati?"

"Well, I had to quarantine her, unfortunately. She'll be out of town for a few weeks, resting on her native island of Corfu."

A group of people swarmed like a school of fish around Phoenix, Gisella, and Rottenmeier. They were led by a tall and lean figure in a white shirt with a ruffled front and an elaborate lace collar, a slim-fitting red coat, a triangular red hat, skin-tight ivory breeches with silk stockings, a long red cape, and red shades. The swarm paused as the lean figure stopped and bowed with a flourish to Rottenmeier.

"Such a delight to see you here, dearest teacher. You and the likes of you make this otherwise worthless and miserable Union shine like a bright star."

"Oh, Arnie, thank you dear, you're so kind," said Rottenmeier. "Let me introduce you to Gisella and Phoenix. Girls, meet Arnie."

"Delighted to meet you ladies," said Arnie in his Royal British accent, nodding his head. "And this is my mob, Doug, Gwladus, and those others whose names I can't for the life of me remember."

Phoenix gave Douglas Anderson a cursory nod, quite sure that the famed lawyer wouldn't recognize her in this dress. He briefly made eye contact and nodded back. The stunning Gwladus, on the other hand, was again strangely familiar. She was tall and lean, and wore what might once have been called a little black dress, deceptively simple, exquisitely cut, and accessorized only with diamond drop earrings, a diamond choker, a tiny diamond-studded black purse, and black kitten-heel sandals. The way she wore the dress, however, combined with her flawless poise and innate style, managed to make half the women in the room feel cheap and overdressed in comparison, while the other half felt dowdy and frumpy.

Gwladus moved her shoulders from side to side almost imperceptibly, as if dancing to some private rhythm, then suddenly froze and peeped sideways as if to check whether Arnie had seen her gaffe. At that instant Phoenix recognized her and realized who the man in the red cape was.

Osmund Ledyard Hamilton checked his daily correspondence after a long and tiring day. He had planned to take it easy for the rest of the night, perhaps even have some time for himself. How about that party he'd sponsored? Wouldn't that be a shocker if he were to attend?

Perhaps in another life, he thought. *If such a thing is possible.*

He turned his attention to the night sky surrounding his office. It was a clear and moonless night, exposing all the stars and the Milky Way alike, reminding him of his childhood days and how he loved to lie on the ground and watch the stars in the pitch-dark windy flatlands of his homeland by the stormy sea. He interrupted his own reverie and turned his attention back to his mails, noticing an urgent one from the upper echelon of the Richfield Experiment. And it was signed by Richfield himself! The experiment had been a financial disaster zone, siphoning billions of dollars each year, marred with technical issues with no economically viable product or service on the horizon. Yet it was a project that none of the big conglomerates wanted one of their peers to have exclusive access to, so donations kept flowing in.

Still, it was surprising that he took the time for this mail while being entertained by the academy folk somewhere in town. A twinge of early guilt for an expected scandal the next day, perhaps? Or worry about future donations from GPSN if things turned really sour? The content of the mail, however, was nothing like he had anticipated. It was an uncharacteristically open and clear-cut multi-billion-dollar business proposal, which could save many more billions if implemented. And Richfield was asking for a spectacular test run the next day, for the whole world to see. Richfield loved popular demonstrations that attracted media attention, not only because his project needed the media to receive funding, but also because he liked being at the center of attention himself.

And despite his typical efforts to claim the bulk of the credit for himself, Hamilton could see through to where this proposal must have originated from. It would be impossible to think or to set this up without the help and guidance of his people at the field office, and he knew exactly who would dare to do such a thing without consulting the management. The curious feeling he had about her following the meeting with the obese chairman of the IAW was now turning into one of serious concern. How could she know so much about the Richfield Experiment? Where did her information come from? Who was behind her, pulling her strings? Could she be a spy of another conglomerate, like his nemesis, the Science and Technology Foundation, or, as a disaster scenario, one for the IAW? And he'd appointed her as the lead of the murder case with his own hands, to be an expendable asset at a moment of his choosing. Now that seemingly expendable asset had quickly turned into a volatile and explosive one.

The first thing that came to his mind was to reject the proposal and grill this senior agent himself to expose her puppet-masters, but he changed his mind quickly, as many things didn't add up. He had run a thorough background check on her before entrusting the murder case, through the Psychological Warfare Unit of GPSN and his own spy network, and the comprehensive profiling had shown that she was an intelligent and loyal agent with no risk of being exposed to any outside influences. He had also assigned his most trusted staff in the field office to subtly keep an eye her, receiving no alarming reports so far.

Moreover, the request from Richfield was perfectly in line with his strategy that he had been implementing over the last three years, with its climax the coming day. Actually, it was going to make it even easier to achieve the overall objective. The climate was perfect to implement such cooperation with the Richfield Experiment, and as a part of his strategy and design, global attention had already been focused on the incompetence of the immigration academies around the world, all week long. This cooperation would only improve the resolution and make it even more applauded by the press and the masses, further enhancing his glory. And the senior agent was the connection that bound it all together; she had to be there to make it all work. Once his objective was reached, he could always find other ways to discard her at a timing of his choosing. He needed to talk to that trusted staff of his in order to make arrangements.

He didn't like the unknowns that came with her, as there were just too many of them for a man who prided himself in knowing everything there is to know, and perhaps she was as bad as a bringer of chaos and devastation as her director claimed her to be. In the top-level competitive environment, calm and tranquility were not a favorable climate for the likes of him. If one knew how to harness the hurricane and the devastation it brought, one could reap huge benefits from it by channeling it in the right direction. Didn't the Supreme Selfs do the same during the Great Meltdown? Just like that late-nineteenth-century inventor who had managed to harness waves in the air to transmit energy to wherever he wanted. Hamilton shared his nickname with that genius.

They were both known as *The Wizard*.

"Ms. Kassel?"

Until that moment, she had stood there like a fashion icon, way out there, out of reach for any ordinary folk. But the moment she opened her mouth, the flawless poise was destroyed, and Gladys made a crashing return to among the mortal living. "Oh, have we met before?" she said in her unmistakable nasal tone.

"Yes, I came to your salon to ask for a meeting with Mr. Arnett here, and you arranged me an appointment on Monday, four weeks from now."

"Was that you? I thought that was a peace agent."

"I am that peace agent, and I need to talk to Mr. Arnett about—"

"Call me Arnie, sweetie pie. And Gwladus, why don't you arrange a meeting with this prettiness here for some time tomorrow afternoon? We shouldn't make our dear teacher's companion wait *four weeks*. That would be so uncool, wouldn't you say?"

"Yes, Arnie," said Gladys with a forced smile.

"Oh, well, time to move on," said Arnett, throwing his hands in the air. "Need to make some purchases for the benefit from the trash there which they shamelessly refer to as *art*. Always such a pleasure to see you, dear teacher. We'd be all lost without your love and guidance."

"Always a pleasure to see you, too, Arnie."

And off went Roger Arnett and his entourage. Phoenix watched behind them as they made way for themselves in the crowd. She noticed Headperson Valkoinen at a distance, squeezed into an uncomfortable-looking crushed-velvet black sheath, exposing just a little too much of her masculine calves. It appeared like she was entertaining a delegation with the help of Ion, in an all-white tunic with thick-rimmed white spectacles, and her angels in matching dresses with the headperson. The man at the center of attention was a short man with long dark hair, greeting everyone with a big smile, wearing a neon-green tunic.

She excused herself from Rottenmeier and Gisella and kept moving again, searching for the mysterious DeVille. She glanced at Sandra from a distance— she appeared bored and annoyed, yet unable to shake off the sticky journalist. She also noticed Dr. Capello, draped in a flowing black dress, with a layer of floaty black chiffon over a fluid black silk empire gown, standing in a slightly elevated corner and observing everybody with her tilted head.

"Looking for me?" drawled someone from behind her.

The Crane watched the party with amusement, imagining the reaction he would receive if he were to show up there with his traditional costume and hat. He could be quite cool, if he played it right, and if that flamboyant dude dressed like a nineteenth-century British prince could pull it off, why couldn't he? He and the Toboggan Hat could be a real hit there!

Following recent developments, the grandmasters had revealed the identity of the Mantis to him a few hours previously and had asked him to monitor his activities twenty-four seven until the plan was completed. To get the job done, he had hacked into the surveillance mainframe of the city; he could now observe any public place he pleased. So far, the Mantis appeared to be behaving normally and within accepted limits. As he casually switched through the cameras to monitor the activity in the party, he jumped from his seat to get closer to the screen. It was *her*, the woman he had run into and had felt all those incredible feelings for, the one he hadn't been able stop thinking about. His eyes glued to the screen, he watched her move around the crowds in grace.

"Wanna dance, Nix?"

Phoenix glared at Julio blankly for a moment or two. He'd wrapped his body in a tight mauve tunic that highlighted his fake muscles. She opened her mouth to say something scathing, and out popped a giggle that escalated into full-blown laughter. "You want to dance," she said in between spurts of laughter, "with me?"

"Sure, why not?" he said with a shrug. "What's so funny?"

"You."

"I'm glad you finally noticed my humorous side," he said with an attempt to touch her arm. "See, I ain't such a bad guy after all."

Phoenix avoided his touch skillfully as she swayed away. "No," she said, shaking her head. "You're not bad. But you're the most annoying self-serving sleazebag that I've ever met in my entire life."

"Self-serving, I am. Annoying, I could be at times. But I'm not a sleazebag, babe. And you are definitely one hell of a babe tonight. Actually make that a babe and a half. Now how about that dance?"

She found herself quite flattered by the compliments she was receiving from him, regardless of the tasteless and crude way they were delivered. She could feel, even smell, the testosterone flowing in his body and the attraction he felt for her, and it might—just might—have been a turn-on for the old Phoenix, but definitely not for the new one. He was just another sleazebag looking for an easy lay, to dump soon afterwards, a crude male version of Sandra, running on greed and testosterone and nothing else. There was no room for appreciating and treasuring any feelings or emotions behind that shell, only to consume them and to throw them in the trash, just like a fifth grader with a cheap toy. She moved close to him with a smile as if she were playing along and leaned close to his ear.

"Not in a million years, even if you were the last man on earth," she whispered and pushed him out of her way, leaving Julio mouthing silently.

She made her way towards the back of the building, by the art displays, to look for DeVille, and there he was. She slowly edged closer, as if she were getting close to a rare wild bird. She wasn't sure how to approach him, but the encounter with Julio had given her an idea.

"Pierre, how are you?"

"I fine, sugar. How're you?" replied DeVille with a grin.

"Don't you remember me? I was at your house yesterday."

"Oh, you," said DeVille and sighed. "What do you want?"

"I needed to talk to you, but you've been avoiding me," she said in a playful childish voice. "You made my heart nearly explode, you know."

"I did, didn't I?" grinned DeVille. "I know I'm hot 'n all, but I've never made a chick faint before."

"I want you to make me feel the same way, Pierre," she said in a whisper. "I want you to be explosive and deadly."

"Oh yeah, sugar," said Pierre, visibly salivating. "I'm gonna light your fire. Let's get outta here and go to your place."

"Oh, no," said Phoenix, pouting. "I wanna ride you surrounded by your fine art and feel that chill all over again."

"Oh, ride me you will. Let's get outta here now."

"Oh, yes, please. But I need to talk to my date first. I wouldn't wanna ditch him like that, you know. Can we meet outside in twenty?"

"Hey, don't you be ditchin' me either, now, you hear?"

It was around two in the morning, and the party was in full swing. Music was a lot louder, the place was jam-packed, and Phoenix could barely find her way back to Sandra. Astonishingly enough, Ainsworth was still with her.

"Powder room?"

"Powder room," Sandra replied, with a flash of anger in her eyes. They left Ainsworth and cut through the swarming crowds.

"I can't believe you left me like that, you slut. The guy wouldn't leave me alone for a moment."

"Hey, you're a grown-up and can take care of yourself. Why didn't you tell him to piss off?"

"Are you kidding? He's press. He can make up all kinds of shit stories about me if I piss him off."

"So you're gonna sleep with him so he doesn't badmouth you?"

"Do I have any other choice?" said Sandra through gritted teeth.

"Sure you do. Now let's powder up, and lemme take care of it."

As they left the powder room, they ran into Beverly. She was dressed in an outfit identical to Valkoinen's, but while the headperson looked faintly ridiculous and uncomfortable, Beverly looked like a million dollars, as the same crushed-velvet black bodice pushed her creamy breasts up and out, the same below-the-knee skirt revealed flawlessly toned elegant calves with ballerina ankles, and identical delicate sandals enhanced the exquisite arch of her finely boned tiny feet.

"Hey, Beverly. Look at you!"

"No, look at *you!*" said Beverly, scanning her top to toe over and over. "You look amazing, sis."

"Beverly, this is Sandra, my friend. Sandra, meet Beverly."

"Hey," said Beverly and turned to Phoenix. "We uploaded all the data; the rest depends on their end."

"I know," nodded Phoenix. "Where have you been all this time? Don't tell me you tended the upload."

"Nah," said Beverly, with a grin. "That's a job for the likes of Harold. Had other stuff to take care of. So what are you girls up to?"

"We're actually about to take off. I finally caught up with this DeVille guy, and I gotta go after him. Then I need to prepare for the morning."

"Be careful with him, you hear? Want me to alert a rapid action team?"

"No, I can handle him. Gonna be there tomorrow?"

"Would I ever miss it? I'm gonna root for you, girl, and with the stuff you're doing with those Richfield people, you'll be saving me so much future headache."

"If all goes as planned."

"Oh, trust me, it will. Now, if you girls excuse me, I gotta party."

"I didn't like her manners," said Sandra. "She's not polite."

"She's my only ally at work," said Phoenix as they squeezed through the crowds.

"So I hear."

"From your secret buddy at my office?"

"Sure, and I don't understand why you feel so apprehensive about that. I got buddies in every big office in town, baby. Who's in, who's out, what's up, what's down. This is my only trade secret."

They went back to Ainsworth, who was idly waiting at the same spot. He produced his trademark smile as they approached.

"Ladies."

"Well, the ladies are beat, and they're leaving," said Phoenix.

"But the party just started swinging, and I barely got acquainted with you two."

"Well, I'm afraid we'll need to do that some other time. We gotta go. And you need to produce that footage for me tomorrow."

"I don't know if I can."

"I know you can, and you will," said Phoenix, her gray gaze cold as ice. "Or else I'll make sure neither you nor your channel get any cooperation from GPSN Peace Corps in the foreseeable future."

Ainsworth cleared his throat, avoiding Phoenix's stare. "You can't do that," he said, with yet another smile. "I mean, no offense, but you're just a senior agent. You can't have that kind of clout."

"You wanna try me?" said Phoenix, with sudden fire sparking in her green-gray stare. "I'm just a senior agent with a ten-million-dollar negative-risk credit line, who will make a thirty-minute interview worth of tens of billions of dollars in settlement and a multi-billion-dollar annual contract tomorrow. So, wanna try me?"

Ainsworth fell silent and swallowed. Following a few seconds of silence, he shook his head slowly.

"I didn't think so. Now, were leaving, and I expect that footage on my desk tomorrow," said Phoenix, and she turned to walk away.

"Wait," said Ainsworth behind her.

Phoenix turned and crossed her arms. "What?"

"Can I quote you on what you just said about that interview?"

"So, sugar, here we are," said DeVille. "Wanna take a bed now?"

DeVille's house was as disgusting as ever. Phoenix carefully moved around the piles of dirt and trash, so as not to taint her beautiful gown.

"Oh, no," she said with simulated enthusiasm. "I need to get the chills first." She walked over to the pile of art lying on the floor by the firearm collection. The pile appeared to be untouched. She kneeled down and started to flip through the canvasses.

"This is all your work, right?" she asked as she flipped. "More light, please."

"That's right, sugar. Computer: Lights to evening mode. So you like being bare and stark, sugar?"

Phoenix continued flipping through the pictures, and she froze when she saw it again, a giant snake ripping through the abdomen of a blonde woman just like herself and shooting towards the sky. A jolt of electricity went through her body, erasing her pretention of playfulness. She pulled the picture out and stood up.

"Did you paint this? Did you?" she said, her hands trembling.

"I painted all of them, sugar," said DeVille, still grinning. "Chill out, now."

"I said did you paint this? Tell me when? Answer me!"

"I—I don't know. I must've painted it some years ago. I don't remember."

"You painted it, not someone else?"

"It's in my pile, isn't it? Hey, what's going on here?"

"You were being ripped off by Bogdanov, that's what's going on! Are *you* getting the chills?"

"What the hell are you talking about, bitch?"

"He made hundreds of grand in your even-steven, dream-team art biz. That's what I'm talking about."

"Get outta here! Nobody can make a six-figure art consultancy in this town. You're full of shit!"

She dropped the art on the floor and took slow steps towards DeVille like a carnivore about to pounce on its prey. He took a couple of steps back as she advanced, hitting his desk, spilling piles of junk on the floor. She noticed the little red packages that fell on the floor but focused back on him.

"I have the bank records to prove it," she hissed. "He was cheating you. He was cheating you big time, and you knew it."

"I don't believe you, Agent Bitch."

"Oh yeah? PA: Upload Vassily Bogdanov's financial information to Pierre DeVille's PA." DeVille turned his PA on as Phoenix zoomed in and checked out the pile of junk on the desk up close and the red items on the floor.

"Oh, that teacher-fucking fat wanker," he shrieked. "He sure got what he deserved, that son of a bitch. I want my money!"

"You can sue his estate. Now, don't be pretending that you didn't know about this before."

"Of course I didn't. I can't believe that fat bastard was filling his own pockets like that."

"Did you rat him out to the Dinastiya?"

"Did I rat him out to who?"

"The Russian mob. He was bragging to you about them, wasn't he?"

"Say what? I know no mafia, man! And I want you to get outta here, now."

"He said he'd let you in on it, didn't he?"

"Let me in on what? I think you're cracking up, bitch. Nothing you say makes sense. And I had such plans for you tonight. Now get outta here."

"All right," said Phoenix, moving towards the door. "But make no mistake. I'll be back with a warrant."

"You do that," sneered DeVille behind her. "I dare you! I'll get my lawyer to kick your ass."

Phoenix left DeVille's apartment smiling. She was still feeling somewhat unsettled because of the painting, but it was all under control. Besides, she wasn't worried about nightmares tonight. She had other plans.

"Tess."

"Hey, Phoenix, so many encounters tonight."

"Yep. You've seen it all, yes?"

"All of it, including DeVille's interesting house."

"I saw some evidence in there, and I'll need to examine the footage later. But we have more urgent matters at hand. How's the processing going?"

"With the current level of processing allocation, I expect it to be complete on time. And our request for a test run this morning was approved by your executives late last night. We're all set to proceed."

"Bravo! I've got just enough time to change and go back to work."

"You don't plan to rest tonight?"

"Nope. I have only a few hours to go over the resulting information with you. You will help me, right?"

"Of course," nodded Tess. "I'm cleared to be with you and assist you all the way, including the procedure. You're sure you don't want to rest for an hour or two beforehand? I can start the study and fill you in."

"Thanks, but no. I need to understand this through and through before I walk in there. Besides, rest usually means unrest to me, these days."

FRIDAY

CHAPTER 27

"**Hey**, sis, ready to become a rock star?"

Beverly stared at her by the door, her arms folded and grinning, as Phoenix checked her makeup one last time.

"I'm not sure; I don't even like rock music. Is that what they think of me? Some outdated woman who uses her talents in an irresponsible way?"

"They're afraid of you. You're the guy they love to hate."

"Are you talking about the academy people or my beloved field office coworkers?"

"I'm talking about those incompetent bastards, who else? They're swarming the hallways en masse as we speak."

"Dunno what they're afraid of," said Phoenix as she touched up. "Alex is right, you know. If I were to approve this student now, I'll be scrutinized. If I were to strike her out, the scrutiny will be even worse. I can't even imagine what might happen if I fail to complete the damn thing. From all angles it's a lose-lose situation. Then I'll get fired."

She felt some comfort thanks to her recent negative risk credit line. She didn't know what kind of strings were attached to it, but at least nobody could deport her from the Union that easily, not until her HDI plummeted. Quarterly reviews started at birth, then they were reviewed every three months. With her last one a few days before on April fifth, she had at least another three months to figure out something.

"Stop thinking about that. You'll be great. Did I tell you that I have my money on you?"

"Seriously?"

"You got the charm, sis. C'mon, there are people who wanna meet you."

There was quite a turnout from the academy camp in the hallways, and tension was in the air, with a mixture of both supportive and hostile feelings emanating from the crowd. The Viewers' Lounge was more crowded than the hallway, with many familiar faces. Director Morssen motioned for them to join. She was with Valkoinen, Ion, Alex, a man, and a woman in expensive designer suits whom she vaguely remembered from the night before, and the smiley short man with long hair that she distinctly remembered.

"I'd like you to meet the lady and gentleman from the board of Immigration Academies Worldwide, and your watchdog, Mr. Richfield."

Richfield took a few steps and extended his hand.

"So very pleased to meet you, Agent Wallis. Tess talks about you all the time. She likes you very much, you know."

"I know, sir," said Phoenix and smiled. "And the feelings are mutual. Pleased to meet you all," she added formally with a brief nod at the others.

"I didn't know that you two were acquainted," said the tall black man from the IAW board.

"We're not," said Phoenix, not giving Richfield a chance to explain. "We just have a mutual friend." Richfield smiled and nodded.

"I can't say that I'm pleased to meet you at all," said the Board Man. "You appear to be nothing but a troublemaker."

"I apologize for any trouble I caused you, sir, but don't take it personally. Everyone around me gets wind of it, not just you."

The director could barely suppress a smile at the answer.

"I notice that you haven't managed to conceal your red eyes," said the Board Woman in a deep voice. "Couldn't sleep from the worries?"

"Actually, it was more like the other way around," said Phoenix.

The woman first nodded at the answer, then got a curious expression on her face as she tried to make sense of Phoenix's strange choice of words.

"Now if you'll excuse me, I need to make some final preparations before Ms. Rana Shah arrives," Phoenix said and turned.

"No coercion this time, please, Agent Wallis," said a cold squeaky voice from behind her. Phoenix turned back and fixed her gaze on the headperson.

"And how does one exactly coerce another into something she's not in a matter of thirty minutes? With a hypothetical mind-altering weapon, or are you accusing me of, excuse the jargon, jinxing or putting the whammy on Ms. Al-Hayani?"

"I accuse you of forcibly convincing a weaker mind that she's something she's not."

"Excuse me, but isn't that exactly what you do with your students any given day?" Phoenix turned and left without giving anyone a chance to reply. She could hear the squeaking behind her as she walked out, her mind imprinted with her fleeting glimpse of the headperson's expression of stunned outrage. The crowds were more intense outside. Ainsworth and some camera crew were setting their equipment up. She walked up to him.

"I told you last night that everything I said was off the record. What are you doing here?"

"Relax, Phoenix," he said, taking a few steps back. "I'm here not because of anything you told me but because we received an invitation from Mr. Richfield for a press announcement in one hour."

"From Richfield?"

"And here's your footage. It came early this morning. Does this news conference have something to do with your billion-dollar interview?"

"No comment," said Phoenix, grabbed the disk, and walked off.

The interview room was empty, but Phoenix felt uneasy, thinking of all the eyes spying on her from behind the big mirror on the wall. She initiated all the computers and expert systems to make sure that the procedural updates were in place. Everything seemed to be in order and good to go.

"Tess."

"Right here, Phoenix. Ready?"

"As ready as I can ever be. Will you be online?"

"I'll be fully integrated with the main servers of the field office during the entire procedure and have access to anything you need. Just call me as usual."

"Respond with audio only, if I call."

The doors opened, and Rana Shah entered with two junior agents at her side. Phoenix watched as she took her seat, mumbling something about her seat being uncomfortable. She was a petite woman in her mid-thirties weighing forty-five kilos at most, her dark and bulky academy uniform making her look even daintier. She had features typical of a woman from the Indian continent: ponytailed long straight black hair, golden brown skin, a slim oval face with a small nose and full lips, and big dark brown eyes reflecting many years of suffering but also deep intelligence.

"Good morning, Ms. Shah. I'm Senior Agent Phoenix Wallis, and I'll be conducting your security interview today."

"I know who you are. You're so famous and feared on the other side of these walls, with big Fs. I wouldn't wanna be famous, you know. It would be such a pain in the ass to be famous."

"Really? And if you share the same fear, I assure you—"

"I don't fear you. But I can't say that I like you, either. You're the biggest obstacle between me and my dream to come true. And I hate obstacles. Who would like obstacles? Nobody!"

"Sweet. Before we begin, I need to make an announcement and inform you of a last-minute procedural change to this interview."

"If it's a last-moment change, why bother? I know I'm at your mercy here, so it really doesn't matter to me. Why should it matter if I'm at your mercy? I read about what you did to Patel, you know. Terrible guy, Patel. Did he deserve what he got? He did. He was at your mercy. I'm at your mercy, so why bother?"

"It may matter to you, actually. According to this change, this interview will begin with already-established baseline behavior patterns for you. I did it by analyzing the footage of your entire tenure at the academy."

"Are you telling me you sat down and watched my entire six months at the academy?" said Rana, with a curious nod. "Thousands of hours of footage? Who would watch my footage? I wouldn't watch my footage."

"It was more than ten thousand, actually. But it wasn't me who watched it. The footage of your entire tenure was processed by the behavioral expert systems of the Richfield Experiment."

"Oh, gee, that's such a relief. I had to confess to so many things, I bet those expert programs had a field day. Actually, it was more fun being observed by so many people during these six months, not that I'm an exhibitionist or anything. You can be only an exhibitionist if humans are watching you. Can you imagine being an exhibitionist in front of a cat or a dog? I don't think so. Some computers doing the same doesn't really matter to me."

"But it matters to me. I will be able to ask you more relevant questions about possible security risks, as opposed to asking irrelevant ones to establish a baseline first. This is also a much healthier way to achieve such a baseline level for you or anyone else, since it's based on thousands of behaviors on a wide variety of situations, as opposed to just a few based on questions asked in an artificial setting."

"You have the duty to ask me what you believe to be a relevant question, and I have the option to answer as I see best."

"Are you trying to say that you will not give straight answers to my questions?"

"Did I say that? No, I didn't! Are you trying to put words in my mouth? I think you are. And I warn you, don't ever put words in my mouth, just because you happen to be a *famous feared agent*, with double Fs!"

"This is outrageous!" said Valkoinen. "Your monster's attempting to psych out and coerce my student again, Dagmar. Is there no limit to her appetite for destruction? Stop this charade before the interview begins."

"I don't know what's going on, either. Mr. Richfield, do you have any knowledge of this procedural change Agent Wallis is talking about?"

"Actually, I do," said the man, smiling expansively. "I personally requested it from your executives, Director Morssen."

"You requested what?"

"Can someone explain to us what's going on here?" said the Board Man from behind. "Valkoinen, what's this procedure change?"

"I have no idea, sir. But this monster disguised as an agent is attempting to skip the compulsory establishment of the baseline behavior patterns and is turning her interview into a mockery again."

A tense silence enveloped the Viewers' Lounge, as the members of the opposing camps glared at each other. All of a sudden, the room erupted. Academy people were on the attack to their field office counterparts, with Valkoinen demanding answers from a stunned director, Ion from a clueless Alex, and others from Fred, Beverly, and Julio. Fred fidgeted nervously, Julio tried to calm them down by being flirtatious, and Beverly yelled back. Simon Richfield was trying to calm everyone down, but with all the loud accusations and shouting, the lounge was ready to crack.

"How could you not know about such a change?" said Valkoinen to the director. "You're lying, you miserable angry goat!"

"Watch your language, Ingrid. I told you I know nothing of it."

"How could you pull something behind our backs, after the hundreds of millions we just donated to your cause, Richfield?" yelled the Board Woman.

"It's for the good of all your academies, too, I assure you," said Richfield, with a nervous smile.

"If this is for the good of the academies, why not inform us? And you're the one who informed the press of it? You'll pay for this, Richfield."

"I intend to stop this charade now," said Valkoinen. "I'll get my student out of there before the procedure begins and inform the press about this scandal."

The director watched her leave, not knowing what to do. But a figure that moved swiftly from the shadowy part of the wall blocked her way.

Valkoinen froze before the man who came with an Arrivee tattoo, and looked over her shoulder at the board people for support. The room quieted down straightaway.

"Do you have an explanation for all this, Hamilton?" said the Board Man.

"Of course. You will be witnessing the future of the security interview process, a procedure that leaves no room for manipulation and error, lifting the burden off my agents from the incompetence and corruption of your academy staff."

"How dare you make such accusations!" said the Board Woman.

"I dare because I can. I approved of this procedural change late last night, after a brilliant last-moment request from Richfield here, suggesting we test-run this brainchild of mine today, as this particular interview seemed like the perfect opportunity, with you, valued board members of the IAW, present, and with Richfield as the globally accredited expert in behavioral field as your watchdog." Richfield smiled and opened his arms towards Hamilton, showing his appreciation for the praise. "If any of you would like to leave, they may do so and be escorted to wait in another room until this interview is over. But I strongly urge you to follow this interview in an orderly fashion and learn something. It has already started. Now, sit down, all of you."

The crowd took their seats quietly and turned their attention to the other room. Hamilton ushered the two board members to the isolated reserved seats in the back row, pointing one to his left and the other to his right.

"Take your seats, please. We have business to discuss."

"I examined your time at the academy thoroughly, Ms. Shah, and I have to tell you that one of the biggest worries I have is your preference to be a loner. Were you always a loner?"

"Me, being a loner out of preference?" said Rana, with a *duh* face. "My biological parents died when I was little, Agent F, during a riot right about when I was three. Did I get a chance to know them? I didn't. Then I was cast out by my society. Why? Because I wasn't bio-kin. So racist of them to choose who to care based on bloodline! So what preference are you talking about? I wanted people around me all my life."

"I understand. I noticed that you felt some irritation and discomfort while the subject of nation-state taxation systems was being discussed in your classes."

"It wasn't discomfort, Agent F, it was contempt. Why would anyone like taxes? Would you like taxes? Can you imagine anybody liking taxes? I don't think so."

"Why did you feel contempt? Because you knew their ways to be fatally wrong all along?"

"Of course I knew," said Rana, rolling her eyes. "Why wouldn't I know? Why wouldn't anyone know? You don't need the academy training to know that taxation with representation was the biggest flaw of the nation-state system. Masses were allowed to bribe central governments and to push them into populist choices, which seldom made any sense. Bloated governments with a huge appetite for spending people's product of labor forced higher taxes onto the rich and destroyed the economic natural selection process by favoring the meek, and by punishing those with a healthy greed. Can you believe that? Can anyone get more stupid than that? Hah! And those governments all claimed to be *for the people*, and yet they never allowed anyone to be greedier than themselves. Public needs and happiness were relegated to a second-tier target. Can you believe that, huh? I couldn't believe that."

"I guess you didn't enjoy paying taxes there."

"No, I didn't," said Rana, shaking her head irritably. "And I never paid. Why should I pay taxes? Why should anybody pay taxes? Would you pay taxes, if you were in my shoes? But you couldn't be in my shoes. They're only size thirty-four."

"You could get away with that? I heard that the nation states always jealously guarded their tax collection and even claimed taxes to be the only other inescapable reality of life other than death."

"They have to intimidate citizens in order to be able to collect these taxes," shrugged Rana. "It would be signing their own death warrant if they failed. I can't think of a setup where a nation state wouldn't intimidate its citizens one way or the other. But I had enough with all that intimidation. I decided that nobody would intimidate me. I wouldn't let you intimidate me, if you tried to intimidate me."

"During your tenure, you voiced your hatred for the nation-state system in general on many occasions. This isn't very common among immigrants from a rogue state, as most people feel some form of loyalty until they are convinced otherwise by being exposed to indisputable facts about fallacies and shortcomings of these governments. Why wasn't this the case with you?"

"Why should it be the case with me? I'm not stupid like the others. It's so obvious that nation states, empires, and everything before them inherited every habit from the hunter-gatherer society. Do I look like a hunter-gatherer to you? I wouldn't know the first thing about hunting or gathering if you left me in a jungle. Nation states had a great chance in setting things straight for the society because of the Industrial Revolution, but instead they brought greater misery, war, and economic destruction. I've seen war, I've seen destruction. Did you see destruction? And anybody who saw what I saw would know what I'm talking about."

"So you don't believe in a nation-state form of democracy either?"

"Hah," grunted Rana. "A democracy where all beggars can beg for more handouts. A democracy where voting is a birthright, so that looters can erode the democracy by democratic means. Gimme a break! Is that democracy? Would you live in a democracy like that? Nobody would wanna live in a democracy like that. Would I wanna live in a democracy like that? I don't think so."

"What about the World Union? What about our geniocracy here?"

"No offense, but I couldn't care less about the geniocracy or how the tranquility was established here. All I want is some peace of mind, some quiet. I'm so sick and tired of hostile and non-caring crowds and noise and all. How would you like to work in a hostile, crowded, and noisy environ-ment like that? I bet you wouldn't last a minute. Especially a *famous feared agent* like you. I want personal peace. I want to be able to do my work. I don't want any trouble from anyone. Would you want trouble from anyone? You wouldn't, of course."

Phoenix checked the indicators before her: The expert computers had de-ducted five points from the overall score for an unfavorable comment on the Union system. She was impressed that the expert system could filter out and decipher such comments from the verbal bombardment from Rana.

"And what work do you plan to do here?"

"Computers and network security. I used to do lots of hacking, Agent F. I know how a hacker mind works, and I know how to stop it. I bet you couldn't tell a hacker mind if you saw one. Do you really think you could do that? I don't think so. Only a hacker would know another hacker mind."

Indeed Rana's personal confessions were full of hacking incidents. Evidently she had accumulated the money for the academy through hacking, as well, and worked part time at the academy network center.

"Do you still have a hacker mind?"

"Of course I still have a hacker mind. But having a hacker mind doesn't mean that I'll be doing hacking in the Union. Why would I do hacking in the Union? If you were me, you wouldn't do hacking in the Union, would you? Of course not. For your information, there is no way I would do hacking in the Union, just because you'd expect me to do hacking in the Union."

"Of course not," said Phoenix racing between following Rana's train of thought and checking the indicators before her. The overall score was now down to eighty-nine, and it appeared that if she kept asking questions along the same line, Rana's score would eventually drop below seventy before the gong struck thirty. Phoenix didn't understand what her game was, and her mind was numbed from her verbal bombardment.

"Five minutes' timeout," she declared and got up. She had added this timeout clause to the procedural changes she had requested as a precaution, and it was approved as is. It never occurred to her that she would be actually using it in her first interview. The main computer suspended the thirty-minute clock, to be resumed at Phoenix's command.

"A timeout? May I take a stroll?" said Rana, with an attempt to get up.

"I'm afraid not. You can't leave the room. I'll be right back."

"If I can't stroll, what's the point of a timeout? How can she call this a timeout and not let me chill out for a while? What's a timeout without a stroll?"

Phoenix went to the dark corner of the room, next to the big mirror, ignoring the grumbling. "Tess," she whispered.

"Right here. Some wordy woman she is. Need something?"

"Yes, I need you to check something for me."

The viewers in the first and second row of the Viewers' Lounge got up and leaned close to the window to see what Phoenix was doing in the dark corner nearby. It appeared like she was facing the corner and talking.

"What the hell?" said Ion. "Is she psyching herself up or what?"

"Don't know," said Alex. "Maybe she has a headache or something."

Ion was truly mad at Phoenix for taking a big shortcut with this shit procedural change, dumping all his plans in the garbage. It was decided that they would throw the biggest troublemaker of the academy before Phoenix, and Ion exactly knew who to pick. This argumentative, picky, and annoying student with a long list of confessions would drive Phoenix over the edge and make her do crazy stuff in front of everyone.

Phoenix's biggest drawback was her inexperience, and Ion had told Rana to never give a straight answer when asked about her childhood or the Supreme Bill, or similar stuff. If Rana could manage to invalidate the interview by stalling and never allowing Phoenix to establish a baseline behavior pattern, her reward would be a very easy interview with Julio next, which would almost certainly guarantee her citizenship, as no female student had gotten less than ninety points from him, ever. But all of that was yesterday's news with this procedural change that the GPSN had cooked up.

"Bill is not telling you everything," whispered Hamilton to the Board Man and Woman. "His personal hatred for me is getting ahead of his greed."

"I can't say that I blame him for that," said the Board Woman. "If someone was to target me as much as you targeted him, I'd be pissed, too."

"I did it because he's the weakest link, yet he remains in the driver seat. You both know that IAW cannot make it through this year without outside help. I made numerous decent offers for IAW's salvation, but he keeps pushing them away on personal grounds."

"There is one thing that I don't understand, Hamilton," said the Board Man. "Why do you want to buy us out so badly?"

"Because it's my job to secure the borders of the Union, and the declining quality of your academies is my biggest security threat. The scandal at the Hong Kong academy is only the tip of the iceberg. It will only get worse in coming years, and unless I put a stop to it, I'll need to deal with a flood of subpar immigrants prone to crime, hitting my share price along with yours."

"But this settlement with you will help us get through our financial troubles. Then we can focus on reforming the academies."

"What settlement? I never agreed to one. I know Bill convinced all of you that he could twist my arm for such a thing, but he's wrong. I will make a big media spectacle out of this collaboration with Simon and why we needed to resort to it, and openly challenge the fitness of your academies."

"Before the press?" gaped the Board Woman. "Are you crazy? That would start a public outcry devastating both of our companies. It would give your nemesis the Science and Technology Foundation a golden opportunity to shred you into pieces before the public and the CDC Corporation to destroy us."

"You're leaving me no choice," shrugged Hamilton. "I haven't the luxury of waiting for you to pull your act together. I'd rather have you destroyed by the CDC and shut your doors than to continue with your existing level of incompetence. I can deal with the heat from the science geeks. GPSN is prepared to take this as far as it can go, and you both know that we can afford to do it. With the boost that I'll get from this collaboration with the Richfield Experiment, and the hit that you get from Simpson vs. Cain, I'll bury you. You won't make it till the end of third quarter."

"What's your offer?" hissed the Board Man.

"Eleven dollars per share."

"Are you out of your mind? You were offering us forty yesterday!"

"I know. But like I told Bill, that offer was only good yesterday, but he decided to turn it down for all of you and said we'd settle today. He had the idea that it would be under better terms for some reason. Maybe he was drunk, maybe he was high, maybe both, I don't know."

The two board members looked at each other, their faces white, with cold sweat beading on Board Man's temples.

"Regardless of the outcome of this interview, I guarantee you that your share price will be below ten in the Far Eastern markets within the hour. By the time our obese friend wakes up on the other side of the world, it will be all over. But in case it isn't over and I've been overestimating the drop in your share price, I will personally cover any losses you two might incur from my own pocket, up to forty dollars per share."

"If you're guaranteeing to match the market price on the coming Monday for all of my shares, I'm in," said the Board Woman.

"I'm guaranteeing the price beginning one hour from now, following Mr. Show-Off's press conference at ten local time," said Hamilton, looking at his old-style mechanical wristwatch, "until the end of trading today in European markets, and only if we complete the transaction before the end of the interview."

The Board Man and Woman looked at each other one more time.

"Done," said the Board Man.

"So tell me about your hacking days. Did you have a nickname or an online name?"

"What kinda question is that, Agent F?" said Rana, with a sour face. "Of course I had a nickname. What's a hacker without a nick?"

"Were you generally a contractor, or did you act alone?"

"I was contracted out, I acted alone," shrugged Rana. "What's the difference? It was all for money. I wore no color hat. I followed no code of conduct. I did it so I could be free, I could be protected. You have no idea how hard it is to stay safe in a rogue state. Nobody could know that without living in one. Could you know that without living in one? I don't think so."

"No, I couldn't," said Phoenix, shaking her head. "Where did you receive your education? Where did you learn how to hack?"

"Education?" smirked Rana. "Hah, education is a myth. They cram poor kids into some room, drill all that junk into their heads through some loser who has no idea how to approach them, and they shamelessly call that education! Who needs that? Would you want that? I wouldn't want that."

"So you are self-taught? What was your online name, anyway?"

"Of course I was self-taught," said Rana, folding her arms. "Every hacker is self-taught. You think you can learn all this from books or something? Who would write a book like that, huh? I wouldn't write a book like that."

"And your online name was?"

"So you gotta know, huh, Agent Famous," sneered Rana. "All right, I'll enlighten you. I was known as a Ghost. I moved through networks like a ghost, dancing around anti-spyware software, giving them the finger."

"So you'd write spy programs to hack?"

"Of course I wrote spyware. Every hacker writes spyware. Can't think of a hacker who wouldn't. I couldn't hack anywhere if I didn't write spyware."

"All right, Ghost, I got the message. Which was the highest tier you could hack into with your *spyware?*"

Rana paused for a moment. Phoenix noticed a slight elevation in heart rate and blood pressure. Brain activity showed that a lie could be imminent.

"Do you want the absolute Ghost truth or the version of the truth on the net?" she whispered, suddenly looking concerned.

"Absolute Ghost truth, please," said Phoenix, with a *duh* look on her face.

"None," said Rana, chin down. "But this is strictly between you and I. I know that the hacker days of the Ghost are already over, but I would like the name to live on as a legend in the depths of the digital universe."

"Don't worry about the immortality of the name Ghost, if there was ever such a hacker, that is. You see, my problem is, I know of so many incidents and reports about those notorious hackers, yet I've never heard of a hacker known as the Ghost."

"Not all of us leave behind a business card. Tell me, Agent F, if you were a hacker, would you leave your credentials behind? I'm not dumb enough to do that. I did it for the money, not for the glory, not for the hat."

Phoenix noticed a blink on the monitor in front of her. It was a message from Tess. She glanced at the contents of the message as she kept talking to Rana. "Still, there are rumors and legends," she said, then she directly looked into Rana's eyes. "So tell me, have you ever attempted a hack in the Union?"

"I've never been in the Union. How can I attempt a hack in the Union?"

"That's not true," said Phoenix, with a grin.

"How can it not be true? I'm not lying to you. I wouldn't lie to you, even if I wanted to lie to you."

"I didn't say that you were. Technically speaking, you're in World Union right now. Your answer was not true, but you didn't lie, either, because you didn't think about this technicality. Regardless of all that, you're very good at fending off questions. I asked you if you had hacked any Union network, and you skillfully diverted the question and concentrated on physical location. Because you knew my next question would be about your last hack, which I know for a fact was just a couple of days ago."

"What hack are you talking about, Agent F?"

"A mail that you sent from one of the student issue network nodes at the academy. It was rerouted and appeared to have been tagged by Tier Zero itself and found its way to our field office's network admin desk. I bet its attachment is nothing like what our network experts would expect. You knew that nobody would be suspicious about a mail from the Zero, because it's every admin's dream come true."

Rana attempted to say something only to back down at the last moment.

"And you were very careful with your words, when you asked me if I wanted 'the Ghost version of the truth.' There was no hacking in the Ghost version, simply because there was no hacker named the Ghost."

"But, how could that be? I told you my online alias, and the expert systems would catch my lie, if it was the case."

"Again, you were very careful with your wording. You said you were 'known as a Ghost.' You didn't necessarily lie, and this kind of ambiguity is hard to trace for our expert systems. They seem to work much better with event-based lies, lies people tell about actual events to conceal the truth. So I asked for some help to decipher your wording during the break, and a program specifically designed to break down and expose such ambiguities from the Richfield Experiment came to my aid. The analysis before me is clear: You didn't say what your hacking alias was, and you didn't say that your hacking alias was the Ghost. So, Ms. Ghost, tell me. What is your hacking alias?"

Rana stayed quiet and kept her head down. The visuals reflecting Rana's thoughts in the background had been all garbled Internet coding since the hacking dialogue started.

"You can't keep quiet forever, but I'll help you. The word ghost was another planned ambiguity, wasn't it? You said you could roam networks like a ghost, and nobody could tell if you were ever there or not, a reality or a fantasy. So your real alias had to be a word that would create just enough ambiguity in a computer's algorithm for you to get away with it. Perhaps *Mirage?*"

Rana kept quiet, looking down.

"Are you known as the Mirage? Answer me!"

"Yes, I am." Silence filled the room for long seconds.

"Did you send that message to field office admin with spyware?"

"Yes, I did." The chatterbox was gone, giving way to a calmer and less animated woman underneath.

"For what purpose?"

"For money. My end of the bargain for a deal that made it possible for me to attend the academy."

"A deal with who?"

"The Russian mob. They provided me a hundred thousand dollars and safe passage. They needed someone who had access to the Internet from within the World Union so that the mail wouldn't get rejected by the Union firewalls. I was to find the memory chip containing the spyware in my locker, and that's what happened. Routing the mail while inside the Union part of the cloud was easy. I didn't write the spyware, so I don't know what it does. How could you tell that I sent that mail?"

"By comparing the timing of the arrival of the mail to the field office admin desk and trace-routing the mail back to the academy computer lab. It was a simple but brilliant idea to route the mail and mimic its origin to be Tier Zero. A simple tracing would've exposed it, but who would suspect such a thing? Your video log at the academy computer lab proved that it originated from you. You were the only one in the lab at that time."

"For obvious reasons," said Rana, with the same eerie calm.

"Tell me, why did you want to infiltrate the World Union? Were you planning to hack our systems from the inside?"

Rana didn't answer, just kept staring into Phoenix's eyes.

"Have it your way, Mirage or Rana Shah or whatever your real name is. The indicators before me show your final score as *zero*. I hereby declare that you failed this security interview. You will be taken into custody as a wanted criminal and interrogated further by our Psychological Warfare Unit to disclose your real intent in coming to the Union. After your psychological checkup and possible treatment, you will be permanently deported. Goodbye, Mirage."

CHAPTER 28

"**DEVELOPMENTS** this morning herald a brand-new collaboration between our companies, the Richfield Foundation and GPSN," said Richfield with his broad smile. "Today we performed a test run for merging technologies of the Richfield Experiment with GPSN's security interview process. I have to admit, I didn't expect such spectacular results in our test run."

"Which results are you referring to, Mr. Richfield?" said a journalist.

"With crucial help and information provided by our neural network, a GPSN senior agent caught a known terrorist who was trying to infiltrate into the Union in disguise as an academy student in a security interview. I always knew that the research we did in the experiment would be priceless when the time came. Now I would like to ask those skeptics: How do you measure the value of catching a known terrorist who was about to make her way into our Union?"

The Board Man walked quietly next to Hamilton in the hallway, watching Richfield rejoicing before the press, thinking this worst-case scenario pushed the boundaries of the plausible. He had no idea how that squeaky bitch managed to put psychopaths or criminals before that smart-ass disaster zone, in no less than two times out of three stinkin' interviews. What kind of incompetence would produce such stupidities in the span of just one week? But it didn't matter anymore, and the *former* Board Man was sure that he had made the right call by selling his shares at eleven dollars. Under the circumstances, it would be considered a steal. He checked the face of the former Board Woman, and it was clear that her thoughts were the same.

"It was good that you could come today, so that you could witness with your own eyes how bad it is," said Hamilton. "It will be all over in a few hours, and my takeover of IAW will be complete. Your share sale was flash news in the Tokyo market just before it closed. I heard that in Hong Kong prices are currently around five dollars, Coalition dollars that is, with a massive stampede to sell."

Phoenix received an ovation from the waiting crowd when she came out of the interview room. Beverly reached her first and gave a warm hug.

"You did it, sis, you earned me five hundred smackers!"

"Well done, Phoenix," said Alex, shaking her hand with both of his. "I don't know how you end up with these crooks all the time, but I'm glad that it's you they face, because you have a natural talent for unmasking them."

"And cracking them, too," added Fred. "I guess I kinda owe you one, Phoenix, you saved my ass with that mail from the *Zero* business. Now, how the hell did you know it had spyware?"

"I didn't. But it all added up that it should."

"I can't believe you caught the famed Mirage," said Fred. "She'd been under the same roof with us all those months, wow. Tell you what, I'm gonna treasure that mail from her like a souvenir, like the *end of an era* kinda thing, like '*Here people, this was the last-ever hack attempt by the Mirage*'."

"Congratulations, Phoenix," said Sean. She appeared a bit down, not exactly joining in the celebration. Perhaps things were not as happy as she had hoped with her new sex partner.

"Thanks, Sean."

The crowd parted and gave way to a small figure. Director Morssen walked to the front with a flat and expressionless face. "Come with me to my office."

The director didn't speak for a while, pressing her palms to her eyes. Then she opened them, and the stern woman was back. "First of all, I'd like to congratulate you. No matter how it came about, you managed to identify and capture a known terrorist who was about to slip into the Union right under our noses, with heck knows what agenda. In doing so, you brought glory and success to this field office."

"Thank you."

"I don't know how all these improbable events are finding you each and every time. But so far, you've managed slip through and outmaneuver everything that came your way. I don't know if it's a coincidence, or luck, or sheer brilliance, or what. I'm not even sure if I really want to know at this point." She paused. "Computer: Stop logging the meeting. Now tell me. How did you learn about this protocol change? Mr. Hamilton mentioned answering some last-moment request from Richfield yesterday evening. Was it late last night after the party that they contacted you?"

"No, not exactly. I—I knew it before that."

"When? Did Mr. Hamilton contact you?"

"No, he didn't."

"Then talk to me: Who was it? Who did this behind my back and made me look like a fool before everyone in there?"

"I did it," hissed a deep voice and filled the room through the speakers on the walls. "Wallis learned about the procedure and was told to keep quiet through my organization. So stop interrogating her on matters she's not supposed to talk about."

The oblivious expression on Phoenix's face made it evident that she had never spoken to Hamilton nor heard him speak before. That hiss was unmistakable: once heard, never forgotten. Everybody joked about how Hamilton had eyes and ears everywhere, but it was the first time the director was witnessing something like this.

"I see, sir. May I ask why I was left out of all this?"

"Wallis, go and fetch Lubosh, Berger, and Blackmore in here," said Hamilton. Phoenix looked at the director and got a nod in approval. She exited the room with hurried steps, bewildered.

"I left you out because I needed the academy folk to walk into my trap without any suspicions. You needed to play your part as a genuinely clueless director, complementing my role of genuinely cornered and helpless top executive, and I didn't want to take a gamble on your acting skills. But all the credit belongs to Wallis for unveiling the Mirage. However, I expect the Bogdanov case to be wrapped up by Monday, so make her get results.

"I'm suspending all security interviews worldwide as of this moment. Some things are definitely not right with those academies, and I've been smelling something putrid there for a long time now. This triple Strike-Out by Wallis cannot be a coincidence. But we need to do our own homework, too. I want a full investigation of the interview process first. I want know its flaws, shortcomings, issues, problems. You have one week to fully implement the new procedure and train all agents and other personnel. This field office will be the showcase of our new interview technology. After that, we'll streamline the interview process and then it will be implemented in every field office across six continents. I also want our network and security systems to be fully integrated with the academy side, with full access granted to Richfield neural network, understood?"

"Yes, sir. Will the academy side cooperate and support this initiative?"

"Don't worry about that, Dagmar," whispered Hamilton, with the hint of a smile. "They'll be as obedient as a dog on a leash. My takeover of IAW will be complete before the markets close today."

Director Morssen brooded about all the strings that had been pulled behind her back, her conversations being monitored, and who knew what other tricks and manipulations Hamilton had been concocting without her knowledge. She didn't expect him to reveal all his corporate plans to her or anything like that, but being a lab rat and cast as the clueless dunce of the field office was definitely not something she had deserved. Hamilton must have contacted Phoenix through an intermediary, someone on her staff that Hamilton knew, like Alex or Beverly. And it could only be Beverly, because her involvement was needed to make all the data available for the neural network's analysis and she was on very friendly terms with Phoenix. She was sunk in her seat, shaking her head, running both hands through her hair in frustration, when Phoenix and the others walked in.

"Well, how about that Strike-Out, Boss?" said Beverly, with a grin.

The director's reply was a cold glare. "Sit down. Hamilton suspended all interviews worldwide. He wants to switch to this new interviewing system he designed as soon as possible. We are to streamline the interview process and integrate the Richfield technology with it within a week, and this field office will be the showcase for all offices around the world. Alex, you'll examine and determine the flaws of the existing interview process, with support from Wallis. You know the existing setup inside out. But perhaps we've been looking at this thing from the wrong angle all along."

Alex nodded and made eye contact with Phoenix, who didn't appear thrilled.

"Beverly, I want you to prepare a manual as to how this technology can assist the interview process, and then write the procedure for it, with feedback from Alex. You'll also need to train all interviewers for it, so arrange a seminar and simulation workshops. Get Phoenix's help if necessary."

"Sure, Boss," nodded Beverly.

"Fred, I need you to extend our full network coverage to the entire building. Also build a firewall to prevent students from doing any form of hacking in the Union. I don't want that 'fake mails from Tier Zero' comedy repeated."

Fred attempted to say something but chickened out at the last instant and watched his hands in his lap.

"Will we get the academy to support that, Boss?" said Beverly.

"I don't think we'll need to worry about hostilities from the academy side anymore. Hamilton is taking over the IAW."

"Really?" said Beverly, agape. "So this is what it was all about; we've been pawns in a way bigger scheme."

"He'd planned it all, I'm not sure how long ago. Luring them to pick Simon Richfield as the watchdog was a part of his plan. So was this neural network support for the security interview. But we have to thank Agent Wallis for catching the Mirage and making it the icing on the cake."

"That'll save me a lot of headache," said Beverly. "I was sick and tired of finding myself at loggerheads with them on every issue. And I knew he was cooking up something, right Alex?"

"You sure did," said Alex, wagging his finger.

"I guess you're already a lot more informed about this new procedure than I am, Beverly."

"Ehm, I think I am, Boss."

"And the hero of the moment," said the director, and turned to Phoenix. "Your job will be even harder now, believe it or not, because Hamilton will be watching you, and he wants results in the Bogdanov case before the next week begins. You have no more excuses of orientation or interviews. I have a feeling that a lot will be changed here in the coming week."

"I know, Director," said Phoenix. "And I have a pocket full of evidence, which can potentially make a break in the case."

Julio thought hard about where he had miscalculated. This mess with the academy was to be his moment of glory, and that was precisely why he had loosened his manipulating grip on Phoenix, even letting go his valuable spy at her side. Now that action proved to be too rash and too premature. He needed to regroup and recycle his plans according to the new equilibrium.

Now it was all obvious that leaving the old bag out of the loop was all part of Hamilton's design. He had left the old bag out in the open so that the likes of himself, Julio, would pick on her like a hyena picking on an incapacitated zebra, letting everybody see that she was a lame duck. And he, Julio, had misinterpreted this message from the very beginning, thinking it was a message for the likes of him, greedy enough to run for the old bag's position. But he had been dead wrong. The message was meant for the academy people, exposing the weak leadership at the field office so that they would be lured into closing in for the kill. Didn't they look like a band of invaders, or a school of piranhas, parading around all arrogant and cocky, as if they owned the damn field office, so sure of themselves before the interview? They were so blindly sure of their victory, none of them realized how Hamilton had pulled the rug from underneath their feet.

Phoenix was under Hamilton's wing, too hot to touch or to mess with until she made a major fuck-up. The direct attack had only made her raise her shields higher, and her defense and counterattack proved to be more effective than anybody could have imagined. Neanderthal or not, this bitch knew how to pick a fight and how to dress up for a party, incidentally. Julio felt lucky that he hadn't been in the target range when she charged. And if she could destroy her opponents the way she did, despite her handicap of being a Neanderthal, Julio didn't want to be near her if she were to think and act by contemporary standards.

He had studied Hamilton's pattern for appointing management and noticed that he had picked people for the job, not the other way around. He needed a provocative angry bitch like the old bag in order to provoke and anger the idiots on the academy side. Then he had made her a lame duck so that they attacked her in blind confidence. And now, looking at the faces of the Board Man and Woman after the interview was over, it appeared like he had decapitated the IAW completely. Now the field office would shift to a new reality, a new equilibrium, and this new equilibrium had no room for the old bag, or for Alex for that matter. The Neanderthal bitch definitely didn't fit the profile, as she was too volatile and knew nothing about greed or corporate politics. The only contender was he, unless Hamilton intended to bring in someone from the outside. But if he was planning to make a shining example of this field office following the Neanderthal's unbelievable triple Strike-Out, he couldn't bring in anyone from the outside, either.

If only he could make one good impression on the *Wizard*.

Phoenix had mixed feelings about the way things had turned out. She was glad that she didn't need to explain all the stuff she had done behind the director's back. But she wasn't happy with how the big boss skillfully claimed the credit that was rightfully hers by taking so many risks under the threat of being fired and deported. On the other hand, if all had been exposed, it would have put tremendous strain on her relations with everyone in the office.

She turned her attention back to the footage from Ainsworth. It was raw and dark, and she couldn't tell anything from it. She had tried to enhance the image several times, but the result had been far worse. The situation called for some expert help.

The moment she walked out she ran into Ray, who was lurking by her office door. "Hey, Ray, how are you today?"

"A storm is brewing," whispered Ray, scrutinizing the ceiling.

"A storm outside, you mean?"

"Oh, no," he whispered. "In here, a terrible, devastating storm."

"Who told you to say this to me? Was it Julio?"

Ray kept looking at the ceiling and the high walls.

"Julio told you to call me by one of those dark nicknames?" said Phoenix and touched his arm to get his attention. "Ground control to General Ray."

"Who?" shrieked Ray. "I know no Julio."

"Then who made you say this?"

"The *me* inside me, deep down in me. A giant storm is brewing, and you need to take cover. And your PA cannot warn you about this."

"This deep thing deep inside you, is it an instinct?"

"An instinct!" said Ray, with widened eyes. "That's what it is, an instinct told me about it. Do you know them?"

"Do I know who? Your instincts?"

"No, *your* instincts. Do you know them?"

Sudden panic invaded Phoenix, rendering her speechless for a few moments. To admit or not to admit? There was no telling where Ray would go and repeat what she might reveal to him. On the other hand, nobody really took Ray seriously, other than herself, that was.

"I'm learning to know them."

"That's wonderful," said Ray, with a big smile, exposing his dire need of dental attention. "They will help you with the coming storm, tell you where you can hide and take cover. But to know them will take an entire life."

"Why is this storm coming, Ray?"

"Because I am calling it," said Ray, widening his eyes. "I am the great general, bringer of storms, destroyer of my enemies. I will demolish all the evil forces, bring them to their knees, and make them surrender!"

Ray kept babbling about the great general and slowly walked away, mopping the floor as usual while Phoenix watched him from behind. There was something about this old man, perhaps so much pain hidden deep inside that made Phoenix *feel* him and perceive him with sympathy. But why she would bother to listen to him this carefully, she had no idea. Perhaps it was the *her* inside her, deep down in her.

"There she is guys, c'mon," said Beverly, and every junior agent at the Monitoring Room gave Phoenix a standing ovation.

"Hey, what's going on? My birthday's not for another six months."

"We congratulate you not only for your un-freakin'-believable triple Strike-Out, but also for your efforts in saving all of us the tedious task of following student behaviors and actions even when they take a piss or wipe their asses," said Beverly with a face-splitting grin.

"Yeah!" said Harold and clapped his hands, initiating another ovation.

"And how about that *zero* as the score?" said Beverly to the mob. "Have any of you ever seen or heard such a thing in a security interview?"

"Not in the history of this planet," yelled someone from the back.

"Oh, you guys, quit the back-patting, please. I need your help." She produced the disc from Ainsworth from her pocket. "I need to make some sense out of the footage on this disc. It's very dark and murky."

"Harold, get your ass here and get this raw footage to work for the lady," said Beverly, checking out the disc. Harold took the disc and plugged it into a network node with a giant screen, then used some tools to adjust the color histogram. "This tool is the next generation of video processing," said Beverly. "We just got it." The dark and murky images became clearer with much better contrast, exposing a crashed plane in flames in the dark of the night. "Whoa," said Beverly. "It's a military plane!"

"I know," said Phoenix, scratching her head. "Too bad its resolution's not high enough. I'd love to see some more detail."

"Who said you couldn't? Are you looking for something in particular?"

"Some contraband maybe?"

"Contraband? Where was this shot, anyway?"

"In the rogue territories."

"Shot down?"

"No, no, I have reason to believe that the pilot of that aircraft, Captain Perez, had been involved in a smuggling ring with my murder victim."

"Computer: You micro-voltaged dimwit, move your lazy electrons and search for contraband in the footage," said Beverly, shaking her head. "Smuggling in a military plane? It's unbelievable. You're sure about this, sis?"

"Pretty sure. I hope this footage will have some positive proof of my theory."

A vertical white line appeared on the screen and moved rapidly back and forth on the image horizontally. It left little dots on the image, and those dots blew up into larger windows, becoming larger and clearer. The image showed hundreds of rectangular red packages spilled on the ground, part burned, part intact.

"Holy shit, you were right. Those are cigarettes. Now what?"

"Now, we log this onto the case database and call for a meeting at once. And I know exactly where I can find similar contraband here in the city."

"Is this authentic?" said the director, her face frozen. Alex, Julio, and Sean watched the processed footage in shock and disbelief.

"Authentic enough that the military asked Ainsworth to keep it hush-hush."

"Okay, let's assume this footage is the real deal and those illegal tobacco products are on their way to the Union," said Julio. "How can you be sure that this is related to the Bogdanov murder?"

"By the fact that Perez's name was on the list made by Bogdanov, and he suffered similar emotional fluctuations as Bogdanov, and I've interviewed this third sales clerk at the Thing Store, who swears that boxes of stuff came to his office and were *rented* to affluent customers. By the way, Sean, did you get a chance to contact the Thing Store headquarters?"

"Yes, I did. They told me that have no rental policies and Bogdanov couldn't have rented anything that was displayed at the store."

"In other words, he had to be renting out something else, which I suspect to be something like the deadly device that killed Dr. Spencer."

"But nobody on that list admits to renting anything," said Sean. "They're all Devotees and insisting that they received art consultancy."

"You talked to all of them? They all said that?"

"All except one," nodded Sean. "I couldn't reach Lena Vanderbilt because her PA was in Silent Mode. Then I searched and found her at the rehab center. She is in intensive care and can't be reached at the moment."

"She was the one who paid Bogdanov hundreds of thousands of dollars in one month," said Phoenix. "Did all of them tell it to you with a straight face?"

"What do you mean? They weren't laughing when they talked."

"Did you get the impression that they were hiding something or lying?"

"I don't know. But most of them seemed quite uncomfortable about my questions. A few hung up on me."

"Understandably, considering what you've been accusing them of," said Julio. "Why don't you just admit that you had no idea how to talk to these Devotees?" Sean said nothing and looked down.

"How about that artist guy?" said the director. "You had some wild theories about him. Any progress on that?"

"I confronted him. He appeared outraged when I told him that Bogdanov had been cheating on him big time, but he denied my accusations, claiming he had no prior knowledge. I'm pretty sure that he's a part of the whole deal, because I saw the same tobacco products in his house."

"What? When?"

"Last night, after the party, I went to his flat to confront him. The illegal tobacco packages that I saw in his house are the same brand as these ones in the plane crash footage. It's all in the case database."

"I hope you didn't initiate any emergency procedure to enter his house this time."

"No, Director Morssen. I've been behaving."

"Those are pretty well-known brand products in the rogue states," said Alex, gazing at the crash footage. "Are you sure it wasn't a coincidence that DeVille had them in his house? Perhaps the man has strange taste when it comes to the articles he likes to display in his flat. Maybe he was just displaying those packages, too."

"I don't think so. I think he got those from Bogdanov. Actually I'm pretty sure about it. Director, I'd like to get a search warrant for Pierre DeVille's house. Also, I'd like to interview him here at the field office."

All eyes turned to the director. It was very difficult to turn down a request from Phoenix at this precise moment. The woman had just saved the entire field office's, even the GPSN's reputation, and she seemed to be acting with an excess of confidence brought on by that success. The director knew that Hamilton would be closely monitoring the developments in the Bogdanov case from now on, and if this DeVille connection proved to be a mistake, there could be an opportunity for her to win back at least some of her control over this field office. However, if Phoenix was right again—

"Granted," she said. "I'll talk to a judge. If the judge agrees, it should be issued within twenty-four hours. Dismissed."

Phoenix received a message the moment the director ended the meeting, and she switched her PA from Busy Mode back to Normal Mode. It was an invitation from someone she had wanted to meet all week long.

CHAPTER 29

"Tess."

"Hey," said Tess, with her surreally dazzling smile. "Congratulations on your amazing Strike-Out."

"Couldn't have done it without your help. It would have been impossible to decipher Mirage's jumbled wording without an analysis on the spot. Thanks, dear."

"My pleasure," winked Tess. "Actually, if she didn't harbor any designs against the Supreme Bill, I would like this Mirage."

"I'm sure you would. Who knows, perhaps even more than you like me. The woman possesses amazing skills in logic, and she's unbelievably quick-witted. Too bad that she's on the wrong side of the law. I don't know. Perhaps if I were in her size thirty-four shoes, I'd be doing the exact same thing."

"You really think so? Would you care to elaborate?"

"Her life and mine seem to have started in a very similar way. Similar riots, similar losses, same scars. But I was fortunate that I ended up being on the right side of the border when it happened. Whether they succeeded or not is another matter, but many people tried to help me and heal me. I had a great teacher-mother in Ms. Rottenmeier. Poor Mirage wasn't that fortunate. She was abandoned. She had no one to turn to, nobody to guide her, nowhere to seek refuge. It's actually amazing that she managed to survive, only to become a dangerous terrorist, of course."

"Do I sense a hint of admiration in there?"

"Oh, no. All I'm saying is that, if I were in her place, I may have had no chance other than to become what she is, in order to survive."

"If you happened to be born over there, I wouldn't want you to be stuck on the other side of the border forever. And that's exactly why our Union gives even criminals like her a second chance, doesn't it?"

"That's true. But I'm not sure how successful our Union has been in educating and filtering out these immigrants. Something is not right here, and I'm not referring to the incompetence of the academies."

"You mean a general problem with the way the World Union deals with the immigration applicants?"

"Yes, but not only that. I don't think the immigration academies have been serving a purpose in line with the interests of the Union."

"Instincts again?"

"Yep," nodded Phoenix. "I wonder what Mirage will reveal when she is questioned by the PWU about her real intentions in the Union."

"PWU?"

"Psychological Warfare Unit, a counter-terrorism unit of the GPSN."

"Never heard of that."

"Because it's a very secret unit. No one at the GPSN knows their member list, except for Hamilton himself."

"In that case, perhaps we'll find out her real intention soon," said Tess. "Now where are you off to?"

"I got an invitation from the Arnett Salon. Lucky coincidence that he paid his respects to Ms. Rottenmeier while I was in her company."

"I know human eyes can be a bit inadequate when it comes to identifying geometric shapes in disguise, but I think you did real well to identify a totally unrecognizable Gladys Kassel. Do you think what an image maker knows can help shed light on the case?"

"I don't know. I'm hoping that Bogdanov might have mentioned a thing or two about his plans, and even bragged about his Mafia past, who knows?"

"Why do you think he'd confess something that secret not to his lawyer but his image maker?"

"Who said he didn't? Maybe Bogdanov told Anderson about his criminal past in confidence without your sister instance noticing it. Besides, I have a feeling that there aren't many secrets between Mr. Anderson and Mr. Arnett—excuse me, *Arnie*."

"Ms. Kassel, hi."

"Oh, Phoenix, I almost didn't recognize you," said Gladys, popping her eyes out. "You look so *ordinary* in those clothes."

"Well, what can I do, comes with the job. Ms. Kassel—"

"Call me Gladys, please," she said, rubbing Phoenix's arm.

"Gladys, Mr. Arnett, I mean Arnie, called you by another name last night."

"You mean Gwladus? It's supposedly the original form of my name. Not that I care or anything, but apparently it's an ancient Celtic name."

"Really? I have some Celtic origins, too."

"You don't say," said Gladys with a fake interest. "So, can I offer you a complimentary M & M?"

"I prefer not to eat candy during the afternoons, but thanks all the same."

Gladys burst into loud laughter abruptly. "My goodness," she gasped at last. "I haven't laughed like that for a long time now. I didn't know GPSN agents could be so humorous. You're so *funny!*"

"I didn't intend to make you laugh, but I'm glad that I could," said Phoenix, still clueless. "We're here to protect and to amuse."

"Oh, that wasn't on purpose?"

"Nope."

"Ah, and I was beginning to think that you were more quick-witted than you looked. I meant a Magical Makeover, not candy."

"You know that I'm not here for a makeover, Gladys."

"But Arnie's not available right this moment, and I'd like to offer you a Magical Makeover with compliments from the salon, while you wait."

"How long do I have to wait? I haven't got all day."

"Oh, not long, Phoenix, dear. Now, how about that makeover?"

"What does a Magical Makeover involve exactly? Does it hurt?"

"Ha, ha, ha." Gladys's laughter was less natural this time. "That was funny, too. Last night who could've told that you were a peace agent. And look at you now. It can only get better, you know."

"Like you said, it's the uniform, dear," said Phoenix, with a fake grin. "So tell me, what exactly do you intend to do?"

"We're going to give you a new hairstyle and do a makeover for your face with top–of–the–line cosmetic products, using our intelligent software."

Perhaps the old Phoenix wouldn't be interested in such an offer, but the emerging new Phoenix enjoyed looking good. Theodora had given her great advice; she could even get better tips from a famed salon like Roger Arnett's. After all, they had designed Tess's clothing and makeup, and she always looked stunning. "All right, I'll take you up on your offer."

"So glad to hear that," said Gladys, wreathed in smiles and clapping her hands. "We won't disappoint you."

"You're still gonna let me see Arnie, right? I mean, I wouldn't wanna miss my chance to see him while being made over."

"I assure you, Phoenix, dear, I'll personally see to it that you have your time with Arnie."

Everybody was ecstatic about the magnificent triple and the fruits that it would bear in the Monitoring Room. Following the integration of the Richfield technology, the bulk of the manual observation work was to become obsolete, and the monitoring was to be confined to suspicious activities based on the neural net's observations and assessment. The neural net was to act like a boundless observer with an unlimited attention span, deep knowledge of human behavior, more than a thousand eyes, ears, and even noses watching over the students twenty-four seven.

Sean was in no mood for a celebration, however, as feelings of being used and betrayed had been eating her up inside. She was feeling utterly stupid that it had taken her so long to realize she had been in a dream world for the last few days. She didn't feel angry at Julio, but angry at herself, because when she thought about all that had been said and done, it was evident that Julio had been using her, but at the same time he had been perfectly clear about his intent and the limits to his relationship potential from the very beginning. But worse than anything else, she had failed Phoenix.

Perhaps making some headway in this murder case could remedy it a bit and make her feel better about herself. Before her were the visual logs that Phoenix had made the night before, with all those illegal tobacco products visible on a disgusting table and a floor full of trash at the DeVille residence. She had viewed this video again and again, searching for details that might have been overlooked, as she had been sure that something didn't add up somehow since the moment she first glanced at the video. She couldn't tell what it was, and she couldn't focus well because of the noise, but there was something in that video that nobody had noticed but her. Yet the thought had been hiding somewhere in one corner of her mind, refusing to surface, and she didn't know why. Could it be because it was something so out of the box? Could it be something unthinkable? Or could she be feeling this way because she contracted some communicable mental disease from Phoenix, as Julio had suggested?

Actually, if Phoenix had some mental disease that made her so smart and talented, she wouldn't mind contracting it. Because all her life she had felt like a misfit with her openness and honesty, taken advantage of immeasurably in the process, and no matter how much she had wished to act and be like Julio and his kind, she had always fallen flat on her face, becoming an emotional ruin. But now she could see that there was another way just by watching Phoenix. She was *so* different from the others. Maybe she was as primitive as Julio had claimed her to be, but she knew how to take risks and how to bend the system to her favor.

She knew how to defy the odds and the laws of statistics, didn't care if she didn't have help, never complained, never brown-nosed, and never sucked it up. She was determined to make her own path, clear it with her bare hands if necessary, and it appeared like nothing and no one could stand in the way of the tsunami she would create.

Sean had no idea if she was as gifted as Phoenix. The odds were she wasn't even close. But she could at least try to learn from her own mistakes, try to defend her own rights, try to build her own path, and try to find herself and be herself for a change. All she needed was a little encouragement, and the best encouragement would come from within herself. If only she could make a little difference in this murder case, she would have all the encouragement she needed. That one glance from Phoenix, a nod of approval, a brief smile of appreciation would be worth a lifetime's achievement.

If only she could figure out what was wrong in the video before her.

"Oh, my goodness, Phoenix," said Gladys, clapping. "You look like a million bucks! I would never have guessed that a makeover could improve you so much!"

"Lemme see."

"Ta da!" Gladys enabled the surrounding mirrors in a true reality show manner. Phoenix tried to blink at her own hideous reflection, but her eyelashes were too heavy to move that quickly.

She looked as if she had been the victim of a schizophrenic toddler's face-painting session. Random patches of her face, not just eyelids and cheeks, had been daubed with an eclectic assortment of garish colors. She could see fuchsia and turquoise and lemon streaks fighting for attention on one cheekbone alone. Her own eyebrows had been airily dismissed, apparently, and she had been given brand-new ones that reached as far as her hairline, shaped like boomerangs and colored a terrifyingly lurid shade of purple. She had been given two new sets of eyelashes, one bile green and the other orange. Her lips had been concealed under the thick layer of whitish base that had been slapped all over her face, and a new mouth had been drawn on with what looked like a pink highlighter pen. The piece de resistance was probably her right eye, which had apparently been painted to look like she'd just been knocked about by a renegade academy student, the splotches of green, purple, and dark blue extended to fill her entire eye socket.

"I'm completely surprised and overwhelmed," said Phoenix, somebody else's mouth moving as she spoke. "I never thought such a makeover was even possible."

"That's what we're here for. We can do wonders with anybody's face. You look sensational. So postmodern, so *object d'art*."

"Evidently," said Phoenix. "Now that we had our fun, can we—"

"Oh, by the way, Arnie's ready to see you, and he's only got like fifteen minutes."

Phoenix swallowed the first ten words she was about to say. It was evident from the proud grin in her stupid face that she hadn't performed this atrocity on purpose. "He is? Fine."

Gladys led her inside and left, closing the door, and the blaring music disappeared with her. Natural light streamed in from outside, exposing beautiful classical paintings and some artifacts from sub-Saharan Africa on the walls, complemented by perfect artificial lighting. Arnett was sitting on an antique chair and working at an antique desk made of English oak, scribbling with pencil and paper, reminding her of DeVille and his disgusting flat. The strange thing was that there were no network nodes, no computers of any sort, not even a PA attached to Arnett's ear. The serene mood of the office was enhanced by freely resonating sounds from the nature in the background, which appeared to be bouncing off the walls and moving in every direction, giving the sensation of being in a secret garden. The gorgeous Oriental carpet on the floor appeared antique and handmade, and Phoenix walked along its perimeter, avoiding stepping on the exquisite designs.

Arnett was in a royal-blue single piece sleeveless suit that tightly wrapped his body, highlighting his toned muscles. His eyes were lined flawlessly in black, his eyelashes coated in black mascara, accentuating his royal-blue eyes. His facial structure was fine and determined and came with a regal nose. He had some faint pink lip gloss and was humming a tune as he sketched. He lifted his head up, and his curious and scrutinizing gaze observed Phoenix thoroughly, making her feel like she had been stripped to the bone and that Arnett could read the depths of her soul. She shivered at the thought.

"Hello, Arnie. My name's Phoenix Wallis, and we met last night at the party. I was with Director Rottenmeier."

"Oh, right, right, the one with the pink dress. I didn't recognize you, sweetie. It must be the uniform."

"Yes, my uniform can do that."

"All right, then, Phoenix of Uniform, what can I do for you today? What kind of image change do you have in mind? I have to tell you, the road's significantly steeper in your line of business."

"But I'm not here to change my image. I'm here to discuss peace business."

"Peace business? Gwladus didn't say anything about any peace business. I thought you were here for an image change, a makeover."

"But I've just had a makeover. You mean you can't tell?"

"Your face looks atrocious," said Arnett, with a sour face. "The color set's all wrong, and the—who did this crappy job anyway?"

"It was *Gwladus*, your assistant," said Phoenix, with a sour face of her own, or at least she tried.

"Oh, is that right? You lucky devil! She must have been trying one of those beta program scripts, experimenting for her term assignment. Obviously she's chosen the wrong color set for you. Anyway, what kind of peace business do you have with me?"

"It's about one of your clients, Vassily Bogdanov."

"Who? Oh, you're talking about VeeBee," nodded Arnett.

"VeeBee? I don't know. Are we talking about the same man?"

"A short, dumpy, bald chap, right? He was one of my very new customers. I never even had a chance to implement the latest makeover that I designed for him. Such a shame."

"I assume you're aware of his untimely death."

"But of course I am, sweetie pie. And such an untimely death it was."

"How do you mean?"

"VeeBee was a dream case for any image maker. There was so much to be done with him. If I'd had enough time to successfully transform that man, I would have been the star of every fashion show on the planet."

"Quite," sighed Phoenix. "I guess I've never looked at it that way."

"Oh really?" said Arnett, examining his perfectly manicured nails. "You investigate his murder, I presume. Wouldn't you be on the cover of every other *Murderous Intent Weekly*, if you were to successfully, whatever success means in such things, solve his barbaric death?"

"Perhaps I would. But why do I get the impression that you don't like my line of work?"

"Because I don't, sweetie pie. I wonder if his death is in any way linked to his sudden wealth."

"Indeed," said Phoenix, her eyes widened at the unexpected insight. "Like my line of work or not, you could make an excellent agent."

"What an atrocious idea," murmured Arnett, frowning as if he had just found a flaw in his manicure. "It's such a crude and dull job. I'm out there to create people, not to destroy them."

"I destroy people in my line of work? I'm a peace agent, not a marine."

"But of course you do. You destroy people's lives, and you have to live with that. Did you ever consider the consequences of wrong decisions in your line of work?"

"Our procedures, protocols, and technology ensure that no harm can come to innocent people, I assure you."

"Oh, dearie, quit reciting from the official website and think about it a little bit," said Arnie, lifting his head up with a gaze full of boredom. "To the likes of you, what shapes a criminal's mind is irrelevant. You think you have all the technology—and perhaps you do—to catch a criminal. But tell me, what good does it do to catch a criminal once the crime has been committed and people are hurt? Who cares if you can understand the criminal mind when it's already too late? How much better are you in that sense from those impotent police forces in those rogue states? Anyway, you're probably too inexperienced to understand and appreciate what I'm talking about. Perhaps you're not even *smart* enough, hmm?"

Phoenix had expected this conversation to go many different ways, but she had never imagined that Arnett would openly assault her career choice and intelligence. It appeared like he was playing some kind of a mind game with her, perhaps in an effort to provoke her and to make her react, for whatever twisted reason he had in mind. One thing was for sure: This man was smarter and bolder than anyone Phoenix had interviewed so far. Her instincts told her to keep her cool no matter what.

"Could we stick to the subject of Bogdanov, please?"

"Suit yourself," said Arnett, his eyes narrowing as he looked into hers, smiling faintly as if he were peering through the windows of somebody's residence and seeing something extremely private going on. "Many people have to pay truckloads of dollars to hear my comments, insights, and suggestions. You just got an earful, *pro bono.*"

"Do you think Bogdanov's business was going well?"

"It certainly seemed to be. I got the feeling that his financial status was improving rapidly."

"And how could you tell that?"

"From the very basic fact that he could afford my services, sweetie pie. It's very unusual for me to have a client with an HDI of only seventy. But he was definitely going to make a giant leap in his next quarterly review."

"What makes you so sure?"

"Let's just say it's my professional intuition. I have to understand my clients well and get into their heads *before* I help them with their images, not after like in certain other lines of business."

"This prediction of yours is purely intuition based?"

"Not only. In my line of business, you always need to support your intuition with a plausible rumor."

"In my line of business, we tend to ignore rumors. We look for the facts."

"Oh, really?" said Arnett, with his faint smile and condescending gaze. "In that case, let me just say that my plausible rumors can be more reliable than your *facts.*"

"Did Bogdanov ever mention to you any of his business ventures?"

"You mean outside of his involvement at that tasteless store where they sell all that junk as hot objects? He'd mentioned an art consultancy business with some young artist he claimed to have discovered, but I just filtered it out."

"You mean to say you ignored it, assuming he had lied to you?"

"I'm exposed to so much hearsay in my line of business, sweetie pie, I just filter out the ones that don't seem plausible. And this art business of VeeBee's was hard to fathom."

"You don't think he had any appreciation for art?"

"Definitely not. Besides, to be an art consultant you need more than just an appreciation of art. You need to know how to implement art."

"You're talking about art as if it has some kind of a magical formula."

"Sure it has," said Arnett, suddenly animated. "It has the most complex formula in the universe. And only a select few have the eyes and ears to understand and apply it."

"Did you know he was going to Russia?"

"No, I didn't. Is that where he died?"

"Yes. Do you know what might have possessed him to go there?"

"For all I know, he might have gone there to cheat for his much-desired weight loss," said Arnett, sketching a few lines on paper. "You know about the barbaric and futile methods they use there to get rid of excess fat, don't you?"

"Yes, I know," nodded Phoenix. "So, he never mentioned to you that he was a recent immigrant?

"He was a Russian immigrant?" said Arnett, lifting his head with the first hint of interest he had betrayed so far. "I guess I should have known. He certainly possessed the characteristics of one."

"And what characteristics would those be?"

"The sloppy dress, poor physical condition, horrible hairstyle, terrible taste in shoes, colors, and the way he carried himself when he walked. Oh, he had such *horrible* posture. I can just remember him sitting where you are, sulking with sunken shoulders, miserable and unhappy."

"So, you don't think that Bogdanov was happy in the Union?"

"He pretended to be. But deep down he wasn't."

"How can you be so sure?"

"I was his image maker, sweetie pie. My job is to make people feel good about themselves and flourish. I know the signs of a genuinely unhappy person. Then again, who isn't?"

"You don't believe people are happy in the Union?"

"Of course not," said Arnett and looked deep into Phoenix's green-gray eyes. "Let's consider you for a moment: You're professionally disillusioned and personally very lonely, just like everybody else."

"To your knowledge, did Bogdanov have many friends?"

"No, he didn't. His interpersonal skills were severely underdeveloped and lacked refinement. I'm sure this was nothing new, and I bet he was the same way where he came from."

"You make him sound like a real outcast. But I have eyewitness accounts that he was a social butterfly among the city's elite Devotees."

"I don't know what else other than a laughingstock he could've been for an average Devotee in his current condition. I guess he could have acted with politically correct manners in those circles in short bursts, only because he was excessively greedy and possessed some willpower. I could say he had the right foundations to become a success story. Otherwise I wouldn't have taken him on."

"Greed and willpower would be the conditions for accepting a case like him?"

"Greed and willpower are the basic ingredients for success in any society, sweetie pie. If you possess those, you have the potential to become anyone you want, provided that you're ready to make sacrifices, of course."

"Was Bogdanov ready to make such sacrifices?"

"That, I'm not sure about. He was supposed to make some important decisions this week regarding my proposed makeover, but—"

"How about enemies? In your opinion, did he have any enemies?"

"You're asking this to the wrong person, aren't you? This is something *you* should be figuring out, not me. Looks like you're truly desperate."

"Let's assume that I am. What would your answer be?"

"So you're willing to stamp on your pride to find answers. How interesting," said Arnett, his smile widening until it was almost wolfish. "But I doubt that he had any enemies here."

"What makes you say that?"

"Because, my dear, our little VeeBee had no wings. He was just learning to walk in the business world."

"His lack of experience in the business world has kept him from developing enemies?"

"Oh, but she's learning," said Arnett, in mock surprise. "Let me elaborate better so you don't need to push those gray cells into a futile overdrive: It's more like he was an ant in the land of elephants. Nobody would notice his presence, no matter how much noise he might make."

"So what made him so unnoticeable?"

"How about the fact that half of the Union is made up of ants just like him, sharing his HDI?"

"Then how do you explain his murder?"

"Sweetie pie, I only told you about the dynamics of *our* society. VeeBee was murdered in a rogue state. It's a completely different ball game there. And I have no idea if he was an ant, elephant, or a zebra in that society."

It was really surprising that Arnett could make such deductions based on the little information she had revealed to him. And it appeared that as long as she let him play his mind games, he would be willing to participate in her brainstorming.

"So, in your opinion, his murder may have links to his rogue-state past?"

"If you're just a teeny bit good at your awful job, you would have deduced that by now," yawned Arnett. "So why do you ask me questions that you already know the answers to? Looking for reassurance, little girl?"

Phoenix swallowed, counted to ten in her head, then continued.

"So, in your opinion, the World Union has no connection to his murder?"

"How can I be sure about that based on the fragments of information you chose to share with me?" he said in mock innocence. "But you know what? Sometimes elephants unknowingly stomp on ants, too."

"Do you know if Bogdanov had any duties in Anti Chaos Society or Amnesty Global, or similar NGOs, which might have led him to leave the country and allow his past to have a chance to catch up with him?"

"Oh, I tried so hard to get him interested in Amnesty Global," said Arnett, shaking his head. "I explained it all to him that it was very important, for public relations purposes, every affluent man needed to be involved in at least one NGO duty, yet he didn't care."

"Couldn't he understand that it was part of his debt to society?"

"Oh, goodness gracious," sniggered Arnett. "Where do you get these philosophical lines? Those are for college kids. You cannot expect a man at VeeBee's stage in life to fall for such ridiculous ideas."

"You don't believe that you're indebted to our system?"

"Look, dearie," he said in a tone of weary exasperation. "To get a man to change takes a lot of convincing. If you feed him the same bullshit that he's been exposed to all his life, you're not going to get anywhere. You need to use words that will touch his subconscious, words that he thinks of but could never utter."

Phoenix felt so strange that she was in the position of defending the World Union system against this arrogant man. It was only yesterday that she'd been feeling totally discarded and abandoned by the same system. Yes, the system was ruthless and had many shortcomings, perhaps wasn't the best place for her to be and live. But it had a working formula for the masses. Yet this insolent man was shamelessly attacking its core principles. "Are you saying that some people don't feel they have any debt to the Union?"

"That is exactly what I'm saying."

"Who? Are you referring to new immigrants and that the immigration academies are doing a bad job?"

"Oh, who cares about what a global disaster immigration academies have been, spitting out losers that were supposed to contribute to this society. I'm talking about people with high HDIs, not low. It's as simple as one, two, three to those of intelligence. As one climbs up the ladders in a society, one starts feeling more and more like an owner, less like a member of it."

"An owner of the society?"

"Society, company, system, you name it. I'm not saying this is how these affluent people think. This is how they *feel*. And to an owner of the society, a debt to the society has no meaning. And I need to talk to these people along these lines in order to reach them. Are there enough gray cells under that neglected hair of yours to understand what I'm talking about?"

She wasn't sure how much of it reflected in her face, but Phoenix was stunned by the way Arnett openly challenged an important founding principle of the World Union, calling it a farce. World Union was built to stand on a society that glorified civil associations or NGOs and relied on the involvement of its citizens in them. In the absence of a traditional political system and strong government, these Non-Governmental Organizations were responsible for uniting people under common causes, pursuing common rights, and procuring the loyalty of the masses to avoid chaos and anarchy.

"You're questioning some of the basic foundations of our system, Arnie, and you could be prosecuted for violating our constitution."

"Then take me to court, if you can, sweetie pie. But you can never prove any violation of the Supreme Bill. Besides, the founders of our system believe in the importance of our thoughts and services. And that's why we have a special deal with the GPSN. See?"

"Are you trying to say that you're immune to such prosecution?"

"Let's just say that I like walking on the fine line between lawful and unlawful," grinned Arnett. "Another reason why I have a helluva lawyer, who knows your company rules and the Supreme Bill inside out."

"Sweet. And the other reason would be?"

"A much more personal reason that I'm sure you wouldn't care to know."

Suddenly a loud sound filled the room, coming from her PA. It was a non-maskable interrupt, and it could be only coming from one person.

"Ah, I hate those devices," said Arnett, turning his head away. "Who needs them, anyway?"

"What is it, Sandra?"

"Phoenix, come to the ZAP store! It's life or death, quick!"

"On my way," she said and hung up. "I need to leave now, Arnie."

"Oh, good. And don't forget not to come back. I have no time to spare for peace agents seeking reassurance."

Phoenix sprinted from the Pyramid metro station to the ZAP store, overtaking several others on the way running in the same direction. She reached the entrance panting, only to see utter chaos inside, with crowds swarming in the aisles, pushing and shoving each other. She noticed the tall figure of Sandra in one of the aisles, trying to hold her ground. She noticed Phoenix and waved her hand frantically.

"Phoenix, is that you? Quick, I got only a minute and fifteen left!"

"One-fifteen for what?"

"Get your curvy ass here, now!"

Phoenix made her way towards the aisle, pushing her way through the hysterical crowds to reach Sandra. "What is it?" she said, still panting.

"The red one or the black one?" Sandra was holding two dresses in her hand with time-tickers, which counted down from one hour, the maximum extent she was able to hold them. Several others were waiting for her time to expire so that they could grab the garments from Sandra.

"You called me all the way here for this?"

"The red or black? Answer now, I only got fifteen seconds left."

Phoenix looked at the garments quickly, trying to withstand the pushing and shoving around her. "Red."

Sandra dropped the black garment, and another woman quickly grabbed it in mid-air. "PA: Scan and purchase the garment in my hand," said Sandra to complete the transaction. "Yay, it was on sale, 80 percent off!"

They made their way out of the packed aisle, towards a calmer area of the store. Phoenix wiped the sweat off her forehead, and a large stain of makeup came off in her hands. Sandra smiled like a little child, kept staring at the garment. Phoenix took out the makeup removal cloth that she had grabbed on her way out of the Arnett Salon and started wiping her makeup off.

"I can't believe you called me here for my opinion on that dress," she said. "I was in the middle of a very important meeting."

"Phoenix Wallis, get a hold on yourself. You can always finish your important business later. You know these spring sales only last for one hour, and I needed your opinion on that dress. What the hell happened to your face, anyway? You look like a renegade clown from one of them rogue state circuses."

"Why couldn't you just call someone else?" said Phoenix, moving in front of a mirror to finish off her cleansing. "You have plenty of friends at work who leisurely plan parties all day long and parade at expensive salons and do nothing else."

"What, I should call the competition to help pick a dress?" said Sandra, with a *duh* expression in her face. "Would you share the tricks of your trade or ask advice about how to conduct one of your famous interviews from that Don Juan or whatever his name is? Hello! This is the ZAP store. I work here, remember? The moment I ask someone's opinion here, the word gets out that I'm losing my edge. And you showed some real potential last night, with the dress and the makeup you applied at home all by yourself. I even felt jealous, you know. So I thought I could try your advice. But look at you now: worse than the old Phoenix."

"It wasn't me," snorted Phoenix. "It was the Arnett Salon."

Sandra burst out laughing, unable to stop for a while, compounding Phoenix's anger at the entire incident. This woman was supposed to be her best friend in town, yet her appetite for selfishness knew no limits.

"You know how crucial the Bogdanov case is. Unlike you, I can't afford to take shopping breaks like this from my work right now. Don't you understand?"

"So you think my work is less important than yours? C'mon, you're a GPSN agent. You should know better than anyone that our system's and economy's well-being depends on responsible people like me, who make the effort to discover and rush to these sales. As far as our economic system is concerned, no business can be more important than a spring sale!"

As she was about to reply to Sandra in a manner that she truly deserved using a choice of words she would be all too familiar with, Phoenix saw him, lurking outside the store, and started to push her way back out through the sea of spring sale shoppers without wasting a word, leaving Sandra standing there with her mouth open and with her sexy red garment dangling from her hand.

CHAPTER 30

THE Mantis was beginning to feel truly frustrated and couldn't understand how Phoenix could still be as mentally fit as she appeared. He had swapped her mood stabilizers the day before, replacing them with his custom eraser-psychedelic cocktail containing a twenty-four-hour rapid-action eraser drug to quickly eliminate the effects of the mood stabilizers in her bloodstream and a strong psychedelic to flood Phoenix's subconscious and push it into the conscious level at full strength. This cocktail was designed for phase one of his plan, where he would drive Phoenix from being an introvert and dormant loner to an unstable and hallucinating monster. She had been already having a lot of difficulty sleeping even with the stabilizers she took. With his cocktail, the contents of her night terrors would be greatly amplified and would spill over to her consciousness in the form of hallucinations, completely swamping her rational thought, making her act crazy and delirious.

The Mantis had also produced a second set of drugs for phase two of his plan, consisting of pure psychedelic, to be planted in Phoenix's house before everything was over. When discovered after his end game, everything about her behavior, how and why she had done what she had done, would become meaningful in any investigator's eyes. Depending on the way certain details would unfold, the Mantis planned either to disgrace Phoenix and turn her into a ruin for the rest of her life or to arrange her death along with a disgrace, perhaps the less painful of the two alternatives.

Phoenix took her drugs in the evening, before going to bed. With the rapid-action release property of the cocktail, the timing should have been perfect, resulting in a magnificent night terror, making her empty and disoriented the next day. But unfortunately the desired effect was nowhere to be seen yet; on the contrary, she had appeared more lucid and in control than the days before. The only explanation that the Mantis could think of was that Phoenix had not slept at all the night before. She had had a very late night at the party, and from there she had gone to DeVille's house, then she had somehow got prepared for the surprise procedure change that Hamilton had shocked everyone with.

The situation was still under control, as the Mantis had considered this unexpected contingency and was prepared for it. Right now she was feeling high from her temporary and undeserved success with the interview. But the day that her world would collapse and destroy her conclusively was planned to be the next day. The Mantis had meticulously designed Saturday to be the worst day of her life, leading to her eventual ruin, or death, or perhaps both.

Phoenix got herself out of the packed ZAP store on the tail of the man she thought she saw. Her senses were totally haywire, her mind was thoroughly confused, and her heart was racing as if running the home stretch in a dash race. Could it be him? Could it be the intruder? *Her* intruder? It was just a fleeting glimpse, a millisecond that she had seen him, when their eyes met momentarily, as he walked off casually. He had appeared totally unaware, perhaps not seeing her inside the store, even though he was exposed to her gaze where he stood outside. Phoenix didn't know what to do, as she could in no way be sure whether it was him or not, so she had decided to follow him, hoping to get an idea about his identity.

Her feelings had just shattered her own emotional ceiling, yet she managed to remain outwardly calm and maintain a distance as she followed him, while he strolled as if he couldn't care less if the whole world was after him. She had thought about confronting him but dismissed the idea immediately, as he might be still equipped with that mind-altering weapon, and a confrontation might result in losing him completely.

He walked down the central metro station below the Pyramid, casually taking the path to the Omega line. The empty train came into the station, and crowds boarded the cars, Phoenix taking the car behind the one that he took, observing his casual moves out of the corner of her eye. She tried to keep him in her visual field at all times, ready to exit the train the moment he did. She couldn't stop the ringing in her ears or calm her heart rate down, barely managing to maintain focus on the task at the same time. She had instructed her PA to record everything, hoping to get a clear image of the man as she discreetly observed him from a distance.

The stations passed one by one, and the cars got emptier and emptier as the train approached its final stop at Omega Ten. Anxiety started filling Phoenix. What if he were to get off at the last station and simply walk into the field office? Her heart was beating faster and faster, her temples chill from perspiration, emotions racing, mind desperately trying to retain control. It was impossible for her to analyze her feelings at the moment, as the entire spectrum of them was numbed by the bombardment of emotions, making her feel dizzy and defocused.

After Omega Nine, just the two of them were left on the train. He was idly sitting in the car at front, with his back to Phoenix. Could he be turning himself in? Could he be someone else, just a figment of her non-mood-stabilized imagination? Could she have been hallucinating all along? Or could this be just another daydream, and she would wake up, surrounded by spring sale shoppers and her utterly self-centered best friend laughing scornfully at her? Trying to contain her flood of emotions, Phoenix's energy was beginning to wear off, and the fatigue of the night before and insomnia of nearly two weeks was beginning to weigh in again. She was in no shape to confront the man, if she had to; in fact, she realized she was barely holding it together.

The train slowed down and stopped at Omega Ten, with Phoenix holding her breath, utterly immobile. The man casually got up and walked out of the car, leaving Phoenix's field of vision. She wasn't sure how to follow him, now that there were just the two of them. She waited for a few more seconds and got out of the car. To her surprise, the man was gone—vanished. She looked at the long empty platform before her, with the closest exit at least twenty meters away. He would need to dash real hard to cover that distance in the span of a few seconds.

With a sudden burst of adrenaline, she sprinted towards the exit. She climbed the escalator quickly, reaching the totally empty main station area. She walked hurriedly and glanced at the kiosks, dispensers, public lavatories, and every other crevice where he might have hidden. But there was nobody other than the annoying 3D bot-ads jumping before her to get her attention from every direction. She glanced once again at the ad she kept seeing, "Where do you want to go today?" thinking that she wanted to go where *he* was going.

After being reasonably sure that the station was totally empty, Phoenix climbed up the stairs to the surface. It was a bright and sunny day, with a soft wind from the east. The cool wind made her feel calmer for a while and help her focus on the task at hand. Where was he?

Beverly felt inordinately proud of her newest creation. She hadn't wasted any time and had immediately contacted the Richfield people, initiating the integration process between the field office network and the Richfield neural net. The people on the Richfield side had responded rapidly and forwarded an installer, which had customized itself to her specific preferences through a quick questionnaire, and the result was Bud, a humanoid character resembling a rock star of the good ol' 1970s, speaking the way she liked. He was a dream come true!

"Bud."

Bud appeared in the middle of the Monitoring Room, projected by one of the Holovisions. He produced a gorgeous smile in his tank top and skin-tight black leather jacket, leather pants, and boots. He was in his mid-forties, had a chiseled face, long dark hair that was somewhat straggly in line with the style of the era, a strong nose, and deep-brown eyes. Many of the junior agents couldn't help but giggle.

"Tell me, gorgeous," said Bud, with a kinky smile. "Whatcha need? Other than my unlimited virility, of course."

"Oh, shuddup," said Beverly with a grin. "Just make sure that the data flow from the cams in the field office is streaming to you properly. We've just enabled all of the surveillance cams."

"The data stream is online and flowing," said Bud and blew a kiss. "Care for a date?"

"Oh, go and short-circuit yourself. Hold on, I got a call. Hey, sis," she answered Phoenix's call. "What's up?"

"I need live coverage," said Phoenix, panting.

"Again?" said Beverly, with wide eyes. "Where?"

"Field office. West gardens."

"Oh, no. Don't tell me it's another student."

"Not a student. Caucasian male in late thirties and one eighty in height."

"Wait a minute. Is this who I think it is?"

"I don't know, I think it was him," exhaled Phoenix. "My head's such a mess. Could you initiate the live coverage, please?"

Any other day, Beverly would definitely ask for the boss's approval for such a hesitant request. But circumstances were hardly normal, with boss being out of the loop. She couldn't tell why this was the case, but it didn't really matter to her. Besides, it would be nice to carry out a live test run of surveillance camera coverage with Bud.

"Stand by," she said and turned to Bud. "Hey, dude, initiate a full sweep of the field office gardens ASAP. Track everyone and everything not in a uniform, and tell me right away, *capische?*"

"Certainly, gorgeous," said Bud and went to work, his pupils moving rapidly.

Beverly turned her attention back to Phoenix.

"Who was that? New staff?"

"You could say that," grinned Beverly. "My new network interface and bud-dy, Bud."

"Lucky you! Make sure all cameras are working. You know how he is with them."

"Gotcha. Bud, report current camera feed statistics."

"The current feed rate is at 100 percent, with live feed from every camera on the compound. Data stream steady and within acceptable parameters."

"Report any activity."

"No activity in the west gardens, save a few occasional rodents."

"Okay, keep monitoring," said Beverly and turned to Phoenix. "Did you hear that, sis? No sign of him here, and all cameras are working."

"Can you do a sweep of the last fifteen minutes?"

"Bud, sweep the last fifteen minutes also," said Beverly, then she turned back to Phoenix, "I don't think we'll find anything. You know how slick this guy is."

"I know. Speaking of slick, can you access the cameras at Omega Ten? I bet he disabled some cameras there."

"I can check that real quickly. Harold, get the surveillance stats for Omega Ten, and report any outages in the last half hour." She turned back to Phoenix in a few seconds. "The only malfunction reported was at the platform level. Sorry, sis, I'll also get Bud to check the surveillance footage there in the last half hour, but I doubt that we'll catch a glimpse of that smooth operator of yours."

If he was nowhere to be found outside, he would need to be still somewhere at the station, unless she had been hallucinating it all. Phoenix quickly pushed away the idea that she could be losing it. She was pretty sure that she had looked almost everywhere at the station, but there were plenty of locked doors, and be-ing as slick as he was, she didn't think they would stop him.

"Tess."

"Hey, Phoenix," said Tess with her trademark smile.

"So you have an instance helping Beverly?"

"Not exactly. Despite his adjustable mood properties and command-inter-preting skills, Bud's comprehension and elaboration algorithms and subroutines only conform to Class C parameters."

"In English, please."

"Bud's coding is a simplified version of mine, and he can allocate only a very limited amount of processing time to non-task-related activities."

"Sweet," said Phoenix and smiled, thinking that even a digital character was capable of a superiority complex. She was feeling significantly calmer now, with her anxiety and heartbeat at relatively normal levels. She walked around the station above platform level with the ad characters in hot pursuit. She tried to open several locked doors, but they all appeared tightly shut. She kept glancing at the slogan "Where do you want to go today" again and again, as if her subconscious was trying to tell something to her.

If only the cameras at the platform level were out, it might have also meant that the man had never gone up to the main station level. But where would he go from there? Where did she want to go? She wanted to find him. She turned and looked at the slogan again. The slogan was suspended in the air and segueing from one font and color to another to attract attention. The morphing was very quick, but it seemed to be turning into another shape momentarily before becoming another font.

"Tess, can you tell me if the ad asking where I wanna go switches into another form in between morphing?"

"Sure. I can detect a butterfly image, showing for only fifty milliseconds, with different angles each time."

"Show it to me."

"It's different each time. Which one?"

"Any one, just show me."

The image Tess displayed on the screen of her PA was unmistakably the same butterfly. At that instant, the slogan made all the sense in the world. The butterfly was the key, it was to lead her somewhere, not as a message but as a pointer to a specific location. Perhaps it was him who'd been hacking into her PA and sending all these butterfly images. Perhaps her PA had never really been damaged. But why would he do such a thing? Could it be an open challenge? A game? Or a trap?

Her emotions went haywire once again. It was the excitement of almost solving the puzzle that was put before her, addressing her subconscious. She had to find him. She had to look into his eyes once again and to find out what she would feel. The butterflies were pointing to a location. But which location? Where did she want to go? To him. Where did the butterflies point? Where did they want her to go? Where were they coming from, and where were they going? At that instant, it all clicked, and everything became crystal clear. She knew where the man had been hiding.

"I'm glad you finally got up," said Hamilton.

The other man appeared as if he was trying to recover from a terrible hangover, with his face bathed in sweat, his hair in disarray, and his pink clothing looking like remnants from the night before. "Listen, Osmund, you know that I truly respect you," he said, with a fake smile. "I know that I used many unfortunate words to provoke you from time to time, but it was all part of business."

"So is this. The going rate at Frankfurt right now is around two fifty. I can offer you two sixty if you wish, for the little percentage you still own."

"But I don't wanna sell," said the fat man. "I know I won't be sitting on that chairman seat coming Monday, but I'm not stupid. I know you'll turn around the company and eventually raise the share price."

"Sure I will. But only after a massive restructuring of its technology as well as its debt. With the money I spared from purchasing your company at an inflated price, I'll refinance and improve its human and technological capital. My guess is this process will last at least another year. Do you think you can hold on that far?"

"One year?" said the obese man, wiping the fresh sweat that poured down his face. "What do you expect the share price will be in the meantime?"

"Who knows?" shrugged Hamilton. "My guess would be between five and ten."

The obese man started sniveling and covered his eyes with his fat hands.

"Worried about your upcoming debt payments, Bill? With all that gambling debt you accumulated all over the world, who in their right mind would wanna bail you out, I don't know. I don't think you'll be even able to make the payments for your Second Culpa next month."

"Help me, Osmund, please. You're my largest creditor. If you were to hold on to your debt and agree on refinancing, everybody would follow your lead."

"Refinance you, so that you can go and gamble it all away again? I don't think so. I work hard for my money. I take calculated risks but never resort to shortcuts or gambling with my companies or my personal wealth."

"I promise that I'll quit, go into real rehab. I'll get cured once and for all. I'll go totally dry, no ethanol, no gambling! We go back a long way, Osmund. You made one of your first partnerships in the Union with me, when you emigrated from Hong Kong."

"That was twenty years ago. You used to be smart and fit then. But you've always had a weakness for gambling, Bill, even then. And look at you now: obese beyond recognition, a notorious narcotic and ethanol abuser, and still a gambler."

"I know, but I'll get back in shape. Please, Oz, give me another chance. This is Bill, goddammit, your old partner, the one that gave you your nickname. We go back a long way, Oz, please don't do this to me."

"We do go back a long way, indeed, and all I can remember from those days is how hard I used to work and how hard you used to play. You made a lot of money when we were partners, Bill, but you never had the urge to work and build wealth, only to erode and destroy. Your entire wealth was hanging in the balance this week. Yet you were so carefree and blindly sure of yourself, you didn't mind going out and gambling again, did you, Bill? And I have a strong feeling that you won, you won like never before and nothing could stop your winning, could it? You were so blindly obsessed with your winnings, you had no idea what was going at the markets on the other side of the world."

The fat man tried to follow what Hamilton was saying. No pill could erase the hangover he was experiencing. He had made more than ten million dollars on the gambling table the night before. It had been an incredible night, as if there were no way he could lose. It was surreal, and he had interpreted it as a sign that his gambling fortunes had been finally reversed once and for all.

"Are you trying to say?" he said and put his fat head between his plump hands, shaking it violently. "Oh no, oh my God, no, you, you couldn't—"

"I could, and I rigged your poker game. You were expecting me to bribe Simon or at least try to influence him. You got Simon under close supervision, rear guarded by two of your most trusted board members. You also took precautions about certain large shareholders that you thought I might try to buy out or influence. But you were so sure of yourself, it didn't occur to you that I could actually buy you out of the equation."

"Oh, no," said the fat man and sobbed for long seconds. Then he lifted his gaze up, fixing his reddened eyes to Hamilton's. "If you don't help me with my debt, I'll definitely be bankrupted before the end of this quarter. I may even get deported, failing to pay the security premium. Don't do this to me, Oz, please."

Hamilton stayed silent for a few seconds then sighed. "I'll tell you what I can do. I'll foot the bill for your security premium and find you a job at one of my field offices on the North American continent, as something like, say a janitor. I'll keep your debt floating, but your HDI will drop to an even seventy, and you'll really start detoxing. Because, for a hardcore gambler and substance abuser like you, the only cure is to have a dry bank account."

Phoenix ran downstairs to the platform level.

"What's going on?" said Tess. "Where are you running?"

"To the tunnels, the metro tunnel, that's where he is."

"And how did you deduce that?"

"He was hacking into my PA, sending me butterflies, playing a game, I don't know. But I'm sure he'd been calling me, or someone had. That ad slogan lingered in my mind every time I saw it. On a subconscious level, I could see those butterfly frames and link them to the images that popped up in my PA after every crash. But I kept thinking about where those butterflies would go, because that's what the slogan had asked: where to go."

"And? I don't follow."

"But the slogan was asking where *I* wanted to go, not the butterflies. And I wanted to go to where butterflies came from, originated from, because they were sent to me by him!"

"I still don't follow."

"Then I remembered a detail: My PA actually had crashed at different days, at different times, but always exactly at the same spot, somewhere between stations Omega Nine and Ten. That's where the butterflies came from and where I wanted to go."

"Uh-huh."

Conceivably, her thought process was way too human for Tess to follow. Tess could easily see the single frame of a butterfly image that was displayed for a fraction of a second, but she didn't have the rational depth to connect the dots. She felt something akin to relief that Tess could not and would not uncover and reverse-engineer certain characteristics of the human mind, for a long time to come. She was well into the dark tunnel now, using the light of her PA to light her way, keeping to the side as much as possible in an effort to avoid the rails and electrical current on them.

"I'll explain later, Tess," she said. There was no reply. "Tess? PA: Activate."

The PA menu was displayed as usual, and everything appeared normal, except for the signal level at zero. She could access the menus on her PA but could not make a call, record what she saw, or do anything else that required connectivity. The metro cars had it, but apparently the tunnels didn't.

She could see a door on the other side of the tracks. Could she cross? Should she cross? It was very dangerous, but she had come this far, and she was determined to see it through to the end. She needed to see him and look into his eyes. She needed to! She closed her eyes and took a few deep breaths, remembering the days she used to run 5k at the CDC. They'd used to run in the field with plenty of natural obstacles. She'd used to jump over those so easily. Her body was significantly curvier these days, but she knew she could do it if she could focus. *Here goes,* she thought. *One, two, three, jump.*

She made it to the other side easier than she expected. She approached the door, only to see that it didn't even have a handle. If there had ever been a trail of breadcrumbs, it appeared like she had reached the end of it. But there had to be something. It couldn't be just a coincidence that she had figured out this much of the mystery and ended up in this dark tunnel. He had to be here somewhere. He had to be! An idea came into her head.

"PA: Light off." The tunnel suddenly plunged into absolute darkness. She was almost precisely halfway between two stations, but because of the curve that the tunnel made, she couldn't see either station from where she stood. She waited for her eyes to adjust to the dark and noticed that a faint light was coming from under the door. She paid attention to the side with the hinges and tried to open the door from the other side. But it was shut tight. Suddenly a wave of helplessness and disappointment flooded her body, but she fought it off and focused back. She kneeled and tried to see if she could get a grip on the door from the bottom. Her fingers accumulated dirt and dust as she rubbed them to the bottom looking for a grip to pull. Suddenly she heard a click, and the door opened. She must have tripped a light detector of some sort.

She pulled the door gently and entered a room full of construction material. There was a big pile of sand on one side, with bricks on the other. She carefully moved around the rusty barrels before her. She was afraid to turn her light on, thinking it might trigger other trap doors. Instead, she carefully walked towards the faint light that was coming from the depths of the room, reaching a brick wall. Something was carved on the bricks, perhaps with a chisel, but it was too dark to read. She examined the wall with her hands and found an opening towards its center, where the faint light appeared to be coming from. Once she squeezed through the opening, she reached a dim modern-looking hallway with a synthetic floor and walls. She walked along the hallway gently on her toes, reaching a dimly lit room full of computers. The walls were covered with monitors displaying various pieces of what appeared to be computer-programming code, geological maps, surveillance videos, and scenes from the solar system.

She could see two figures sitting next to each other at the far end of the room, with their backs to her. In the dim lighting, she could tell that the larger figure looked like her intruder, the fugitive of her daydreams. She wasn't sure who the other small figure was. She took a few deep breaths and focused as best as she could, trying to control her feelings going haywire once again and the anxiety that she had been feeling due to the anticipation of the moment.

"Hey, you two! Can you tell me who you are and what you're doing here?"

The man turned to her, with his intense brown eyes looking directly into hers and probing her soul. It was him. It was her intruder, the one that made her heart race, shiver, have goose bumps. There was no mistaking those eyes. It was in those eyes that she had felt all there was to feel in a single instant. It was those eyes that she had needed to see so desperately all this time. She knew her happiness was behind those eyes. Then she glanced at the other person who had turned towards her.

Now, this was a combination that she wouldn't dare to dream of, even in her worst nightmare.

CHAPTER 31

"**DAMMIT**, why doesn't any software ever work the first try?"

"I'll fix it, darling," said Bud, with a smile. "You just hold your horses."

The data flow from the surveillance cams to the neural net was achieved without a problem, but the net couldn't process the data for some reason, perhaps due to some data format issue, or compatibility issue, or who-knew-what issue, which didn't interest Beverly in the slightest. She was a psychologist and a deception expert for the human population, not for a neural network, no matter how cute he was in appearance.

"I like your new friend," said a voice from behind. "Care to introduce me to him?" Beverly turned towards the familiar nasal voice.

"What do you want, Julio?" she said, with her arms crossed. "I'm busy."

"Oh, I just strolled by to say hi and see if you needed any help with the Richfield stuff."

"I'm fine, thank you. Your presence is not needed here, nor desired."

"You'll need help to settle the new interview procedure in place, Bev. And I don't think the junior staff can be of much help with that, or your new digital friend."

"Alex will help me with it. He's working on an analysis about the existing interview procedure as we speak."

"C'mon, you know that there is no place for Alex in the new and improved reality of the field office. He can do a hell of a job with analyzing the existing procedure, but I doubt that he'll be much help with the new one. He's a great guy, but he's just a modern guy, out of his depth with the technology of the future."

"You keep underestimating those around you, and it keeps blowing up in your smirking face. You've been coming at Phoenix at every chance you got, but it got your fingers burned, didn't it? Now, you're turning and plotting behind the back of one of your supporters, actually your only supporter in this field office, I should say."

"Hey, I'm not plotting behind anyone's back. I'm just protecting my interests, nothing more."

"I know you are. But I'm curious to see whether you'll protect your interests by doing some actual work at some point or not. You can only rise so far by climbing on others' shoulders, you know."

"And that's exactly why I'm here," said Julio with a grin. "To do some actual work and help you with that new procedure."

"So that you can hang around here, flirt with a few girls, and then claim the whole credit for it? Not on my watch!"

"Suit yourself," shrugged Julio. "It was just a peace offer. You and I seem to be the only ones who have a place in the future of this field office."

"Again, you and your underestimations," said Beverly, grinning and shaking her head. "How about our heroine of the moment?"

"I admit that she's surprised me quite a bit with her unexpected and rather over-glorified triumphs. But you have to remember that she would never have defeated Mirage without Hamilton's procedure change. And I don't think she's cut out for a management position, just doesn't fit the profile."

"And you'd fit that profile?"

"Absolutely. There isn't much chance that an outsider would be chosen for the director's chair, either, which brings it down to two people: You and me."

"Wow!" said Beverly, in mock surprise. "So you got this all figured out. Go and share your musings with Hamilton if you dare and if you can find his office, I got work to do."

"Mirage! Stay where you are. You're under arrest."

"And just when I thought it was so quiet and peaceful here." Mirage was out of the academy uniform now, wearing a skintight glossy black bodysuit. She had also put her hair up and applied some light makeup that accentuated her big brown eyes and plump lips, and the overall image was like that of an agent-operative from a turn-of-the-century spy movie. Even the expression in her eyes was different somehow, a lot smarter and more focused.

"What are you doing here, Mirage? Answer me!"

"You're talking to me, right? Actually, I don't wanna share, and you don't wanna know what I'm doing here. Trust me."

As Phoenix fought incredulity and shock, the Crane remained silent and almost unnoticed. He had been observing Phoenix's every single move, memorizing her face, her eyes, the specks on her hair, her curves, and her gracefully moving beautiful, beautiful hands. He instantly fell madly in love with those perfectly shaped, perfectly manicured hands with their long slender fingers. He kept watching her quietly. He didn't need any words, he only needed to feel her. He was even scared to breathe in case he lost the moment's concentration and focus, as he didn't know how long it would last, and when he could do it again: quaff her with his eyes, inhale her soul, smell her beauty, and imagine her touch.

"Don't play games with me, Mirage," said Phoenix, with a shaky voice. "I'm prepared to take you down by force."

"Suit yourself. You can certainly give it a try. But for you to know, I actually managed to survive the streets without any big muscles, and I have to tell you that your method of picking a fight is far less imaginative than any I've seen."

Phoenix couldn't even imagine how Mirage could have ended up here. Her emotions were already through the roof, and she was barely retaining control. She switched her attention to the intruder. He was just idly standing there, with the serenest expression on his face, as if reading exquisite poetry. His looks were full of admiration and understanding, as if he were trying to inhale her soul and breathe out his own. At that instant, she knew that her own feelings for him were perfectly reciprocated. Suddenly a brief and involuntary smile tugged at the corners of her mouth, as their eyes locked onto each other.

"And she thinks she can actually take me on," said Mirage to the intruder. "Only because they issued her some meaningless diploma of some sort for a simulated combat training. I have fabulous news for you, darling. You're about to learn the lesson of a lifetime from a seasoned street fighter."

She was torn between her sense of duty and overwhelming joy at being in the presence of him He had definitely broken the law, and she had no idea how to deal with that. But Mirage was a known terrorist who had been under GPSN custody until that moment not too long ago, and she somehow must have broken free.

She slowly closed in on Mirage, who adopted a defensive stance, as the intruder watched, spellbound, frozen, and unable to take his eyes off Phoenix. Phoenix's heart was racing at full speed, partly due to her encounter with him, partly due to Mirage. But right before the physical confrontation began, something bizarre happened. A butterfly about the size of a mockingbird appeared, gently flitting its wings and darting in between the two women on the brink of attack. It was the butterfly from the *"Where do you want to go?"* ad back at Omega Ten. But there was more to it. By looking at the way it flitted its wings and radiated light, she knew that she had seen this butterfly before, somewhere buried deep in her subconscious. She tried to remember, but it was impossible to think with the bombardment of emotions between her and her intruder. The butterfly was sprinkling points of light behind it as it gently flew. She wasn't sure if the other two were seeing the butterfly, because judging by her hesitant expression, it appeared that the Mirage was only standing down because of Phoenix's own totally awestruck face.

The butterfly gently flew up to hover before Phoenix's face, throbbing light in sync with her heartbeat. "*There will be no fighting today,*" it whispered.

Did that butterfly just speak? Did she really hear something? Or was it another day-dream, another hallucination? "Who are you? What are you?" she found herself saying.

"*O lost Daughter of Corona Borealis and the Castle of the Silver Circle,*" the voice echoed in her head. "*We've met before, and we'll meet again soon.*"

"We've met before? Where?"

"*But not now.*"

Then it started spinning around her, gently at the beginning, then faster and faster, accelerating, creating a vortex at an incredible speed with a blur of light streaking behind it. She was beyond wondering whether this was a dream or a hallucination or whatever, but she suddenly felt nauseous with a feeling of weightlessness. She could barely see through the blur Mirage and her intruder looking at her as if they were watching the launch of a rocket to the moon.

Phoenix managed to look up, expecting to see the ceiling of the room, but instead she saw the open skies of a moonless night and found herself shooting to the stars at the speed of light.

Phoenix opened her eyes only to realize that opening her eyes didn't end the darkness surrounding her. She sat up in panic, turning left and right to see a glimpse of light, closed and opened her eyes again and again to be able to see something, anything, and to end the panic that was flooding her entire body. Could she be blinded? Or was this another night terror? She couldn't help but think that even a night terror would be preferable to the alternative: real life.

"PA: Light!"

The light of the PA suddenly filled the dark void before her, only to reveal that she was back in the room with the sand, the bricks, and the disgusting barrels. She exhaled in relief and realized that she was weeping. It was just too much. Too much mind-throbbing emotion, too much fatigue, too much confusion, too much happiness at finding her intruder, too much sadness at not knowing when she would see him again, too much of not having a clue what was going on or what was happening to her.

She felt betrayed by a system that she had sworn to protect, she was in love with a man who defied law and order, she had been confronted by a terrorist only a few hours after her well-publicized apprehension, she had been a pawn in a much bigger game where she had no idea who the puppet-master was, and she was feeling very, very lonely. She sobbed for many minutes in the safety and security of the room, knowing that she was far beyond anyone or anything's curious observation. She was disillusioned and alone, just like Arnett had said. Nobody understood her; nobody even tried to understand her. And when she tried to understand others, she could see a big rift between her and them, where certain concepts were a total mismatch, or it was more like they had been substituted by others.

She could see how greed made so many people around her happy, such as Julio and Sandra. They felt happy simply because they possessed greed and had the ability to follow their greed-motivated urges. Like with gluttony, there would be no end to these urges, simply because by definition a healthy greed knew no boundaries. But the laws of economics dictated that only a select few could reach the heights that would satisfy a healthy greed. If everyone had greed or strived to have greed like Julio or Sandra, Arnett was absolutely right: They were all doomed and had to be miserably unhappy and lonely until the day that they died.

The New World Order had prided itself on its claim that it had advanced the human race by defeating three-quarters of a catchphrase that used to define the misery of human life only half a millennium ago:

Conception is sin,
Birth is pain,
Life is toil,
And death is inevitable.

It was claimed that the first three had already been conquered, with just the last one to go. But Phoenix wasn't sure anymore if this was really the case. By looking at the way that immigrant woman Cain violated the Supreme Bill on no less than three articles, conception was most certainly still a sin. And birth was still painful, not for the mother anymore perhaps, but definitely for the newborn, with the inborn debt of Culpa Innata around her neck. And despite all the ability to consume, life still seemed to be comprised of toil for the likes of her, because the system's definition of happiness and her own was a total mismatch.

She slowly got up from the mud and dirt on the floor. It was all over her, in her clothing, her hair, her face, everywhere. She wiped the tears off with the back of her hand and tried to clean herself as best as possible then looked around. She was right by the wall, where she had found the opening that led to the room with Mirage and her intruder inside. The opening was no more, and the brick wall was shut tight. She could see the carving on the wall now, which read: "Don't fear chaos." In light of her recent confusion regarding meanings of popular concepts, she thought *why not*, shaking her head.

She exited the room to the metro tunnel—there was a knob on this side of the door—and thought about what had happened to her. Was it another one of her daydreams, or did someone use a mind-altering weapon against her? She knew that she saw her intruder; there was no doubt in her mind about that. He had been on the train; he had disabled the cameras at the platform level and the ones in the train, she was sure. But one question was lingering in her mind, making her frontal cortex ache: Was Mirage really there? Could she have imagined her involvement, or could it be that some mind-altering weapon had created the illusion for her? The butterfly had to be the work of some device, some weapon, perhaps a reflection created by her subconscious by the probing of the weapon. Her instincts, on the other hand, pointed at the reality of Mirage. Why would anyone force the image of Mirage into her head anyway, so that she could bring the muscle from the GPSN down to these disgusting tunnels to tear apart the place?

As she walked back to Omega Ten, she knew what she had to do.

"Is there ever no end to your surprises? You're making me dizzy."

Director Morssen took a hard look at Phoenix. Her eyes were red, her uniform had been torn up in parts and soaked in dust and dirt, with more smudges on her face and hair, and a strange lilac stain on her throat. Under normal circumstances, she would conclude that Phoenix had been on a very strong mind-altering hallucinogen and dreamed about Alice's rabbit hole. Yet the circumstances were not normal, and she couldn't just ignore her story. She had to be taken seriously, especially because it was involving a known terrorist that this woman had apprehended only the same morning. So many things had been going on behind her back, and she wouldn't be surprised if this episode was the continuation of the whole charade. But if it was true, and Mirage had really escaped somehow, it would be a huge scandal, and she wasn't intending to take any risks on this issue.

"All right," she said. "I'll make arrangements. You go clean up."

Phoenix had a spare uniform, an older issue and not as revealing and as sexy as the current one. She changed into it and realized how much weight she had lost over the past week, as she could barely fill it. She wondered if the placebo had any part in this, as well as her insomnia.

She took out the real pills, the ones that Gisella had given the day before, from the torn uniform's pocket. She hadn't had time to think about them the night before, but she would need to decide if she wanted to take them or not for the coming night. But for now, there were more urgent matters at hand. She checked that the tape on her forehead was still holding and applied some light makeup. Her eyes were still reddened from crying, but she couldn't do much about that for the time being. She went back to the director's office.

"Where did you get that uniform?"

"It's my old uniform. I never got rid of it. It isn't disposable like the current ones. I actually feel better in it."

The director just grunted and shook her head with a wince. "What drug are you on?" she said all of a sudden.

Phoenix turned red at the implication, and anger and panic simultaneously swept through her body. "Absolutely nothing. What do you mean?"

"Because I just got a message back from the PWU, and they assured me that Mirage was under their supervision, in questioning. That's what I mean!"

Self-doubt seeped into her mind once again. She tried to refocus and think clearly. Somebody must have been playing mind games with her. Was it Mirage, or maybe someone else that resembled her? The woman had never admitted that she was Mirage. No, no, it had to be a mind game, or a mind weapon, or, was she, Phoenix, ever there at the metro tunnels? Where did the mind game begin? When was the weapon fired? When did it end? Who had pulled the trigger? Could her intruder be a part of it? Her love? Could he be a part of all this? No, no, no, no, he couldn't be! But, what if he was also a figment of her imagination? Was she hallucinating now, right this very instant?

Phoenix Wallis commanded her mind to stop racing for a moment, for one lousy moment. All these questions were driving her insane. Her conscious mind needed to stick to reality somehow, hold onto one version of reality that made some sense and was plausible or at least possible. If she was already hallucinating and couldn't tell where the dream ended and reality began, it was time to give up, and there was no point in pushing forward. But if it wasn't her, but certain external factors causing all these seemingly impossible situations, she somehow needed to retain self-control and to defend her own sanity.

"I saw her," she said. "And it wasn't just her there, Director, I told you, the intruder at Bogdanov's house was in there, too."

"How about that Patel? Are you sure he wasn't there as well? He'd definitely fit the gang profile!"

Her fragile self-control was being eroded by the director's blatant disbelief. She needed to control her self-doubt, which was mounting by the second, somehow, as her entire life was disintegrating along with her rational thought. She sunk into her seat and put her head between her hands. "No, no, no!" she muttered then looked up again. "I saw her, you understand? I saw her! It was the Mirage. She was down there in an all-black, shiny, skintight suit."

"Mirage in a black shiny suit? You know what? I might have concluded that you've been attacked by a mind-altering weapon, but I don't think any weapon could be blamed for making you see Mirage in tights down there."

Phoenix heard the director with ringing in her ears, her voice distorted, as if coming from the bottom of a well. It was her who was in the well, and with every passing second the walls of the well were towering higher and higher. She didn't dare to make eye contact with the director and kept her head between her hands, her palms slowly rubbing her temples, unwilling to believe this was happening and not knowing what to think.

"I seriously believe that either you're on some kind of a narcotic or suffering from the lack of one. After my discovery about the *Mirage* you saw down in the tunnels, I accessed your medical history. How long have you been on mood stabilizers?"

Phoenix stopped rubbing her temples and raised her eyes to meet the director's. Her piercing gaze didn't matter anymore. Nothing mattered anymore. "All my life," she whispered then lowered her gaze, blankly staring at her knees.

The director had been feeling no remorse for Phoenix's suffering up to that moment, but her heart sank at that answer. There were so many commonalities between her life and this woman's, she couldn't help but feel a deep sympathy. She knew how it was to be on such drugs all too well, she knew about their side effects and how hard it was to deal with those side effects. She knew many people who resorted to all kinds of stimulants to counter those side effects, and she was now seriously wondering if Phoenix was one of them.

"Have you been taking your pills regularly?"

"Yes," whispered Phoenix. "But they weren't real."

"What's that supposed to mean?"

"I've been on a placebo for the last three months. I just learned yesterday, during my neuro-checkup. She gave me real pills again. But I didn't have time to take them yet."

"Are you positive that you're not on something else? A stimulant, perhaps, to offset the side effects?"

"I took those pills all my life," whispered Phoenix then looked up to the director. "Those drugs shaped my personality until a few months ago. How could I know what is a side effect and what is not?"

"So you never experienced such things before?"

Phoenix just shook her head, her blank eyes still lowered.

"In that case, it appears like you're in dire need of this mood stabilizer of yours. Go home and take your pills, and get some rest. You're of no use to anyone like this, including yourself. You know, there are a whole bunch of people here that would love to hear all this and tear you apart in public. But I'll do you a great favor and strike this dialogue out from the record. Not because I like you or respect you, but because I've had enough of the havoc and devastation you keep causing this field office and your destruction of its balance. And I need to retain control."

Phoenix got up and left director's office without saying another word.

"Tess."

"What happened? We were talking and then the line was cut and you went in Silent Mode again."

Phoenix kept idly staring at the Holovision. Nothing seemed to help raise her spirits, and the bath she had taken had actually made her even more tired and dizzy. "There is no reception in the metro tunnels. And I thought I saw the Mirage down there, but I'm not sure."

"Mirage? How could that be possible?"

"I don't know, Tess. I can't be sure of anything anymore. I'm so tired. So tired."

"You've been severely deprived of REM sleep. It can cause all kinds of malfunctions at your frontal cortex, even hallucination."

"I wasn't hallucinating!"

"But what other explanation is there?"

"I don't know! I don't know anything anymore."

She kept thinking of her mood stabilizers, representing a lifelong habit, one that molded her personality, diminishing her skills and abilities, reducing her to mediocrity, creating an outcast who thought that her life's story would be spent on the sidelines, observing others. The bottle in the drawer and in her pocket had defined her past, who she had been, but not necessarily who she was destined to be. If she were to take the pills, she knew there was no way she could be happy, not even pretend to be happy, now that she had seen a glimpse of her true potential, despite the chaos, confusion, and devastation that came with it.

If she were to not take the pills, on the other hand, the cognitive chaos would continue, the confusion would penetrate her mind even deeper, the wall between dream and reality would continue to rupture, and she wasn't sure if she could remain in control long enough without going insane to bring all of her new senses and abilities under the control of her conscious mind. Her subconscious had been under a pressure lid of mood stabilizers for such a long time, now it was creating a hurricane in her mind, destroying every thought in its path, leaving behind a thick dust cloud of confusion, and she just didn't know what would remain standing when this hurricane abated.

She liked who she was becoming, despite the pain and frustration it brought. But could her mind take the pressure until her new, her real, non-artificial personality had time to settle in? Or would the invasion of the subconscious overwhelm her mind and drive her insane? She had the ability to thrive under pressure, and it appeared that recently this ability had been reaching unprecedented heights. But would it be enough for her to weather this mental storm and prevent her from tumbling over the Niagara Falls of insanity?

Or, could there be a third option?

She looks up at the stars, so many of them, and so bright on a moonless night, blinking in the sky, as if they are trying to convey a secret but universal message.

What could that message be? Is the message identical for everyone, or is she supposed to decipher her own version from it? Is her mind equipped with the ability to understand this message? Is anybody's? Perhaps the message is meant to be understood only by those who are able to attain divine knowledge. She wonders where that divine knowledge could be hidden. Could it be far, as far away as the stars, at the ends of the universe? Or could it be squeezed inside an atom? Or perhaps it is coded in the minds of people waiting to be discovered, unlocked by that special key that everyone possesses without being aware? Could it be this simple, this trivial?

Suddenly she realizes how cold it is, as a deep shiver overwhelms her body. She looks down to check her surroundings. She can see the silhouette of a mountain in the background. Before the mountain, there are some dark objects in the shape of small buildings. She slowly walks towards them with the hope of finding some kind of shelter, only to run into a thorny bush, piercing her bare feet and legs. The sharp pain permeates her entire body, as the cold begins to penetrate through the wet mud on the ground. She needs to find shelter soon, or she won't survive the night.

She takes little steps on tender bare feet, stumbling over more bushes and rocks on her way to the shacks. Then her foot hits something very hard on the ground. It's solid but smooth, with a groove running along it. She kneels to touch it, only to feel the coldness of the metal that stabs her soul. She steps over the cold metal, only to hit another one a couple of steps later. She desperately tries to control the sharp pain in her feet and convulsive shaking from the cold. She tries to retain her focus. The shacks are not far anymore, only a few more steps.

She reaches one of the shacks, only to realize that it is a total ruin, offering no real shelter. And from the smell and the sharp fragments of stone piercing her exposed feet, she can tell that it has probably been demolished by an explosion. She feels desperate and lonely, quietly weeps, not knowing what to do. Her tears warm her face and her heart momentarily, giving her a glimmer of hope.

No, she refuses to expire like this. She still has so much to do, so many things to learn and understand. There is a reason for her existence, and she needs to know what that reason is. She needs to satisfy that urge to prove herself and to be someone, to show all of them, everyone, but most of all, show herself. Suddenly an idea comes to her. She turns and slowly walks back to the smooth metal that her feet had collided with earlier. She reaches it and gets between the two metal pieces on the ground and begins walking along them towards the dark mountain before her. As she had hoped, there are no obstacles between these long pieces of metal on the ground. She still walks with care, avoiding the occasional horizontal pieces that connect the two lengths of metal.

She reaches the skirts of the mountain, to see that the metal line continues inside it. She walks through the rectangular entry way and takes fearful steps into the absolute darkness inside. It should at least be dry inside, and there shouldn't be any wind, but she finds out that it's even colder inside. She takes a few steps to reach the side wall, touching it with her hands, looking for it. She breathes rapidly as her panic increases in the absolute darkness, but she cannot find it. She turns and runs to the opposing wall, only to trip over the metal line and fall on the hard and rocky ground, scraping her arms and legs. She gets up with the adrenaline pumping from anxiety and fear, feeling the wall with her hands. She needs to find it, and it has to be here. It better be here!

Finally she finds a lever that resembles it, as her heart races. What if it doesn't work? She pushes the lever up, and to her relief, dim weak lights come on, illuminating the inside of an abandoned mine and the rails that led her there. She takes deep breaths of gratitude and tries to calm herself down. Then she begins to walk towards the depths of the cold mine in hope of finding some warm clothing or anything to cover herself, only to find her way blocked by a big boulder, with a strange slogan chiseled on it: "Chaos is Peace."

She gets closer to the boulder and tries to make sense out of this oxymoronic expression, when suddenly the boulder begins moving with a ground-shaking rumble. She jumps back in fear behind one of the fallen wooden beams and watches the boulder give way. She tries to see what will come out from behind the boulder, as the lights blink on and off with the vibration created by the big rock's movement. The boulder stops and the dust settles, with no movement or sound other than the whistle of the wind from the outside. She eventually comes out from her place of hiding and walks towards the opening, reluctantly passes through it, and takes a few hesitant steps into the depths of the dimly lit mine. Suddenly she feels the same ground-shaking rumble; as the boulder closes, she dashes back in an attempt to squeeze through before it fully shuts but is too late.

She bangs her hands on the huge rock in vain, screams helplessly, yet the boulder refuses to budge. She desperately looks for levers or triggers or anything and everything that could make this damn rock move. She screams again for help, cursing her fate, feeling totally helpless and insignificant in the greater design of things. Refusing to give up, she tries to control herself, focusing on her options, if there are any left. She concludes that there is only one thing she can do, and that is to go forward.

She drags her feet towards the depths of the cave that she is trapped in, exerting a herculean effort to retain focus. After a short walk, she finds an old elevator that terminates the gallery, with a big rusty butterfly shape made from iron on it. A wave of simultaneous excitement and trepidation hits her: She knows this butterfly. She doesn't know where, but she knows that she has seen it before. She can hear her pulse beat in her ears, as her discovery ignites a tiny spark of hope within her. She knows that there is something at the bottom of the elevator, and she needs to know what it is.

She hesitantly opens the rusty grilled metal gates and enters the elevator. There is just one button, yet she is reluctant to press it. She knows that going down is her only option. She closes the gate and presses the red button. The elevator creaks and makes the unmistakable sound of metal rubbing against metal, then slowly begins *its descent. She just stands anxiously in the middle of the large freight elevator, not knowing how long the descent is, or who or what is waiting for her down there, if anything. She hears the sound of more metal scraping against metal, starting as a very high-pitched sound, gradually going to a lower and lower pitch, only to be followed by a sharp and very loud snapping.*

She momentarily feels that the ground has just moved under her feet then the fall begins. She doesn't know what to do or what to think or what to feel, but she cannot believe this could be the end.

Not like this, not her life, not now.

SATURDAY

CHAPTER 32

DESPITE the weekend, the field office was humming with activity, preparing for the next generation of interviews. There was also a tangible sense of excitement in the air since her third Strike-Out, an excitement that wasn't shared by its architect anymore. Her only remaining hope was to get DeVille to confess. She wanted to reexamine the DeVille files before the judge's approval of her warrant request, get him under custody, make him confess, and close this damn case for good, and perhaps then she could get a good night's sleep.

She went to the cafeteria, resigned to the fact that it was to be another day endured with support from the big C. She got an oversized black coffee from the dispenser and poured in loads of sugar, only to notice Sean sitting quietly at one of the tables, gulping down her own, her eyes reddened.

"Mind if I join you?"

Daydreaming, it was Sean's turn to be startled; she almost spilled her coffee. "Please," she said and stood up. "Take a seat."

"How are you, Sean? It looks like you didn't get much sleep last night."

"I don't deserve sleep. I did so little to help you with this case."

"You did okay."

"No, I didn't," she said, looking away. "You presented me an opportunity of a lifetime on a golden platter, and I messed it up completely. I became a pawn in Julio's scheming."

"Ah, well, that can happen to anyone, I guess. The important thing is that you eventually realized it."

"Only too late," murmured Sean. "I was dumb enough not to realize anything until he gave me the cold shoulder. How could I be so—? *Damn*."

"So he used you. Everybody uses everybody, nothing new."

"I know only too well. But I'd hoped that it would be different this time."

"It never is," said Phoenix and sighed. "Until that one time it really is."

Sean turned and looked at her, momentarily seeing a glimpse of a tiny smile and a spark in Phoenix's green-gray eyes, a spark of hope for true happiness. For a moment, Sean could feel it too and produced a tiny smile of her own, then wondered if hope could be also communicable. If diseases like neurosis and psychosis were contagious, why not?

Then suddenly the smile on her face gave way to a poignant sadness as she thought of the harsh reality. No matter how hard she tried, she just couldn't be like Phoenix, plowing away obstacles, problems, and negativities. She lacked the energy, wits, creativity, and perhaps even inspiration. Or could it be that there was simply no hope for some people, just like that evil Patel had said in his graduation speech, and she happened to be one of them? She looked down into her coffee mug, her mouth grim.

"Hey, cheer up! You're not the first one with a broken pride, or the last. So if you weren't sleeping, what did you do all night?"

"I examined that footage from DeVille's house. There's something in there that we're missing, but I couldn't find it. I guess I'll never be a good investigator like you. I don't think I have the eye for it."

"C'mon," said Phoenix and reached out to her arm. "Don't be so hard on yourself. This is your first week at being a case assistant. Did you expect some instant miracle?"

"You seem to be performing miracles on a daily basis," said Sean, looking up to meet Phoenix's eyes. "Well, I also did something else. I took your original advice and went through GPSN protocols and regulations all night long. How much of it stayed in my head, however, remains to be seen."

"Good for you. Gotta start from somewhere, and those will eventually come in handy."

"You look like you didn't sleep, either. Working on the case?"

"Nope. Just at my nightly routine of playing catch with my subconscious."

"And here I was, smugly thinking that I'd show you all these reasons why you shouldn't be quitting this week," said the director, wincing. "Look at me now: couldn't even foresee my own fate with too much focus on accomplishments and recognition, too blind for corporate games, and too trusting to the intent and judgment of certain executives."

"Who could have guessed any of this?" said Alex and shook his head. "But don't be unfair on yourself. There's still lots of juice in you, Dagmar."

"Hah, juice to do what? There is no way I can lead the rabble here anymore. Not after being left out like a clueless idiot, when even a newcomer was a centerpiece of corporate plans. I need to wrap up a few cases and get a new life, some new career, I don't know, academics or something, finish my postdoc work. And your fortunes will be reversing with my departure. I guess your worth to this field office will be proven as promised after all."

"Nah," said Alex and lowered his eyes. "Don't want it. I'm too old for all this."

"So you're still seriously considering leaving?"

"Sure," nodded Alex. "More so than at the beginning of the week. All that's been happening is too much for me. I'm tired. I wanna be happy, you know. I think I deserve some peace and happiness, and so do you."

The director felt the depth of Alex's admiring gaze. She had been so busy and so wrapped up with her work lately, emotions of all kinds, particularly love, had been down at the very bottom of her lengthy to-do list.

"So your plan is to move back to your native Pannonia?"

"I think so. You know me, I have a simple life. I've always had a simple life. I have plenty of money in my retirement account and a few good stocks in my portfolio, enough to let me live in contentment for the rest of my days. Hey, I might even give some seminars at the local university about the ancient craft of barrel building."

"Barrel building? I had no idea you had such a skill."

"Well, I learned from my bio-old-man," said Alex and smiled. "He was a winemaker before the invention of these tasteless syntho-wines and all that other stuff. And I used to work for him ever since I could remember. We used to make our own barrels from white oak. Now it's a useless skill, just like most of my other skills."

"C'mon, you're nowhere near obsolete, Alex. And if this is going to make you happy, why not?"

"It sure would."

"Tell me," she said with a smile of her own. "At that local university of yours, do you think they'd be looking for a faculty member with a background in criminology?"

As Alex was rendered momentarily speechless, a high-priority message came to the director's network node. She opened and read the message quickly and looked back up to Alex. The stern director was back.

"It's time we call an immediate meeting."

"We have a problem," said the Black Hat. "We need to make some major course correction."

"And just when I thought we were ready to sail into the sunset," said the Toboggan Hat. "What correction? Everything will be over within the next twenty-four hours; what kind of a correction can we afford?"

"We have a loose cannon on our hands. Following the developments of last night, it was time to suspend the Mantis's operations. The Prefect tried to put him back in his dormant state, only to avoid a trap at the last moment, then he had to withdraw. The Mantis is now completely out of our control."

"In the name of all the souls lost during the Danish Resistance," sighed the Toboggan Hat. "Now we're in deep shit. Don't tell me the Prefect was exposed in the process."

"No. The Prefect let go of all controls just before being exposed."

"Oh, thank God," said the Toboggan Hat, with a sigh of relief. "But how could the Mantis get so powerful all of a sudden?"

"I have a farfetched idea. And I hope that it isn't the other way around and the Prefect is actually getting weaker, unable to control the Mantis."

"I'd certainly sense such a change, and the Mantis would definitely turn against the Prefect, should such a thing happen."

"The Prefect has managed to stay unscathed so far. But it still doesn't solve our dilemma. Mantis is strong, and he can completely block us. We cannot control him without exposing ourselves, which we cannot do unless we intend to kill him."

"We've created and unleashed a monster!" said the Toboggan Hat, shaking his head. "Only I can stop him now. Perhaps I could find a way to control him and turn him dormant again without—"

"Forget that. Too much risk for you. Everything could be ruined en route."

"What do we do, then? We just ran out of alternatives, and soon we're gonna run out of time."

The Black Hat didn't answer and kept looking at a point on the wall. Following a silence of few but long seconds, he turned to the other man with an ice-cold gaze. "We'll do the unthinkable. But first, tell me what happened yesterday. Why was the encounter so short with her? Did something go wrong?"

"A contingency we couldn't anticipate."

"What contingency?"

"A very natural one. An emotional reaction made the Crane freeze."

"In the name of—" hissed the Black Hat. "One goes berserk, the other falls in love. Perhaps we should re-evaluate our stock of masters when we get a chance! So the bottom line is, the influence that you managed to exert on her was minimal?"

"Weak."

"Exactly how weak?"

"I'm hoping strong enough for her to feel an urge to come back here," shrugged the Toboggan Hat. "Not that it matters anymore. She's as good as dead at the hands of the Mantis. He won't stop until he destroys her first, then only God knows what he'd be up to next."

"The comment you made about her the other day might be actually true. Once again, she is moving to the eye of the impending hurricane."

"How so?"

"According to our original plan, she was supposed to be destroyed along with the murder investigation she was carrying out. But through a surprise initiative, she created a storm to clear the path before her and forced us to change our plans more than once, first to a position where one of our three masters would be dragged into the path of destruction along with her. I have no idea where her strength and determination comes from. Could it be—? No, it couldn't."

"Could it be what?"

"Nothing," said the Black Hat. "Just making a mental note for later. Anyway, now it appears that this wasn't enough for her, because she somehow provoked the Mantis beyond expectations, without even being aware of his existence. I think he inadvertently got stronger and eventually broke free from the Prefect's grip while trying to deal with her. Perhaps she possesses some kind of an energy that makes people around her react in unexpected ways. Otherwise, how could you explain our purebred geek turning into a Romeo following an encounter that lasted a fraction of a second? I think we can make her energy work to our advantage. She could become our centerpiece to neutralize the Mantis, if we can manage to focus the storm she creates on him."

"What an intriguing idea," said the Toboggan Hat, raising his eyebrows. "Totally worthy of the cunningness and the riskiness the Black Hat is known for: turn the prey on its hunter."

"Do you think she has enough chutzpah to pull off such a thing?"

"She'll be under tremendous pressure from the Mantis," said the Toboggan Hat, scratching his long beard. "But she might be able to pull it off with some outside help, especially if she comes back today before the Mantis makes a move."

"And if she doesn't come back?"

"She might crack under the pressure. But I have faith in her. She'll come back and pull through. I can tell how gifted she is from the way she left a mark on the Crane."

"Then let's help her use whatever gifts she possesses to contain and stop the Mantis."

"And the murder case?"

"After the developments yesterday, irrelevant right now," shrugged the Black Hat. "That's why we wanted to pull the Mantis back to his dormant state."

"In that case, I have an idea," said the Toboggan Hat, his eyes glowing. "What would make the Mantis so furious that it would force him to get out of his meticulous routine and make a mistake?"

"A stain on his precious ego, of course," said the Black Hat. "Of course," he said with a rare cold smile. "We help her to solve the murder prematurely, and that should drive the Mantis crazy, forcing him to go on the defensive, making unplanned moves and exposing himself, only to be caught by the GPSN, saving us the trouble of neutralizing him ourselves at the great risk of exposure."

"Precisely. Can you achieve that in a subtle enough way from the outside? Help her solve the case?"

"I can try. The time frame is short, to be sure. But we've still got the Russian. And in the meantime, it would be a good idea to remind the field office of the Mantis's existence, don't you think? Our storm-bringer needs to become aware of her nemesis."

"Absolutely," nodded the Toboggan Hat. "I'll get the Crane to create some upheaval. On the downside, putting the Mantis on the defensive will create mayhem, and he might harm many people in his way. You know that he'll fight back hard, right?"

"I know, but it can't be helped. This is our only chance to keep everything under control. It would be far worse if we tried to deal with him out there. He hides in the open, and his untimely disappearance would rouse a lot of suspicion. And with his new power and abilities, it might be downright dangerous even for us."

"True enough. Well, at least we have one operative on the case who touched our storm-bringer and yet remained unharmed and unchanged."

"One out of three is not exactly up to our standards," said the Black Hat. "But still, we shouldn't take away the credit that the Mount deserves."

"She still has a tight grip on the Russian, yes?"

"Of course. She did her part admirably right from the beginning, including her dealings with the Russians to contain the mess created by the murder. The

Russian is a bird in the cage, and she has the key, ready to be served up at will, and in no way can he be traced back to us."

"Then there is no reason that our storm-bringer shouldn't solve her murder case by tonight," said the Toboggan Hat. "We just need to make sure that she has enough grit and mental strength to tackle the Mantis. If only I could think of a way to lure her back here…"

"Your warrant is here, but I'm still not fully convinced that this is the correct way to solve the Bogdanov murder. Are you positive about this?"

"Yes, Director. I'm sure DeVille is involved in Bogdanov's murder. The least I suspect is he ratted Bogdanov out to the Dinastiya."

"Have it your way," shrugged the director. "Your investigation, your call. But be aware of the consequences if you're wrong."

Julio shook his head in disbelief. This woman was known for her micro-management and hands-on approach for taking any decision in the field office, and exercising a search-and-seizure warrant for a World Union citizen in a murder case definitely constituted a *very* important call. And despite his deep urge to get involved and expose their stupidity to their faces, Julio was determined to stay out of this one and let the skies collapse on both of them. He crossed his arms and observed the dialogue with a smirk, checking out Alex's reaction. That was another thing. One would expect some kind of reaction from Alex, but it appeared that he had decided to use some good sense about this one, too. Perhaps he wasn't as valiant and as old-fashioned modern as he appeared to be.

"I know what I'm doing, Director."

"Fine. Have you assembled your search team?"

"Erm, I didn't have time to think about that. But if I can just take Sean, I think it should be enough. I don't think we'll find DeVille in his apartment. We might need to get a locator on him and get him apprehended."

"All right," said the director. "I'll arrange his apprehension, the moment you locate those tobacco products and any other evidence that would link him to the murder in his residence."

"Computer: Execute emergency access."

It was her third in the same week, but this one came with a court order. She couldn't help but think of her feelings following the first one at Bogdanov's house. It felt like the incident took place ages ago. Thinking of her intruder, she felt a sudden rush of emotions, as if he were thinking of her at that very moment, longing for her presence, needing to know her scent and the touch of her hands. She closed her eyes, imagining his presence, his touch, the way his body would feel, and tried to anticipate her own reaction to it.

"How do we proceed?" said Sean, suddenly right in her face.

"What? Oh, okay," she said, straightening herself. "You know what the place looks like. It's a complete mess. We'll walk as carefully as possible, scan for DNA and heat signatures like we did in Bogdanov's house. Only this time we'll take some evidence with us."

They started scanning the rooms in a pattern similar to the one they had followed in Bogdanov's flat, looking for DNA and other identifiable objects and fibers. It was very difficult to do this, given the filthy nature of the place, and Phoenix was hoping to get Tess's help with identifying their findings later. She carefully moved to the disgusting table with the pile of junk. The tobacco packs were still there, waiting to be picked up.

"You don't wanna go in there," said Sean, coming out from DeVille's bedroom.

"I don't intend to. That's your job. You need to finish his bathroom, too."

"I know," said Sean, her shoulders slumping. "It will be the experience of a lifetime."

Phoenix examined the pile on the table and removed objects one by one, as she continuously recorded and verbally tagged every item. She didn't need to take these items back to the field office, unless the item was to be presented as evidence, because she could completely reconstruct the hologram of the scene later. She scanned and tagged the tobacco packs before placing them in the synthetic evidence bags. Then she turned to the pile of art on the floor. Her heart raced and ears burned as she saw the painting with the blonde woman and the serpent. She picked it up, her hands trembling.

She wasn't sure what to do with this painting. It had a great significance for her personally, but was it really an item worth taking back to the field office in connection with the murder? It clearly wasn't, and she knew that. But she couldn't leave it here, as this painting was a clear evidence for her own sanity, and she had to figure out where it came from. She had to ask DeVille its origin under the testimony device. She—

"What a strange painting."

Phoenix jolted back, bumping against Sean behind her, who stumbled. Visibly shaking, she turned and looked at Sean, her eyes emerald ice. "Don't ever do that again," she said with terrifying calm, stressing every word.

"I—I didn't mean to startle you. So sorry. Are you okay?"

"I'm fine. Did you finish up the bathroom?"

"I guess. His collection of urine in jars wouldn't have any relevance to our case, would it?"

Phoenix snorted then laughed properly, a relieved Sean joining her.

"I think we're done here, don't you think?"

"I don't wanna spend another second in here. Taking that painting, too?"

"Yep. I think this one was inspired by me."

I'm free! thought the Mantis.

He had barely managed to wrench himself away from the influence of his despised controller, but the victory had been decisive. He still didn't know who his controller was, but one thing was for sure: no more seclusion. Now that he was free, he could do whatever he wanted, wherever he wanted. His pride wouldn't let him leave any unfinished business behind, of course, but still he felt the liberty to complete this mission as he saw fit, not necessarily the way *they* wanted. Things had been going as planned so far, and Phoenix was walking right into his trap. She still didn't show the effects of his ingenious drug swap, but the Mantis was expecting it to be imminent, especially in the following few hours.

He was beginning to think that he had severely misjudged Phoenix from the very beginning, not his fault as he had been acting on the provided profile information. She appeared to be more, a lot more, than what the records indicated, turning into a true worthy opponent, promising his eventual success to be sweeter. But he had to be even more careful now. She was showing a totally unexpected resistance to the attack on her rational side; moreover, he could sense that her emotional side was also showing some rapid development. But she was to receive the big blow very soon, and the Mantis was expecting everything to go downhill after that. The adult Phoenix would collapse under the insurmountable pressure from the little girl inside, and she'd be ready for the spectacular end the Mantis prepared for her.

After that, it would be time to settle the score with that controller and the others behind him, whoever they were. He would show them all what the Mantis was made of.

"Mr. DeVille, you're here today on suspicion of being linked to the murder of Vassily Bogdanov, a citizen of the World Union, in the city of Odessa, in the rogue nation state of Russian Federation. I'll be asking you questions about the case, and I expect relevant answers. If you insist on presenting non-relevant information, this will attract more suspicion to your position and be perceived as admission of guilt."

"Whatever, Agent Dumb-Bitch," said DeVille shaking his head. "I'll make you pay dearly for this. My lawyer will kick your ass."

Phoenix momentarily felt nervous thinking about the lawyer sitting on the other side of the mirror but quickly shook it off. The questioning process was to be fairly straightforward in her mind; she had no intent of wasting any time with any baseline questions. She exactly knew what questions to ask, and the Holo-Projected Testimony Device would ensure the rest.

"How would you describe your relationship with late Mr. Bogdanov?"

"As I told you before, Agent Nosy. We were partners, even-steven, in an art business."

Phoenix looked up at the visuals to see a vague figure of an obese man with a big round face. But there was something wrong with the picture; its colors were fluctuating and solid…as if it were a placeholder? *Some artist, with way-below-average visual skills,* she thought.

"And what was your contribution to this *even-steven* partnership?"

"Why do you people always ask questions that you already know the answers to? I create *objects d'art*, woman!"

"For the record, Mr. DeVille. Now, when did you become aware of the fact that Bogdanov was cheating you?"

"When you tricked me and confronted me after that party, when else? And you didn't even have sex with me, wasting my potential for the night. Remind me to ask my lawyer if I can sue you for that, too."

Phoenix looked at the sundial-shaped object behind DeVille. It appeared to be moving with extending tentacles and was colored pink. It must have been her, in her pink dress, but evidently DeVille only focused on the sundial part of her body and nothing else. "When did you first contact the Dinastiya about Bogdanov's smuggling ring?"

"What smuggling ring? What the hell are you talking about?"

"The smuggling ring that you and a captain of our armed forces were a member of, along with Bogdanov. The smuggling ring that brought illegal tobacco products here to be sold."

"First of all, I know no captain of any armed force, understand? And if you happen to be referring to them cigarette packs in my house, Vassily gave them to me as souvenirs. He knew my interest in displaying such explosive and deadly stuff. That ain't a crime!"

Phoenix quickly checked the indicators before her then the visuals. She could see a blob, presumably Bogdanov, extending some red rectangular package to DeVille. And shockingly enough, indicators concurred that he was not lying. Panic hit her as she considered the possibility that her theory was totally wrong. Or could this man have somehow found a way to fool the hardware? "Are you also denying knowledge of his involvement with the Dinastiya crime organization?"

"Whoa, wait a minute. You keep talking about some people you refer as Dinastiya and call them a crime organization. Is this a new reality show, shot in one of them rogue states that I'm not aware of?"

"No, I mean a crime organization as in mafia. You know what mafia means, right, Mr. DeVille?"

"You mean to tell me Vassily was a part of a notorious gang? Cool, if only I'd known before the wanker got snuffed. Still, he got what he deserved, that cheating cock-sucker."

"You had no knowledge of this?"

"Of course not! If I'd known, I'd treat the guy with more respect, if you know what I mean. Not that he deserved any, but whatever."

The indicators before her showed no deceptive patterns so far, nor did his physical signs show any sign of an imminent lie. Cold sweat started beading on her temples. Her only option was to push through until the end.

"Tell me about the illegal devices Bogdanov was renting out to affluent customers at the Thing Store."

"Wa-wa-wait a minute. Are you trying to tell me that the Thing Store is actually a cover for selling other stuff and not Things?"

"No, that's not what I mean," said Phoenix and cleared her throat. "I'm sure they really sell those famous *Things* there as they advertise."

"Aha." DeVille leaned back. "You scared me for a moment there, sugar."

"What I meant was that Bogdanov had been using his supervisor privileges at the Thing Store for other sinister purposes."

"Now, I know what you're talking about," said DeVille with a sly grin. "He had them on rotation, you know."

"Excuse me?"

"Those sales clerks at the Thing Store, man, them college girls. He couldn't stop talking about how he'd screw one of them one day, and the other the next day, and the other on the third. See? On rotation."

DeVille was either the dumbest man on the planet or one incredible actor who came with the ability to fool the billion-dollar hardware before her. It was impossible for a human to control his thoughts so that the Testimony Device would project fake or false images on the screen. But what if someone hacked into it? That could explain the overly simplistic placeholder figures in the hologram. Or could these thoughts be a desperate attempt to cover up her own error in judgment? What about the fact that none of the other sensors observing every signal of his body showed signs of any deception? Could there be another explanation?

Her hopes of wrapping up the case right there were quickly waning every passing minute, as she was running out of things to ask. She knew she had only one more attempt to make.

CHAPTER 33

DOUGLAS D. Anderson watched the proceedings next to Director Morssen in the front row of the Viewers' Lounge grimly, while Julio struggled not to laugh a few rows back, occasionally unable to suppress a snort.

"Shhh," whispered Alex. "What's so funny?"

"It's just this DeVille guy. He's hilarious, man."

Julio knew him. He had never cared about his name, but he knew this guy. He was regarded as a total joke in the art circles, known for his ineptness and acute lack of skill. This man was so bad at art, he was famous for being a scavenger who would pick up other people's rejects and garbage and pretend that they were his. He'd heard so many stories how his buddies would mail their garbage to him, and he'd just add their rejects in his pile. Moreover, he would sleep with any woman who came his way, no matter what she looked like. Julio had no idea where Phoenix had found this loser, but he was sure that she was about to get her fingers burned.

"Why do you think he's funny?"

"Just the way he looks and the way he's talking to Nix. He should be a comedian, not an artist."

And the even funnier thing was, when he had been pushing and cornering her with his manipulations and clever tactics, Phoenix had shown a lot of resolve and fought back hard. Evidently all he had to do was not to stand in her way and allow her to self-destruct from the very beginning. So, for these greed-deprived and ego-rich Neanderthal bitches like Phoenix, the best remedy was to let them blindly charge into any nearby wall like a myopic rhino or allow them to run off the cliff like those Scandinavian rats or rodents or whatever they were. In a twisted kind of way, it was actually ironic. Nevertheless, it was a valuable lesson learned, and it came totally free of charge. Then he saw the blobs on the display screen behind DeVille, representing heck knows who. He started laughing uncontrollably and found his way out of the lounge.

"Computer: Display item alpha, one, six, three, four, four." The hologram of a painting appeared above the table. "Did you paint this?"

"I don't know," he said as looked at the image, his eyes narrow. "Did you take it from my flat?"

"You know that I did. Did you paint it or not?"

"How the heck would I know? You think I have the memory of some elephant or something? I've designed thousands of things."

Phoenix checked the indicators before her, only to add to her existing frustrations. This man was as comfortable as if watching a Holovision show and eating popcorn in his disgusting house.

"Try to remember," she hissed. "Did you make it, or did someone put it there for you?"

"I don't remember. If it's that important to you, you can keep it."

"How could you know about that!?" She stood up suddenly, her chair crashing on the ground. "How could anyone know about it? I only—"

"Agent Wallis," said a stern voice from the speakers. She turned at the mirror. "Agent Wallis, this questioning is over," said the director. "Mr. DeVille, you're free to go."

"Damn right I am," said DeVille, with a grin. "I told you not to mess with me, sugar. But you couldn't see the train coming full speed in your face, could you? Now it's time to make you pay."

"Just get the fuck out of here," she whispered, her eyes stinging.

DeVille didn't reply. He just turned to walk out.

That moment it dawned on her. This whole mess was all because of something she didn't see, some detail she missed, while all the evidence was right before her eyes all this time. Now she was angrier at herself than at him.

"Hey, Pierre." DeVille stopped and turned, wearing a slimy grin.

"Now, if you're gonna apologize and confess that you did all this out of jealousy, I'd understand, sugar. But I'm still gonna sue your ass off."

"Just that, you better get those eyes of yours checked. You're so blind, I bet you couldn't see a train coming full speed in *your* face. And, apology? Huh, I don't even know the meaning of the word."

"Well I'm not sure if I should consider it a success or not, but I managed to keep the damage under eight figures," said the director. "I told him that the mistake was made by a mere senior agent and that the settlement should be proportional to her rank, and he somehow bought it. Who knows? Maybe he knew of something in our company rules that even we're not aware of."

Barely listening to anything being said, Phoenix was in deep thought, desperately trying to figure out where she had made the mistake and where her instincts had been when she was making her move on DeVille. The biggest factor for her to charge so decisively on DeVille had been that painting. On top of that, the man had appeared so idiotic, so blind, and out of touch with the reality, it was just suspicious. Nobody in the postmodern world could be or should be this clueless. It had never occurred to Phoenix that his blindness could be a physical condition, not a mental one. Now he was rewarded for his blindness, clueless naivety, and idiocy with a large sum of cash, with compliments from the mighty GPSN.

"It's my fault," she muttered. "I acted rashly under the time pressure."

"Yes, you did. And with every such act, you drag not just yourself but a whole bunch of us down. What happened to you since yesterday afternoon, anyway? Your seemingly blind convictions proved to be true on many occasions this week. But since your encounter at the metro tunnels, your confidence—"

"I saw her," said Phoenix, looking down. "I don't know how to explain it now, but anyway. Am I still the lead in Bogdanov case?"

"For the time being, yes," shrugged the director. "Only because I don't want to take it over myself, and I couldn't stomach giving certain people the satisfaction of replacing you. It would be regarded as another weakness from my side, and I've had too much of that already this week."

"Thank you."

"Don't thank me. I'm simply acting out of self-interest. Besides, our fates have been tied together in this since the beginning."

"What do you mean by that? Tied by someone else?"

"You were handpicked as the lead for the Bogdanov case by Hamilton himself, with heaven knows which plot in mind. The reason he muttered to me then made little sense, but I was in no position to argue with him."

"So you've never been instrumental in my installment as the lead?"

"Not the least bit. If it was up to me, the lead would directly go to Alex. But this wasn't good enough for Hamilton. And now here we are, our fates tied together, whether we like it or not."

Why would the director share such critical details about her installment as case lead, and why now, Phoenix wasn't sure. Nor she had any idea why she wouldn't reprimand her before her colleagues. Perhaps the director was really fed up with the constant chaos that ensued during the week. Still, her case was her only way for her salvation. All necessary clues were already in her head, and she could solve everything if only she could get some decent rest. But it was a typical chicken-and-egg dilemma, as she knew rest wouldn't come until she could solve this damn murder. She inadvertently found herself in front of the Monitoring Room. Perhaps her subconscious was telling her that she needed support and knew where she could find it.

"Hey, sis." Beverly greeted her from her seat. "You're okay?"

"I feel like shit."

"Hey, you did a lot for us this week," said Beverly. "And everyone's allowed to make mistakes here and there, especially with a weirdo like that."

"That picture messed up my mind."

"Yeah, I was gonna ask you about that. What did that painting have to do with anything?"

"I had a nightmare just like that."

"Say what? You have nightmares like that?"

"On a nightly basis since I moved here."

"Oh my God! Now that I think about it, the woman in that crude image resembled you so much." Beverly looked at the horizon with deep intensity. "Actually it *was* you, sis. But how could it be possible?"

"I don't know. That's why I insisted on asking about it. But the guy desperately needs eye care. Anybody who's been to his disgusting apartment could have dropped it there, and he wouldn't have a clue."

"Right. So tell me, who exactly knew about this nightmare of yours?"

"Now that you ask—"

"Hi, Phoenix," said Sean, standing behind her. "Am I interrupting?"

"No, no, it was just gossip," said Phoenix. "How are you?"

"I'm okay, I guess. So what do we do now?"

"We'll try to solve the murder, still, what else? By the way, any news from that woman in rehab? We don't have many leads left."

"Lena Vanderbilt? Not yet. But even if she were out of the rehab, we may not be able to talk to her."

"Why not?"

"It's something that I came by last night, as I was going through the GPSN manuals, a special deal that GPSN has with her company, mentioned in the footnotes."

"Don't tell me she's with WIMA."

"How could you guess? She's the regional coordinator for WIMA."

"You cannot interview her unless she agrees to it." Beverly completed her sentence.

"I know," nodded Phoenix. "I had the same problem talking to Arnie, I mean, Roger Arnett."

"She's the only possible lead that can help us establish a link between Bogdanov and the mysterious device. But I don't think there's much chance that we can reach her in short notice. What do we do, Phoenix?"

"Actually, there might be a way to reach her. But before that, why don't we pamper ourselves a bit?"

"So, tell me about Lena Vanderbilt, Arnie."

"I prefer to call her the *annoying and overbearing tasteless chatterbox who comes with an undeserved title*," said Arnett, sketching a few lines on the pad before him, totally uninterested.

"A rather long nickname."

"But fully deserved. You got my attention at the urging of our dear teacher, sweetie pie, so please get on with it. What do you want to know about her, and why?"

"I need to talk to her."

"So go talk to her. Do I look like her assistant to you?"

"She's been at rehab all week. I can't reach her."

"So that's why this has felt like the best week in years," said Arnett and looked up with a spark in his eyes. "You aren't referring to a detox by any chance, are you?"

"No. She's recovering from some kind of a mental illness. And that's actually what I need to talk to her about."

"Oh, how awful," said Arnett and grinned. "I hope she gets well soon. Tell me about this mental illness."

"I believe an illegal device she used made her ill." She paused. "Can you arrange a meeting with her for me today, please? It's very urgent."

"Oh, come, come, little pussycat. You know that I'm talking to you completely on a voluntary and pro bono basis. If you want my help, you have to share all. Otherwise, I'm not playing."

Phoenix glanced Arnett's scrutinizing gaze momentarily then lowered her eyes. *What do I have to lose*, she thought. *The situation is already beyond merely desperate.* "Everything I say to you about this murder case—"

"Would remain in the confines of these walls," said Arnett, pointing at the walls with a flourish. "For purely entertainment purposes."

"All right," said Phoenix and took a deep breath. "I believe your dream case was heading an illegal formation with an Air Force captain and undetermined others in order to smuggle contraband into the World Union, including the mysterious device that killed Dr. Melvyn Phillip Spencer from Adrianopolis University. Same device, I suspect, that made Vanderbilt ill. I think Bogdanov also collaborated with some group of hackers, one of which I ran into first at his house, then in what appeared to be a computer center accessible from the metro tunnel between stations Omega Nine and Ten, together with another terrorist hacker, Mirage."

"You don't say! So my dear VeeBee was trying to be someone after all. Do you know if he's been involved in such illegalities in his previous life?"

"Yes. He used to work for a notorious mafia group called the Dinastiya."

"Ah, that explains it, then. But he's been here for a while, no? So why wait for all those years? What was he waiting for all this time, sweetie pie?"

"Not sure. An opportunity, perhaps?"

"Come on, think, think, think. What happened? What triggered him? What made him change? What gave him the audacity to come and seek my services?"

"That's one thing that keeps puzzling me. This man had a character shift all of a sudden about two months ago and never looked back. I suspect a similar shift occurred in his partner, the Air Force captain. According to eyewitness accounts, both of them appeared emotionally imbalanced during the same time period."

"A former mafioso and an Air Force captain displaying similar emotional reactions as well as borrowing from each other's personality: one acting like a mafioso by running contraband and the other behaving as audacious as a captain of the Air Force. What a charming combination. Someone or something had to free them from their built-in fears and ingrained code of conduct at a fundamental level and flood them with all that misguided greed and daring, putting our little ant VeeBee on a fast-track to become an elephant on this side of the border."

"Until the Russian mafia eventually caught up with him."

"Eventually caught up with him?" echoed Arnie, frowning. "Are you trying to tell me that he had no contact with them all those years?"

"He couldn't have, because he stole their money and ran away from them, seeking refuge in the Union. I suspect that he'd been stealing from them consistently before he ran away, along with his nuptial spouse."

"He ran away from mafia with his nuptial spouse?" said Arnett and cackled. "Well, I don't find that very convincing, sweetie pie. What mafioso would run away from his notorious past with his wife, only to settle in a border city, tell me?"

"Hmm, sweet, you're right, I suppose he couldn't have had a reason to hide, after all."

"That's right. So either he wasn't running away, or he had protection. Tell me about those hackers."

Phoenix felt a rush at the mention of her intruder. She just hoped that she managed to conceal her feelings from Arnett's soul-stripping gaze. "I ran into one of them at Bogdanov's house. He managed to incapacitate me and ran past me. Then we couldn't even trace him with the surveillance camera network we have in the city. It was unbelievable."

"Fascinating! So the entire might of the *Geeee Peeee Essss Ennnn* couldn't track one simple hacker. Truly fascinating. How do you know that he is a hacker, by the way?"

"Because he hacked his way into Bogdanov's house, imitating him. Then there were all these PA crashes that I experienced with recovered butterfly images, subtly leading me to this elaborate computer room in the metro tunnels with him and Mirage."

"Who is this Mirage? You speak of him with so much contempt."

"It's a she. And I saw her with the intruder from Bogdanov's house in that computer room in the metro tunnels only a few hours after I managed to apprehend her during a security interview at the field office."

"Ahhh, that explains it," grinned Arnett. "It's a she, a she that you could be potentially jealous of, I suspect."

"What jealousy are you talking about? The woman's a known terrorist!"

"Is she now?" said Arnett with his gaze probing. "So *you're* the one who created this havoc at the academy by striking out those poor suffering souls from the rogue lands and helping the Wizard to take over Immigration Academies Worldwide."

"Helping who?"

"The Wizard of *Oz*. Goodness gracious, girl, don't you know the nickname of your big boss, hero of a hostile takeover at a yummy price? So did you manage to catch this jealousy-worthy woman, in that pit where you found her?"

"I didn't."

"How come, pussycat? You two had a catfight to claim your man, and you've lost?"

Phoenix turned red at the suggestion, barely suppressing the urge to get up and leave. She knew that it would eventually come to mind games with Arnett, and she needed to play along to get what she wanted. "No, a rainbow-colored butterfly came out and talked to me. Then it created a vortex, which shot me to the stars, then I gained consciousness in the adjoining room."

"Congratulations, that's what I call an original encounter," said Arnett and clapped. "Go on."

"You find my explanation plausible?"

"Of course I do. You're not the kind to make up such an outrageous lie on the spot, nor do you possess this kind of wild imagination. It appears like someone just zapped your mind. But why didn't you get your GPSN to make that cave of theirs to collapse on their heads?"

"I tried. But they didn't believe me."

"Who? Your supervisor didn't believe you?"

"My director accused me of being on a mind-altering drug, or lack of one, and told me that Mirage was still under GPSN custody."

"Are you on such drugs, or lack thereof, pussycat?"

"Actually, I was put on placebo a few months back after using mood stabilizers since my childhood. I was on drugs most of my life after surviving the Bloodbath." She looked down.

"So we have a true survivor on our hands," grinned Arnett. "How exciting. So tell me, is this here before my eyes the true you? Or is there another you, inside you?"

She felt goose bumps at the question. Arnett's intense gaze was compelling her to reply immediately, not allowing her to think about anything else. This dialogue was fast becoming more about her than about the murder case. On the other hand, Arnett was providing invaluable insight with his extraordinary observation and analytical skills. She had to endure his mental torture a little longer and maintain a face as straight as possible.

"What do you mean?" she said and swallowed.

"This is the third time I'm seeing you. The first time you looked quite decent for an amateur, perceptibly with considerable outside help, the second time you had strokes of someone's masturbation on your face, and this time I look at a plain Jane who has no regard for her appearance. So which one is you? Which is the survivor? Is what I look at now the true you?"

"They are all me, parts and reflections of me. The survivor is in here, ready to be unleashed when needed."

"Oh my word, how thrilling," applauded Arnett. "I wish I could see you at your catfight with that hacker nemesis of yours. I bet the survivor was there at full strength. Speaking of which, tell me why you backed down so easily."

"I already explained that. A butterfly came and—"

"I'm not referring to the whammy part. With your supervisor, he told you that this nemesis of yours was still under custody. Why did you back down?"

"And that's also a she. I don't understand what you mean."

"Come, come, come, you are the hero of the moment. The spotlights are on you. Thanks to you, GPSN signs a multibillion-dollar annual contract with those computer brain people and wrestles to take over those useless academies, and no one will be jealous of that? What century are you living in, pussycat?"

"You mean to say the director would lie to me? But why?"

"To mess with your not-so-quick mind, of course. Her or whoever told her about the whereabouts of that she-nemesis of yours."

Could it be possible? Could the director lie to her about such a thing in order to play mind games? Or, could someone at the Psychological Warfare Unit lie to the director about it?

"From the bepuzzlement on your dry and neglected face, I can tell you're seriously considering the possibility," said Arnett with a wolfish smile. "Good, now we're pushing the boundaries of thought and getting somewhere. Have you ever considered what certain departments of your GPSN would need to do, or what kind of people they would need to employ, to be successful in the real world? I wouldn't be surprised if that she-nemesis of yours was recruited by them on the spot, right after your spectacular revelation of her true identity."

"Mirage to work for the GPSN? I don't think—"

"Oh, come, come, come. Do you think our peace and tranquility at home comes from a giant figure in the sky with a magical wand? It's manmade. Of course it'll come with loads of flaws, dirty tricks, and plausible lies and denials, expertly swept under the carpet. The place you discovered down there may even be a place of gathering for renegades like that she-nemesis and intruder of yours, conveniently under the protection of your precious, über-giant corporation."

"You mean like a safe house? Being so far away from the curious eyes, and even from network coverage, it certainly possessed many characteristics of one. But still, I don't think it was a hideout or a safe house of some GPSN covert team."

"And how might you conclude that? You saw a disclaimer at the door?"

"Not a disclaimer at the door, but writing on the wall," shrugged Phoenix. *"Don't Fear Chaos."*

"Now it's getting *really* intriguing," said Arnett, rubbing his hands. "So, you *did* see a disclaimer after all. If I were running one of those clandestine units of that company of yours, I'd definitely put *that* on my wall as my disclaimer."

"A matter of perspective I guess. I wonder if it could be a mafia hideout."

"Now mafia and imagination are two words that don't go very well together, sweetie pie, much like I feel about you, unfortunately. When you asked me for reasons of VeeBee's sudden departure to the rogue lands, I didn't give your ineptness much thought. But now that I know the instrumental role you played in that hostile takeover, I feel that it's truly disappointing. Where are you from, anyway?"

"I already mentioned the Bloodbath. Experiencing memory loss, Arnie?"

"Oh, cut out the feistiness, sweetie pie," said Arnett, rolling his eyes. "Doesn't go with the color of your neglected hair. I'm not asking about your birthplace. Tell me about your origins."

"As my last name implies, I'm nearly 70 percent Cambrian."

"I'm never good with names, you see," said Arnett, leaning back and checking out his manicure. "Especially the ones that come after the first one. Any particular area of Cambria?"

"Anglesey."

"Anglesey?" said Arnett with a jolt of interest. "Now isn't that fascinating! Our little pussycat is from the island of druids."

"What does that have to do with anything?"

"Don't get nervous just because I happen to show interest in your genetic whereabouts. It's only professional curiosity. Those barbaric ancestors of yours possessed the most impressive interpersonal skills. Shame they were never passed down to you."

For the second time, Phoenix had an overwhelming urge to leave. But a strong instinct made her stay and keep her composure under the increasing mental pressure from the image maker. "Actually, you have no idea if I inherited any skills from them or not," she said with a sudden spurt of confidence. "I finally discovered my instincts only a few days ago, and they already got me here."

"You don't say," said Arnett and narrowed his eyes at her. "Instincts are mere genetic jokes that have no place in postmodern world."

"And you don't believe a word of what you've just said."

Arnett's cool indifferent façade was dented by surprise as if he just heard something unheard of, but only momentarily. He quickly snapped out of it and looked at Phoenix with a renewed interest as if he were trying to see what was behind those green-gray eyes. He leaned over his beautiful wooden desk towards her.

"Is that you or your instincts talking now?"

"We're one and the same. They can't talk for me, if that's what you're asking. But they can be very convincing when they need to be. Now why did you conclude that I was inept, just because I once asked you about Bogdanov's reason to visit Russia?"

"Because you have no idea why and how he got there, do you? So what do your precious instincts tell you about his inexplicable departure to those wretched, rogue, and hostile lands?"

"Nothing. They don't like answering direct questions."

"And yet your confidence in them fills my eyes with tears, pussycat. Still the question remains: Why did VeeBee get to those wretched lands?"

"To be honest, I don't have a clue," said Phoenix and shrugged. "We don't even have a record of him leaving the country. And I don't know if I have to tell you how strong our border controls are."

"Oh, don't even bother. I'm sure they got you to memorize every single attribute of all those insurmountable and impenetrable border security systems from ay to zee, and I have no stomach to listen to any explanation about the indelible deterministic nature of the security apparatuses. Yet, by their very nature they'd have to have gaps and loopholes embedded in them. Remember what I said about manmade earlier?"

"You think somebody outsmarted our security systems? But how?"

"*How* is the critical question here, so let's start with the basic assumptions. Our VeeBee was smuggled out of the Union into the rogue lands, agreed?"

"That's one way to look at it," nodded Phoenix.

"Now tell me how most cases of smuggling are being done nowadays."

"Through official channels and falsified records."

"Indeed. So loading a mule and crossing the mountain passes in dark, no more. What does this tell us?"

"That Bogdanov had to be smuggled through some falsified records? But that's impossible. We check the biometric information of every citizen at every entry and exit to the Union, so that no alien can pretend to be them. Nobody can fool or replicate a strand of DNA."

"Now, now," said Arnett, wagging his finger. "What did I tell you about pushing the boundaries of thought? Again you're diving into the sea of assumption prematurely. Now, tell me about those aliens, those extraterrestrials, those rogue stators. How do we deal with them, when they try to enter our ripe, precious, and innocent promised lands?"

"Every rogue stator has to apply for a visa in one of our embassies or consulates in their country. Then our consulate makes an exhaustive background check, interviews the person face to face, makes sure that the person has touristic intent or business and no intent for remaining in the Union illegally."

"I see that you know your company rules inside and out, sweetie pie. Let's see if your analytical skills are as good as your memorizing skills. What happens if an alien over-stays in the Union?"

"He gets detected and deported to the rogue state he or she comes from, at that rogue state's expense."

"And how do you detect this rogue stator?"

"They have limited stay periods in each entry, based on their visa type. If an over-stay is detected, that visiting alien gets on the persona non grata list. In most cases, they are caught through the expert systems that search for them through the surveillance cameras in public areas."

"So we have the biometric information for these aliens, too?"

"Of course we do. One of the requirements to apply for a visa is to submit biometric data. Unless—"

"Unless?"

"Unless—" Some little detail appeared in her head, and it had the potential to be a major loophole in World Union's border security system. If this was the case, it was an unbelievable void and security risk for the entire Union. But it was so trivial, it should have been impossible not to have been considered before. She needed to check a few things before she could be sure, but potentially this could explain everything, the whole process of how Bogdanov had disappeared, along with the existence of a hideout.

"Hello," trilled Arnett. "Is there anybody in there?"

"We're all here," smiled Phoenix. "And I think we just figured out how your VeeBee vanished from the surface here, only to reappear at the rogue lands. And it all happened in *plain sight*."

CHAPTER 34

PHOENIX left Arnett's office worn out but with a renewed energy. Now she had a theory about Bogdanov's mysterious disappearance, but she had to check and verify a few things before she could be sure. That glimmer of light was still there, and she felt she could still crack this case wide open very soon. With his condescending attitude and soul-probing remarks, Arnett was a very difficult and annoying man to deal with, but he possessed a true gift for provoking one's mind—on top of being a great analyzer himself. Moreover, he seemed to be developing some kind of an interest in her, or else why would he tell her to call anytime if she needed more help? Could he be running his own experiment on human behavior? Perhaps she could introduce Arnett to Tess. She'd be curious to know who'd manage to analyze the other.

She walked down the ramp to the image-making station that Gladys was standing beside. Gladys clapped her hands with excitement as she watched her latest creation with great pride, another attempt to make history in facial art, which happened to fall way short.

"You look sensational, dear. Ready to see yourself now?"

"I—I'm not so sure," said Sean, after seeing Phoenix suppress a snort.

"Ta da!"

Sean's first reaction was that of horror, and her hands moved towards her face.

"No, no, no, don't mess it up," said Gladys. "Wait until it totally dries."

"What are you talking about? It's already messed up!"

"This is a color scheme directly from Milano," said Gladys and folded her arms. "You don't have the luxury of not liking it. And you got it for free. What more can a woman like you expect from life?"

"A woman like me? And what does that—"

"All Gladys is trying to tell you is to enjoy her complimentary services, while they last," said Phoenix. "Right, Gladys?"

"Yeah," said Gladys. "I guess—"

"Okay, time to go," said Phoenix, dragging Sean by the arm.

"This is atrocious," grumbled Sean, as they walked. "I can't believe she did this to me. This is supposed to be a very respected salon."

"Grab a few of those."

"Did you know she would turn me into a clown like this?" She grabbed the cleaning wipes. "You knew, didn't you? Don't tell me she did it to you, too."

"How else would I know to bring my assistant to assist me?"

The Mantis was completely thrown off following his discovery of the reason Phoenix's drugs still didn't work. But how could this happen? How could Phoenix sense something and not take the drugs? How could his replacement of her drugs at home overlap with her discovery of the placebo, a placebo that nobody in the city had been aware of, including the Mantis himself? Or, could her banging of the head and visit to the rehab for a neurological check be a part of some plot that he wasn't aware of? Could the plot be that deep? And if so, how many more layers were there? And if not, what kind of a cosmic coincidence or fate could engineer such delicate timing?

The Mantis firmly believed in logic and science. In his thinking, there was no place for any random chance, and his plans had always reflected that fact. He didn't believe in coincidences and never left any space for such incidents in his meticulous designs. But now, the situation seemed to be pushing the boundaries of the plausible. He was still sure that there was some kind of explanation to this *seeming* coincidence, but not knowing what it was was driving him crazy. What was his controller up to now? It had to be her. This had to be designed by that controller of his, who never shared anything with him and always left him in the dark. But the Mantis knew that the time was running out for his controller. Now he had the freedom to mess up her plans and force her to reveal her identity, or him.

But now he had to evaluate and plan for this contingency. His strategy depended on driving Phoenix over the edge by first manipulating people, events, and circumstances around her and then by getting the hallucinogens into her system. Despite her devastating failure with DeVille, Phoenix had managed to keep her calm so far, and the Mantis wasn't sure how long it would take for her to crack up without a nudge from his specially designed drug cocktail.

He had to think about this and come up with a plan, quickly.

"You need to be very delicate with Ms. Vanderbilt," said Gisella. "She's still recovering and in need of time to shake off all the ill effects."

Arnett had called the WIMA headquarters at Geneva in the Swiss Alps and asked a favor from some high executive, who in turn had called the European director in order to forward the request. This European director had called the case physician at the rehab center at Adrianopolis, who happened to be Gisella, in order to let Phoenix see Vanderbilt for a very urgent WIMA matter. Gisella had okay'ed the request on the condition that the interviewer followed her strict guidelines. And all of this communication was already completed by the time Phoenix and Sean had traveled from the business district to the rehab center.

"Can you tell me what happened to her?"

"I cannot discuss her case specifics with you due to confidentiality," said Gisella with a smirk. "I'm sure you'd understand that."

"Sure," nodded Phoenix. "Actually, you being the case doctor tells me a lot already. Just tell us what you can; she'll fill in the rest."

"When she was first admitted, her case was initially reviewed by our psychiatrists, thinking that she had a breakdown. Only after her personal revelation did the case come to my attention."

"A revelation? First of all, can you tell me when she was admitted?"

"Last week, on Friday. But the case came to my attention only yesterday, a full week after."

"I'm guessing this revelation involved a device. Do you think her condition could be caused by the same one supposed to have caused Spencer's death?"

"Of course, that was my first guess. But in the absence of this *nonexistent* and *mysterious* device, my hands are still tied."

"You still don't have access to it?"

"No, and I'm getting tired of this game of hide-and-seek."

"Can't blame you. What can you tell me about her condition?"

"She's lucid enough to talk," shrugged Gisella. "And her mood swings are more manageable."

"Mood swings?"

"Yes, she's been displaying typical mild-level manic-depressive behavior so far. We think it might be associated with her claimed usage of a device."

"*Claimed* usage? You have suspicions that she might have lied about it?"

"According to some of my colleagues, she might have. The fact is, she didn't tell us about the device until yesterday. It's a remote possibility, and I don't agree with him, but her psychiatrist thinks she might have made up her usage of the device after seeing the news about Spencer on Holovision, in order to save face."

"To save face with her colleagues, you mean? Showing that she didn't suc-cumb to neurotic stuff due to job pressures or genetics or whatever else, but external factors? Sweet. I'd claim a mind-altering weapon if I were her."

"If she thought that it would be a credible explanation or excuse, I'm sure she'd claim it. You think such things really exist?"

The events of the week crossed Phoenix's mind, and she felt a desperate urge to share the things she had seen and witnessed with Gisella. She wanted to ad-mit that the existence of such weapons was the only way to prove her sanity, she wanted to talk about her intruder and how she had been zapped by him, she wanted to confess how a butterfly shot her up to the skies, she wanted and needed to, so much, just to get it off her chest. She wanted to scream to the whole world that she was in love! But she couldn't, despite the fact that her instincts were fully trusting Gisella, at least not yet, and not until she got to the bottom of this damn case once and for all.

"Well, those are classified subjects. But you're part of a criminal task force, so I don't see any reason why I shouldn't share them with you." Clarification was more for Sean, who had been quietly listening to them.

"I'm glad," said Gisella with a wink. "Go on."

"There have been cases of such incidents, and I believe such weapons exist. Actually, we might have been exposed to one on Monday, right, Sean?"

"Yes," nodded Sean, suddenly animated. "It was actually like—"

"You think it was some kind of a hardware that zapped you?"

"Is there any other way? We ran into this intruder, and he froze us momen-tarily to gain advantage for escaping."

"Did you catch him?"

"Nope, he vanished."

"Wow. I'd love to get my hands on one of these weapons, you know, and fig-ure out how they work. Did I tell you I also have a background in electronics?"

"Seriously?"

"I aspired to be an engineer before I fell in love with my field," said Gisella and grinned. "So I majored in double-E before going to med school." She checked the screen of her network node and looked up. "Ms. Vanderbilt is out of her therapy session. The nurse will take you to her room."

"All right," said Phoenix and walked out.

Sean watched Phoenix leave, unsure what to do. Then she hesitantly turned to Gisella, only to see her staring at her with a curious gaze. She cleared her throat. "You're not gonna offer some complimentary neurological test now, are you?"

The therapy room was stylishly furnished with several comfortable couches and armchairs, illuminated by soft light. Lena Vanderbilt was standing by the tall window watching the garden, as immaculate as the one in Versailles Palace, below.

"Ms. Vanderbilt?"

Vanderbilt turned to Phoenix brusquely, her body language hostile. She was a tall, lanky woman in her mid-forties with platinum hair and a strangely rodent-like face with a sharp nose and receding chin. No amount of carefully applied makeup could conceal the smallness of her close-set ditchwater-colored gray eyes, nor had she quite managed to cover the liberal sprinkling of little red veins around her nose and across her cheeks. She gazed at Phoenix top to toe then turned back towards the window, watching outside, shifting her weight from one leg to other impatiently.

"What do you want?" she said in a deep voice.

"I need your help about a very important case that I'm investigating."

"What case? I was told that it was an important WIMA matter."

"It's not about WIMA, Ms. Vanderbilt, but it concerns you a great deal."

"My health concerns me a great deal," said Vanderbilt, still facing the window. "And you have no jurisdiction over anything that concerns me. Good-bye."

"It's about Vassily Bogdanov. He's dead."

"He's dead?" said the woman and turned with a tiny smirk at the corner of her mouth.

"Yes, and I'm investigating his death. Is it your position that you paid hundreds of thousands of dollars to him for art consultancy?"

Vanderbilt just stood there looking down upon Phoenix with her chin up. Her face was totally expressionless, but Phoenix could tell that she was trying to figure out how to position herself with Bogdanov's death and her association with him.

"Or would you rather help me determine how Bogdanov coerced you into using this smuggled illegal device that drew you over the edge?"

"You know about the device?"

"I know of the device," nodded Phoenix. "And I also know he was no art consultant. There are eyewitness accounts that he was renting items secretly through his office at the Thing Store. Is that where you met him?"

"Yes," nodded the woman. "I was there to see those *Things*, and my assistant had organized a private viewing during the afterhours. I hate crowds and crowded places. Bogdanov personally attended to my tour."

"Did he mention the device to you during that private tour?"

Vanderbilt didn't answer but just stood there in grim silence with her murky gray eyes locked onto Phoenix's green-gray ones. Then she scrutinized Phoenix's curves with an envious gaze.

"Ms. Vanderbilt, I can only prove how Bogdanov tricked you into using that device if you're open with me. We know he'd established a criminal ring to bring contraband into the Union in collaboration with a captain from our Air Force."

"An Air Force pilot? I thought those people were incorruptible."

"If you'd be kind enough to tell me about how this device came into your possession and how it drove you over the edge, it would be so much easier for me to expose how you have been victimized by an evil plot."

"He—" she said and sighed. "He mentioned it that day I had that private tour. He was so full of himself and so energetic, that repulsive creature, he said that there was a brand-new device, produced by an undisclosed but reputable company, and that he was authorized to test market it."

"And, of course, you had no reason to suspect such an offer which came at a reputable company like the Thing Store."

"Why would I? I'm a very respectable executive, and I only have contact with upright people. I thought it was another product in their catalog, reserved for the likes of me. I had no reason to suspect any foul play."

"Of course not," nodded Phoenix. "Please go on."

"He said I could use it for a week for free, and all I had to do in return was to give him feedback, telling him if I liked it or not."

"What was this device actually for?"

"It was a virtual reality device. You didn't know about this?"

"I only know *of* the device, I've never actually seen it. It's being kept under lock for scientific evaluation. You happen to be the first one to admit to its existence."

"I am?" said the woman, her voice shaking. "In that case, I shouldn't—"

"Relax, Ms. Vanderbilt. Your doctors are already suspicious that you may have made up its involvement. Changing your story would only strengthen their existing suspicions."

"You have no idea what I'm dealing with here. It's highway robbery!" said the woman, her eyes bulging. "My insurance is refusing to pay my bills, on the grounds that I had a preexisting neurological condition since birth. How absurd is that?"

"It sounds downright farfetched and fallacious. I intend to show that you're a victim in this situation so that you can salvage your reputation unscathed, as well as your wallet, provided that you cooperate with me."

"That would be a beneficial arrangement," said the woman, with a tiny smile on her stony face, "provided that you can deliver."

"Believe me, if there is anyone that could deliver this to you, it's me."

"So you say. And why is that?"

"Because my personal reputation also depends on me proving Bogdanov's criminal ring, as well as the damaging effects of the device in question. I can't get my hands on the device due to safety reasons, but a testimony from a respectable member of our society, such as yourself, would definitely fill that void."

"It looks like our fates are tied together, Agent. I hope that you're smart enough to deliver your promise."

Vanderbilt was the second person to make the same remark in the same day, and Phoenix knew that the two weren't the only ones. Somehow, she had moved into a position where the fates of many people had been tied to hers.

"You will see that I am. I have to remind you that all of your comments will be recorded in my case file."

"So be it," murmured the woman. "What do you want to know?"

"Bogdanov approached you during your initial visit at the Thing Store and gave you the device for a week to try out. What happened after that?"

"I didn't really give it a second thought for a while. But later, my curiosity overpowered my skepticism, and I decided to give it a try." The woman paused for a moment, her murky eyes drifting to somewhere on the horizon. "Then I had the most tantalizing experience of my life."

"Did you check if the device had appropriate authorization seals?"

"I noticed much later. By that time, it was already too late."

"Too late for what?"

"I was already addicted. After my first try, I used the device with increasing frequency. When I told that scum pretending to be a human being that I wanted to keep it a little longer, he said 'Sure, for a price.' He introduced a weekly rental rate which doubled every week. Within a month, the rental price was so high, it made no economic sense whatsoever. But I didn't care. I had to have it."

"What made it so addictive?"

"I used to be a hardcore gamer, and I had my share of experience with all kinds of virtual reality apparatuses during those years. But this device was so unique in so many ways, it isolated you from the real world completely. I don't know how they did it, but I couldn't see or hear anything else while the damn thing was on. Sometimes it was even hard to remember that this was just a simulation. I didn't wanna switch it off. I couldn't switch it off." Vanderbilt turned to the window and gazed down to the immaculate garden.

"Please go on."

"I'm not sure if I want to explain further and relive the same thing right now," she whispered over her shoulder.

"Why? Because the experiences were painful?"

"On the contrary. I cannot remember many details due to my treatment here, but there was so much pleasure. But it was just so intense."

"Intense? How so?"

"Intense as in deep, real deep, sensations," said Vanderbilt and turned to Phoenix with widened murky eyes. "The device came with many preset routines, and my favorite was this one involving sex. It was the most tantalizing experience I have ever encountered." She turned back to the garden.

"As in realism?"

"Hah! What's realism? This was beyond realism. Anyone who experiences anything like this is bound to forget about any sexual act and become addicted to this new experience, at least in my case, because I have yet to experience any emotions so overpowering. After every session, I was ready for more. So my sessions quickly became longer and more frequent."

"Was there any other side effect of the device, other than the addiction?"

"None. Actually, I was feeling very strong and confident. I was so full of greed, a misguided greed focused only on having it. I had to have it, I couldn't stop thinking about it."

"Have you ever heard of the Dinastiya, Ms. Vanderbilt?"

"No. Was I supposed to?"

"It's the name of the Russian criminal group who I suspect to have murdered Bogdanov. You wouldn't happen to have any contact with them, would you?"

The woman turned and took a few steps to come face to face. "How dare you insinuate such a thing, you little piece of shit? I am a respectable executive at one of the most important guilds in this world. And I'm immune to such accusations from you!"

"I already told you that I know about your immunity," said Phoenix, standing firmly in an at-ease position. "But you need my help to salvage your reputation, I need yours to solve my case, and this question needs to be answered, for the record."

"Of course I have no contact with such despicable groups. Who do you think I am?"

"Thank you. Now, can you explain to me why you waited so long before telling your doctors about the device?"

"You have no idea the shape I was in when I got here! The last days I had it, I'd been using that thing every day at work, and one day I simply collapsed, my body unable keep up with the emotional overdrive. I had no idea where I was and whether it was just another routine or not. Because of all that accumulated emotional fatigue, I couldn't tell which was reality and which was dream until just a few days ago."

Phoenix froze, and panic almost swamped her. She fought back to retain her cool in front of her. But the question was already lingering in her mind, and she knew that it would remain there like a splinter, causing pain every time she thought about something, anything. She *knew* about the feelings Vanderbilt was talking about. She knew about the emotional fatigue. She knew about heightened sensations. She knew about the body finally giving up, as hers was so close to doing.

What if, she thought in panic, *what if the same is true for me? How am I to know that I'm not dreaming any of this right now?*

CHAPTER 35

"So, what did she tell you? Did she use a device?"

Phoenix didn't respond, just looked through the glass bubble of the metro car to the dark void of the tunnels, thinking about them, thinking that since she'd been in them, nothing had been the same and all boundaries were gone. Now the difference between dream and reality was as murky as Vanderbilt's eyes. She felt like she was in a state of constant hallucinating, with fragments of reality sprinkled here and there, simply adding texture to the overall picture. Yet the overall picture was still dark, still in the shadows, and she didn't know how to cast any more light on it; she was afraid to shed light on it. She was afraid that the whole picture would crumble to dust under the intensity of the light, and the reality would be too much to bear. She was afraid that all her new senses and abilities were a part of the dream and that she was addicted to the dream's false sense of ease, like the woman with murky eyes. She was afraid of not being able to pull herself out of the dream world, never waking up, never knowing what really happened, never realizing her goals, her hopes, her dreams.

And here it was, the same word again: dream. All her life she'd fought to realize her dreams, and now she was being drowned in them. Was she born like this? Or was it the fault of the Bloodbath? Was it the treatments they experimented with on her? Was it the drugs? Or was it the absence of drugs? Would it matter if she took them now? Or if she took the whole bottle? Would it kill her to do that? Did it matter? Did anything matter anymore?

"Are you okay?" said Sean and rubbed her arm.

Phoenix leapt up from her seat, her eyes scanning everyone in the car, startling Sean and the few other passengers.

"What's wrong? What happened to you in there?"

Phoenix just stood there, quivering in fight-or-flight mode, her eyes observing every angle, looking for threats. Sean watched her anxiously.

"Phoenix, you're scaring me," she whispered. "What's wrong with you?"

"I don't know. Something is wrong with me?"

"I'm afraid it is. You look like you're on the brink of—"

"What? Insanity?" Phoenix almost smiled.

"How can you talk like that?" she whispered with tears in her eyes. "How can you be so lighthearted about what's happening to you?"

"Why shouldn't I?" shrugged Phoenix. "I don't know if any of this is for real. Do you?"

"Of course it's for real."

Phoenix couldn't answer immediately, sat back down, and continued watching the darkness outside for a while. Every muscle in her body was hard, unable to let go and relax. Her neck was so stiff, she could hardly make it turn. She had to relax, or a collapse would be imminent. With an almost superhuman mental effort, she psyched herself down from the sense of imminent calamity and tried to order her muscles to relax.

"Of course it's real," she said to Sean minutes later, somewhat more relaxed. "I'm better now."

"What happened to you in there?" said Sean, her big brown eyes reddened. "I'm worried sick about you."

"I'm physically, mentally, and emotionally drained. I don't know what I'm running on right now. And all of this makes me feel like—"

At that instant they both received an alarm on their PAs from the field office. All staff was being summoned for an emergency.

"We are under attack by a band of hackers led by a notorious terrorist called the Mantis."

The senior agents listened to the director in stunned silence then looked at each other, puzzled, with the exception of Alex and Beverly, who appeared like the skies just collapsed on them.

"Why do I get the feeling that this isn't the first time," said Julio.

"It isn't. This field office has been attacked by this Mantis before. Actually, he or she managed to control this field office, engage in human trafficking, and enable many spies and terrorists to slip into the Union. We believe he had strong connections with the criminal groups on the other side of the border and that they worked in tandem. One of the reasons for my installment here was to stop the Mantis and his gang and reestablish the order and security of this field office. I thought that I had achieved this through reorganization, yet it appears like this wasn't the case."

"Couldn't it be a copycat?" said Beverly. "Or one of the former members of his gang?"

"That's a possibility, but it doesn't change the fact that we're under a cyber-attack and our network is almost at a halt. Some of our databases are corrupted, and others are inaccessible. We have backups for all, but our existing work is severely disrupted. His involvement may also explain the disappearance of that student."

"How can you be sure that this is the Mantis?" said Alex.

"I'll let Fred explain that."

Fred cleared his throat. "We have a bunch of free-floating programs on the network collectively known as the safety net. Our network is subjected to enormous amounts of data traffic, and these programs act like old-style traffic police, making sure the data is flowing—"

"Can you get to the point?"

"Yes, of course," said Fred and rubbed his hands on his pants. "As our network had started to slow down, the safety net intercepted some irregular activity on a very large scale. I managed to capture the virus code and examined its DNA, so to speak, and discovered the same pattern we'd found years ago, bearing the name of the Mantis."

"So the Mantis *is* back," said Beverly with sunken shoulders.

"If he was ever gone, that is," said the director. "I've been receiving intelligence challenging that for some time now, and it seems like this intelligence had merit."

"So even if it is a copycat, this person or people actually have access to the original hacking source-codes used by the Mantis?" said Beverly.

"That appears to be the case," nodded the director.

"There's one thing that I don't get," said Julio. "From what I can gather from the chitchat between you, the experienced folk, this Mantis was never caught or apprehended, right?"

"No, he wasn't," said the director.

"Then, how can you even tell that it was a he or a she, or a real person for that matter?" said Julio with a smirk. "For all I understand, the character could be just a myth, created as a decoy in order to generate a misplaced target. I remember reading about such terrorists before the Great Meltdown; one came in form of an indestructible religious fanatic or something."

"It is true that we never verified the existence of the Mantis," said the director. "But he or she was making its presence felt through many different ways, little details, misplaced items, unexplained breaches."

"You make it sound like the Mantis could be good ol' wacko Ray," said Julio and grinned. "You're sure he comes in a human form, or should we resort to our own imagination to see what this Mantis looks like? What does it mean, anyway?"

"Mantis is an insect that can imitate a plant and hide in plain sight from its prey, you moron," said Beverly. "It was his hacker nick."

"Excuse me for not studying my etno-whatever-the-name-of-that-science-is. So if this Mantis can hide in plain sight, it might be among us right here, right now, couldn't it? I mean, she said it!"

The room fell quiet very suddenly, with all eyes swiveling first to Julio and then to each other.

"We can sit on our asses and argue about the existence of the Mantis all day long," said the director. "But it's irrelevant. With or without the Mantis, the threat is real, people. Someone is messing up our network and leaving a calling card behind. This is an open challenge, and we need to show we're up to the challenge by neutralizing this Mantis, or whoever is behind it, once and for all."

Everyone nodded grimly and looked at each other with wariness.

"And how are we supposed to do that exactly?" said Julio and crossed his arms. "We're no network experts, we're investigators. Don't tell me we're opening a case of investigation for a bogeyman."

The director fixed her icicled gaze on Julio for a few seconds then spoke in a whisper. "Actually, we are opening such an investigation," she said. "And I hereby appoint *you* as the lead."

"Me?" said Julio, leaning over the table. "You gotta be kidding me!"

"You better believe that I'm not," said the director and leaned over to match his move. "Unless, of course, you're declining my offer. What's wrong, Julio, not feeling up to a *real* challenge?"

"I—I do. Fine, whatever, I'll take it."

"Good," nodded the director with a rare grin. "Now as the lead senior agent responsible, I want you to work closely with Fred and enlighten us about how this hacking was carried out and how to stop it. Who knows, maybe you can trace a lead to the identity and whereabouts of the Mantis or the copycat, which we experienced folk failed to catch all these years, and shove it in our faces. Wouldn't that be swell?"

Julio nodded quietly with a flash of hostility in his little dark eyes.

"I expect you to work around the clock until this hack attack is neutralized, understand? You've been all talk so far. It's about time you showed all of us what you're made of. I hope you make the best of this opportunity. Additionally, I want all of you to check the information related to your work and ensure its integrity. If you cannot access your data, report it to our new case lead, Julio. Dismissed."

Phoenix watched the meeting from behind a frosted glass, unable to focus. She appeared calm on the outside, but there was a storm raging inside her mind. She couldn't care less about the hack attack, or the Mantis, or whoever or whatever was behind it. It wouldn't even matter to her if this Mantis was sitting next to her. Why should it, if she couldn't be sure if any of this was real or not? She had to know if this was all a dream, yet she didn't know how. She had to be able to discern the edge between reality and fantasy. She had to do something and find a way.

"Hey, sis," said Beverly and kneeled next to her. "You okay? The meeting's over. C'mon, let's get some coffee."

Beverly's words couldn't pierce Phoenix's consciousness. They came from the bottom of a well, with a lot of echo, words blending into each other, losing their meaning. Beverly had a lot of compassion in her clear blue eyes. But her eyes were behind the frosted glass, too, like everything else, and Phoenix wondered if Beverly was really aware how far away she was right now. Perhaps not, for sure not. How could she expect others to understand what she was sensing, or feeling, or doing, if she wasn't able to understand it herself? And all this fake sympathy and good intent in the absence of genuine understanding made her sick. She needed to get out of here. She didn't know where, but she needed to run away and protect herself.

She took off without a word.

"What are you doing in my domain?" said a weary voice. "Are you lost?"

Phoenix snapped out of her trance only to realize that she wasn't exactly aware of her whereabouts. From the absence of natural light and the low ceilings, she could only guess that she must have walked down into the bowels of the wretched old field office building, only to run into the real owner of these dungeon hallways. "Ray! What are you doing here?"

"No, the question is, what are *you* doing here?" said Ray in a moment of rare lucidity. "Are you trying to take cover from the storm that I warned you about?"

"I don't know. I don't know anything anymore."

"Now that's my girl," said Ray, embracing her with a little hug. "It all starts with the acceptance. I'm glad that you finally realized what you know and don't know makes no difference."

"What does make a difference, then? Tell me. Why am I here? Why do I live? I feel like I know nothing about myself. I don't know me. I only know the me behind a mask that they made for me."

"Mop, mop, mop it away. Mop, mop, mop it away," mumbled Ray, wiping the floor as usual and moving away from Phoenix.

"Talk to me! Tell me, why am I here?"

"Hiding or seeking?" said Ray, without turning. "Which is it?"

"Huh?"

Ray stopped and turned towards Phoenix, rolling his eyes. "You're deep down in the dungeons of my building. It's like a cave here, yes? Now why do people go to caves?"

"I don't know. Because they are speleologists?"

"I'm not referring to those valiant but crazy souls," said Ray, shaking his head. "But normal people, like you and me."

"Hrrmph—" Phoenix snorted and laughed long and hard. Unfettered by any sense of social obligation, Ray's face remained blank. He tilted his head, a la Capello, trying to make sense of her reaction.

"Normal people, like you and me? You know, Ray, I haven't laughed like that for such a long time. Thank you."

"I don't know why you found my words so funny, but—"

"It's because we're anything but normal, you and I."

"Says who?" shrugged Ray. "I don't know about you, but I find myself very normal, and so are you."

"What I meant was, we're different from others. We think different, we act different, we feel different. We observe the world from a different viewpoint."

"Aha," said Ray and snapped his fingers. "But you're talking about average, not normal. It's true, you and me, we're not average. You see how words can shift in their meanings? Sometimes they do it on purpose."

"You mean, being average to become normal and therefore to be the norm?"

Ray simply nodded and continued wiping the floor, humming. Words shifting meanings, she remembered this from somewhere. But where? Could it be in a—?

"You still didn't answer my question about caves," said Ray over his shoulder.

"I don't know, Ray, you tell me," said Phoenix and folded her arms. "Why do people go to caves?"

"Like I said to you before. Hiding and seeking."

"As in the game, hide-and-seek?"

"What do you think?" said Ray and turned to her, rolling his tired eyes once again. "Do I look like I'm playing a game?"

That moment it dawned on her. She knew why she was down there. She had come down here, subconsciously, looking for answers. The place was the key, the key to another location, the key to the place she would find all the answers, the key to her sanity, and where it all started.

Phoenix planted a big wet kiss on Ray's cheek and took off running.

"Now that's what I call a real dilemma," said the Crane, shaking his head.

He turned his attention back to his array of monitors, where he could see all of his running threads and wares simultaneously. The hack at the field office was still ongoing at full throttle, and the poor souls up there had been totally helpless and inept, having no idea what to do. At first, it was fun and interesting to watch their predictable and fruitless countermeasures. But in time, it became a more and more tedious task to observe and follow up their repeated futile efforts to loosen the grip he had on their network. With all the resources at their disposal, somebody really lacked intelligence and imagination up there. He wished he had some worthy opponent, like that supervisor at the NC Research Triangle, who had come up with the ingenious idea of cutting all the power to the entire network, only too late.

"A dilemma we've been unable to come up with a solution to yet," nodded the Toboggan Hat. "I'm sure she'll do it. My only concern is the timing."

The Crane's heart raced as he thought of her. Despite the criticism he had received concerning his behavior during their encounter, he had no regrets. It was the only way he could have acted, and yet he hadn't known it beforehand. Toboggan Hat understood him completely, but understanding didn't solve their dilemma. They still needed to bring her down.

"She's still somewhere at the field office. Should I send her another PING?"

"I said delicate and subtle, my boy, not head-on and charging like a bull."

"Perhaps I can go up there and kindly invite her with a formal invitation letter, Grandmaster. I'm sure she'd appreciate that."

"Great idea, considering the fact that the field office is on full alert. I'm sure the Mantis would love to see you, too."

"Actually," said the Crane, his eyes glued to something on his giant monitor. "Actually, she's coming down here, running, as we speak."

"Indeed!" Toboggan Hat smiled pleasantly. "I knew it."

"Should I go and greet her?" The Crane sprang to his feet. He couldn't hide his excitement.

"You?" said Toboggan Hat, arching an eyebrow. "I understand your desire to meet her now, but you should be the last one to greet her if we are to salvage our plan, as well as improve the chance of her well-being."

"Why does everything come to me so difficult?" said the Crane and sat down to his chair, his hands on his face.

"Because you're smarter than most, and you usually get what you want readily and quickly, which makes it hard for you to develop patience. So circumstances keep bringing situations requiring patience before you, and it's up to you whether to take up these challenges or to push them away."

"All right, all right. I'll be patient. So you'll greet her?"

"No, no, no. She's coming down to see me, but she doesn't know that. She doesn't know who we are and what we're down here for. In the previous encounter, we thought that we could ease her mind with your presence and then appeal to her strong rational side by explaining certain hard-to-believe facts with the presence of the Mirage. But she had an unexpected emotional reaction to Mirage, and your frozen appearance worsened the situation further, causing a total failure. Now, for all she knows, we're a band of hackers and terrorists. When she sees me, she needs to be in a calm and open mindset, not a tense and resistant one. We need someone who can calm her worries down, make her feel confident and relaxed."

"You're talking about me. I could achieve all this."

"Yes, you potentially could," nodded the Toboggan Hat. "But your presence would also bring the side effects of love, confusion, and anxiety."

"But who else down here could achieve what you're saying without jinxing her?"

"Someone with no jinxing or stunning abilities, someone innocent, someone she'd feel at ease with without hesitation, someone who'd pose no threat to her. I need you, but not you, more like a tiny image of you."

Hide and seek, Phoenix thought as she walked along the metro tunnels. Of course old Ray wasn't talking about a child's game. Caves featured three characteristics that terrified humans over ages: dark mazes, cold, and water. Fear of being trapped in the dark, of hypothermia, of drowning. This led a few people to use caves and the underground for two main purposes: to protect themselves from enemies and to search for divine knowledge in its stark and unearthly solitude. She had found herself in the hallways beneath the field office subconsciously hiding from enemies and looking for answers, then remembered certain details of her last nightmare. She had been trapped underground, yet kept on going deeper, looking for salvation and answers. Again, her subconscious was forcing her to go underground, both to take cover and to seek answers, *hide* and *seek*.

She knew what answers she was seeking but wasn't sure whom or what she was supposed to hide from. Walking in these dark tunnels, an answer emerged in her mind: What if all her confusions, her daydreams, her hallucinations, her insomnia, her fatigue, anything and everything that was slowing her down and not making her think straight, what if all of these were a part of some design? What if she had been the oblivious and unsuspecting target of a deep plot, on top of, or underneath, the one concocted by Hamilton, and had been a target of attacks of an immensely asymmetrical nature? What if these attacks were designed to wear her out and drive her to the edge of insanity? What if these dark tunnels were the only place she was safe from harmful attacks and influence? What if a powerful nemesis was secretly waging a personal war against her? All these thoughts were of a deeply paranoid nature. But what if it was all true?

Arnett was right. She had had a lot of success within a week, and that was drawing lots of attention and negative energy, which translated into deep envy in the postmodern world. The director could have a lot of reasons to lie to her, or the PWU might have more reasons to lie to a lame-duck director. And what if the lies didn't end there? Her dialogue with Arnett was still lingering in her mind, and she was only now beginning to process everything spoken between them. Her mind had to be in good shape, simply because Arnett had spent so much time and energy on her, even leaving an open door for more, all in return for nothing. Arnett was a no-nonsense, brilliant, arrogant prick. He would never waste a second of his time if he were to think that there was something wrong with her head. And Phoenix's instincts had told her that he would be as good as Gisella in telling sane from insane, unless, of course, *he* was also a part of the plot.

She brushed off the thoughts that she considered to be too deep from her mind. She had to maintain focus. She had made two brief calls to Sean and Tess before she had headed down to the tunnels and, losing network connectivity, asked Sean to dig into the GPSN Company Rules and find out something about the border security apparatus and asked Tess to use her expertise for researching a few things in the border-control database.

She could barely speak to either of them, as the communication kept breaking up amid the attack from the Mantis and his hacker chorus. Could her intruder be a part of this attack? Could he be involved with or part of the same gang as Mantis? Could he be the Mantis?

She jumped over the rails easily this time and put her hand under the door to open it. She carefully walked to the back wall. She couldn't remember how the boulder had given her the way in her dream. Could it be another trapdoor? She walked along it touching the bricks, trying to press them and pull them to see if anything would happen. Suddenly she heard a loud rumble and inadvertently jumped back a few steps, her heart beating as if it would explode. The wall opened up from the middle, giving way to the passage she had been through before. Sudden anxiety filled Phoenix as she remembered the similar scene in her nightmare. She had to take this passage, if she was to *seek* her sanity. She gathered all her courage, crawled through it quickly, and got out at the hallway on the other side. She proceeded along the corridor slowly; she could hear her heartbeat in her ears, wondering if she would see the Mirage, her intruder, or anyone else in there. The loud slamming sound from behind multiplied her anxiety, leaving only one direction to go.

The room was empty, yet all the computers seemed to be working. Cables were running on every wall, under the grilled floor and the ceiling, way more than necessary for the machines in the room, as if this was some kind of a connection point, some network hub for many distant locations. She didn't dare touch any of the devices and focused on the back wall, where there appeared to be a metallic door or gateway. Was it there the last time? She pressed the large button on its side, and the door opened, exposing an elevator. She felt a chill in her spine and could hear her heart beating in her ears again. She closed her eyes and told herself to calm down, then desperately tried to go to the place she felt safe. It didn't work.

She took a hesitant step into the elevator. There was just one button, yet she couldn't quite bring herself to press it. She kept thinking of the nightmare and the rusty elevator. She merely touched the button, and the door closed, beginning the long descent. She didn't know why or how, but she knew it would go down to the bowels of the earth.

She tried to count the seconds to be able to guess how deep she was descending, but after the sixtieth second, the count gave way to more anxiety and panic. When would this descent end? Where was she going? Who could have built such a massive shaft with such a long descent? Was she ever going to be able to see the surface again? If something were to happen, with all of its might, could the World Union find and rescue her from down here? World Union, rescuing her? Yeah, right! She smiled, thinking some old habits were hard to eradicate.

At that moment, the descent started to slow down, and in a few seconds the door of the elevator opened, with cold air rushing inside. She found a dimly lit tunnel before her, a kind of tunnel that she had never seen in her life before. It was an orderly semi-circular tunnel carved in the rock, with walls and ceilings partially covered with synthetic material in reflective orange and, in the rest, the dark gray of the solid rock visible. She noticed large metal trays on both sides of the wall, presumably to carry cables. The ground was paved with gray synthetic tartan-like material and was very easy to walk on. The tunnel was empty, leading to a left curve twenty meters ahead.

She took a few hesitant steps and shivered at the damp coldness of the place, watching the vapor from her warm breath. Wasn't the earth's crust supposed to get warmer as one went down? She looked up and wondered how many hundreds of meters of solid rock separated her from the surface. The thought sent another chill down her spine.

An echo of a voice came first, then she saw him turning the bend ahead and approaching with his hands in his pockets, humming a song. He walked with idle and playfully irregular steps, making zigzags as he approached and looked at her with a warm smile, completely melting away her worries. Phoenix smiled back inadvertently and waited until he was closer.

"Now tell me," she said. "What are you doing down here?"

CHAPTER 36

"Hey, Bud, talk to me, dude," said Beverly. "C'mon! And just when I thought I had a good thing going, dammit. The story of my life."

"I—here—gorg—" came Bud's fragmented voice. His visuals were also in distorted jagged movements to match his voice, as both the audio and video lacked sufficient bandwidth due to the ongoing hack. It had been like this for several hours now, and nothing they did seemed to work. Beverly didn't expect much help from Fred in the matter, either, especially now that Julio would stick his little nose into network affairs, too. She had no idea why boss would assign the lazy and arrogant manipulator to lead such a thing, other than to annoy him. And that was so unlike the boss.

"Harold, can't you give me some more bandwidth so I can go on with this process? I need to complete this section of the damn installation or say good-bye to six hours of work."

"Impossible," said Harold. "It's maxed out already. Try voice only."

"Hey, hunky dude, I'm afraid I won't be able to gaze at your gorgeous ass for a while. Let's continue with voice only until this hack is sorted out."

"Sure," said Bud, as his image vanished. "Can you hear me now?"

"Loud and clear," smiled Beverly. "And you?"

"Hear you perfect, gorgeous. Need help with that hack?"

"Afraid not. We already have experts from the HQ working on it remotely along with our local staff. You guys aren't cleared for this kinda thing yet."

"Your loss."

"Oh, shuddup. Not in a playful mood. Got a hold of Phoenix yet?" she turned to Sean.

"No. And she's *silent* again."

"No shit! Computer: Get your lazy micro-voltaged dimwit ass to make a trace to locate Senior Agent Wallis in Greater Adrianopolis area." She turned to Sean. "When did you last talk to her?"

"About an hour ago. She was on her way somewhere, I think."

"What exactly did she say?"

"She asked me to find out certain details about customs and immigration policies from the company rules regarding—"

"I'm not asking about that. Where did she say she was going?"

"She didn't," shrugged Sean. "She just told me to figure it out before she gets back and to be available all night long."

"Lo—tor—race—incon—sive."

"Computer: Widen the search to entire Eastern Europe. It's gotta be a mistake. Probably her PA went wacko again."

"But didn't she receive a new PA recently?"

"She sure did. I wonder if this hack is disabling us from finding her. Computer: Cancel the last request and make a trace to locate Junior Agent Sean Euskara in Adrianopolis city limits."

"Inval—para—eter."

"What the hell? The hack progressed to the micro-codes in the CPUs of our wire-brains, or what? They were already too dumb for their own good, now they're turning total imbeciles."

"Try Ixone," said Sean. It's my official name."

"Oh! Computer: Make a trace to locate Junior Agent *Ixone* Euskara."

"Ix—Eus—ara—room—umber—"

"All right, all right, cancel, we got the picture, it works. And it should work even in the Silent Mode. She's not in any hospital, yet she can't be reached even with a locator. Only two things I can think of: One is her PA being fried. But if this was the case, she couldn't even take the metro, which means she'd need to be in the vicinity, unless her PA wacked out while in transit, like before, or, she could be in the rogue territories, where she'd be out of any kinda coverage."

"It's gotta be the malfunction, right?" said Sean, her voice shaking. "I mean, I saw it happen, her PA acting all weird. She's been acting weird, too. What if she—"

"Stop that!" said Beverly. "There's gotta be an explanation."

"Hello, my name is Konrad," said the little boy, extending his hand.

He was about nine or ten years old, had a heartwarming smile and beautiful dark-brown eyes. He was dressed up pretty warmly in a white woolen shirt, brown woolen breeches, white knee-high woolen socks, black shoes, a brown two-button coat, and a gray wool Trenker hat. Phoenix thought about the cold once again and felt lucky that she had her old uniform on her, which didn't expose her waist area and was better insulated for the cold environments.

"And I'm Phoenix," she said and smiled, shaking his hand. "What are you doing down here, Konrad? Aren't you supposed to be at the CDC?"

"CDC? What's a CDC?"

"You don't know what a Child Development Center is?"

"No, I don't," shrugged the boy. "A place for underdeveloped and naughty kids?"

"You could say that," nodded Phoenix, thinking of the brat with the make-believe Arrivee tattoo. "But who takes care of you here?"

"My parents and my teachers, who else? Are you from World Union or Russia?"

"I—I'm from the World Union, of course. What is this place, Konrad? Who built it? Where does this tunnel lead to?"

"This is the Land of the Renovators," said the boy, then took Phoenix's hand and started walking. "Come with me, I'll show you."

"Who are the Renovators? Is it some new-age religious group?"

"I don't know what that is. Renovators are Renovators. We're all Renovators."

They walked along the tunnel, passing by iron doors on both sides with signs in a foreign language. "What language are those signs?"

"It's Danish."

"You can read them?"

"Sure. That's entrance to a materials lab, this one for the sick bay."

"You speak beautiful English, Konrad. Why go into an effort of learning a language like Danish that makes no economic sense?"

"I don't know. Renovators don't just speak Danish and English. They speak many other languages, too. Some even prefer not to speak in English."

"Why wouldn't they want to speak in English? It's the lingua franca."

"No, it's not," said Konrad, looking up at Phoenix with a mischievous smile.

"I don't know what they teach you here, Konrad, but it is."

"It's obvious you don't speak Latin. If you did, you wouldn't make such a serious mistake."

"As a matter of fact, I don't speak Latin," nodded Phoenix. "And I don't think anyone other than some lingo-historical experts do, either."

The boy stopped and turned to look at Phoenix. "You're wrong, again," he said. "I speak Latin, and I'm not one of those experts that you mentioned, a lingo—"

"Lingo-historical experts: researchers in universities who study old languages."

"Ah, I heard of universities," nodded Konrad. "They are mass-instruction organizations, right?"

"A mass-instruction organization? Never heard of that before."

"And from the way you misremember things, I would guess that you're a graduate of one of those."

"I guess I am."

"Because if you graduated through our academies here, you'd know that in Latin *lingua franca* means 'language of the French people.' So English can't be lingua franca."

"It's an idiom, but technically speaking, you're right, Konrad."

Soon the tunnel ended, and they reached a shaft, a cylindrical opening of about thirty meters wide and more than one hundred meters high. It was a huge natural underground shaft, with a spiral-shaped metal walkway with a mild incline attached to the rock where one could walk and climb up and gates that looked like doors to dwellings. Sounds of running water could be heard up at a distance. The place must have been part of a massive cave system, enhanced with manmade tunnels, like the one they had been in. The shaft was illuminated wonderfully and resembled a mystical ziggurat inside out.

"Whoa! Do people live in those rocks?"

"Yes."

"How many people live here? I mean, how can you survive in underground without natural light?"

"I don't know how many Renovators there are, but our homes and workplaces are installed with solar simulators that provide us with full-spectrum lighting."

"But why do all this? Why live here? And where are all the other people?"

Konrad stopped in front of a metal gate at the end of one of the short tunnels that they took from the shaft and turned to Phoenix.

"I'm just a young apprentice who only knows very few things. I was asked to take you to the one who could answer all your questions."

"To whom?"

"Our Grandmaster. Please enter, he is expecting you. Good-bye, Phoenix."

"You're not coming with me?"

"My duty ends here," said Konrad and smiled. "I hope I see you again, Phoenix. I like you." He turned and left without giving Phoenix a chance to reply, humming a song and walking in zigzags.

Phoenix turned to the metal gate, not exactly sure what to do. There were no buttons or anything else to open it. She took a step towards it, and the metal door silently gave way. It was pitch dark inside. She took a few hesitant steps inside the dark, heard the gate close behind her, jump-starting her anxiety. What was this place? Who were the Renovators? Who could have built all this, and why? Could this be a top-secret World Union facility?

As her eyes got used to the darkness, she noticed a faint trace of light under her feet that was leading forward. She took a few more steps and looked ahead, only to notice the sky on the horizon. Suddenly she looked up and saw millions of stars, brighter than she had ever seen before. But how could she have reached the surface so fast, without climbing? Was this another dream? Could she be hallucinating again? Then she noticed something in the sky. Then she knew that this wasn't a dream or hallucination. It couldn't be.

She held her breath and watched as the stars above started to accelerate. It wasn't just a dark sky and vibrant stars anymore, but orange pulsars, purple nebulae, and galaxies in other striking colors were parading in their galactic grandeur, as if she were traveling in space and time at the speed of thought, exploring the depths of the universe in every dimension imaginable. It was so ironic to witness such a spectacle so far below the ground, but on the other hand, would there be a better place to *seek* the divine knowledge? She took gentle steps along the path marked by the lights and watched the simulation in amazement. Then she saw him, a little old man with a long white beard, dressed in a funny-looking costume. He came with a funny orange hat, the kind that people used to wear to their beds. He kept looking at her intently, along with a twinkling smile. Could he be some kind of an entertainer? But as she got closer, she could tell that this man was no clown.

"Hello, my name is Phoenix," she said and extended her hand. "Are you a Renovator, too?"

"Yes, I am," said the old man with his deep and warm voice, ignoring her hand. "My name is Magnus, and I'm the grandmaster of the Renovators."

"So you're the grandmaster that Konrad was talking about?"

"Yes, lonely-star, I am."

"Lonely-star? Why would you call me such a thing?"

"You have a beautiful name, Phoenix. Do you know what it means?"

"It's the name of one of the most important cities in North America, and a mythological bird, I think, right? Didn't give it much thought."

Toboggan Hat turned and pointed with his arm at the horizon, and suddenly the parade of the stars dimmed down, making a faintly blinking star visible. "And a star cluster in the Southern skies, a cluster where only one star is bright enough to be seen. A far, lonely, and unappreciated star."

"I'm afraid my astronomy is not as good as yours," said Phoenix, looking at the horizon. "Is there any significance to it that I should know?"

"There sure is," nodded the old man. "Do you know what brought you here?"

"You mean the elevator and Konrad? What is this place, anyway? What do Renovators do? Why is Konrad not attending a CDC?"

"I'm not asking about the physical side of your journey. Why are you here?"

"I'm investigating a crime, and some leads brought me here. What's the purpose of Renovators, anyway? Why stay in this freezing place under the ground? Why are you hiding?"

"Because, my dear, we wouldn't feel secure in the World Union or the nation states. Your Union wouldn't let us pursue our path the way we like, and the others we wouldn't be physically safe in. So, for now, we prefer to stick to the sacred solitude of the underground, placing ourselves right in between, in a state of purgatory."

"Why are you afraid of the Union? Is it because you pursue certain intent which would violate the Supreme Bill, or involved in illegal activities? And where are all these other Renovators? I've yet to see anyone other than you and Konrad."

"Everyone was asked to refrain from interfering with your path, as Konrad brought you here, so that you wouldn't seek answers from the wrong people. And, yes, our intents and thoughts would violate your Supreme Bill, as we don't believe in the Supreme Bill. And, although as a peace agent you'd consider some of our activities illegal, I should remind you that same could be said for your own GPSN."

"Excuse me, Grandmaster Magnus, but what kind of illegal activity do you claim that GPSN is supposed to be involved in?"

"Interacting and doing business with mafia and other criminal groups in the rogue states, for one."

"I dealt with across-the-border illegal activities myself. GPSN is there to stop these illegal organizations, not to do business with them."

"But the bottom line is, the GPSN is just another company trying to make a profit, no? So if it were to serve its purpose, the GPSN would do many things to maximize this profit, including using condemned hackers like the Mirage for their needs. You remember seeing Mirage in the tunnels above soon after your ill-fated interview with her, don't you?"

So it wasn't a dream or hallucination after all. It really had been the Mirage. Otherwise how could this old man in his funny clothes, claiming to be a grandmaster of some sort, know about that? Then again, it could be some kind of a trick in order to unsettle her, couldn't it?

"From your hesitant disposition, I can tell that you are unsure about me because you don't know me. But I happen to know a lot about you, Phoenix."

"What do you mean by that? You've been following me?"

"I don't need to follow you to know you, dear one," said the Toboggan Hat, his voice transmitting immense warmth. "I know that you're here, seeking answers. I know about your worries, about your nightmares, about this knot inside you, about your hesitations, about your love, and about your instincts, which are telling you right now that you could and should trust me."

Phoenix just stood there, frozen. She could have reacted to in a million different ways: She could have screamed at the old man, she could have arrested him, she could have run away, she could have questioned him, she could have laughed at him. She could have and perhaps should have reacted in one of these many ways, but somehow, her reaction was not to react in any way but to listen to that voice inside her telling her to be open with him and that he knew more than anybody could in this world, and not only about her, but about anyone. She attempted to answer a few times, only to stop at the last instant, unsure what to say. The old man, on the other hand, just waited for her patiently, allowing her time so that she could listen to all the voices inside her.

"I—I know what you say to me is so fantastical. But somehow, something about the way you say makes them so completely believable."

"What you are referring to, dear one, is called instinctual trust."

"I suppose that's what it is. I appear to trust you for no reason. Yet, I don't even know you."

"You have very strong instincts inside. I can feel that you're just learning how to use them. And it appears they've been lying dormant for a very long time, until they were recently awakened."

"But how could you know all this?" said Phoenix, her voice shaking. "You have some mind-reading apparatus of some sort? Some advanced or secret technology enables you to read my thoughts and feelings?"

"You could say that," smiled the old man. "I possess something to unlock the mysteries of the mind."

The Mantis was angry and frustrated, as the field office hummed with activity in order to stop what they called *his* actions. He knew nothing of the hack, which was still ongoing and severely disrupting all communication, but he had a pretty good idea whose doing this was. It had to be that Crane. He was the hacker type, and perhaps hacking was the only thing he was good at in life. The Mantis felt pity for the Crane. His rashness and inability to be patient would eventually make him pay dearly. And this was to be one of those times.

Perhaps the Crane was doing all this to fool the leaders and to discredit the Mantis so that he could get ahead. But the Crane wasn't aware how much experience, self-discipline, and patient rational thought was needed to become like the Mantis. Deep down, the Crane must have known that he could never be like the Mantis, and this was why he was resorting to these tricks in order to create confusion. But he wasn't aware that, unlike the Crane, the Mantis had broken the constricting will of his controller and the leaders and was now acting alone.

There was also another possibility, a much more plausible one, namely that the Crane could be doing all this with the blessing of his former leaders. If this was the case, the leaders were weaker than he thought. A flood of silent anger spread through him. He had served them all these years with the utmost loyalty, dedication, and respect. And this smear campaign was his reward? How dare they insinuate that such a head-on vulgar attack was created by the Mantis, making him look inept and clumsy? He had to act quickly and swiftly bring an end to all this before everything got out of control.

All he needed to do was to control the boiling rage inside him, maintain focus, and not get distracted. He needed to *eliminate* Phoenix first, then the turn for his controller, the Prefect, and that adolescent-acting Crane would come next. And in time, he would identify and destroy those leaders who took him for granted, one by one, and make them all pay for this charade. But the first target was Phoenix.

Where *was* she, anyway?

Phoenix didn't know what to do or to say, and the thought of being totally naked to an outsider made her shiver. So this was how it felt to be on the other side of the interview table. She tried to think of a way to stop him. Could she run? It didn't appear like this old man could catch up with her, if she did. But would it help? Did his device and technology have a range? Could he read any thoughts? Could he know what she was exactly thinking now?

"What—what device do you use?" she said, her voice shaking. "Where is it hidden? Answer me."

"I have no hidden device, dear one," said the old man and pointed to his temple. "It all happens in my head. I can sense and empathize with your feelings."

"You can sense my feelings? But how?"

"It's an ability I developed during the Danish Resistance," said the old man, his smile vanishing for the first time. "You call it the Blockade of Denmark. In a nutshell, one has to witness humans devolve into grunting pack animals, *creatures* as we used to call them, in order to unlock the mysteries of the human mind and develop such senses, at least in my case."

"You can sense anything that anyone feels?"

"Yes, I can. And I can manipulate those feelings, too."

A little butterfly in rainbow colors appeared at the horizon, gently flitted its wings, and approached her. As she watched its approach, a feeling of pleasure and safety filled inside her, only for her to see a dark silhouette rising on the horizon behind it. The butterfly vanished, the dark evil shape of a giant serpent filling the sky, instigating a deep shiver in her spine. Cold sweat began to accumulate at her temples, with an ever-tightening knot in her stomach. Suddenly both the butterfly and the serpent disappeared, along with the feelings.

"You've just tasted a teeny bit of my jinxing capabilities. I hope you didn't get scared too much."

"You did all that? You created the visions of the butterfly and the serpent?"

"No, no, no," said the grandmaster, shaking his head. "*You* created those visions. I merely amplified your feeling of serenity first, then your fear. Your mind filled in the rest by selecting appropriate objects for representation. I had no idea you saw a butterfly and a serpent."

"I—I see," said Phoenix, not seeing anything.

"You saw a butterfly, signifying happiness," he said and stroked his beard. "Actually, it fits well with your mind and personality."

"What about my mind and personality?"

"Butterfly signifies change, great change brought by seemingly insignificant actions, the deep-down belief that only these great changes against great odds can bring you happiness, as in a Butterfly Effect. Ever heard of it before?"

"Nope."

"Oh well, more about that some other time," sighed the old man. "Now tell me, where are you from?"

"I was born and raised here in Adrianopolis."

"Oh, so you survived the terrible riots here. You must possess very strong survival instincts, too. But where are you originally from?"

"You mean my genetics? I'm Welsh, from an island called Anglesey."

"Anglesey: the island of the druids," said the old man and looked up to the stars with a spark in his eyes. "So that's what it is. It all makes more sense now."

"What makes sense? First about the meaning of my name, and now my genetic origins, you're becoming to sound more and more like an image maker I know."

"What, you don't believe your genetic makeup determines your traits and abilities? I thought this was one of the pillars of your mighty Union, preservation and perpetuation of genes. '*Omne vivum ex ovo*,' no?"

"That it is. I was referring more about your comment regarding the druids and stars and clusters."

"The ancient druids came with amazing survival skills and instincts, dear one. You share their genes, and you're a natural. I had to acquire all this the hard way and at great mental and emotional expense. You're unique in the sense that your instincts didn't get tainted all these years by that Jacobin rational thought and Enlightenment garbage they force-feed into the young fresh minds. I wonder how."

"My mood stabilizers, they suppressed my instincts, protected them from being degraded and spoiled. But why are instincts so important? What about deduction, reasoning, positive science?"

"You think those and your instincts cannot coexist?" said the old man with a twinkle in his eye. "You think Einstein didn't use his instincts, or Tesla, or Newton, or any other scientist who used his intuition? You think human thought is only bound by science, deduction, reason, and the formulae that come with them, limited and confined by the terms, ideas, and formulae that were designed *by* humans, bounded inside a box? Have you heard of the term 'thinking outside the box'?"

"But only the laws of science can lead to understanding the world, the universe. How can one unlock the mysteries of universe with guidance from something as vague as the instincts?"

"And how can a person imagine and solve the mysteries of the universe by locking himself inside a self-made box? Look at them." He pointed to the stars above, and they suddenly all got brighter. "Do they look like they care about our self-indulgent musings in pursuit of unlocking their mysteries during our infinitesimal existence compared to their ages reaching to infinity? They are so much older than us, and yet they'll continue to be here long after we're all gone. And only our instincts could potentially rival them in age and experience. They made us survive the wild, and they represent the experience of more than a billion years, whereas our thinking schools and philosophies are merely of a few thousand. Our instincts are our most dependable assets, and the only assets that we're born with. Yet, almost everywhere around the world, they are savagely destroyed by the time we reach puberty by in-the-box thinking. Tell me, could you ever have found us down here by only rational thought? Or did you need to resort to something of a more internal nature?"

"I have to admit I use my instincts extensively. Perhaps I was just reacting out of habit. But I thought this place was a hideout for some mafiosi and terrorist hackers, not a breeding ground for out-of-the-box thinking."

"We're neither terrorists nor mafia. But we keep in contact and use or interact with them when necessary. I can see how you thought of this place as being a hub for hackers, and we do have excellent hackers here. But can you tell me how you concluded that there might be also members of organized crime here?"

"You already know so much about me, so I assume you already know about the case that I'm working on, right?" The old man simply nodded. "One of the biggest dilemmas I have is the victim's mysterious disappearance from the Union and reappearance in Russia. I think I figured out how they did it, but in order to achieve that, they would need a hideout. And that room in the tunnels above looked like a perfect hideout, especially after seeing the Mirage there."

"Ah, Mirage and Crane were waiting for you there. But the Crane unpredictably froze after seeing you, due to now-obvious reasons, and you acted more rashly than expected in his presence, perhaps compensating for his dormancy, and so did the Mirage. I had to interfere to end the confrontation."

Phoenix's heart started racing as she heard the name of her intruder for the first time, the Crane. She tried to contain her excitement as best as possible, despite knowing that there was no way she could hide it from the grandmaster. "So you did that," she said. "You jinxed me and dumped me on the other side of the wall. Do the Crane and Mirage also have your jinxing capabilities?"

"Mirage doesn't. Our journeywomen and men don't have stunning abilities. Crane does have some stunning capability, not jinxing, as he's recently been promoted to a master. You experienced his first-ever attempt at it, in the victim's house."

"I experienced more than that, heck of a lot more."

"I know," shrugged the old man. "A side effect none of us could anticipate. The little butterfly was flitting her wings, and I'm sure there was a reason for it; *God need not play dice*."

"But what was he doing there in the victim's house?"

"Covering our tracks."

"You mean to tell me that you were a part of his smuggling ring?"

"No. But he may have had some crucial information in his possession, without even knowing it, which might have exposed us, and we had to check. I cannot explain more than that at this point."

"And how did the Crane stun the security cameras?"

"He doesn't need to stun those," smiled the old man. "He's a world-class technology expert, and this tiny gadget he designed can jam the networking ability of any camera in a certain radius."

"Sweet. What about the Mirage? How did she manage to get free?"

"The Mirage was installed at the immigration academy in accordance with a contract we received from the GPSN."

"What!? The GPSN contracted you out for what purpose?"

"For getting a hacker in the academy, so he or she could be exposed at an appropriate timing. We were hired by the Psychological Warfare Unit."

"The PWU? Do they know you're down here?"

"Of course not. We can only be contacted through intermediaries in the nation states, and nobody knows our hiding place."

So Arnett had gotten so close to guessing the connection between Mirage and GPSN, but according to this grandmaster, the PWU had been acting a lot more heinously than that.

"And Talayman? Is he also one of yours?"

"Indeed he is," nodded the grandmaster. "As a part of the same plan, he was supposed to be captured by someone, anyone other than you, that morning. But the little butterfly was fluttering its wings again, and you happened to be the one first out of that metro. He panicked and stunned you, and you banged your head. Our scenario of him being caught collapsed. We needed to make many changes to our plans because of that, including erasing your dash race from the surveillance footage."

"What about this Mantis?"

"The Mantis is a sociopath who's controlled by the Russian mafia," sighed the old man. "We believe he was instructed by them in order to slow your investigation, but the way he launched an attack to your network, he appears to be getting out of control."

"You know about that?"

"Of course. We closely follow what goes on above. Actually, we've been contacted by your regional headquarters at Munich in order to fight off the attack. If we can come to an agreement, our hackers will launch countermeasures to stop the hack by the Mantis's band."

"After all the stuff you told me, that wouldn't be a surprise," said Phoenix, shaking her head. "But everything you told me is so farfetched, why should I believe any of it?"

"Because deep down you know that everything I told you here is for your own good. I don't want any harm to come to you. And for that, you need to expose the Mantis. We believe he's been plotting against you to stop your murder investigation."

"Plotting against me? How?"

"From what we know, the Mantis resorts to psychological warfare and might be equipped with mind-altering weapons. We think he was trying to unsettle you mentally."

Now that she thought about it, there had been many subtle signs of such an attack. Being led in the direction of DeVille had been one of them. Now she was sure that the picture of her nightmare in his flat had been planted there by the Mantis in order to drive her to the edge of insanity. But how could he know about that? "I think he has been. So the Mantis is a he?"

"We don't know," shrugged the old man. "All we know is he or she can—"

"Hide in plain sight, I know. So why help me? Why did you expose yourself so much to me? You hide yourselves from everyone. I could go up there and blow your cover."

"You tried that once, and what happened? You couldn't find anyone to believe your story, could you, surrounded by the walls of plausible deniability in every direction? What do you think would happen if you try it again, hmm?"

"I'll lose all my credibility, whatever's left of it. But you still haven't answered my question."

"We operate in a gray area, where your GPSN allows us to exist, as long as we're out of sight. And we couldn't be more out of sight than these caves, could we now? We help you because we have a common enemy in the Mantis. His aim is to destroy you first, and then he'll come after us."

"Why would he come after you, if you're so careful about your hideout and nobody knows your existence?"

"We're at loggerheads with the Russian mafia group the Dinastiya. We were involved in a business deal with them, but the deal turned sour due to an assortment of reasons. They murdered your victim and are now aiming to derail your investigation, so they unleashed the Mantis on you. Once he's done with you, he'll most certainly come after us."

"I already know about the involvement of the Dinastiya. It appears that my murder victim double-crossed them before he came to the Union."

"The Dinastiya's entire power is behind the Mantis right now. And the best way for us to fight him off is to help you solve your murder mystery and expose the Dinastiya as culprits."

"But I need to find out their hideout for that. Can you help me locate it?"

"I can do better than that," said the old man with a wink. "I can give you the one who can lead you to their hideout and everything else you'd need."

"Who is it, and where can I find him?"

"He's up there, protected by the mightiest of stars," said the old man, pointing to the sky. "Waiting for you."

Suddenly mental numbness and fatigue invaded her body, with the weight of all the revelations starting to sink in. Her mind was beginning to relax, knowing she wasn't going insane, and adrenaline was fading. There was still a tiny thought at the back of her mind, taunting her, *What if this is also a dream?* But with such an amazing dream, she wouldn't mind being controlled by its puppet master. "So many things, Grandmaster, my mind is so full, I—I can't think straight right now. I'm so tired, so tired."

"I know your mind is like a room filled with dust by a strong wind. But all the dust will fall into place, and you'll come to understand everything. Now you need to leave, as you have things to do. And trust me, you'll wake up with renewed energy."

The little butterfly appeared once again, flitting its wings and spinning around Phoenix. But this time she was as calm as she had ever been, just letting herself be lifted by the vortex that the little animal created and be shot to the stars.

Phoenix opened her eyes in her bed and sprang up. Was it another dream? It couldn't be, as she could remember every detail of the conversation she had with that grandmaster; it wasn't even a nightmare. She felt energetic, and the dust was beginning to settle in her head. As it settled, a place emerged in her mind where she would find the one she needed to solve her case, the one protected by the stars. But first she had to get prepared. She needed to create her own stunning effect, to outshine those stars.

CHAPTER 37

"**W**HY so many lies, Grandmaster?"

The Crane idly managed the ongoing hack at the field office, neutralizing their weak efforts at countermeasures and initiating fresh attacks.

"Because she mustn't know that the Mantis is, *was,* one of us," said the old man. "If she did, I'd need to reveal the identity of the Mantis to her, and she'd want to apprehend him. Even if I could convince her to hold back until the murder is solved, the Mantis would sense her awareness and move to kill her promptly to protect his identity and anyone else on his way. We'd lose any hope of gaining control of the situation."

The Crane shivered at the thought of losing her. It would be simply unbearable.

"Not knowing will keep her safe for a while. Also, exposing the Mantis prematurely could endanger the Prefect, his controller, and this is something we need to avoid at any cost."

"I know, I know. I wish there was a way that we could make her aware of the imminent danger."

"I understand your concern, Sandor. But now she's a lot stronger than she's ever been before. Now she knows that she wasn't on the brink of insanity and hallucinating, she's aware that she'd been targeted by a notorious tormentor, and she possesses the vital clue to solve her murder. Moreover, I think she'll feel a lot more comfortable about trusting her instincts now and understand that they are her only true defense mechanism."

"How could you permit such an evil thing as the Mantis to be a part of us all this time?"

"The balances of nature and the winds that shape the events of our lives," said the old man, looking down. "In the early years, such ruthlessness was essential for survival. Still, we kept his sociopath side under close scrutiny and pressure so that he couldn't escalate and cause more harm than necessary. In the recent years, we've been resorting to him less and less, last time being the great hack you made several months back. We had no idea his emergence from the dormant mode would be so powerful. Perhaps it has to do with your love interest."

"With her?" He turned to the Toboggan Hat. "How?"

"She's blessed with the strength and instincts of the original dissidents."

"The original dissidents?"

"Systematic indoctrination of norms and culture, and eradication of those who don't conform isn't anything new, Sandor; it was invented two millennia ago. Her ancestors put up the original battle against it and lost; as a result, their mark in history and culture was totally eradicated by the sinister evil that beat them. Now she carries the untainted heritage of those people in an age of total order and indoctrination, bringing instability and chaos as she moves along, as the system has no clue how to deal with her. Hers is a very difficult journey, involving carving a path for herself and bulldozing forward at any cost. In doing so, she inadvertently brings many changes to people in her close proximity, sort of jolting their steady states through her entropic ability. Some respond weakly to the instability and disequilibrium she brings, the others strongly. I think the Mantis has gained strength from his encounters with her so far, in order to be able to cope with her, gaining momentum through being pulled by her wake, so to speak."

"I hope he doesn't get so strong as to cause her any harm."

"He won't, simply because there isn't enough time. It will be all over tonight."

"Tess."

"Hey, you were off the planet again. Where have you been?"

"Off the planet," said Phoenix, grinning. "Did you check the border-control databases for what I asked?"

"I found one person matching the parameters you provided. This man came to the Union as a part of a tourist group."

"Perfect. Contact your bro-instance Bud and relay a message for Beverly."

"Sure, what's the message? By the way, what's the occasion?"

"If I told you I have an important business meeting, would you believe me?"

"I'd believe everything you'd say to me. But I'd also consider the possibility that this time you might be pulling my leg."

"Actually, I *am* on my way to an important meeting. And I might need some support in the form of muscle. Can you make sure Beverly arranges a security team to be at standby at this location within the next hour?"

"Any specific reason you don't ask her directly?"

"Well, I didn't exactly leave her side in a graceful way a few hours back, and I don't have time for answering worrisome questions about my sanity."

"Your sanity? Why would she worry about your sanity?"

"Her and Sean saw me in a very depressed mood. I can't blame them."

"You don't appear depressed now. Something was wrong before?"

"Let's say I had a very hard time following the interview with Vanderbilt."

"Her depression or neurosis infected you?"

"That could very well be the case. But don't worry." She produced a dazzling smile. "I've already got the perfect inoculation."

Phoenix paused and observed the atmosphere of the Stardust from the higher entrance area, wearing her new dress with poise.

The moment she had woken up in her bed, she'd known where she would find the man with the answers Grandmaster had been talking about. This man had to be Russian, and a Russian that she would know of; it had to be the same man that Piper and Fabian had mentioned. And there was only one place he could be on a Saturday night, the night that the famed Mata Hari, the mightiest of stars of the club named after stars, would perform her show.

She appeared to have arrived at the perfect time, as the place was jampacked with people—men—and there was eager anticipation in the air. She took slow elegant steps down the stairs to the main floor, the clicking of her steel heels attracting the attention of the Devotees leisurely chatting at the back tables. Her presence literally turned all heads and hushed conversation as she passed by until the only thing audible other than the easy background music was the clicking of her heels. All gazes were on her, but it didn't bother her at all. She grinned mischievously at the thought, thinking how old Phoenix would feel, and kept on walking, looking straight at the horizon without making eye contact with anyone.

As she approached the bar, the crowd standing by the bar got uneasy then gave way. A gaping Fabian approached her at the other side. "Agent Wallis?"

"How are you tonight, Fabian?" she said with a mischievous smile.

"I'm quite well, but you look incredible!" said Fabian, observing her from top to toe. "Ehm, would you like a refreshing cocktail?"

"I'd love a refreshing cocktail. Busy evening."

"This is the evening that Mata Hari is to premiere her new show," said Fabian and went to work. "Actually, you made it just in time, but I'm afraid we don't have any tables to offer you. They're all taken from months before."

"Finding a table is the least of my worries," she said, with her eyes fixed on his. "I'm looking for one *special* man."

Fabian froze at her words; the juice he had been adding to the shaker spilled everywhere. The wet feeling on his leg jolted him. He cleared his throat and put the shaker and the juice away, cleaning up his tuxedo. "I—I'm sorry."

"You're not used to seeing women here, are you? Would you be disappointed if I told you that you're not *him?*"

"I—I'm not sure what you're referring to, Agent Wallis."

"I'm here for the man that I first heard of from you, and I'm sure that he is here tonight. Do you know who I'm talking about, Fabian?"

"I think so. He's seated at the front row, close to the stage."

"Good. Please bring my cocktail there and put it on my tab."

Phoenix left the bar and slowly walked towards the stage, once again with all heads turning, with men parting to make way for her, only to gaze behind her and to curiously whisper to each other. She found her man, the one she'd first seen with Mata Hari, at the center table nearest to the stage, sitting with three others. The conversation paused as she approached. Phoenix pointed at the chubby man in the ill-fitted but very elaborate magenta tunic.

"I want you."

The man's brief surprised gaze gave way to a randy grin, and he turned and made an '*I'm the man*' gesture to his buddies at the table. The buddies got the message and stood up with remarks of surprise, wagging their fingers at him, then showed a place for Phoenix to sit next to him. The man briefly stood up as she took her seat, pressed his receding combed-back blond hair into place with his fat fingers. He had a full face and a big nose in the shape of a hook. His thin lips and eyes appeared too small for the face dominated by the nose. His small pale-blue eyes twinkled with a certain devilish sparkle.

"Have we met before, or are you coming with compliments from one of my business contacts, beauty?" he said with his heavily accented deep voice.

"Not one or the other. I'm here to talk to you, Mr. Mancheek."

"Ilya Manchik at your service. Are you sure talk is all you want to do with me tonight, beauty?"

"Perhaps I'll take you to a historic and quiet place at the outskirts of the city, if I like what you say to me," said Phoenix, with her eyes fixed on his.

"Just tell me what I need to say, beauty," said Manchik and swallowed. "So that you can take me to your quiet place."

"You're that sure you'd like it there?"

"I'm positive that I would," said the man with his eyes dropping to her breasts. "If you'd be kind enough to share your name with—"

At that instant, the lights dimmed with the sound from a giant gong, and the dark-red curtains that separated the stage from the rest of the club made way. A strange music filled the place in darkness, an instrumental piece originating from the Middle East, with familiar classical instruments being played to a bizarre, offbeat tune.

Following a short overture in complete darkness, a couple of spotlights came on from the ceiling and exposed Mata Hari in an amazing costume. A snug-fitting gold headpiece framed her flawless bone structure, caressing every sculpted curve and rising to a glittering crest on top of her head. The crest was mirrored by a huge golden teardrop pointing midway between her eyebrows and balanced by a pair of golden discs dangling on either side like earrings. A translucent sarong flowed like water from a jewel-encrusted gold belt. Her torso was naked apart from her breasts, only restrained by a kind of barely-there bodice, comprising shallow gold cups studded with more oversized jewels linked by flimsy scraps of emerald-beaded silk. Heavy bands of gold encircled her wrists, upper arms, and calves.

Mata Hari's body flowed with the music, bending, curving, her arms and legs moving with the offbeat waves created. It wasn't exactly what one would call the old-style belly dancing, as it had many classical, modern, and postmodern moves involved. The dance was all about reflection of feelings. She could see the pain and suffering in Mata Hari's face, as if she were witnessing the Armageddon and the Genesis at the same time. The performance was totally hypnotic; she just watched it her eyes glued to the dancer. She peeked at the man sitting next to her with the corner of her eye, only to witness his intense gape and focus on Mata Hari as if—

Then everything fell into place. This man had been made to wait here for her, compelled by a force he couldn't and wouldn't resist, a *stunning* mightiest of the stars, so that she could solve her case. At that instant, Mata Hari made eye contact with her, with the briefest of smiles, before resorting back to her act of agonizing expression.

"Where were we? Ah, yes, would you like to share your name with me, beauty?"

Mata Hari's dance was over, and life was getting back to normal at the Stardust club. Now there was the buzz of reactions to the amazing performance and excitement about Mata Hari's expected appearance on the club floor.

"My name's Phoenix Wallis, a senior agent from the GPSN Peace Corps."

"Really?" he almost purred. "And I thought gorgeous peace agents took second jobs in the evenings only in your field offices in Russia. Or is this some make-believe appearance of an agent? And aren't you supposed to be in one of those sexy uniforms?"

"This is no make-believe kiss-o-gram, Mr. Manchik, I'm a real agent."

"You don't happen to be one of those actors in them sexy ZAP commercials, are you now, beauty?" grinned Manchik. "You'd be my second after Holly Love."

"Tess, send them in now."

"Oooh, more beauties coming to join us? I love this World Union hospitality. But you guys are gonna spoil me, and I'll want this all the time."

"A couple colleagues of mine will be joining us," said Phoenix and stood up.

"I'm, how do you say, *game*, beauty," said the man, standing up and rubbing his hands excitedly. "And I'll go *anywhere* with you."

"You might regret what you're wishing for, Mr. Manchik."

A stir in the crowds standing around them ensued, with curious gazes looking towards the back of the main floor, and murmuring. Manchik eagerly waited for two more women to appear, but to his chagrin two tall men in orange riot uniforms, riot helmets, and dark shades, only to be seen in documentaries, made a truly rare appearance in public and stood on both sides of Phoenix. There was a certain surreal texture to the combination of the orange two-meter-tall Robo-Cops on her sides and the immaculately dressed Phoenix in pink with her relatively tiny stature between them.

"But, I don't understand! For your information, I don't like orgies involving many men, beauty, and I'm not one of those who enjoy only watching, either."

"The only thing you'll watch will be your own reflection on a big mirror, Mr. Manchik. You're under arrest for suspicion of illegal activities in the World Union and involvement in the murder of a Union citizen in your rogue nation state."

"This must be joke, right? I mean, it can't be for real." Manchik looked at his buddies, who just stood there shocked and speechless. The two Robo-Cops moved to either side of Manchik, grabbing him by the arms. The crowd hushed and watched in astonishment as Phoenix led them slowly towards the club's exit. Then suddenly the side door opened and Mata Hari appeared, immediately grabbing the entire attention of a frozen clientele. Her attention, however, was completely on Phoenix, who glanced back at her while she walked and their eyes locked. The entire crowd held their breath, and once again the only audible thing in the entire club was Phoenix's clicking heels. Phoenix kept her gaze on Mata Hari, absorbing the new emotions in the dancer's spellbinding gaze, a certain serenity and calmness as if, as if she was *proud* of Phoenix.

"What a show," said Mata Hari in a husky whisper and initiated an ovation as Phoenix reached the end of the floor. She replied back with a nod then climbed the stairs leading outside. She could hear a roar of excitement erupting behind, and she didn't need to look back to know that now Mata Hari had taken the center of the floor.

"Where have you been, sis? We were so worried about you!"

"I'm fine, Beverly. Is the director here?"

"No, but I'm sure she'll drop by shortly with your spectacular return with an alien in tow. Where did you find him, anyway?"

"At the most prestigious table of the most prestigious club in town."

"You look incredible," said a gaping Sean. "I had no idea. Do you always dress up this vibrant, this beautiful, when you're not in uniform?"

"Sometimes," said Phoenix and winked. "Did you check what I asked from you?"

"Yes, I did. And just like you thought, it is possible for an alien to—"

"What the hell do you think you're doing?" said Julio and entered the scene. "Where did you find this rogue stator, and with what authority did you arrest him without a court order?"

"I arrested him with the authority vested to me as the lead of my murder investigation. If you had read your company rules through and through, you'd know that I don't need a court order to make the arrest of an alien if I suspect ongoing conspiratorial activity."

"That's a lame technicality. And if you think your sexy appearance will make me go softer about this, you're dead wrong. The man screams bloody murder, claiming diplomatic immunity."

"It's irrelevant," said Phoenix with an icy gaze. "And so is your opinion."

"Mr. Manchik, you were arrested on suspicion of illegal smuggling activity, aiding and hiding suspects, and involvement in a Union citizen's murder. I'll be questioning you using the hardware above your head, which will determine whether you're lying to me or not."

"I protest my arrest," said Manchik as he briefly checked out the cylindrical device above his head. "You have no jurisdiction. I have diplomatic immunity."

"Your protests are noted, and your nearest consulate in Vienna has been notified of your arrest. You're not one of the diplomats who were accredited by our Council of Foreign Relations, Mr. Manchik. You only carry a diplomatic passport, which is a necessary but not sufficient condition for you to claim any immunity from the GPSN. Now, if you could calm down, we can proceed with the questioning."

"I'm not answering any questions from you, you slut," said Manchik, rising from his seat and leaning over the table towards Phoenix with a menacing glare.

The two Robo-Cops, who stood behind Manchik, made an attempt to reach out to him, only to be stopped by eye contact and a slight head shake from Phoenix. She slowly stood up, fixed her gaze on Manchik's, and leaned over the table, matching his posture.

"You think you can intimidate me with your male theatrics, mafia man? I'm not one of those submissive women pretending to be peace agents in your rogue state that you're used to bullying. Now, sit."

Manchik looked away and swallowed. The energy radiating from her chilling whisper turned his wolfish face into a grim one. Sweat beaded up on his forehead, and he found himself complying with the order.

Phoenix quickly initialized the expert systems. She was going to do this her way, again, and ignore those useless baseline questions. With the network at a grinding halt, she couldn't expect much help from the computers anyway. And if those expert systems couldn't keep up with her, it would be their problem. She knew she'd make him sing.

"Do you know a Vassily Bogdanov?"

Manchik crossed his arms and pressed his lips together in a slimy grin.

"So you *do* know Vassily Bogdanov," said Phoenix with a grin of her own. "Thank you for your admission in silence."

The Mantis watched them from the Viewers' Lounge, exerting tremendous amounts of energy to control his inner rage. The woman had fallen off the face of the earth for several hours, only to reemerge with this, this Russian. He had no idea who the man was or how Phoenix could find him, but what if he shed a light on the murder and ruined all efforts of the Mantis? His best option was to wait until an appropriate moment to stun him, if it proved necessary. It was all in the timing, and he wasn't sure how powerful his attack would be from behind these thick walls and glass. He was a lot stronger with his defenses now since he had broken free from his controller, but stunning and influencing somebody's mind was a whole different ball game. It was also possible that the controller was in the room observing him, hiding among the crowd, but the Mantis didn't think this controller would dare to stop him and risk exposure if he were to launch an attack on the Russian. But everything aside, he had to contain his rage and be patient for the right moment. And all this unplanned, improvised activity he had to do was making him feel sick.

Manchik had no idea what this immaculately dressed slut was talking about. He hadn't admitted to anything, nor was he planning to.

"Check out the visuals behind you."

Manchik turned back and saw a lifelike hologram of Bogdanov talking with no sound. The place appeared like Bogdanov's office, but why was that furniture in bright orange and blue? Bogdanov was sitting behind his desk, banging his fist on the table, looking directly at the camera and giving a tough talk. Could this footage have been taped when talked to him the last time? If so, they had messed it up and couldn't get him in the frame. Then the footage slowly faded out, giving way to another that showed the dressed-up whore with a badge before him, up close.

"You appeared to have your recordings mixed up," he said and folded his arms. He had heard of all that hype about World Union having incredible technologies for catching lies, but what if he didn't talk? No talk, no lies.

"That's no recording, Mr. Manchik, it's live from your frontal cortex. You see, I ask you questions and these billion-dollar gadgets trace your thoughts to be displayed in a hologram. And by showing us here what Vassily Bogdanov looked like, following my question, you tacitly admitted that you knew the man. Actually it appears from the footage that you've been to his office at the Thing Store. See, you can shut your mouth, but you cannot shut your brain, *wise guy*."

Manchik felt a knot in his big belly. Could this be for real? He'd seen similar "mind-reading" devices in movies, but they existed only in movies, right? Yet the footage behind him looked very real. What was he to do? He knew how sensitive the Union authorities were on lies.

"All right, so I do know Vassily Bogdanov."

"Are you a member of the Dinastiya crime organization?"

"Wait, wait, wait, I understand that lying and even not speaking is not an option anymore. And I can reveal everything openly, if you give me a deal."

"If you'd like to take your chances in your rogue state, I can provide you with a quick repatriation, following your full, court-approved deposition, of course."

"Yes, yes," nodded Manchik. "I'll take my chances there. But please no rehab treatment or any interrogation by your Psychological Warfare Unit."

"The rehab treatment is up to my report, whether I detect any signs of neurosis or psychosis. If you don't lie to me or attempt to deceive me here, I see no reason why not. If I detect even one lie, however, you'd pay a visit to first PWU, then to the rehab for treatment. Understood?"

"Yes, yes," he said breathing heavily. "I'll tell you everything."

"Actually, let me ask you a question first. I already know that you're a Dinastiya member of importance. Now tell me: Where is your safe house or hideout?"

"How could you know about that?"

"By figuring out how you smuggled Bogdanov out. You switched him with a lookalike, didn't you?"

"I actually have no idea how he was brought back. He was switched?"

"Someone in your organization found a loophole in our border security apparatus. You see, we check and verify the biometric information of our citizens entering and exiting the Union each and every time. However, for aliens who enter the Union, the procedure is somewhat different. We collect their biometric information during the visa process and make sure the intended and approved person enters the Union by comparing the biometrics of the actual person to the one in the visa at the border. But on their way out—"

"You don't check for anything other than overstaying."

"And why should we? Who in their right mind would want to exit the Union using fake alien credentials? And this was the perfect cover to sneak Bogdanov out. A very effective lookalike of Bogdanov entered the Union using a good visa and good credentials as a part of a tourist group. Bogdanov was sneaked out using his credentials as a part of the same group."

"So that's how it was done. I knew Verolomniy was good. But I didn't know he was this good."

"Is that the name of your operative?"

"Verolomniy is one of our most notorious and secret mercenaries. He's only called in for impossible tasks like this."

"Perhaps not impossible, but it puzzled me for a long time, that's for sure. Now tell me. Why did you murder Bogdanov? Because he stole your money and fled?"

"Well, well," he said with a grin. "You haven't figured everything out after all. We eliminated Bogdanov because he double-crossed us."

"He wasn't running away from you?"

"Once with Dinastiya, always with Dinastiya," he said in a whisper. "We gave him the money to immigrate into the Union so that we had a legitimate presence here for opportunities. We used our contacts at the Thing Store Corporation so that he would have a favorable position at the store here. We wanted him to have access to elite clientele for future needs."

"And his former nuptial partner also came because…?" said Phoenix, only to realize the truth as soon as her words ended. "You are her biological sibling, aren't you? The sibling she had mentioned to me as being very close to the top in Dinastiya command structure, something I can tell from the way you have access to certain niceties in this city. And in a strange way, you resemble her."

"Yes, I am Larissa's brother. It was my idea to send her here with him. I knew she'd be devastated if Vassily immigrated here alone under the cover of being a thief. Actually, Vassily never wanted her to come along. We argued several times about it."

"So how did he double-cross you? It was about those devices, wasn't it?"

"Yes," nodded Manchik. "We got those virtual reality gadgets from a supplier under the protection of the Triads in Hong Kong. They asked us to smuggle the items to the Union for test marketing."

"Why didn't they resort to regular channels for that? There is no reason to smuggle an item to test market in the Union. You can simply consign and ship it."

"The devices were somewhat controversial, and the designers didn't want their technology to be scrutinized by Union authorities. It was a cutting-edge device, and they were afraid that its technology might get stolen."

"I'll give you a more plausible explanation," grinned Phoenix. "What if this technology was stolen from the Union by these Triad-protected *developers* to begin with? They were worried that their theft might have been exposed under close scrutiny by the Union experts, weren't they?"

The director watched the interrogation in silent awe. She had been hanging out with Alex and having a good time for a change when the call came regarding Phoenix's latest activity. Being used to dark and ill-fitting academy uniforms and peace agent ones, it was such a strange sight to see Phoenix in her stunning night outfit interrogating a man in an expensive designer tunic in that room. But to her credit, it appeared like she had finally made a major break in the case.

The Viewers' Lounge was packed once again, and everyone watched the interrogation breathlessly. There was one more person she would expect to be here but wasn't. She activated her PA and quietly sent a priority one invite.

"You think the technology of the device was stolen?"

"I'm sure it was. Otherwise why hide such a commercial product from the exhaustive World Union testing standards? Those tests would most certainly avoid the death of a prominent university professor in the city."

"What? You're talking about that man they mention on Holovision, the one with the fried brain?"

"Him and at least one other person who almost ended up like him."

"Unbelievable! I had no idea that those gadgets were dangerous."

"How did Bogdanov double-cross you?"

"He was to test market the devices to the affluent clients that frequented the store, then to report us the results. At first, everything was as it should be, but I could sense an ever-rising cockiness and assertiveness in him. I was his very old friend, but also his superior in the organization, yet he would act in disrespectful ways."

"Such as?"

"He downplayed the progress with the rentals, but at the same time took me to expensive hangouts like the Stardust to impress me, only to pretend to be my superior behind my back. He thought he could fool me, but I knew everything. On the positive note, I ended up meeting the irresistible Mata Hari with his minor involvement and made such an impression on the woman, she came all the way to the motherland to invite me back here for her new show and hosted me in her house for almost a week now."

"You must be the one with the charm," said Phoenix, arching an eyebrow. "Have you ever used these devices?"

"No, but I know Vassily tried them. He couldn't stop talking about how incredible they were for a while."

"I know. The catalyst that converted your mellow accountant into the monster of greed was those virtual reality devices, Mr. Manchik. They gave him feelings of enormous confidence and audacity."

"You're saying these gadgets shifted his personality? But how?"

"*How* is a puzzle that technical experts need to answer with their analysis of the device. The fact remains that these devices were addictive and harmful, causing an emotional overdrive and an eventual shift in personality, changing

Bogdanov so much and so suddenly, making him dare to take on an entire mafia organization."

"True enough," nodded Manchik. "And we needed to do something about that. He was openly daring us while he formed his own organization with some contacts he made in your military."

"I know about Perez. Is that why you killed him?"

"We didn't intend to kill him," said Manchik and sighed. "It would be such a scandal to murder a World Union military officer, one that would potentially threaten the very existence of our organization. Instead, first we wanted to switch him to our side. But no matter how much bribe we offered, he turned us down and told us that we couldn't touch him."

"He had a good reason," nodded Phoenix. "He was addicted, too."

"Huh," said Manchik and shrugged. "That would explain why he turned down an eight-figure sum for switching! So when that didn't work, we sneaked a man into his cargo plane in one of his missions, one we knew that he carried contraband in, in order to expose and discredit him upon his arrival to the base. We're not sure what happened in that plane, but it crashed, which turned out to be the best scenario for us, as your military decided to keep it under wraps."

"How did you notice that he was renting out the devices without your knowledge or consent?"

"How could we not? He was spending so much money, and it couldn't come from his puny Thing Store paycheck or his newly established ring running cigarettes. I knew he was making deals behind our back, extorting money from those rich clients, but it wasn't like I could report him to you or deal with him the way he deserved."

"Why not? Afraid of being caught by us?"

"Not exactly," grinned the man. "You can ask that question to your executives; they should have an answer for you."

"Meaning?"

"Meaning, our tsar has connections in high places at your GPSN. After the plane crash, he took the matter into his hands and in no time we were fully informed of Vassily's dealings and finances, and even a banker's check was prepared so that we could transfer the rental funds to Russia around the same time he was delivered."

"And who murdered Bogdanov?"

"I don't know who he was. One of our henchmen, I guess. But the order for his public execution to set an example came directly from Moscow."

Manchik gazed at the horizon, and a dark and rainy scene appeared behind him, seemingly of a sea port or similar, with giant cranes and containers in the background and a crowd whose faces were mostly in shade or in vibrant colors. Vassily Bogdanov was in the middle, his colorful tunic a sharp contrast to the dark dull trench coats of the men surrounding him. He was on his knees, with a man behind him holding a gun aimed at his neck. The man pulled the trigger, and suddenly there was a sea of blood all over the place.

"We'll try to identify all people involved from our databases, including the man who actually pulled the trigger. Now, onto another important topic. How deep has your organization penetrated the GPSN, and especially this field office?"

"I'm not sure. I know there are other operatives under deep cover in the Union, but the one that I've been in contact was only Vassily. We place these people in cell setups, and no cell has knowledge of the other."

"Really?" said Phoenix with an intense gaze. "Will you also deny the existence of another secret operative of yours, known as the Mantis, who has launched an ongoing attack on this field office?"

"The Mantis?" said Manchik, his eyes widened. "But I—" He abruptly grabbed his head with both hands, as if trying to stop an excruciating migraine or some high-pitched sound, and collapsed on the table, groaning something like "Stop it, please stop it" and some other words in his native tongue. Phoenix and the security detail immediately tended him, only to see that he had passed out. She turned and gave a hell-freezing look at the big mirror, knowing full well that the Mantis was back there, somewhere, hiding in plain sight.

But not for long.

"Is he all right?" said the director, overlooking the Russian, now lying on a couch in the staff room. "How does he look, Alex?"

Following Manchik's unexpected fainting, Phoenix had suspended the interrogation, and everyone in the Viewers' Lounge had flooded the interview room. At someone's suggestion, the director had ordered the two Robo-Cop security guards to carry him to the windowless staff room at the back parts of the floor and put him on the couch. Alex moved his eyelids up with his thumbs, and then checked his pulse.

"He appears stable," he said with a shrug. "In some deep sleep, it seems."

"Shouldn't we call an ambulance, Boss?" said Beverly.

Phoenix could sense the director's hesitation about letting this man out of sight, perhaps thinking along the same line with her that a mind-altering weapon had been used here. Almost everyone from the field office was in the room, from Sean to Julio, Fred to Harold. And *he* was here, somewhere, right before her, she could feel it. The answer to the Mantis's identity was hidden somewhere in her mind, and it would eventually come to her. But *eventually* was the key word here. If it didn't happen in a timely manner, it could cost lives, including her own.

"No, not yet," said the director. "This man is a very important eyewitness to a case of utmost importance, making wild accusations about our organization, and we can't afford the press to get wind of this. If he were to show up in a rehab facility, we couldn't avoid a scandal. I feel uneasy about speculating what might have happened to him, but I know one thing for sure: We shouldn't let him out of our sight and send him in some rehab care unless we have to. For all we know, he could be acting. In the meantime, we can get some experts with security clearance here. Alex, can you contact that neurologist from the Spencer investigation and kindly ask her to come here at once, discreetly?"

Alex nodded and left the room to make the urgent call.

"Until the doctor arrives, we should clear this room and leave him to sleep, right, Director?" said Phoenix, directly looking into her eyes. "And we can leave these two security experts at the door for precaution, so he won't try to escape if he wakes up or if he is faking all this."

As far as Phoenix was concerned, the two Robo-Cops were the only people who had no connection to the field office and couldn't be the Mantis.

The director looked at her for a few seconds and nodded subtly. "Right, okay, everybody out. And you two, wait at the door and do not let anyone in or out until further notice."

The Mantis felt so frustrated and angry at himself. He couldn't understand why he had reacted in such a way the moment his name was mentioned, almost in *panic*. He had to contain his urges and not let things get out of hand. He had to control the rage continuously building inside. But what had happened had happened, and at least he had managed to shut the Russian down temporarily, at the cost of considerable mental energy.

He wasn't sure how quickly he would regain his full stunning strength, but it needed to be quick, as his controller was about, perhaps in this very room, waiting for any opportunity, any weakness from him. And although his stun ability was exhausted, he didn't feel any diminishment in his defenses, and they appeared to be as strong as before. Besides the situation was under control, with the Russian confined in the staff room. This gave him a boost of confidence for his next task.

And he didn't need any mental strength for this one.

"He's right here, among us," said Phoenix. "I know it, Beverly. And he did something to that creep, with some mind-altering weapon or technique or something. And I think the director knows it, too."

"No shit! You're sure, sis?"

"Quite sure. Tell me, was the Mantis as daring then as he is now?"

"He sure was," nodded Beverly. "He'd rampage the place, and we wouldn't do shit about it. The director then was a clueless idiot. He was so relaxed and at ease, one would have thought he was the director of some remote mountain post at the Swiss Alps."

"Sweet. What if, maybe, just maybe, what if he was influenced by a mind-altering weapon, too? Tell me, do you remember anything, *anything* from those days which might have given you an impression that such a thing could be going on?"

"Heck, I remember everything from those days," shrugged Beverly. "But a monster memory can be a curse, too, sometimes, too many details to sift through."

"Did you know the former director before he arrived, or did he display some personality change of any kind?"

"No. When he arrived, he was as clueless as when he left."

Sean knocked on the door and came in Phoenix's office with their coffees and took the seat opposite from Beverly. Phoenix could feel her fear and apprehension and gave her a warm smile of assurance. She replied with a tiny smile of her own but resorted back to her nervous mood.

"I know that I've been under attack by this Mantis all week long."

Both Sean and Beverly looked at her in disbelief. Beverly managed to break the silence after several seconds. "Mantis attacking you? For what purpose?"

"To crash the murder case so I couldn't expose his employer, the Russian mafia. Couldn't you guys tell from my eroding and fluctuating disposition?"

"I could tell that something was going on with you. But I didn't know if this was your normal self or not. I've only known you for two weeks, sis."

"That's true," said Phoenix and smiled. "Two long sleepless weeks that felt like two years to me. But trust me on this. He laid deceptive leads before me, tried to disrupt my sleep patterns and rest, and heaven knows what else. Someone had been snooping around, and I could feel it, perhaps even here or in my apartment. And I'm not talking about Ray."

The tired-looking Sean suddenly looked animated, as if she'd just remembered something. Her expression turned into one of horror, she briefly made eye contact with both Phoenix and Beverly, then she muttered "*Jaungoikoa!*" and dashed out of the room.

"Now, what's with her? Infected by you, perhaps?"

"I don't know if it's me. But I could feel that something had been bothering her and kept lingering in her mind for a few days now."

"She sure looked like she was scared shitless," said Beverly.

Phoenix's energy levels suddenly slumped. The adrenaline that had been keeping her going was fading away. She had gone through so much in the last half a day, from being at the brink of a total collapse all the way up to new peaks of self-belief and confidence, and she'd had no food. She betrayed herself with a long yawn.

"You look tired, sis. Why don't you change into something more comfortable and take a power nap? I'll wake you up the moment that doc arrives or the mafia dude wakes up."

"I'm so tired. And unfortunately I already used up my spare uniform, so I'm stuck with this until I can get home. And to be honest, now that the Mantis is launching a full attack here, I don't know what might happen if I fall asleep."

Director Morssen sat at her desk with both hands on her temples, staring into the void. He was back, and he was here, if he ever left, that was. He was inside them, among her staff, *her staff,* lurking inside her building right now, and Phoenix knew it, too. She felt so stupid not to admit to it all this time, despite little signs here and there, warnings from her executives. And now he was bold enough to openly challenge them by hacking into their network and neutralizing a suspect, who was about to confess, perhaps to his secret identity.

Maybe she wasn't as good at her work as she always thought she was, or maybe it was too much hard work for her own good. Or maybe she just needed a break. Oh, she needed a break so much. She needed to get out of this place, this damn, depressing building where she felt she was rotting inside. She needed to leave this city, she needed some fresh air, some peace!

Regardless, she had to push these thoughts out of her head and focus on the task at hand. The neurologist was on her way, and the Russian mafioso was still sleeping when she had checked five minutes before. She connected back to that camera to see if he was still asleep, only to be surprised with what she saw. Then panic ensued.

The director rushed out of her office and ran down the main hallway, towards the back hallways of the floor.

"You're all right, Sean?" said Beverly, from her desk at the Monitoring Room.

She appeared to be working on something and seemed so focused, she didn't hear the repeated pleas from Beverly, which were getting louder each time. "Sean!"

Everyone in the room jumped except Sean. She just lifted her head from her network node briefly with big and worried eyes, only to dive back to her monitor as if she were working on something that the entire world depended on. Irritated by the non-response, Beverly got up and walked towards her then she froze halfway. Something had dawned on her about what she and Phoenix had been talking about just minutes before about the old director. She had been thinking about that ever since, trying to sift through the memories, and in doing so not seeing something obvious, so obvious, that they had talked about so many times, only to attribute other reasons for it.

Beverly left the Monitoring Room and ran towards the elevators.

Director Morssen walked hurriedly through the hallways, thinking about what she'd seen on the monitor, or hadn't seen, with the cameras in the staff room having outages. Despite the ongoing hack, she'd managed to get a frame or two a few minutes before, but now the cameras were reporting completely out. It was probably nothing, but she had to go there to check and verify. Perhaps it was also best to ask one of those Robo-Cops to stay inside the room until the doctor arrived, just in case. But when she reached the entrance of the room, neither of them were there. She made a quick call to the Rapid Action Center and asked for the badge numbers of the Robo-Cops, then called them. "What are you doing, leaving your posts?"

"—didn't leave—you—to escort—from the station—"

"Get back here immediately, wherever you are," she said and hung up. "Computer: Did anyone enter inside this room since we left as a group?"

"Ne—tive."

The reply dampened her anxiety a bit, and she turned back, walking towards her office, thinking who she could ask to stand guard until those Robo-Cops' return. The Door Bot was already instructed to notify her if the door were to open for any reason, but she kept thinking of the intruder breaking into Bogdanov's house and the loophole Phoenix found in Door Bot logic, an incident that felt like it happened ages ago. It sure had been part of a different reality, and so many things had changed since then. Things that were unimaginable to her only a week ago, such as thinking about quitting this field office and GPSN once and for all, were so real and so appealing.

Then it all clicked, and everything fell into place in her mind: She was going to pursue that crazy thought; she was going to quit! It was such a relief that her mind was finally up, and she felt a glimmer of hope thinking maybe, just maybe, everything would be better for her in the future than in the past. And it seemed like a silly stuttering Door Bot had helped her realize all this. She could never be sure what kind of life lay ahead of her or what surprises the coming week would bring, but one thing was she was sure of: No matter how much advancement was made, no matter how smart neural networks were to become, the Door Bots would always be stupid. She smiled at the thought only to be perplexed by it a moment later. What if the intruder and the Mantis were one and the same?

A horrified Director Morssen dashed back to the staff room.

The Mantis squeezed through the secret opening and entered the staff room. He might not be as well-equipped and as capable at hacking as that show-off Crane, as he'd never resorted to such crude methods in his immaculate career, but he'd still kept a few useful tricks up his sleeve, which proved to be crucial in tonight's annoying yet unavoidable improvised action. He had jammed the cameras of the staff room, something that would be hardly noticed in the ongoing mayhem. Sending a message to the clueless XL security guys and sending them away from their posts in case the Russian was awake had been even easier than fooling a Door Bot. Now it appeared like his extra precaution had been unnecessary, and the Russian was still in deep sleep. He could feel that his stunning ability was coming back even stronger, and now he could sense the feelings of the Russian having a horrific nightmare. *Good,* the Mantis thought. He was here to end all of his nightmares, once and for all.

He'd never been one to resort to physical violence, but sometimes the circumstances had left no alternative. He had to get rid of this Russian and eliminate the only witness of the murder that the GPSN held. His interrogation was already on record, but the GPSN would be hesitant to pursue such leads in the absence of a solid and living eyewitness. Besides, he was curious as to how he were to feel after killing someone, if any at all, his curiosity about this roused since Monday. Moreover, an unexplainable death or murder of a Russian with a diplomatic passport would cause such a stir in the field office, the Mantis would easily hide in the resulting chaos. Then that wretched Phoenix would be next.

The Mantis took a nearby pillow and placed it on the face of the deeply sleeping Russian. He must have stunned him quite hard, as the man didn't react to him at all. He held the pillow down for several minutes, then removed it and checked his pulse. He was dead. The Mantis smiled and turned to get back to the secret passage. At that moment he heard the click from behind, only to see Director Morssen entering the room.

She raises her eyes momentarily, only to lower them again at the sight of the horror surrounding her. It's dark in the dungeon, but her eyes are used to the dark, enough to see what is being done to the girl next to her. She doesn't scream or cry for help, only tries to ignore it all and bites her lip to subdue the pain until it's over; her eyes are vacant as if what's being done to her is of no consequence. After all, it's just an ordinary day.

She is used to this routine now, as it rarely changes over time. How long she has been here now, she cannot remember. She only remembers that she stopped counting the days a long time ago. From the faint light that comes from the outside, she can tell the days are longer. What does that mean again? Winter or summer? And who cares, anyway? It's always cold in the dungeon. She cannot even remember if she had been anywhere else.

Was there ever another life for her? Is there, could there be in the future? No, she shouldn't think about those things anymore. Hope is the worst tormentor of all. It's worse than the daily torture they receive from the Creatures. Are they human? Is she? Isn't her presence merely that of an animal's, not a human's, as she is kept in bondage all the time, she isn't allowed to talk to anyone, she pees and shits in the same place she eats, she has lesions on her skin as large as her bare chest, and the dirt accumulated among the hair at her head and at her crotch includes mud, blood, semen, pee, shit, and every other disgusting substance that found its way into this, this hell?

Time passes slowly in the dungeon, but routine never changes. One day, she notices that the girl next to her doesn't move anymore. Her eyes are open and soulless as ever, staring at a spot ahead as usual, but there is an unusual stillness to her. Two of the grunting Creatures come down and take the dead girl away, not even bothering with keys, tearing the corpse from its chains, dragging her off from her foot. She is now all alone in the dungeon. She can barely open her eyes from lack of food and energy. She remembers the older woman across from her taken away in a similar fashion, which coincided with some uncooked bones that they dumped before her to eat. When was it that she last ate? Two days ago? Or three? Some soft tissue and cartilage of God knows what.

Speaking of God, where is He these days?

The Creatures' visits are less and less, and so is the food. There is a damp spot in the dungeon that she can reach so that she can drink some water. She doesn't need much of it anyway. Her body is little, tiny, skinny. What was it they called it? Aha, she remembers: a kilo. She wonders how many kilos she is. Five? No, no, it can't be five, it's too little, even for her. How about, fifty-five? Could that be more accurate? Or how about a hundred and five? Wow, that sounds so rich and full.

She hears some strange noises outside, then the door opens, here they come again. But, no, it's not them, it's some other creatures! And, they are even clothed, in dark color, all over, including their heads and faces. Only their eyes are visible. They even look at her and talk! What are they saying? She cannot understand; it's all too complex. It's been a long time she heard anything other than grunts and screams. They force open and unlock her chains. She looks at her wrists and ankles. Are they supposed to be this color, black? They lean over to touch her. She doesn't want to be touched by them, what if the Creatures come back? What if they get mad? She belongs to them. She needs to find them and tell them that it's not her fault.

She gets up with a superhuman effort and pushes the clothed ones away. She bites one that tries to stop her. She screams! It's a she! And she has no chains? She has clothes? How is that possible? She drags her feet and limps past them up the steps as they try to say something. She always wondered what was up those steps. She painfully climbs them, only to see more clothed ones, leaning over and making clicks and lightning with little strange boxes. It's the Creatures, lying on the ground, dead. Could they be killed by this lightning? She makes an inadvertent sound as one blinds her eyes. Was that a scream? She has a voice? She has a voice!

The clothed ones slowly advance on her, making sounds and waving their hands. She knows they want to hurt her. No, she will not give up easy; she will resist. She sees more steps and climbs them, just one more, and another, and another. Her legs hurt like never before. But she has to climb. One more step, one more, and another, and a gate to an opening. Is it outside? Is she supposed to go out there? But the Creatures are down there, dead. Could they really die?

She walks out to darkness and can see bright spots above her. Could those be stars? And there are so many of them. And it's warm outside. Does this mean it's summer? Then she sees a bright light in the horizon, and a walkway emerges, all white, so white that she cannot look at it. She closes her eyes, but a voice inside her head tells her to come. She drags her bare feet to the side of the building towards the walkway, only to hear another voice coming from a distance. She turns and sees a man at the door leading to the building. He is one of the clothed ones. The voice inside her head tells her not to trust him. He is clothed all in black, and in disguise he is evil. He is there to harm her and inflict her more pain.

She doesn't want pain anymore. She is outside now, and she begs that it's not another dream that will end in shattered hope that will burn her from the inside. The voice inside her head says that it is not. But the far voice from behind, the voice of the clothed one, keeps saying something. She cannot understand what, but he doesn't stop. She glances back at him, once more, to see that he has removed his mask. He extends his hand, which is also not clothed anymore, to reach her. His old and tired eyes have a soft and familiar expression. She knows those eyes from somewhere, long time ago, or could they be from the future? The voice inside her head tells her to walk to the bright path, to her salvation, to happiness. Happiness? Is she supposed to be happy?

Then she hears some sound from behind, an awfully familiar sound. She turns back one more time to see the clothed one with the soft eyes making those sounds. She remembers it's a song, a song from long time ago. She can even hear and understand the words. "I will count the stars," *he sings, and she tries to sing with him, as much as her weak lungs and cracking voice allows, faintly pointing up to the stars above with him. The song ends, and the clothed one extends his hand one more time.*

"Come with me, hurting one," *he says.* "Come with me, and we'll heal your wounds one by one. I promise you that I'll never leave your side."

The voice inside her head tells her that she can only be happy if she walks to the bright path, leaving that building, that prison, that hell of hers behind, once and for all. She trusts the voice inside her head. She cannot go back to that building. She cannot see those Creatures again, she just cannot.

"I—I—" *she tries to talk and clears her throat violently.* "I can't go back there— I can't—"

"You can, and you must. It's the only way out of here. Reach out and hold my hand, hurting one. Let me walk with you outside and heal your wounds. There is no instant salvation."

She takes a few more slow steps towards the bright path, coming to the edge of the building. The voice in her head tells her to take the path and ascend to the stars, to be cleansed of all the filth, dirt, and shame that had accumulated on her skin and her soul for more than five years.

"Don't go there, please," says the clothed one. "You lived through it, survived. Let me help you heal and find yourself back."

"I can't go with you."

"Yes, you can," says the clothed one with gentle eyes. "Tell me your name. Could you please tell me your name?"

She stops and thinks for a while. What is her name? Did she ever have one? The Creatures never asked for it. But she must have; otherwise why would this clothed one ask for it?

"D—D—I can't—remember. But—you know what?"

"Tell me anything, everything," says the clothed one. "I'll listen to everything you say. But please don't go there. Just reach over and grab my hand."

"I—I am—one hundred—and five—kilos," she says and produces a bitter smile. And she turns and takes that final step towards the bright path. But suddenly the bright path disappears, and she falls from the edge of the building, her hopes shattering one last time. What was she thinking? Her being happy is too good to be true anyway. Then her momentary fear gives way to the relief that it is over, this never-ending torture they call life is finally over. Her face lights up with a beautiful smile, and she embraces the end as her fragile body smashes to the ground.

SUNDAY

CHAPTER 38

"**WAKE** up, sis, I think I got something."

Phoenix opened her eyes and just stared, as if she were trying to unfreeze her mind from a state of suspension. Had she been sleeping? Apparently so, and with no nightmares.

"We kept focusing on the wrong director. It's the director now who's been acting not herself before our eyes. What if the Mantis has been attacking not only you but also her?"

"Morssen?" Phoenix slowly got up from her seat. "Where is she now?"

"Don't know, must be in her office or something. Computer: Locate Director Dagmar Morssen."

"Direc—Morss—in—lent—ode."

Phoenix and Beverly looked at each other. "Could she be having a meeting with the corporate?" said Beverly. "I know they tend to put you in Silent from time to time."

"I doubt it. So, you think she could be under the influence of the Mantis?"

"She's been acting strange all week. Now that I think about it, I've never seen her so unbalanced and hesitant during her three-year tenure here."

"As in, I could be a decoy, and she'd be the real target?"

Beverly nodded. "Alex told me about a meeting he had with Hamilton, soon after the installation of Morssen as the new director. Hamilton told him that he and I should be the ones to maintain equilibrium at the field office, should the boss become incapacitated due to some crisis."

"Hamilton said that to Alex three years ago?"

"Alex told me on Wednesday. We interpreted it as the crisis between us and the academy. It made sense. So we jointly decided to keep a lid on the staff and not allow jerks like Julio to provoke anyone. But now when I think about it, we may have reached that conclusion prematurely."

"You're thinking perhaps the previous director was under the influence of the Mantis, and Hamilton had discreetly warned Alex about a similar thing happening to the current one?"

"You just read my mind, sis," nodded Beverly. "What if the Mantis had always had a grip on the boss? What if he did the same with the previous one? And what if his grip on her tightened considerably this past week to reach a peak tonight, so that he could manipulate her into doing something unthinkable?"

"Such as?"

"Computer: Trace location of Director Morssen, priority zero! I don't know, sis, something for the Mantis to cover his tracks, perhaps? Erase evidence of his presence or existence?"

"Or to get her to do his dirty work, like he did with the previous director, when he blindly laundered all those criminals into ordinary Union citizens?"

"Something like that, or perhaps worse. Computer: Where is the result of that damn locator trace? Acknowledge."

"Loca—tor—ace—incon—sive."

They looked at each other agape.

"The Russian!"

The message from the director of the field office had been delivered almost an hour ago, but he hadn't noticed it in between other things. She wasn't one to send meaningless or unnecessary invites, and it appeared that something of importance was going on. The message didn't contain any clues as to what. It was a simple, yet firm, invite.

Already half an hour past midnight, and he was nowhere near done. But there was something in that message, something between the lines. He could feel it, a mute plea, perhaps even desperation, as if she needed help. Under the circumstances, a last-minute visit to the outskirts of the city seemed unavoidable.

He quickly went to his private elevator and started the long descent.

"Computer: Emergency access to staff room at third floor. Execute!"

Following the loud click, they rushed to the Russian. Beverly checked for a pulse at his throat then checked it on the other side of the throat, then back again.

"Too late," said Phoenix.

"No sign of a struggle. Could it be due to natural causes?"

"I don't think so. Any other day, I'd say *maybe*. But not today."

"Computer: This is Supervisor Beverly Blackmore. There's a code twenty-one on the premises. Initiate emergency lock-down procedure. We're going into red alert."

A loud buzzing sounded in the rooms and hallways of the field office, once again. All exits to the outside and to the academy were sealed off with impenetrable metal doors, isolating the field office from the rest of the world. Beverly walked up and down the room nervously, as Phoenix took a few deep breaths in order to focus and clear her mind. She thought of the place she felt safe, and surprisingly she could get there instantly. She opened her eyes again a few seconds later, refreshed and ready for action.

"PA: Initiate crime scene mode—"

"Forget that," said Phoenix. "Almost everyone has been here in the last hour. We'd be swamped with DNA evidence."

"All right, then let's go back to the Monitoring Room. Maybe we can see what happened in the surveillance cams."

"It would be a waste of time. I'm sure the cams here had been inactivated."

"But we need to do something, sis!"

"The director is the key. We need to find her. Call everyone to her office for a meeting."

Beverly's face turned as pale as the stones on the wall. She swallowed. "You think the boss is capable of doing something like this?"

"Any other day, I'd say absolutely not. But today—"

"We have a murder on our hands," said Beverly. "The Russian is dead, and the director's gone missing."

All senior agents were gathered at the director's office. They froze for a few seconds and then started a loud murmur.

"Quiet, quiet," said Beverly, standing behind the director's desk. "We need to find the boss first, so I'd like to organize search parties."

"Wait, wait a minute," said Julio. "Based on what evidence do you claim that the Russian was murdered?"

"Based on the fact that he doesn't breathe and his heart doesn't beat."

"So what? Doesn't necessarily mean he's been murdered. By the way, did you happen to perform a crime scene sweep in the so-called *crime room* and find any evidence to that effect? And for all we know, the director might be pursuing a secret vice on a Saturday night instead of wasting her time here like us. Besides, who gives you the authority to—"

"For all we know, the Mantis is in this room," said a calm and soft voice from behind, and everyone turned their attention to Phoenix.

"Not that Mantis crap again," said Julio, rolling his eyes. "I don't even believe the man exists. Show me a tiny fraction of scientific proof to his existence."

"Scientific proof, I don't have. But there are just too many convenient coincidences, an abnormal number of security camera outages, terrorists and psychopaths about to slip into the Union, security interviewers with perfect approval percentages, clueless deception experts unable to see liars before their very eyes, students vanishing without a trace, ongoing hack attacks to our network, and finally, suspects fainting when asked about the Mantis's existence and identity, and then all of a sudden, dying, all very *conveniently*."

"If you're insinuating stuff about me, talking about interviewers with perfect scores, I'm proud of my perfect record, you Neand—"

"Enough!" Alex reached the center of the group. "The fact remains that Director Morssen is missing and that she is unreachable and untraceable. We don't have time for petty squabbling. I say we take Beverly's advice and find her first. I believe the staff room with the dead Russian is already sealed. We can check for evidence there later."

The crowd murmured in approval and started talking about organizing the search parties.

"Speaking of wild theories, I have one of my own," said Julio with a smirk. "We have this legendary Mantis, who floats in the high and dark hallways of this haunted field office, putting a whammy here, and another one on the network there, and we have a missing director. I say, what if the two were one and the same?"

Julio walked to the center of the room as the crowd watched him, agape.

"Think about it for a moment. She's been acting all strange throughout the week. A week which started with the spectacular Strike-Out of our precious colleague here, then continued with more Strike-Outs and scandals which rocked the very foundation of this field office. Then all of a sudden a myth got resurrected: the Mantis was back. So the 'blame everything on the myth' game was on."

"How can you even suggest that the boss is the Mantis? said Beverly. "The Mantis existed way before she got here, and it's a he."

"And what better cover than hiding behind the wrong gender? I'm not suggesting that Chief *is* the Mantis. Frankly, I don't believe the dude even exists; he's a myth. But I also believe that our good director took the opportunity to resurrect the myth in order to cover up all the mess going on in this field office and her evident shortcomings."

"Are you suggesting that the boss would fake the presence of the Mantis by hiring some hackers, to cover her ass?" said Beverly. "You're so full of shit!"

"Bingo," said Julio and clapped his hands a few times. "You finally got it, Bev. That's *exactly* what I'm suggesting."

"How can you even suggest such a thing!?" Alex approached Julio, fists clenched. "You have no idea about her past, what she went through in a dungeon for five years, how she suffered, how she survived, and what a proud person she is."

Harold and a few others came between Alex and Julio in order to prevent a physical confrontation, Fred tried to calm Alex down.

"Hey, hey, take it easy, pal," said Julio. "You know I really like you, Alex, but your soft spot for the chief is making you blind to her shortcomings."

"Then let's get on with it," said Phoenix. "Let's find her, so that she can answer Julio's accusations in person. I'm really curious to hear what she'd have to say about being or imitating the Mantis."

The Mantis smiled to himself, gleeful that his improvised plan was working to near perfection so far. Aided by a few fortunate circumstances, he had managed to shift the attention away from himself to the director. And if things progressed as he had expected, there was a good chance that he could get away with everything he had done.

The director's appearance at the staff room had been a total surprise. Yet he had managed to turn the situation to his advantage by using his growing stun ability to push her to the extreme end of her negative emotional spectrum. It had been very easy to do, as the woman had already been fighting to control her inner demons and chronic depression her entire life and the Mantis had been playing mind games with her all week long. His final push had sent her headlong into the worst memories of her life, forcing her to take that final step to permanent seclusion, literally speaking. The Mantis couldn't feel prouder about his growing stun ability, almost at jinx levels.

Another unexpected development was the involvement of his controller, the Prefect, during his final torment of the director in an effort to save her from the

Mantis's grip. Foolishly, the Prefect had gotten close to them physically and used his jinxing powers to stop the director from taking that final step to oblivion by intervening in the nightmare induced by the Mantis, perhaps even appearing in the nightmare in vain, only to be exposed to the Mantis. What could be the point of trying to salvage the director at the risk of a thought pattern exposure? Being a lame duck, strategically she was of no value anymore. Could there be an emotional reason? Could this controller be amateur enough to prompt actions based on primitive urges such as fondness, love, or lust, like that adolescent Crane, only to be fended off by an even stronger Mantis and be exposed in the process? Evidently, yes!

Unbelievable, the Mantis thought. All this weakness, low energy, and amateur moves, there could be only one explanation: This couldn't be his original ruthless and exacting controller. This was a new and inexperienced one pretending to be the Prefect, a total amateur, possibly perpetrated by the manipulations of that Crane. And he had been intimidated and kept under pressure and control by this premature and amateur bunch all these years, but no more. Now he possessed the power to defeat and torment the lot of them.

As a part of the massive search party, the Mantis had one purpose only. The Prefect was trapped somewhere in the building, just like he was. Now his mind was working like radar, seeking the thought signature of the controller. The only way to avoid giving away the signature was to abstain from thinking, hardly something the controller could do while on the run. And if he could get physically close enough, the Mantis could terminate the Prefect once and for all.

All three floors of the old building were being swept by the search parties. Every room, every stairway, every crevice, every turn, the tiniest corridor, even the roof, was to be searched and reported. Every staff member was given a certain section of the building's grid and asked to sweep it then help the others. Given the inconvenience of her attire, Phoenix had decided not to take part in the search and remained instead with Beverly in the Monitoring Room to oversee. Following the meeting at the director's office, she had come into her office to tend to the blisters caused by the heels of her shoes. Where were those wonderful transparent skin-adaptive Band-Aids when you needed one?

"Tess."

"Right here."

"I need your help: I need you to go through the surveillance database and trace Director Morssen's movements, going two hours back. I'm pretty sure there will be many inconvenient camera outages which might hamper your search, but do your best, extrapolate, something. We need to locate her."

"Of course. It will take longer than usual, given the state of the network."

"Do what you can, and keep on standby. I may need you any moment."

She put her shoes back on and went to the Monitoring Room down on the second floor, catching Beverly in the middle of berating Sean.

"What do you mean you're onto something crucial, dammit? We need every pair of legs to do this search."

"What's going on?"

"This Ms. *Know It All* here refuses to be a part of the search!"

"Phoenix, I need to talk to you."

"Is this true?" said Phoenix.

"Yes, but, there is this—"

"There are no buts," said Beverly. "We need to find the boss, don't you get it?"

"This is not a good time to argue, but time to act, Sean, can't you see?"

"But you gotta listen to me—"

An incoming call with no caller ID buzzed from Phoenix's PA.

"Who is this?"

"Phoe—it's—sella—" said the voice. "Down—er—now."

"Who is this? I can't hear you."

"West—dens—" said the familiar voice. "Com—d—now."

"Oh my God," gasped Phoenix, kicking her shoes away and dashing out of the Monitoring Room.

The Crane took a sip from his coffee and kept watching the dance of the threads on his giant monitor. Some people danced for their missions, and others, like himself, only watched these binary hacking threads dancing, and life was supposed to be fair. He supposed he shouldn't complain, as he was pretty sure that he wouldn't be that good of a dancer.

There was a significant decrease in the weak countermeasures the field office geeks had been launching for the past half hour. He wasn't sure why this might be the case and checked out their surveillance cameras, noticing the red alert and a lockdown. Moreover, they appeared to be looking for something or someone all over the building. He couldn't hear what they were talking about, as the surveillance cams didn't come with any audio capability. Nevertheless, the situation was highly unusual, and something must have happened. He quietly opened a communication thread and sent a message to the grandmaster to come at once.

Then he saw *her* dashing down the hallway in her long dress. Bare feet?

"Tess, I need the main gate to the west gardens open, now."

"I don't have the authority—"

"I don't care what you do, just open the damn gate!" she said and banged on the gate.

"I'll try. Stand by."

She could hear the calls of Beverly behind her, who had dashed out following her but had fallen behind waiting for the elevator, while she took the ancient and treacherous stairs. She kept banging on it then suddenly a miracle happened: She heard a loud click, and the gate opened. She dashed out into the pitch-dark moonless night.

"Gisella! Where are you?"

"Over here!"

She couldn't see Gisella, but the two missing Robo-Cops in their orange reflective overalls were easy to spot, standing by the stone wall of the building looking at something on the ground. She knew what they were looking at, and she was late, too late. She stopped running and approached them with her eyes locked on the ground, without a word, and went down on her knees next to Gisella.

Director Dagmar Morssen's twisted lifeless body was lying on the ground, with a rare serene expression on her beautiful yet still hard and pain-etched face.

CHAPTER 39

THE search party was called off, and almost everyone was outside at the scene of the incident. With some portable lighting, the area was flooded with bright light. The clear moonless night was turning into a stormy one, as the wind was picking up.

Gisella examined the director's corpse on her knees while Phoenix observed and helped her with quiet competence, not allowing the prevalent feeling of anxiety to pierce her self-constructed bubble of neutrality. She scanned the director's lifeless body with the blue ray from her PA. She had already declared the area a crime scene and had asked the onlooking field office staff not to get closer than five meters. She was sure she was to find no trace evidence, but it was a part of the protocol, and it needed to be done.

Quiet tears were flowing down Beverly's cheeks, with many of the other agents either crying or barely holding the tears back. Even Julio appeared to be shocked and saddened at the unexpected nature of the incident. But clearly the person who took the hardest hit was Alex. He was just standing there in disbelief, unable to say anything, his face wet with tears, occasionally shaking his head and wiping the tears with the back of his hand. Fred was standing next to him, trying to support him with murmurs, rubbing his back, not even fidgeting.

"Anything suspicious?"

"Nothing so far," said Gisella as she probed the body with a handheld MRI device. "Everything seems consistent with a fall from up there."

"What about those dark marks on her wrists?"

"I think those have been there for a long time," sighed Gisella. "But I can't be sure until a full body scan determines if there are any recent pre-mortem injuries. If there are, those might tell a different story, but everything so far points to an accident. Or a suicide?"

"You are aware of what you're saying, right?"

"I know suicides in the Union are virtually nonexistent," shrugged Gisella. "But here we are, looking at one tragedy or other. Or would you prefer it to be a homicide? Because accident is a bit of a far stretch. What, she went up on the roof barefoot just to look at the stars?"

Phoenix took a deep breath. It would take hours, if not days, to get any kind of useful information from the director's body to determine the nature of the incident. But, no matter how unbelievable it seemed, her instincts told her that she had two murders at hand. Two murders by that heinous Mantis within less than an hour of each other.

"Can you tell me anything about the time of death?"

"Based on the temperature of the liver, about half an hour ago."

"And why are you out here?" Phoenix turned and said to the Robo-Cops. "You were supposed to be standing guard at the staff room."

"We were sent a message ordering us to escort Dr. Nemeth from the metro station."

"By who?"

"By her," said the Robo-Cop, pointing to the dead director.

Phoenix nodded grimly. With the full-scale hack going on at the field office, anyone from the Mantis's band could easily send a message to these guys that mimicked the director's digital ID.

"How's the other guy doing?"

"He's dead, too."

Gisella stopped her work and turned to Phoenix. "We have our work cut out for us, don't we? What was the occasion, by the way?"

"Let's just say that there was a strict dress code at the place that I apprehended the dead guy, and I needed to look my best to be able to unmask him."

"And I'm sure you did, a few hours ago," said Gisella and winked.

"Well, this explains everything," said Julio loudly, shaking off his sad disposition. "And my theory about our late chief seems to be holding."

"What are you talking about?" said Phoenix, without moving her head from her scan.

"That our dead director here was pretending to be that legendary Mantis. She realized that the mafia dude upstairs was about to shatter her story by denying the existence of the Mantis, so she decided to silence him to cover her tracks. But it seems like she was flooded by an overpowering guilt and opted for a quick end."

"Then how do you explain the Russian's fainting the moment I asked him about the Mantis?" said Phoenix with fire in her eyes. "She used her mind-altering weapon?"

"Why not?" shrugged Julio. "We all agree that such weapons exist, right? I mean, she was the one who told us that whole story with that man in that black oversized hat who whammied a whole bunch of them."

"Tell me one reason that it shouldn't be you who's doing all this, you fucking asshole!" said Beverly with tears in her eyes.

"I got no reason to get rid of the Russian, for one," said Julio with a smirk. "And I'm not the one who's been running this place like crap, causing rifts with the academy, treating us like dirt, and eventually falling out of the loop with the corporate bigwigs. I think she was halfway cracking up anyway. I mean, c'mon, who could live through all that torture and be normal? So this week too much pressure must have just cracked her wide open."

"I can't—" Alex left the scene in tears, with Fred behind him.

"Sorry, I'm not the sentimental type, okay?" said Julio. "It all adds up to me: She cracked up, mimicked an attack from Mantis, got freaked out by the Russian, killed the Russian, climbed up onto the roof, and jumped off in panic and/or guilt. Case solved. You guys can fill in the incident log, and I'll approve it when I return tomorrow. Still got a fragment of a Saturday night to catch."

"You're not going anywhere," hissed Phoenix, slowly standing up. "Nobody will leave the premises until further notice, and the lockdown will continue. Everyone inside, now! I will interview each and every person following the examination of this body and the other body in the staff room."

"Oh yeah? On whose authority?" said Julio. "Besides, there's no evidence of foul play here. It could even have been an accident."

"Perhaps she really jumped off, or maybe she was pushed off, or maybe she was a secret astronomy nut and this is how we finally found out. Unless we find evidence to the contrary, *this* is a crime scene, my crime scene, as the first senior agent arriving. And as far as I'm concerned, everyone here is a suspect and won't leave the building until I interview them."

"Hey, who is to say that you're not him?"

"I happen to be the newest agent here," said Phoenix with a cold smile. "The one with the least possibility of being mixed up with any mafia or the Mantis. And I have reason to believe that was precisely why I was chosen to lead the Bogdanov case."

"Says who?"

"Said she," said Phoenix motioning to the corpse. "She revealed that I was picked by the high executives to avoid any foul play or mafia involvement. I suppose they don't share your sentiments regarding the Mantis, Julio."

"Spoken through the lips of a dead woman," said Julio and shook his head. "C'mon, Nix, you can do better than that."

"Speaking of which, same could be said about your claims regarding her, too," said Phoenix, her lip curling. "But in my case, there's one more person who can confirm what I just said."

"And who would that be?" said Julio and crossed his arms. "Your nut-job buddy Ray?"

"Nope. Why don't you call and ask Hamilton?"

"The Mantis is on the counterattack," said the grandmaster. "He has managed to distract the attention by creating a shocking diversion up there. But our dear one seems to retain control." He watched the incident with the Crane through the security camera feeds. "How's the Prefect?"

"He seems to be doing okay so far. Should we be worried about him?"

"Not yet," said the grandmaster. "I'm hoping that she'll pick up the leads and unmask the Mantis soon. The Prefect is not in any danger right now."

"That Mantis, he's definitely cooking up something, Grandmaster, and I don't like it. Should I withdraw the hack? That would give them one less thing to worry about and perhaps focus better on the case."

"No, not yet," said the old man. "She still has the Russian. Let's closely observe what she'll do. Where is the Russian, anyway?"

"What do you think?"

"It could be a murder. There's subconjunctival hemorrhaging in his eyes, burst blood vessels. But I can't conclude that the cause of death is asphyxiation just by observing the eyes or scanning his body."

After the examination was over, an ambulance had removed the director's body. Then they had gone to the staff room to examine the other body. Phoenix had asked the two Robo-Cops to stand outside until the postmortem of the Russian was concluded. She had also asked Sean to scan the area for evidence, despite knowing it would reveal nothing useful. And, of course, the surveillance camera in the room had been out.

"Where's everyone?" said Gisella. "Where will you question them?"

"There's an ongoing hack at the field office, so everyone's at their posts. I'll call them one by one when I need them. And I don't know where to talk. The best place is the interview room, of course, but I don't want to make everyone sit under all that hardware as if they were all suspected criminals."

"That would be so unpolitical. You'd have a handful of enemies."

"Things are already bad as they are," sighed Phoenix. "I can't say that I have many friends here."

Sean turned and looked at Phoenix following the comment, her big brown eyes betraying frustration and disappointment, then turned her head away quickly and continued her work.

"How is it going, Sean?"

"Slow."

"You've been acting preoccupied all evening. I want you to do this scan carefully without missing anything, understand?"

"No, I don't understand! If you're so keen on doing this crap and not focusing on real leads, why don't you do it yourself?" Sean turned and left the room, leaving a gaping Phoenix behind.

"Now I understand what you mean by 'not having many allies' here," said Gisella, watching Sean leave. "If your case assistant is acting like this—"

Phoenix got up and stormed out of the room, her bare feet making barely a sound on the cold stone floors of the building. She caught up with Sean in the hallway and grabbed her by the shoulder, feeling a childish satisfaction at her little shriek. "Now you know how it feels when you sneak up behind me. What's going on with you, Sean? What happened to you? You're not following requests and orders."

"It's because you don't listen to me! I know who he is."

Phoenix felt a big knot in her stomach tightening as she watched Sean's disposition shift from frustration to fear. "Convince me."

"You mean, you're not gonna shut me up again?"

"I said, convince me!"

"I'll try."

"Come with me." They ran down the hallway as quiet as a couple of cats.

"The death of the Russian will put a lot of strain on her, and now I cannot locate the Mantis," said Crane. "But how can he disable the surveillance cams? As if—" He looked down and shook his head. "He has one of my gadgets, doesn't he? I can't believe it!"

"He was given one of the older versions of your designs for you to be able to make that great hack a few months back," nodded the grandmaster. "I guess he kept good care of it all this time."

"Grandmaster, he can access anywhere in the Union, open any door, and disable pretty much any countermeasure. Didn't it occur to anyone to ask for the damn thing back? What if it fell in the wrong hands there, someone from GPSN discovered it?"

"You know the special situation with the Mantis," said the old man. "He isn't one of those operatives we can call in here from time to time. We needed to keep him isolated because of his circumstances, only to be maintained and controlled by the tight grip of the Prefect."

"Which is no longer the case. I have a really bad feeling about this."

"C'mon, tell me, I'm all ears."

Sean made an attempt to open her mouth, only to close it again.

"Talk to me, Sean, we're running out of time!"

"What if—what if I'm wrong? What if there is a totally plausible explanation to all of it?"

"Then you're wrong. But talk to me now, and let me be the judge of that."

"All right," said Sean and took a deep breath. "It all started when I remembered something, when you mentioned Mantis being in your apartment."

"Yes, it's a feeling I still have."

"I don't know about your apartment, but I think he's been in your office. I noticed him going towards your end of the third-floor hallway, but I got distracted by someone else, a call or something, and simply assumed that he was on his way to the director's office."

"What made you change your mind?"

"That part of the hallway ends with your office or the director's. You were out in the city for your interviews. Normally I'd think that he'd be on his way to the director's, but there was something strange in his disposition, I don't know. There was also something about DeVille's house. I kept watching the footage you recorded there, but I couldn't figure it out. Then today, when you mentioned Mantis being in your place, I decided to check the surveillance footage for your room during that day of the incident. It took forever because of all the network issues. And I found out that the cameras in your office during that time frame were conveniently offline."

"I almost checked the visual logs of my office a couple of days back to see if Ray had been in my room to switch my new PA and my old one."

"I know. I did a sweep of the entire week. He'd been to your office three times last week and took your PA on his first visit."

"I already know about that. I'm sorry to disappoint you if you think that Ray is the Mantis, because—"

"If I thought he was the Mantis, I wouldn't hesitate this much."

"Tell me, then, who?"

The Mantis was walking down the hallways of the building in search of the controller's unique thought signature when suddenly he sensed a faint tingle in his mind. The signature was on and off, like drops in a pond, but consistent enough for him to tell the direction. The controller was definitely trying to hide his or her thoughts, but he or she wasn't aware of Mantis's growing strength and sensitivity. He shifted his direction to follow the tingle, using trial and error in order to see which hallway was to lead to a better reception. None of them did; therefore he must have been on the wrong floor. He took the elevator to one floor below and walked quickly to the same area to see if the pattern was stronger. Yes, it was.

He searched all hallways and rooms in the surrounding area, but still there was no sight of the controller. *Perhaps one more floor down,* he thought. He took the elevator again and walked to the same point deep in the hallways. The sensation was even stronger now, and it was moving away from him; the controller was running away. His *controller* was running away from him, unable to hide his thoughts! The Mantis felt a rush of confidence, thinking that the Prefect was even weaker than he had thought. But he couldn't attribute everything to weakness of his adversary—it also had to do with his growing strength, increasing by the minute.

He searched the maze of hallways to get a better sensation, only to find himself facing a stone wall. The Prefect couldn't be on the other side of the wall unless—. So that's what it was, the controller knew about the secret passages, too. He went to the end of one of the hallways, which he knew had access to the secret labyrinth behind the walls. He pressed the appropriate stone to reveal an opening and entered.

The hunt was on.

Following Sean's revelation, Phoenix felt a strange serenity about it, as if she had known it all along and wasn't surprised at all. She didn't possess the photographic memory that Beverly had, nor did she have the time to resort to the databases like Sean did, but she possessed something else. To her, it was about the feelings, how she felt after each encounter, how each encounter influenced her emotional pattern, her reactions, her ups and downs, her senses, her instincts. When she thought about many such instances in the past week, they all seemed to fit with well with Sean's revelation.

Then her mind got stuck on a detail about DeVille's house following Sean's mention. She worked on her network node and made queries to the central database. Then it was time to make a quick but intrusive call.

Sandra wasn't sure what to do with her life anymore. Her uphill battle to gain a better position in her organization was going nowhere. She had planned to make a big break at the Anti-Chaos party, but because of her so-called best friend, not only was the party ruined but her entire weekend turned into a nightmare. The guy just didn't understand a polite no, and she couldn't just bluntly reject some journalist and risk being badmouthed by the press. Things were bad enough as they were. And why couldn't he be some journalist with some real clout, instead of being a petty reporter?

One crazy thought came into her head: Perhaps she could ask for her best buddy's help. She had known how to handle him during that party, and with the recent acquisition of the immigration academy by GPSN, her luck may have turned. Then again, maybe not, as she definitely wasn't the executive type. The woman didn't even know how to have fun, so how could she be a good executive? Sandra was sure that she was probably sitting alone in her house, watching that dumb Court Network, not even thinking of a date on a Saturday night. But, then again, who could Phoenix have had a date with, when Sandra had covered all the bases?

At that instant, her PA started making an atrocious noise, a sound both urgent and jarring, something she had never heard before.

"What the hell is that?" said the marine. "I thought we agreed to put our PAs in Busy Mode."

"I did, baby. Lemme see what's wrong with it."

The marine pulled out and moved aside so that she could reach the nightstand. Sandra had felt so down, for distraction she had popped a couple of libido enhancer pills and called him directly to her apartment late at night, as she had no intention of being seen with him in public. And he had come to her apartment, set out to prove his worth, going at it again, and again, and again, for whatever reason men had this urge to prove their manliness to women. Why couldn't they accept the fact that women didn't really care about it or enjoy it and just pretended? She grabbed her PA, only to see that it was an NMI from none other than her best friend.

"What's going on? Can't you see I'm busy?"

"Sorry to spoil your party, but I need to know who your buddy in my office is."

"My buddy? You called me with an NMI in the middle of the night for that? I told you, those are my only trade secrets!"

"I couldn't care less about your secrets in trade, unless, of course, you'd prefer to explain all this to me at the field office."

"You wouldn't dare, you cunt!"

"Don't test my patience, Sandra. Did you tell him about my nightmares? I need to know *now!*"

"All right, all right, so I did mention a few scenarios concocted by your freaky mind, so what? Wait, wait, you're not gonna sue me for copyright infringement, are you?"

"Just tell me who he is, and I won't."

Sandra gave the name, eliciting no reaction on Phoenix's part.

"That's all I needed to verify. Thank you for your time."

"By the way, the marine here says hi to you."

"Really? So you couldn't even get a date with the sticky journalist and had to settle with a barebones HDI marine? Business must be really down," said Phoenix and hung up.

"Who was that?"

"Ah, just my best friend. I think you're right."

"Really?" said Sean and produced a beautiful smile, which faded seconds later. "What do we do now?"

"First, we have to find him. Tess, I want you to find someone for me in the building, and I have a gut feeling that it won't be easy."

"There's more trouble," said the Crane. "I lost the Mantis. I think he's taking the secret passageways again."

"Where's the Prefect?" said the grandmaster.

"I can't find him, either," said the Crane, relentlessly working on his computer. "I think he's in the passageways, too. Could it be—"

"Dear God, I think the Mantis is onto him. I don't know how, but I think he knows the Prefect's identity."

"We need to help him!"

"Terminate the hack. He's using the slow network to his advantage to hide. The Prefect is trapped. The only place he can escape is through the emergency hatch. But I'm not sure if—"

"There!" said the Crane and terminated the digital attack at the press of a button. "Nobody will be up by that hatch at this time of night. I'll do it."

The Crane grabbed his PA-like gadget and dashed out of the network center into the tunnel outside, en route to the shaft. His little device would keep him connected to the network and maintain his access to the GPSN surveillance system so that he could try to follow what was going on up there and intervene if necessary. The emergency hatch connected the Land of Renovators to the dungeons under the old monastery and was accessible from the natural cave area on top of the shaft. The Crane needed to run up the shaft and enter one of the small cave subsidiaries that only masters and grandmasters had access to. He could only think of one trouble that he might encounter.

He didn't know if the hatch would work.

"Can't find him anywhere," said Tess. "The last time I could detect him in surveillance logs is from the west gardens."

"After we discovered the body of the director. He must have a gadget to disable the surveillance cameras. How about his PA?"

"That was the first thing I checked," said Tess. "It's on his desk, one thing that I could visually verify. The network connectivity seems to be back to normal, by the way."

"It is? Good. Now, this is what I want you to do."

Sean watched Phoenix as she explained to Tess her idea for tracking the Mantis. "And who was that?" she said when Phoenix finally turned to her. "You have another assistant that I don't know about?"

"Nope, this one is more like a guardian angel. And she'll help us to find the demon."

The Mantis was enjoying this hunt immensely. His controller was using the secret passageways skillfully, going out to hallways from time to time, only to submerge into another passageway nearby, and making the Mantis lose time with each exit and entry. So far he or she had managed to maintain distance between them, but this didn't worry the Mantis at all. He was moving in methodically, taking into account all the escape routes, and pushing the Prefect towards an inescapable corner. The Mantis's glee mounted, knowing that this hide-and-seek would be over soon and that he would end the misery of this fearful and weak controller. He was looking forward to the encounter to test his ever-growing powers and abilities. *Only a few more minutes,* he thought. Soon it would be all over.

Down on the first floor, Phoenix and Sean dashed eastwards along the main hallway, towards the immigration academy part of the building. Tess was screening
the pattern of the surveillance camera outages in real time and extrapolating the
direction the Mantis was going. They reached the main gate that separated the
field office from the academy. Phoenix remembered how she rushed through this
gate to attend the graduation ceremony, nearly a lifetime ago. But the gate was
sealed this time, due to the ongoing lockdown.

"Tess, unlock the gate."

"I'll try, but I'm not sure how. We may need Beverly or Fred for an override."

"Do something," said Phoenix, banging her hand on the gate. "We have no
time. He's running away, perhaps to Russia. Do what you did with the gate to the
west gardens. C'mon!"

"That wasn't me."

"That wasn't you? Then who—?"

There was a loud warning beep then the metal seal of the gate slowly lifted
up and gave way. Ringing and buzzing flooded the entire building, startling both
Phoenix and Sean.

Their eyes met momentarily, and they dashed to the academy side.

The Crane squeezed through the narrow tunnel, the dampness on the walls penetrating his clothes. The thick walls of the cave had a negative influence on his
PA-like network gadget, but the disruption wasn't as bad as he feared it would
be. The same gadget provided him light and visuals from the camera feeds in
the field office. And when he'd seen her desperately trying to get to the academy
side, he hadn't hesitated to open the gate, knowing that it would trigger an alarm.
Actually he hoped that the alarm would distract the Mantis for a while, buying
some time.

The cave subsidiary was narrow, and it twisted left and right, with a sixty-
degree incline. The Crane could see the end of it, which was still some ten meters
away. He'd never climbed all the way up here before, off-limits to Renovator kids,
but now he could see why it was called an emergency hatch. It was an oval metal
door with a circular release, the kind one would find in ships and submarines.
He had a pretty good idea where this door might have come from. The hatch
was sealed from the Renovator side, and there was no way of opening it from the
other side, where it appeared as a stone wall. He punched a few codes into the
nearby keypad to enable his access and, as the light turned green, he tested the
circular release to see if it would move. It didn't.

Now what? he thought.

"This is not a drill!" said Phoenix to curious students in the academy hallway. "There is a security breach. Go back to your rooms and stay there!"

The trail led them to the basement levels of the building, and the only way to get down there was to use the narrow circular stairs with very high steps and no railing to protect from falling to the void in the center. Phoenix ran down the stairs with Sean at her heels.

"Are you sure he'll be at the bottom level, Tess?"

"The extrapolation points to the bottom basement floor. My signal is getting weak. You may lose network connectivity down there."

"Understood." Phoenix had ripped up her long dress some time ago for freedom of movement. But there was one strand of cloth that was hanging on one side, and she inadvertently stepped on it as she was trying to illuminate the stairs and pay maximum attention to the incline. She lost her balance, tripping towards the void in the middle of the circular stairs, nearly three meters down. She managed to fall on her feet, but the right one buckled beneath her. Sean let out an involuntary cry and hurried to her side.

"Are you okay?"

"Still in one piece," said Phoenix and tried to get up. "Oh, shit, I think I sprained my ankle."

"Can you walk?"

"I think so. Tess, we're on the lowest floor. Which direction do we go?"

"Can't tell until the next outage," said Tess. "Are you okay? There was a loud noise on the microphone."

"I'm fine. What do we do now?"

"We wait for him to surface. Whoops, here we go, heading east."

"We can't let him run away. I'll catch him." Sean dashed to the long dark corridor leading eastwards.

"Wait." Phoenix attempted to take a few steps behind her, but her ankle bucked once more, and she collapsed on the cold stone floor in pain.

He entered the GPSN building amid the ringing alarms. He'd been already notified about the director's death, and the main gate at the west gardens was overridden for him. A security detail was running towards the academy side.

"What's going on? Where are you running to?"

The detail stopped and stood fast. He swallowed, his eyes wide. "The lockdown of the main gate to the academy side is breached, sir! Someone hacked into it. We have to secure the gate manually."

"At ease, soldier. On whose orders?"

"His," said the security detail and pointed at the tall figure dashing towards the academy.

The Mantis reached the end of the secret passageway and pressed the unlocking stone. This was it. There was no way out for the controller; he or she couldn't hide anymore without being exposed. He pushed the heavy wall to make enough of an opening to squeeze through, only to hear a shriek echoing down the dark hallway.

He held his breath and closed the secret door softly, then turned his attention to the place that the sound had come from. The shriek had been pretty high-pitched, perhaps from a female? It wouldn't surprise him if the controller was a woman. The Mantis tried to sense the thought signature, but there was nothing. Perhaps the Prefect was hiding again by abstaining from active thought.

He took a few soft steps down the narrow hallway towards the sound but then decided to wait for a while at one of the sharp turns. He could hear the alarm bells still ringing in the distance, but it didn't matter. He had the Prefect walking into a trap, as he could see light from a PA approaching the corner. He patiently waited until the source of the light reached the corner, then yanked her and covered her mouth with his hand, unable to prevent another shriek.

From her evident weakness and illogical, emotional attempts to save the director, he had already worked out that the controller could be an inexperienced female. But this was the last woman he had expected her to be.

The Crane braced his left leg on the side wall and pulled at the circular release with all his strength. His muscles felt as if they were tearing apart fiber by fiber, but he couldn't let go. He had to open this hatch; the Prefect was on the other side. After long seconds of pulling, he let go for a few moments to gather his strength. He thought of asking for help, but there was barely enough room for one person to operate in the narrow cave branch. Sweat was leaking out of every pore in his body, and he was breathing as if he had just finished a marathon, yet he had to try again. This time he didn't try to turn the circular release with his arms but held it with an iron grip and applied both of his legs to the wall, pushing the release with them. He silently asked all those grandmasters why this hatch had never been cared for all these years.

Then he thought about her. She was somewhere just on the other side of this wall, and she might be needing help. Extra strength surged through his body at the thought, and the metal creaked and moved. He kept pushing with his legs and turning the rusty release until he reached a dead stop. Only then did he loosen his grip and lower his legs to the ground, panting heavily, then he pushed the hatch, opening it surprisingly easily and quietly. The Prefect was waiting on the other side in a state of some kind of trance, his eyes closed. The Crane got into the hallway and paused for an instant, trying to understand what was going on.

Then he heard the scream echoing down the narrow hallway. As he was about to dash in the direction of the scream, the Prefect gripped his arm, and he turned to be caught in a spellbinding gaze.

Phoenix limped down the hallway dragging her right leg, which now had a very swollen ankle. After Sean dashed off down the hallway, she had barely managed to get up, and it stabbed at her painfully every time she stepped on it. Her ability to move was severely hampered, but she had to push on, as she knew Sean was in trouble from her scream. And why wouldn't she listen to her when she told her to wait? What was she trying to prove? She wished she had her uniform on, as there would be a nerve disrupter in one of its pockets. But now she didn't know what she could do if she needed to physically confront the Mantis. And from the scream she had just heard, Sean needed help desperately. "Tess, alert Beverly, alert everyone to come down here, quick," she whispered into her PA.

"Are you okay?" said Tess, her voice breaking up. "The signal is too weak. I can't get a lock on your position. Wait for backup to arrive."

"I can't," whispered Phoenix. "Sean needs help. I can't leave her."

She limped down the dark hallway as fast as possible. She could hear some breathing in the distance, heavy breathing, like the one during the Patel interview. It could only mean one thing. She ran down the hallway, ignoring the pain, and turned the corner to see the Mantis strangling Sean on the cold stone floor. The expression in the eyes of Sean merged in her mind with the expression of the woman Patel had strangled. She sprang on the Mantis with sudden savagery, pushing him to the side and rolling on top of him. But the Mantis responded with a rage she had never thought possible on that face, and he punched her violently, the jab connecting with her chin. She fell back, nearly unconscious, trying to keep it together and shake off the spinning.

Sean was gagging and desperately trying to breathe, coughing, making inhuman sounds in the meantime. The Mantis turned his attention back to Sean and set out to finish what he had started. He squeezed her neck viciously, and a few seconds later Phoenix heard a snapping sound and saw a spinning image of the Mantis discarding Sean's lifeless body like a rag doll.

"So much for the infamous controller," he hissed. "What an amateur and a weakling she proved to be. Not even a trace of mental resistance. Now, let's see what you're made of!"

CHAPTER 40

"LET me go," whispered the Crane with tears in his eyes.

It wasn't the physical strength that kept the Crane in place, but the Prefect's quiet willpower and the deep suggestion in his eyes that told him to stay put. It was the first time ever that the Crane was seeing the Prefect in person, and he could tell that this man was nothing like what he had seen in those videos from security cameras.

"Please," he said. "I know how important you are. Just go and lock the hatch behind you. But please leave me here. I cannot leave her in the hands of that monster. I just *can't*. And I don't know if the willpower brought by her love would give me enough strength to overpower you, but I'll have to try with everything I got. Please understand me, Grandmaster."

The Prefect looked hard into the eyes of the Crane. He could sense the depth of the love inside the Crane, and it felt so good as he inhaled that love, like a fresh bunch of wildflowers, like a beautiful sunset, like the rainbow after the rain, like butterflies flitting their wings in the field, elevating his spirit and senses. This love radiating from the Crane was beyond any other feeling he had witnessed in a long time, and it was perfectly complementary to the one growing inside her. It was so beautiful to be able to witness this, right in the middle of all the ugliness and evil around.

The Prefect had felt so many powerful emotions from others in his life, most of which were at the other extreme from love. There was so much negative energy in the world, so much hatred, so much despair, envy, pain, so much of it, it was hard for him to bear it all. The Black Hat and the Toboggan Hat had total control and command of their emotions. The Prefect was not like them. He sensed them all and felt happy with the good feelings and sad with the bad ones. It was his duty to deal with and manage all that bad energy, the worst of which emanated from the Mantis.

The Mantis despised every living soul who had feelings, only because he lacked them. He took pleasure in tormenting those in his way, and many times the Prefect had had to witness and do nothing to prevent it in order to control him. And the guilt of losing control of the Mantis had been giving him so much pain. Now that soulless creature full of hatred was on the loose, on a killing spree. He had tried to save the poor director by interfering in her dream, yet the Mantis had proven to be unexpectedly strong and took him by surprise, rendering his efforts from a distance useless and detecting his thought signature in the process.

The Prefect had known what he had to do in order to lure the evil being to an unanticipated trap: He would make himself the bait. He could hide his thought signature anytime he wanted, and he had exposed himself briefly from time to time, dragging the evil down near the emergency hatch to neutralize him and to bring him into the Renovator side. He had been on the field for so long, for so many years, that he was exhausted and desperately needed to come in. And he would bring in the troublemaker Mantis with him so that he could be terminated once and for all, if only Phoenix and Sean hadn't showed up in the hallway prematurely.

The Prefect knew how important he was for the overall mission, but he felt totally depleted. He had managed to keep going at the urging of the other grandmasters, but his energy had been diminishing steadily, passing a critical threshold with his inability against the Mantis. He couldn't carry on like this anymore, acting as controlled, ruthless, and as exacting as the other two. And if they were doing all of this for the good of the world, for people to have real choices, real freedoms, real pursuit of happiness, to expose the lies, and for love to flourish again in this crazy world, what good was it to let this powerful and real love, which had miraculously managed to flourish in the surrounding ugliness like a flower in the desert, be destroyed to reach that overall good? Wouldn't that lower the Renovators to the same level that they had been struggling against for decades?

It had to start somewhere; it had to start right now and here. He had to let this precious love between the Crane and Phoenix stand a chance, no matter what the consequences. He had to let this butterfly flutter its wings and generate a wave of change. And if this meant that Renovators' years of preparation were to fail, causing chaos, then so be it. After all, he could see the strength and courage needed to build everything from scratch, perhaps in a much better way, in the Crane's tearful eyes.

And the Prefect had never feared chaos.

She looks up, only to see the sky from the bottom of a bottle. Why is the sky so far away? And why is the sun's image being refracted as if she is seeing a mirage? She attempts to move, only to feel the resistance from the medium around her, allowing her to move in slow motion alone. Then she realizes that she is underwater, a big body of water, and she cannot breathe. And it's cold, so cold, down here. A deep and profound fear invades her body, so powerful, a wave of helplessness like she never felt before.

She desperately tries to swim up to the sky, to the sun, but she cannot. She is bound to the bottom of the sea. With every movement, she exhausts a little more of her energy, as well as hope to see the sun again. So this is how it ends, her biggest fear, a large body of water surrounding her, suffocating her?

Then she sees a shadow on the surface, calling for her. It's him, her intruder, diving into the depths of the sea to come to her rescue. He swims to her and releases her from bondage and drags her up. She feels like her lungs are about to explode, but she hangs on.

Swim—up—quick!

Phoenix opened her eyes and took a deep breath as if she hadn't breathed for a lifetime. She coughed and gagged as the air rushed in and out of her depleted lungs, and she rubbed her throat gently in an attempt to ease the severe pain. She slowly tilted her head towards the noise, the sound of a struggle, and she saw blurred images of two figures, one of which was in a GPSN uniform…and the other was in a strange costume? It was her intruder!

She tried to move, but she wasn't able to. Her entire body was shaking with cold and aching in pain, her vision still blurred. She turned her head to the other side as the two men's struggle continued, only to see a pair of bulging, lifeless eyes staring back at her. She could see the struggle in the reflection of the eye. She slowly turned her head back and saw her intruder fell the other with a cracking head-butt, a head-butt she remembered only too well.

He rushed to her and kneeled down, his worry turning to relief after seeing that she was conscious. He gently helped her sit up and pressed her to his chest.

Phoenix closed her eyes and tried to absorb the overwhelming feelings that the physical contact brought. It felt like many shades of color and the dominant color for the moment was that of peace, a peaceful feeling that could sweep away all the worries, all the fears, all the insecurities, a peace that she longed for her entire life without knowing, a peace that she needed in order to better under-stand who she was, a peace to make her mind more focused and more deter-mined for whatever she set out to achieve. No feeling would ever compare to this inner peace of knowing that he was here and he was for real.

She opened her eyes as he loosened his hug so the two could look at one another. She watched his soft brown eyes absorbing every detail of her battered face with deep compassion. Other than the beautiful lips that she noticed before, this man came with beautiful brown eyes that had so much depth and so many things to tell.

She wanted to say something, but her throat betrayed her, and she could only cough once more in pain. She was so focused on the moment, she didn't notice another figure entering the scene behind him.

She felt a strange pain in her entire body then there was darkness.

"Alex, are you all right, buddy?" said Julio. "When the students told me these two went down to the dungeons, I wasn't sure if I should follow, to be honest. I was lost and swearing at myself for following when I heard sounds of struggle. What the hell happened here?"

The Mantis nodded quietly, as he breathed heavily and tried to sit up straight. Julio leaned down to tend to Sean's lifeless body, only to get back up in shock.

"She's dead! And Nix is barely alive. PA: Relay my location—shit, no coverage, lemme get back to the stairs to call for backup."

"Wait," said the Mantis in between breaths. "Help me get up. I'll explain what happened."

"Yeah, that would be swell," said Julio and helped the Mantis to his feet. "It seems like this dude gave you some hard time. Is he who I think he is?"

The Mantis slowly straightened up and nodded. His uniform was torn up, and he could feel that he had several bruises on his face and body, as well as some missing front teeth. The Crane had fought like a vicious animal and had bested him with sheer willpower and determination; no stunning or jinxing had worked.

"It's a good thing I had my nerve disrupter handy," said Julio with a grin. "Kept it in my pocket just in case after the freaky events of the night, man. Never used the damn thing before. I don't even know how to calibrate its levels. Yet I'll be remembered forever as the man who caught the great Mantis! Wish our dead director could witness this, my lightning triumph in the impossible mission she dumped on me just a few hours ago. I think he was about put some serious whammy on Nix. Too bad the disrupter's stun carried through to her as well. Gotta be the physical contact."

"Let me have a look," said the Mantis, still heavily breathing. "I hope it wasn't set too high, or it might cause permanent damage to her."

"Here, buddy," said Julio and handed over the little gadget. "PA: Tag this location as a crime sce—" The Mantis activated, adjusted, and pressed the disrupter to Julio's chest. Julio froze and fell on the floor like a stone.

"Actually, it was set to minimum," he shrugged, "but not anymore."

Phoenix slowly opened her eyes, as the indirect influence of the disrupter waned out, only to see a dark shadow looming over her. The Mantis kneeled down and sat on her abdomen and gripped her throat once again.

"I'm back, you little troublemaker shit! So glad you gained consciousness for one last time. And this time, no nightmares for you. No nightmare I invoke can be worse than the ones you already had. This time, I want you to witness and feel your own death through and through. I want to see the ultimate terror in those beautiful eyes when they look at me for one last time."

Phoenix weakly grabbed his arms and made an ineffectual effort to push him away.

"Good, I like it when you struggle," said the Mantis and sniggered. "And don't worry, your amateur boyfriend will be following right behind you wherever you go."

As he squeezed her throat, the Mantis looked deep into Phoenix's eyes. He wanted to see the same fear and pain he'd seen in that woman that Patel was strangling. The Mantis had watched the visuals from that interview again and again privately in his office, vowing to do it for himself to see how it would feel. He had no idea that this chance would come so soon, with someone so rewarding.

Then he noticed a supernatural glow in Phoenix's green-gray eyes, surely some side effect of the strangling. He watched it curiously for a while, and he could feel her strength slowly diminishing just like that Indian woman. Or could this glow be a reflection? A reflection of what? Suddenly he sensed a strong presence behind him, and warmth?

He turned and saw a blinding light emanating from an approaching figure. He let Phoenix go and got up to take cover from it. It was as if the figure's entire body was blazing with light, and it was so bright, it was impossible to see what or who the figure was. He put his arm before his eyes to shield them, but he was frozen, unable to move, just like a little insect. The only thing he could feel was the intensifying heat and the light that made him burn and go blind. He cried out in primeval fear and went down on his knees, then collapsed on the ground, the light dimming out and falling along with him.

Phoenix saw two bright figures collapse, but her vision was blurred and she was unable to grasp what had happened. She could hear another set of soft footsteps approaching, but she had no energy to see who it was. Then it all became dark again.

The Man with the Black Hat arrived on the scene moments later and immediately ran to the Prefect's side.

Slowly recovering from the disrupter's effect, Crane saw the Prefect whispering and his head falling to the side in Black Hat's arms. He crawled towards Phoenix under the intense gaze of the Black Hat.

"How the hell did this happen? How could this happen? Explain!"

"My—my fault," said the Crane as he crawled. "I—"

"No. On second thoughts, I don't even wanna hear," said the Black Hat and turned to the lifeless body of the Prefect. "It's all irrelevant now."

The Crane checked the pulse of her and sighed in relief, stroking her hair gently.

"How is she?"

"Alive."

"Prefect's loss is a devastating and unrecoverable one," said the Black Hat and shook his head. "It will create a setback of I-don't-know-how-many years. We don't have much time. Can you get up?"

"I can." The Crane managed to get up and stand on his still-numb feet.

"Help me, quickly." They lifted up the Prefect's lifeless body, carried it to the hatch, and crossed to the cave side. The Black Hat attempted to close the heavy hatch.

"Wait," said the Crane. "The Mantis has something that belongs to me."

He walked as fast as he could with his stiff legs, went through the Mantis's pockets, and found his gadget. This was one thing that he couldn't leave to the World Unioners. Then he went to her side and gave her one last hug, whispering his love into her beautiful little ear. He had no idea when he would see her again, but he knew it was time to leave, as he could hear footsteps and voices getting closer. He quickly went back to the hatch. "What did he say to you?" he said as he closed the hatch.

"Who?"

"The Prefect. I saw him whispering something into your ear."

"The senseless babbling of a dying old lunatic, not that he was any different in real life," shrugged the Black Hat. "It will come, and your world will change."

Phoenix opened her eyes and winced at a sharp light piercing them.

"Noster nostri!"

"Easy," said someone. "You're safe."

The light moved to the side, exposing the grinning face of Gisella. "Phoenix is coming round," she said to somebody behind.

Phoenix attempted to sit up and see what had happened. She needed to see him, make sure that he was okay. But her own body failed her.

"Hey, take it easy, I said," said Gisella, turning back to her. "Your body temp is down to thirty-six degrees. Lemme give you a condensed IV shot first. It will improve your energy level in no time."

Phoenix felt a tingle on her leg. Beverly approached and kneeled next to her, her eyes reddened. "Oh, thank God. You're okay, sis?"

"I guess," croaked Phoenix, then she coughed a few times.

An unfamiliar silhouette appeared above her, and she could see the serious demeanor of a middle-aged man in a long blue-and-white striped tunic. Then she noticed the tattoo on his forehead, as she tried to straighten herself one more time to see if her intruder was okay.

"At ease, Agent. Get some more blankets here and a uniform. She is freezing," he ordered behind. "Do you remember what happened?"

"I—I think so," said Phoenix, unsure what to say, and coughed again.

"Drink some water," said Gisella and gave her a small cup.

Phoenix took a couple of sips and cleared her throat once more. She needed to know that her intruder was fine. Her instincts had been calm about it, but she couldn't stop the ever-increasing worry inside her about his well-being. "Sean?"

Beverly looked on, her reddened blue eyes avoiding contact with Phoenix's. Hamilton shook his head slowly.

"I can't breathe easily like this," she said. "Help me straighten up."

They held her arms and pulled her up gently. Only then Phoenix realized how busy the narrow corridor was, with medics, agents recording the crime scene. She was wrapped in several survival blankets in her underwear and bra, her beautiful costume completely destroyed. She saw the lifeless body of Sean examined by the crime scene beam of Harold. She could also see Alex and Julio lying unconscious, with two Robo-Cops standing by them. There were more Robo-Cops armed with nerve disputers along the hallway and several repeater hubs to ensure network connectivity. With Hamilton on the stage, she could easily assume the perimeter to be completely secured by military troops. Yet, she couldn't see her intruder anywhere. She felt relief and anxiety simultaneously, relief that he wasn't here, but anxiety because she didn't know where he was. Could they have just taken him away already?

The presence of Hamilton was making things a lot harder, as it was evident from his ruthless gaze that he was becoming impatient for answers, yet she wasn't sure where to start, as she didn't know how much they knew. It went against everything she had been taught, but she couldn't, just couldn't, mention her intruder here and risk putting him in harm's way, no matter how deeply he was involved in any crime. She had to improvise.

"We were chasing the Mantis. We had a strong hunch that it was Alex Lubosh. We managed to follow him all the way down here. I sprained my ankle coming down the stairs, and Sean surged ahead of me, ignoring my instruction to wait. When I got here, he was already strangling her. We had a fight, but he got the best of me."

Beverly shook her head, the tears still flowing. Gisella was trying to remain cool, but she was also quite shaken. Hamilton remained as stony faced as ever.

"You're sure it was Lubosh you saw strangling Euskara, and not this young agent here, Dominguez?"

Phoenix felt relief at the question. It seemed that none of them were aware of her intruder's presence. Not yet, at least. Where could he be?

"I'm positive, sir. We had considerable circumstantial evidence against Alex being the Mantis and decided to confront him. But he had found a way to disable the security cameras in the building, so we managed to track him by following the pattern in camera outages. I suspect he was attempting to escape to the other side of the border."

Hamilton intensified his X-ray glare on Phoenix for a few seconds. She blinked a few times and looked down to avoid it. He turned to Gisella and nodded. Gisella cleared her throat.

"She's fully conscious, lucid, and seems to be remembering the events clearly, sir," she said, then turned to Phoenix. "You have a very nasty bruise on your left cheek. And I'm not even gonna comment on the bruises on your throat. But nothing I can't fix, don't worry," she added with a grin.

"What happened next?"

"I witnessed Alex—Alex murder Sean, while trying to remain conscious after he punched me. Then he attacked me in earnest. I was struggling for my life and barely noticed someone else arriving on the scene. It must have been Julio. I was knocked on the ground, but I vaguely remember someone leaning over me and saying something, something nice."

"It appears that Dominguez came to your rescue and gave a brave fight against Lubosh, managing to incapacitate him. But Lubosh, the Mantis, somehow managed to use Dominguez's own nerve disrupter against him at the last moment. Perhaps Dominguez can enlighten us as to how that happened when he comes round."

Phoenix could remember all of the incidents, including being underwater and being saved by her intruder from the depths of the sea, but she had no idea what he was doing down here in the basement of the academy. Could all of it have been a part of a nightmare engineered by the Mantis? Could it have been really Julio in the fight and not her intruder, the Crane? Then, there was that light that appeared and stopped the Mantis. Could that also be a dream?

"The Mantis, he has a mind-altering weapon. Keep him under, I urge you!"

"We didn't find any weapon or device on either one of them other than the disrupter set at maximum on the ground. Are you sure?"

"I'm positive, sir. Gisella, please check and see if he has an implant."

Gisella turned to Hamilton. Following his nod, she walked by Alex. She took out her wand-like device and moved it around Alex's head.

"He has some implant in his head. But no way of knowing what it is until a comprehensive scan."

"That's good enough for the time being," said Hamilton. "Keep Lubosh under, Doctor. And how's, what's his name, Dominguez?"

"He shows some signs of movement, sir. The disrupter's effect is fading. He should gain consciousness fairly soon."

"Sir, you are aware of the other deaths, yes?"

The man nodded, with his intense gaze fixed on Phoenix's green-gray eyes.

"I know that Alex committed those murders, too."

"Are you sure those are also murders and that he is the Mantis?"

"Yes, sir, I am. Let me interrogate him. I'll make him confess. Let me do it now, while the events are still warm and I can catch him off guard."

"How could you interrogate him if you believe that he has an active mind-altering implant?"

"I'll find a way, sir." She felt a lot better now, her energy level rapidly coming back to normal. She attempted to stand up, only to sit back down as intense pain pervaded her ankle.

"Hey, you need to go easy on that ankle," said Gisella. "No quick fix for that one."

Hamilton's stony expression didn't change. But if a slight twitch in his eyebrow was an indication, he appeared to be impressed by Phoenix's determination and nodded in approval.

"All right, Wallis, you've got two hours. Blackmore, help Wallis to prepare the interview room to her specifications. Doctor, keep Lubosh out until you get a nod from Wallis. I'm curious to see how you'll manage this."

"Ahhh, I should have known that it would be you, sweetie pie," said Arnett and grinned. "And who should you need to reach at WIMA this time, in the middle of this utterly inanimate Saturday night?"

Phoenix's biggest problem was how to tackle Mantis's mind-altering abilities in that interview room. Her instincts told her that it could be done, but she hadn't the slightest clue as to how. Beverly and Harold had already made a thorough search on such weapons, but there was nothing in GPSN databases, not on the ones they had clearance for, at least. She needed to find a way, and she needed it quick. She wasn't the lead of the Mantis case, and she'd only have a chance to interrogate him while Julio was still incapacitated.

The only other person she could think that might, just might, have some information on the subject was Arnett. She vividly remembered how he had bragged about his interest in those druids and their powers of persuasion then talked about mind altering. His deep interest in understanding the human nature was also evident in the unorthodox, and perhaps even unconstitutional, methods he used to reach out to his clients. Phoenix could feel that he would go to any lengths in pursuit of this knowledge. Rousing his interest and prying the information out of him, on the other hand, was a totally different story.

"I *am* talking to the one that I need from WIMA already. I need your help Arnie, in a *very* curious matter."

"All right, enlighten me about your *curiosity,* and I'll be the judge as to whether it makes me curious enough to deal with you in the middle of the night," said Arnett, sitting on the side of his bed, checking his nails. There was also some movement under the sheets. "C'mon, c'mon, I haven't all night. Don't you see? I've got company." He got up and started roaming the room fully naked, except for his fluffy lilac slippers.

"I need to interrogate a murder suspect who has a mind-altering implant in his head."

Arnett stopped roaming and turned to her. "Goodness gracious, how fascinating! Is this a suspect for the murder of our little VeeBee?"

"No. I've already solved that murder. But this guy went on a spree tonight, killing my prime witness for the Bogdanov murder, my case assistant, as well as my director here at the field office, and almost managed to kill me."

"Come again? A triple homicide, here in the city?"

"Yes. And I need to interrogate this man, the famed terrorist Mantis, who was under deep cover as a senior agent here at the field office for decades."

"Oh—my—God! How did you manage to catch this monster? Looking at the shape your face is in, it looks like you had to resort to violence in order to stop him."

"I don't have time to explain, Arnie. Do you know any way to stop or slow down or disable such a mind-altering weapon, or is there someone you know or have access to in the next hour who could give us some information about this?"

"Actually, I did quite a bit of research about such curiosities some time ago, sweetie pie," said Arnett with a sly grin. "What do you know, it's your lucky night, and I'm willing to come where you are to give you a hand. I'd love to see that monster you caught up close."

"Ah well, I guess it's all right to come here, if you think you can be of help. But we're very short on time. I need to be ready in an hour and a half."

"Splendid!" said Arnett and clapped his hands. "We'll be there in no time, sweetie pie. Just get one of your electronic experts to install a couple of old-fashioned wave generators in your interrogation room, adjustable to subsonic frequency range, so that we can *entrain* your juggernaut's mind. I can bring Doug with me, can't I?"

"*Entertain* his mind? Sweet," said Phoenix, having no idea what he was talking about. "I want to remind you that you are bound by confidentiality agreements between your guild and the GPSN. But I'm not sure if it's a good idea—"

"Come, come, little pussycat. Do you think I'd set foot in your territory without my lawyer on a night like this? I'm sure it's already infested with high-level security professionals and executives from every part of the world to see and analyze that monster, and I've been known to step on toes. Besides, now that you're blessed with a ten-million credit line, I'm sure you and Doug would have a lot to discuss."

"You know about that?"

"It's a part of my art to follow such developments, sweetie pie, and a rare thing such as a negative credit line is hard to miss. I even know who's behind it and why."

"Who? Tell me!"

"Actually Doug did all the research for me. He knows all the details. How about us three have an early morning tea, once we're finished with your monster?"

"As a respected member of our legal community, there's no reason for Mr. Anderson not to be here, I suppose, and I'd like to hear what he found out about that credit line."

"Marvelous," said Arnett and clapped again. "But unlike me, Dougie is allergic to pro bono. You'll need to pay him a certain fee for his time and connections for that information, and in return you'll have the privilege of retaining the finest barrister in town, something you can certainly afford now."

Phoenix just stared at the naked Arnett, standing before his bed with his arms folded, waiting for an answer, and marveled at his negotiation skills.

"Do you always negotiate this well when you're naked?"

"My favorite business meeting outfit. So, do we have a deal, sweetie pie?"

"Yes, we do. I've seen what he can do. And if he's gonna come to the field office with you anyway, I'd rather have him on my payroll rather than on Mantis's."

"Well, well," said Arnett, arching an eyebrow. "You might have some gray cells under that neglected hair of yours after all." Then he turned back. "Doug, did you hear that, dear? This Saturday night might not be a bore after all!"

Phoenix tried to straighten out the uniform she had been provided with, but it was just too long as well as too tight around the chest.

The sound oscillators were already set to Arnett's specification in the interview room by Harold, and they were making some final preparations of the expert systems, when Arnett arrived with not only Douglas Anderson in tow, but also a languorous Gladys, both of whom had their arms full of some expensive-looking purple upholstery.

"Ah, here we are, sweetie pie. My goodness, so many security checks coming into your building tonight. Were those some marines and green berets down there?"

"Yep. Hamilton doesn't want to take any chances with this terrorist."

"Ahhh, how exciting," sang Arnett with a little clap of hands in elbow-length gloves. "So this is where the show will take place, good. Doug, Gwladus, place the material over there, please. And we'll have to fix you up, darling, you look terrible, and look at that awful uniform! Tell me, why do you have to shock me with your appearance every time I see you? Do you do it on purpose?"

"We have little time to get ready for the interrogation. I can't waste time on my makeup and make Hamilton wait. We've only got twenty more minutes to prepare."

"Oh, don't speak such nonsense, sweetie. An interview, an interrogation, is all about domination psychology and how you force your will and presence on the other person. You need to look best and feel best, even if your interviewee will not see you, *capische?*"

"What do you mean by, 'he'll not see me'?"

"Ah, come, come, think! You can't be in the same room as him, even with my preparations. You don't want to be whammied, now, do you?"

"Of course I don't plan to be in the same room with him. But I planned to project my 3D image to the room, and—"

"Oh, don't be so naive. Looking at the marks on your face and throat, I can tell that it's personal between you and your troublemaking psychopath. He'd immediately know that you're not in the room, and you'd lose all of your dominant edge, your charisma, and any chance you possess in subduing him. Believe me, even interrogating with voice only would work much better. Can somebody explain to her how POV cameras and angles work in a nutshell?"

"Ehm, unless there is a camera exactly located in the place of your projected image's eyes, and that camera moved with your projected image, there is no way to make your projected image to have an eye contact with him," said Harold.

"Excellent, young man," said Arnett and winked.

"I didn't understand a word of what he just said."

"The point is, you can't simply project your image and expect a highly intelligent homicidal maniac to be fooled by it," said Arnett then turned to the upholstery pile. "And we need to put these velvet sheets up. I picked royal purple, thinking that it would go well with the gray stone walls. I always keep a pile of these handy, for parties and stuff."

"Arnie, we don't have time—" She paused. "You didn't bring these here for decoration, did you?"

"She's learning, Dougie," said Arnett and winked at him. Anderson's face was as expressionless as ever. "Those are to block the ultra-gamma waves from his mind or implant or whatever he has, in case his whammying power were to penetrate these thick walls."

"And the generators?"

"Set one of those at a constant hundred and thirty Hertz on this side, and the other at hundred and twenty on the other side," said Arnett, turning to Harold. "Set the amplitude to blend in well with the background noise of the computers. But the sounds need to be channeled directly to his ears from both sides, understand?"

"How will that help?" said Phoenix.

"Let's just hope that it will put him in a fairly submissive mode. Can we remotely control those oscillators?"

"Yes, sir," said Harold.

"Good," nodded Arnett. "Now we'll fix you up all pretty, sweetie pie, and I have an idea for our projection problem. Does this room come with a spherical sound system, young man?"

"No, sir," said Harold. "But I can set it up quickly."

"Excellent! Actually, you'll be amazed at how great you'll look and you'll sound before that psycho of yours, sweetie pie."

CHAPTER 41

ALEX regained consciousness on the interviewee chair, only to find that he was bound to the chair by plastic straps on his arms and legs. He tried to move his limbs, merely succeeding in making the straps even tighter. He moved his head to avoid the strong light from above in an attempt to identify the figure on the other side of the table.

"Phoenix, is that you? What am I doing here? Is this some kind of, how do you call, a prank?"

"Alex Lubosh, you're being interrogated for the murder of Junior Agent Ixone Euskara, attempted murders of senior agents Julio Dominguez, and myself, Phoenix Wallis, and possible murders of Director Dagmar Morssen, and one Ilya Manchik of alien origin."

"What?" said Alex, his eyes bulging. "What the hell are you talking about? Dagmar is dead? All right, the joke went too far, and it's not funny."

"Don't play games with me! You know full well that she's dead, and so are the others. I want you to tell me how long you've been under deep cover here at the field office. How many years has it been, Alex, that you've been the Mantis?"

"Me, the Mantis? What are you talking about? Dagmar can't be dead. Please tell me she is not. Please tell me this is a cruel joke, I beg you—"

Phoenix checked the indicators before her. The expert computers showed that Alex was in a state of genuine shock. *Great acting skills*, she thought. *Good enough to fool the expert hardware in absence of baseline behavior patterns.*

Tess was examining visual logs of meetings at the field office in order to determine his baseline patterns. She had processed as many visuals as possible in the limited time frame, and Phoenix had been using the preliminary baseline patterns determined from those, while Tess was still processing meeting logs in a reverse chronological order.

The strange thing was that there were no holograms from Alex's frontal cortex, as if he had no recollection of the incidents. How could Alex, the Mantis, hide his thoughts like that? The only thing she could come up with was that the mind-altering implant had something to do with it, or hacking.

"Computer: Display crime scene footage from cases of Morssen and Euskara. Project it before the interviewee."

Holograms of a dead director appeared above the interviewing table. Alex was first irked, then watched the images gapingly, then started sobbing.

"It can't be—it can't be true. Please, tell me this is just a make-believe hologram."

"The only thing make-believe in this room is your theatrics in an attempt to fool me. Are you denying your involvement in this incident?"

"I loved her," he said, with fresh tears gushing down his cheeks. "How could you even suggest that I killed her?"

"And how about her?" said Phoenix, motioning to the footage with a dead Sean. "Are you also denying your involvement in her death?"

"Oh, my God, no! I can't believe this is happening. You—you know me, Phoenix. How can you even think that I could be a part of such monstrosities?"

"I can think because I saw this particular monstrosity firsthand. I saw you murder Sean."

"You're doing fine, sweetie pie," whispered Arnett to Phoenix. "Keep jogging his memory. Eventually something should leak. With the soothing effect from my waves, he cannot resist forever."

Phoenix couldn't talk back at Arnett, as her voice and mimics were captured and applied to a virtual movie actor, created in her image, one with perfect makeup and hair. Arnett's idea had been to scan her face and body to create an animation-ready model of her, like they used in the movies. This was the same technology that gave Tess and Bud their virtual bodies, which Arnett had stylized. This model could then be fed movement in real time from Phoenix's movements and facial mimics through a camera pointed at her face.

Phoenix's virtual actor was programmed to copy every movement Phoenix made, except for the eyes, which were programmed to be fixed on Alex's face or on the holograms. In reality, she was sitting at a table in another room with a big monitor before her, watching the room through a camera directly behind her projected image. As long as she didn't try to get up and walk, everything would appear to Alex as realistic as digitally possible.

Holograms from the crime scenes hovered over the table as Alex watched them in evident devastation, while Phoenix continued her relentless verbal assault.

"I went back as far as two weeks, examining the visuals of Alex Lubosh so far," reported Tess, in text mode on the screen before Phoenix. "There are strange discrepancies in his behavior, and it's been hard to get a baseline behavior pattern for him so far. I need more time to analyze more visuals in order to achieve a statistically viable result."

Tess's inability to get a baseline pattern was quite disturbing. She needed those to prove deceptions and lies. But, independent of any baseline pattern, there were no visuals behind Alex. It was just blank, meaning no memories. But how could it be? She had witnessed Alex murdering Sean. Heck, the monster had even tried to murder her. How could there be no memories of it? They couldn't be just erased somehow, could they? Or—

A rush of deep anxiety swept through Phoenix. What if all of what she saw was another nightmare? What if all this was a part of the plan by the real Mantis? What if the real Mantis was sitting in the Viewers' Lounge and watching with amusement her desperate attempts to break an innocent man? Suddenly she remembered the question Hamilton had asked. What if it wasn't Alex, but Julio? She felt like she was trapped in the mine of her nightmares all over again. She could feel that her face was beginning to turn white, and the knot in her stomach was tightening. Good thing that her model didn't reflect such details.

She couldn't just stop the interview and admit defeat in front of everyone, but her time was running out. She had volunteered for this interrogation. She had rushed it so that the Mantis couldn't prepare any additional defenses or use his mind-altering weapon and slip away. On the other hand, her instincts were persistent that she was on the right track. If they were right and this wasn't another horrific nightmare, there had to be some other explanation, some improbable, yet plausible, explanation.

As her mind raced in overdrive to find the solution to her dilemma, she remembered something, an old movie she saw a long time ago, one of those early ones with no color. What if she had a similar case before her? It would explain so many things, why there were no images and why Tess couldn't get a pattern for baseline behaviors, but also require her to completely alter her line of questioning and try something totally radical. She thought of what Vanderbilt had told her, affecting her so deeply. Could she do a similar thing here? Did she dare?

Once again, salvation lay in the depths of the dark mine, and she had to go forward, taking the tunnel down, deep down into Alex's subconscious. She stopped her verbal bombardment abruptly and let out a long psychopathic laugh, shocking the desperate and weeping Alex, along with everyone in the Viewers' Lounge.

She had one final revelation to make in order to unsettle everything and to unleash one last wave of chaos.

Julio discreetly peeked at the man sitting next to him. *He* was sitting next to *the man himself!* His body was still quite stiff from the disrupter, and his talking had been one notch above gibberish, yet there he was, being honored by the big boss's presence. He had been told about the events and was congratulated for bravely saving Nix and incapacitating the Mantis.

The events, as they were described to him, were not exactly as he remembered them. He definitely remembered another dude with strange clothes who he zapped and then being zapped by Alex. He didn't remember fighting Alex, but that could have happened after the fucker used the disrupter against him, as his recollection was still vague. But either way, he wasn't about to confess to the wrong thing and ruin the party at this point. As ever, the Neanderthal bitch was at center stage, and despite the fact that he should have been interrogating Alex or the Mantis as the case lead, he was happy to watch Nix destroy herself, running full speed into some solid wall.

Her cornering of Alex hadn't worked, and she wasn't asking any questions to him anymore and was acting all strange. Maybe she was finally cracking up, or she was cooking up something further. Either way, Hamilton was here, intensely watching the procedure in the Viewers' Lounge, and he wasn't known to be a patient man. Perhaps he could say a word or two to encourage the impatient side of the top executive?

"I fink Niksh ish looshing it, shir," was what came out of his mouth.

Hamilton looked at him in faint surprise, only to ignore him and to focus back on the adjoining room. Julio sank back in his seat, silently vowing not to attempt to move his disobedient and useless tongue again until it was all over. Now he knew only too well how Alex and others with thick accents felt.

He checked out the others in the room in order to see if anyone shared his reaction to this ridiculous *questioning*. Beverly was on the other side of Hamilton and was watching everything intently, and so were that hotshot lawyer, the cute petite doctor, and Fred. He checked the back seats out of the corner of his eye, only to see everyone fully focused, with the exception of that awfully tired babe who came with the image-making guru. Julio had no idea why Arnett was here and what he could be doing in the field office in the middle of the night. He made a mental note to check out the babe after it all ended. He was sure that she would fill him in on all the details.

"You're playing a very dangerous game, sweetie pie," whispered Arnett with a sly grin. "I hope you know what you're doing."

"I know all of what you remember from the incidents, Mantis," she said, shaking her head, with a grin. "But what you remember is not what really happened."

"I don't remember anything," said Alex in tears, desperately shaking his head. "What the hell are you talking about?"

Phoenix leaned on her elbows towards Alex, with a cold smile, exposing a better view of her face to him.

"You're good, Mantis, I'll give you that. Your hiding capability is truly admirable. And I thought I'd seen it all. But being good at hiding in plain sight will not change the fact that you've been hiding in the wrong place at the wrong time. You see, being well aware of your mind-altering capabilities, I decided to play your game, but with my rules. I tricked you. You've been under the control of *my* mind-altering weapon all this time."

"What are you talking about? What weapon?"

"You think these weapons existed all this time, without GPSN getting its hands on it? We've been aware of this for more than a decade and pursuing our own technology secretly. You think you're in the interview room of the field office, right? But you're dead wrong. You're only in a prison, which I designed for your mind, where I've been allowing your imagination to run amok!"

The devices indicated a slight increase in heart rate and blood pressure, not consistent with Alex's mood. Her wild tactic might, just might, be paying off. It was still too early to know for sure, but this was the first inconsistency she had managed to squeeze out. Now it was time to drop the bomb.

"I work for the Psychological Warfare Unit. I have no reason to hide this from you anymore as I've just been playing a game now, only to see how far you can manage to hide the Mantis inside. My mission was to catch you red-handed. We've already known that you were the Mantis for a good while now. I came to this field office, pretending to be a *fragile* senior agent hired in *such a rush*. By the way, didn't it occur to you that it was strange that nobody even interviewed me? It's because nobody knew about me. I came here directly under the orders of none other than Hamilton himself."

Beverly turned to Hamilton in shock, only to see her feelings reflected in Julio's face. She wanted to ask zillions of questions to the big boss but stopped short of making an attempt. She checked the reaction of the others and noted similar gapes of disbelief, with the exception of Arnett's sleeping assistant—even the stony-faced lawyer had flinched. But she couldn't catch even a tiniest expression on Hamilton's face. And this was the second time Phoenix had dropped the name of Hamilton in the last few hours. Beverly looked on, crossed her arms, and shook her head. PWU people worked under deep cover, only to reveal themselves and their real intent under the rarest of circumstances. Phoenix seemed to confess to this a little too quickly and too publicly. Could this be another attempt to unsettle Alex?

On the other hand, she couldn't help but think all the evidence, her request to prepare the Richfield technology demo behind the late boss's back, but with blessing of the Wizard... Her corporate-level assignment to the Bogdanov case, her miraculous successes at unmasking Patel and the Mirage, her unorthodox methods and disregard for procedure, her quiet and distant demeanor... It all seemed to add up. Perhaps she had been sent as a spy to unmask this Mantis under the protection of the Wizard.

Alex froze, staring blankly at the wall behind Phoenix's image. Irregular spikes flooded his brain activity. Phoenix quickly typed something into the terminal before her. Arnett looked at the message and smiled.

"So our good girl wants to play hardball," he whispered. "And hardball she'll get." He pushed the controls of the oscillators to the exact opposite extreme, converting the alpha waves into gamma to spur brain activity to maximum levels.

"I've been playing a game with you and the others all this time," grinned Phoenix. "And you've been under my control for nearly a week. I wanted to see the extent of your network, but it's obvious that they don't tell you much, do they?"

Alex jerked in the seat, and all indicators spiked before Phoenix. A hologram of darkness appeared all of a sudden, with flashes of images coming and going as if there was severe static in the air. Then an image started appearing, a long dark face with little dark eyes, small nose, and a small mouth, totally void of any expression.

"Well, hello there, Mantis. Glad to finally see a face to match the name."

Alex turned behind and shrieked in terror at the face he saw. It appeared to be saying something.

"Can't hear a thing, Mantis," said Phoenix. "Are you trying to say something to me? Why not speak through Alex?"

Alex suddenly calmed and dropped his eyes, then slowly turned towards Phoenix with a completely blank face, reflecting the expression on the hologram a moment ago, whereas Alex's panic-ridden face was now in the hologram, looking around as if he was in pitch darkness, screaming something. The Mantis in Alex's body turned around and looked at the images behind.

"Poor ol' Alex. What would I do without him? Now, it's your turn!"

Having seen the same inhuman expression on his face while squeezing her throat, Phoenix gasped for air momentarily. But this time there was no feeling of weightlessness or being under the water. She kept her resolve and launched her counterattack with another manic laugh.

"Nice try, Mantis," she said, still smiling. "But the game is over. You cannot jinx or strangle anyone in this virtual world I designed for you, unless I allow it. Aren't you supposed to look at a Phoenix with reddened eyes and bruises all over her face? You don't, because this is what the real Phoenix looks like. The other was only designed for your sick mind."

The intensity on the Mantis's face slowly faded, his body relaxed. "So it was all a game. And who was the dungeon master, you?"

"Who else could it be? But I gave you a lot of latitude so that I could discover more about you and your organization."

"Where are we now? Where is the stage set?"

"The stage is set at the rehab center in room twenty-five oh-eight. The only other real person you've been interacting with was Dr. Gisella Nemeth. I had to include her for control purposes. I invented the murder of Spencer so that she could make a plausible entry onto the scene. All the others were computer-controlled characters, which we painstakingly programmed for months. And I have to confess, some characters were easier to emulate than others. I know our portrayal of Director Morssen was barely up to par, with many discrepancies, but Julio's was easy; the likes of him are so predictable."

"I see. It was my powers, they felt so good, and I felt so strong. But I should have known. That controller of mine proved to be such a weakling, making such poor and emotional judgment calls. It just didn't make sense. Then she broke like a twig in my hands."

Suddenly a scene filled the background, with a pair of eyes staring in utter horror. The scene zoomed out slowly and exposed Sean's terrorized face and her long beautiful neck being squeezed by powerful hands. Phoenix inadvertently moved her eyes away from it, focusing back on the Mantis.

"Can't look at it, huh? Even when you know it's virtual reality."

"Why did you opt to kill the Russian?"

"I have to admit I momentarily panicked. I was so disappointed in myself. But that awful hack attack, which used my name, distracted me. Making the Russian faint was too rash an action for my taste, but it was already done, and I needed to follow through."

"Killing the director was also stupid."

"As if I had a choice," shrugged the Mantis. "Or did I have a choice?"

"No, you didn't. I purposefully put her in your way to see how you'd deal with Alex."

"Oh, dealing with Alex is easy. You see, the poor soul has no idea about what's going on. I can see everything he does through his eyes, but he cannot see what I do. He only gets suspicious from time to time, after waking up in the morning with bruises and fatigue he cannot explain, or loss of time he cannot account for. But you see, poor Alex is too afraid of doctors and rehab centers to consult, and who can blame him. Because he's convinced that this field office is haunted by ghosts that control his body from time to time, and he desperately wants to retire. But his *love* for the director stops him short every time he tries to make a decision. Actually, I did him a great favor by killing Morssen and ending his terrible dilemma, in the virtual world at least. How come you got the controller to interfere in Morssen's final dream to the bright light? In order to bait me to follow her? To put me under pressure?"

"Why else?"

"I had to improvise so much all day," said the Mantis, shaking his head. "And I was beginning to think that I was getting good at it."

"They were all plots to reveal the identity of your controller. How come you had no idea who she was?"

"Because she'd always kept me under pressure and control. She had the power of sending me away to sleep and to stay dormant as long as she or he wished. I only knew that her mission name was the Prefect. Why did you program the Prefect to be Sean? It makes little sense."

"In order to make you get suspicious and contact your real controller," shrugged Phoenix. "I had no idea that you despised her and wanted to kill her. And I'm back to square one now."

"Sorry, I couldn't help you with that. I should have known that Sean was way too young and weak to be a controller like the Prefect." He shrugged. "Oh well, she became a part of the collateral damage."

"And your sponsor? I suspect the Dinastiya crime organization has been using you."

"I can't help you with that, either," shrugged the Mantis. "I assume so. I only know the names of a few operatives that I worked in tandem with, like the Mount and the Crane, whom I suspected of launching the hack in my name. You must know about the Crane. Not by name perhaps, but he was in the—" The Mantis cut his own words off, looking intently at Phoenix. He could see the surprise, even behind the virtual mask.

Phoenix was completely overwhelmed at hearing her intruder's nickname mentioned by this evil man. She quickly checked the indicators before her, but it was not a lie. Could the Mantis deceive the hardware? But why lie about this, after confessing everything? It had to be true. So the Mantis had been a part of these Renovators, and that self-proclaimed grandmaster had been lying through his teeth. What else did he lie about? She felt so devastated, she couldn't maintain her façade anymore. And as her mask slipped, the Mantis understood.

"Oh, no! No, you—you worthless piece of shit, you—you tricked me! Now you'll see my real power!" The Mantis let out a ground-shaking scream and freed himself from the plastic wrist cuffs by pulling his hands and dislocating his thumbs. He got up with superhuman power and broke the chair under him, freeing his legs and attempting to attack Phoenix. Diving through the hologram, he fell on the ground in utter astonishment. He scrambled to his feet looking totally out of control and disoriented.

"How did you know it was me?" he yelled at the walls, banging on the mirror. "How did you know?"

"Too many little coincidences," said Phoenix, regrouping herself. "Calm down, and I'll tell you. You know better than anyone else that you cannot get out of this room."

The Mantis calmed down a bit and moaned with pain as blood ran down from his cut wrists. He walked back and leaned on the table, where his chair used to be, letting out another scream of agony and anger.

"I remember feeling down and negative after every meeting I had with you," said Phoenix's virtual reflection. "It was just a little thing here, another there, but they were all adding up somewhere back in my mind. Through Alex's soft style, you wore me out with your orientations. You brought me down with the crude jokes supposedly due to your poor knowledge of English idioms. You even had me almost convinced that I coerced that poor Shakira into something she wasn't. And all that time, I had assumed it was Julio who was the origin of all the negativity towards me. But it was you who put that idea in Ion's head about the mind-control weapon. You leaked all the gossip about my darkest secrets by being in constant contact with my best friend. And you used the information about my nightmares to unsettle me and divert my attention to that half-blind DeVille as a red herring."

"I even swapped your mood stabilizers with a hallucinogen," groaned the Mantis. "How could you have noticed the swap?"

"I didn't. Evidently some doctor decided to do that for me some months ago. Do you believe in fate, Mantis?"

"So what you told to Morssen about your stabilizers was the truth? I can't believe you admitted something you've been hiding for so long to her like that."

"You've been deceiving people for so long, you can only see more deception when things go wrong, don't you? I confessed to Director Morssen about that, being aware of her past. If there was one person in this field office to understand my issues, it had to be her. Poor woman was struggling with her internal demons all her life, and you did your worst to make her slip further into the oblivion."

"You think Mantis to be fool enough to launch a direct attack on his prey? Of course I used my influence on all those around you, not only on that stupid and arrogant Julio, but also on Beverly, Fred, Sandra, and especially on Morssen. With others, it was just a few words here and a juicy tidbit of gossip there. But with Morssen, my plan was to unsettle you further by degrading her mentally and forcing her to make up unbalanced and irrational stuff. I even put words in Hamilton's mouth to get Beverly on my side to further incapacitate her. After slipping to the brink of insanity, Morssen was meant to make the final strike that would destroy you completely, and she'd be destroyed along with you. It was all planned and executed to perfection. How did you manage to break free from my impeccable web of deception?"

"By going through hell. There were so many fragments in my mind, lying here and there without any meaning, but I could hardly focus on anything from insomnia, thanks to you. Then Sean told me of her suspicions about you after noticing you going to my office. After a brief check with my so-called best friend and the interview logs, I realized that you were behind every corner, in each and every detail, like you somehow knew what kind of objects DeVille would display in his filthy flat *before* seeing the footage of it."

The Mantis remained mute.

"I can't deny that I felt anxious earlier, until that moment I realized your split personality. I had to provoke you to come out of hiding. Then I remembered how one of the victims of the deadly device, Vanderbilt, explained to me that she couldn't tell reality from fantasy. Actually, her confessions had deeply depressed me, as I still wasn't aware that my mental prowess and stability was being targeted by you in order to drive me to insanity. Then I thought of playing your own trick back at you, Mantis. And it proved to be easier than I thought. I had no idea that you were so clueless that you didn't even know who your controller was, thinking she was poor Sean. You are a total disgrace to the human race. And the only place you'll go from here is to that rehab center, with no comebacks."

The Mantis looked at Phoenix's vision with a chilling calm then he leaned towards it.

"Me, clueless?" he said grinning. "You think you know me, don't you? You know nothing of me, but I know everything about you. I know about your nightmares, I know about your little pink diary, I know all of your fears, your worries, your weaknesses, your hopeless love, even your dirty secret of treason that you successfully managed to hide all these years. You think the Mantis to be a fool? I know they sent you here to destroy me. Do you think I don't know that you're a sleeper agent for the Dinastiya and the recent negative credit line they provided to you worth millions of dollars to destroy me?"

Hamilton flinched at Mantis's words. It was the first visible reaction he had produced since the beginning of the interview. He turned to Beverly and whispered something, who in turn nodded and quickly got up and left the room.

"Desperate last-minute smear campaign, huh, Mantis? Don't think you can frighten me or anyone else with such hollow accusations."

"We'll see if that's the case, little girl," said the Mantis with a strange grin. "So long, until the next time."

Then suddenly tears started flowing down his cheeks, with his face now twisted in agony once again. Alex was back. He dashed around the table helplessly in the room screaming "No." It appeared like this time the Mantis had allowed Alex to see through the eyes of the Mantis. He dashed towards the big mirror and banged his head on the thick glass, leaving a smear of blood behind.

"Alex, stop, we can help you."

"I don't deserve to live! We don't deserve to live! I killed her! I murdered the woman I love and so many others!"

Then he banged his head a few more times against the mirror, weeping in agony both physical and mental. Then he knelt down and grabbed one of the power cables with both hands, thumbs dangling, then looked up.

"Forgive me."

He bit the cable as hard as he could, not letting go. Power surged through his body, the computers in the room flickered and reset, as Phoenix, Hamilton, and the others burst into the room at the same instant.

"Stay back," said Hamilton. "Cut the circuit breakers, quick."

They watched helplessly as the current went through Alex's lifeless body for several long seconds, with a disgusting smell of burnt flesh wafting through the air, and somebody finally ended the show by cutting the power.

Alex Lubosh and the Mantis were gone for good.

Beverly arrived on the scene and shrieked in horror at the sight of the burnt body. Hamilton turned to her. She shot an anxious glance at Phoenix then turned to Hamilton and slowly nodded at him.

Hamilton knew that Phoenix had been hiding something all along and that something wasn't right with this senior agent from the very beginning. It was in the way she was hired, the way she had acted with a bizarre confidence, the way took risks, made unusual friends and connections, manipulated those around her, the way she lied about her connection to the PWU and himself, and the audacious way she had conducted this interrogation. He'd been letting her get away with it, hoping to find out more about who was behind those pretty green eyes or who had been pulling her strings. It could be those useless Dinastiya guys playing tricks behind his back, or she could be a spy for those science geeks, but it didn't matter anymore. He'd already known about her ten-million-dollar negative credit line through a whole bunch of intermediaries, as his finance people were still hard at work trying to determine who the real culprit was. But that didn't matter, either. This was the perfect opportunity to arrest her, accused of corruption before her coworkers, with the coworker closest to her discovering her negative credit line to be true, the opportunity he'd been waiting for since that evening he'd received that cooperation letter from Richfield.

Her closest coworker, Beverly, had befriended her under his orders to keep an eye on her, but it didn't escape his attention that she had also developed a deep fondness for her as well. Perhaps this one came with some special subtle jinxing powers of her own. All of that and the details of her puppet masters would be exhaustively explored by PWU's interrogators.

"You're under arrest for treason, conspiracy, impersonating a PWU agent, and violating two articles of the Supreme Bill. Take her away," he hissed to the standing Robo-Cops.

Phoenix just stood there, completely thunderstruck. She scanned the faces of the people there quickly, only to see them turning their heads away, avoiding any eye contact, including Beverly! *Beverly?*

Then she saw Gisella observing her with a curious smirk, Arnett rolling his eyes and shaking his head then whispering something to Anderson's ear, and Anderson raising an eyebrow. Anderson raising an eyebrow? What could *that* mean? Hell freezing over?

Then the knees buckled and lights went out. She collapsed out of exhaustion, tumbling headlong into a much-needed deep sleep.

CHAPTER 42

"**KNOCK**, knock."

Phoenix opened her eyes and sprang up. What had happened? How long had she been asleep? Suddenly she felt pain in her throat and ankle. She couldn't see her throat, but her right ankle appeared double the size of her left, bandaged tightly. She was in a dim, windowless room with stone walls and minimal furniture, wearing one of those bulky academy uniforms, sitting on a very hard bed. She noticed the sink and the toilet across from the bed and turned her attention to the tall man in navy tunic with a large briefcase.

"Mr. Anderson?"

"Douglas," he said with a rare smile.

"Douglas, what happened to me?"

"You've been totally out for almost eighteen hours now. How do you feel?"

"Uhm, rested," she said, surprising herself.

"Good, because we're good to go. I've got some clothes for you, with compliments from Arnie."

She glanced at the old stone building one last time as the limo pulled off. Then she turned to check out the inside. The seats were white leather with dark purple pillows. Anderson had arranged a small velvet ottoman and had helped her rest her swollen ankle on it. There were several monitors before them, displaying news and media of all sorts. A soft music similar to her music played in the background. The lilac tunic Anderson brought for her was one of amazing quality and comfort, something even beyond the platinum line of the ZAP. So this was how Devotees with HDIs way above eighty lived.

Anderson reached out for the fridge from his seat across from Phoenix, took out a bottle of champagne, and poured two glasses. He handed one of them to Phoenix.

"Are we celebrating my release?"

"And your good fortunes."

"You mean, they're not gonna to prosecute me!?"

"No."

"That's great news," she said with a radiant smile, only to sink back into gloom a few moments later. "Still, I'm not sure what to do now. It will be very hard for me to find a job in the Union. I can go back to school for a new career or seek my fortunes in the rogue states. Considering the negative effect my discharge will create on my HDI, I'd say I have less than three months to make a pick. And I don't think my now-world-famous negative credit line will be of any use, following my less-than-honorable discharge."

"You had an honorable discharge," shrugged Anderson and took a sip of his champagne, gazing outside.

"I did? How did you manage to pull that off?"

"It's my job."

"Thank you, Mr. A—Douglas, so much," she said with a warm smile.

Anderson just nodded and kept gazing outside.

"But I don't know how I'm gonna be able to pay for your services. I'm out of a job, with no good prospects on the horizon anytime soon. I know I have a decent credit line and all, but I have no idea what kind of strings are attached to it. Is that why you appear so worried?"

"Oh, no," said Anderson. "I'm already paid, well paid."

"But how? Don't tell me Arnie did it. And now I'm gonna pay him by being a lab rat for his and Gladys's futile attempts at making art history?"

"Hrmphhh." Anderson sprayed the champagne out of his mouth and burst into booming laughter, as Phoenix watched him in utter astonishment.

"And what's so funny, law man? Where are we going, anyway? This isn't the way to my apartment."

"I didn't think you'd wanna go there, Ms. Wallis."

"Phoenix. So where do you think I'd want to go, Douglas?"

"I thought one of the seven-star hotels in the business district would be a good idea, so I reserved a suite for you with private maids and help, so that you'd be comfortable until your ankle gets better."

"A nice thought, thank you, but I don't think so," grimaced Phoenix. "All of this is way out of my league," she said, pointing at her surroundings.

"Actually, it's not. As your lawyer, I took the liberty of leasing this limo for you. I hope it's comfortable enough and the interior is to your satisfaction."

"You did what? With what money? Don't tell me you took from that credit line without my authorization. Who was behind that, anyway? Arnie told me that you've done research on it."

"I did. Behind several layers of intermediaries, I discovered several investors in the Richfield Experiment."

"But why?"

"For your invention of the new security interview process using their neural network technology. They were well aware that it wasn't Hamilton but you who invented it. And that's when I realized that Arnie was right about you."

"What did he say about me?"

"That they'd come after you to steal your invention and possibly destroy you in the process."

"Seriously? But why would he care?"

"Arnie has a strange talent in finding seemingly lost situations, or people, and turning them around. He thought I could benefit from it, if I were to do my homework."

"About me?"

"I know all of your accomplishments, especially in the last week. I verified them through independent eyewitnesses. A thoroughly impressive week, I should add."

"And how do you expect to make a profit from all this?"

"I already have," said Anderson and turned to her, "in nine figures."

"The what!? Who? How?"

"You," he said and pointed at her. "Hamilton attempted to arrest you under false pretense in order to destroy you and to steal your invention. And he attempted the arrest himself, such a grave mistake from such a brilliant man. I suppose he felt invincible under his own roof. According to the fine print of GPSN Company Rules, the company agrees to make severance payments based on the rank of the officer in question. It's typical military ranking mentality. So if we were to sue GPSN for such a gross violation of the Supreme Bill by no less than their number two, we'd win somewhere around eleven figures. But that would take months, even years. Knowing that you like taking shortcuts, I thought you'd want results quickly and made Hamilton a settlement offer he couldn't refuse."

"How much!?"

"For a round ten-figure sum."

Phoenix froze and just kept staring at the lawyer.

"You're a rich woman, Phoenix, not only with lots of credit, but also with lots of capital. Now, tell me: What do you want to do? Where do you want to go today?"

EPILOGUE

FEELS *so warm,* she thought, a blissfully content smile spreading across her face.

Phoenix's feet sank into the hot, fine sand as she walked. She reveled in this heat, which permeated all the way to her bones, whether she was strolling along the beach, idly watching the surreally turquoise waters, resting in the shade, sleeping in her little bungalow, or venturing slightly further than the beach to satisfy her newly ravenous appetite for healthy food, simple, non-engineered, delicious, *real* food.

She abandoned her lavender-rose sarong beneath a nearby coconut tree and changed direction, continuing her leisurely walk towards the aquamarine serenity of the bay. It had been about ten days since the last time she had looked at that ad, which she had kept seeing at the metro station Omega Ten.

"Where do you want to go today?" it had said.

She remembered thinking, *Anywhere but here,* during the mayhem of those terrible days but never giving a second thought about actually doing something about it. Then Anderson had used the exact same words. Phoenix couldn't have cared less about all that money she had acquired suddenly and unexpectedly. All she had cared about at that moment was to get out of there and go somewhere far, far away, somewhere too far for her to catch even a whiff of the stench of the World Union, somewhere she would be immune from its aggressive bombardment of ideals, norms, and those annoying bot ads. Then she'd remembered something that heinous Patel had mentioned in his graduation speech: a faraway, warm, peaceful place.

Along with the warmth from the sun and sand, she felt so warm and content inside. The blocks of ice that had kept her frozen, numbing her feelings and skin alike—they had melted. She had realized that she had been seeing the entire world in black and white, with no room for color. She had realized that she had been unable to breathe in because of being surrounded by an unbearable smell. She had realized that she was in a waking nightmare and desperately needed to wake up. She had realized that the source of the spine-chilling cold was not only her scarred childhood, but her adult life like a long dark tunnel stretching ahead of her without any light beckoning from afar.

But no more.

The warmth in her heart was spreading to the rest of her body, complementing the unrestricted heat coming from the sun that permeated her skin. She felt like a butterfly, happily flitting through the air with the sole purpose of appreciating the universe around her. Or was that a *phoenix*, stretching her colorful, glorious wings after rising from her own ashes?

She looked at the sky and breathed in all the colors of the rainbow, allowed the smell of the fresh grass and salt of the sea to fill her nostrils. She listened to the cry of the gulls and the whispering of the sea, without any subconscious anticipation of those artificial sounds from a PA or any other similar gadget. Old Ray had been right all along: She didn't need a PA for anything. And she knew she would never use one again in her life.

What was she to do with her new disposition, she wasn't sure.

It will come to me, she thought, *as I surf this wave.*

Luxuriating, wallowing in this warmth, she noticed a familiar figure on the horizon.

She produced a beautiful smile and waved, then watched him approach.